To,

Mick & Dot.

I met you in the 60's
and we're still laughing! May
it continue.

Regards,

signature

(DAVE to you!)

David Newham was born in the small hamlet of Miningsby in Lincolnshire. After grammar school education, he joined the RAF as a Boy Entrant and served 24 years as a photographer.

On leaving the RAF, he started his own commercial photography business but really wanted to combine writing and photography and so became a freelance photojournalist. In 1991, he was struck down by cancer and was given very little time to live. The oncologists helped him defy the surgeon's prognosis and, from that moment, he decided life was too short and precious to waste conforming to life's expectancies and so he'd do just what he damn well pleased for the rest of his life. He now lives on the edge of the beautiful Cotswolds shooting stock photography for an international agency and enjoying his new profession as an author of thrillers.

'Winter of Spies' is his debut novel but there are two more books already in the pipeline for future release.

WINTER OF SPIES

David Newham

Winter Of Spies

Vanguard Press

A CIP catalogue record for this title is
available from the British Library

ISBN 1 84386 185 2

*Vanguard Press is an imprint of
Pegasus Elliot MacKenzie Publishers Ltd.*

www.pegasuspublishers.com

First Published in 2005
Vanguard Press
Sheraton House Castle Park
Cambridge England

Printed & Bound in Great Britain

Dedication

This book is dedicated to the memory of

Norman Christopher

Brother-in-law, friend
and Lancaster rear-gunner, 630 Sqdn
RAF East Kirkby

Grateful acknowledgement is made to friend, author and military historian Mike Hodgson, who sowed the seeds of the idea in the first place and helped me keep the story historically credible.

Also many thanks go to Dutch friend and aviation fanatic, Gerrit Bouma, who furnished me with hospitality, information and contacts during my research in Holland.

My heartfelt appreciation to supporters Gill Christopher, John Powell and Len and Eirlys Braybrook who gave me the courage to go ahead with the project.

Any mistakes are all mine.

PREFACE

Black snow? Now there was a thing. The flurries of snowflakes, drifting through the thick smoke from the locomotive, were actually turning black. It was discernable only in the lurid glow from the open furnace as I hurried past the cab. The fireman on the footplate had paused in the backbreaking task of stoking his ever-hungry boilers. I saw him wipe his sweat and soot-stained brow with an equally dirty rag. The heat from his panting charge was palpable in the bitterly cold wind knifing in from the North Sea.

Did I say I was hurrying? If I was it was purely involuntary. The truth was that I, along with my heavy and numerous bags, was being carried along by a coughing, yawning tide of uniformed humanity that surged towards the shadowy portals of the station exit and the even darker forecourt beyond. I tried for a last glimpse of the train – it was my last link with civilisation. Alas, my efforts were in vain as the press of bodies carried me relentlessly and reluctantly forward to a new and unfamiliar life.

CHAPTER ONE

I'd joined the Royal Air Force straight from university. I'd wanted to be a steely-eyed fighter pilot 'hacking the Hun' from the sky, but my eyes lacked the necessary requisites to be 'steely' and so I'd ended up as an intelligence officer. It seems my classical degree determined my wartime future – recruiters are always impressed by a classical degree. At first I was very disappointed at not being accepted for aircrew, but once I'd become aware of the attrition rate of steely-eyed young men, I began to feel I might last a little longer serving out my time on the ground.

On completion of my Officer Training, or 'Knife, Fork and Spoon School', at RAF Cosford in Staffordshire and an intense week of 'Intelligence Training' in Harrow, I was posted to that god-forsaken part of England, the Lincolnshire Fens.

In the December of 1942, I arrived at Boston station on what was known as the milk train. It was an ungodly hour of the morning, still dark, and there were uniforms everywhere. It seemed operations had been scrubbed the night before, so all and sundry had headed for the hot spots of London. The detritus that now surrounded me on the platform was returning from that night out, the crumpled greatcoats and unshaven faces evidence of their night on the town. Hungover personnel now had to get back to their bases dotted around the fenland wastes. Although all were wrapped in shapeless greatcoats and it was impossible to see their brevets, it was pretty easy to pick out who were from Bomber Command and those who were Fighter Command. The bomber guys were in groups of five to seven. There was an obvious affinity between these men and they soon gravitated towards other crews as they fought their way out of the station and on to the trucks parked on the station forecourt. The fighter men seemed a little aloof. No more than two in any one bunch and they seemed to leave their greatcoat lapels open, so everyone could see the top button of their tunic jacket underneath had been left undone. It was obviously 'not on' to be mistaken for somebody who flew 'heavies'.

I stood out like a sore thumb. My shoes were gleaming and my officer's greatcoat immaculate. Other officers on the platform, not wearing forage caps, wore hats that looked as if they had been run over by an oily convoy. In contrast, mine was a beacon of rigidity and innocence. I dragged my bags along in the wake of the hungover revellers and tried to find a truck going to RAF West Fen. The men around me, well used to the chaos, began milling around and bleating like sheep. The transport drivers, most of them WAAFs, had seen it all before. A large masculine looking WAAF, the driver of a truck at the front of the queue of vehicles, decided she'd had enough.

"West Fen little lambs this bleedin' way!" she roared as she clapped her arms around her ample bosom in an attempt to get warm.

"Fuckin' hell!" said a sergeant crushed up against me in the crowd. "Little Bo Peep."

As if by magic the crowd began to sort itself out into RAF stations and soon everybody had boarded their respective trucks apart from me. I was doing a very good impression of a little lost lamb with far too many suitcases. I struggled towards the patiently waiting Amazon-like driver from RAF West Fen whilst the occupants of the other trucks looked on with bored amusement. My masculine WAAF driver gave an exaggerated sigh of impatience.

"There's a little black sheep in every fuckin' family but why does it always have to be one of mine?" By now I was getting pissed off with sheep. I began to have a growing suspicion that many people in Lincolnshire had an indecent interest in the ovine. Maybe I should have brought my Wellington boots.

"West Fen, Petal?" Her Geordie accent was now very pronounced.

"Yes, please." I panted with the exertion of hauling my luggage.

She stepped forward and, with a flick of her wrist, my bags flew effortlessly through the air and over the tailboard into the dark interior of the truck, the occupants scattering to avoid the lethal missiles.

"You, my little Petal," grinned the WAAF, "can come up front with me in the warm."

There was a roar of mirth from the occupants of the truck. I stood like an idiot staring at the black hole into which my luggage had so easily flown. Not only that, never before had a WAAF dared call me "Petal". This was not the RAF I was used to. Obviously Lincolnshire had a detrimental effect on the mentality of service personnel. Maybe I could get a nice posting to somewhere civilised - like Surrey.

"Get a bleedin' move on!" The voice came from one of the other trucks.

I pulled my startled thoughts together and climbed quickly up into the cab. It was not much warmer than the station forecourt but at least it cut out the bitterly cold east wind. My driver rubbed furiously at the inside of the windscreen as our warm breath threatened to freeze on the cold glass. She was wearing a pair of huge leather gauntlets and they looked as if she wiped her nose on them as many times as she did oil changes.

"American trucks have heaters," she panted in protest. She gave up on the windscreen and stomped on the clutch. There was a loud grating sound from the gearbox. "They've got friggin' synchromesh gears as well!"

Nevertheless, as spartan as our vehicle seemed, we lurched forward and began to lead a convoy through the narrow, deserted streets of Boston.

It was still dark and beginning to snow again. I'd no idea what Boston looked like in daylight but it held out little promise of improvement from the miserable sight that met my eyes. I glimpsed, in the dismal light from our hooded headlights, shabby shops, a cinema and a deserted marketplace. A large church loomed on our left. It had the tallest vertical tower I had ever seen. It thrust up into the dark, snow-laden sky with an air of defiance.

"'St Botolph's," shouted the WAAF over the roar of the engine. "It's known locally as The Stump."

I was very impressed and tried to show my appreciation of her knowledge in things both ecclesiastical and local.

"Really?" I shouted. "Jolly interesting."

"Reminds me of a big dick," she shouted in return and shattered my illusion that she was not really as bad as I'd first thought. I'd never met a woman like this. All my experience, which I'm afraid to say was not very extensive up to that time, had been with intelligent, demure young ladies. This one was more masculine than some of my male friends at university! In fact when I recalled Rodney Rowbottom, I began to see a little more clearly why I'd felt rather uneasy in his presence. All the WAAFs I'd met up to now had saluted and called me 'sir'. I was only a mere acting pilot officer but my commission still warranted due service respect. I was now confronted with a female who not only made me feel totally inadequate, but who had completely undermined my already shaky confidence as a leader of men. Strewth! If this was an example of the women, what the hell were the men like?

"Aircrew, Petal?" she bawled at me across the cab.

I didn't really want to carry on a conversation with 'Foghorn Fanny' but it seemed churlish to ignore her after she'd shared her cab with me.

"No," I screamed in reply. "Intelligence."

She turned to stare at me and I withered under her unwavering gaze. Just as I was about to grab the wheel in panic, as we were now out of town and the road was bordered each side by huge water-filled dykes, she returned her eyes to the road and yanked us back from the brink of certain death.

I saw a sardonic smile play across her manly face before she replied. "Really?" she howled. "Jolly interesting." The accent was no longer Geordie. It was a bloody good imitation of my own clipped tones. To make matters worse, her face well and truly belied the veracity of her 'Jolly interesting'. She'd won. I felt a complete arsehole and she obviously had no doubts as to the reality of that fact.

I was saved any sort of retort as she braked hard and swung the truck to the left over a small bridge and headed deeper into the wilderness to the west. The other trucks followed our change of course.

I inclined my head to the headlights following. "Surely not all these men are going to West Fen?" I was getting pissed off with screaming.

"Coningsby and Woodhall Spa," she yelled.

The names were familiar to me as neighbouring airfields to RAF West Fen. They were all part of Bomber Command's Five Group and formed just a small clutch of airfields in the county that had become, damned nearly, one huge airfield.

On learning of my posting to West Fen, I'd studied a map of the area and I couldn't believe so many airfields could be so close together. Surely their circuits must overlap? How could they avoid the tragedy of collisions? I was to learn, all too soon, they did collide and not infrequently. Just another statistic in the terrible loss of young aircrew lives in Bomber Command.

My own life seemed in jeopardy as Foghorn Fanny waved the other trucks past and then stamped on the brakes. We slithered to a halt on the edge of a small copse and she seemed oblivious to the thud of bodies hitting the back of the cab and the muffled epithets. She wound down the driver's window and bawled, "SIX SITE!"

This meant nothing to me but then I could just make out a huddle of Nissen huts among the trees. It was obviously one of several domestic sites dispersed well clear of the airfield. It was to protect personnel in the event of enemy air raids but often meant a bloody long walk to the mess and other amenities. I heard men tumbling over the tailboard. They risked their lives night after night and all they had to come back to was a freezing bloody Nissen hut down a muddy track. I began to appreciate that my failing the aircrew medical was not the end of the world. But the shouted and varied threats to my driver from the unfortunates in the rear of the lorry did portend her early demise.

"Bollocks!" she shouted cheerily in reply and wound up the window. She glanced at me and grinned as she let the clutch out with a jerk. There was another crash of bodies from the rear and much hammering of fists on the cab roof.

"Next stop, Fuckup Fen!" she yelled and used both hands on the gear stick to yank the non-synchronised box into another gear. There was a grinding of cogs as she struggled manfully. "There's only four of the bastards - you'd think I could find at least one!" she bawled. Find it she finally did and we lurched on our way to arrive a few minutes later at the main gate to RAF West Fen.

It did nothing to raise my spirits. Yet another Nissen hut beyond the barrier, this time serving as a guardroom. As it was finally getting a little lighter, I could make out the dim shapes of two RAF policemen. I could hear the rear occupants of the lorry debussing into the cold dawn and I made to open the cab door. Foghorn laid a filthy gauntlet on my nice new greatcoat and restrained my reluctant progress.

"Stay here, Petal. I'll fix the snowdrops and give you a ride to the Henry House."

As the others filed past one of the RAF policemen, the other 'snowdrop' walked over to my side of the cab. I wound down the window and had my identity card ready in my hand but before the poor guy could take it from me, Foghorn leaned across.

"Allo, darlin'!" she yelled to the snowdrop. "Give us a snog then!"

I swear the poor guy nearly expired on the spot. I distinctly saw his face turn a ghastly pallor at the sight of Foghorn Fanny. He grabbed my card, gave it a cursory glance and shoved it back through the window.

"Thank you, sir!" he stammered and quickly withdrew to the safety of the guardroom.

Foghorn screamed with laughter. "Doesn't know what he's missin'!"

I'd the distinct impression that the poor chap knew exactly what he was missing and was very grateful of the fact.

The other policeman raised the barrier and waved us on to begin a drive through the most derelict RAF station I'd seen to date. There were few permanent buildings. It was either small Nissen huts or large Nissen huts. From every hut there were plumes of white smoke issuing from metal pipes serving as chimneys. The acrid smell of smoke seemed to permeate the cab of the lorry. There was a dusting of snow on the corrugated surfaces of the huts but where the chimneys emerged there was a wet ring of slush, slowly expanding to drip mournfully down to the ground. Bicycles were everywhere, all chained to any solid structure that could be found. This was obviously the main source of transport and jealously guarded from any predators who had carelessly lost their own bikes. God! It was all so depressing. My first priority would be to get a posting. ASAP!

Foghorn, much to my surprise, braked to a gentle halt outside a clutch of large Nissen huts. They were all joined together to form a larger complex.

"Here we are, Petal - the Henry House."

I didn't want to believe it but I couldn't mistake the tatty sign declaring this was indeed the Officers' Mess. I momentarily forgot myself and actually turned to her in despair.

She saw the pained expression on my face and roared with laughter. "Never mind, Petal. You should see the shithouse we live in. Lap of bleedin' luxury this!"

I looked at this Amazon sitting next to me. She had smudges of grease on her face. Her uniform, the part of it that could be seen under the layers of sweaters and the leather jerkin, was a disaster. Her boots were filthy and I swear her cap badge had an inch of verdigris committing treason by hiding the King's crown. But, for one incredible second, in Foghorn Fanny I saw the quality one needed to survive in this hellhole - a sense of humour. In spite of myself I started to grin. A rueful grin, but at least it was a start. To my dismay the smile on Foghorn's quickly disappeared. She raised her gauntleted hands in mock defence.

"Whoa! Whoa!" she said in a surprisingly quiet voice. "If there is one thing that gets me worried it's when a bloody officer starts to smile after meeting me. What have I done wrong? By this time they're usually having a fit and putting me on so many charges the SWO has to get his big book out to see if anybody can commit those particular offences and still be a member of the human race!"

"Don't worry," I laughed. "You've done everything wrong but I expect you always do. How the hell do you survive?"

"By the skin of my teeth most of the time," she grinned. "Although I reckon my magnetic charm has got something to do with it." She burst out laughing.

"What do they call you?" I asked.

"Do you want my real name or the ones I'm usually given?"

"I think I'd better have your real name - I've had a sheltered upbringing."

"Airwoman Bourne, sir."

I couldn't help showing my surprise at the 'sir'.

She laughed. "Oh, I can do it right when I have to. Anyway, you're the first bloody person who actually asked for my name without clutching a fistful of two-five-twos."

In spite of the laughter, I could see a glimmer of hurt in her eyes. I quickly looked away. It wouldn't be wise to let Bourne know I had seen the chink in her armour.

I jumped down from the cab but she beat me to the back of the truck and was already heaving my bags down to the ground. "Thanks for the lift." I meant it.

"My pleasure, Petal."

She jumped down from the back of the truck. She hesitated and then spoke quietly. "This bloody place looks a right shithole, and it is, but you've got worse to come."

I was puzzled by her remark but decided to keep silent and let her take her time.

She took my silence as a tacit agreement to continue. "You've got a wing commander in charge of your section. Watch him – he's a right bastard. Beware the smile on the face of the tiger, as they say." She looked uncomfortable and turned back to the cab.

"Thanks, Petal," I said.

She grinned as she climbed into the truck. "We'll make a Geordie of you yet, sir!"

The truck roared off into the dawn in a cloud of petrol fumes and grating gears.

I turned and looked at the tatty portals of my new home, sighed and picked up my bags. Might as well get on with it.

I walked into the dim interior and looked around me. On the wall in front of me there were two large squadron crests plus the inevitable notice board. Station Routine Orders, Mess Rules and all the other paraphernalia covered the board. A sign informed mess members the mail rack was down the corridor to the right. The floor was covered with the same dingy brown linoleum that had covered every RAF floor I'd seen to date. There was a bouquet of floor polish and cooked vegetables lingering on the air with more than a hint of stale tobacco smoke. What a bloody dump.

To my right there was a counter of sorts and a door to its rear led to a small office. There was a bell on the counter but I ignored it.

"Anyone at home?" I called.

There was a rustle of paper from the office and a voice called, "Coming."

The door opened and a trim, elderly man with a bald head emerged. He was wiping his mouth with a handkerchief. I'd obviously interrupted his breakfast. He was wearing a pair of dark trousers, white shirt, bow tie and a pair of half-moons perched precariously on the end of his nose. He pushed the handkerchief into his pocket and peered at me over the half-moons.

"Good morning, sir. What can I do for you?"

"Pilot Officer Carver. Just posted in."

"My condolences, sir."

"It's as bad as it looks, huh?"

"Not really, sir. Every station is what you make it. One just has to try a little harder at West Fen."

There was no smile from the little man.

I handed over my papers and he scanned them quickly.

"I see you're posted to the Intelligence Section."

I nodded. "That's right."

"In a way that is fortunate, sir. There's another officer from your section living in the mess and there's a spare bed in his room." He glanced up at me. "Two to a room may not be your ideal but at least it is better than being billeted out on one of the dispersal sites."

"I totally agree with you," I replied with feeling.

He grinned and his whole face lit up like a mischievous gnome. "Well, at least we can already agree on something and you haven't been here more than five minutes. A good start, sir." He riffled through a sheaf of papers secured to a clipboard with a bulldog clip. "Here we are, sir, room thirty-seven. You'll be sharing with Mr Hammond. He's a flying officer and about your age. My name is Bates, sir, and I've already heard the old joke at least a thousand times. Yes, I do have a son and Master Bates is up in Scotland training with the Commandos." He paused and spread his hands to emphasise his slight build. "Fortunately for the Commandos he takes after his mother. I also have a daughter but she's safely ensconced with an elderly aunt in Wales, well away from the menaces posed by young gentlemen such as yourself, sir."

It was well rehearsed and he uttered it all without taking a breath. I got the point.

We were suddenly interrupted by the corridor door crashing back against its stops as a very rotund figure, clad in dressing gown and slippers, burst into the lobby. The apparition had at least three chins and was gasping from exertion and anger.

"Bates!" he cried. "Where the bloody hell is Crawford this morning?"

Bates didn't even look up from his clipboard as he wrote my name into the slot for room thirty-seven.

"It is his day off, sir."

"Bloody day off?" bawled the dressing gown. "The bastard didn't deliver my laundry yesterday. How the hell am I supposed to wear a clean shirt if my bloody batman can't organise my sodding laundry?" He was virtually stamping his foot in rage and his face had become so suffused with blood I began to fear I might soon be tested in my shaky knowledge of first-aid.

"Normally I'd suggest one borrowed a shirt from a friend," replied Bates, his head still down as he stamped and signed my mess card. "But I'm afraid in your case, sir, we've no other gentlemen who can match your degree of corpulence. It will have to be the shirt you wore yesterday."

Three officers, huddled up in their greatcoats, emerged from the other corridor. They stared at the fuming apparition in the dressing gown and pushed out of the doors into the cold morning air. The doors swung to behind them but not before one of the three asked a question of the others.

"Did I just see a Paisley-pattern bell tent in the lobby or was it a dream?"

Mercifully, the closing doors cut off any rejoinder but we heard their roar of laughter.

The subject of their mirth was now a volcano nearing eruption, but I think the

18

humiliation had got to him.

"What a fucking way to run a mess," he blustered. He slammed back through the door and we could hear him stomping furiously back down the corridor to his room.

"Nice chap," I commented, not without a degree of sarcasm.

"I'm pleased you think so, sir," replied Bates. He finally raised his head and his eyes met mine. Neither he nor his eyes were smiling. "Because he's the commanding officer of the Intelligence Section, sir."

I felt my already dismal spirits sink to a new nadir. It must have shown on my face.

"May an old man give you a little advice, sir?"

"Of course, Mr Bates." At this point I was ready for all the help I could get.

"Bullies are invariably cowards, sir. You've to stand up to them or they will walk all over you. The young officer in your section who preceded Mr Hammond appreciated that fact and he stood his ground. He didn't allow that rather unpleasant gentleman, your CO, to demoralise him."

"He was posted on to greater things?" I suggested with a smile.

Bates avoided my eyes and busied himself with some papers on the counter. "Actually, no, sir, he was posted to Reykjavik." He added lamely. "I do believe that is in Iceland."

"Oh, well," I answered glumly, "it can't be worse than this damned place."

Bates brightened. "Ah, but it is, sir. Here, you're not just seeing bad weather, you're also seeing the worst part of the county of Lincolnshire." He leaned across the counter. "I live only a short distance from here, but it is as if I live in a different county. I live in the small town of Spilsby. Not a lot of entertainment, I grant you, but the scenery is totally different. Rolling hills, forests and even the odd thatched cottage." He paused and then stood back and folded his arms across his chest. His chin rose slightly and his eyes wrinkled in a quizzical expression.

"How many famous Belgians can you name, sir?" he asked.

I grinned and for the life of me, I couldn't think of one. "None, I'm afraid," I eventually conceded.

"Ah, but how about the famous people of Lincolnshire?"

I pondered for a few moments and then inspiration struck. "Sir Isaac Newton," I announced proudly.

"Well done, sir," he laughed. "But don't forget Sir John Franklin, Alfred Lord Tennyson and the naturalist Sir Joseph Banks, to name but a few. You must get up into the Wolds and see Tennyson's birthplace. It's beautiful and the countryside will knock you for six. Please don't judge Lincolnshire by the starkness of the fens."

"I'll take your advice," I grinned. "Mind you, I think I'll reserve judgement on the bit about standing up to old 'dressing gown'. Somehow even this place seems preferable to ice and volcanoes."

The mess was beginning to come alive and officers in every form of dress one could imagine were heading out into the cold morning. All seemed to be talking at once and more than one called out,

"Morning, Batey!"

Bates acknowledged them all with a smile and a wave. I was getting the feeling that this little man was very popular and it would pay me to stay on his good side.

"Right, sir. If you take the corridor to the left you'll find your room. If Mr Hammond is still in bed, do give him a kick up the backside or he'll be late for work."

I picked up my bags. "Thank you, Mr Bates. You've been a great help."

"My pleasure, sir. Oh, by the way...." He stooped under the counter and came out with a sheet of foolscap paper. "This is a map of the station to help you find your way around when you do your arrival procedure. Bit limited on information but we do have to think of security."

"Thank you," I replied and headed off towards my room and, for the first time in my life, a roommate!

I staggered down the corridor muttering apologies to all and sundry as everybody seemed to be heading in the opposite direction to their places of work and the narrow corridor was not conducive to two-way traffic. The wooden floor echoed and thudded to the sound of hurried footfalls and I dreaded to think what it was going to be like trying to sleep after doing a night shift. At last - room thirty-seven.

I let my bags clatter to the floor and knocked. There was no response. I knocked again and this time I thought I detected a muffled reply. I slowly opened the door and peered into the gloom. I could just make out a couple of beds and a sparse collection of furniture. One of the beds was occupied and the occupant obviously didn't take kindly to being woken from his slumbers. There was a strong smell of beer.

"Piss off, Thomas. I've a hangover and I'm not on duty until this evening."

It seemed I'd been mistaken for a mess attendant or batman.

"According to Bates, you're on duty and I've to kick you up the arse to make sure you get there on time."

The head came slowly out from under the bedclothes and the man with whom I was to share my domestic life peered at me across the darkened room. I stepped over to the window and drew the curtains which apparently was a bad move for a man with a hangover.

"For crying out loud, who the fuck are you and where is Thomas?"

"The answer to your first question is Sam Carver, just posted in. I'm afraid you'll have to give me a clue for me to answer the second question. You must be Hammond."

Hammond sat up and rubbed his eyes. "I thought having a room to myself was too good to be true. Bloody place is so overcrowded it's like living in a madhouse." He pointed to the other bed. "That is obviously yours and I'll remove my stuff from your locker later."

He stretched and swung his legs out of bed. He sat there scratching and yawning. Suddenly, he sat bolt upright. "Christ! Did you say Bates said I was on duty this morning?"

"He certainly did."

Hammond leapt to his feet and started scrabbling into his clothes, which were strewn all over the room. "Shit, if he says I'm on duty I must be. The old bugger is never wrong and if I'm late again that bastard Janner will have my guts for garters."

I started dragging my bags into the room and I called to him over my shoulder.

"I really hate to piss on your parade but I've just met Janner and he was in a foul temper about his laundry."

"Oh no!" Hammond howled. "Out of my bloody way, Cleaver, or whatever your name is - I am a man in a hurry. See you later."

I'd no chance to reply. He was already far away in his quest to reach the Intelligence Section before the dreaded Janner. I looked at the debris-strewn room and tried to find a space in which I could start to unpack, but gave it up as a bad job.

I decided to have a quick wash and shave before beginning my trudge around the station, starting with the General Office. The sooner I started my 'Arrivals' procedure the better, although I felt I'd be much happier with a 'Departures' procedure. I already hated RAF West Fen and I'd only been in the bloody place for a few minutes. Things didn't bode well for the future.

A Merlin engine crackled into life somewhere out on the airfield and I moved to the window, but all I could see was yet another bloody Nissen hut. The snow had stopped and a weak, watery sun was trying to break through the thinning cloud. What a depressing scene, but it summed up my mood. I was thoroughly pissed off!

CHAPTER TWO

Hammond's rapid departure had left me with nowhere to store my kit, so I dumped my bags in the corner of the room. After a quick wash and shave, to remove the LNER soot and a twenty-four hour stubble, I left the mess and began my Arrivals procedure.

Several signatures later, one of which was for the ubiquitous RAF bicycle, I arrived at yet another collection of Nissen huts. These huts formed the Operations Centre and the Intelligence Section was part of that complex. I propped my bike up against a telephone pole that seemed to attract every cable ever invented and entered the building. The inevitable brown linoleum floor and green and cream walls of the corridor finally led me to a tatty, green-painted door. According to the sign on the door, this was the Intelligence Section. It was hardly what I'd expected. Okay, there was a war on, but everything looked so shoddy and temporary. Of course, my service here might be very short-lived. I wasn't even a fully-fledged pilot officer. Mine was an 'acting' rank and I'd been posted in as a 'supernumerary'. I'd have just three months to learn and prove I could do the job. At the end of that period, if I were successful, my rank would become substantive. It would make damn all difference to my paltry ten shillings and sixpence a day but at least I'd be regarded as a productive member of the team. I knew that eventually I'd have to brief and debrief aircrews on their operations. How would seasoned aircrew look upon a penguin in the eyrie like myself? It was a sobering thought. A thought that was abruptly interrupted as the tatty green door was opened sharply from within and I was face to face with the most beautiful girl I'd ever seen in my life.

She jumped back with a delightful little exclamation of surprise. "Good Lord! You scared the life out of me."

I felt as if I'd been caught peeping through the keyhole. "Sorry!" I said quickly. I was just making sure I'd got the right place." I saw the single ring on her sleeve denoting a WAAF section officer and added, "I've just been posted in from Harrow."

"You must be Carver," she grinned. "We've been expecting you." She opened the door wider and beckoned me through. "Come in and meet the gang - well, at least some of them."

Her hand lightly touched my arm as she ushered me into the room and momentarily I felt an inordinate sense of pleasure at her touch. I glanced at her and saw she was regarding me with a quizzical air. She was no doubt wondering what the heck I was going to be like as a trainee intelligence officer. I secretly hoped she was also quietly considering what I'd be like as a friend.

The room was warm and large and as I looked around me, I could see the other occupants of the room giving me a secretive once-over. Folding tables were all over the place. Some in isolation, others pushed together to make large surfaces on which to roll out maps and charts. Folding wooden chairs also littered the room but there was an area off to one side where a number of battered easy chairs formed a hollow square. That had to be the rest area. It seemed space was at a premium here at West

Fen and when one added the map cabinets, there was not a lot of room to spare.

Dominating the whole room, on the longest wall, was a massive map. On the left of the map was eastern England, studded with multi-coloured pins and to the right, across the North Sea, was the whole of Europe. Coloured acetates covered areas denoting heavy enemy flak concentrations, nightfighter airfields and the hundreds of other hazards that faced the bomber crews. A young airwoman was standing on a small stepladder making amendments to the map and two airmen were sorting through a pile of maps on top of one of the cabinets. They barely glanced at me. We would get to know each other soon enough.

The section officer pointed to a row of greatcoats and service hats already hung on hooks behind the door. "Sling your things over there and take a pew in one of those old chairs. I'll rustle you up a cup of tea." She opened a door marked 'Watchkeepers'. "Sarge," she called. "Would you let the squadron leader know our new officer has arrived and ask when he will be free to meet him?"

She closed the door and looked up at the airwoman on the stepladder by the operations map.

" Roberts, would you make a cuppa for Pilot Officer Carver, please?"

"Yes, ma'am. Sugar and milk, sir?" she asked as she climbed down from the steps.

"Thank you," I nodded.

I turned to the section officer. "I'm impressed by your hospitality but I'm afraid I still don't know your name."

She grinned and held out a hand. "Natalie Cowen and your first name is...?"

"Sam," I replied as I returned her firm handshake.

"Have a seat, Sam." She waved to one of the easy chairs and as I dropped rather ungainly into its battered shape, she perched on the arm of the chair opposite. She really was beautiful. Her fair hair was gathered tightly into a bun and it seemed to accentuate her high cheekbones and slim face. She wore no make-up and didn't need it. Her blue eyes and natural rose-coloured lips were all she needed. Even the shapeless WAAF uniform couldn't disguise her perfect figure and, as she sat there, she had neatly crossed her ankles. It was the pose of a professional model but her smile, as she watched my obvious visual assessment, was perfectly genuine.

"Do I pass the inspection?"

"I'm sorry," I grinned with embarrassment. "The first female I met on my arrival rather coloured my expectations as to what might follow. Not only that, she called me 'Petal', would you believe?"

There was a muffled snort from one of the two airmen and Natalie glanced over at him.

"Hoare, you shouldn't be listening," she chided, but there was a smile on her face.

Hoare, a leading aircraftsman, looked up from his map. "Sorry, ma'am, but it had to be Rhoda Bourne." He turned his gaze to me. "We call her Blad the Impaler."

The other airman joined in the discussion. "Actually, I've heard she eats her young."

The surprise came not from what the second airman said but from the way he spoke. He'd a deep, cultured 'brandy and cigar' sort of voice and was a complete contrast to Hoare's cockney accent.

I looked at Natalie in surprise as she gave a slight warning shake of her head and opened her mouth to reply, but I got there first.

"Which of you two would be prepared to make those comments to her face?"

23

Hoare didn't hesitate. "Nobody on this station is that suicidal, sir. Try that and she'd rip your arms off and thrash you to death with the soggy ends."

I'd not looked round but the silence from his friend spoke volumes. He was more astute and had recognised the slight edge to my voice as I'd posed the question. I couldn't see him but I knew he was watching me carefully.

Natalie sensed the slight tension and decided to put a prompt end to the discussion.

"Back to work, the pair of you."

I heard the rustle as they resumed their task. It was strange. I'd not even looked at Hoare's colleague but I sensed he and I were not going to get along. I was given no time to ponder on my inner feelings as the young WAAF re-entered with a tray and two large mugs of tea.

"I thought you might like one, ma'am," she said to Natalie as she put the mugs on the table.

"Thank you, Roberts." Natalie smiled her thanks.

The WAAF turned to go but then remembered something. "Oh, by the way, ma'am, Sarge says the squadron leader will see the pilot officer in about fifteen minutes."

Natalie nodded her thanks and Roberts headed off back to the huge map.

"What sort of chap is the squadron leader?" I asked Natalie.

There was no hesitation. "He's a really nice man. He's firm but fair and you always know where you stand with him. His name is Jake Houseman and I don't think there is a better intelligence officer in the command. The aircrew respect him and therefore don't try to give him a hard time."

"How do you mean?"

"Well, you know…when they land from an op, it is usually early morning and they are dog tired. At the debrief, the last thing they want is people like us asking them a seemingly endless list of questions. All they want to do is get their breakfast and then off to bed. So, sometimes they will give you some rather strange positional references when you ask them where a certain fighter combat took place or where they saw an aircraft going down in flames." She grinned at me. "You'd better make sure you've the night's target entry and exit routes firmly fixed in your mind before you start the debrief. Or, later, when you come to collate all the information, you're likely to find a navigator has given you a position in the middle of Outer Mongolia!"

I sighed. "I'm dreading doing my first briefing. A sprog officer, giving those experienced aircrew blokes a lecture on what to bomb, what to avoid, how to get there and back and all the rest of the gen. How the hell do you do it?"

"I don't know. I've yet to give a briefing," Natalie said quietly.

I looked at her in amazement. "What? How long have you been here?"

"Seven months."

"Why no briefing? Surely you know the job pretty well by now?"

Natalie lifted her head sharply. At first it seemed she was tossing an imaginary curl from her eyes but I realised she was angry. She glanced quickly at the others in the room and lowered her voice. "The wing commander doesn't think a woman has a sufficient air of authority to lead a briefing."

"Bollocks!" I said with feeling.

"You think that, the squadron leader thinks that, but Wing Commander Janner thinks otherwise. He's of the opinion that a woman's place is in the home - not in the services."

"How the hell does he think we'd manage without all the women? For Christ's sake, we'd never find sufficient manpower without the women - even if that does sound a bit Irish." I finished lamely and grinned to hide my embarrassment.

Natalie was about to answer but was abruptly interrupted as the outer door crashed open and Wing Commander Janner heaved his bulk into the room. It was pretty obvious he was not in a good mood. Both Natalie and myself made to stand but before we could make it to our feet, Janner had taken in our half-drunk mugs of tea and put his own interpretation on our little tête-à-tête. He stormed off in the direction of his office, which meant he had to pass through the watchkeepers' room. He yanked furiously at his snow-speckled greatcoat.

"Section Officer Cowen." He spat the words over his shoulder. "My office - now!" The watchkeepers' door crashed shut behind him and there was total silence in his wake. The airmen and Roberts studiously kept their heads down and tried to pretend they had not heard a word.

For my part, I was bloody furious. How the hell could he speak to another officer in that manner in front of subordinates? I was about to make my feelings known but Natalie, obviously with more sense than myself, raised a warning hand and gave me a tight little smile.

"It's okay. We get quite used to it in this place. See you in a few minutes."

I watched her leave the room and my initial reaction was to run after her and sort the fat bastard out but that would only result in a court-martial and other unpleasant things. Hitler had just been demoted to second place on my shit list.

I ambled over to the operations map and, for a few minutes, tried to make sense of what I saw there, but all I could think about was what sort of ordeal Natalie was being subjected to by 'The Lump'. I'd decided 'The Lump' was a good name for Janner, or even 'The Blob'. Hardly the musings of an educated man but there was something juvenile about the RAF and it was bringing out the worst in me. Before I could invent any more childish names for Janner, Natalie put her head round the door. She looked angry and flushed but she smiled and nodded in the direction from which she had just come.

"Your turn," she said quietly.

As I was about to speak she put a finger to her lips and laid a gentle hand on my arm as I made to pass her in the narrow doorway. "Don't be a fool, Sam. Just let him do his big boss act and keep your mouth shut. Okay?"

I nodded. "I may need fifty stitches in my tongue but I'll keep biting on it until I'm safely back out here."

She squeezed my arm. "Good man!"

I put my cap on and straightened my tie. "Will I do?"

"Straight out of Officer Training Unit," she grinned.

"Christ! That bad?"

"Just get a move on, you silly clot." She pushed me towards Janner's office.

I seemed to be getting on great with Natalie and, as that was of paramount importance to my morale, Janner paled into insignificance. I reached his door and knocked. At first there was no response but finally Janner's voice boomed from within.

"Turn the bloody knob and the door will open."

I wondered what the bastard would have said if I had not knocked and just walked straight in. As I reached for the knob, a door further down the corridor opened and a tall, grey-haired squadron leader quickly emerged and raised a hand in my direction.

"Hold it, Carver," he said. "I'd like to see the wingco for a sec."

In the time it took him to reach me and enter Janner's office, I felt he'd read my character and probed my very soul with just a glance. I don't think I'd ever met a man like him. His face was pale and strained but he had a presence, which without any effort on his part demanded instant respect. He wore a pilot's brevet on his chest and a row of medal ribbons but, in spite of the grey hair, I estimated his age to be no more than early thirties. Life had not been easy for Squadron Leader Jake Houseman.

I stood back as he entered the office, closing the door quietly behind him. I waited and strained to hear what was being said behind the closed door but all I could hear was Houseman's low voice. I could detect urgency in the tone. There was a short, sharp exclamation from Janner and then I heard footsteps approaching the door. It opened wide as Houseman held it open for me.

"Come in, Carver."

I marched in and came to a halt in front of Janner's desk. He looked like a large toad wearing an officer's service cap. I was pleased to see his shirt collar looked distinctly grubby.

I saluted. "Pilot Officer Carver, sir. I've just been posted in from Harrow."

Houseman positioned himself to the right of Janner's chair. I knew he was watching me carefully.

Janner scrutinized me from under his heavy eyelids. I now thought the toad had changed into a lizard. He'd distinct reptilian features. When he finally spoke, much to my surprise his tone was quiet and reasonable.

"Tell me, Carver, what do you think your role will be here at West Fen?"

I shot a quick glance at Houseman but he regarded me impassively. I switched my gaze back to Janner. "Well, sir, as I've only one week of experience in intelligence to date, initially I'll be of little productive use to the section. Having said that, I hope I can pick up the job quickly and soon be a useful member of the team. I'm looking forward to the new challenge."

There was no beating Pilot Officer Carver for bullshit. I sneaked another glance at Houseman. He seemed carved from marble and his eyes were still locked on me. Janner spoke and I switched my eyes back to him.

"Very laudable, Carver." He paused for effect but it was all a bit 'hammy' and he signalled his next move well in advance. "So you think that all this expertise you so desire to learn will just happen?"

"Certainly not, sir. I'm under no illusion as to the task ahead of me." Bullshit? This was 'creepy-crawly' at its best.

Then it came and it was like something out of a bad movie. Janner crashed his fist down on the desk but as he had hammed it so badly, I knew it was coming and so I didn't even flinch. This seemed to infuriate him. "So you think lolling around drinking tea with the WAAFs is the perfect way to start off in your new posting?" His voice was deafening.

I dropped my chin and fixed the fat bastard with a stare that would have had Goebbels running for cover in the Reichstag. But, just as I was about to open my mouth, out of the corner of my eye I saw a flicker of movement from Houseman's right hand.

I took the hint and, after a deep breath, I said meekly. "No, sir."

Janner was now in full swing. "Let me tell you something, Acting Pilot Officer Carver." The stress was on the word 'acting'. "You're so bloody supernumerary as to be actually unwanted. Whoever decided to post you here was a perfect ass. We're fully established and have no need for another bloody university educated amateur. I suggest you don't unpack your bags because I'll be on to Records Office today and insist they find somewhere you can be of more use, although my personal feeling is that no such place exists. I'll make no bones about it, Carver, I don't like you. I think you're arrogant and I think you expect to stroll through this war in your own sweet way. Well, you're not going to do that in my section. Is that clear?"

I couldn't trust myself to answer immediately. My tongue was firmly clamped between my teeth and it was hurting. Again I saw the flicker of Houseman's hand and remembered my promise to Natalie. I opened my teeth and the blood began flowing back into my tongue. I decided to try a strategy of my own. He wanted arrogance? I'd give him bloody arrogance!

"Perfectly clear, sir," I replied languidly and with a lightness of tone that belied my inner rage. "You must do whatever you judge to be correct under the circumstances. One can ask for no more than that."

There was a stunned silence and I could see a flurry of warnings from Houseman's right hand but I kept my gaze firmly on Janner.

"Don't you patronise me, Carver." He hissed like a snake.

I'd hit the target and was beginning to enjoy myself. "I didn't dream of such an indiscretion, sir. Although, if I may say so, I did feel you were a little harsh over what was simply a welcoming cup of tea after a difficult night of travel. I thought Section Officer Cowen's actions were merely that expected of an officer and a lady."

Janner's huge bulk seemed to deflate and then reflate.

Houseman suddenly turned to look at the miserable scene out of the window and thrust his hands deep into his trouser pockets. I was on my own.

"So, Pilot Officer Carver," Janner was spitting with rage. "You think I'm harsh. You also feel I'm unreasonable, do you?"

"A little, sir." I used a conciliatory tone. "But of course, perfectly understandable under the circumstances."

There was the longest silence yet. Janner's face seemed to suffuse with blood. "What circumstances?" he finally ground out.

"The fact you've been working all night and you're extremely tired, sir. I'm sure fatigue can affect the judgement of even the most senior of officers." I was into my stride. In the silence I glanced up as Houseman turned from the window to once more fix me with his unwavering stare. But this time his eyebrows had a slightly quizzical expression and I could see something else in his face - humour maybe?

As for Janner, this was the point where he should have used his authority to grind me into the office carpet or, in this case, linoleum. But I reckoned I was a pretty good judge of character and he'd already missed the point where he could have made his move. He was a bully and, like most bullies, he only picked on subordinates. He was now out of his depth. So was I but I was determined to finish what he had started.

Janner leaned forward across the desk, his words dripping sarcasm. "I seem to recall, Carver, from your records, which actually managed to get here before you, there was no mention of you reading psychology at university."

"Nothing so grand, sir. I've a classical degree but my observations are based on common sense. At Harrow they told us we would spend so much time looking for the unusual we must not miss the obvious." I stopped and feigned an eagerness to explain by leaning forward slightly towards Janner.

Houseman's eyebrows had moved up another millimetre.

Somebody had to break the silence so I rushed on with my revelation. "The obvious being, sir, the state of the collar of your shirt. No self-respecting senior officer would come on duty with a collar as filthy as yours. Hence, my deduction is to the effect that you've obviously been on duty all night."

I beamed at them both as if delighted with my powers of deduction but inside I was quaking. This whole bloody thing had gone too far and I was unsure how it was going to end. My hatred of Janner had led me into a trap of my own making. 'Big Gob' Carver strikes again.

To try and describe Janner's reaction defied words. His face had drained of all the blood that had rushed there earlier. His hands were clenched into fists on the desk. I noticed that his spectacles case was protruding slightly from the side pocket of his uniform jacket. The case was wedged under the arm of his chair. If he launched himself to his feet now he was going to throw the chair backward through the window.

Houseman rescued both of us. "Pilot Officer Carver," he said quietly. "My office is just up the corridor to the right. It is clearly signed. Go there and wait outside for me...now!"

"Yes, sir."

I saluted, about turned and left the office. I damned nearly collapsed against the wall of the corridor but I breathed deeply and walked down to the door of Houseman's office. I was now a marked man and it was entirely my own bloody fault. I knew what service life was all about by now. I should have listened to Natalie and to hell with my stupid bloody pride. Good start, Carver. Good start!

A stockily built sergeant entered the corridor and looked at me in surprise. He walked up and peered through the open door into Houseman's office.

"Are you still waiting to see the squadron leader, sir?"

"Yes, Sarge. The wing commander wanted to see me first. The squadron leader asked me to wait for him here."

There was an awkward silence as we tried not to notice Janner's raised voice as he raged at Houseman in the office up the corridor.

The sergeant gave me an embarrassed glance. "Right, sir, I'll leave you to it." He stole another quick glance up the corridor in the direction of the raised voices and turned to go but then put out his hand. "Welcome to West Fen, sir. I'm Sergeant Powell. I run the admin side of things in this section. Any time you need help just give me a shout."

I returned his firm handshake. "Thanks, Sarge." I nodded down the corridor. "I may need all the help I can get."

He grinned and shook his head. "The impossible I can achieve, sir. Miracles are another thing entirely and that sounds like somebody is in need of a miracle. Best of luck, sir."

He walked away just as Janner's door opened and Houseman emerged. The tall squadron leader walked briskly towards me and nodded impatiently towards his own office.

"In!" he said shortly.

It was pretty obvious from his expression that this was not going to be a friendly little officer-to-officer chat. I was in deep shit and it was going to take a big shovelful of luck to come out smelling of roses. I stood to attention in front of his desk as he sat in the chair. He sat up straight and fixed me with a stare that passed through me and burned a hole in the wall behind me.

"That," he said finally, "was the most stupid piece of bravado I've ever witnessed. So you think you scored points, do you?"

"I didn't enjoy the exchange, if that is what you mean, sir."

"Of course you fucking well enjoyed it." He spat the words in frustration at my stalling. "You're either so arrogant as to be impervious to all the crap around you, or you're innocent to the point of full-blown stupidity. What the hell did you think you were doing in there? The wing commander has a reputation for intolerance, which, even at the best of times, is difficult to accept. But your life, from this moment on, will be misery. He's not a man to 'forgive and forget' and you just made him look a complete arsehole."

I'd been staring over his head but the tone of his voice made me look down at him in surprise. I couldn't believe my eyes - he was grinning from ear to ear and some of the tension seemed to have drained out of him. He waved an arm vaguely at an empty chair and slumped back in his own.

"For goodness sake, take your bloody hat off and pull up a chair. You and I've a lot to talk about if you're going to remain at West Fen - and don't tell me you want to leave because I'll squash all orders to that effect."

I pulled the chair over to the front of his desk and sat down. "I'm sorry I was a bit of a twit in there, sir. I'm afraid I let my pride get the better of me."

He grinned. "Not much good apologising to me. I can't do much to save you from his revenge and, believe me, he'll try to exact his revenge so you'd better watch your back. Anyway, don't be so bloody hypocritical - you meant every word of it, didn't you?"

"I'm afraid I did, sir."

"Good man. I like a chap who believes in his own rhetoric, even if it does drop him in the mire. Where are you from?"

The change of tack took me by surprise. "Brighton, sir. Well, Patcham actually."

"How did you end up in intelligence?"

"I failed the aircrew medical and they seem to think there's a niche for me in this branch. Actually, what I've seen of it so far, which is only one week at Harrow, I'm looking forward to getting started. Having already had a quick word with Section Officer Cowen, the only aspects I'm dreading are the briefings. I'll feel like a cuckoo in the nest."

Houseman regarded me seriously. "Don't underrate yourself just because you haven't got a brevet on your uniform. If it's experience you're worried about, forget it. Too few of the aircrew lads live long enough to become experienced in anything other than sheer bloody fear. If you let them they'll give you a hard time, but do your job properly and they'll respect you. They rely on us to help keep them informed on what they can expect to have thrown at them by the Jerries. We do our best to keep updating all the latest info on flak concentrations, new radar, new weapons and tactics. I personally think it very important for them to be given a thorough profile of the target. Early in this war, we were often sent off to targets without being told the reason for going there. It's nice to know that you're putting your life on the line for something worthwhile, not just a pin in a map."

"How long have you been flying a desk, sir?" I asked.

"Too bloody long," he replied grimly. "But at least this job is interesting and very rewarding at times." He shuffled some papers on his desk." I'll team you up with Section Officer Cowen for the time being. I feel that putting you with Flying Officer Hammond would be a bad mistake. He's rather like you but I'm afraid to say, after watching your little session with the wing commander, I feel he does not have your mental gifts. The end result would be the pair of you forever in the shit and you having to expend all your energies getting both yourself and Hammond out of it."

"It seems I'm to share a room with him in the mess," I said carefully, watching his reaction.

Houseman shrugged. "No problems there. Just don't be led astray. He's a bright lad but the light of understanding has a slow wick." He stood up and stretched. I took the hint. The interview was over.

"The first things to get to grips with are the security procedures here in the section, then I want you to spend a little time over at the station Photo Section. We work closely with the photographers. We like to get target photos back here as quickly as possible after a raid for assessment by the photographic interpreters. The crews can always see the results of their bombing before they go out on the next raid. We run an unofficial competition and the crew that achieves the best bombing results get their target photo pinned up in the intelligence library for all to see. Speaking of the library, I think that could be your secondary duty. Once you know the job I'll put you in charge of keeping the library up to date. Aircrews spend a lot of time in there. Anything to give them an edge over Jerry."

The last words were spoken quietly, as if to himself. He seemed to pull his thoughts back to the present. "Right," he resumed briskly. "Nip out and see Sergeant Powell and he'll get you sorted out with all the necessary admin for your arrival chit plus clue you in on section security." He held out his hand. "Welcome to West Fen."

"Thank you, sir." I shook his hand and for the first time I could feel the tension in Houseman. It was palpable. He sensed my surprise and quickly withdrew his hand. I turned to go but just as I opened the door he spoke again.

"Carver, just two things before you go."

"Yes, sir?"

"Firstly, whatever happens between you and the wing commander is between the two of you. He's my commanding officer too and you know how the service works on such things. No matter what my feelings may be I must back my commanding officer so you'll get no special favours. I feel he's misjudged you but that was your own damned fault. It's up to you to prove him wrong, but I feel you may well be on a loser there." He ran a hand through his grey hair. "Secondly, you don't have to feel like a knight in shining armour where Section Officer Cowen is concerned. She's a very resourceful girl and can handle herself in the most trying of situations. She doesn't need your help. In fact if you display an alliance to her causes, you'll make life very difficult for her too. Is that clear?"

"Perfectly, sir."

"Good man." His face lit up in another of those boyish grins. "I'll let you buy me a beer in the mess this evening."

"It'll be my pleasure, sir."

He laughed. "You don't know how much I can drink! Away with you or you'll still be a supernumerary when this bloody war ends." He was already at work on some files before I'd closed the door. I liked Houseman.

I spent the next hour in the company of Sergeant Powell. He guided me through the shift system as worked in the section and made sure I was fully conversant with section security. He introduced me to the two watchkeepers on duty - WAAF Sergeants Trudi Collins and Ann Carter. They and other watchkeepers were responsible for manning the switchboard twenty-four hours a day, ready for the latest ops orders from Group HQ. These orders could change at a moment's notice and last minute changes of targets and take-off times could have the groundcrews sweating to change fuel and bomb loads to meet the new ops order.

Sometimes the crews would be in the aircraft with engines running and about to taxi when an operation would be scrubbed. That was the cruellest scrub of all. Seven men in each aircraft, wound up to face the horrors of the night, only to be told the raid was off and they had to face the preparation and waiting all over again. For some it was a sheer relief but to others it was a cruel disappointment. They just wanted to get their thirty trips over and done with as soon as possible. The longer it took, the worse the waiting became.

Natalie had left the section before I emerged from Houseman's office and when I asked Sergeant Powell about Hammond, he told me my new roommate was over at the Photo Section picking up some target reprints for the files. So, having nothing better to do and wanting to get the damned chore over, I cycled around the station and collected all the remaining signatures on my arrival chit. I finally handed it in at the General Office and I was now officially on the strength of RAF West Fen.

In spite of what old Bates had told me I was pretty sure I was not going to like Lincolnshire. Not only that, I felt sure that Janner was going to make sure I hated more than Lincolnshire. The future didn't look rosy.

CHAPTER THREE

My feet hardly touched the ground during the following week. Houseman didn't assign me to any particular shift, he simply made sure I was available at all times. He intended me to learn the job as quickly as possible and sleep would not be a priority until I could do the job standing on my head.

In spite of Houseman's determination to keep us apart, I found myself understudying Steve Hammond on flak and searchlight concentrations. We'd first evaluate all the latest reports from the Photographic Reconnaissance Unit and then add in our own aircrews' visual reports from the debriefings. We'd access to other reports that obviously came from inside enemy territory but of course we could only guess as to who might be sending those. We then collated all the information in order to update the intelligence maps and the main briefing room board. I was also given more and more responsibility for updating data and information sheets available to the crews in the Intelligence Library.

I saw a lot of Natalie during this period but we'd no chance to meet socially. I'd no free time and what little time I had I spent in bed, desperately trying to catch up on lost sleep.

Natalie's intelligence speciality seemed to be target decoys, dummies, smoke screens and POW camps. The Germans were past masters at the art of camouflage and had set up decoy sites as large as a city. When our bombers neared the target, the Germans would start huge fires and use pyrotechnics to simulate the dropping of target indicators. They would round that off with ground-triggered exploding bombs and throw up plenty of searchlights to help in the deception. In the early years of the war they were very successful and the combination of their success and our poor navigation systems ensured that many of our bombers wasted their bomb loads on dummy sites and crews sacrificed their lives bombing waste ground. Towards the end of 1941, Bomber Command received its first trial GEE sets. This was a navigation aid only, but at least the crews could, if high enough, get a decent navigation fix even when deep inside Germany. They could then correct for variations in the strength and direction of the winds and drop the bombs with more accuracy. The first real success using GEE had been a raid on Cologne early in March of 1942 and now all of West Fen's Lancasters had GEE. Eventually we were to get a new navigation and bombing system called OBOE, but that was still on trial.

Also, every aircraft now carried an F24 camera to record the aiming point and the fall of bombs of each individual aircraft. It was unpopular with the crews because it meant they had to fly straight and level after releasing their bombs until the photoflash bombs exploded over the target. We, along with the Pis, would interpret these photos. A photographer was always present in the debriefing room when the crews returned and he'd take the film magazine from each bomb aimer and take it away for processing. Those photos were soon in our section for us to study and add our findings to the station's report for Command HQ.

The West Fen squadrons carried out two raids during my first week. We'd actually been briefed for four operations, only to have two scrubbed due to lousy weather. We were lucky that week. On the two raids the squadrons did fly, all our crews returned safely.

Houseman led all the briefings and he was good at the job. He knew what operations were like and, as a result, he'd a special rapport with the crews. The medal ribbons on his chest told them that he'd done his bit. Not once did I see him consult his notes. He knew the target routes, the hazards and the target information off by heart. He always stood well to one side of the huge map and used the pointer to good effect. There were no cries of 'Let the dog see the rabbit!' - the cry often heard when others did their section of the briefing and stood in front of the map, hiding it from the crews. He answered all questions quietly, confidently and concisely. The crews knew they were getting the best information to help them survive the hazards that faced them and they needed all the help they could get.

My intensive training during that first week meant I got to meet all the other members of the team. We were nineteen in all, plus we had Flight Lieutenant Max Shearing as our resident photographic interpreter. He was a tall, schoolmasterly young man with thin-framed spectacles. He reminded me of a secretary bird with his sharp features and quick movements but he was to become a great help to me in the weeks ahead.

Houseman went out of his way to keep me well away from Janner but inevitably our paths would cross and he'd go out of his way to remind me that he intended to have me posted at the first available opportunity. Twice, with no justification whatsoever, he criticised my work in front of the others, but both times Houseman caught my eye and I bit my tongue. I welcomed criticism from Houseman as it was always fair and constructive. From Janner, who seemed to do nothing around the section, I found it galling. Janner's whole day seemed to be spent making calls to Command HQ or trying to 'bump' into the station commander. His calls to Command were usually with reference to ideas he had plagiarised from the real workers on the team. His whole reason for existence, or so it seemed to me, was self-enhancement at the expense of the real experts. He was so thick-skinned he could't see the ridicule and contempt in which he was held.

The end of my second week at West Fen coincided with Christmas, although it made little difference to those of us in Five Group. Both our squadrons operated on the twenty-third and landed in the early hours of Christmas Eve. It seemed the AOC, Bomber Harris, was determined to deprive the Jerries of any chance to recharge their batteries. In spite of bad weather there were no signals from Command for a Christmas Day stand-down. Not a popular state of affairs to be sure!

Lunchtime on Christmas Day found Steve, Max and myself carrying out the annual duty of all officers at that festive time - serving Christmas lunch to the airmen and airwomen in the Airmen's Mess. It went pretty well really, with lots of good-natured banter. To my surprise, Foghorn Fanny was not there and I confess to a certain relief. We'd just served pudding when the tannoy crackled into life.

"Stand by for broadcast. All crews to report to briefing at fifteen hundred hours. All crews to briefing at fifteen hundred hours. End of broadcast."

Hundreds of voices roared their protest. Many of the groundcrews had just come in from frozen aircraft dispersals and now faced the task of going back out there. I wondered about those who'd missed their Christmas lunch - I guessed there must be a special session for them. They certainly wouldn't get back to the mess for some hours if there were an operation.

Intelligence would now know the target and aircraft would have to be refuelled and bombed up. I didn't envy the groundcrews but they seemed resigned to their lot as their chatter and laughter in no way decreased in volume or content. Already, some were washing their knives, forks and spoons in the steaming hot water trough just inside the mess hallway and dragging on their cold weather gear. Christmas Day or not, it was life as usual for the groundcrews.

We finished serving pud and ditched our paper hats. It was time to get back to the section.

As we rushed in, Houseman greeted us with a grin. "Ho! Ho! Ho! Happy Christmas and all that."

"With the greatest of respect, sir...bollocks!" Max was the only one who could get away with that.

Natalie's voice called out from somewhere behind a map cabinet. "Thank you, Max - just remember there are ladies in the room."

She popped her head up over the cabinet. Her hair had come loose from its bun and her face was flushed with the effort of whatever she had been struggling to do. I thought she looked beautiful and I knew there was no doubt about it - I was in love. At least I think it was love, although we'd drunk a few beers before serving the airmen's lunch and it may have been lust.

"Ladies?... Where?" Max demanded with mock surprise.

"Well, let me see...erm," replied Houseman, looking around the room. He let his gaze pass over Natalie and finally his eyes settled on Aircraftswoman Sammi Keans who was helping Hoare sort out some large-scale maps.

"Ah, there we are," said Houseman. "Young Keans is a lady."

"Oh, thank you very much, sir," Natalie panted as she scrambled to her feet.

Hammond laughed and turned to Keans. "Is this true, Keans? Are you really a lady?"

Keans, a good looking, well-spoken girl from a prosperous Norfolk farming family, looked at Steve, curved her lip and, in a fair imitation of Mrs Mop from ITMA, shouted. "Course I bleedin' are, sir!"

We roared. It was totally unexpected from the normally quiet young girl. She blushed with pleasure at the effect she had caused but it was to be short-lived. The outer door crashed open and Janner stood there, his face red with fury.

"What the hell is going on in here?" Then he spotted Houseman and bit off whatever he was going to say next.

"A little Christmas joke, sir," replied Houseman quietly, but his eyes gave away his true feelings.

Janner ushered his bulk towards his office. "I'll be leading the briefing today. I want all info ready by fourteen hundred in the main briefing room for a run-through." He bustled out and there was a long silence. We all looked at each other in amazement. Since when had Janner taken a briefing? Before anybody could make a disparaging remark, Houseman took charge of the situation. His face was impassive.

"Right! Ladies and gentlemen, let's get to work." He moved over to Keans and Hoare. "Let the dog see the rabbit." He began to unroll the maps on the table. He glanced up at Steve and myself and beckoned us over. "We've got an odd one." He opened a chart covering the Channel area. "A recce pilot from Benson reckoned he caught a glimpse of two large warships heading for the Channel. He knew we've nothing in that area but the weather was thick clag and he couldn't even attempt to get pictures. He was so certain of what he saw he broke radio silence. He knew the consequences of two German raiders getting out into the Atlantic." Houseman ran his hand through his grey hair. "God knows where they are now but we've been tasked to send one squadron on a search and destroy operation."

We looked at him in amazement.

"Yeah, I know. Crap weather means they'll be lucky to even see the sea never mind two bloody warships. Even if they do find them, they'll have to attack at low level and that will be sheer bloody suicide."

"Who thought up this little disaster?" asked Steve.

"Not Butch Harris," replied Houseman. "That's for sure."

"What about Beauforts with torpedoes?" asked Natalie. "Or even the Navy - surely they are far more suited to this kind of operation?"

Houseman nodded. "I agree. It seems somebody has panicked but somehow I don't think they'll go ahead with this. I reckon it'll be scrubbed but we must carry on as if it is going ahead. Okay?"

We nodded and started to get the operation together. We were well into it when Houseman was called into the watchkeepers' office. He emerged smiling but didn't speak. He simply walked over to the prepared charts and began to roll them up. We all cheered. Sense had prevailed and the op had been scrubbed. Christmas was back on.

Sergeant Paula Tyde popped her head round the door from the watchkeepers' office and called over to Houseman. "The AOC has just called, sir. He's cancelled his visit for today and will arrange to come over next week."

Houseman's face was impassive. "Thanks, Sarge." He glanced up at us but he didn't need to say anything. That explained why Janner had suddenly taken an interest in briefings. The AOC would have been there to see him perform. The creepy bastard!

Janner suddenly emerged through the door from his office, stalked through the section and, without a word, wrenched open the outer door.

"Happy Christmas, sir!" called out Hoare with barely concealed sarcasm.

Janner paused only momentarily and then slammed the door to behind him. There was an embarrassed silence until Houseman suddenly clapped his hands and beckoned over to Hoare.

"Hoare. Here are the keys to the 'Unrestricted' filing cabinet in my office. Open it up and bring back here what you find in the second drawer down. Okay?"

"Yes, sir," replied a mystified Hoare as he headed off with the keys.

Natalie opened the watchkeepers' office door and called, "Bring out Christmas, girls!"

The two WAAF sergeants emerged carrying a few Christmas decorations and a small Christmas tree planted in a wastepaper basket lined with coloured paper. As they hung the sparse decorations around the section, Hoare emerged with four bottles held close to his chest.

"Strewth, sir! Where did you get these?" He placed four bottles of American bourbon on the table.

"From the Americans at Shipdham in Norfolk. I went there on liaison last month and they were very generous. I thought they might come in handy." He opened one of the bottles. "I'm sorry we've no mixers but what the heck, I'm sure we will manage." He turned to Keans. "Come on, Mrs Mop, grab enough mugs for us all!"

Before long we were actually celebrating Christmas. Well, not just Christmas - we were also celebrating the fact that we didn't have to send the aircrew out on this special day. The whole station could now have a bit of a 'knees-up'. I watched Houseman as he exchanged banter with the others. Some of the strain seemed to have left his face and his easy, friendly manner was genuine.

Time passed quickly and when Inext looked at my watch I looked at my watch, it was time to put up the blackout boards at the windows. We had just finished blacking out when Sergeant Trudi Collins walked in, shaking the snow from her greatcoat.

"Christmas drink, Sarge?" asked Hammond, who was already overfull of Christmas spirit.

"Love to, sir," she replied, "but I'm on duty all night, so I'm afraid no booze for me or I might miss a very important telephone call - like notice the war has ended."

"Come on, Sarge, one won't hurt you," slurred Hammond but then caught Houseman's eye and read the silent rebuke therein. He tried to make light of his gaffe.

"Ah, well - what a pity. Never mind, we'll save you some for the New Year." The door slammed as he staggered out to the toilets.

Natalie moved to my side. "I think I'm going to call it a day," she said quietly. "There is a dance in the mess tonight and, if I am to do my duty, I must be clear of head and prepared for the fray."

"May I walk you to the Waafery?" I asked.

"Why not?" she smiled and went to get her coat.

I saw Houseman watching us out of his eye corners and I saw him smile. I shrugged into my greatcoat and walked over to him.

"Don't get the wrong idea, sir," I said quietly.

He just grinned and grabbed his own coat. "In that case, Carver, you won't mind if I walk back to the mess with you both."

"Just as long as you don't insist on accompanying us to the Waafery," I laughed.

"Carver! Do I look like a gooseberry?"

"No, sir - but you might try to pull rank," I answered as I drained the last drop of bourbon from my mug.

"Sorry, Carver, just because I'm an officer does not mean I'm a gentleman. Pulling rank would not even come into it. I'd just kick you in the balls, grab her and whisk her off to my den."

He thought for a second. "Actually, I'd have to whisk her off somewhere else tonight as my so-called den is full of dirty, unwashed squash kit - hardly an ambience conducive to passion."

I laughed. "Mine is not much better. Living with Steve Hammond is rather like living in a second-hand shop - tatty clothes everywhere and none of them mine!"

"I can imagine," answered Houseman. He turned to watch Natalie as she joined us. "We were just discussing which of us was going to whisk you off on a huge white charger but decided it would have to be a rusty old RAF bike, sorry!"

Natalie grinned. "If that's all you can manage, I shall throw myself to the wolves at the dance tonight."

"Heaven help you and God bless the wolves," laughed Houseman.

We walked outside and paused on the front step. It was getting very cold again but the bourbon seemed to have given me a sort of in-built heating system.

I turned to Houseman. "Thank you, sir, for the unexpected Christmas drink."

"My pleasure." He rubbed his hands together vigorously. "I think I'll pop over to the tower and see who the poor old duty pilot is for tonight. Happy Christmas to you both." He raised a hand in a farewell gesture and disappeared into the gloom.

My bourbon-induced central heating was beginning to wear off. "Come on!" I urged Natalie as my teeth started chattering. "Let's get you back to your quarters."

"Are you coming to the dance tonight?" she asked.

"If I do, do I get a dance?"

"Probably only one. Females are a bit scarce at the moment and it would be a bit of a 'no-no' to dance with the same man all night."

"Good God!" I exclaimed. " Don't tell me even dancing is rationed. Is there no end to the shortages in this war? I think I'll stay in my room and sulk."

"Poor old thing," she laughed as she slipped her arm through mine and gave me a little hug.

Nobody was going to see us in the dark so we stayed arm in arm. We walked in a silence broken only by the crunch of our feet in the freezing snow. We reached the path leading to the WAAF officers' quarters. It was strictly out of bounds from this point on. To my surprise, Natalie leaned forward and gave me a little kiss on the cheek and took both my hands in hers.

"I'm very glad you were posted to West Fen, Sam."

"So am I - now!" I answered truthfully.

She looked at me intently for a few seconds then the moment was gone.

"See you later," she said and hurried off up the path. I turned and headed for the wreck that was my room.

I went to the Christmas bash that night and had not one but two dances with Natalie. She looked beautiful but unfortunately not just to me - all the other guys could see it too. Natalie danced every dance. A girl as beautiful as her would not get a chance to sit out even one dance and I was as jealous as hell. Every time my eyes sought her in the crush she'd be in the arms of yet another young officer. I'd suddenly had enough of warm beer, cigarette smoke so thick you could walk on it and the strangled tones of the bosomy dance band singer. The band was even worse but everybody was so pissed they didn't care. This was Christmas and everybody was determined to have a good time and there has never been anything worse than the British enjoying themselves!

Bloody hell! I was feeling very sorry for myself. I was also well and truly drunk. I'd been drowning my sorrows without even realising it. I lurched off to my room and crashed out. For once I slept right though the night totally oblivious to Hammond's return. This time it was my bloody clothes all over the place.

Boxing Day dawned clear and bright but I didn't! My head refused to stop throbbing and my mouth felt like a gorilla's armpit.

Hammond was on the floor snoring like a castrated grampus. He was still fully dressed and I wondered idly if that was because this time there was nowhere for him to throw his discarded clothes – I'd got there first. I located most of my clothes and threw them on my bed. I was shivering. The room was freezing and I dreaded going down to the communal washing and toilet area. It was even colder in there and the water would be tepid. I'd cut myself shaving and somebody would be farting like a bull elephant in one of the sit-downs. There was always somebody in there. Maybe it was the same chap every morning. More likely it was an Irish navvy, with the galloping craps, who had been in there since they built the bloody bogs. God! How I hated this stinking place!

"Stand by for broadcast!" Even the announcer on the tannoy sounded hungover.

Oh no! For fuck's sake, not today!

"Aircrews to report to briefing at fourteen hundred hours. All aircrew to briefing at fourteen hundred hours. End of broadcast."

I hauled my trousers on and hopped over the cold linoleum to where Hammond lay on the floor. I kicked him in the ribs.

"Come on, sleeping beauty - ops are on."

All I got in reply was a grunt and a muffled fart.

That was it as far as I was concerned and I stamped off in a rage to carry out my ablutions. Hammond could stay where he was for all I cared. Let him take his chances with Janner. Bollocks to them all!

My mood had not improved by the time I reached the section but I was soon hard at work. It was all to no avail, as once more ops were scrubbed and a stand-down announced for the next forty-eight hours. Not that it affected me - I was duty officer for the week. No nipping off home to see the folks, but Natalie managed to get a lift home for the pass period and I felt really miserable. Max also had deserted me and even Hammond had found somebody to take him in.

Cold, dank and miserable. That description applied to both West Fen and myself. Roll on 1943!

CHAPTER FOUR

It was not quite 1943 when we went back on operations. On the night of the 28/29 December the squadrons were tasked with minelaying. This kind of op was known as 'gardening' and we were to provide twenty Lancs to lay mines in the mouth of the Gironde river.

Houseman had already been to a briefing with the navigation leader and they'd planned the route to and back from the target. He asked me to help him pin the coloured route tape on the master briefing map. The tape stretched from West Fen down to Cornwall then headed south, skirting the French coast at Brest and down to the Gironde. There would be no moans when the curtain went back tonight. If any op could be called a 'milk run', this should be one.

We checked the friendly signal flare colours for the day and also the 'sisters', which was the code name for the enemy equivalent. Don't ask me how we got those, but we did and they saved many a crew when fired in a last ditch effort to get away from fighters or searchlights. Our colours were used mainly to deter our own Royal Navy convoy escorts who were notoriously trigger-happy.

I was unable to sit in on the briefing at 14.00 hours but I'd finished all my tasks when Houseman came over to me and handed me an envelope. Twice takeoff time had been delayed and it was now dark and rainy.

"Carver, pop this over to the duty pilot in the tower." He looked at his watch. "You might as well stay for the takeoffs. You'll not see much but at least you'll get an idea of what goes on down there."

I nodded and grabbed my coat.

"Okay if I go with him, sir?" asked Natalie.

Houseman grinned and headed for his office. "Oh, I think we can spare you now."

"Thank you, sir."

She shot off to get her coat and as I glanced round I suddenly saw one of the airmen make a crude sign to the others. It was the well-spoken airman who had, on my first day in the section, made the remark about Bourne eating her young.

"If you've a desire to masturbate, Christian, I suggest you go out to the toilets." I said coldly.

He glanced up at me guiltily but didn't say a word. He looked down, unable to meet my stare, but I could see the traces of a smirk on his face. I decided it was time to sort this arrogant bastard out.

"Christian! Come here... Now!" I ordered quietly.

He glanced round at the other two airmen but his smirk died when he saw they were studiously avoiding eye contact. He looked distinctly uneasy as he approached and I was going to make the bastard even more uneasy.

"Stand to attention, man!" I snapped and he quickly obeyed.

I stood and stared at him but he didn't meet my eyes. He just stared straight ahead but the smirk had not returned. I walked forward until I was virtually nose-to-

39

nose with him.

"If I ever see you making signs like that again I'll put you on a two-five-two quicker than you could commit the act you were miming. Therefore, you disgusting little arsehole, I'll be watching you very closely from now on." I paused to let the words sink in and to make sure everybody else in the room got the message.

I stepped back a pace and lowered my voice slightly. "Actually, Christian, I want you to make that sign again because I don't like you. I find you an arrogant shit and nothing will please me more than if I can put you on a charge. You'll never have had punishment such as I'll devise for you and you'll regret that you and I ever met. Is that clear?"

"Yes, sir." He whispered the reply and the hate was visible in his face.

"What did you say, airman?" I shouted and he jumped as if shot.

"Yes, sir!" he said louder.

"Good!" I answered. "Now get back to your work."

He did a passable about-turn and marched off back to his desk. Hoare, the cockney, glanced at me and I thought I could see approval in his face. Maybe I was not the only one who disliked friend Christian. I turned back to see if Natalie was ready and was surprised to see both her and Houseman standing just by the watchkeepers' door. They had obviously watched the whole scene.

"Ready?" I asked and felt embarrassed when I heard the anger still in my voice.

She gave no impression of noticing my anger. "Yes, I'm ready when you are."

I picked up the envelope for the duty pilot. "Let's go."

When we reached the darkness outside I was surprised to find Houseman was with us.

"Hang on a minute, Carver." He put a restraining hand on my shoulder. "What was that all about?"

"Christian was making crude gestures with reference to Natalie and myself, sir. I thought it was in bad taste and decided to make it clear that I'd have no more of his nonsense."

"You certainly did that," he laughed. "I was quite impressed - didn't know you had it in you. You were quite right, he's an arrogant sod. He seems to think he's on a higher intellectual plane than the rest of us and it was good to see you bring him down a peg."

"It's that bloody affected accent of his," I said bitterly.

"Public school," answered Houseman.

"What?" I asked in surprise. "Then why didn't he try for a commission when he was called up for service? If he's so bloody clever, why is he still an airman?"

"Doesn't want the responsibility," Houseman answered.

"In other words," Natalie interjected, "he's not as big as his mouth."

"Succinct and to the point, young lady." Houseman grinned and made a slight bow to Natalie. He suddenly shivered. "Right, get over to the tower before you miss all the fun."

In spite of Houseman's shiver, the weather was actually a little warmer but there was a heavy drizzle. The Met man said it should have cleared by the time the crews reached the enemy coast. He'd called in at the section earlier and had complained, without being too serious, that the crews always hooted with derision when he told them such good news. I guess his was an inexact science, but it was getting better now as Mosquitos were being sent out on Met reconnaissance flights well in advance of the main bomber stream.

By the time we reached the tower, Merlin engines were crackling into life from their dispersals all around the airfield. It was a lonely and frightening sound that created a heightened sense of tension in everybody on the station. We pushed our way through the blackout at the entrance and I immediately saw a door marked 'Duty Pilot' but the room was empty. A WAAF corporal sat at a teleprinter in the next room.

"Duty pilot's upstairs, sir. Flying Officer Tait."

I thanked her and we trotted up the stone steps to the main control room. In the centre of the room was a series of consoles - mainly radio and telephones. There was a plan of the airfield and runway indicator board showing the runway in use plus the QFE, wind direction and speed.

I found Tait with a young WAAF section officer. They were discussing the aircraft-state board and I handed him the envelope.

He ripped it open and quickly scanned the contents. "Thanks a lot." He glanced up at us. "Staying for the takeoffs?"

"As long as we're not in the way," I replied.

Tait pointed. "See that door? If you go out there on to the balcony, you'll see a set of metal stairs going up to the roof. If you don't mind the inclement weather, you'll at least see the airfield lights and the aircraft nav lights as they takeoff."

I glanced at Natalie and she nodded her assent.

"Thank you," I said to Tait and we turned up our greatcoat collars ready for the wet night outside.

Once on the roof we positioned ourselves in the lee of a small cabin with windows in all four sides. Inside, a flying officer and a sergeant, huddled in their greatcoats, were checking over a couple of Aldis lamps, a brace of Very pistols and a rack of flares.

We could see the blue lights that marked the perimeter track but the main runway lights were not yet on. The damp night air throbbed with the muted rumble of twenty Lancasters and I could feel their thunder reverberate in my chest cavity. It was weird and quite disturbing. Eighty mighty Rolls Royce Merlin engines powered the twenty Lancasters and every now and then the flickering blue flame from their exhaust stubs would merge with the blue lights of the peritrack. Red, green and white navigation lights also found their place in the darkness of the airfield. The duty runway was Two-Seven, so the aircraft would just be airborne as they passed the tower. I knew the crews would be pleased as it was the longest runway and each Lanc would be heavy with the six 1,500lb mines on board.

I'd read in the intelligence reports that our mining operations tied up some twenty thousand German personnel - men who would have normally been used in an offensive role.

The mutter of voices and the sweet smell of tobacco smoke broke my train of thought as three more officers joined us. I couldn't see who they were in the darkness but the taller man of the three laughed at a comment made by one of his colleagues.

Natalie tapped my arm. "Watch what you say," she cautioned. "That is the station commander."

Even though I'd been on the station just over three weeks, I'd not yet met the great man. I'd been told he made a point of interviewing every new officer but he'd been on leave so my interview had yet to be announced.

Suddenly runway 27 lit up along its length and the light reflected back off the lowering cloud. I glanced at my watch and saw it was already 21.00 hours. Takeoff had originally been scheduled for 17.30 but it had been delayed twice. The crews had been pretty edgy when they were finally bussed out to the aircraft and, although I didn't have to go through the hell they experienced night after night, I thought I knew

41

how they felt.

There was a rising crescendo from the far end of the field as the first Lanc started its takeoff roll. It roared nearer and nearer until finally there was a subtle change in the engine timbre and, although I could only see the green starboard navigation light and the blue flames from the engines, I knew it was airborne. It bellowed past us, ripping the moist air apart with its thunder as it clawed its way up into the night. A second aircraft followed and soon I'd lost count.

About half of the aircraft had taken off when I heard a strange echo of engines. It seemed to come from my left and pass to my rear. I half turned in surprise to seek the source of the echo but the main servicing hangers were too far away to give an audio soundboard to the roar from the bombers. I turned fully to face the direction of the departing Lancs and, just for a second, I thought I saw the fleeting shadow of an aircraft going the wrong way in the circuit.

I blinked my eyes hard and wiped the rain's moisture away. Another Lanc bellowed past and I watched its navigation lights floating upwards as the pilot nursed the heavily laden aircraft in pursuit of his squadron colleagues. I spun to my right - there was that bloody noise again and, for some unaccountable reason, the hairs on the back of my neck prickled with a frisson of fear. What the bloody hell was the matter with me? Natalie and the other observers didn't seem in the least perturbed.

I was just going to turn back to the airfield, when a stream of intermittent light seem to hose through the darkness and pursue the last Lanc to takeoff. Over the sound of engines there was a strange rattle and then the speeding lights caught up with the Lanc. There was a sudden blossom of flame and, in its evil light, I could see the Lancaster quite clearly against the dark sky. It seemed to stagger in the air as flames poured from its port wing and then, with frightening suddenness, it had gone in a huge explosion of fire which lit up the countryside for miles.

The other occupants of the roof were now etched on the retinas of my eyes. They were, like myself, frozen into immobility by the horror of the incident they'd just witnessed. Their shocked faces flickered as a myriad of burning aircraft fragments fell from the sky like a huge Roman candle.

Then the blast hit us and the tower shook. Panes of glass in the little cabin shattered and scythed into the two men inside and I saw them clutching their faces as blood flowed through their fingers. Yet, instead of rushing to their aid, my eyes were drawn back to the glow that seemed to have spread across the horizon. Seven young men had died in front of my eyes and I felt sick with horror. I could do nothing, not even when Natalie sobbed and clutched my arm.

It was one of the officers with the station commander who was the first to recover his wits. He ran towards the wreckage of the little cabin.

"Intruders!" he screamed. "Intruders! Get those fucking airfield lights off and halt the takeoffs."

He reached into the cabin and grabbed one of the Very pistols, checked the colour of the loaded flare and ran to the front of the tower. He raised the pistol high in the air and fired a red flare.

The instant he fired, the controllers beneath our feet cut all the power to the airfield lights and, apart from the glow out to the west, we were in total darkness. All aircraft still on the airfield had switched off their nav lights. Somewhere out there was an enemy intruder who had tasted blood and would want more before he went home.

"Oh! Fucking hell, no!" muttered the officer with the Very pistol and we turned to follow his gaze.

Once more those devastating lights were hurtling through the night and another

Lancaster, somewhere in the vicinity of Boston, burst into flames. It trailed flames for what seemed like a lifetime but it could only have been a matter of seconds before it too crashed in a mushroom of silent fire. The dull and distant thud of the explosion caused a few more shards of glass to fall from the small cabin.

I felt myself shaking with both fear and anger. Natalie had buried her head in my shoulder and I could feel her sobs through the thickness of my damp greatcoat. I suddenly realised I was gently pounding my fists on her back in sheer frustration. By the time I'd regained my senses, I realised only Natalie and myself remained on the roof – even the injured men had been taken below. She raised her head from my shoulder and turned to watch the dying glow in the west where the first Lanc had gone in. We didn't speak - what could we say?

We were brought back to reality and the urgency of getting the bombers airborne by the sudden glow of the runway lights. Somebody fired a green Very from the balcony below. The risk had to be taken.

Once more, a Lancaster started to roll down the runway, the noise of the Merlins now sounding defiant and vengeful. I noticed that the nav lights were off just in case the raider was still around. We watched with bated breath as the remaining Lancs roared into the night sky but, thank God, they all got off safely. We stayed until the last murmur of Merlins had faded into the wet night.

Natalie shivered and I pulled her close.

"Cold?" I whispered.

"Not really," she said quietly. "Just miserable."

I held her tighter for a few seconds and then kissed her gently. "Come on, we'd better get back to the section and see if there is anything we can do."

We groped our way down the metal steps in the dark. The runway lights were off again, denying us their reflection from the clouds to light our way. We pushed into the dimly lit control room, adjusting our eyes to the light.

The station commander, Group Captain Edmund, was standing with Wing Commander Brady, the CO of 552 Squadron, and the Church of England padre, Squadron Leader Dai Lewis. Dai had introduced himself to me in the mess the previous evening and I'd taken an immediate liking to him. He was no 'Holy Joe' and he felt his task was to comfort, not convert. He was a stocky little man with grey hair and a face so red one could take him for a farmer.

The station commander was tall, well over six feet, and with the sort of face that could put the fear of God into lowly junior officers such as myself. He'd medals from the last war and I guessed his age at mid fifties, although his white hair and lined face suggested a much older man.

The padre spotted us and gave a little wave. He muttered a quick apology to the other two officers and headed over to us.

"Hello, young Carver, Natalie - bit of a dicey do!"

I nodded. "Jerry pulled a real flanker there, didn't he? Really caught us with our pants down."

"He certainly did," agreed Dai. "Of all the damned luck! Caught the lads at their most vulnerable. Poor devils didn't stand an earthly. Thank God the weather was duff because I hate to think what the carnage would have been like if it had been a clear night."

Before we could reply, the door burst open and Wing Commander Janner heaved his panting bulk through the door, his eyes eagerly searching for the station commander. He located his target.

"God! How awful, sir," he gasped. "I got here as quickly as I could."

Of all the people who was of sod all use at a time like this, it was Janner. We stood dumbstruck whilst he puffed away like a leaky old tank-engine. His stance was that of a puppy eagerly awaiting a congratulatory bone. Somebody had to break the silence and the only man who could do that was the station commander but he was still looking as baffled as the rest of us.

Edmund finally shook his head as if to clear it, paused to collect his thoughts and then spoke. His voice was quiet and even, but one could detect the suppressed anger and contempt.

"How thoughtful of you, Wing Commander Janner. I'm sure we need all the help we can get at this moment." He looked round at the rest of us as if seeking help, but all we could give him were blank looks. The great man was lost for words but he was the guy who got paid a group captain's salary and he was on his own. Even Dai Lewis was speechless.

Out of my eye corner, I could see a WAAF sergeant sitting at a typewriter. She was desperately trying to keep her composure. I looked straight at her and when she saw my eyes on her, the smile died on her face. I should've left it there but I couldn't resist giving her a big wink. It was a disastrous thing to do. She erupted into a cauldron of suppressed laughter, coughing and counterfeit sneezing in a wretched effort to conceal her mirth.

Everybody in the room spun round to locate the source of the interruption and that is when Janner spotted Natalie and myself. He took a half pace towards us and it was pretty obvious the sight of me displeased him.

"Carver! What the hell are you doing here? Why are you not in your own section?"

He was seething at the reception he had been given and here was a whipping boy - good old Carver!

All eyes were now on me, much to the relief of the WAAF sergeant!

"I came to deliver a signal to the duty pilot, sir," I answered quietly.

"Well, at last you've found your true vocation, Carver," he sneered. "Messenger boy is about your level, I'd say."

I was not the only one struck dumb by the remark and the vitriol with which it was delivered.

Janner realised that his rage had taken him over the top. The remark delivered in private would have been bad enough, but openly and in front of the group captain it was, from an officer of his rank, totally unforgivable. He turned to the group captain, desperate to retrieve the situation, but a face hewn in stone confronted him.

"Thank you, Wing Commander Janner," said Edmund quietly. "I suggest you return to your office. I'll send for you ...eventually." The last word was spoken with a slight hesitation and was dripping with an ominous portent.

Janner looked as if he had been slapped in the face with a wet haddock. He began to wring his hands and for a moment I thought he was going to drop to his knees. This was Wing Commander Uriah Heep at his best and embarrassing in the extreme. He was so bloody pathetic I nearly felt sorry for him.

"Of course, sir," Janner stammered. "Of course. I'll be in my office."

He began to make his exit and it reminded me of, in days of yore, the old courtiers to the monarch. The poor minions had to reverse backwards across the whole court so as not to turn their backs on the king. Janner went backwards groping for the door handle. He turned a blistering glare on me and made an attempt to retrieve his shattered authority.

"Pilot Officer Carver. I want you in my office - now!"

Groupie was just about at the end of his patience but when he spoke it was pitched in a tone that was pleasant and quite calm.

"Pilot Officer Carver was a witness to tonight's incident, Wing Commander. I want him here so that we might discuss what he saw and his opinion on what happened. He'll not be available until I release him and that will not be until tomorrow."

Wing Commander Brady gave me a quick grin and joined us in watching Janner disappear backwards out of the door with a squeak that could have been a strangled retort. At least he had the decency to close the door quietly behind him.

For a few moments nobody dared speak.

Groupie looked at his watch. "Right! It's time we got down to business." He turned to the WAAF control officer. "Do we know who the downed crews were?"

"Yes, sir. Flight Lieutenant Park, Cakewalk S-Sugar and Flight Sergeant Chapman, Cakewalk F-Freddie."

Wing Commander Brady rubbed a hand across his eyes but it didn't wipe the strain from his face. He was just twenty-six years old but he looked much older. "Oh God, both my crews." He turned to us as if willing us to understand and suddenly, in spite of his rank and responsibility, he really looked what he was - a vulnerable young man. "Chapman and his crew had only one more trip to complete their tour," he said bitterly.

Groupie moved forward and placed a hand on Brady's arm. "Come on, Tom, let's get back to my office and see what we can make of things." He turned to Natalie and myself. "Carver, I'd like you and the section officer to accompany us. Maybe we can get a few answers on what has happened tonight."

We left the tower and Groupie drove us to Station HQ. Once in his office we took off our caps and coats and sank gratefully into the easy chairs. Groupie offered us a cigarette but only Brady accepted. He'd regained his composure and it was difficult to imagine him as we had seen him in the tower. Aircrews died damned nearly every day and he couldn't afford to dwell on their fate - at least not in public, but I'd have hated to have the dreams he took to bed.

"Just give me a minute," said Groupie and he left the office to reappear a short time later with four mugs of coffee on a tray. Natalie and I looked at each other in amazement.

Brady, spotting our quizzical expressions, grinned. "I can assure you the group captain makes excellent coffee."

Groupie looked up in surprise. "Damned well have to. I sent my PA off duty when I came over to the tower but you'll have to help yourselves, I draw the line at being 'mother'."

We all laughed and helped ourselves to the coffee. Then, before we got down to business, something occurred to me.

"Excuse me, sir," I addressed Groupie. "I really ought to let Squadron Leader Houseman know where I am."

"Already done, Carver. Did it myself whilst the kettle boiled. I also felt I'd better put him in the picture as to what was said to you in the tower by Wing Commander Janner. He's now fully aware of all the facts and he let me in on a few too. I think I must look into the situation in your section and get things sorted out. Now, how about a few thoughts on tonight's disaster?"

"The first I knew anything was amiss was when the bastard opened fire," said Brady. He put a hand to his forehead in dismay. "I'm sorry, young lady," he apologised to Natalie.

Nat just nodded and smiled her acceptance of the apology.

Groupie looked at us in turn. "Did any of you see or hear the intruder? I hear damned all these days - too much time in open cockpits and noisy engines. I heard the Lancs but nothing else."

"Strange thing about his method of attack," mused Brady. "Surely the best method of attack was straight down the runway, behind the bombers as they were silhouetted against the runway lights? Where the hell did he come from?"

"From the north, then he curved round to the west to come up behind his target." I spoke more or less to myself and I suddenly realised that the others were staring at me.

"Good Lord!" exclaimed Groupie as he stood up in surprise. "Did you actually see him?"

I opened my arms in frustration. "I heard him rather than saw him, sir. I first heard what I thought was an echo from the aircraft taking off but the hangers were too far away to be the source of the reverberation."

"But did you actually see him?" persisted Brady.

"A fleeting shadow maybe, but it all happened so fast I can't be sure of anything." I closed my eyes, desperately trying to bring that darting shadow into some kind of focus, but real shape and form evaded me. Then realisation hit me like a bolt from the blue. I jumped out of my chair and began to pace the office. The others just stared at me in surprise.

"Oh God! That's it." As I uttered the words, I got that prickly feeling at the back of my neck again. I walked up to Groupie Edmund where he sat on the edge of his desk.

"Of course we didn't hear the bloody thing. We didn't hear it because it had a Merlin engine!"

There was a long silence and I could feel Brady staring at me, but I kept my eyes on the Groupie. Edmund returned my stare for a long time and I could sense I was quickly losing an ally.

He exhaled loudly and folded his arms. "Careful, Carver. I want you to think carefully about what you're saying. There was so much noise how the hell could you hear another Merlin?"

"But, sir! That's the whole point. I heard only Merlins. Surely I'd have noticed if it had been a Daimler-Benz or a BMW engine? I heard only Merlins and I'll swear to that."

Groupie continued to regard me with a doubtful look then he turned to Brady. "Tom, did you hear anything other than Merlins?"

Brady shook his head. "No, sir, but I'm damned sure I would have done if there had been anything else airborne." He fiddled with his cigarette lighter for a few moments then gave a reluctant sigh. "I'm afraid Carver is right, sir. Well, at least he's sown a seed of doubt in my mind."

Groupie turned and shuffled some papers on his desk then he thumped the desk with his fist. His voice was sharp with exasperation. "For Christ's sake! Do you realise what you're both saying?"

Brady and I looked at each other but didn't reply.

Natalie cleared her throat. "Are you trying to say that our aircraft were shot down by one of our own fighters?"

Groupie nodded angrily. "That's exactly what they're saying."

Natalie looked to me as if for an explanation but I didn't have one. What I did have was yet another idea that was not going to find favour. I started pacing the office again.

"For Pete's sake, Carver - stop walking up and down!" snapped Groupie.

I looked at him in surprise and he immediately jumped off the desk and put a hand on my arm. "Sorry, boy. That was uncalled for and I apologise. Tonight has rattled me more than I'd care to admit."

"I'm afraid I'm going to rattle you a little more, sir."

He sat back down on the desk and looked at me grimly. "Go on, get it over with."

I paused for a second. This was not going to be easy. "How did he just manage to be there at the right time?" I asked.

Brady shook his head. "Now what the hell are you getting at?"

I started to pace the office again and then remembered what Groupie had said a few moments ago. I stopped and gave him a self-conscious glance but he just smiled slightly and shook his head. I stood still but my mind was racing.

"Takeoff time was delayed twice. If he'd prior knowledge from a radio leak or whatever, how could he have stood around waiting for the revised takeoffs? If he'd flown from France, Belgium or Holland He'd not have had that sort of endurance. It was not a large aircraft, I'm pretty sure of that from my quick glimpse, so he wouldn't have had the range."

"Oh, come on, Carver!" protested Brady. "It had to be chance. Our fighters do the same on 'Rhubarbs'. It is simply down to targets of opportunity."

"Has this happened before?" I asked.

Groupie nodded. "Yes, a few weeks past at Coningsby."

"Was takeoff time delayed?"

"I've no idea," replied Groupie. "I can soon find out in the morning."

"I can see the way your mind is going, Sam," Natalie joined in. "But for your logic to be on target, there would have to be an enemy agent operating locally - maybe even here on West Fen."

"Oh, bloody hell!" exclaimed Brady. "Surely we're getting into the realms of fantasy? This was a chap who, unfortunately for us, got lucky."

I knew I really ought to agree with him. Common sense said it was chance the intruder got here at the right time but somehow I didn't believe that scenario.

Groupie got to his feet and stood with his legs apart, hands clasped behind his back. "I think we must leave it there for the moment and I must ask you not to say a word to anybody. Is that clear?"

"Goes without saying, sir," replied Brady on our behalf.

"Good," replied Groupie. "We cannot afford to let rumours start flying around and if we've a fox in the chicken coop, we must not startle him into making a run for it."

We nodded in agreement but before we could take our leave, we heard footsteps running down the corridor and entering the outer office where Edmund's PA normally worked.

"Who the hell is that?" asked Groupie with a frown of annoyance. "See who it is, would you, Tom?"

Brady nodded and went through to the office. We heard a murmur of voices and then Brady returned. There was a small smile on his face. "That was one of Tim Wareham's policemen, sir. A farmer out at a place called Wyberton has just phoned the guardroom to say he's seven airmen sitting in his front room. They are badly shaken but all in one piece. It's Chapman and his crew - they managed to bale out."

"Bloody good show!" exclaimed Groupie and he clapped his hands together in delight but stopped when he realised Brady had not finished. "Go on, Tom."

"I'm afraid there were no survivors from Park's kite, sir."

"Damn and blast," Edmund muttered. The smile had gone from his face but he pulled his thoughts together and faced us. "Right," he said. "Don't forget what I just said. Not a word to anybody."

We assured him the secret would stay within our small group.

"Good!" sighed Edmund. "Tom, you and the young lady can go but I'd like Carver to stay."

Brady nodded. "Okay, sir. I'll escort Cowen back to her quarters and then get over to the squadron. I want to be there when Chapman and his crew get back. I also have seven letters to write to the families of Park and his lads." His voice was strained.

"Make sure Chapman and his crew see the MO, Tom," Groupie said quietly.

Brady was once again the professional. "Squadron Leader Jameson went with the transport to pick them up, sir. The policeman just told me."

"Fine. Let me know as soon as they get back and I'll pop over to see them. It will be interesting to see if they can shed any light on Carver's mystery kite. Maybe the gunners saw something."

Brady looked at me and grinned. "You've put forward quite a theory, Carver. I must admit you've set me thinking, but I'm pretty certain this will all boil down to a lucky night for the Jerries."

He was thoughtful for a few seconds before he added a rider. "There again, your theory could explain why he stayed out of the airfield lights. He wouldn't be afraid of being shot down but he could have been afraid of somebody identifying the type of kite he was flying." He ran a hand through his hair. "Carver, I hope you're wrong."

"I hope so too, sir."

Brady and Natalie collected their caps and coats, saluted and left me with the group captain who promptly sank wearily into one of the easy chairs. He waved a tired hand towards the chair next to him.

"Come and sit down, Carver. You and I have a bit of talking to do. The trouble is, I don't know where to start."

I sat and waited patiently as he drummed his fingers on the arm of his chair. His head was tilted back as he stared thoughtfully at the ceiling as if the answer might be written there. Finally he slapped his thighs with his hands and fixed me with a keen stare.

"Carver! I gather, from the little episode in the tower and from a short conversation with Squadron Leader Houseman, that you and Wing Commander Janner don't exactly see eye to eye."

"I'm afraid not, sir."

"Nothing to be afraid of, Carver. The man's a bloody cretin."

I looked at him in surprise.

He waved a hand irritably in my direction. "Don't look so shocked. I know he's one of my senior officers but he's bloody useless and the sooner I get Houseman in charge the better. The CO of your section should be a squadron leader but somehow I got saddled with that bloody clot, Janner. I've tried umpteen times to get him posted but for some reason Command won't wear it. How do you get on with Houseman?"

The change of tack took me by surprise. "Fine, sir. He's an excellent officer and knows the job inside out. He's also a good man-manager. He keeps a tight grip on us but we all like him because he's fair. I've him to thank for getting me out of a couple of court - martial situations."

"By falling foul of the wing commander?"

"Yes, sir. I'm afraid I don't always engage my brain before I open my mouth. I could also do with a few lessons in the art of swallowing one's pride."

Groupie grinned. "I can imagine. I used to be just the same as a junior officer - always in the shit! But, young man, that is water under the bridge. I understand you're surplus to establishment?"

There was that sudden change of tack again.

I nodded. "So the wing commander keeps telling me, sir."

"Right, in that case, let's see if we can keep you out of his way for a while. I want you to quietly investigate your suspicions about this intruder."

I looked at him in amazement.

"I know, I know!" he said with a sigh. "I don't know how the hell you're going to go about it. I don't know where to start but you've youth on your side and a very vivid imagination. I watched you tonight as you tried to explain your feelings and I know you're totally convinced your theory is correct. Okay, maybe you're barking up a gum tree, but I feel there is a vestige of possibility in your theory and I want you to bring the whole thing to a conclusion - one way or another. If there is a rogue aircraft out there, find it! If there is an agent, find him or her too!"

I tried to visualise the enormity of the task he'd set me but it was too much for me to take in. I stood up and collected my hat and coat and began to put them on.

"What about my normal duties, sir?"

"Don't worry, I'll fix things up with Squadron Leader Houseman in the morning. I'll have to bring him in on this. It would be most unfair to pinch one of his blokes without telling him why. The wing commander, on the other hand, will be told nothing. I'll have him in to see me in the morning and tell him you're on temporary attachment as my personal liaison officer with Command Intelligence. That should impress the hell out of him but if he tries to give you a hard time, just tell me and I'll sort him out."

I grinned. "Thank you for your confidence in me, sir. I just hope I can come up to your expectations."

"Oh, you will Carver. I've just given you all the motivation you need. No more daily contact with the bogey man in the confines of the Intelligence Section."

I laughed. "For that act of kindness, sir, I'll wrestle the mad Hun from the skies with my bare hands."

Edmund laughed with me but then his face became serious as he held out his hand. "Just be very careful, Carver. There may be more to this than even you think. I lose enough of my aircrew lads so I don't want to start losing my ground officers as well. Just be very wary of who you trust until this whole thing is wrapped up one way or another."

I shook his hand, stepped back a pace and saluted. "I'll do my best, sir."

As I left his office and walked out into the darkness I could feel those hairs on the back of my neck start to tingle again. What the hell had I started? Big mouth Carver strikes again!

CHAPTER FIVE

Operations were scrubbed the night after the visit of the intruder and I accepted an offer from Max to accompany him out to the village of New Bolingbroke for a pint. A small, ribbon development each side of a road known to the locals as the 'Seven Mile Straight', it was only a few miles north of Boston and its four pubs were pretty well packed on nights when there were no operations. Max had decided we'd start at the Lancaster Arms. He had been there a few times and got on pretty well with the landlord, Harry Woods and his wife Ethel.

By the time we got there, in Max's old MG, it was well past opening time and the pub was heaving with people. We managed to get a pint but there was nowhere to sit so we stood in the corridor leading to the pub's living quarters. Even in the corridor, space was at a premium and we pressed ourselves up against the wall as a tall woman, carrying pints of beer on a tray, tried to squeeze her way through to the main room. She spotted Max and the frown of concentration left her face.

"Now then, Max," she shouted above the noise. "How are you doing, duck?"

"Very well thank you, Mrs Woods," replied Max.

"Mrs Woods? What sort of greeting is that?" she laughed. "I suppose Ethel is too familiar for you officer types."

A corporal, further down the corridor, overheard her comment and decided to get in on the act. "I'd get familiar with you any time, Ethel."

Ethel grinned. "Aye, I know you would Charlie, but I'm surprised you've got any energy left after going out with Big Bertha. She's a big lass and if her dad catches you, you'll find out he's even bigger!"

"A man's gotta do what a man's gotta do, Ethel." The corporal laughed.

"Aye, I know," said Ethel with a wink at us. "But you're no man yet, so stop boasting."

Charlie and his mates roared a chorus of approval and Ethel continued the obstacle course to the taproom.

Somebody was hammering away on a piano in the taproom but either the piano needed tuning or the pianist was pissed. I suspected it was probably a bit of both.

With all the cigarette smoke, the roaring fire in the taproom and the press of bodies, quite a fug was building up.

Max handed me his glass. "Hang on to that for a minute, I need to take a pee!" He headed off through the crush and made his way in the direction of the outside toilets.

I was standing there, with a pint in each hand, when a shortish chap headed past with a tray of empties. He looked at my two pints - one bitter and one mild.

"What's up, mate, can't you make your mind up?"

I gave him a puzzled look and then the penny dropped. "It's not what it seems. This is mine and this is my friend's. He's just gone to the bog."

The man stopped and looked me up and down. "You new?"

"Pretty much. Just a few weeks actually."

"Like it?" he asked with a sardonic grin.

"I've been to better places," I answered carefully. It wouldn't do to upset the locals on my first night off camp.

"Aircrew?"

I was still sweltering in my greatcoat and he couldn't see my jacket. "No..." I found myself hesitating. "Ground wallah." That would do for now.

He waved his arm around at the crush of bodies, most of them aircrew. "You can't all be bloody heroes."

A very young navigator passing by put his arm around the man's shoulders. "Have to be a bloody hero to drink your beer, Woody."

"You mind your bloody manners, Mr Sawyer," grinned the man who I now realised was the landlord. "Any more of your lip and I'll have the missus throw you out."

"Sorry, Woody, you can't throw me out because I'm holding the crew kitty for the night. Where I go they go. Kick me out and it would be a bloody economic disaster for you, old boy."

Woody turned to me. "They've always got you by the balls, this lot."

The navigator held up his hands in mock horror. "I've got to know you well, Woody, but I don't want to get that close. Got to draw the line somewhere, old boy."

"Keep the conversation above the belt if you please, Mr Sawyer" called out Ethel as she arrived at the end of the conversation.."Whatever is down there will remain as secret as your aerodrome."

It was pretty obvious that Ethel had a way with words. Most of the others in the corridor had now got into what should be done with Woody's balls and things were going from risqué humour to outright crudity. Ethel just roared with laughter, grabbed the empties from her husband and headed back to the cellar.

I held out my hand to Woody. "I'm Sam Carver. You must be Harry. I've heard about you from Max."

Harry Woods shook my hand. "So that's who you're with. He's a good lad, is Max. I'm pleased he's found a friend because he's usually by himself and looking a bit like a fish out of water."

Somehow I couldn't see that description fitting Max. Having said that, the humour was loud, brash and crude. Highly educated Max would find it hard to join in. The subject of my musings interrupted me as he returned from the toilet and retrieved his pint.

Harry touched my arm. "I hear you had a bad night at West Fen last night."

I just nodded and hoped he'd change the subject.

"Oh, it's okay," he said. "I know you can't talk about it but I'd just like to say how sorry I was to hear about it."

We squeezed back against the wall as yet more newcomers tried to find space to park themselves and their beer.

"Bloody hell, Harry!" I remarked. "You've got a very popular pub."

I winced as a rather large 'erk managed to stand on my foot.

"Sorry, sir," he said quickly and I nodded at his apology.

One of his friends looked back. "Wot you do that for, you prat? He's a bleedin Henry - no bleedin' sense, no bleedin' feelin'."

Harry was smiling. "Servicemen never change, do they. Yes, sir - no, sir, three bags full, sir. A few pints later and they can take on the whole world. As to me having a popular pub, young man, to go back to what you were saying before we were interrupted, don't get the wrong idea. It's not my superior beer or even my magical charm that draws them in. It just happens there's a Land Army Girls camp just down the road at Carrington. They're due in any minute now and you know what they say - where the crumpet goes, the RAF goes. Actually we get a lot of army lads in here some nights but that can get a bit difficult at closing time. Usually ends up as the RAF versus the Squaddies. The MPs usually pop round to keep an eye on things until they have all staggered off home."

"You mean the local lads don't get a look in?" Max asked.

Harry laughed. "There's not many of those girls who would swap a chap in uniform for a chap in wellies."

Max suddenly shoved his pint into my hand again. "Excuse me for a minute - someone is murdering that piano. I must go and rescue the poor old thing."

I shoved his pint back at him. "Take your pint, you might not get out to get another!"

"Good idea." Max grabbed his pint back and forced his way towards the taproom.

Harry looked at me in astonishment. "Well, that's a bloody first! He's never done that before. I didn't even know he could play."

"Neither did I."

We both listened as the dreadful rendition of 'Roll out the Barrel' stuttered to a halt. There was a pause and then Harry and I stared at each other in amazement as the most beautiful jazz piano riffs cascaded from the taproom. There was a surge of bodies as every man and his dog tried to get a view of who was playing such superb music.

"Well, I'll be buggered," Harry said in amazement. "Would you credit it?"

I shook my head and just listened. No longer would Max be like a fish out of water, he was going to be in great demand. I was so carried away with the music I nearly missed what Harry was saying.

"Sorry Harry, what did you say?"

"I said, you nearly lost another plane last night. I saw old Stan Cornish at lunchtime today over at the shop. He said it was lost and circling really low around his place."

I was only half listening as Max had started to play a fantastic slow blues number that had reduced the clamour of the pub to total silence. There was nothing wrong with Harry's piano now - the notes fell through the smoke-laden air like golden rain.

Ethel dashed into the corridor. "What the heck's happened?" she asked in alarm. "Have they all cleared off?" Then she heard the piano. "Blimey! Who's that?"

"Max," Harry whispered.

Ethel strained to peer into the taproom. "The little tinker. He's never even played darts before, let alone the piano." She listened for a few more seconds. "By heck, he's good. I've never seen anybody shut this lot up before." She turned as two young boys in pyjamas appeared in the doorway from the living quarters of the pub and peered round Ethel to see what was going on.

Then Harry spotted them. "Come on, you two. You know you're not allowed in here. Back to bed with you - now!"

"Can we have some crisps?" asked the eldest.

"No, you bloody well can't. Bed! I won't tell you again."

Ethel grabbed them both and hustled them away.

"Your two?" I asked Harry.

"Aye. That was Eric and Keith. The other one, Alan, is only just eighteen months old."

"How the hell do they sleep with all this racket?" I asked.

Harry laughed. "Normally they could sleep through a bloody earthquake but you see what happens when things change? It was the silence that woke them up. They're not used to it."

I could see the logic in his explanation and was just going to comment when I was struck as if with a blinding flash of light.

"What did you just say, Harry?" I whispered urgently as I grabbed his arm.

Harry was startled by my action and it showed in his face. "I just said they're not used to the silence."

"No! No!" I gabbled. "Before that. Something about a lost plane."

I could see I was losing him. I'd unsettled him by my strange behaviour but I'd got that prickly feeling again. I took a deep breath and started again. "Sorry, Harry. You said something about a plane flying low as if lost?"

He looked somewhat mollified. "I just said that Stan Cornish had a lost plane over his place last night."

"What sort of plane?" I asked without even thinking.

"How the bloody hell should I know, you daft bugger?" Harry had obviously had enough of me.

"Where does this chap live?" I managed to get a little more calmness into my voice.

"Out in the wilderness the other side of Eastville."

Where's Eastville?" I asked patiently.

"To the east of West Fen." Harry was getting pissed off but I stuck at it.

"What's his name again?"

"Cornish. Stan Cornish."

I fished out a little notebook and a pencil. "What's his address?"

"Bloody hell, I don't know," snapped Harry. "His place is called Chestnut Farm. That's all I know and it's out beyond Eastville."

I closed my notebook. "I'm sorry, Harry. I got a bit carried away."

"What's so interesting in that?" he asked.

"Oh, nothing really." I tried to sound nonchalant. "We just like to know these things."

Harry gave me a very old-fashioned look. Countryman he may be but he was no bloody fool.

There was a burst of prolonged applause and cheers from the taproom as Max finished his performance.

As if on cue, the door crashed open and in poured a crowd of young girls. The Land Army had arrived to brighten up the lives of all the hot-blooded males in the Lancaster Arms.

"Evening girls!" shouted Harry. "The wife's away tonight, so I'm all yours."

"No, I'm not, Harry Woods!" shouted Ethel from out back. "And you're not."

Harry shrugged his shoulders. "It's like living with Old Mother Riley." As he turned to go he tapped my arm. "Nice to meet you, mate, even if you're a daft bugger. Come again."

Max reappeared from the direction of the taproom and the piano submitted once more to torture by unseen hands.

"Bloody fantastic," I exclaimed. "Where did you learn to play like that?"

"Royal Academy of Music." A very self-conscious grin came with his reply.

I grinned. "You dark horse!" Suddenly, I had had enough of the pub. "Max, do

53

you mind if we move on?"

He shook his head. "Not at all, it's getting like a sardine can in here. Anywhere special you want to go?"

I wanted to go to Chestnut Farm and meet Mr Cornish but I couldn't say that to Max. I thought for a moment. "How about back to camp?"

"You can't be serious," he protested. "Why not the Red Lion at Revesby?"

I shook my head. "Sorry to be a wet blanket, Max. I could say that I'm a bit out of practice when it comes to socialising - all work and no play since I arrived at West Fen. To tell you the truth, something has come up and I'd like to get back to camp as soon as possible."

Max gave me a curious look. "What could possibly come up in a place like the Lancaster Arms?" He looked around at the melee of bodies and then back to me. "Has this anything to do with your so-called detachment?"

I looked at him with astonishment. "How on earth do you know about that?"

"Houseman came back from seeing the Groupie this morning and told us that you'd not be on the section strength full-time. He said you were getting a jammy little detachment and every now and then you'd be popping off on other duties."

I'd not seen Houseman in the section that day. I'd been stood down in order to get some sleep after the previous night's events. By the time I had got in for duty in the afternoon, Houseman had gone on a liaison visit to Coningsby. He'd obviously started my cover story going.

I shrugged. "Well, it probably has something to do with my new temporary job but, there again, I could be tilting at windmills."

"It all sounds very mysterious but if you want to get back, it's no problem."

"You sure?" I was feeling very guilty at ruining his evening.

"Course not! We can save the petrol for another evening." He drained his pint, dumped the glass on a nearby window ledge and we pushed our way outside to the car.

"Funny thing," he said as he started the MG. "Janner went to see the Groupie this morning too. When he came back he was bloody furious. He bollocked me, he bollocked Natalie and just about everybody else who came within range. I swear he was really looking for you as he was in and out of our office like a Jack in the Box. He asked Natalie why you were not on duty and when she said you had been stood down he told her to send somebody to kick you out of bed and back to your place of duty. Fortunately, Houseman came back and cancelled the whole thing. He was in with Janner for some time and we could hear Janner shouting and raging. Finally he buggered off back to the mess and we didn't see him again for the rest of the day. He was so bloody mad I'm surprised he didn't come and kick you out of bed himself."

I shook my head in disbelief. "But none of you said anything when I came in later."

"Houseman swore us all to secrecy. The other ranks know nothing anyway. The rest of us have been told to co-operate with you but not to ask questions. As I said before, it all sounds a bit mysterious!"

I took a chamois out of the door pocket and tried to wipe the condensation from the windscreen.

"Well, it's not as mysterious as it sounds, but at least it will keep Janner off my back." I started to think about the intruder again. "Can we go straight to the section when we get back?"

"Bloody hell, Carver! I thought you were fed up with work."

"I am, but I've got a bit of a bee in my bonnet and it'll not go away until I've

54

satisfied my curiosity."

Max laughed. "Okay. Back to work it is. Do you want me to stick around?"

"No, I'll be fine. I can think better on my own. Anyway, I've buggered up your evening out, but you'll still be able to get a beer in the mess."

A little later, Sergeant Ann Carter, the duty watchkeeper, let me into the section. I found a large-scale map of the local area plus a couple more to cover the east coast of Lincolnshire. Sergeant Carter brought me a cup of tea and I settled down to try out a theory.

I soon found Eastville and it was, as Harry had said, pretty sparsely populated between the village and the coast. Why would an aircraft be lost in that area? He could have called a number of airfields in the area and he'd have been given a diversion to the one with the best weather. Maybe he had radio failure? Why was he so low? Why fly a circular pattern? None of it added up. Although, there were so many young men under training in Lincolnshire, anything could happen. Aircraft wreckage littered the county as a testimony to the dangers facing student pilots in worn-out aircraft and the vagaries of the Lincolnshire weather. It was not just the students who were caught out. Many an experienced crew had arrived back at base low on fuel and in rapidly deteriorating weather. Not all of them survived, in spite of their experience. Something told me I was looking at a totally different situation. This one didn't add up and I knew I was going to have to go out and find this chap Stan Cornish. I glanced at my watch. There was still time to catch Houseman in the mess. I thanked Carter for the tea, wished her a quiet night and left for the mess.

I dumped my hat and coat in my room and then went through to the bar. I spotted Houseman with three other aircrew chaps, standing in front of the open fire. Before I could approach him, I saw him murmur quick apologies to his friends and head in my direction.

He smiled. "Carver! you have the look of a man on a mission."

"And here I was, thinking I was already the calm, inscrutable but deadly spy."

He laughed. "One thing I know for sure, Carver, you'll never be inscrutable. One can see what you're thinking from ten thousand feet on a foggy night."

I laughed and knew he was right. "Sorry to interrupt your evening, sir. I wanted to ask a favour for tomorrow."

"You've not interrupted anything. Just me, and three more boring old farts, talking about flying."

I looked at the other 'old farts'. The eldest could have been no more than twenty-eight. Wartime attrition in aircrew didn't permit many to reach even middle age. Thirty was definitely old in their game.

"Come on then." He prompted me back to the matter in hand. "What can I do for you?"

"It may be nothing, sir, but I overheard something tonight in a pub that set me thinking. I won't say anything at this stage, because it may be a load of balls but I need to visit a farmer who lives a few miles from here. Somewhere out towards the coast. I wonder if you could get the MTO to let me have a service vehicle?"

There was no hesitation. "Of course, I'll ring him first thing in the morning. Do you have a service driving licence?"

"Yes, sir. I was able to take a test at Cosford."

"No sooner said than done. The station commander put me in the picture this morning. It seems you threw a real spanner in the works last night. He's very impressed with you, but he did have a few reservations about your lack of service experience. I told him that what you lack in experience you make up for with

55

inventiveness."

I laughed. "You mean I make it up as I go along."

"You said that, Carver, not me! Fancy a beer?"

"Not for me, sir. I've got a bit of thinking to do and I've no experience of flying to help me keep up my end of the conversation."

He looked at me carefully. "We'll have to do something about that in the near future. Well, good night to you and try not to get too engrossed in your little problem. Remember to step well back and look at the problem from all angles - not just the one you thought of first."

I wished him 'good night' and headed for my room. Hammond must have been on a forty-eight hour pass as he didn't return that night. For once I'd the chance to get an undisturbed night but, try as I might, sleep would not come. All I could think about was the 'lost' aircraft. What the hell was an old farmer going to be able to tell me? He'd certainly have no idea of aircraft types. Anyway, it had been dark and drizzling with rain. I knew it was going to be a wasted trip but I had to start somewhere. I began to feel like Harry and Ethel's kids. They had woken because the pub, for once, had been too quiet. Maybe I was missing Hammond's raucous snores and his disgusting flatulence! I was certainly missing answers to all the questions whirling around in my brain. It was going to be a long night.

CHAPTER SIX

Houseman was as good as his word and next morning I picked up a service Hillman 'Tilly' from the MT section and set off on my quest to find Chestnut Farm.

I passed through the village of Eastville and also passed the entrances to several farms but none seemed to be Chestnut Farm. The landscape and the weather were dreary in the extreme. I hadn't seen a soul since I spotted an old woman in Eastville, peddling with great difficulty against the wind on a 'sit-up-and-beg' bike. All the roads were dead straight and gave the impression of disappearing forever into the leaden horizon. If I'd been an artist, I'd have needed no palette - just a tube of grey! Man-made drains, like large canals, criss-crossed the flat landscape in evidence of Dutch aid in the reclamation of this part of Lincolnshire from the sea. Lincolnshire was split into three areas, Lindsey, Kesteven and Holland. I didn't need a map to tell me which bit I was driving through.

Eventually, another farm appeared on my left. There had been little in the way of habitation for some time, so I slowed in the hope that this one also had a sign on the gatepost. The house was redbrick, small and plain. Three windows upstairs and two downstairs, with a door plonked symmetrically in the centre. The grey slates gleamed in the damp morning light.

I gently braked to a halt. Was this Chestnut Farm? If it was, the farmer who'd named it had fanciful notions or his trees had failed to flourish. There was not a chestnut in sight. In fact, as far as the eye could see, there were no trees of any description. I shivered as I tried to imagine living in this godforsaken place. It was not just the fact it was surrounded by the dismal fenlands - it just looked the epitome of loneliness. Somehow I knew this was going to be the place. With my luck it just had to be. Then I saw it. The sign was battered and weathered but it confirmed my worst fears – 'Chestnut Farm'.

I sighed, eased out the clutch and began to drive slowly down the potholed track. It was a long track as the house was at least two fields from the road. The Hillman creaked and groaned in protest at the dreadful surface. This track may be fine for horses and tractors but not for one of Mr Rootes's finest. As I neared the farmhouse and its sparse collection of outbuildings, a large black Labrador dog came bounding down the drive to greet me. In a strange way, the sight of the friendly dog raised my spirits. Alas, although it seemed friendly, it also appeared to be very stupid as it stood directly in front of the Hillman and I had to brake to a stop to avoid running over the damned thing. I contemplated getting out and walking the rest of the way to the farm but the muddy track was not the ideal surface for my shiny RAF shoes. It seemed we were at an impasse but I was rescued from my dilemma as a wiry little man emerged from one of the outhouses and shouted at the dog. The Labrador promptly turned and trotted back to the house, with just the occasional glance at me over his shoulder. I followed and parked on a small concrete area in front of the outhouse. At least my shoes would stay clean.

I climbed out of the Hillman and the little man watched my approach, but he made no move to intercept me. His unruly, thick grey hair stuck out in all directions from under his flat cap and his hands were thrust deep into his overall pockets. He wore very muddy wellingtons and his feet were planted firmly apart in an overt defensive stance. I felt somewhat overdressed!

I put out my hand. "Mr Cornish?"

He ignored my hand and his blue eyes regarded me from under bushy eyebrows. "Aye."

Our conversation was getting off to a slow start but I plugged on regardless. "My name is Pilot Officer Sam Carver from RAF West Fen. I wonder if I might have a few words with you?" A little pompous, I thought, but to the point.

"Aye?" No beating about the bush with this guy.

"I was chatting with Harry Woods from the Lancaster Arms in New Bolingbroke last night. He mentioned something you had told him in passing and it interested me very much."

"Oh, aye?" The blue eyes never wavered.

"The lost plane?" I said hopefully. "A few nights ago?"

"Aye."

The fact he was a man of few words was beginning to get my bloody goat and, in spite of my determination to hold up my end of this interrogation with dignity, I lost my temper.

"Mr Cornish!" I said desperately, my voice growing in volume with my anger. "This is very important. For fuck's sake, try to give me some help!"

The only discernible change in Cornish's demeanour was a sudden sparkle in the eyes and a small twitch at the corner of his mouth. Both signs were soon gone and his lined, weather-beaten face resumed its mask. He regarded me for what seemed an age then he suddenly walked past me and headed for the house.

"You'd better come in and have a cup of tea then," he called over his shoulder.

I stared at his departing figure in amazement and it was at this moment that the dog did a very strange thing. He moved forward and quickly took my gloved left hand in his mouth and began to slowly pull me towards the house. I'd never known a dog do this before and, although I was intrigued, my progress was somewhat undignified. The dog was pulling me in a slight stoop to the left and I had to walk sideways to avoid treading on the damned thing's paws. I arrived at the farmhouse door looking like a cross between Quasimodo and a bloody crab. I felt, yet again, a complete arsehole!

Cornish had stopped to kick his Wellington boots off just inside the door and he watched our approach. I could swear the little bastard was struggling not to laugh.

"Novel behavioural trait for a dog." I know it sounded prattish but it always happens to me when I find myself embarrassed. I always end up feeling an even bigger prat!

"He likes you," said Cornish with a straight face but he finally lost his composure and dissolved into helpless laughter. The dog released my hand and I regained a more normal posture as I waited for Cornish to pull himself together.

"I hate to think what he'd do if he didn't like me," I muttered in a fit of pique.

Cornish wiped the tears from his eyes with oil-stained hands. "You'd have no use for a glove on that side."

I knew he meant it.

He turned into the house. "Come on in and I'll get the kettle on."

I followed him down the hallway, which ran through the heart of the house, to where the kitchen was situated at the rear. A small fire burned happily in the grate and two comfortable, albeit slightly battered, armchairs were positioned each side of the fireplace. An old Ultra wireless set sat on a shelf to one side of the fireplace, its accumulator perched precariously on the edge of the shelf. The remaining furniture comprised a small dining table covered with a neatly embroidered cloth, two high-backed chairs, and a small Welsh-style dresser. Small vases adorned the mantelpiece and a large ornamental clock ticked loudly from the wall. The kitchen obviously was also used as a small sitting room and dining room. The only oddity was something akin to a village pump standing to one side of the sink. I suddenly realised this was the only supply of water to the house. No mains water here and that also meant an outside toilet. Indeed, as I glanced out of the window I spotted the unmistakable edifice of an outside privy at the bottom of the garden.

Cornish had taken a tea caddy and teapot from another shelf near the fireplace. He picked up the kettle from the draining board and, sure enough, he pumped fresh water from the pump by means of the carved, wooden handle. He placed the kettle on a hook over the fire and then motioned me to one of the two easy chairs.

"Take your coat off and sit down. The kettle will be a while boiling so you'll have plenty of time to tell me what you're so het up about."

He took my greatcoat and cap and hung them on a hook behind the door. When he sat in the chair opposite I saw his eyes flick to my tunic breast and then back to my face. He was obviously disappointed he saw no aircrew brevet there. I knew I'd suddenly plummeted even further in his estimation but as he slid his slight frame into the chair, I noticed his feet barely touched the snip-rug covering the quarry-tiled floor. For some reason, known only to my inner rationale, it gave me a slightly superior feeling. He quickly deflated my newfound sense of self-assurance.

"Have you got a name other than that high-faluting rubbish you gave me out in the yard?" he asked.

"Sam," I said eagerly. "And you?"

He remained totally impassive. "Mr Cornish."

I'd no answer to that and I had to look away from that penetrating gaze. There was a pregnant silence.

"Well?" he finally asked. "What about the lost plane, I haven't got all day?"

I was smarting from being made to look such a clown but relieved to get back to the reason for my visit. "Harry Woods told me you'd noticed a plane flying around here in circles as if the pilot was lost. When was that?"

"Night before last."

I felt a small frisson of excitement. "What time was that?"

"Quarter to nine 'til nine." No movement from him, just that stare. Even the damned dog was now in on the act. He was sitting between my legs with his head tilted upwards, his eyes unwaveringly on mine.

I glanced quickly back up to Cornish. "You mean it flew around for a whole fifteen minutes?"

He just nodded.

"Which way did it head when it finally flew off?"

"West."

"Towards West Fen?" I prompted.

"That's right."

"How could you tell? It was pitch dark and drizzling with rain."

"I'm not a bloody idiot."

I jumped as the dog suddenly licked my hand. I glanced down and idly stroked the animal's ears. As I glanced up, I saw a little smile quickly disappear from Cornish's face. We were back to impassive mode.

"You could tell it was a Jerry?" I asked.

"Who said it was a Jerry?"

I looked at him carefully. This next bit would take a bit of careful handling. The dog nuzzled his nose into my palm. "Well, Mr Cornish, just after the time you mentioned, an intruder came over West Fen and shot down two of our Lancasters. I admit it's a bit of a long shot but I've to assume it was our Jerry."

"You can assume all you like, young feller. It was one of ours."

"How could you tell? It was dark."

"Merlin." Just the one word set my heart beating a little faster.

"Sorry?" I wanted to be damned sure he'd say it again.

"It had a Merlin engine," he answered as if talking to a complete idiot.

I gave him a long look but his gaze didn't waver an inch. Either he was an arrogant bastard who thought he knew it all, or he really did know a Merlin from a Hercules, Vulture or whatever.

As if in answer to my prayers, there was a sudden roar of engines and I saw, through the small window by the sink, a Mosquito at about a hundred to two hundred feet. It was in a hard bank to the right and was completely out of Cornish's line of sight. I glanced behind me to see if there was a mirror on the wall but the wall was bare. I turned back to Cornish but before I could ask my question he said just one word.

"Mossie."

"How do you know it was a Mosquito?" I asked in disbelief. "It could have been a Spitfire, a Hurricane, a Halifax or a Lancaster."

He looked at me with barely suppressed contempt. "It would have to have been two Spits or Hurricanes because there was more than one Merlin. The sound was here and gone too fast to be a Lanc or a Halibag - they lumber along. That was really shifting so it had to be a Mossie."

I stared at him in astonishment and he smiled a small smile but there was no smugness there. He rose to his feet. The kettle was boiling merrily and he removed it from the fire. He poured a little boiling water into the teapot to warm it and popped the kettle back on the fire. The water from the teapot he swirled around and disposed of in the sink. He spooned three teaspoons of tea from the caddy into the teapot and carried it over to the hearth. He filled the teapot from the kettle and walked back to the table. His movements were deft, precise and gentle. Not what one would expect from such a hard little devil.

As he waited patiently for the tea to brew, I began to notice how spotlessly clean everything was in the room. Even the windowpanes were clean. No cobwebs and no dust but I had yet to meet the wife. I suddenly realised there were no photographs. No snaps of a wife and children. The kitchen had become very quiet and I glanced quickly up at Cornish. He was watching me.

"I never married," he said quietly.

I got that tingle at the nape of my neck again. How the hell did he know what I was thinking?

He walked over to the dresser and took down two beautiful china cups and saucers. This man was a walking, breathing, living contradiction. I estimated his age to be mid - sixties. He was physically strong, no doubt about that. He was also incredibly perceptive and, I was beginning to realise, a very intelligent man. This was no hick from the sticks but there was a conflicting character trait that puzzled me.

There was an element of the fastidious about him. When he held the cup and saucer it was done in a smooth and gentle way. His hands were rough and careworn but he handled everything gently. I felt I had to break the silence.

"Never met the right girl?" I suggested lamely.

"I met plenty, in spite of living in this godforsaken place."

"But none of them appealed to you as a potential wife?"

He handed me the cup of tea and held out a small sugar bowl. I shook my head and he replaced the bowl on the table. He picked up his own cup and saucer and lowered himself carefully into his chair.

"What do you know about epilepsy?" he asked. He didn't look up but concentrated on stirring his tea.

I wasn't ready for the sudden change of tack in our conversation. "Not a lot," I replied carefully. "It must be very debilitating for the sufferer and unfortunately it seems to carry a social stigma. I had a distant aunt who suffered from it and she was virtually an outcast, even from our own family. I felt very sorry for her."

"I'm an epileptic," said Cornish quietly. He was watching carefully for my reaction.

"I'm sorry." It was totally inadequate but I was lost for a sensible answer.

He took a sip of tea and placed his cup and saucer on a small occasional table down by his chair. "Actually, that's not quite true. I used to suffer from epilepsy when I was a small boy and it lasted into my twenties. Then, either I grew out of it or the medicines my doctor prescribed did the trick. I've not had an attack in forty years."

I watched him in silence because I could still not assemble a reply that was not pitying or patronising.

"But you were right about the stigma," he said suddenly. "No young girl in her right mind would want to marry an idiot who could, without warning, collapse into a twitching, frothing fool. Every girl, without exception, once she learned of my malady, would avoid me like the plague. Kids thought it great entertainment to watch me have an attack. I became a sort of sick celebrity - good for a laugh."

He'd spoken in a perfectly controlled voice. There was no hatred or self-pity; in fact no emotion at all. He just made simple statements in a matter-of-fact voice.

"Surely, once you were well again, it didn't matter?"

"People around here have long memories. Would you let your daughter marry a chap with my medical history? The chance of your grandchildren being epileptics?"

I'd no answer.

The dog moved away from me and went over to Cornish as if sensing a sadness I couldn't recognise. Cornish looked down at the dog and smiled. He gently cupped the dog's muzzle in both hands - again there was that gentleness. He spoke as if to the dog. "I'd have left the area but my father died and I was left to look after the farm. Mother died shortly afterwards so I became a reluctant farmer."

"You've lived here all your life?" I asked gently.

He nodded and gave a small sigh. "Yes. I've become not just a farmer but somebody who can sew, darn, launder, iron and cook. It's now second nature to me."

"Do you enjoy your solitude?" I think I knew the answer before he spoke.

"Enjoy my solitude?" He laughed and for the first time there was a hint of bitterness. "I'd solitude forced on me and I've not enjoyed it." He suddenly sat forward in his chair. "Do you know what the greatest thing in my life has been?"

I shook my head.

"The war," he said quietly. "If it had not been for Hitler, I'd have died a lonely old man, without having known anybody outside of this bloody fenland desert. When the first RAF blokes began coming into the Lancaster Arms at New Bolingbroke, my whole life changed. Suddenly I didn't have to rely on the wireless and books for my knowledge of the outside world, it was all around me, any night I wanted to go to the pub. I was now meeting men and women from all walks of life who knew nothing of my past, yet they would laugh and joke with me as an equal. I found I could hold my own in conversation and people were prepared to listen. For the first time in my life I was alive."

He sat back in the chair and the tension had gone from him as quickly as it came. "Do you know?" he said. "If I had tried to hold a conversation with the local so-called gentleman farmers, they would have cut me dead. I'm just a small tenant farmer. They'd have seen it as a local yokel trying to get above his station. But to all the servicemen, I'm just Stan. We discuss politics, religion, war and even sex. Nobody gives a damn what my station in life is. They don't even realise that the feudal system is still alive and kicking in Lincolnshire. For once in my life I belong." He paused. "That must be difficult for a young chap like you to understand."

"Not at all," I replied quietly. At last I was beginning to understand the little man but I knew I'd lose him if I showed even the slightest hint of sympathy. "I understand perfectly. As a young lad I didn't fit in. I wasn't the footballing type and I loathed cricket. It wasn't until I went up to university and I met other people like myself that I found my niche."

"Do you like the RAF?" he asked.

"Not particularly," I replied with a rueful grin. "Unlike you, Hitler has done me no favours."

He suddenly grinned and his whole face was transformed. The blue eyes sparkled and a myriad small laugh lines appeared all over his face. "Sorry," he said. "I want to see that bastard blown sky-high with the rest of his Nazi friends, but it is strange how it took a war to bring Stan Cornish out of his shell."

I found myself laughing heartily with him.

He rose and held out a hand to me. I took his hand and, to my surprise, he pulled me to my feet.

"I've work to do, young man. So, if you're finished with the questions, I must get back to my chores."

I clasped his hand in both of mine. "Mr Cornish, thank you for your help. You've helped me more than you could ever realise."

"So have you, lad," he said quietly." I think you must be a very good intelligence officer because I've told you things I've never told anyone before. You've a good technique."

I stared at him in amazement.

He laughed and pushed me towards the door. "No brevet, Mr Carver. Dead give away. Who else would be so interested in a strange aircraft?"

He made perfect sense and I marvelled again at this astute little man.

We reached the Hillman and, as I opened the door, an aircraft passed high overhead. Cornish never even looked up.

"Beaufighter," he said with a grin.

I looked up and watched the aircraft disappear into the now thinning cloud. It was indeed a Beaufighter. I brought my eyes back down to meet his. "You really do know your aircraft."

"I told you, the war has opened up a whole new world for me. I've a rabid interest in everything military. Aircraft, our land forces, the U-boat war in the Atlantic - everything!"

I eased myself into the driving seat and wound down the window before closing the door.

"Mr Cornish," I said and looked him straight in the eye. "Would you care to join me for a pint one evening in the Lancaster Arms?"

"Anytime you like, Mr Carver."

He turned away to get on with his chores but before I could ask my question, he answered it. "I'm in the telephone book!" he shouted over his shoulder.

I drove slowly out of the farmyard and began to think again about that strange aircraft with a Merlin engine!

When I arrived back at West Fen I drove straight to the section. Natalie was helping the other pilot officer in our little gang, David Jones, to sort out a pile of signals from Command. Norman was a tubby little guy with a red face and was already losing his hair although he was no older than me. We'd not yet met although Natalie had spoken of him. He looked up as I entered the room and grinned with anticipation.

"Ah! Is this the poor sod taking over from me as chief whipping boy?"

"It certainly is," answered Natalie. "Hi, Sam. How are things in the higher echelons?"

I hung up my hat and coat and ran a hand through my hair. "Pretty good, pretty good, but I could murder a cup of tea."

ACW Roberts jumped up from her desk. "I'll get you a cup, sir. Anybody else for a brew?"

"Might as well do a brew for all of us, Roberts," replied Natalie.

"Where have you been skiving off to, you crafty sod?" asked Dave.

I shot a quick look at Natalie and saw the slight shake of her head. "I've just been running an errand for the Groupie," I said lightly. "I'm his whipping boy now."

"Bloody hell!" exclaimed Dave and turned a pleading face to Natalie. "How's that for bloody snobbery? I get crap from a wing commander but he gets it from a group captain. This lad will go a long way!"

I laughed but I knew that we both had no illusions. Poor old Dave would get all of Janner's vitriol in my absence.

Tom Powell entered carrying a pile of amendments for the section's Air Publications.

"Sarge, is the squadron leader in?" I asked him.

"I'm afraid he's with the wingco at the moment, sir. As soon as he's back in his office I'll give you a shout."

I nodded. "Thanks, Sarge."

Powell turned to Dave. "Mr Cox, sir!"

"Oh God!" Dave turned to us with a pained expression. "When he calls me 'Mr', I know I'm in the shit."

There was a malicious grin on Tom Powell's face. "Not at all, sir, but I do believe you're now responsible for all the section's Air Publications?"

Dave nodded glumly. "I'm afraid so, Sarge. Don't tell me, somebody farted at Command HQ and they have written two thousand amendments on the subject."

"No, sir. I've just a few here but I couldn't help but notice rather a lot hidden in the cupboard over there." Powell's voice was light and humorous but there was no mistaking the thinly veiled reproof.

Dave looked more than a little embarrassed. "Sorry, Sarge. You've made your point. I promise they'll all be up to date by the end of this week."

"Thank you, sir." There was a hint of a smile on the sergeant's face as he headed back to his office.

I began to see what people meant when they said it was the NCOs who ran the air force. Tom Powell was always on top of the job and was a master of tact when chivvying us 'hostilities only' guys to keep our mind on the job.

He popped his head back round the door. "The squadron leader is in his office, sir."

I followed him through, picking up my cuppa from Roberts on the way. I knocked on Houseman's door.

"Come in!"

I popped my head round the door. "Okay if I bring my cuppa in with me, sir?"

"Carver! Of course you can, man. Come on in and take a seat. How did your visit go?"

"Very well, sir." I settled back in a chair. "He's a remarkable little chap."

"Really?" Houseman was surprised. "Not your average hayseed?"

"Anything but, sir. He's a sharp little devil and I've no doubts about his abilities at aircraft recognition. I'm afraid that what he told me did nothing to allay my fears that this was a 'friendly' kite."

"Oh, shit!" Houseman swore as he flopped back in his chair. "I was hoping you were wrong but Groupie was convinced you knew what you were talking about. I must admit, I didn't think an echo could have fooled you. What did the farmer say?"

I told him about my meeting with Cornish. He didn't interrupt me at any time and when I'd finished, he stood up and walked over to the office window. He stood with his hands behind his back and didn't turn round when he spoke.

"So, where do we go from here?"

I took a contemplative sip of my now cold tea. "If we've got ourselves a Trojan horse, the next question we must ask ourselves is 'where is it based?' "

Houseman turned. "You sound as if you already have your suspicions."

I nodded. "What is the range of a Spitfire or a Hurricane?"

He thought for a moment but then realisation dawned. "Bloody hell, Carver! I hope you're not going to say what I think you're going to say."

I stood and began to pace the small office as I spoke. "Let's look at it this way. Neither a Spit nor a Hurricane could fly from enemy-held territory to this country, loiter for some hours because of delayed takeoffs, carry out an attack and fly all the way back to France, Belgium, Holland or wherever it should be based."

Houseman shook his head in disbelief. "Surely not in this country? For God's sake, the place is crawling with airfields and radar. Maybe it was just coincidence he got here at the right time"

I shook my head. "The aircraft Cornish heard was definitely waiting for something. A radio codeword, a visual signal or just simply the runway lights I don't know. He was low and flying a precise circuit until he suddenly made off to the west."

Houseman nodded. "The chap was either very good or very stupid. The visibility was crap that night, especially for a single-seater at low level." He shook his head and turned back to the window. "I cannot believe what we're talking ourselves into. It's too fantastic for words."

I sat down again. "Is it really impossible for a rogue kite to be hidden in this area?"

Houseman shrugged his shoulders. "If you'd asked me that last year, I'd've said it was totally impossible. The whole coast was being patrolled day and night because of the expected invasion. There were troops everywhere, backed up by the Home

Guard. Now the threat is over, I suppose it is a different story. Even if it still has token patrols, the area is very sparsely populated. There are some very isolated areas but most of it is marshland and mud flats."

"Sounds pretty impossible, doesn't it?" I said glumly.

Houseman shook his head as if a thought had just occurred to him. He turned to face me.

"Well, no, not really. I remember that in the October of Forty-One, 97 Squadron, over at Coningsby, had a Manchester go down on the way back from a raid on Bremen. Flak had holed the fuel tanks and they just didn't have enough juice to make it the last few miles, so they crash-landed near Friskney on the East Coast. It was still dark and they thought they were coming down over flat fenland but it turned out to be the marshes and instead, they found themselves in the water. Thankfully, it was only about chest deep and as soon as it began to get light, one of them set off to wade to the shore to get help. The others stayed put and fired off all their emergency flares trying, in vain as it turned out, to attract attention. In the end they followed their crew mate and waded to dry land. The only person in sight, away in the distance, was an old chap ploughing with his horses. They found an isolated house a little further up the coast and were finally taken in by the owner and given a cup of tea. While they were waiting for transport back to Coningsby, they asked the lady of the house if she'd seen their flares. She said she had, but thought it was ships out at sea and had taken no notice. They discovered that although there was still the threat of invasion, there were no mines, no beach obstacles and no troops. In fact, there were no defences at all. If that could happen then, I'm coming to the conclusion that maybe it is possible for somebody to squirrel away a rogue kite and remain undetected."

He picked up a pencil from his desk and began to lightly tap out a rhythm on his teeth. I waited in silence. I didn't want to interrupt his train of thought. He suddenly threw the pencil down and strode to the door. He opened it and stood in the corridor. "Sergeant Powell!" he shouted.

There was a pause and then Powell came trotting down the corridor. Houseman turned quickly to me. "Natalie knows a little about what is going on, doesn't she?"

I nodded and he turned back to Powell. "Sarge, ask Miss Cowen to find some large scale maps of the East Coast from the Humber Estuary to Yarmouth and bring them here."

"Yessir!" Tom shot off on his errand.

Houseman rubbed his hands and I knew he was enjoying himself. "Right, let's get down to work. When we get the charts we'll try to plot likely areas for a secret airstrip. We know the length of runway needed by all of our fighters and we can use that as a scale for likely fields or flat areas. It sounds crazy but I'm beginning to think you're right."

"Sir, can you give me a rundown of the takeoff times and delays?" I asked, as another thought occurred to me.

Houseman gave me a puzzled look but lifted a sheet of typed paper from a tray on his desk. He studied it for a moment then began to give me a précis of the times.

"Takeoff should have been at 17.30. Crews told at 16.30 takeoff had been delayed until 18.00. Then they were told at 17.30 that takeoff would now be at 20.30. They were already in the aircraft with engines running when, at 20.15, they had to shut down as takeoff had been delayed yet again. New time was 21.00. That became the actual." He looked up from the piece of paper. "What are you trying to make of that?"

I sat and tried to get my whirling thoughts into some sort of order. There was another theory forming in my brain, but I had to reason it out before committing it to Houseman's scrutiny. As I began to talk, I marked each point by a long pause.

"Right," I said slowly. "Let's look at the timing. The crews get one hour's warning before the first scrub. Even better, they get three hour's notice of the second scrub. But, they only got fifteen minute's warning of the third and last scrub." I paused and glanced at Houseman to see if he was beginning to see what I was getting at. His face told me that he was with me all the way. He finished my train of thought for me.

"Whoever is controlling our intruder had plenty of time to warn the pilot of the first two scrubs but not the third. Our pilot would've been airborne and wondering what had happened to the bloody runway lights. His first reaction would be to give it up as a bad job but our joker on the ground must have been able to give him the revised time whilst he was actually in the air. He now just had to stick around until they switched on the runway lights." For the first time since I'd met him, Houseman looked rattled. "Carver, what have you started?"

"I'm afraid I don't know, sir. Whatever it is, it scares the shit out of me. If we believe in what we're saying, then we must have an enemy agent on West Fen. Or, even worse, at Five Group HQ."

"Shitty death!" Houseman swore.

"The wing commander is going to have a field day if we let this out and then find it's all a load of balls," I warned, inwardly praying that my instincts were not letting me down.

Houseman held a finger to his lips. "The Group Captain was adamant that no matter what happens, Wing Commander Janner is to be kept right out of this affair. If he caught just a sniff of it, he'd be on to Group every five minutes offering his superior intellect on the matter and insisting he take command. If this is a real situation, then it is a very serious situation. We cannot afford to have a leak in the system or our prey will make a run for it and that, as they say, will be that. We must catch the bastards in the act."

I was just going to reply, when there was a knock at the door. Houseman walked over and opened it. "Oh thanks, Natalie. Just pop them on my desk."

Natalie entered with her arms full of maps. She flashed me a little smile and dumped the charts.

"Anything else, sir?"

"No, Natalie. Those should be fine."

As she turned to go, Houseman put a hand on her arm. "Natalie, I'm sorry we're keeping this from you all at the moment. We've got to keep this under wraps until we know we're doing the right thing. Okay?"

Natalie nodded. "I understand, sir. The best of luck with whatever it is you're doing."

After she had closed the door behind her, Houseman grabbed the charts and began to sort them into some sort of order. "Right! Let's see... Ah, here we are ... the Humber estuary. This is where we will start our search. Unless you've a better idea?"

I shook my head. It was as good a place to start as any and for the next hour we discussed, argued and rejected site after site. We were getting nowhere.

"Oh, bollocks!" fumed Houseman as he slumped in his chair. "This is bloody useless. We can't get an impression from these bloody things. It is like looking for a needle in a haystack. The real problem is, we can't see the topography. What looks like a nice big, flat field could be ridged, furrowed or even covered in bloody rocks." He put his hands behind his head and started a tuneless whistle through his teeth. This went on for some minutes and then he jumped to his feet. "Bloody photographs!" he cried. "What we need is oblique photos of the area immediately inland of this east coast."

"You mean get PRU in on the act?" I asked.

"They're too busy," answered Houseman. "Plus we'd have to wait ages to get the pics. No, I've a better idea. We've an old Anson on Station Flight that is used as a station hack. I use it regularly to keep my hand in. I reckon I could get Sergeant Lamont, from the Photo Section, to jury-rig an oblique aerial camera in the old Annie and we could fly a sortie from the Humber down to Norfolk. We may be able to spot something visually but, as a bonus, we would have photos to interpret at our leisure."

"Max Shearing is our man for that, sir. He can see things on a photo that just look like a smudge to me."

Houseman nodded. "You're right – we're just amateurs. Problem is, that's another person to be let in on our theory before we're sure we've got something. There again, without his expertise, we could miss the very thing we're looking for. Also, I'll have to get Groupie's permission to use the Annie but I can't see that will be a problem."

I grinned. "He'll probably want to come with you."

"What's all this 'you' business, Carver?" asked Houseman. "I can't do the bloody job on my own. You'll have to come along as camera operator."

Although I was secretly pleased at getting a chance to fly for the first time in my life, I tried not to appear too eager. " I know damn all about cameras, sir"

"Sergeant Lamont will soon get you up to scratch on that little problem, Carver. A sly smile came over his face. "Actually, there are one hundred and sixty good reasons why I want you along."

I wondered at the precise number of reasons but he was already picking up the telephone and I heard him get through to the Photo Section. He asked the person on the other end to hang on a minute, put his hand over the mouthpiece and turned to me. "Carver, could you go back to your farmer friend and try to get a bit more out of him? Did he see our kites explode? Had he heard the damned thing before that night? You know the sort of thing."

"I'll get on to it right away, sir."

I was heading for the door when something occurred to me. I turned and Houseman spoke into the phone.

"Hang on again would you, Sarge? Yes, Carver - what is it?"

"Mr Cornish is a very astute man, sir. I reckon he's going to figure this all out for himself. I'm sure he'd normally talk about it, but a few pints in the pub could be a different scenario."

Houseman rubbed his chin thoughtfully. "Hmm, I see what you mean." He scratched his head. He could see the inherent danger of an outsider putting it all together and then discussing it with all and sundry in the pub.

"Can we get him to sign the Official Secrets Act?" he asked in exasperation.

"Don't know how it works, sir. He's not a government employee, he's just a farmer."

"Leave it with me," Houseman ordered. "I'll have a chat with the legal chaps at Command. Just carry on for now. If the little sod blabs, I'll personally shoot the bastard."

As I closed his office door behind me, I knew he meant it!

Natalie met me in the plans room. "Were the charts what you wanted?"

"I'm afraid they didn't really tell us anything," I answered wearily. "But

Houseman has an alternative plan. He's very enthusiastic. I just hope I'm not making a bloody idiot of us both."

"I'm sure you're big enough to take it," Natalie quipped. "Anyway, I think I know what you suspect and I'm sure you're on the right track."

I grinned. "Clever old you and don't try the old adage of 'you're not just a pretty face'. I think you've a beautiful face."

"Shh!" She put a finger to her lips and looked quickly around the room but I'd kept my voice low and the others seemed totally unaware of my indiscretion.

"Ops on tonight?" I asked to change the subject.

She groaned. "Certainly are. Poor devils have got Berlin."

"Ouch!" I replied with feeling. I looked at my watch. "Hell! I must get that blasted Hillman back to the MT Section."

"Personal service car now, eh?" Natalie tutted quietly. "Even Wing Commander Janner hasn't got one of those."

"Don't go stirring it up, Cowen, or I'll not invite you out to sample the delights of George Formby at one of the Boston fleapits."

She raised herself to her full height. "I have, in the past, received rather more elegantly worded invitations but, in spite of my reservations as to your lack of innate charm, I accept." She lifted her chin and gazed at me with those bright eyes. "If only for the novelty value," she added with a mischievous smirk.

"Rowlocks, Cowen!"

She burst out laughing. "I rest my case. Go and mount your fiery MT steed and disappear into a setting sun."

I took a quick look around the room. Nobody appeared to be watching so I leaned forward and kissed her on the nose. I didn't wait for her response. I just headed for the door with a cry of "Geronimo!"

I departed with her parting word in my ear. "Namedropper!"

It was already getting dusk and Lancasters were rumbling into life all around the airfield. I thought of the mystery fighter that could be out there, lurking like a predatory shark just waiting for its prey. I was so deep in thought, I'd forgotten the high kerbstone on the edge of the parking area. I hit the kerb full force with my leading foot and fell arse over tit onto the rough concrete. I felt a sharp pain in my left wrist as I hit the ground but managed to wrench myself into a sideways roll to prevent my head smashing into the rear wheel of the vehicle. I lay there for a few moments - all the breath knocked out of me. My wrist hurt like hell.

"Oh, fuck it!" I grunted out aloud.

"Not a bad circuit, old boy, and you'd pegged your approach speed, but I'm afraid you flared a little too high and stalled in." The voice boomed out of the darkness and I peered up into the gloom. I saw a large figure bending over me and I felt his hand on my shoulder. "Think you can get up?"

"Yes, I think so, although I seem to have done something to my wrist."

"Good God!" exclaimed my rescuer. "That could be very serious."

"What do you mean - 'it could be serious'?" I winced with pain.

"Well, if it's your right wrist, that could seriously affect your ability to lift a full pint pot of the venerable mead." He stooped to get an arm under my shoulders.

"It's my left wrist," I reassured him.

"God! That's even worse, old chap," he said in a voice of doom, as if I was about to expire on the spot. "That's your wanking arm."

I couldn't believe the incongruity of such a conversation, whilst lying on the car park with a stranger's arm round my shoulder, but I felt I had to have the last word.

"Why can't I use my right hand?"

"It's just not the same, old boy." He was beginning to shake with laughter. "My old friend at prep school, Batty Bartholt, said it was better with the left hand because it felt like somebody else was doing it."

I'd had enough of this. "Oh, for fuck's sake, you daft bugger, are you going to get me on my feet or not?"

"Undercart serviceable?" he asked.

"Apart from a badly stubbed toe."

"Super! Have you up in no time."

I winced as he hauled me to my feet. My wrist hurt like hell and my toe throbbed, but at least I was now able to get a better look at the man who had come to my aid. The first thing I spotted was a huge walrus moustache. He was wearing a leather flying-jacket and he had a very colourful scarf at his throat.

He pointed to the Hillman. "This your bus?"

I nodded and winced as I tried to take a step forward.

He opened the passenger door and took my arm. "Come on, hop in. Sorry, old boy, no pun intended. I'll run you over to sick quarters and let them take a look at you."

I managed to get into the seat and we were soon on our way.

I turned to my rescuer. "Thanks for going to all this trouble. My own stupid fault. Deep in thought and not looking where I was going."

"No problem, old boy. You're just one more blackout casualty. It's more bloody dangerous walking, cycling and driving round this place at night than it is flying over Berlin. That's where I should be heading off to at the moment but I've only just got back from survivor leave and two of my crew are still in hospital."

"Shit!" I replied and felt a bit of a fake. "What happened?"

"Are you actually interested, old boy, or are you just indulging your innate sense of the Good Samaritan?"

"Of course I'm interested, you twit."

He roared with laughter. "Keep your ruddy shirt on. I just don't want you going all over the station telling everybody what a bloody line-shooter I am, that's all."

"I haven't been in the air force long enough to know when somebody is shooting a line or just telling the truth. You're on pretty safe ground with me."

"Okay, if you really want to know. We were 'gardening' off the Friesian Islands. Never liked the job, always too low. It didn't help when we started dropping the bloody mines in an area where a Sperrbrecher was operating. Bastard tore us to shreds. Didn't see him until he opened fire. We made it as far as the Yorkshire coast. The crew had decided to stick it out in the hope we would make dry land. Paddling in the North Sea in December is not to be recommended! Two of them had been pretty badly shot up anyway, so we really had no choice but to hope we made terra firma. Just over the coast I parked the old girl in a field."

We were just pulling up outside Station Sick Quarters and I wanted to hear the end of the story.

"Did you all get out?"

"More or less." He applied the handbrake and switched off the engine. "I got off very lightly compared to the lads but they're all on the mend and we should be back together again soon."

The levity had gone from his voice and I could detect the concern he felt for his crew. The dropping of his guard was only momentary and he was soon back into the 'old boy' and 'wizard prang' mode.

"What's your name, old boy? I assume you're from intelligence as, not only did I pick you up from outside their very warren, but no self-respecting aircrew bod has a lovely clean greatcoat like yours."

I laughed. "You're right, I'm in intelligence. Got here just before Christmas and the name is Carver - Sam Carver."

He held out a hand. "Jack Barclay, old boy. 552 Squadron. Pilot, raconteur, bon viveur and deflowerer of virgins."

"Nice to meet you, Jack. Thanks for all your help. Maybe I can buy you a beer in the mess sometime" I shook his hand before he leapt out to open the passenger door.

"Accepted with alacrity, old chap. Now, let's get you inside."

As we entered Sick Quarters, a tall squadron leader was walking towards us. He had grey hair and a very long, aquiline nose. It should have given him a rather aloof air but the big grin on his face banished any coldness before it had a chance to affect his features.

"Harry, old boy!" called out Barclay. "I've got a chap here who just made a determined effort to throw himself off a very high kerb."

The senior medical officer shook his head. "Are you sure you didn't push the poor bod, Barclay?"

"You've a very low opinion of me, doc. I promise you he did it all by himself." He turned to me. "I don't think you'll be driving the old bus again today, old chap. Would you like me to return it to your section or the mess?"

"I was actually going to return it to the MT section."

"Okay, I'll take it back for you. It's not far out of my way. Best of luck, old boy. Oh, another thing, don't let old sawbones here and his cronies get too carried away with your injuries. They kill far more than they cure. Bloke came in here last week and said he felt circumspect. Ten minutes later they made him a member of the Jewish faith."

"Bugger off, Barclay!" said the SMO lightly and showed him to the door. Barclay was gone with a final grin and a wave to me.

"Nice chap," I said to the SMO as he returned.

"Bloody nice chap," he replied. "And a very lucky young man."

"You mean to survive his prang?"

"You know about that, do you?" asked the SMO, watching me carefully.

"Well, he just told me he had to park it in a field in Yorkshire. 'Park' was his word, not mine."

"That's typical of young Barclay." The SMO shook his head. "That man is the master of understatement. He pulled off a miracle getting the bloody thing back at all. It was like a colander. He and his flight engineer spent three hours pulling the control column back and to the left to stop the kite from spinning in. They tried tying the yoke in place but they ended up hauling for all their might with their feet braced on the instrument panel. When they finally hit the deck, the kite broke up all over the field. Barclay and the engineer were thrown through a gap in the fuselage as the nose broke off. The rest of the crew managed to drag themselves and each other clear. In a normal world they should all be dead but they are very much alive. Mind you, it was touch and go for a couple of them."

"Bloody hell!" I said quietly. "I'd no idea."

The SMO gave me a grim smile. "He'll never tell you what really happened. I can tell you this though – he's been recommended for the DFC and he bloody well deserves it."

He started to walk towards his office. "Think you can hobble into here and I'll take a look at that wrist and see what you've done to your foot."

After examining the damage he felt pretty certain I'd only sprained and bruised my wrist. The toe was just bruising. Both would be painful for a few days.

"I've a suspected appendicitis leaving for Boston hospital any minute," said the SMO looking at his watch. "I think you'd better go over there in the same ambulance and get your wrist X-rayed. Tell them your case is urgent and they should process the plates tonight and let you bring them back with you. I'll be in the mess, so just call me and I'll have a look at them to make sure my diagnosis is correct."

"That's very kind of you, sir. I've got a lot on my plate at the moment and the last thing I want is to be off sick."

He grinned. "Sounds like you're trying to win the war all by yourself." He pulled a form from a pad on his desk. "Let's have your name and you can take this form with you to Boston."

"Pilot Officer Carver, sir. Intelligence section."

He paused from his writing. "Ah, you're the new lad. I was talking to that lovely lass, Natalie. It was at the Christmas dance in the mess." His eyes twinkled. "She spoke quite highly of you."

There was not a lot I could say to that and, to my embarrassment, I felt myself begin to blush.

The SMO laughed and helped me to my feet. "Oh, the innocence of youth. I didn't know there was any left." He pointed to the door at the rear of sick quarters. "You'll find the ambulance waiting out the back. The first thing you must do tomorrow is let the MTO know you'll need a driver. You'll not be driving yourself for at least a week."

I felt really pissed off and it must have shown.

"Never mind, Carver," he called after me. "Just make sure you let them know that you're for an X-ray, not an appendectomy."

I waved a resigned hand and limped out to the ambulance.

It was late when I finally got to bed. The doctors and nurses at Boston hospital had been very helpful and kind. As the SMO had predicted, I'd only sprained my wrist and bruised my toe. I'd managed to catch Houseman in the mess on my return and he told me not to worry. He'd make sure the MTO knew I needed a driver for the following day.

Actually, that was the only bright spot on the horizon. I was really looking forward to meeting the little farmer again.

CHAPTER SEVEN

Next morning I hobbled down to the MT Section, hoping fervently that Houseman had kept his word and arranged something with the MTO, an elderly flight lieutenant who'd once been an NCO. The fact that there were squadron leaders and wing commanders in the mess who were at least twenty years younger seemed to bother him not one bit. He was happy with his lot and greeted me with a big grin.

"Good God! Carver. What the hell have you been doing to yourself?"

"Fell over the bloody kerb," I answered sheepishly. I was getting a bit fed up having to confess that my injury had been sheer carelessness.

"Pissed I suppose?"

"No such luck. Forgot to engage my brain before mobilising my legs."

"Well, don't you go engaging the gears on my vehicle without engaging your brain. Ah! I've just remembered. Squadron Leader Houseman called and told me you'd need a driver. That right?"

"That's about it," I replied.

He turned round in his chair and consulted a large board on the wall behind him. It listed every vehicle in his charge. Normally, an officer would rely on an NCO to organise the transport roster but with this man, old habits obviously died hard. He wanted to have the overall picture at his fingertips and there it was, on the board behind his desk.

He scratched his chin. "You can have the Hillman again but who can I spare as a driver?"

To this day, I've no idea what made me say what I did - it came blurting out quite involuntarily.

"How about, Bourne?" I squeaked as my throat tightened with shock as the enormity of my response dawned on me.

The MTO spun round and stared at me as if I was stark, staring mad. There was a crash in the adjoining office as the warrant officer knocked a china mug, full of tea, off his desk. The MTO slowly slid back into his chair but his knuckles still showed white as he gripped the arms of that chair. His voice was hoarse with shock. "It is at this point, in a good novel, where shock is indicated by the words 'there was a pregnant pause'. There will now be such a pregnant pause whilst you gather your thoughts and reassess your ill-judged request."

I stared at him helplessly. I swear I'd not given Foghorn Fanny a second thought. Obviously evil powers were at work. Maybe I should make an urgent telephone call for a priest to exorcise the pagan spirits Oh yes, it was all running through my brain as I continued to stare at the horrified officer on the other side of the desk. In the silence I distinctly heard the warrant officer whisper loudly to somebody in the outer office.

"Some daft twat just asked for Bourne as his driver!"

I couldn't fail to hear the response. "Fuckin' hell!" or the incredulity with which it was expressed. I felt my face redden but I couldn't back down now. The Carver pride was once more at stake.

"No! No!" I was still squeaking.

"Ah! Thank God!" said the MTO, relief evident on his face. "I thought for a minute I was going to have to send for the men in white coats driving the little green van."

"No! No!" I tried to sound more like a man with a full set of gonads. "Bourne will be fine, if she's available."

The MTO snorted. "She's always bloody available as far as I'm concerned. Don't forget, young man, you asked for her, this was nothing to do with me." He turned towards the door of the next office. "Mr Baldwin, would you kindly escort this raving lunatic outside and when you've located Bourne, inform her she'll be driving this officer until further notice - station commander's orders."

I raised my eyebrows in surprise. Houseman must have cleared things with the Groupie.

The warrant officer appeared in the doorway and beckoned for me to follow him. "This way, sir."

As I walked behind him he kept glancing over his shoulder at me as if I had six legs and nine eyes. When we were out in the middle of the vehicle yard, the warrant officer screamed just one word.

"BOURNE!"

" 'Allo!" came the reply. It was the raucous tone of Foghorn Fanny and she loomed into view around the rear of a large mobile crane. She was clutching a huge grease gun in her hands as if it were a Tommy gun.

"What's up then?"

The warrant officer's next action took me totally by surprise. He simply pointed at me and started running for the safety of his office. He managed to throw three words over his shoulder as, with indecent haste, he made good his escape. "He wants you."

Foghorn's eyes lit up. "Well, if it isn't old Pe..."

I quickly interrupted before she could finish. "You call me 'Petal', Bourne, and I'll wrap that bloody grease gun round your head."

She grimaced and it was not a pretty sight. "Fair do's."

I could sense the heads of airmen and WAAFs popping up surreptitiously from behind vehicles all over the yard. Word was getting around! I looked Bourne up and down. "Any chance you might have a clean uniform back at the WAAF quarters?"

"For you, sir, anything." She was not going down without a fight.

"Never mind the crap," I said quietly but there was enough menace in my voice to make sure she knew I wasn't going to be pissed about. "You're going to be my driver for the next few days, so I suggest you sign out the vehicle and our first stop will be the WAAF block. There you'll change into something more suitable for a visit to a civilian establishment."

"Don't tell me you're taking me out to lunch, sir."

"Just do it," I snapped.

She sensed she'd gone as far as she dared. "Alright, sir. Just get yourself into the vehicle and we'll be on our way. Which one is it by the way?"

"The Hillman utility, over there." I pointed across the yard.

"I'll get the keys and we will roar off on our mystery tour."

"No mystery about the first stop," I said with feeling. "The bloody WAAF block for a clean uniform."

She gave me an evil leer and ran off to the despatch office. She was soon back with the keys and, after a quick check of fuel, oil and water, we were on our way. We stopped at the WAAF block and, to my surprise, Foghorn emerged looking quite smart. Well, as smart as she ever would.

"Where to now, sir?" Her tone was surprisingly demure.

"Do you know Eastville?"

She nodded.

"We're going to a farm a few miles to the east of the village. I'll let you know when we are getting close."

"What are we going to do when we get there?"

"None of your business." I sounded like a prim old schoolmistress. I'd no intention of sounding that way but Foghorn had the ability to winkle out these silly reactions from me.

"I only bleedin' asked," she muttered grumpily and we travelled the rest of the way to Stan Cornish's farm in an uncomfortable silence.

Cornish emerged from the house as we approached down the drive. He still wore the old flat cap, overalls and Wellington boots. Strangely, there was no dog.

"Bleedin' hell!" yelled Foghorn. "It's old Stan."

I looked at her in amazement. "You know him?" A bit of a pointless question but I wasn't an intelligence officer for nothing!

" 'Course I do," she grinned. "See him regular in the Lancaster Arms." She leapt out of the cab. "Hallo, you old bugger. How are you?"

Cornish's face lit up when he saw her. He came forward and actually attempted to give her a big hug but it was a hopeless effort from a man of his slight stature. Foghorn responded by throwing her arms around him, lifting him off his feet and whirling him around like a rag doll.

"Hey! Put me down, you daft bat," he gasped. "You'll crack my bloody ribs."

She lowered him to the ground with surprising gentleness and I was beginning to feel a bit left out of things. They obviously had a rapport that I was unlikely to achieve with either of them.

"What the hell are you doing here?" Cornish gasped as he massaged his ribcage.

Foghorn nodded in my direction. "I've brought Petal to see you."

"Petal?" Cornish regarded me with a little smile at the corners of his mouth. "Petal?"

"Her little joke," I answered shortly.

The farmer decided not to pursue the issue of my title and turned towards the house. "You'd better come in for a cup of tea, although I can think of a thousand other things I should be doing."

"Stop moaning, you miserable old twat," chided Foghorn.

Cornish roared with laughter. "By heck, you really know how to charm a bloke."

As we entered the warm little room at the rear of the house, I was once more struck by the absence of the dog.

"Where's the dog?" I asked.

"He's in bloody disgrace, that's where he is," grunted Cornish. "If you want to see him, he's through there." He pointed to a door leading to the very back of the house.

I gently opened the door and peered into the room. It was obviously a sort of utility room. There was a dolly tub and peg, a washboard and an old wringer. In the corner stood a big old copper used for supplying hot water for washday. There was no fire in the furnace today but hot water had come from somewhere because there, in the middle of the room, stood a large tin bath with steam rising into the cold air of the unheated room. In the bath stood the dog. Forlorn and dejected described his

74

demeanour. He looked pleadingly at me but made no move to jump out of the bath. There was just a faint twitch of his tail.

"What's this?" I called over my shoulder. "Bath day?"

"It's an unscheduled bath day," answered Cornish. "He's in disgrace."

Foghorn came and peered over my shoulder. "Oh! The poor little bugger. What's he done wrong?"

"For some strange reason, known only unto himself, he rolled in a pile of fresh cow shit," said Cornish in disgust. "He ponged so much I had to give him a bath before he stank the house out."

As he spoke I caught a whiff of something very alien to a man brought up in urban surroundings.

"What do you call him?" I asked as I went back to stand in front of the welcoming fire in the grate.

"A mucky bugger," laughed Cornish.

I grinned. "I think I understand what you mean, I just got a whiff of him. Seriously though, what's his name?"

"Dog," he answered as he made the tea.

"Dog? Is that all - not Rover or something?"

"No, just Dog," said the farmer.

I looked hard at him but there was not even a flicker of amusement on his face. He was perfectly serious.

I looked down into the red embers of the fire. "I'm afraid I've come back to ask a few more questions."

"I didn't think it was a social call." He handed me a cup of tea.

I glanced in the direction of the door to the utility room but Foghorn was still in there and it sounded as if she was laundering the dog. "I think we'd better go outside, Mr Cornish."

He looked at me in that strange way of his and then nodded. "Rhoda!" he called. "When you've managed to get him into a more sociable state, keep him in here with you. We've got to pop out for a minute."

"Will do, lover," shouted Foghorn in reply as we walked out into the farmyard.

I smiled to myself at the incongruous sight we must have made as we stood in the harshness of the farmyard drinking from fine china cups and saucers. Me in my RAF uniform and Cornish in his rough, well-worn working clothes.

"What's so secret that Rhoda can't hear about it?"

"I'm afraid the whole damned scenario of your 'lost' aircraft has become very secret."

"I never said it was lost."

I put a restraining hand on his arm. "I know you didn't. We also now suspect it was not lost but just waiting." I turned him to face me and looked straight into those unnerving eyes. "I don't want to sound too officious, Mr Cornish, but I want you to promise me you'll not speak of the aircraft again. Not to civilians or even service personnel. Nobody. Is that clear?"

He returned my stare without even blinking. "Will I ever be told what it's all about?"

I looked down and prodded a pebble with my shoe. "Maybe. Eventually I may be able to tell you what it's all about but I can promise you nothing."

"Fair enough," he said finally. "You've got my promise. I don't want to end up in the Tower of London."

"If I'm wrong about this, I may be in there with you," I answered ruefully. I was beginning to feel the chill wind. "Let's walk for a while and I'll try a few more questions."

"Fire away." We began to stroll slowly through the farmyard.

"Did you see the explosions as our aircraft went down that night?"

"I heard the first and when I came out to see what was going on, I saw the glow of the second going down out towards Boston."

"How long after the strange aircraft headed west, did you hear the first explosion?"

He thought for a minute. "About ten to fifteen minutes."

I mentally calculated the time from the runway lights coming on to the faint sound I had heard from the tower. It was about right. Time for him to see the lights, curve round to the north and then approach West Fen in a southerly direction so he could cut in behind the climbing bombers as they headed out to the west. This would keep him out of the lights and, if he approached the airfield fast in a slight dive and throttled back, when he opened the throttle to climb after his target his own engine sound would blend in with all the other Merlin engines in the sky that night. His timing would have to be perfect but we already knew this guy was no amateur.

"Did you hear the aircraft again after the explosions?" I asked.

He was a long time in replying. I could see him trying to compose an answer without misleading me. "I think...," he said finally, "mind you, I can only say 'think', I heard a single Merlin just after the second crash."

"Any idea which way it may have been heading?" I asked carefully.

"East," he said slowly. "Towards the coast."

I glanced at him and his face was tight with concentration but I knew he was not mistaken. This little man would not have given me that information unless he was pretty sure he was right.

"Had you ever seen or heard it before?"

He shook his head. "No, I'm sure I had never been aware of it until that night."

I put a hand on his shoulder. "Thanks, Mr Cornish. You don't know how much help you've been in this matter. I reckon I owe you more than that pint I promised on my last visit."

He grinned. "Keep talking, lad, I could get to like you."

I laughed. "I hope you do."

He looked at me and held out his hand. "Then, for goodness sake, call me Stan."

I shook his hand. "All right, Stan. My name is Sam."

He nodded. "I know. I haven't forgotten that pompous announcement when you called here the first time."

"Sorry about that," I answered ruefully. "It's all a bit new to me and I'm trying to do something I've not been trained to do. I'm a civvy in disguise really. You'll just have to forgive me until I get a bit more experience."

"Oh, don't worry, lad, you'll do. You must be alright because this is the first time I've seen Rhoda even half-way decent to a man." He chuckled. "My advice is to stay on the right side of her. I've seen her smack a farm boy in the mouth down at the pub and he didn't get back up for another one. He was built like a brick outhouse but he was no match for her."

I sighed. "She's a holy terror, really. Strange thing is though, there is something about her that I like. Mind you, when I find out what it is I'll bottle it and make a fortune."

We started to head back to the house and meandered our way through the chickens and geese that seemed to roam the farm with impunity.

"She's a heart of gold," Cornish said suddenly and with feeling.

I looked at him in surprise. "I'll take your word for it."

He didn't reply but gave me a quick understanding smile.

As we approached the door of the house, the dog bounded out to meet us. His coat was still damp but at least the noisome scent had disappeared.

"Get in, you daft bugger!" shouted Cornish. "You'll get a bloody chill and the last thing I want is veterinary bills."

The dog took no notice whatsoever and the next second his mouth was round my uninjured wrist and I had assumed the Quasimodo walk. Cornish found it highly amusing but I was relieved that the dog had not taken a grip of my other wrist. Then it occurred to me, as I crabbed my way to the rear of the house, that the last time we had gone through this ritual, the dog had taken my other wrist. It seemed the damned animal was as sharp as his owner.

The dog never left my side for the next hour but at last Foghorn and myself took our leave. As we drove off down the track, I glanced back and returned Cornish's farewell wave.

"I like that man," I said to Foghorn.

"So do I," she said. "I'd go so far as to say he's the nicest bloke I've ever met in my life." There was a long pause then, typical of Foghorn, she thrust a damned great wedge into my train of thought. "You realise he's a homo?"

I jerked round in my seat to remonstrate with her. I didn't appreciate her bloody joke. But, as I looked at her, I realised she was perfectly serious and she was simply waiting resignedly for the burst of anger which would follow her comment. I didn't disappoint her.

"What the hell are you talking about? That was a bloody lousy thing to say about a chap who has just made you welcome in his home and I don't reckon there are too many who have done that in your past."

It was a really spiteful thing to say and I regretted it the minute the words left my lips but I was not about to apologise. She was really pissing me off. Her face gave nothing away. If I'd hurt her she was not showing it. She simply edged the Hillman out to pass a farm cart drawn by a horse. She waved her thanks to the waggoner for letting us pass and sighed.

"Maybe I shouldn't have mentioned it, but I didn't want you walking into something with your thumb up your arse and your brain in neutral."

I'll say one thing for old Foghorn, she had a nice turn of phrase, but I was still bloody furious. "If you like the chap so much how the hell can you bring yourself to drag the poor bastard's name in the mud? He could go to prison just on your stupid allegation. He's no bloody homo, I'd be able to tell." I added lamely, knowing full well that my experience of homosexuals was thankfully even less than my sparse knowledge of the opposite sex.

Foghorn was silent for a few moment and then she spoke quietly. "Are you saying that the old adage 'it takes one to know one' doesn't apply in my case?"

The conversation was getting totally out of hand and I was fed up with the whole bloody issue. I liked Stan Cornish and I was not going to have his reputation sullied by a nasty old cow like Foghorn. Then her words finally sank into my thick skull. I stared at her in amazement and searched desperately for suitable words for a response, but my mental thesaurus was empty.

It was Foghorn who broke the silence. "Don't tell me it had never crossed your mind that I was a lesbian? For Pete's sake, Petal, I'm more bloody manly than most of the blokes on the station. Can you see any bloke fancying me?"

She had spoken quietly but, in spite of my whirling thoughts and innate stupidity, I wasn't so insensitive as to miss the bitterness in her voice. I slumped in my seat. I was totally out of my depth. How did one deal with this sort of confession? I was a classical scholar but until now, the island of Lesbos had been the home of the Greek poets Alcaeus and Sappho around 600 BC. I was in no doubt as to their sexuality but had not prepared myself for the eventuality of meeting someone of their predilections. I felt a twinge of guilt too, because I knew I'd had doubts about Foghorn's sexuality right from the start, but I'd never have voiced those suspicions to a soul. Whilst those suspicions were just an idle notion at the back of my mind, they were of little importance. Now, here I was, confronted by a bald confession from the subject of my suspicions and I couldn't cope. I also knew, in my heart, that what she'd said about Cornish was true. Those deft, precise movements and the spotless house. They were not the ways of a rough countryman. Outwardly he looked the part but once he stepped through the door of that farmhouse, he changed. In a way, I felt cheated because I liked the little guy as, inexplicably, I liked Foghorn. I'd no doubts about my own sexuality, so why this affinity? I suddenly realised, to my shame, I felt sorry for them. Both had had a rough deal from life's pack of cards but had done their best to carry on in spite of everything. Damn Foghorn! I wished she'd kept her bloody confession and revelations to herself. There again, in a way, she was right. I'd already forged the first bonds of friendship with Cornish. What if he took my friendship as something more than I intended? I'd be embarrassed and he'd be humiliated. Bloody hell, what a situation! I turned to Foghorn.

"Okay, I know you're right about Stan Cornish. I think I already had thoughts at the back of my mind but it took your bloody nerve to bring them to the front. As for yourself, you've told me and now, as far as I'm concerned, that's it. This conversation will go no further than the cab of this vehicle. Why did you have to tell me?"

She wiped some condensation off the windscreen. "As I said, I could see you liked Stan and he likes you. The unknown factor was how naive you were as to what friendships mean to people like Stan and myself. I've taken so much crap over the years, I'm immune. Stan, on the other hand, is a different kettle of fish. In spite of the tough exterior, inside he's a gentle and kind man - very easily hurt."

I sat and stared at the contradiction sitting next to me in the driver's seat. Crude, scruffy, rude, insolent - all these words could describe Foghorn, but her simple philosophy, expressed in a manner I wouldn't have thought possible from such a person, made my own deliberations seem shallow and ill-defined.

"You don't think the old chap is getting the wrong idea about me, do you?" I asked.

"Good God, no!" she snorted with laughter. "I bet Stan has never done anything improper in his life. He's discovered what he is and he doesn't like it but he knows he's stuck with it. Nothing the poor little devil can do about it and jail would kill him, if he didn't die of shame first. As for me, I'm a different. I'm going to make the best of it. Any silly little cow who fancies me can have me."

She saw the startled look on my face. "Oh, come on, Petal. I'm ugly enough now, think what I'll look like when I'm older. Get it now while I've got the chance - that's my motto." She began to whistle tunelessly, as if to show me how little she cared. I was not completely fooled by her little act but I was completely out of my depth. I decided it was time we closed this conversation.

"Thanks for being so honest," I said.

"That's all right, sir. I happen to like you and just wanted to get you on the straight and narrow. I reckon we can close the hangar door now and forget the conversation ever happened."

"I agree wholeheartedly," I replied with relief. "If you decide to make any more startling revelations, for goodness sake, break them to me gently."

She turned and gave me a wicked grin. "Subtlety never was my forte."

Not for the first time, I had to agree with her.

When we got back to West Fen, she drove straight to the Intelligence Section and I hurried in to see Houseman. I found him in the main room, holding an informal briefing with some of the staff. Sergeants Collins and Carter, Corporal Maudsley and three of the airmen were gathered around him by one of the map cabinets. He looked up as I entered.

"Carver! How's it going?"

"Not bad, sir. May I have a quick word?"

He glanced at his watch. "Give me another ten minutes. Grab yourself a cuppa and wait in my office."

I nodded and, as I left the room, I could feel the eyes of the others on my departing back. They must be pretty baffled by my new 'liaison job' but they would have to stay baffled for the time being. I made two mugs of tea and took one out to Foghorn. I reckoned she deserved it. Houseman glanced up as I took the cup outside but said nothing. The looks of the others spoke volumes. I walked back in, picked up my own mug and strolled through to Houseman's office. I stood sipping my tea and looking out of the window at the lane beyond the perimeter security wire. Try as I might, I couldn't get my thoughts away from Foghorn's revelations. It was with some relief that I heard Houseman's footsteps coming down the corridor. The door opened but it was not Houseman, it was Janner.

"Houseman, I want you to.....," he broke off when he saw me. His piggy eyes flew open and he slammed the door wide open with a crash. "Carver, what the bloody hell are you doing in this office? Explain yourself, man!"

I'd made a half-hearted attempt to come to attention but it seemed a rather ludicrous stance as I still had a mug of tea in my hand. "Waiting for the squadron leader, sir. He did tell me to wait in his office."

"Did he also tell you to swig bloody tea all day?" he bawled at me.

"He did suggest I brought a brew in with me, yes."

Janner glanced up the corridor and then slid into the room like a big fat lizard. He closed the door behind him. I didn't like the look on his face. Come to think of it, I'd never liked the look on his face.

"I don't know what you're up to, Carver, but I want a report on my desk by tomorrow morning. Liaison bloody officer to the station commander, my arse. You're up to something and I'll not have junior officers going behind my back. I repeat, Carver, I want a report of your activities on my desk, first thing tomorrow morning."

I placed my mug carefully on the desk and then stood back and faced him. I chose my words carefully. "May I use the telephone, sir?"

Janner looked at me. His little piggy eyes took on a baffled glaze. "What the hell are you on about, man?"

"Well, sir, it's like this. You want confidential information from me. The only way I can give you that information is for you to speak with the station commander. Only he can authorise me to release that information to you." I picked up the telephone from Houseman's desk and waited for the switchboard operator in the watchkeepers' office to answer.

There was a click. "Yes, sir?"

I recognised the voice. "Sergeant Tyde, could you put me through to the station commander's PA, please?"

"Station commander's PA. Very good, sir."

I waited with the telephone to my ear and locked eyes with Janner. He suddenly struck out and smashed the telephone from my hand. The receiver flew to the extent of its cable and smashed into smithereens when it struck the wall.

"You arrogant bastard!" he screamed. "I'm going to have you under mess arrest and court-martialled, you over-educated little shit."

I'd had enough. I sat insolently onto the window ledge. "Do you have an inferiority complex with all graduates, sir? Or is it just me you find difficult to accept?"

He tried to get around the desk but he was too fat and there was insufficient room. "I'll have you removed from your so-called special assignment, Carver." His voice shook with fury. "There are better people in this section, far more qualified than you. You may have brown-nosed the station commander but you don't fool me."

"But, sir," I said quietly as I leant towards him over the desk. "How can you say there are better qualified people for the job if you don't know what the job is?"

At this point, he totally control. He gave a hoarse cry and swept Houseman's 'Pending' tray off the desk. It crashed to the floor and papers flew in all directions just as Houseman opened the door and walked in. His eyes went from Janner, to me, to the mess on the floor and finally back to Janner. His eyes were bleak and his mouth a tight slit in his face.

Janner stepped in quickly. "So sorry, Jake. Caught the tray as I turned." He headed quickly for the open door. "I feel sure Carver is well qualified to pick up the mess," he spat, as he stormed out. There was a pause in the proceedings as we listened to his footsteps hurrying down the corridor to his office. We heard his door close with a loud slam and silence reigned once more.

"What the fuck was that all about?" asked Houseman angrily.

"He wanted me to write a full report on my work as liaison officer to the station commander, sir."

Houseman moved round his desk, trying not to step on his papers and flopped into his chair. "Oh, that stupid bloody man. He's been told not to interfere by the group captain, no less. What else did he say?"

"Better you didn't know, sir."

"Like that, eh?"

"I'm afraid so."

He waved to a chair. "Sit down, Sam."

I was surprised at the use of my first name, but I knew I was now accepted as a fellow officer in a conspiracy that could cause problems for the whole section. Janner would need to vent his spleen on somebody and, if he couldn't get at me, somebody else would have to take my place in the crap stakes.

Houseman picked up a framed photograph from his desk. I'd noticed it before and recognised it as a crew snapshot. It was Houseman and four other men standing in front of a twin-engined Whitley bomber. He stared at it for a while and, when he finally spoke, it was as if to himself. "I'm the only one still alive. The others died in the North Sea, but I survived."

I didn't dare speak. For once his guard was down and I could see the hurt in his eyes. The premature grey hair and the lined face were the result of experiences of war that I could only guess at. Suddenly, he looked straight at me and spoke as if seeking some sort of reassurance. "Do you think that is fair, Sam?"

I knew it was no good hesitating. He wanted a straight answer and without the bullshit.

"Fairness has sod all to do with it, sir," I replied. "It is all down to fate. I'm a firm believer in the old adage 'when your time is up, you've had it'. No good fighting it and no good feeling guilty because you made it and your friends died."

It was as if he had not heard. "I put that kite down in the drink as gently as I could. Luckily it was summer and the water wasn't too cold but it was very rough. I saw the others get into the dinghy as I was struggling to get out of the top escape hatch. The line tethering the dinghy to the kite snapped as a rogue wave hit the aircraft and the dinghy was whipped away by the wind and the sea. They disappeared into the darkness and I was left standing on the half-submerged fuselage. It stayed afloat for a surprisingly long time but eventually sank and left me with just my Mae West to keep me afloat. I should have died but eight hours later, against all the odds, a passing trawler picked me up. My crew, on the other hand, were never seen again."

I couldn't reply. I just watched him with his struggle to understand. It was as if he wanted to show some kind of grief but had nothing of that nature left to give. His feeling of guilt came from his lack of grief. He placed the photo back on the desk and ran his finger over the frame as if removing an imaginary layer of dust.

"I've done another tour since then and I'm still here." He stood up and grinned at me. "Maybe you're right, Sam, maybe my time has not yet arrived."

"Not for many more years, sir." I answered with feeling.

He laughed. "Don't you go making promises you've no power to guarantee, Carver. Mind you, if you're in touch with Him up there, I wouldn't mind a few words on my behalf. Right! What did you get from your farmer chappie?"

I related my conversation with Cornish and, as I talked, he made notes on a sheaf of paper. When I'd finished, he consulted his notes for a few moments. Finally he stood and turned to look out of the window.

"Let's see what we've got so far." He stretched as if easing a painful back. "We've a Merlin-powered, presumably captured, aircraft. Timings of its operations suggest it's in touch with ground operators and probably based somewhere in this county. Therefore, we go for the concealed airstrip theory?"

"I can come to no other conclusion, sir," I answered. "It seems too much of a coincidence that the intruder can be in the right place at the right time, in spite of operational delays, weather and cancellations."

Houseman nodded. "In that case, if your farmer is right and he felt it headed east after it hit us, I don't reckon it can be too far away. It adds weight to our theory that it could be hidden in the sparsely populated area of this East Coast."

"I've total faith in Cornish, sir. He really knows what he's talking about."

"Alright, Sam. I'll get the station commander's permission to have Sergeant Lamont fit a camera in the Anson. We need to get airborne and get some pictures just inland of the coast. Could be a wild goose chase but I think not. I can feel it in my water."

"I'm looking forward to my first flight, sir."

He grinned and came round the desk. "That's the spirit! I promise not to throw her around too much. Nothing will put you off flying quicker than airsickness."

I suddenly had an idea pop into my head and, for the second time that day, I spoke without thinking. "Any chance of taking my driver with us, sir?"

"Don't let the wing commander hear you say 'my driver' or he'll explode. Even he doesn't rate his own personal driver and if he finds out you've got one, he'll have a bloody fit!" Houseman was laughing but there was a warning there nonetheless.

"I promise never to mention it again, sir."

"Well, we could do with an extra pair of eyes up there. We could stick him in the turret to keep an eye open for other traffic. It can get a bit crowded up there on a good day. What's his name?"

"Actually, sir, she's a WAAF."

"Lucky old you, my boy. Don't be shy, what is the lovely lady's name?"

I hesitated but, even after clearing my throat a few times, I was back to squeaking mode. "Bourne, sir."

"Bloody hell!" Houseman exclaimed. "Not THE Bourne?"

"I'm afraid so, sir."

"Who was the rotten bastard who landed you with her?"

"I'm afraid, in a moment of pure madness, I actually asked for her by name, sir."

Houseman roared. "You daft twit! Still, if she actually consented to drive you, she must like you. That in itself is a bloody miracle."

"She's not as bad as she's painted, really." I felt I had to somehow qualify my statement. "Actually, to be truthful, she's really pretty awful but I feel a little sorry for her. Everybody calls her crude names and treats her like a piece of dirt. How else is she going to react? She can't help how she looks."

Houseman nodded. "I agree. Okay, Bomber Bourne can come with us. If the Anson is serviceable, I hope Sergeant Lamont can get a camera fitted and operational by the day after tomorrow. One thing though, if we're taking Bourne, we'd better be careful what we say. We don't want her putting two and two together and letting the cat out of the bag."

I walked forward and was about to start picking up the papers from the floor where Janner had thrown them.

"Leave them, Sam." Houseman waved me away. "Just go and tell your driver she's going for a flight. I reckon that'll put you way up at the top of her 'favourites' list. You never know, she may even give you a grateful kiss."

"Heaven forbid," I grimaced.

"That reminds me," chuckled Houseman. "When I flew over to Shipdham the last time, one of the Yanks described his girl friend as the best kisser in the USA. He said her kissing was so powerful she could 'suck the chrome off a trailer hitch'. His words not mine."

"Bloody hell, the mind boggles!" I laughed.

"Away with you, Carver."

So I left him to pick up his own papers and headed out to where I'd left Bourne. She was sitting patiently in the Hillman, reading a rather battered book. The fact that she quickly hid it when I appeared indicated that it was not a book for me to see. When I told her of the impending flight she was ecstatic.

"Bleedin' Nora," she breathed. "This is going to put a few noses out of joint." She started the engine and leaned out of the window. "Sir, you've just made me a very happy little WAAF, or as near as I can get to being a 'little' WAAF."

I looked at her and said quietly. "Don't run yourself down, Bourne. You're just fine - at least when you want to be."

"Smooth talking bastard," she said with an evil grin and drove away before I could reprimand her. Not that I'd intended doing such a thing because she was like a breath of fresh air. She was totally irreverent and I think I envied her ability to not give a shit for anybody. I just hoped the flight happened because I'd seen the look of excitement in her eyes. I didn't want to be yet another person who let her down. She'd had enough of that to last her the rest of her life.

I headed back into the section and to my real job helping out with the preparations for tonight's operations. I hoped Natalie was on duty and suddenly, in spite of my bruised toe, I found a new spring in my step. What love can do to a man!

CHAPTER EIGHT

As it turned out, there was no disappointment for either Bourne or myself. Two days later, just before I staggered off to bed after debriefing the crews from a raid on Essen, Houseman gave me the good news. Our photographic recce flight was on for early the next morning, which just happened to be Sunday. Natalie and I had planned a bit of a cycle ride around the local area but it was not to be. Would I ever get a chance to be alone with the girl? And, no matter how one looked at the situation, Bourne was in no way an adequate substitute. Why the hell had I not suggested Natalie came along for the flight, not old Foghorn Fanny? I guess I knew the answer to that. Foghorn needed a bit of a treat in her life.

Bourne was already waiting for me outside the Officers' Mess at 08.30 that Sunday morning. As we drove down to the station flight dispersal, I tried not to smile at Bourne's barely concealed delight. She was like a little kid who had been given the keys to the goodie shop.

Even the initial sight of the Avro Anson did nothing to dampen her enthusiasm. There was a tatty old Oxford and a rather smart Mosquito sharing the pan but the Anson certainly looked as if she had seen better days. Her camouflage was faded and it was obvious where her fabric had been frequently repaired. Patches were witness to the hard life she'd lived. The result being rather like a drab, aeronautical patchwork quilt. To say the old kite looked a little 'tired' was like saying Goering was a little chubby. She didn't just look tired - she looked positively exhausted. She still had a dorsal gun turret fitted and all the Perspex in her fuselage made her look like an old lady in an indecently short skirt. All this was in stark contrast to the other 'lady' in my life for the day, as Bourne had pulled out all the stops and actually looked quite smart. But I knew better than to congratulate her on her appearance. Don't make a big deal and Bourne would be just fine.

"Which one is ours, sir?" asked Bourne with barely concealed excitement.

"That one." I pointed at the Anson.

"Bloody Nora!" whispered Bourne, which did nothing to allay my own fears for our safety.

A window in the Flight HQ Nissen hut opened and Houseman thrust his head out. "Come on, Carver - chop, chop! This weather isn't going to last all day."

The weather, for once, was bright and sunny with not a cloud in the cobalt blue of the sky but there was no warmth in the sun. The chill factor from the slight wind was making itself felt. We hurried over and Houseman met us in the corridor.

"Nip up to the room at the end there and the lads will fit you up with a couple of old Sidcot suits I've scrounged from the stores. They'll also sort you out a flying helmet and Mae West each. Flying boots I couldn't get, so I hope you're wearing thick socks as it will be bloody cold up there." He was already in his own bulky flying kit and he looked more at home than I'd ever seen him. He stuffed some maps into the top of one of his flying boots. "I'm just nipping out to do a walk around and then I'll be back to sign the Form 700. I want you to be ready by then. Okay?"

"Fine, sir," I replied.

Houseman now looked at Bourne and his eyebrows rose a couple of millimetres as he saw the transformation in my driver. "Morning, Bourne. Looking forward to your flight?"

Foghorn grinned from ear to ear and actually came to attention. "I certainly am, sir."

"Good girl. See you both at the kite but hurry up, Carver, Sergeant Lamont needs to brief you on operating the camera." He ran out of the door, whistling a popular song. It was obvious he was in his element. Even after all he had been through, he still craved to fly.

A leading aircraftsman bundled us into our thickly padded flying suits and tested the helmet headsets. By the time he had shoehorned Bourne into a parachute harness and Mae West, she looked like a Michelin man. The LAC showed us how to clip the chest chutes on to the harness and how to carry them with the carrying handle and not the 'D' ring.

A sergeant, with thickly Brylcremed hair, walked in just as we were ending our dressing session. We were both now wearing our flying helmets and there was no sign of rank. The only thing that was apparent, as we stood there like two trussed up turkeys, was that we were certainly not aircrew. The sergeant looked Bourne up and down and then, with a wink at the LAC, poked Bourne rudely in the stomach.

"Better lay off the old nosh a bit, mate, that's the biggest size we've got!" He smirked at his little joke and looked around at me to see my reaction to his obvious wit.

What he got actually did rhyme with wit but it was unrefined and succinct. Bourne's face, framed by the leather flying helmet, was suddenly just millimetres from his own ugly mug. Her voice dripped vitriol as the words slipped from her tightened lips.

"Do that again, numb nuts, and I'll pull your fuckin' foreskin over your head and shove the excess up your arse."

To say there was a shocked silence would have been the understatement of the year. I took the opportunity to grab Bourne's arm and drag her towards the door but the sergeant was beginning to recover from a state of deep shock.

"I want both your fuckin' names, NOW!" he yelled.

I shoved Bourne out of the door and turned to face the sergeant. "Pilot Officer Carver is my name, sergeant. If you speak to me like that again, I'll have you placed under close arrest and you'll await my return in the guardroom. Is that clear?"

"Yessir!" He was now on the defensive in earnest.

"As to the identity of my companion," I continued. "She's on an assignment authorised by the station commander and that is all you need to know. Is that also clear?"

"Yessir!" He was now standing to attention but I could see he was perplexed by the word 'she'.

I turned to the LAC. This lad, unlike the sergeant, was no fool and he was trying hard not to show his delight at the NCO's plight. I pointed a finger at him. "As for you, airman, you saw and heard nothing. Understood?"

"Yessir!" he snapped in reply but I could see him beginning to lose the struggle with mirth. He knew who Bourne was. Bloody hell, everybody knew Bourne, but nobody expected her in full flying kit.

"Good man," I said and hobbled off after Bourne, the bulky flying kit making a dignified exit impossible.

She was waiting outside and looked crestfallen. "Sorry, sir. I've ballsed it up again, haven't I?"

I looked at her and shook my head in frustration. "For Pete's sake, girl! You've got to get a grip of that bloody temper."

"Sorry, sir." It was genuine contrition. "Shall I go and get out of this kit and wait for you?"

"No you bloody well won't," I said wearily. "If I'm going to get airsick in that bloody death-trap, then so are you."

The big grin returned. "I bet there's carrots in it."

"Carrots in what?" I asked in exasperation.

"When you're sick, there's always carrots in it, even if you haven't eaten any carrots. It is one of life's great mysteries."

"Bourne," I said wearily and pointed towards the Anson. "Just shut up and walk."

"Okay if I hobble?"

Houseman prevented me from giving her a very rude answer. He was on his way back to sign the Form 700. "Speed it up, you two."

We scuttled off in the direction of our destiny with wings and made a pretty ungainly effort at getting aboard through the open door on the starboard side of the fuselage. Our entry was made all the more difficult by the bulk of an F24 aerial camera on a makeshift mounting just inside the door. As we squeezed past I got my first smell of the inside of an aircraft. The whiff of electrics and rubber did nothing for the state of my stomach. Bloody hell, we hadn't even started the engines and I was already feeling sick. Not so Bourne, she was looking around with wide-open eyes. It was only an old Anson but to her it was escape from the drudgery of the MT Section.

A tall, thin sergeant with sandy hair came down from the cockpit area. We recognised each other from the day I'd spent in the photographic section to be trained in the magic of target photography. All target photos came to us for interpretation as to bombing accuracy, so it helped that I knew something about the difficulties of the task.

"Morning, sir." Sergeant Lamont had a strong Scottish accent.

"Morning, Sarge. What have you got for us?"

He pointed to the F24 camera. "We've jury-rigged the camera for you. The squadron leader said it was not to be obvious to observers on the ground with binoculars, that you were taking pictures. We thought a hand-held camera would be too obvious, so we've rigged it to take oblique shots and you'll be able to control it from the second seat up front." He squeezed past us and put his hand on the camera film magazine. "This mag should have enough film to do all you require but if you get carried away, there is another spare mag stowed under the navigator's table." He pointed to where a section of Perspex had been removed from the glazed area immediately in front of the door. "We had a bit of trouble getting the camera angle right. We had to mount it here as, any further forward, the wing and engine nacelle get in the way. We removed the Perspex to give the camera a clear view. The Perspex was scratched to hell and you'd have had very fuzzy pictures. Just to keep the slipstream down through the gap, the riggers have fitted a homemade fairing in front of the hole. That should cut down any slipstream vibration to the camera and the draught to yourselves but it's still going to be bloody cold up there. We've angled the camera so that the pilot will be able to fly straight and level. Anybody seeing an aircraft flying one wing down would soon be suspicious."

He turned and pushed me in front of him up to the cockpit area. He pointed to a piece of metal protruding from the top of the windscreen and then to a wax pencil mark on the Perspex window in the starboard side, just in front of where I'd be sitting. "The pilot will have to use this simple device to get the sighting angle right. If he flies the correct distance from the target and lines up this bit of metal with the pencil mark and the target, the camera will be spot on. Don't worry, we used a chap the same height as the squadron leader to get the calibration right."

I looked at him in amazement. He and his lads had worked miracles to get this Heath Robinson rig together. I should not have been surprised because the groundcrews were forever having to invent and make do. Pity nobody at Command knew how much they had to 'make do'!

"Bloody good job, Sarge." I meant it.

"Thank you, sir."

Jock squeezed past me to sit in the pilot's seat on the left. He motioned for me to raise the back of the seat on the right and slightly to the rear of the pilot's seat. "Plonk yourself down there, sir. I want to show you how to operate the camera control." He reached for a small grey box sitting on the throttle pedestal. "This is a T35 camera control. It is simplicity itself and you should have no trouble but you'll have to hold it in your lap as we didn't have time to mount it anywhere here in the cockpit. We've already calibrated the speed at which the camera will operate. We've told the squadron leader that the optimum speed is one hundred and ten miles per hour at one thousand feet. He'll stick to that criteria and you should get a sixty-percent overlap on the photos. All you have to do is lift and turn this little knob here and the camera will continue to operate until you reverse the action of the knob. There is a green light and a red light. One to tell you that power is going to the camera and the other to flash each time the camera operates. If it stops flashing you've got a mag jam."

He stood up and I rose too, quickly folded the back of my seat flat and he followed me back down the fuselage. He pointed to the two clips at each side of the mag. "These clips are to release the mag. Just remove the cover from the spare mag and clip it into place. Don't worry, sir, my lads have never had a jammed mag yet. Is all that clear or would you like me to go through it for you again?"

"No thanks, Sarge. I think I've taken it all in. Wish you were coming with us though."

Lamont gave me a little smile. "You would't get me up in anything with wings, sir. I reckon I'm much safer down here."

"Are you trying to put me off?" I asked with a grimace.

Lamont laughed. "Would I do that, sir? No - aircrew are volunteers and I never volunteer for anything, especially flying." He clapped a hand on my shoulder. "Have a nice trip, sir." He jumped down to the ground and turned to look up at me. "One of my lads will be here to collect the mag when you land."

"Thanks, Sarge. Now bugger off before I change my mind and volunteer you for this job."

He grinned and gave me a wave as he trotted off. He was a bit of a martinet but his lads thought the world of him and they had done a fantastic job rigging out the old Anson.

Houseman appeared at the door and climbed up into the fuselage. "Had your camera briefing?"

"Yes, sir."

"How's your map reading?"

"Never done it from the air, sir."

"Dead easy. You'll have to make a mark on the map each time you start and stop the camera. That way we will know exactly where the run begins and ends. Don't worry. If you just make sure you let me know when you operate the camera, I'll keep a record at the same time." He turned to Bourne. "Young lady," he said quite seriously and I swear Foghorn glowed with pleasure. "I'm going to ask you to ride in the turret. There are an awful lot of aircraft in the skies over Lincolnshire and it will be wise to have another pair of eyes on watch. Also, if you can hear the camera operate over the noise from the engines, I'd like you to make a rough mark on a map for us each time it starts and stops."

He pulled a map from his boot and spread it on a table in front of some radio kit. He motioned us around him and pointed to the map. "We'll fly north to the Humber but stay inland. Then, over the estuary, we will turn south and follow the coast, from out to sea, right down here to Cromer on the Norfolk coast." He turned to Bourne. "This will be your map. I'll mark where we intend to start photography and I'd like it if you could keep a bit of a log for us but, at the same time, keep a good look out. Think you can manage that?"

It was obvious to me that Bourne would do it even if it meant jumping out and making marks in the sand. Houseman was going to be her hero for ever.

"I'll have a damned good try, sir." It was said with feeling.

"Good girl," replied Houseman. "Now, if you feel a bit queasy, just take a couple of these 'barf' bags up with you." He handed a couple of sick bags to Bourne and tactfully said nothing when he also passed a couple to me. "I'm sure you won't need them. It's a cold day and there should be no turbulence. This is not a fighter so we will be flying straight and level so as not to attract attention. I'll keep the old girl as steady as I can. Okay?"

"Thank you, sir." She was positively beaming with pleasure but nearly ruined it all by giving me a huge wink. Houseman pretended he'd not noticed and when he turned to me there was just a hint of a smile around his mouth.

"Right, young Carver, let's be off!" He turned and called out to one of the three ground crew now standing around the aircraft. "Jones, hop up here and show our passenger how to strap into the turret."

As the airman ran forward, Houseman turned to Bourne. "He'll show you how to strap in and how to move the turret but I'll need you to sit up at the navigator's station for takeoff and landing."

"Right, sir."

We didn't wait to see if the airman would recognise Bourne. If he did I reckoned we would hear his gasp of surprise over the sound of the engines! Houseman climbed into the pilot's seat and I raised the back of my seat, settled myself and strapped in. Once installed I glanced out to the right and stared in amazement. I turned to Houseman and tapped his arm.

"I hate to say this, sir. I've just seen a guy disappear behind the engine nacelle carrying a bloody starting handle."

Houseman laughed. "You'd better hope he is or we'll be sitting here all day. Somebody has to wind up the elastic bands." He motioned to the window on my side of the cockpit. "Would you slide that open, I need to talk with the ground crew."

I slid open the window just as an airman stuck his head up over the engine nacelle.

"Ready to prime, sir," the airman called.

Houseman leaned across me and did something with the fuel cocks down by my right leg. He then moved the starboard throttle forward about three quarters of an inch and I heard him muttering to himself.

"Mixture - normal. Main mags - off. Starter mag - on." He raised his head and gave the airman a thumbs up. There was a flurry of activity on the other side of the nacelle and suddenly the engine burst into life. Obviously the chap with the starting handle had done his job.

Houseman reached up to two switches mounted above the windscreen and flicked one switch down. He then opened up the throttle a little and the whole procedure was repeated for the port engine. He did something with a lever marked 'mixture' and opened up the throttles for a few moments only to move the lever back again and throttle back whilst he watched the various instruments. It was all double Dutch to me. Finally he waved a hand and two of the airmen removed the wheel chocks. We were ready to taxi. West Fen's code name was 'Redstart' and it seemed, from Houseman's brief chat with the tower, that we were 'Station B-Baker'. We were given permission to taxi and Houseman pushed the throttles forward to ease us on our way.

I swear the aircraft started to come apart at the seams. Every instrument danced up and down in the instrument panel and the wings actually flapped as we taxied along the peritrack. The two engines sounded like a couple of bitterns with bronchitis. I sensed a movement behind me as Bourne lowered herself into the vacant navigator's seat. I dared not look at her because I knew she'd see the apprehension in my face. To see her gloat would really spoil my day. Whatever I thought of the state of the aircraft, it seemed to be of no import to Houseman. He whistled tunelessly as we waddled along and finally, after clearance from the tower, we turned on to the runway and roared into the air as if the old bird had shaken her feathers and decided to fly. I found I was gripping the camera control box in a vice-like hold and made myself relax. I started as Houseman tapped me urgently on the arm. There was a click as he switched on the intercom.

"Do you remember me saying that I had one hundred and sixty good reasons for you coming on this flight?"

I flicked my intercom switch. "Yes, sir. I wondered why you were so precise."

He grinned and pointed to a handle by the base of his seat. "The undercarriage is still down and will be until you wind it up with one hundred and sixty turns of this handle. Come along, Carver, chop, chop or we will never get enough speed up to go anywhere."

"You crafty sod." I grinned and then realised what I'd said but I need not have worried, Houseman was helpless with laughter. I glanced round to see if Bourne had seen what was happening but she was already in the turret. I started to wind and by the time the undercarriage was up into the engine nacelles, I was totally knackered and bathed in perspiration. All the time I was winding, we had been in a gentle turn to the right. Houseman pointed out to the left.

"That's Coningsby over there. We'll stay at five hundred feet on the way up north. Give you a chance to see the scenery."

I gave him a thumbs up.

"How's it going back there, Bourne?" he asked.

There was a click and the sound of heavy breathing. "Bloody fantastic, sir," she finally managed to pant in reply.

"Good girl!" Houseman looked at me and winked. I was beginning to think he was getting a real pleasure out of giving Bourne this treat.

I started following my map and spotted a partly constructed airfield out to starboard. I was just going to ask when Houseman anticipated the question.

"East Kirkby. They're building another over near Spilsby. Should make bashing the circuit interesting!"

We were leaving the fens now and were scudding just above the Lincolnshire Wolds. It was a transformation to behold and although it was still a wintry scene, the ground now had texture and form. Maybe old Bates, back at the mess, was right. This could be a place for me to bring Natalie. We could explore the area this coming summer if the war would only let us. Our progress now was virtually from airfield to airfield. Lincolnshire had become a giant aircraft carrier.

Bourne's voice interrupted my reverie. "There's a fighter right behind us, sir."

Houseman looked quickly over at me. "I hope he's one of ours."

"It's a Spitfire, sir." Bourne answered.

"How far back is he?"

"About fifty yards, sir."

"Okay," said Houseman. "Bourne, give him a wave to let him know we've seen him."

There was a pause then Bourne came back on the intercom. "He just waggled his wings and he's coming up on our left side, sir."

Both Houseman and myself craned our heads to look over our left shoulders. It was a magnificent sight as the Spitfire slid into position just feet from our port wing. The pilot had a small degree of flap down, indicating that he was finding it difficult to fly as slow as our Old Annie. The pilot's oxygen mask was hanging down from his face and he grinned across at us and raised two fingers in a very Churchillian salute but not the way Churchill meant it to be used.

"Cheeky bugger," Houseman laughed and replied by miming a jockey whipping a slow horse. The Spitfire pilot shook his head in sympathy and then with a wave and a flash of light blue wing undersurfaces, he was gone. It had been a beautiful sight and I was beginning to see why Houseman was so passionate about flying. I looked up and saw the sun glistening on the waters of the Humber estuary.

"That's Cleethorpes just to the left of the nose." Houseman pointed for me to locate the town.

"I've a Danger Area on my map, sir. It's off to the right."

"Donna Nook bombing range," explained Houseman. "Don't worry, I phoned them all this morning for clearance through their area. We'll have to overfly Theddlethorpe and Wainfleet ranges but they are not expecting any traffic this morning. I've arranged to call each area as we approach. With luck we should get a straight run through the lot."

We did a gentle right turn to the east of Cleethorpes and climbed to one thousand feet. Houseman received clearance from Donna Nook. He next called up Bourne on the intercom. "Bourne. Do you see Spurn Head off to our left?"

There was a slight pause "Yes, sir. I've got it."

"Okay. Now, to our right, do you see the lock gates at Tetney?"

I strained my eyes to pick up the locks but Bourne spotted them before me.

"I see them, sir."

"Good. We'll soon start the camera so get ready to mark your map and try to follow our progress down the coast. Okay?"

"Will do, sir." Bourne was unable to disguise the pride she was feeling as, for once, somebody trusted her and was giving her some responsibility.

We were now at the correct height and speed as we flew parallel to the coast. Houseman pointed out to the right. "That is RAF North Cotes over there, so there's unlikely to be anything in that area, but we'll start once we get near Donna Nook. There are a lot of unpopulated areas inland from the bombing range."

I looked down at North Cotes. There were Beaufighters dispersed around the airfield but the circuit was clear. It soon vanished from view as the range at Donna Nook appeared.

Houseman tapped my arm. "Let's start taking shots here." He sat upright in his seat and I watched him squint his eyes as he lined up the makeshift sight, the pencil mark on my cockpit window and the coast below. He gave me a nod and I started the camera, marking my map as I did so. We flew on in silence as Saltfleet and Theddlethorpe passed below. Finally Mablethorpe hove into view.

Houseman relaxed in his seat. "We might as well switch off until we clear Mablethorpe. Did you hear the camera, Bourne?"

"Yes, sir. It makes quite a racket."

"Managing to mark your map?"

"So far, sir."

"Well done. Keep it up." He tapped my arm and motioned for me to pass him my map. He checked it against his own and gave me a thumbs up. He passed it back and then consulted his own map again. "We'll start again once we clear Sutton-on-Sea."

We started the camera again and kept it running until Skegness pier came into view. Once we were clear of the town we filmed all of the coast down to Boston, along the coast of The Wash, where yet another bombing range was sited at Holbeach. Eventually we reached the mouth of the Great Ouse to the north east of King's Lynn.

Houseman frowned at the horizon. "I reckon the good weather is going to desert us so we'll call a halt at Hunstanton. This haze is building and I don't think it worth our while to go any further than that."

So at Hunstanton I switched off the camera and Houseman wheeled us around to head back to West Fen, taking the direct route across The Wash and climbing to two thousand feet.

"Did you see anything?" he asked.

"Nothing obvious, sir. I reckon we'll have to leave it up to Max, he's the expert in the section. I just hope it hasn't been a waste of time."

Houseman looked across at me. "Have you enjoyed the flight?"

"Yes, sir. Every minute of it." I replied truthfully.

"How about you, Bourne?"

There was a click on the intercom. "Bloody fantastic, sir."

Houseman burst out laughing. "There you are then. How could anything so enjoyable be a waste of time?"

I had to agree with him. I'd enjoyed the flight immensely and all my fears about the state of Old Annie had long since disappeared. The two Cheetah engines roared healthily and, as we flew over the expanse of The Wash she was so stable in the still air, it was as if we were motionless in the sky.

Bourne's intercom clicked into life. "What were we looking for, sir?"

Houseman glanced at me and held up a warning finger. "Archaeological sites," he answered.

"Oh, right, sir." She sounded more than a little mystified as she switched off her mike.

Houseman checked his watch and peered ahead. "Bourne. Time you came forward to the nav's position ready for landing."

"Okay, sir."

All too soon, as far as I was concerned, we were back over West Fen. We were cleared to land after a couple of Lancs that were returning from their NFTs.

Houseman tapped my arm and pointed to the dreaded undercarriage handle.

"Better start winding or we're likely to make a loud grating noise when we land."

I grinned ruefully and started cranking like a mad thing to get the wheels down. I reckon it was Old Annie's way of saying, 'you don't get anything for nothing'.

Houseman was also busy as he pumped down the flaps but finally we slid in over the threshold and he greased Old Annie on to the runway with barely a squeak from the tyres. I glanced across at him but there was no expression of satisfaction at such a superb landing. He was a perfectionist and he expected nothing less than a perfect landing. He began pumping the flaps back up as we started to taxi back to the station flight dispersal.

"I'll go straight back to the section. Would you go to the Photo Section and wait for the first batch of prints? Sergeant Lamont has his lads standing by so it shouldn't take too long. Once you've got them, Bourne can drive you over and we'll start scanning them ourselves. Max will be on duty later today so at least he'll be able to give us a first impression."

An airman marshalled us onto the pan and Houseman shut down the engines. It suddenly seemed very quiet but Old Annie was still alive. Her engines still ticked as they cooled and the gyro was still winding down with a muted whine. I was actually feeling quite fond of the old girl and gave the throttle pedestal a little tap with my fingers as a small personal indication of my gratitude.

As I turned to rise from my seat I saw Houseman observing me with a small smile and a twinkle in his eye.

"It gets to you, doesn't it?"

I felt a little embarrassed at being caught out in such a stupid gesture but I had to admit I was hooked. Then realisation dawned - this was just flying. Men like Houseman didn't just fly, they fought for their lives in these things and suddenly my little flip seemed totally insignificant.

I shrugged and gave him a shamefaced grin. "That was a real pleasure and I thank you for it but your operational flying must be a nightmare. How can you still love to fly?"

He looked down at his hands for a few moments and then back to me. "It's just a job. For every bad fright there are twenty good flights."

"Good God!" I laughed. "Who said that?"

He grinned and shoved me back down the fuselage. "I did. I just made it up."

"Stick to your day job, sir."

"Don't know anything else, Carver." He leapt quickly and nimbly out of the fuselage door but it took Bourne and myself a little longer to descend. Houseman started to trot off to the flight dispersal hut. "See you back at the section."

A young airman approached whom I recognised from the Photo Section. "How was the camera, sir?"

"Great – at least it made all the right noises. We've only used the one mag. The spare is under the nav table."

He jumped up, removed the mag and collected the spare. I signed the reconnaissance report and, dropping the mags in a home-built truck fixed to the back of his service bicycle, he pedalled furiously off in the direction of the Photo Section.

Twenty minutes later, after divesting ourselves of our flying clothing, we walked into the Photo Section to be met by Sergeant Lamont.

"Good trip, sir?"

"Fantastic, Sarge. We covered most of what we wanted but it started to get a bit hazy on the Norfolk coast."

"The filter will take care of most of that, sir. I've just seen the film out of the brew and it looks fine so, once we get it dry, we can start printing. In the meantime, find a couple of chairs in the crewroom and I'll send one of the lads in with some tea."

As he disappeared, Bourne wrinkled her nose and pulled a face. "Cor! It really pongs in here."

"All the chemicals they use. They must process a hell of a lot because every kite carries a camera. It can't be much fun fitting cameras and gear at this time of the year."

Bourne nodded. "I reckon I've got a crap job but when I see the groundcrews, working out in the freezing rain and snow, I thank Jesus for small mercies."

"Hear, hear!" I answered.

We settled ourselves in the crewroom and an airman brought us the tea. I took a sip from my cup and placed it on the table. It was time to ease Bourne into the picture.

"You did well today," I said as an opener.

"Never forget it as long as I live," she replied.

I paused for a few seconds as I tried to formulate my approach to explain what we were doing. She was going to be part of the team and as we progressed we would have to answer more of her questions. I had to impress upon her how serious and confidential the job was going to be. I started carefully.

"Do you not think it rather strange a mere pilot officer should have his own service vehicle and now his own driver?"

"Maybe your dad knows somebody at the Air Ministry, sir," she grinned.

"Bourne! I'm being serious."

She wiped the smile from her face and looked at me expectantly.

"We've a bit of a mystery here at West Fen. As I am surplus to requirement in the Intelligence Section, the task of solving the mystery has fallen to me. For the time being you'll have to curb your voracious curiosity. As we progress, you'll learn a little more at each stage, but I must impress upon you that the whole shebang is confidential. You're not to speak to a soul about anything you may learn. As far as anybody else is concerned, you're just my driver and we're carrying out a community relations task. You know the sort of thing - complaints about low flying and things like that. Do you understand?"

"Yes, sir." To my relief she was taking me seriously.

"No getting pissed or pissed off and letting the cat out of the bag?"

She fixed me with a level stare. "Look, sir, I'd rather cut off my right arm than let you down. I appreciate everything you've done for me and I'm not going to wreck the first job I've ever enjoyed." Her sincerity made me feel uncomfortable but I knew she meant it.

"That's what I wanted to hear," I replied. "Just to reinforce the seriousness of the situation, at some point in the near future, the station commander will have to interview you. You're likely to learn about something known only to a handful of people and he'll want to stress the seriousness of that knowledge. So, best blue, clean shirt and polished shoes. Okay?"

"You're dead worried I'll grab his trinkets."

I held up a warning finger. "Bourne!"

"Sorry, sir. I know what you mean and there will be no problems. I'd be a mug to wreck a doddle of a job like this!"

I was not sure that was the best motive in the world but it would do for now.

Some time later, Jock Lamont popped his head around the door. "The first batch of prints are ready for you, sir. I've filled out a request, so if you'll just pop through and sign it, you can take the prints away with you. It should put the squadron leader out of his misery. He's phoned twice since you landed."

He took us through to his office and I signed for the photos. As I signed I saw him giving the odd glance in Bourne's direction but Jock was a good sergeant and he knew enough to show no reaction or ask questions. I thanked him and we shot off at high speed to the Intelligence Section where I knew Houseman was waiting impatiently for the results of our aerial recce.

I had to leave Bourne in the vehicle because all the staff were in the middle of preparing tonight's operation briefing and that was secret. Natalie was off duty so I just gave a quick acknowledgement to the others and went through to Houseman's office.

He leapt up as I knocked and entered. "How are the pics?"

"I only got a brief glance at them before Sergeant Lamont wrapped them up, sir. What I did see looked pretty good though."

He rubbed his hands in anticipation. "Come on, then, get the bloody things out."

We were both eager to see the results of the flight and, thanks to the superb air clarity that winter morning, they were excellent shots, but after two hours of scrutiny we'd drawn a blank. There was nothing obvious all. We even borrowed the stereo glasses from Max and could see every little undulation, ditch and furrow but to no avail. Max wouldn't be able to look at them properly until much later and we sorely missed his expertise. We were amateurs at this game and were probably missing the obvious. Max was trained in the art of photographic interpretation and he was going to be our real hope for locating a covert airstrip if it existed. Houseman threw the final couple of prints on his desk and slumped dejectedly into his chair.

"I'm going cross-eyed goggling at these bloody things."

I sorted the prints back into sequence and flopped into the chair in front of his desk. "It's like looking for a needle in a haystack. There are plenty of fields big enough for a Hurricane or a Spitfire to operate from, but there must be a hangar or shed or something to hide the bloody thing in. Surely we would spot that?"

Houseman tiredly rubbed a hand over his eyes. "Camouflage to prevent detection from the air would be their first priority. Security on the ground would not be too difficult. A few warning signs of an Air Ministry establishment and the locals would ask no questions. There are sites like that all over this county. Having said that, they must know that the chance of remaining undetected is pretty slim. I bet you that they've planned how long they dare stay in one place before picking up sticks and going somewhere else. I just hope the bastards are not already history in this area."

"You really believe they exist, sir?"

Houseman looked at me grimly. "You started all this, Sam. You've convinced me and you've convinced the Groupie. Don't for Christ's sake start to doubt your judgement now!"

I shook my head slowly. "The more we go into this the more I believe I'm right, sir. Stan Cornish was the man who sold it to me although he didn't know what he was selling at the time. Actually, I'm not so sure about that. He's a sharp little devil and quite capable of working it out for himself."

"I'd like to meet him," said Houseman.

"You'll have to come for a pint at the Lancaster Arms. That way it will look unplanned."

Houseman laughed. "You're becoming quite the spy, Sam."

"God forbid!" I grinned. "I'm still a bloody trainee intelligence wallah and I still can't tell my arse from my elbow!"

Houseman stood, picked up the photos and locked them in his safe. "Don't undersell yourself, young man. It was your penchant for thinking the impossible that put us on the track in the first place. Anyway, let's pack it in for today. I must prepare for this afternoon's briefing. War stops for no man."

"I'll give you a hand." I followed him to the door.

"No, Sam, bugger off for the rest of today. We've enough staff in there to cope. Natalie's off duty. Take her out for a drink or something." He said it so quickly I nearly missed it. I was about to protest when he grabbed me by the shoulder and shoved me out into the corridor. "For goodness sake, man, get out of here before I change my mind."

"Do you normally order your men out on dates?" I laughed.

"Only if they are too slow to catch a bloody cold. Bog off, Carver. I've work to do."

As we walked up the corridor to the watchkeepers' office I heard Janner's door quietly close. I was sure Houseman heard it too but he gave no reaction.

I had to walk back to the mess as I'd long since sent Bourne back to the MT Section. As I entered the foyer, Bates was behind reception and called out to me.

"Mr Carver, sir. Miss Cowen asked me to inform you, if you came in, that she's in the anteroom and she'd like you to join her."

"Thanks, Mr Bates." I turned for the anteroom then turned back to Bates. "I took a look at your Lincolnshire Wolds, from the air, this morning and I must say they are a marked improvement to these fens."

"There you are, sir. I did tell you that they were worth a visit. You actually went flying today, sir?"

"For the very first time, Mr Bates. It was like a dream, but of course it would be, there was nobody shooting at us and it was fantastic weather. Can't really go wrong with that scenario, can you?"

"Indeed not, sir. I envy you. Although I'm not by nature an adventurous man, I'd dearly love to fly in one of your infernal machines. Just to see God's work from a different angle would probably rekindle my waning faith."

I laughed. "Mr Bates, if ever I get the chance, you'll get that opportunity. To save just one of God's wandering flock would be quite satisfying."

"Bless me, sir," he joined in my laughter. "I fear you're another romantic soul who has lost all sense of reality."

"I lost all senses when I was posted here, Mr Bates. I'll see if Miss Cowen can offer me salvation."

His words followed me as I passed through the doors into the corridor. "Succour can always be found in the bosom of a good woman, sir. Your salvation awaits you in the anteroom!" I heard him chuckle and, just as the doors closed, I distinctly heard him softly add the rider. "If you play your cards right!"

Natalie rose from a chair and smiled as I entered the room. "Hi! How was the flight?"

I sighed and motioned her back into her chair. "The flight was fantastic but we didn't get the result we wanted. Well, not so far. Maybe Max can come up with something." I sank tiredly into a chair. I'd only experienced a short flight but I was worn out. How did the crews manage eight or nine hours, night after night? I passed a weary hand over my eyes and yawned. "Bourne enjoyed the trip. She was like a puppy dog with two tails. If you can imagine such an analogy applied to Bourne."

Natalie looked at me in amazement. "You took Bourne with you?"

"Yep."

"How did you get Houseman to sanction that?" She sounded incredulous.

"He was a bit taken aback when I suggested we take her along but he was really great with her. He's now her knight in shining armour and she's ready and waiting with her little tin of Brasso! Actually, she did rather well."

Natalie shook her head in disbelief. "I don't believe it."

"No, seriously," I replied. "She made quite a contribution to the trip. She became a gunner for the day and rode in the gun turret and, before you ask, she didn't wipe out Skegness in a fit of pique as we flew by. Mind you, that was probably because the guns were not loaded. Christ! I hope the guns weren't loaded otherwise we took a hell of a risk." I clapped my hand to my forehead in mock dismay.

"You great twit!" laughed Natalie.

"Sorry about the bike ride," I said quietly changing the subject.

She put a hand on my arm. "I've a feeling we will have plenty of time for that. I can't see the war ending this month."

I glanced at my watch. "Fancy pedalling furiously into New Bolingbroke this evening and grabbing a pint at the Lancaster Arms?"

A smug and secretive look appeared on her face as she reached down into her shoulder bag. She withdrew her hand and dangled a set of car keys in my face. "No pedalling for me, Carver. I've got Max's car for the evening."

"You jammy devil. How come?"

"Max said he'd be on duty all night and, if I could twist your arm into coming out with me, I could use his car."

"You sure he didn't offer it to me?" I asked, pulling her leg.

She pointed at my wrist. "You can't drive so I get the car."

"So you're going to take me out?"

"If you'll come."

"Try and stop me." I took her hand in mine. "I'll go and get changed and meet you in the foyer at about seven. How's that?"

She nodded and grinned. "Don't be late or I'll take somebody else."

I stood and looked down at her, trying not to let her see how much I felt for her. "I'll be there ready and waiting. Anybody else tries to muscle in and I'll bruise my other toes by kicking him up the arse."

She laughed lightly and rose. "Succinct but to the point."

As we strolled towards the door, we passed five aircrew officers seated together immersed in their newspapers. One of them glanced up as we passed and he tut-tutted loudly.

"Damned me if he hasn't pinched the only decent bit of crumpet!"

"Not fair," one of his friends shouted after us. "What've you got that we haven't, old boy?"

"Bollocks!" I called over my shoulder.

There was a roar of laughter and the same voice shouted a rejoinder. "I didn't ask what's keeping your ears apart, old man!"

Thankfully the door closed behind us and muted the resultant laughter. We paused in the foyer and Natalie squeezed my arm. "What a coarse chap you are. I'd no idea of your hidden talent for ribaldry."

I grinned. "In this environment one learns quickly."

"There's no answer to that. See you later." She gave my arm another quick squeeze and was gone.

Bates looked at me from his position behind the counter. "A lovely young lady, sir."

"Indeed she is, Mr Bates, indeed she is," I replied as I headed for my room.

Natalie picked me up about seven and we were soon outside the Lancaster Arms, but all looked deserted. The usual wartime blackout was in force but the whole village gave the impression of a graveyard. There was no noise from the pub and no bikes or cars on the parking area. I stood by the car and listened, but there was only silence. I looked at the darkened pub in disgust.

"Looks like it's closed. Just our ruddy luck!" I heard a strange sound behind me in the darkness and I whirled round in alarm. I could just make out the form of somebody who had approached quietly across the grass in front of the pub. The strange noise had been the panting of a dog as it strained at its leash.

"Who's that?" asked a man's voice and the shielded beam of a small torch flashed briefly on my face and then went out. "Ah, it's the chap who asks all the bloody questions."

"Is that you, Harry?" I asked quickly.

"It is. What are you doing here on a Sunday night?"

"We were under the delusion we'd come out for a drink."

The torch flashed again briefly, this time on Natalie who was still seated in the car.

"By heck!" said Harry. "You're a hell of a lot better looking than Max!"

There was a soft chuckle from Natalie and Harry nudged my arm in the darkness but thankfully didn't say what was on his mind. Instead, he elected to explain the closed pub.

"We only get a delivery from the brewery on Mondays so, by the time we've seen the Saturday night rush, we're out of everything. I've nothing left to sell until the brewer delivers again. Best thing you can do is carry on to Revesby and go to the Red Lion. It's a bigger pub and he gets more beer than we do. If I'd anything at all, you could come into the house and have a drink with me and Ethel but the cellar's as dry as a witch's tit."

"Thanks for the offer anyway, Harry. We'll probably see you one night in the week."

"Did you find old Stan Cornish?" he asked.

"Yes, thank you. It wasn't that difficult. Nice little chap."

Harry laughed quietly. "He is if he likes you, but he can be a clunch old bugger if he doesn't take to you."

"Well, I reckon he must have liked the cut of my jib because, although he was a bit wary, he was fine. He's nobody's fool though."

"He certainly isn't," agreed Harry. He pointed to the north. "Now, if you follow the rest of the seven-mile straight and cross the bridge over the drain, you'll come to a 'tee' junction. That's Revesby and the pub is right across the road from the junction."

I thanked him and we set off for Revesby. This time, as Harry had forecast, we were in luck. The pub was open. It was pretty crowded but we slipped into a couple of vacant chairs in the large front room. There were no servicemen in the pub, which was a bit of a surprise. Local men playing dominoes occupied three tables. Their games punctuated by the click of the pieces and the banging of their fists on the tables as they 'knocked' and cursed their luck.

"All of a sudden, the war seems a long way away," Natalie mused as she looked around her.

It was true. The fire burned brightly in the hearth and the flickering paraffin lamps gave the room a cosy feel.

"Very romantic." I watched her reaction.

She didn't smile or in fact react in any way. She toyed idly with her finger in a small pool of spilt beer, tracing small patterns on the surface of the table. "It's very strange," she said finally. "I see so little of you but I know our relationship is going far beyond that of work colleagues. Do you feel that?"

I placed my hand on hers and stopped the patterns. "Do you mind that?"

She waited a little while before answering. "How about an answer? You always seem to follow a question with yet another question, Sam."

"Sorry," I said quickly. "How do I feel? Bloody marvellous actually. The thing is, am I overreacting and making more of our friendship than actually exists?"

She slowly shook her head. "I don't think so. The very moment I opened the door to you on that first day, I knew you were going to be something special to me."

I felt a small shudder of pleasure at her remark. "That was a lovely thing to say."

"I mean it, Sam." She said it quietly and looked me straight in the eye.

I reached out a hand and gently touched her lips. "All this and it's only our very first date."

She grinned. "I know. Bit of a fast worker, aren't I?"

"Thank God for that!" I laughed. "If you'd left it to me, I'd've probably taken months to pluck up the courage to tell you how much I love you." I looked around the dingy room with its nicotine and paraffin soot - hued walls. "Pity it couldn't be in a more romantic setting."

She gently stroked my bandaged wrist. "Who cares?"

I was about to answer her when there was a disturbance in the corridor outside. All faces in the room turned as a tall, florid-faced young man staggered in. He was already drunk and grinned genially at everybody.

"Evenin' all!" he called loudly and reeled over to the fireplace. "A pint landlord, if you please!" He shouted the request in a strong, local accent but to no avail because there was no bar in the room. To get a drink one had to queue at the hatch in the corridor through which beer was served straight from the barrel. The lad was wearing a tattered old military greatcoat, large boots and a crash helmet. At first I thought he'd come on a motorcycle and was wearing an army despatch rider's helmet. If he'd ridden a bike in that state then he needed his bloody head testing. I turned back to Natalie but I suddenly got the old prickly feeling in the hairs on my neck. I stared hard at her as I tried to prevent myself from taking another look at the helmet. The full implication of what I'd seen was causing my heart to race and I was fighting to keep myself under control.

Natalie's eyes narrowed with concern and she took my hand in hers. "Sam, are you feeling all right?"

I could see the helmet out of my eye corner. The young man was leaning up against the mantelpiece and his thick fair hair was sticking out from under the green shell.

"I've got a bit of a problem," I answered quickly.

She looked mystified. "What on earth is wrong with you?"

I shook my head slightly to warn her to keep her voice down. "You saw the lad who just came in?"

"I could hardly miss him."

"I need to get him outside." I said it in a rush.

"I'm sorry, Sam?" Irritation was creeping into her voice. "What the hell are you talking about?"

I wanted desperately to explain but I knew it was impossible at this stage. How could I tell her that a very drunken young local was wearing a German paratrooper's helmet? I suddenly realised I was becoming paranoid. It was probably a souvenir from a relative serving in the forces, but somehow I knew it was not that simple. How the hell could I get hold of the damned thing? More important, how was I going to get him to tell me where he had got it from? I had to do something.

I rose quickly. "Just nipping out to the little boys' room."

I left Natalie with a look on her face that put our future relations in grave danger.

Outside it was a really cold night. There was no wind but the cold air penetrated even my thick greatcoat. I shivered and turned towards the road as a faint squeak heralded the approach of somebody on a bicycle. The hooded front light wobbled to a halt.

"Evening, sir," said a voice from the darkness.

I couldn't see the uniform but I knew that tone of voice - the local policeman. Shit! He was the last person I wanted in the pub. The chances were high that he'd recognise that helmet and I'd lose the opportunity to talk to the lad. It would also be all over the pub and local area within hours and any chance for a covert investigation would be lost. I thought fast.

"What's all the shooting up that way, constable?" I asked and pointed vaguely in the direction of East Kirkby.

"Shooting, sir?" he queried.

"Yes," I babbled on. "Quite a few shots actually - just as we arrived here." I could sense him mentally comparing the merits of promotion for a job well done with a warm pub fireside. Thankfully, duty won the battle of wills. "Could be poachers up at Revesby Abbey, I'd better take a look. Thank you, sir. Goodnight to you."

I watched as the faint red light wobbled off up the road in pursuit of the imaginary poachers. Two elderly men came out of the pub and headed for the gents' toilets. I was desperate for a plan so I followed them into the smelly and very dark urinal. We stood side by side, our urine splashing noisily into the trough. One of the men broke wind loudly.

"Which way did that bugger go?" his friend laughed.

"Dunno, but it's yours if you can catch it," replied the flatulent one.

It was now or never. As I spoke I tried to modify my accent from its normal clipped tones. Couldn't afford to alienate them from the start.

"The young chap wearing the helmet seems to have had a skinful," I said lightly.

There was a silence as we buttoned up our trouser flies. I thought I was going to get no reply. Fuck these taciturn Lincolnshire countrymen. But, as we walked out into the fresh air, one of them finally spoke.

"He can be a right bloody nuisance," said one of the men.

"He's one of Jack Troutbridge's boys, isn't he?" asked his friend.

"Aye," replied the first. "Young Norman. It's about time he was called up. He needs some army discipline to straighten him out."

That was all I was going to get. They collected their bikes from under a nearby tree and cycled away into the darkness. I could hear them chattering happily together long after they left the pub, their voices carrying on the still, cold air.

I tried to find a piece of paper in the MG but I had no torch. Finally I found a map and, taking a pencil from my pocket, I blindly scrawled the name, 'Troutbridge. Norman,' on the inside of the cover. Where the hell did the family live? I couldn't ask in the pub. I couldn't afford to let anybody see my interest in that damned helmet.

Maybe we could follow him home. Maybe I could offer him money. Rubbish! He'd find it impossible not to tell all and sundry about the idiot who bought old helmets. It was no good clouting him and pinching the bloody thing but I had to know where it came from. It was no good; I'd have to wait until tomorrow. Maybe Harry Woods would know where they lived

I went back into the pub. The lad, still wearing the helmet, was slumped on the floor in the corner of the room, singing quietly to himself. I didn't sit back down at the table.

"Sorry about this, Nat. Do you mind if we leave?"

She rose slowly. "No, of course not." Her voice was light but the look she gave me didn't match her voice for levity.

Once in the car, I stretched out my hand and stopped her from starting the engine. "Look, Nat. I really am sorry I've wrecked the evening but I may have just been given a key to help me solve a problem. I can't say anything now but I promise you it is very important. Can you bear with me until I either find the answer or give up in disgust when it all proves to be a wild goose chase?"

She sighed. "If you were not such a nice chap, Carver, I'd be furious. However, having seen the way you reacted in the pub, I know that whatever you saw gave you a hell of a shock. If you're trying to keep something secret, I hope nobody was watching you at that point. You looked as if you'd seen a ghost. Don't worry, I'll never put you on the spot. You just do whatever you're doing and get it sorted out because, as I said, after seeing your reaction, I know it is something very serious."

I reached out, took her face in my hands, kissed her gently on each eyelid and finally on her mouth.

"I love you, Nat."

She kissed me on the tip of my nose. "I love you too, Mr Carver."

We held each other tight in the confines of the MG and, although my heart was singing with joy with my love for the girl in my arms, the gears in my mind were slipping the odd cog. I must get that helmet and any information that went with it. I'd do it tomorrow. Later, I wished I'd done something more positive that night.

CHAPTER NINE

Natalie drove me back to the mess and, in spite of the cramped conditions of the MG, we managed just one lingering and very gentle kiss. I finally came up for air with the distinct feeling that German helmets were the last things I wanted to occupy my thoughts at this time. Here in my arms I had the most beautiful girl I'd ever met in my life and I was going to have to say 'goodnight'. Bugger Hitler and his little cronies, they were totally destroying my newly found love life. I sighed heavily and disentangled myself from her arms.

"Sorry, I've got to go but I must see Houseman before he turns in."

"I understand, you great clot. But when you've finished playing Ronald Coleman, just remember this heroine is waiting in the wings!"

"I shall return to you on a large white charger and whisk you off into a red, setting sun."

"Knowing you, Carver, you'll turn up on an old RAF bike and whisk me off to the Boston Odeon."

"I see you're accustomed to the high life."

"Only if we sit in the circle!"

I crawled out of the car in a most undignified way, which, it seemed, was the burden of all MG owners and passengers. "I am destroyed," I said, adopting a hurt tone. "Your words have cut me to the quick."

She hooted with laughter and revved the engine. "Oh, do bog off, Carver. See you tomorrow."

She was gone with only the oily smell of a car with worn piston rings lingering on the night air to remind me she had ever been there. God! How romantic!

As I rushed into the mess foyer, Bates called to me from his desk. "Mr Carver, sir. Squadron Leader Houseman's compliments and would you go to his room before you turn in for the night. It is Room forty-six."

I pulled off my gloves and unbuttoned my coat. "Good Lord, Mr Bates, do you ever go home?"

His face was as serious as ever as he peered at me over his specs. "You're beginning to sound like my wife, sir. I don't think I care for the simile."

I laughed. "Sorry, Mr Bates. I promise not to question your affairs again."

"Most kind of you, sir." His face creased into a smile. "Actually, the broken nose and the cauliflower ears are features which would set you apart from my wife."

I halted halfway through the door and turned back to him. "I haven't got a broken nose or cauliflower ears."

"No, indeed, sir, you've not - but my wife has!" His laughter echoed my own mirth as I set off to find Houseman's room.

I found Number forty-six, knocked and Houseman called for me to enter. He was sitting at a small table writing a letter. "Evening, Sam. Just give me a second to finish this and I'll be with you. You'll have to perch on the bed - this is the only chair."

I sat on the edge of the bed and looked around me. The difference between his room and the one I shared with Hammond was a simple matter of tidiness. This room was neat, clean and very spartan, a little like Houseman himself. My room looked like Hamburg after a thousand-bomber raid. On the locker by Houseman's bed there was a snapshot of a serious but beautiful woman with two small children. As he licked the envelope to seal it, he saw me looking at the photo.

"My wife and the two terrors. This is yet another letter to reassure her that I'm still flying a desk and not a Lancaster. I think she actually sleeps at night now she knows I'm no longer operational."

I was a little surprised, as he had not previously mentioned his wife. "Where are they living, sir?"

He hammered a stamp onto the envelope with his fist and switched off the desk light. "With her sister in Hereford. We lived in London when the war started but I persuaded her to move when the raids started. She loves the Hereford area and I've a sneaking feeling that we will end up there when the war is over. Hereford is a lovely place, full of beautiful old buildings and, of course, the cathedral. Such a pleasant change from the serried ranks of houses in London's suburbia." He paused and then spoke almost to himself. "Those serried ranks are now full of black holes - rather like decaying teeth." He looked up quickly. "Sorry, got a bit carried away there!"

I just shook my head to show that I was not unable to understand the sentiment.

He looked at me curiously. "Sam, I'm afraid I've some rather unfortunate news for you."

"Don't tell me, sir, Command have heard of my pie in the sky?"

"Strewth, no! Although, it has to do with Command. Wing Commander Janner has been at work and has volunteered you for an operational trip."

"Blimey!" It was all I could think of to say. This was serious stuff. Taking on the Germans in this country was one thing but flying around over their territory could seriously damage one's health.

"Exactly my feelings," replied Houseman without a smile. "He's wangled it with Command that you fly on an operation as an observer."

A rather large knot of fear was beginning to make itself felt in the pit of my stomach and I wished I'd not missed dinner. I tried to make light of the situation. "How am I going to observe anything, sir? I'll have my eyes tightly shut from the moment we takeoff until we're back home again!"

Houseman gave a small smile but it was soon gone. "You don't have to go, you know that don't you? Volunteers carry out aircrew duties and you've not volunteered. Neither I, the wing commander, or anybody else can make you go. I think the risk is too great. You're more valuable here at the moment and I don't want to lose the impetus of our investigation."

I looked down at my shoes and tried to fully grasp the fact that I was, for the first time in my life, going to put my life on the line. It was a sobering thought but I knew what I was going to say, even while I deliberated the possible outcome. "I'd like to go, sir."

He looked at me and shook his head. "How did I know you were going to say that?"

I tried to justify my decision. "If I'm going to spend the rest of the war briefing others, I reckon I ought to see first hand what I'm sending them into, sir."

"You're not sending anybody anywhere," he said quietly. "Command does that."

"At least I'll get an idea of what the crews are going through, sir."

"Carver, you're a damned fool but, as I already suspected as much, I've arranged for you to fly with Squadron Leader Mason - he's 'A' Flight Commander on 629

Squadron. He and his crew are very experienced and in the middle of their second tour."

"How does he feel about having a ground wallah on board?" I asked.

Houseman grinned. "I told him you've flown before."

"One trip in an Anson hardly makes me an albatross, other than around his neck!"

Houseman laughed. "Sammy Mason is a bloody good type but he's very strict with his crew. Believe you me, he'll not let you get away with a free ride."

"Maybe that will be a good thing, sir. The more I've to do the less scared I'll be."

Houseman became quite serious. "You haven't asked me how the wing commander managed to get you on this trip."

"Surprise me, sir," I prompted resignedly.

Houseman sat up straight and fiddled with the pen he'd picked up from the desk. "He was at a meeting over at Command and the idea was mooted, probably by the wing commander himself with you already in mind, that somebody from Intelligence should fly on a sortie to assess a new type of target indicator. It seems the Pathfinders are going to experiment with markers that will indicate precise points on the run in, to give the bombers a visual update of their position in relation to the target. He suggested you and nobody even gave it a second thought that you probably didn't wish to go." He paused and looked at me carefully. "He really doesn't like you, does he?"

"I'm afraid not, sir."

"Right!" Houseman said as he stood. "That's the story for now. Just do your best and shake him with a report to knock his bloody socks off." He grinned and placed a finger to the side of his nose in a conspiratorial gesture. "I'll help you write it!"

"When do I fly, sir?"

"After tonight's operations, the crews are stood down for the next two nights. I imagine they will pick a French target so as to limit the risk. Although they are all bloody dangerous. I was terrified on my first and it didn't get any better."

"You were scared every trip?" I asked in amazement.

"Bloody terrified, but it was better than flying a desk or circuit bashing with ham-fisted students."

I looked at him carefully as I asked my next question. "How many actually go LMF?"

He shrugged. "No official figures are released for obvious reasons - bad for morale. Half way through my first tour our rear gunner twice sabotaged his turret so we had to turn back. Of course we didn't know it was sabotage at first but then the armourers came up with the evidence. He was stripped of his rank and posted with the dreaded words 'Lack of Moral Fibre' on his records for all to see. A couple of Canadians in another crew refused to co-operate with the pilot as they were taxiing out and he had to scrub. They both disappeared very quickly. The problem is this - who is qualified to accuse anybody of cowardice? Nobody knows how he's going to react to danger until he actually experiences it. Then, after all the expensive training, it's a bit late to say you'd rather go and change your library books. On the other hand, how much can a man take? I've known guys who have flown their bloody hearts out and gone through hell. Finally they broke and could take no more. It didn't matter to the powers-that-be; they were still classed as LMF, even though they had done more than was humanly expected of them." He moved, sat on the edge of the small table and grinned at me sheepishly. "Sorry, getting carried away again."

"No problem, sir. Thank you for the candid answer. I can see it on some of their faces in the mess and I'm under no illusions as to what I'm undertaking."

"Just as long as you do, young man. Now, I've another bit of bad news. Max could find nothing out of the ordinary on our photos."

I jumped to my feet. "Shit! I was so preoccupied with your news, I forgot I've something to tell you." I paused and tried to form the words to tell him but, no matter which way I looked at it, it was going to sound ludicrous. Ah well, shit or bust - go for it, Carver.

"I saw a chap tonight, in a pub, wearing a German paratrooper's helmet."

I was right, it did sound ludicrous and Houseman regarded me in silence with the quizzical expression on his face of one who has been denied a punch line.

"Where?" he finally asked.

"The Red Lion at Revesby, sir. A few miles from here."

"Where is the helmet now?"

A bloody good question and I found myself stuttering the answer. "Well... actually...I mean he was pretty pissed and I couldn't sort of get near him, sir. If I had approached him in the pub, everybody would have wondered why I was so interested in the damned thing."

Houseman nodded. "Do you know who he is?"

"Norman Troutbridge, sir. I don't actually know where he lives but I'm sure it's pretty close to Revesby as everybody seemed to know him. I intend to ask Stan Cornish – he'll probably know the name. I'd like to get down there in the morning and get the helmet. I also hope to find out where he got it from."

"Could be a wartime souvenir."

"That had occurred to me, sir. Somehow though, I think not. It was in good condition and I'm sure he'd no idea of its origin or, more importantly, its significance."

"Anybody else recognise it for what it was?"

"Nobody made a move as far as I could tell."

"Okay, let's hope you can sort it out in the morning." He tapped his teeth thoughtfully with the pen.

"Bloody hell! You certainly know how to throw spanners in the works. If your conjecture is correct, an enemy agent could have actually been inserted into this area, right in the middle of the biggest collection of airfields in the country."

"Well, that was the hurried conclusion I came to, sir. Of course, like the covert airfield, it could be a load of balls."

"Who said the covert airfield was a load of balls?" he asked me quickly.

"Well, sir, you did say that Max saw nothing unusual in the photos."

"Max hasn't been able to give them a thorough going over. He may find something yet."

I nodded and hoped fervently that this was not all a load of bollocks. I sat back down on the bed. "You know, sir, if the agent, assuming there was an agent, discarded the helmet then he must have had to get rid of his parachute. Find the location where Troutbridge found the helmet and we may find the chute."

Houseman stood and I followed suit. "Get on it tomorrow, Sam," he said. "I'll inform Groupie of this latest development and suggest to him that we may soon have to call in the security services. If both the airstrip and the helmet leads prove positive, then we'll be well out of our depth. It'll be time to call in the experts."

I opened the door. "I'll get out there first thing, sir."

"You've done well, Sam." He glanced at his watch. "I'd better be going as the first aircraft are due back about oh-one hundred."

He grabbed his cap and greatcoat and we walked out to the foyer together. We parted as he headed out into the night and I to my room. I was soon in bed but sleep was a long time coming. My preoccupation with the helmet was bad enough but now I had the extra worry of actually flying on a raid. Would I let the side down by showing my fear and becoming a gibbering liability at twenty thousand feet? I began to wonder how the hell I'd got myself into all this. I was only an insignificant pilot officer, not even fully trained, yet I had all this on my plate. Oh well, shouldn't have joined if you can't take a joke. With the transition of that ambiguous phrase through my mind, I fell into a deep sleep.

I was in a field of waving, golden corn. The sun was warm on my naked body and the sky above, as I lay on my back, was sprinkled with white, fluffy clouds. I felt a movement by my side and Natalie's hand gently brushed my shoulder.

"Sir!" she said in a strangely gruff voice. "Sir!" she said again and shook me with surprising force. I couldn't understand how her beautiful mouth could form and emit such a coarse sound. Why was she calling me 'sir'? The fact we were both naked indicated we had reached a level of intimacy that far outstripped any archaic service etiquette! I couldn't understand but at the same time I didn't care. I was naked and so was Natalie. What could be more important than that? Maybe she was hoarse with excitement?

I slowly rolled over and tightly gripped her arm, barely able to control my rising passion. "Yes, my darling?"

"Cor! Fuckin' 'ell!" said Natalie with feeling.

I woke with a violent start and saw the dim light of a hooded torch flashing wildly around the dark room. It was held by a large airman, muffled up in greatcoat, scarf and gloves, fighting to free himself from the grip I had on his arm.

"What the fuck is going on?" I muttered, quickly removing my hand from his arm.

The poor chap struggled to pull himself together and, after taking two quick paces away from my bed, whispered loudly. "Pilot Officer Carver, sir?"

"Yes." I grunted the reply.

"You're to report to 629 Squadron, sir. Commander 'A' Flight, Squadron Leader Mason will see you in his office at 05.00, sir."

"What the hell for?" I protested.

"No idea, sir." The airman muttered the reply as he backed hurriedly towards the door. Poor sod, it was not his fault. He was just the messenger and, as far as he was concerned, he'd damned nearly been sexually assaulted into the bargain!

"Very well. Thanks for the call." I whispered.

He left the room quickly, as my uncle up in Yorkshire would say, 'like a frog up a pump!' Talking of frogs, Hammond was snoring away in the darkness, oblivious to my rude awakening. I felt like opening all the bloody windows and letting in the sub-zero Lincolnshire equivalent of the Russian steppes. I thought better of it and stumbled off to the washroom.

Later, as I groped my way through the darkness to 629 Squadron HQ, I wondered what this was all about. Houseman had told me the squadrons were stood down for the next two nights. Surely my operational trip had not arrived already! My bowels gave a quick twitch as fear began to rouse my sleep-befuddled brain. Maybe I should damage my other wrist. Surely they couldn't ask me to fly with two bandaged wrists?

I entered the 629 Squadron HQ hut and located the door with the usual stencilled white letters indicating 'A' Flight Commander. There was a light shining from under the door and I could hear the murmur of voices. I knocked and was bidden to enter.

The room was small and behind the desk sat a short, stocky squadron leader. Perched on the corner of his desk was a tall, lanky flight lieutenant with dark wavy hair. He wore the brevet of a flight engineer on his battledress jacket.

I saluted "Pilot Officer Carver, sir."

The squadron leader rose to his feet and held out his hand. "Morning, Carver. My name is Mason, sorry about the early start but Jake Houseman told me you'd been volunteered for an operational trip."

I shook the extended hand. "That's right, sir. Our wing commander put me forward as an observer for some new markers."

The two men exchanged knowing looks before Mason indicated the other officer. "This is my flight engineer, Jock Bryant."

"Welcome aboard," said Bryant as we shook hands and he actually sounded as if he meant it. "What's your first name?"

"Sam," I answered and warmed instantly to the engineer. I turned to Mason. "Have the op orders changed, sir? I thought you were stood down for the next two nights. Well, at least you were when I finally got to sleep last night."

Mason grinned. "We are and no change to the orders, are the answers to your questions. The reason for me calling you out at this unearthly time of the morning is to give both you and myself the chance to find out how you'll cope on a long trip in a Lancaster. I understand you've flown before?"

"One quick trip in the station flight Anson, sir."

"Well, at least it is a start," said Mason. "How did it go?"

"Fine, sir. Hardly time to get sick and it was so smooth as to be unreal. I must say, I'll be pleased to get the chance to try a flight before going on an actual mission. My biggest fear has been letting the side down by being so ill as to be a bloody handicap to you and your crew."

Mason looked at me long and hard. "If that is all you're scared of Carver, you've nothing further to worry about. You've debriefed crews and you've seen the photos so you know something of what to expect. Does that not scare you?"

"Shitless, sir."

They both roared with laughter.

"Thank God for that!" said Mason, wiping his eyes with a handkerchief. "I thought we'd found a bloody hero."

I grinned with embarrassment. "I'm afraid not, sir. I think they removed the brave bits at Cosford, as I've discovered a marked lack of enthusiasm for war since the day I walked through the gates of the damned place."

"Good Lord!" Mason exclaimed. "An honest man at last. I know just what you mean. Anyway, down to business." He waved me to sit on a typically basic RAF issue chair. "We've to flight-test a bit of new navigation equipment today and we're going to combine it with a sea search for two downed crews. My crew and myself were not flying last night but one of our crews, who were on ops, ditched into the North Sea. We've their last reported position and that of a Coningsby crew who are also down. No need to tell you that unless they got into their dinghies, there will be no survivors. On the other hand, we'll look on the bright side and assume the ditchings went well and they are alive and afloat. Even with that scenario, we need to find them fast so I've arranged transport to pick us up from kitting out at 06.00. Jock here will get you fitted up with all the necessary gear and fill you in on the emergency procedures." His eyes went to my bandaged wrist. "Are you right handed?"

"Yes, sir. Only the left is giving me problems."

"Well, at least you should be able to pull the ripcord in the event of a bale-out situation occurring. We've not had to do that yet so don't worry. Anything you didn't like about your trip in the Anson?"

"Only having to crank the undercart up and down, sir."

They both laughed and it was Bryant who spoke. "Well, that is one thing you won't have to do in the Lanc."

"But, young man," said Mason waving a cautionary finger. "Don't think you're coming on a 'jolly'. Everybody in my crew has a job to do and they know and appreciate my standards. You'll be just as busy on this sea search as you'll be on the actual trip. I'll make sure of that. Is that clear?"

I nodded and rose to my feet. "Perfectly, sir. The more I've to do the better I'll like it - less time to think!"

"Good man!" Mason turned to Jock Bryant. "Right, Jock. Get him kitted out and we'll get the show on the road." He stood. "See you at D-Dog's dispersal. I'm going over, as soon as I've changed, to see how Ted is getting on setting up the new kit."

We left the building together and he disappeared into the darkness as we made our way to the kitting-out hut and the parachute section. All I could think about was the fact I had had no bloody breakfast. There again, maybe that was a blessing in disguise. Mason's crew would not welcome regurgitated eggs and bacon as we searched for survivors in the empty, freezing wastes of the North Sea. Mason had obviously, before actually meeting me, decided not to take 'no' for an answer as there was already a full set of flying kit waiting for me in the kitting-out hut. This time there was even a choice of different size flying boots.

Jock dressed himself from his own locker and we let a young LAC test our oxygen masks and helmet headsets.

"Where are the rest of the crew?" I asked.

"They went earlier to help Ted, our navigator, get the test kit rigged."

"The crew that ditched - are they friends of yours?"

Jock grimaced. "We haven't had a chance to meet them. They are on 'B' Flight and this was their first operation."

"Poor bastards!" I said quietly. "What a start to a tour."

Jock nodded. "I just hope the poor devil got the kite down in one piece. The Skipper is only twenty years old which is also the average age of the crew. They don't have a lot of experience."

I followed him through to collect our parachutes. A very tired looking young WAAF handed two over and we signed for them.

"I'm going to feel like a spare prick at a wedding on this trip," I remarked glumly.

Jock laughed. "Remember what the Skipper said, 'no passengers'? Well, he meant it. You'll be kept very busy as an extra lookout. We'll be pretty much on our own out there in broad daylight and there could be German fighters on the prowl. We'll also be looking for two needles in a giant haystack. Two small specks in the ocean. Each speck, if we're lucky, will contain seven hungry, cold and very tired airmen. They'll be desperate to get home and let their families know they're still alive. Their kit will already have been removed from their rooms and bed spaces and it will not be long before the first telegrams are going out to report them missing. Let's hope we can find them and spare at least fourteen families the grief those bloody telegrams bring."

I looked at Jock in surprise. I'd not expected that depth of feeling from the Scotsman. "I'm sorry, Jock. I'm afraid I've a lot to learn." I looked around me. "If I can find a phone, I'll get one of the watchkeepers to bring my binoculars over from the section. If we've time, that is?"

"We can nip round there in the transport before we go out to the kite," he said, glancing at his watch. "But, whatever you do, don't stare through the glasses too long at one time or you really will get airsick."

"I'll take your advice," I answered with feeling.

An airman put his head around the door. "Your transport is outside, sir."

I slipped on my leather gloves and followed Jock outside to where the bulk of the aircrew bus loomed in the darkness. I blinked in surprise as a hooded torch flashed in my face.

"Bloody hell, Petal! Where the hell are you going?"

I stopped dead in my tracks. Oh no! Bloody Foghorn had reverted to type. I turned quickly to look at Jock but he was already convulsed with laughter. Fat lot of help he was going to be. The torch blinked out and I said weakly into the darkness.

"Flying." I could think of nothing else to say.

"Flying?" Foghorn roared. "You're a bloody telly, not a soddin' shitehawk! Got a spare parachute 'cos I reckon you're going to need me up there to look after you?"

I turned to Jock, desperate for help, but he was leaning weakly up against the bus muttering the word, 'Petal', over and over again. I threw up my arms in disgust and Foghorn hooted with mirth.

"All aboard! All aboard!" she roared as she revved the engine.

Jock opened the back doors and clambered in. I followed and pulled the doors closed behind me. Only just in time as the bus lurched into motion. The flight engineer was drying his eyes with the sleeve of his flying suit as I staggered to a seat. He kept glancing at me and dissolving into gales of laughter. I was thoroughly pissed off. Bloody woman, she'd done it again. I fumed in silence as we lurched our way around the peritrack to D-Dog's dispersal. Finally, the bus lurched hard over to the left, then whipped back upright and slithered to a halt.

We clambered down into the beginnings of a false dawn and I could see Mason and the rest of the crew waiting under the nose of the huge Lancaster. I tried to ignore Foghorn and manoeuvred myself to keep the bus between her and me. She was having none of that and drove slowly forward until she could see me skulking away like a dog with its tail between its legs. She called out in a sweet voice that was so alien to her.

"Have a nice trip, Mr Carver, sir," she cooed and then roared off into the gloom at high speed.

I saw the looks of sheer disbelief on the faces of Mason and his crew. Their mouths were open and they were staring at me as if I was some sort of film star.

"Mr Carver, SIR?" Mason said in a shocked voice. "I've never heard her call any officer 'SIR' before. What the hell have you got, Carver, that makes you stand out from the rest of us undistinguished mortals?"

I humped my parachute over to my other hand and was about to reply. Jock, back to wiping his eyes, got in before me.

"That was just for your benefit, Skip. Privately, she calls him 'Petal'." He dissolved into yet more strangled spasms of mirth.

"PETAL?" they all choroused in disbelief.

One of the NCO gunners spoke with awe. "Bloody hell, the only thing she's called me to date is 'Bog Brains'."

"A natural and relevant assumption," replied the oldest-looking member of the crew but he couldn't have been more than his late twenties. Mason himself was only twenty-six. Promotion was quick in Bomber Command.

"Right, Petal," grinned Mason. "Come and meet the rest of the crew."

He introduced me quickly to the two gunners, Jimmy Tait and Bill Bedford. Then it was Tommy Burns the wireless operator, Phil Jolly the bomb aimer and Ted Lowry the navigator. All but the two gunners were officers. All greeted me warmly but, no matter what form their salutation took, without exception and with a big grin, they all ended their greeting with the word 'Petal'. I smiled ruefully at the repetition of the name but I was determined to strangle bloody Foghorn when we got back.

Mason turned to the flight engineer. "Jock, I've done my walk around. We'll get aboard whilst you do yours and I'll get Petal settled in."

I cringed but followed Mason to the fuselage door just in front of the starboard fin and tailplane. I followed him up the steps but somehow got my parachute jammed in the doorway. It took me a while to free the damned thing and the crew were not going to let a good leg pull die until they had milked it for all it was worth.

They all laughed as one of them shouted. "Do get a move on, Petal! We haven't got all day."

I turned and looked down at them. "I'll kill that bloody woman!"

"No you won't, old chap," Ted Lowry contradicted me. "She'd beat seven kinds of shit out of you."

I laughed with the others. "The sad thing is, you're bloody right."

"Come on, Petal," Mason cried from the darkness of the fuselage. "We've got to go flying."

I scrambled into the sloping fuselage and tried to follow the pilot up towards the cockpit. It was like an obstacle race as I smacked my head on every bit of metal between the door and the wing main spar. The main spar traversed the whole fuselage just before one reached the 'front office', as the cockpit area was known to the crew. I clambered over in Mason's wake and hoped that I'd not have to climb over the damned thing again until we landed. I watched Mason settle into his seat on the left side of the cockpit and shuddered at the implication of the armour plate at his back. Phil Jolly tapped me on the shoulder and motioned me into the navigator's position so that he could get by and down into the nose. Next came Jock and I had to vacate the nav's position when Ted arrived to take up his rightful place. I could just see Tommy Burns easing himself into his seat just ahead of the main spar.

Jock put a hand on my shoulder and pointed back down the fuselage. "You can get down by the main spar for takeoff if you like, it's supposed to be the safest place. Or you can stay up here and watch the fun. Just stay out of my way though until we're airborne and sorted."

I nodded. "I'll stay out of your way and I'd like to stay up here."

Mason turned to me and grinned. "We're pretty light today, just lots of fuel, so we should be off pretty quick. Different story with a full bomb load. The end of the runway gets closer and closer and there we are, still on the ground. It scares the shit out of me and I'm the pilot." He stooped and pulled something from a small satchel at his side. "I borrowed these from the tower," he said, handing me a pair of binoculars. "Like I said, no passengers in my kite!"

I grinned with relief. The horror of seeing Foghorn had completely put my own binos out of my mind.

Mason and Jock now had well-thumbed checklists in their hands. First Mason called up each member of the crew on the intercom, finally coming to me." I guess we'd better drop the Petal tag or the Jerries, if they're listening in, will think we're all a bunch of fairies. How about 'Telly'?"

"A blessed relief, sir. Thank you."

"I like him better as Petal," called one of the gunners.

"I've always had my suspicions about you, Bedford." Mason grinned at Jock and myself. "Now wrap up the chit-chat or we'll never get off the bloody ground."

Suddenly, it was as if he was a different man. Gone were the humour and the joshing as he leaned forward in his seat. "Ready for start-up, Eng?"

"Ready, Skip" replied Jock as he consulted his checklist.

"Number Two tank - ON. Booster coil - ON. Pulsometer power - ON. Master cock - ON. Ignition - ON. Contact starboard inner!" Mason stuck his left, gloved hand out of the sliding window on his side and waved his hand in a circular motion to the ground crew marshaller.

The propeller on the starboard-inner engine jerked spasmodically a few times then the engine burst into life. Blue smoke was whipped away astern in the propwash. The engine settled into a steady roar and soon all four Merlins were bellowing away only feet from where I stood. Even though I was wearing a thick leather helmet, the noise was mind numbing. What the hell was it going to be like at full throttle? There was a whining sound as the hydraulic system closed the huge bomb doors.

"Navigator to pilot. Five minutes to takeoff. Runway is two-seven, wind two-four-zero at ten knots. QFE 1008."

"Roger, Nav." Mason looked to his left and then craned to peer across Jock. "All clear your side, Eng?"

Jock checked out beyond the starboard wing and as far to the rear as he could see in the dimness of the dawn. "All clear, Skip."

Mason eased the four throttles forward and, watching the marshaller out to port, he nosed D-Dog out on to the peritrack. The wings seemed to stretch forever. How the hell did these great leviathans get off the ground? It didn't take D-Dog long to allay my fears. We reached the runway, only a short distance from the dispersal and lined up. On the steady green light from the runway controller's caravan, Mason began to pour on the power.

"Here we go, lads." He released the brakes. Slowly we gathered momentum and I watched Mason's right hand as he covered the four throttles. It was not a straight application of power. He seemed to wriggle his wrist, favouring the port outer engine with his thumb. It suddenly occurred to me why. Those huge engines, their props all turning the same way, must generate a lot of torque doing its best to pull the aircraft to one side. Until we reached a speed high enough for the rudders to become effective, he was having to steer with the throttles. I just stood there and marvelled at the balancing act that was taking place. I felt the tail come up and we were now hurtling down the runway, the huge aircraft balanced on just two wheels and being steered by a man's thumb. Jock took over the throttles once Mason could steer with the rudders and the pilot used both hands to lift us gently off the runway and into the dark sky ahead.

"Brakes - ON. Brakes - OFF. Undercarriage - UP." Mason called. It was exactly 06.31.

Mason hauled D-Dog into a turn to port to avoid Coningsby and held the turn until Boston appeared dead ahead. There was a livid pink band of sunrise on the eastern horizon and it glistened on the waters of The Wash. I could just make out the tower of The Stump, or 'The Big Dick' as Foghorn had described it as she drove me through Boston that first morning. Already, it seemed so long ago. The glow of the

110

compass in front of Mason, if I was reading it correctly, was showing a heading of zero-nine-zero.

"Skip," called Ted. "You need to turn on to 045 degrees in one minute."

"Roger," intoned Mason and exactly one minute later, he dipped the port wing on to the new course and we headed out into the North Sea.

Jock was standing close to the instrument panel by the entrance to the bomb aimer's position. He refolded a map, waved me forward and indicated a cross in the expanse of the North Sea. He pulled his oxygen mask up to his face and keyed the intercom switch.

"The nearest ditching was plotted as being around eighty to a hundred miles due east of Flamborough Head. When we reach that position we'll start a square search. Ted will be busy as he not only has to keep us from searching the same area twice but he also has to test the new kit. We'll stay on station for about two hours. Let's hope we get lucky and spot the dinghy or, even better, the dinghies. The other was plotted much further north but 3 Group are doing a search in that area."

Mason cut in. "That reminds me everybody. Look hard for the dinghies but don't forget to keep your eyes open for Jerry fighters. They shot a Shagbat down out here a couple of weeks ago."

Shagbat I knew to be the aircrew nickname for the Walrus, a rather ungainly, single-engined, amphibious biplane. They were used to pick up downed airmen and were crewed by very brave men who deserved far more recognition than they were getting. At least the aircrews appreciated what those men were doing for them even if the powers-that-be were ignorant of their heroism.

It was now much lighter and the pink and gold dawn was mirrored on the sea below. It looked beautiful but I knew from our briefings how deceptively deadly it was from up here. At this time of the year, if a ditched crew failed to get out of the water and into the shelter and relative safety of their dinghy within three minutes, the cold would kill them. Perhaps the men we were looking for were already dead. To ditch a Lancaster in the dark, already damaged by flak or fighters, was no mean feat in itself. For the aircraft to remain intact when it hit the water and the crew to survive the impact would be a miracle. Within forty-five minutes, when we reached the target area, we'd be able to see if that miracle had come to pass.

Exactly forty-five minutes later, the search had begun. Jimmy and Bill were in their turrets, Phil was down in the nose and Tommy had gone up with his head in the astrodome. Jock covered the port side from abeam of the nose to the leading edge of the port wing and I got the same field of search out to starboard.

As we roared on and on, the excitement of flying in a Lancaster began to pall and was replaced by a sense of tedium. The air was smooth and the sun shone from a cobalt blue sky. The sea looked grey but calm. Luckily we seemed to have the sky to ourselves and we had maintained radio silence to try and keep it that way. It wasn't far to enemy airfields equipped with the dreaded Junkers 88. A couple of those could be here in no time and really piss on our parade.

We drank coffee from the crew Thermos flasks and ate bully beef sandwiches but we never let our eyes drift away from the grey sea below.

Two hours passed but Mason seemed loath to give up the search. Every now and then my adrenaline would pump into action, only for me to discover that what I'd thought was a dinghy was just another whitecap.

Mason keyed his mike and surprised me by dropping his previous strict crew formality. "I make that two hours and fifteen, Ted."

"Correct, Skip."

"Jock. How's the fuel?"

"Enough for about another fifteen minutes on station but then we'll have to head for home."

"Roger." Mason's shoulders seemed to sag with despair. He glanced round at me and switched his mike. "How's it going, Telly? You've been very quiet."

"Just thinking of the poor sods down there, sir."

"Yeah, I know what you mean but we've given it a good shot. I don't reckon...."

He got no further because I banged him hard on his right shoulder with my gloved left fist. I kept my eyes glued to the speck that had appeared at the very limit of my vision. I panicked as I suddenly realised it would soon disappear behind the starboard wing.

"Come right! Come right!" I yelled.

Mason didn't hesitate and slowly dropped the right wing to keep my field of view clear. I stared intensely at the speck. My eyes began to water but I didn't dare wipe the tears away for fear of losing that little dot on the surface of the sea. It actually kept disappearing but to my immense relief it would reappear.

"What have you got, Telly?" It was Mason.

"Object in the water at about two-o'clock. If you hold off the turn now, we should pass right by whatever it is."

"Use your binoculars," Jock urged.

"I daren't," I said quickly. "I daren't take my eyes off the bloody thing or I'll lose it."

"Good thinking, Telly," Mason replied. "I'll bring her down to about one hundred feet. If you think the angle is going to be wrong to maintain your sighting, for Christ's sake yell out."

The nose dropped slightly as he eased back the throttles.

"Got it!" a voice yelled.

"Who was that?" Mason barked. "Remember your drill!"

"Sorry, Skip. Bomb aimer. There is definitely something out there."

"I've got it now, Skip!" Jock pointed excitedly.

"Can I use the binos? " I asked. "You both seem to have a fix on it now."

"Go ahead," Jock replied. "I've got it."

I raised the binos and felt a surge of panic as I scoured the surface of the sea but couldn't locate the object. Then, there it was - blurred but there. I focussed the glasses and, to my sheer joy, I could make out the unmistakable shape of an aircrew dinghy. Five men were sitting around its outer wall and two lay in the well. I saw a puff of smoke arc up into the air towards us.

"They've fired a flare!" I yelled.

"Easy, Telly," Mason remonstrated with me. "You've left your ruddy mike on - you'll deafen us."

"Sorry, Skip." I quickly switched off the mike.

"I've got them now," called Mason. "Navigator! Get a fix on our position. Wireless Op, get down out of the astrodome ready to transmit the fix."

"Already down and waiting, Skip."

"What can you see through the glasses, Telly?"

"Seven men, sir. Five look in good shape but the other two are down in the well of the dinghy. Hang on a minute..." I peered intently at the wavering image. "One of the survivors in the bottom of the dinghy just waved. He seems to be supporting the other bloke."

"Rear gunner, Skip."

"Yes, Jimmy?"

"Skip, I can see a small vessel about three miles out to the west."

Mason glanced at Jock and myself. "Any chance of telling whether it is ours or Jerry?"

"Sorry, Skip. I can't see it that well. One thing's for sure, it's military. No civvy vessel can move that fast."

Mason rubbed a gloved hand over his eyes as he thought for a moment. "Right! All of you that can, keep an eye on the dinghy - we've to take a look at that bloody ship. It could be an E-Boat."

He banked hard left and pushed the throttles hard forward until the Merlins were screaming their protest at such treatment. He rolled out of the turn and hauled the nose up hard. I felt my legs buckle as the floor rose to meet me but I soon stabilised and peered hard to try and locate the boat.

"Bomb aimer, Skip. You can go down again. It is one of our ASR launches."

"You sure, Phil?" demanded Mason.

"Yeah, Skip. I can definitely see the roundel on the foredeck."

Mason responded by chopping the throttles and dropping the nose into a fairly steep descent. This time, for just a second or two, I found my feet leaving the floor and I grabbed quickly to stop myself heading up to the Perspex roof of the cockpit.

Jock spotted my sudden movement out of his eye corner. When he saw the cause, he grinned and winked in reassurance.

Mason keyed his mike. "Tommy! Get up here with the Aldis lamp so that we can signal the dinghy's position to the launch."

I had the feeling that the wireless operator was a mind reader because the words were no sooner out of Mason's mouth, than I found myself having to squeeze back to let Tommy through to the cockpit. We were now down to about five hundred feet again and Mason put us into a tight orbit over the launch, increasing the power again as he did so. He nodded to Jock to take over the throttles and he concentrated on the turn. Tommy was already flashing the day's code to the launch with the Aldis. He consulted a piece of paper in his hand on which Ted had written the position of the dinghy. He lowered the Aldis and waited. A light began flashing rapidly from the launch and I watched as Tommy's lips moved slightly as he read the message. His face suddenly lit up with a huge grin and he punched Mason on the shoulder.

"Fuckin' great, Skip!" he yelled. "They've picked up the other crew all in one piece."

There were shouts of approval from the gunners down the back end.

"Okay, cut it out," ordered Mason but he was grinning from ear to ear. "I hope some of you guys still have a bead on that dinghy."

We didn't need to worry about that as the survivors were firing off flares like it was Guy Fawkes night and the launch had altered course to intercept the dinghy.

"Rear gunner, Skip! Two twin-engine aircraft at five o'clock, same height, three miles, closing fast."

It was as if somebody had thrown a bucket of iced water over us all in the cockpit. When Mason responded, we could hear the tension in his voice. We were a long way from home and very vulnerable. So were the launch and the survivors.

"Can you identify them, Jimmy?"

"Mid upper, Skip. I can see them now and they're Mosquitoes."

"Rear gunner, Skip. Bill's right – they're Mosquitoes."

"Thank God for that." Mason's breathing was heavy over the intercom. "I'll fly a course straight for the dinghy and hope the launch soon gets here."

"Mid upper, Skip. Two Mosquitoes coming up on our port side."

Mason glanced over his left shoulder. "Okay, I've got them."

The two Mosquitoes slid into view, the nearest about fifty feet from our port wingtip. We were slowly descending towards the dinghy and Mason was pointing down and forwards to indicate what we were up to. The Mosquitoes sheared away in a graceful curve to see what Mason was pointing at down below. We flashed over the dinghy at about fifty feet and Mason began a gentle climb back to altitude.

A Mosquito once more joined off our wingtip and the pilot and navigator were both giving 'thumbs up' signs. Mason made a sign with his hand by his mouth as if drinking a cup of tea. He then raised his left wrist and tapped his watch to indicate we had to be getting back to base. Another wave from the Mosquito navigator before the aircraft whipped into a tight left turn and disappeared from our sight.

"Skip to rear gunner. What are they doing now, Jimmy?"

"One's orbiting the dinghy, Skip. The other kite is flying a direct line between launch and dinghy. No problems, they're as good as home."

"Thank God for that," replied Mason. Suddenly, he was the professional again. "Navigator! The course for home, please. Engineer! Fuel state?"

We were back in business again and the flight back to West Fen was very much an anti-climax. There was still a little snow on the ground, particularly in the shady areas, but the sun was shining and we were feeling rather pleased with ourselves.

"Hello, Redstart. Casino D-Dog. Landing instructions, please." Mason glanced around the sky in the never-ending search for conflicting traffic.

"Redstart to Casino D-Dog. Join at two thousand feet upwind. The circuit is clear. Runway two-seven. QFE 1008. Wind 230 at 5 knots. Call when downwind."

"Redstart. D-Dog Wilco." Mason wriggled himself more firmly into his seat. "Engineer. Flaps 20 degrees."

"Flaps 20, Skip."

Mason scanned the instruments and eased on a little more power to bring our speed to 160. He pressed the RT switch. "Hello Redstart. D-Dog downwind."

"Redstart to D-Dog. You're cleared to land."

"Undercarriage down."

"Undercarriage down and locked, Skip."

The engines now sounded strained as if protesting at having to drag the flaps and huge wheels out into the cold air. The airframe shuddered slightly with the disturbed airflow around the wheels and flaps. Mason brought us round on to finals, slid us down the funnel as if on rails and dropped us on to the runway with the faintest of audible protest from the huge tyres. We moved slowly off the runway and started the long taxi to our dispersal.

"D-Dog. Landed and clear."

"Roger, D-Dog."

As we finally approached the dispersal, Jock closed down the two outer engines. We were marshalled into place and, at last, silence reigned as the last two engines clanked into silence. It seemed like heaven. Silence - after five hours aloft in close company with those four huge Merlin engines.

I pulled off my flying helmet and ran a hand through my hair. Mason and Jock were going through the ritual of shutting down. My ears were still ringing from the noise and my mouth tasted like a gorilla's jockstrap. The cockpit suddenly seemed crowded and I headed for the main spar to collect my parachute. This time I managed not to bang my head on every bit of projecting metal and hopped down the ladder to the ground. My legs nearly buckled under me and only then did I realise I'd been on my feet for the whole trip. My bladder was also giving me urgent messages that it was full. The two gunners were already relieving themselves off to the side of the pan and I staggered over to join them. I shivered violently as I peed. The wind was straight off the North Sea and I realised how much I'd sweated during the flight. That sweat was now cooling rapidly and my teeth began to chatter as I walked over to join the others standing by the rear door.

Jimmy grinned. "Feeling a bit chilly, Telly? Now you know how we gunners feel most of the time."

Tommy Burns laughed. "Stop trying for the sympathy vote, Tait."

"Well, it's all right for you lot up front," complained Jimmy. "Especially our esteemed wireless operator, he gets all the bloody heat. I reckon we should put him down the back and the guns up front. What do you say, Skip?"

Mason grinned. "Sorry, Jimmy. I've an aversion to things that go 'bang'. I'm afraid you'll have to stay down the back."

Bill Bedford put an arm round his colleague. "It's no good, Jim, we'll have to become Henrys. Only officers get the perks in this job."

Jimmy shook his head mournfully. "It's no good, mate, I'll never make the grade. Every time I try to keep me little finger raised when drinking me tea, me finger goes up me nose."

We laughed and they all produced cigarettes and lit up. The smell of smoke was really sweet on the cold air and I thought that maybe I ought to take up smoking. I turned and looked at D-Dog. She was still ticking away as the engines cooled and already the ground crew were beginning to pull on turret covers and attend to her other needs.

When I'd first seen her bulk in the gloom that morning, she'd seemed ugly. Now, in my eyes, she was a thing of great beauty. She'd just brought eight men home safe and sound and played her part in the rescue of others. She'd probably taken hundreds of lives in her role as a harbinger of death but today she had saved lives. Suddenly, I felt an empathy with D-Dog. The feeling was palpable and I felt uncomfortable at the realisation that I, sensible old Carver, actually had feelings for a huge mass of metal and rivets.

I jerked back to reality as a hand touched my shoulder and I realised with surprise that, whilst I had been away in dreamland, I'd walked away from the others and right up to D-Dog. I was actually standing so close I was having to crane my neck to look at her.

"Gets to you, doesn't it?" Mason was watching me with a small smile.

I looked at him and then back up at D-Dog. "It's as if I am now part of her," I replied slowly.

"Does that surprise you?" he asked quietly

"If I told anybody about it other than you, they'd think I was nuts." I looked at him quickly to check his expression. "You probably think that too."

The small smile was still on his face. He glanced up at the aircraft and then across the barren wastes of the airfield. Although, with the sun shining, even that was beginning to look more hospitable.

"It's like a drug, Carver. I watched you up there today and you were loving every minute of it. I'm pleased - it bodes well for your operation with us." He turned back to me and the smile had gone. "That will be a different kettle of fish. Today you heard me call the crew by their first names and there was a lot of chatter on the intercom. On an operational sortie, I insist on nothing but the highest standards of airmanship and professionalism. I'll boil in oil anybody who leaves his mike switched on or yells incoherently over the intercom."

I nodded. "I promise to remember that, sir."

The rest of the crew sensed our private little discussion was over and they joined us.

"Where's the bloody transport?" complained Bill. "I'm freezing."

Ted Lowry put out his hand to me. "Well done, Telly. You did a bloody good job up there today."

There was a chorus of approval from the others and I felt more than a little embarrassed at being the centre of their attention. I was just a 'foreigner' to this crew.

"Yeah, well done, Telly." Jimmy patted me on the back.

"How come you're a ground wallah?" asked Bill.

"I failed the aircrew medical."

"What was the problem?" asked Mason.

"My eyesight!" I answered sheepishly.

They all burst into incredulous laughter.

Jock walked over and put his arm around my shoulders. "Well, I'll tell you one thing, Telly, there are seven men alive today who would disagree with that bloody medical board. How the hell you spotted that dinghy I'll never know. It took me ages to locate it even though you'd told me where to look. When I did find it I kept losing it. I reckon you must have eyes like a hawk and it will be a comfort to have you on board when we take you on the op. An extra pair of eyes is always welcome."

The others all voiced their approval and I felt quietly pleased. I might not ever be one of these men but at least my association with them was satisfying.

My thoughts were interrupted by the sound of grinding gears and an asthmatic internal combustion engine. The truck which ground onto the dispersal must have been the oldest vehicle in RAF service.

"Mr Carver, sir!" boomed a familiar voice as the driver's door was flung open. "Nice to have you back, sir."

"Oh, no!" I groaned. D-Dog's crew were already convulsed with silent laughter.

Foghorn was determined to lay it on thick. She walked to the back of the truck, lowered the tailboard and watched my approach with an evil glint in her eye.

"Feeling fine, sir? No honky-poos?"

"Fine thank you, Bourne. Lovely flight actually."

"Oh, jolly good show, sir." She used my own accent.

I reached the truck and was about to attempt the difficult scramble to get aboard when Foghorn suddenly half crouched and cupped her hands between her thighs. I didn't even stop to think. I just put my right foot in her hands and she catapulted me up into the truck as if I was a feather. It was so swift and deft that I was in the truck before I realised what she'd done. I gave her a startled look of surprise but only received a sly wink in return.

"Come along, gentlemen," she cooed. "All aboard The Skylark."

The others had to make their own way aboard, which was not an easy task when encumbered by heavy flying kit. No stirrup for them!

Jimmy, who was last to board, gave a startled howl and fell face down on the floor of the truck. There was a roar of mirth from Foghorn as she slammed the tailboard back into place.

"What the hell's wrong with you?" asked Mason as he grabbed for one of the hoops that held up the canvas tilt.

"She grabbed my nuts!" complained Jimmy.

"Lucky old you," laughed Mason.

"Did she give them back?" I asked.

116

Jimmy felt gingerly between his legs and raised his eyes to the tilt as if concentrating on the matter in hand. "One, two...yeah! They're all here."

"Then it's a case of 'lucky old you," I replied. "If you'd really upset her, they'd be pinned up in the cab as a trophy."

Mine was not the only suggestion as to what Foghorn would do with a full set of gonads but we arrived intact for the debrief.

I did the debrief with Hammond, who was duty intelligence officer, and it was the easiest yet. I'd seen it all for myself. All I needed to do was verify the relevant position fixes with Ted and we were finished. As I drank tea and joked with Mason and his lads, I felt a coldness from Hammond. He soon made an excuse and disappeared. Finally we too went our separate ways. The crew to change for lunch and me to file the debrief report.

When I got into the main office, the only occupants were Hammond and AC Christian. They were sitting in the easy chairs and stopped talking when I walked in.

"How come you were unlucky enough to get duty officer?" I asked Steve Hammond pleasantly, just to break the silence.

"Well, some of us have to work for a living," he replied sarcastically. "Not all of us can be 'Boys Own' heroes and swan about all over the bloody place at the beck and call of the station commander. You're not dropping your trousers for him by any chance, are you?"

I calmly signed the report and filed it. I screwed the top back on my pen as I walked towards them. I stood and looked down at Christian. His head was down in an attempt to hide the supercilious smirk on his face.

"Find yourself something to do outside, Christian," I said quietly.

He stayed where he was and looked at Hammond for support but Hammond was a coward and avoided his eye.

"Don't look at him, Christian," I ordered quietly. "I'm speaking to you and you'll do as you're bloody well told. Get out and get out now!"

The airman rose and looked at me with open contempt. There was a slight curl to his lip but he couldn't hold my gaze and he left the room.

I leant over Hammond and put my face right up to his. "You speak to me like that again in front of subordinates, you useless bastard, and you'll have a chance to make that observation to the station commander personally." I stepped back, raised my right foot and rammed it into his groin as he sat in the chair. He gave a sharp yelp of pain and his face turned ashen.

"I've the unfortunate luck to share a room with you, Hammond. You keep the place like a bloody pigsty and I'm fed up with your drunken racket nearly every bloody night." I pressed my foot harder into his nether regions and a sweat began to break out on his forehead. "When you get back to the mess, you'll ask Batey to find you another room. I care not what fucking excuse you use because I accept you'll have to save face. Just do it! Do I make myself clear?"

He wrenched my foot away and leapt to his feet. All his bravado had gone and he was on the verge of tears. Tears of anger and humiliation. He pushed me violently out of the way and stormed out of the room. The door slammed behind him. Now for the other bastard.

I found Christian washing his hands in the airmens' toilet block outside. This time I wasted no time on speeches or warnings. I just grabbed him by the front of his uniform jacket, wrenched him round to face me and punched him hard in the stomach. He hit the floor retching and croaking for breath. I'd just committed a serious offence but I knew he wasn't going to tell anybody. There were no witnesses and he knew my lies would be believed no matter what the truth. Hammond was right to a certain extent. I was the blue-eyed boy, and bugger me if I was not going to use that advantageous position to sort a few people out.

I crouched down beside Christian as he struggled upright. "You now know me better than anybody else in this section, Christian. You can be under no illusion as to what I stand for and what I expect. This is the second time you and I've crossed swords. Get it into your thick, arrogant skull that I'll always win because I'm the nasty bastard. If you wanted to be superior and take on people like myself, you should have gone for that King's commission when it was offered to you. As a little airman, you're on a loser from the start. I can't stand the sight of you and you'll be my target from this moment on. Just pick your snotty little nose and I'll be there, right behind you, holding a charge sheet for infringement of good service hygiene." I stood up and walked to the door. "Now, get up, clean up and get back to work."

I left him to sort himself out. I glanced up and down the corridor when I re-entered the section but there was nobody to be seen. I was very relieved because what I'd just done was professional suicide.

I was surprised to see Houseman waiting in the main office. "Hi!" he called. "How did it go?"

I couldn't help grinning. "Fantastic, sir. We got both dinghies. Well, we found one and the ASR lads had already picked up the other."

"So I gather. Sammy Mason called me over at the mess a few minutes ago. I thought I'd come and get the story first hand. I hear you got on well with him and his crew."

I nodded. "They were great, sir. Squadron Leader Mason made it clear I wasn't there for a 'jolly' and I enjoyed every minute."

The door opened and Hammond walked in.

Houseman glanced round. "There you are, Hammond. I was wondering where you'd got to."

"Had to nip over to the tower, sir," Hammond answered without stopping as he headed for the watchkeepers' office.

Houseman asked quickly, "Why are you limping?"

Hammond didn't even turn round. "Fell off my bike, sir."

The door closed behind him. Houseman had a puzzled expression on his face. "Strange lad. Somehow I don't think his heart is in it." He turned and looked at me for a moment. "I think he feels a bit put out at all the attention you're getting. If he causes any trouble, just let me know."

I had to look away from his gaze. "I'm sure he'll be no problem, sir."

Houseman stood as if waiting for more and I was sure he sensed something had passed between Hammond and myself. He took a quick breath. "Fancy a late lunch? I booked a couple with the mess chef. You know what he's like about late meals."

"Good idea, sir. I'm ravenous."

He laughed. "Flying does that to you."

We'd walked some way towards the mess when Houseman said, "Anything you want to tell me, Carver?"

He took me by surprise and, before I could stop myself, I shot him a startled look. "Like what, sir?" I asked quickly.

He looked a little nonplussed at my reaction. "Like who spotted the dinghy."

Relief coursed through me. "Oh that! We all saw it, sir."

"Eventually you all saw the damned thing," he protested. "Sammy Mason said they'd have missed it if it had not been for you."

"Pure luck, sir," I stuttered in embarrassment.

"Bollocks!" replied Houseman heartily. "Sammy phoned me to tell me how well you'd carried out your role in the sea search. He'll also be having a word with Wing Commander Janner - that should go down well! He told me he'll be very happy to have you on board for the next op. From Sammy, that is great praise indeed."

I sighed. "Well, one thing is for sure. If I've to fly operationally, there's not a man I'd rather fly with, sir."

"I couldn't agree more," Houseman concurred. "By the way, he was also full of praise for the way you handle a certain heavyweight WAAF driver." I could hear the suppressed humour in his voice.

"Oh, no!" I complained. "Not Foghorn Fanny again. I can't get away from the bloody woman. She always succeeds in making me look a complete twat."

Houseman laughed. "Don't think you've the twat club exclusively to yourself. She's succeeded in bringing greater men than you to their knees. At least she does what you tell her!"

"Only when it bloody well pleases her."

"Maybe she fancies you"

"You can't be serious." I was horrified at the thought.

"Well, you never know with women. I must say though, she was great on the trip in the Anson. I thought you'd gone cuckoo when you suggested taking her. She could've ruined the whole trip."

I kicked idly at a pebble as we walked. "I think there is more to Bourne than she's given credit for. She's ridiculed by all and sundry because of her looks and her size. Can you blame her for fighting back?"

"I do believe you feel sorry for her," admonished Houseman in surprise.

"I suppose I do, sir. Then she makes me look like a complete twerp again and I could kill her."

"You're a strange young man, Carver. You can be a bastard when you want to be and yet you feel sorry for lame ducks. Don't ever let your heart get in the way of professionalism." He started to trot the last few yards to the mess. "Come on, I'm starving. You've got all night to dream of Basher Bourne."

I trotted after him. "Am I allowed to say 'bollocks' to a squadron leader, sir?"

"Only when I'm more interested in food than discipline," he called over his shoulder.

"As food seems to be your priority at the moment - bollocks, sir."

"Same to you, Carver. Do get a move on, man!"

We dumped our coats and I followed him to the dining room. It had been a bloody good day.

CHAPTER TEN

The next morning, when I arrived in the section, Houseman beckoned me to follow him to his office. He closed the door and waved me into a chair. "Can you get on with the task of finding your man with the taste for German headgear?" he asked.

I nodded. "That's what I intended to do this morning, sir. One thing though, I don't think it would be good policy for me to turn up in uniform."

"Good point," Houseman agreed. "Foghorn and yourself, in full regalia and driving an RAF Hillman Tilly, would certainly rouse more than a little interest. That also means you'll need a civilian car. Max is the only chap on the section with his own car and he's always prepared to loan it when he's not using it. But, having said that, I'd hate to compromise him when he's not yet fully part of the investigation. The wrong people may start taking notice of his car and he'd be totally unprepared for any form of threat that may come his way."

He thought for a few moments and then picked up the telephone. "Put me through to the station commander's PA, please." He put his hand over the mouthpiece. "There are seven cars parked over by the ASF hangar which will soon be coming up for disposal at the station auction."

I didn't immediately grasp the significance of his remark and I made a questioning movement with my head.

Houseman's face clouded and the tired look came back into his eyes. "All the owners of the cars have got the chop - dead, missing or POWs. We auction the cars and send the proceeds to the ex-owner's next-of-kin." He removed his hand from the mouthpiece and held it up to warn me to keep quiet. "Oh, good morning. This is Squadron Leader Houseman from Intelligence. May I speak with the station commander, please?" He paused for a few seconds. "Thank you."

He turned and gazed out of the window, his fingers tapping on his desk as he waited for Groupie. Suddenly he swivelled back round to his desk. "Good morning, sir. Sorry to bother you but Carver is making progress with our little affair but we've encountered a snag."

He stopped and listened for a few seconds and then raised his eyebrows questioningly at me. "Now, sir?" he said into the telephone. Another pause, then "We're on our way."

He rang off and moved around his desk. "Come on, he wants to see us, right away."

We dashed over to SHQ and were shown into the station commander's office by his PA.

"Come in, Houseman. Morning, Carver." Groupie rose from his desk as we entered and saluted. "Dump your caps and find yourselves a seat."

He waited until we were settled then came round his desk to offer us a cigarette. We both declined but he lit up and blew the smoke towards the ceiling. "Right," he said. "What's the story so far and what is the snag?"

Houseman turned to me. "I'll let Carver tell it, sir. He's the one doing all the work."

Groupie sat back in his chair and eyed me expectantly.

I was really not prepared for an impromptu briefing but quickly put my thoughts together.

"The first part of the programme has gone cold, sir. As you know, I flew a recce with Squadron Leader Houseman but so far the photos have told us nothing. Although, to be fair, the photographic interpreter has been so busy, he's yet to make our shots a priority."

Groupie interrupted. "Who is the PI - Shearing?"

I nodded. "Yes, sir."

He made a note on the pad on his desk and then nodded for me to continue.

"Well, sir, a bit of luck came my way in a local pub. A chap staggered in, very much the worse for drink, wearing a German parachutist's helmet."

I paused as Groupie's eyebrows shot up in astonishment but rushed quickly on before he could say anything. "There could be a perfectly innocent explanation. Still, the squadron leader and myself feel I ought to check the chap out as soon as possible. So, this morning, I hope to find out where he lives and how he came by the helmet. One thing was for sure, the man himself had no clue as to the import of what he was wearing on his head."

"And that's where we came up against the snag, sir," Houseman interjected.

"Which is?" asked Groupie.

"Transport, sir," replied Houseman. "We don't think it a good idea for Carver and his driver to turn up in both uniform and service car and start asking questions. Shearing is the only chap on our section with a car but I don't feel I can ask to use his car and fuel for a purpose which, for security reasons, I cannot reveal to him."

Groupie studied us for a few moments and then, once more, scribbled on his pad as he spoke. "I can see where your train of thought is leading you - the cars over at ASF. Am I correct?"

"Yes, sir," Houseman nodded.

"Mmmm...." Groupie pondered the problem. "The thing is, we're having the auction this week and it's only fair that the next-of-kin get their money as soon as possible." He paused and scratched his head. "There again, I believe I can raise enough from sources available to me to buy one of the cars for your use. We can always re-auction the car when you've finished with it."

He stood up. "Leave it with me. I suggest you get over to the hangar, choose a suitable vehicle and get it registered at the guardroom in Carver's name." He suddenly slapped a hand to his forehead. "Oh, bloody hell!"

We looked at him in amazement. He turned back to his desk. "You'll need petrol but you'd never get enough privately. The only way around the problem is to make it an official car so that you can draw fuel from the station MT supply. That would raise a few eyebrows and if the RAF police caught you with service fuel in a civilian car, you'd be in the guardroom before you could blink."

He rammed his hands hard down into his trouser pockets. "Damn it! It is too early to take this to Command and get their help." He paced the room as he pondered the problem. We waited for an age before he suddenly seemed to make up his mind.

"Carver, I can get you the petrol but you cannot be seen fuelling a civilian car in the MT section."

"What would the fuel be supplied in, sir?" I asked.

"Jerrycans would be the most suitable, surely?"

"Okay, sir. I think I know a way round the refuelling problem. Whenever

Foghorn and myself take the Tilly out ..."

"Who the hell is Foghorn?" Groupie exploded in surprise.

I cursed myself for the slip but had to answer. "I'm afraid it is the nickname I've given my driver, sir - Aircraftswoman Bourne."

I swear his face turned white. "My God!" he took a deep breath to steady himself. "That bloody woman is not involved in this, surely? Please tell me she's not involved." I couldn't believe it. Here was a man with medals all over his chest and he was scared shitless of Foghorn Fanny. What kind of monster lurked under her lumpy frame and oil-stained uniform that could reduce a man like this to pleading for reassurance?

Houseman leapt quickly in to answer for me. "She's well and truly in, sir. She flew with us on the recce and did a damned good job. She also knows the locals and the local area. In spite of her reputation, she's been a real asset." He glanced at me and a twinkle came into his eye as he spoke. "Not only that, sir, she fancies young Carver here."

Groupie dropped into his chair as if drained of all energy. "Oh God, Carver, I'm so sorry to hear that." For a moment he kept a perfectly straight face but then exploded into hoots of mirth. It was infectious and soon the three of us were helpless with laughter. We finally subsided into occasional snorts and Groupie wiped his eyes with a handkerchief. He suppressed another snort of laughter. "How on earth did you get landed with her?"

There was a long silence as I found myself totally unable to confess my stupidity.

Houseman answered for me. "He asked for her personally, sir."

Groupie studied me for a while. "You know, Carver," he said finally, "you've just posed a real problem for Jake here. On your annual assessment record he'll have to decide whether to rate you as 'extremely brave' or 'a raving bloody lunatic'." He started to shake with laughter again but fought it like a man and finally got a grip of himself. "I'm sorry, Carver. Please finish what you were trying to say."

"Well, sir, Bourne and I can take the jerrycans out to Stan Cornish's farm in the Tilly. When I need fuel for the car, I can just drive it into the barn and fill up without anybody being any the wiser."

"Cornish?" Groupie screwed up his face in thought. "Is that the chap who told you about the mystery fighter?"

"That's the man, sir."

"What's to stop him using our petrol in his tractors or whatever?"

"He only has an old Fordson tractor and he starts that on petrol but, once its warm, it runs on paraffin. Another thing, sir, I'd trust him with my last penny. He may be cantankerous but he's an honourable man."

Groupie stood up from his desk. "You're doing a good job, Carver. Go with Jake and sort out a vehicle. In the meantime, I'll draft an official letter for you to carry at all times. It will help you in the event of being stopped by a police fuel check."

"Thank you, sir."

We stood, donned our caps and saluted.

As we headed for the door, Groupie called out to me. "Oh, Carver."

I turned. "Yes, sir?"

"You're turning into a good intelligence officer but, by heck, you've got a terrible taste in women!" His laughter followed us down the corridor as we headed off to choose my mode of transport.

The seven cars were parked on the grass by the blast bank at the side of the ASF hangar. Two were quite clean and recently polished but the others had already been old before they had found a new life with aircrew bods at West Fen. They were, shall we say, past their best! Five were saloons, well, if you can call an Austin Ruby a saloon, but the other two were cabriolets. One was a beautiful green Jaguar with the biggest chrome headlamps I'd ever seen. The other was modest to the point of being totally overshadowed by the Jaguar. It was small, maroon and had definitely been at the back of the queue when headlights were handed out. Whereas the Jag's were enormous, this car had two little black bumps each side of the radiator grill. I moved back to the Jag and stroked its chrome grill.

"Forget it, Carver," Houseman grinned. "Your cover must be subtle and unremarkable. This is more the thing for you." He grasped the door handle of the little maroon cabriolet.

"What the hell is it?" I asked as I gave the Jag a last reluctant pat.

"Damned if I know." Houseman walked round to peer at the radiator grille. "Ah, a Fiat no less."

"Oh, not a bloody Eyetie, sir," I protested.

"I'm afraid so, old boy. A Fiat Topolino."

"Sounds like a bloody ice cream," I grunted.

He laughed as he reached into the car and brought out an owner's manual. He leafed quickly through the pages. "Well, one thing's for sure, you won't be breaking any speed records or slurping up too much service fuel."

"How come?" I asked.

He gave me a malicious grin. "Because, young Carver, it only has a five hundred cubic capacity engine."

"Bloody hell!" I exclaimed. "Does it come with pedals?"

"No. Just a hole in the floor to put your feet through."

I opened the driver's door and eased myself into the black leather upholstery. Actually, it was quite comfortable and I liked the canvas hood - it opened all the way back to the boot. Boot? Did I say boot? Did it even have a boot? I climbed back out and surveyed the little car. It was tiny but the deep colour gave it an appearance of strength. I could just visualise the coming summer months - tootling along country lanes, the sun warm on my head, the breeze rippling through my hair and Natalie by my side. Keep your mind on the job, Carver. Then my delight at having a car quickly faded as I thought of the man who had been its owner.

Houseman sensed my change of mood. "Don't worry, Sam. I know the guy who owns this. He's a prisoner of war and should safely see the rest of the war out."

"Are you just saying that to cheer me up, sir?"

He shook his head. "No, I'm telling you the truth. Take a tip, Sam, don't let aircrew attrition get to you. We know the risks. Don't feel sorry for us or you'll never survive the war."

I nodded. "You're quite right, of course. Sorry, it just gets to me at times."

We both turned as a Hillman Tilly pulled up at the end of the hangar and an RAF police corporal came towards us. He saluted. "Squadron Leader Houseman, sir?"

"Yes, corporal." Houseman returned the salute.

"Station commander asked us to bring you the keys to the cars awaiting auction. I understand you're going to choose one?"

Houseman nodded. "That's right. Do you have keys there for this little Fiat?"

" 'Alf a mo, sir." The corporal shuffled through the bunches of keys he'd brought with him and finally selected one set. "Here we are, sir. Well, the label matches the registration. Try these."

Houseman took the keys and climbed into the driver's seat. He pulled out the choke and pumped the accelerator. A few hesitant turns of the starter and the engine burst into life - albeit a bit of a smoky birth.

"Thanks, corp," I said and returned his salute as he left to return to the guardroom.

"How's that wrist of yours?" shouted Houseman from the interior of the car.

"Still bloody painful but it's getting better."

"What a pity," he laughed. "That means I'll have to drive."

I grimaced my disappointment and climbed in beside him. He gunned the motor and we were off. The car sounded healthy and, by the time we reached the section, the exhaust smoke had dwindled to a blue haze. We squeaked to a halt as the brakes telegraphed their recent lack of use and Houseman switched off the engine. "Well, I can't drive you this morning and, as you'll need to look a couple, I feel Bourne will be totally unsuitable." He was careful not to look at me. "I think I'd better detail Natalie to accompany you."

I gave him a quick look to see if he was smiling but he was impassive. "I think that is a very good idea, sir."

Now he grinned. "I thought you'd say that."

We climbed out and walked through to his office.

"May I make a call to Stan Cornish from here, sir?"

He nodded. "Ask the watchkeeper on duty to get the number for you. Do you know the number?"

"Yes, sir. Foghorn gave it to me."

"Quite a mine of information, your Foghorn."

"I think 'mine' is the operative word, sir. Likely to detonate at any moment."

Houseman guffawed and headed for the door. "Make your call and I'll get us both a mug of tea."

I picked up the telephone and asked Trudi Collins to get me Cornish's number. As I waited I heard Janner's door open and his footsteps approach Houseman's office. There was a perfunctory knock and Janner walked straight in. I was sitting on the corner of the desk and, although I attempted to stand as he entered the room, the telephone cable was too short. I ended up bent over the desk trying not to drag the telephone to the floor. Janner, of course, was not amused.

"Is this your office, Carver? It seems you've access to every other facility on the station."

This was one of those occasions when 'dripping sarcasm' fitted the bill. I actually could see no point in answering, as he knew perfectly well in whose office we were standing. We'd been through it all before. I also gave up my one-sided struggle with the telephone and sat back down on the desk. My action seemed to infuriate him. Out of the window went the dripping sarcasm and in flew rage to take its place.

"What the hell do you think you're doing?" he bawled.

It's funny how when one wishes to appear intelligent, one's brain and mouth fail to obey the rules.

"Making a telephone call, sir?" I could've chosen my words better and placated him with some bullshit or another but no, I chose the very words to incense him to the point of apoplexy.

"Put that telephone down when I am speaking to you!" His mouth quivered over a mass of chins and he began to move towards me.

At that moment I heard Trudi. "You're through, sir."

I heard Cornish shout. "Hello?"

"Hang on, Stan," I shouted back and turned back to Janner to try to reason with him.

"You insolent bastard," he bawled and tried to knock the telephone from my hand. I managed to avoid his clumsy rush and was highly relieved to see Houseman appear in the doorway with two mugs of tea.

"Can I help you, sir?" he shouted at Janner's back.

Janner whipped round in surprise and cannoned straight into Houseman, sending the mugs flying. Tea splashed over them both and dripped down the wall. There was a loud crash as one of the mugs shattered on the floor. Houseman's face turned white and whilst Janner stood like a gaping fish, trying to gargle an excuse, Houseman grabbed him by the tie and yanked him out into the corridor.

"Carver," Houseman said quietly although he was breathing heavily with anger. "Make your call."

He slammed the door shut and there was another crash as the other mug was splintered between the door and the jamb.

"Hello!" The cry came from the phone. Stan was getting angry.

"Stan?" I gasped as I leant on my sprained wrist.

"Aye."

"It's Sam Carver."

"Oh, aye."

"Do you know a family called Troutbridge?"

"Aye."

I lost my temper. "Don't start that crap again, Stan. For fuck's sake, talk to me."

I heard him chuckle. "By heck, lad. Things don't sound too good over there - all that banging and shouting."

"Never mind about that." I spoke in a more moderate tone. "Stan, please help me. Where do the Troutbridge family live?"

"I suppose if I asked you why you wanted to know, you wouldn't tell me."

"Correct," I answered but then I felt the little guy had a right to an answer of some kind.

"Look, Stan, I'll tell you more when it's all over but for now it's yet another secret between just you and me. Can you accept that?"

"Aye, alright. I appreciate your confidence in me and I won't let you down. They live in a little cottage set back in the woods out near Tumby. The woods are on each side of the Mareham-le-Fen to Coningsby road. You want the wood on the left-hand side of the road. There's old Tommy, the father, his wife May and six lads. God knows how they've all managed in that small cottage but they're a nice couple and a very close-knit family. The lads get in the local pubs and are really well behaved although the youngest, Norman, has been kicking over the traces recently. I think he wants to join the army but his dad is keeping him in a reserved occupation. I don't know for sure but I reckon the old man could be a conscientious objector. He lost a brother in the Great War."

What would I do without this little man? "Stan, you're a real trouper."

His laughter echoed down the phone. "I'll take your word for it. Anyway, you can't miss the cottage; it's the only one on the left after you pass between the two woods. Can I get back to work now?"

"Of course and thanks again, Stan. That's another pint I owe you."

"Oh, don't you worry, I'm writing them all down on a slate in the barn. Cheers, lad."

I put the phone down and glanced at my watch; it was ten-thirty. Where was the bloody morning going? I paused and listened but there was no noise from the corridor or from Janner's office. I opened the door and peered down the corridor, only to see Sergeant Powell peering back at me from around the door at the top. We continued to stare at each other for some time, both desperately thinking of something to say.

I broke the silence. "Are we going to spend the rest of the day playing peek-a-bloody-boo, Sarge?"

He grinned sheepishly, opened the door fully and came down the corridor. "Sorry, sir. I heard a bit of a commotion and then the squadron leader and the wing commander rushed straight out of the section without a word. I just wondered what was going on."

"I think," I answered carefully, "there's been a slight disagreement of policy."

"I am surprised," replied Powell with a straight face.

I grinned. "If I didn't know you better, Sergeant Powell, I'd say that was a cynical remark."

He laughed. "Heaven forbid, sir."

I changed the subject. "Do we know tomorrow night's target yet?"

"Not yet, sir, but the wing commander is going to give the main briefing. It seems a couple of staff officers and the senior intelligence officer are coming down from Command to see how we do things at West Fen."

"Should be interesting."

"Now who's the cynic?" asked Powell. "Oh, don't you worry, sir, the wing commander will make sure he's word perfect, or at least make sure that you all make sure he's word perfect. If that makes sense"

"I bet he doesn't ask 'Any Questions?' at the end and yes, Sergeant Powell, that was a cynical remark."

"People like the wing commander are experts at covering their arses, sir."

"Makes a change from talking out of them," I replied sourly.

Powell laughed. "Not having a good day, sir?"

"Bloody awful, Sarge, and I've a feeling it is going to get worse." I glanced again at my watch. "Is Section Officer Cowen in?"

"Yes, sir. Last I saw of her, she was in the Intelligence Library setting up some new Escape and Evasion exhibits."

"Would you ask her to come to Squadron Leader Houseman's office?"

"Of course, sir." He headed off to find her.

I walked back into the office and looked out of the window. If Houseman and Janner had left the section, where the hell had they gone? I'd been staggered to see Houseman grab the fat bastard and yank him out into the corridor. I just hoped Janner was not now bleating about being physically attacked by a subordinate. Somehow, I couldn't see Janner losing face to that extent. He was a useless bastard but a crafty one. He'd bide his time but he had no friends on West Fen so he'd have to have a pretty watertight case to get his own back on somebody as well liked as Houseman.

"Penny for your thoughts."

I spun round at that familiar voice. Natalie stood in the doorway.

"No click of high heels to warn me?" I smiled at her.

"WAAF shoes are not made for 'clicking', more like 'shuffling'."

"Come and sit down, Nat." I held a chair for her.

"Got your own office now?"

"Oh, don't you start."

"Janner got there first?"

"Naturally."

"Have you heard he's taking the briefing tomorrow?" she asked in disbelief.

I nodded. "Tom Powell told me."

"Should be interesting."

"Could be he'll make a cock up of it and we'll be able to get rid of him," I suggested hopefully.

"Fat chance," Natalie sighed. "Nobody will have him."

I glanced yet again at my watch. Time was hurtling by this morning and I was getting worried.

"Nat, can you be spared for a couple of hours?"

"Yes, I think so. Why?"

"Houseman wants you to drive me out to find that lad I saw wearing the German helmet."

"What's happened to Foghorn?"

"Nothing, but we need to be in civvies and we need to look like a couple."

"A couple of what?" she asked without a glimmer of a smile.

"Bloody hell! Everybody is a comedian this morning," I said in exasperation.

"Whoops! Sorry."

I took her hands and pulled her to her feet. "Sorry. Even Groupie got in on the act this morning. Houseman told him Foghorn fancies me. I swear we could still hear him laughing when we were over at ASF."

"I can see I'm going to have to keep an eye on old Foghorn. If she fancies you I hate to think of what she'd do to a rival!"

I sighed. "Can we get off the subject of bloody Foghorn and get back to the job in hand?"

"Yes, sir. Of course, sir." She stood to attention and waved a hand in a salute – the kind of salute that didn't become a young lady of her background. Her background? What did I know about her background? I was off at a tangent again. Get on track again, Carver.

"I want to arrive at this guy's house and give him the impression I'm a dealer in war artefacts or something. I need a lovely young lady as cover. As Foghorn was busy I've had to settle for you."

I ducked the friendly clout she aimed at my head but totally failed to anticipate the sharp rap of her foot on my anklebone.

"Ow! That hurt, Cowen."

"You shouldn't get clever, Carver. Now, please continue with the briefing on how we're going to enter this nest of German master spies."

"Don't joke. I've no idea where this is leading and I hope Houseman soon calls in the cavalry."

"You're really serious, aren't you."

I nodded. "Yes, I am serious. I've a feeling that we're beginning to pick the lock on Pandora's box and I don't want to be on my own when it springs open."

She sat on the corner of the desk as I continued.

"So, we find this lad's house and pretend we're interested in the old helmet because we collect such things. I reckon if we offer him enough for it, he'll part with it without any questions. What does a farm labourer earn?"

"Not a lot. The farmers give them a tied cottage and damned all else. You keep on the good side of the farmer or you're on your way without a roof over your head. Bit bloody feudal."

I thought for a second. "What if we offer him ten bob? Do you think that is about a week's wage for a labourer?"

"I've no idea," answered Natalie. "Is there nobody you can ask?"

I thought of Stan. "Yes, there is actually but I've already called him once this morning and he's a busy man. I don't want to spoil a friendship that has paid dividends in this investigation. No, we'll stick with ten bob. I'll get it back." I looked up at her to see a small smile was flickering around her mouth. I could feel my heart begin to beat faster. I tried to make light of the situation before it all went too far too soon.

"Why is it," I asked, "when I get near you I want to gather you up into my arms and whisk you off to the hills on a fiery white charger?"

She raised her hands to my shoulders. "Do you have a fiery white charger?"

I grinned ruefully. "Not exactly, but I do have a Topolino."

"What the heck is a Topolino?" she laughed.

"You'll see." I kissed her quickly on the end of her nose. "Come on, before I get carried away."

"I thought I was the one about to get carried away, even if it was on something that sounds like an ice cream." She gave me a mischievous grin and I couldn't help thinking that even our minds were in tune. Ice cream had been my reaction to the name Topolino. A good omen for the future? I hoped so.

I grabbed my hat. "Cowen, will you get a bloody move on, we haven't got all day." I grabbed her hand and hauled her out into the corridor, remembering to release her before we reached the watchkeepers' office. Just as we entered the main office, Houseman came in from outside.

"Ah, Carver. Have you explained the situation to Cowen?"

"I have, sir. Is it convenient for us to leave now?"

"Of course. Get this sorted as quickly as you can. Report to me when you get back." He strode away in the direction of his office.

Natalie gave me a questioning look. "Bit short and sweet, wasn't he? Anything wrong?"

"Problem with Janner."

"What's new?"

As we turned to leave, I noticed that in spite of there being a stand down, Hammond was actually working. I thought I'd better reinforce my previous threat but let him retain a little of his pride.

"I hear you're moving out into another room, Stephen."

He glared at me but he knew what I was doing and I think he actually appreciated it but his reply was not quite without sarcasm.

"Yes, I am. I hope you don't feel I'm moving because of you."

"Not at all," I replied brightly. "I'm hoping Max will be able to take your place as we seem to be working together a lot these days. See you later."

Natalie waited until we were outside. "What was all that crap?"

"A little matter of helping somebody save his reputation and you'll do yours no good by using words like that."

She was not to be put off. "Have you had a go at him?"

"I don't know what you're rabbiting on about."

She was about to continue the interrogation when she realised we'd stopped by the little Italian car. She looked it over carefully. "Is this your fiery steed?"

"It is. 'Fiery' being the operative word as we left quite a trail of smoke when we drove down here."

I handed her the keys and we climbed in. She ran her hand over the little leather seats and grasped the steering wheel.

"It's a little cracker."

"Let's hope it doesn't turn out to be a bloody damp squib."

"Don't be such a wet blanket, Carver. It's a great little car." She tapped the fuel gauge and the glass fell out into her lap. "Ah, I see it is not going to allay any doubts we may have about the reliability of an Italian car."

"Oh, shit! How much fuel does it say we've got in the tank?" I asked.

She peered closely at the gauge. "Bone dry, but I don't think this gauge has worked for some time."

I jumped out, dashed into the section and came back with an old wooden ruler. I removed the petrol cap and dipped the ruler in the tank. To my surprise it was three-quarters full. I threw the ruler over by the dustbin compound and jumped back into the car.

"Plenty of juice for the mileage we will do today. We're going to a village out near Coningsby. Come on, let's go and get changed into our civvies and pretend we've the day off."

"I'm all for that," she laughed as she started the engine and pulled away from the car park. As if to boost our sense of freedom, the sun came out. At last things were getting better.

We were soon changed and on our hunt for the Troutbridge family. The little Fiat hummed along nicely and, with the bonus of Natalie by my side, I was on top of the world.

We reached the Red Lion at Revesby and turned left for Mareham-le-Fen. It was deserted as we drove through the little village and it just seemed to be one street with a few houses each side of the road. The isolation of the place seemed to dampen my spirits and, to add to my misery, it began to rain again. At least the canvas hood of the Fiat seemed waterproof and, in spite of the sudden heavy downfall, we remained dry. The rain ceased as quickly as it started and, at the end of a longish straight stretch of road, I could see the two woods Stan had mentioned.

"Slow down, it's somewhere near here."

As she slowed, the cottage came into view, set back on the left of the road.

"In here!" I said quickly.

As we drove slowly up the muddy track, I began to doubt we had the right place. The cottage was not just small - it was tiny. How could eight grown-ups live in this little place? I shifted my gaze to an area to the side of the cottage where an elderly man was chopping wood. He was hacking small logs into kindling with a hatchet. He turned and lowered the hatchet to his side to watch our approach. Natalie switched off the engine and I climbed out.

"Mr Troutbridge?" I asked as I walked towards him.

He didn't reply and I sensed he seemed to take a firmer grip on the hatchet.

"Mr Troutbridge?" I asked again as I halted in front of him.

He didn't move a muscle. He had thick grey hair and the colour matched the washed-out grey of his eyes. The skin on his face was lined and creased like well-worn leather and, although he was not a small man he looked frail, swathed as he was in a huge old overcoat. The Wellington boots added to his general appearance as the relic of what had once been a proud man.

"Who wants to know?" he finally asked. Even his voice sounded devoid of spirit.

I was puzzled. I'd experienced the typical Lincolnshire response from Cornish - taciturn to the point of rudeness. From this old man it was more than that. Although he looked tired and beaten, there was a hostility about him as if he was looking to find somebody to blame for his demeanour.

I extended my hand. "My name is Carpenter, Mr Troutbridge. I am an antique and curio collector from Nottingham. I'd like to speak with your son Norman if that is possible?"

It was as if I had struck him. He took a half step backwards and his eyes began to blaze with a fire I'd never before seen in a man. Alarm bells began to ring in my head but I held my ground.

"What does somebody like you want with our Norman?" he rasped.

I forced a light laugh to try to defuse the situation. "He has an old helmet that I'm interested in. He had it with him in the Red Lion at Revesby the evening before last and I'm prepared to pay a fair price for it. If he's willing to sell, that is"

His cold grey eyes were locked with mine. He stood like that for what seemed an age. Then, quite suddenly, his composure seemed to collapse inwards and his lips began to tremble.

"You cold, unfeeling bastard!" he hissed. His next move took me totally by surprise. He swung his fist, thankfully not the one holding the hatchet, in an almighty haymaker. It connected with the side of my head and I went flying. I hit the muddy ground with a bone-jarring thud and could feel myself losing consciousness. I could vaguely hear somebody screaming and then I joined in the screaming as the old man kicked me in the ribs as I lay on the ground. He may only have been wearing Wellington boots but I felt every vestige of breath leave my lungs. I was barely conscious but it didn't do a thing to alleviate the pain coursing through my body. I heard a voice, as if from the depths of a huge well.

"Dad! Dad!" It didn't seem to concern me but the pain did. I was so pleased when oblivion finally came.

I could only have been out for a few seconds and when I began to once more take an interest in proceedings, I could feel an arm supporting my head and there was the odour of stale tobacco. I opened my eyes and blinked blearily into the eyes of a man in his thirties. He had a ruddy complexion and red hair to match. His breath, as he leaned over me, smelt strongly of tobacco smoke. I could sense him warding somebody off with his other arm.

"Hang on a minute, miss, give me a chance to see how he's doing." He pushed my hair out of my eyes with a rough hand. "How are you feeling, mate?"

My head was pounding, my vision was blurred and my ribs protested violently with every intake of breath. "Bloody awful," I croaked.

"Think you can sit up?"

A smooth albeit cold hand now stroked my forehead and I felt so relieved to hear Natalie's voice.

"Sam, try to sit up if you can."

I tried and, in spite of a couple of gasps of agony, I made it into a sitting position. I could feel the cold, slushy mud soaking through my trousers and I swallowed hard to stop the bile from flooding into my mouth. As I suppressed the acrid taste trying to force its way up from my stomach, I was taken by surprise by the sudden feeling of rage that coursed through me. I was going to kill that old bastard. I was going to wrench his fucking head off his shoulders and feed it to the dogs. I felt the rage exploding in my head and it seemed to anaesthetise the pain to the extent that I staggered to my feet unaided. I turned to locate the old bastard who had caused me all this suffering. I wanted to kill him so badly, I was shaking with the sheer anticipation of getting satisfaction. My heart was pounding in my chest as I sought my target. Then I saw him and the fury and hatred that had taken control simply dissipated as suddenly as it had arrived. Now, as the pain returned, I could feel only bewilderment. The old man was slumped on a pile of logs. A careworn and elderly lady stood with her arms around him as he sobbed with an intensity that shook every fibre in his spare frame. I turned to the others for an explanation.

Natalie threw her arms around me and said quietly. "Hi, Carver, it's me." She held me tight and I could feel the tears on her cold cheek as she pressed her face to mine.

"What the hell happened?" I whispered hoarsely.

"I don't know," she replied. "We walked into something with our eyes closed." She held me tighter and I shuddered as I felt the last of my rage return to its lair.

The chap with the red hair separated us and took us both by an arm. "Come on, let's get you inside and get you a cup of hot tea."

I didn't protest as my legs were beginning to tremble and I could feel myself heading for the cold, wet ground again.

He led us into the cottage, which seemed to be just one large room. To my relief there was a good fire burning in the grate. The room was tidy and clean but the furniture was heavy and old. A brass paraffin lamp, beautifully polished, stood on the sideboard along with a number of silver trophies. A few old, framed prints hung on the wall and among them was a large, black deep frame. It contained a photo of a man in army uniform. As he was wearing long puttees and carrying a swagger stick, it had to be a soldier of the Great War. Also, inside the frame, there was a plaque from the War Ministry, a number of medals and a small silver matchbox holder. Obviously a shrine to a relative killed in the fourteen-eighteen war. The man and Natalie eased me down into a chair but not before he'd spread a newspaper over the chair cushions. The cottage may have been tiny but the contents were spotlessly clean and he was not going to let my muddy clothes change that. The old lady I had seen outside, comforting my attacker, entered the cottage and came over to me as I sat in the chair by the fireplace.

She took my hand and stroked it gently. "I'm sorry, duck," she said sadly. "He's so full of grief he doesn't know what he's doing."

I looked at her lined and tired face. The lack of lustre in the eyes of the old man was repeated here. Her face was drawn and empty of expression. As she moved out of my line of vision, the word 'grief' kept echoing in my mind. I could hear the word but couldn't understand its importance.

"Here you are, mate." It was the red-haired man again. He was carrying a glass of water and had a couple of white pills in the palm of his hand. "Aspirin," he explained.

Natalie helped me take the tablets. I began to feel sick again but breathed deeply a few times and the nausea subsided. Warmth was slowly coming back into my veins and I began to felt sleepy. The closing of my eyes alarmed Natalie.

"Sam? - Sam?" She shook my arm.

I opened my eyes and looked up at her. "Don't worry, kid. I'm not dying and I've no intention of doing so."

She stroked my hair as she spoke to the red-haired man. "Why did your father do this to him?"

"The name is Frank," said the man. "I'm afraid you asked the wrong questions at the wrong time. Grief does strange things to people."

There it was again - the word 'grief'. Surely I was the only one suffering any 'grief'? I raised a hand in protest as I spoke. "I only asked if I could talk to your brother Norman about the helmet."

There was a long silence from Frank Troutbridge. Finally, with a catch in his voice, he spoke. "Norman's dead."

It was as if the old boy was back kicking me in the ribs again. I felt the breath leave my body in a rush and I struggled to breathe.

I heard the shock and incredulity in Natalie's voice. "Dead?"

"Aye," replied Frank. "Yesterday morning. I found him in a drain - what you folks would call a canal. He'd fallen off his pushbike and drowned."

I managed to breathe again. "I saw him the previous night. He was in the Red Lion at Revesby. That's when I saw the helmet."

"Why the hell do you keep going on about that bloody helmet?" Frank snapped.

I raised a placating hand. "I'm sorry, Frank, but that's what started all this. Norman was pretty drunk when I saw him so I thought I'd try to find out where he lived and do a deal with him when he was sober." I paused but I was desperate to know more. "Where exactly did you find him?"

Frank ran a hand over his eyes. "When he didn't come home that night, we thought he'd stayed with a mate who lives on a farm not far from here. He often did that when they'd had a few too many. They would play cards damned nearly till dawn. There's not much else to do around here." His voice was grim with more than a hint of bitterness.

"Where did you find him?" I asked again patiently.

Frank had averted his face and I could sense rather than see the struggle he was having to control his own grief. We waited for him to regain his composure.

"We were worried when he didn't turn up for work in the morning. We were even more worried when we found out he'd not stayed with his mates. We split up, me, my other four brothers and dad, to search for him. We were all supposed to be at work and round here, you don't take time off to look for a drunken brother; you'll soon find yourself and your belongings on a cart heading up the road. Anyway, we found nothing and I decided to check with a lad who lives out at New Bolingbroke. I went via the back road and about half a mile before the doctor's place on the bridge, I saw a body face down in the drain. Even from up on the road I could see it was Norman. The back wheel of his bike was sticking up out of the water just a few feet away." He paused and fought to get a grip of his emotions. "I managed to drag him to the bank and I ran with him to the doctor's. I knew it was a waste of time but I was nearly out of my mind. The doctor was pretty good to me and he called the police. He also drove over to our place and got the rest of the family. It was the worst day of my life."

His voice had sunk to a whisper and he clenched and unclenched his hands.

Natalie crouched in front of him as he sat in the chair with his head bowed. She took his hands in hers. "Frank, we're so sorry, we'd no idea."

That is how we were when May Troutbridge came in with the tea. She cast a quick look at her son and I saw her shoulders sag as she too began to weep but she made no sound. The tears flowed silently down her lined cheeks. I tried to get to my feet but she raised a hand to stop me and, lifting the hem of her apron, she wiped the tears from her eyes. She quickly straightened her shoulders and poured the tea. From the determined stance and the way she moved, I knew this was a woman who had suffered a lot but still had a fire in her to help her cope when the chips were down.

She handed a cup to Natalie and then to me. "Frank's told you, has he?"

"Yes," I said. "I cannot tell you how sorry we are at the loss of your son."

She looked blankly out of the window and we had to strain to hear her words. "If he'd been killed fighting in the war, maybe it would've been easier to accept, but to die from a stupid accident ... it is such a waste of a life." The tears began again but, as before, there was no sound, not even a change in her facial expression. Just those silent tears as if she no longer had the strength to cry properly.

Natalie moved forward and placed a comforting arm around the old lady's shoulders. It seemed to bring her back to the present and she briskly brushed the tears from her eyes.

"Thank you, my dear," she said to Natalie. "I'd better go and see how father is doing. This has just about done for him. I'm frightened we'll lose him as well." She seemed to drag herself from the room.

"Father?" I gave Frank a perplexed look.

His eyes, red and swollen from crying, turned to look at me. He actually gave me a small smile. "That's usual in Lincolnshire. The husband usually calls the wife 'Mother' and she calls her husband 'Father'. I think it starts after the first child has been born. It's just the way we do it here."

I nodded my understanding but I wanted so desperately to ask him about the helmet, though I knew there was no way under the present circumstances. I stared helplessly at the flames in the hearth.

"Who are you?" Frank suddenly asked.

My head came up with a jolt that made my senses swim. "I'm sorry?"

He stared at me and then threw the 'yorker'. "Don't give me the old crap you tried out there in the yard. You don't have the look, mate. I bet the only thing you've collected in your life is cigarette cards when you were a kid. You're no more an antique dealer than I'm a brain surgeon."

I glanced quickly at Natalie.

Frank sighed. "Don't look at her for answers. I just know there is something about you two that is not right. So - who are you really?"

I was beginning to learn that the Lincolnshire people were a crafty lot. They might look a bit rustic and rural but there was a sharp brain behind the 'local yokel' exterior. I'd no choice. If I wanted to get the conversation back around to the helmet, I was going to have to tell the truth and risk the consequences.

"We're both intelligence officers in the Royal Air Force."

His expression didn't change. "So, what had you and Norman got in common?"

"The helmet," I answered simply.

It was his turn to stare at the flames in the hearth as he tried to gather his thoughts.

I felt I had to prompt him. "We're interested in the helmet. He was wearing it in the Red Lion that night I saw him. It was a German helmet and we would like to know how it came into his possession."

Frank rose to his feet and although he seemed to move in a casual way, I noticed he had intentionally blocked the only way out of the room. Once again, the farm labourer appearance totally belied a shrewdness that most outsiders would never suspect. I'd learned a lot from my short acquaintance with Stan Cornish.

"Do you have any identification?" he asked quietly.

I nodded and fished my twelve-fifty out of my wallet. He checked it carefully and handed it back.

"Alright, you're who you say you are. Tell me about the helmet."

I explained the origins of the helmet and he listened carefully. When I'd finished he stood immobile in the centre of the room and I could see him mentally putting all the facts together. He eventually sat back in his chair. "Are you telling me that a

German could have parachuted into this area - like a spy or something?"

Strewth! I hoped he was going to keep this quiet.

"I don't know. It depends on how Norman got his hands on the helmet."

Frank seemed to make up his mind. "He found it not far from here. He was doing a bit of poaching out at Tumby Woodside and he had to hide in a culvert when he saw the head gamekeeper on his rounds. That's where he found the helmet - in the culvert."

I felt my heart miss a beat and those hairs on the back of my neck began to tingle.

"Whose farm was he on?" Natalie asked, her voice taking me by surprise.

"Meacher's place. It's not a big place from the point of view of arable land but there's a lot of woodland. The culvert was under a little bridge on the southern end of a large wood. You can see the bridge from the road. That's how I know where it is because Norman pointed it out to me. He found the helmet there one evening last week."

"Could you tell us the actual road you were on?" Natalie was taking over and I could see that Frank accepted her probing more than he would have if I'd been asking the questions.

He got up and fetched a pencil from the sideboard and I offered him my notebook. He quickly and skilfully drew a map of how to find the bridge.

"Any chance you'd accompany us, Frank, just to make certain we get the right place?" asked Natalie.

"No problem," he answered. "But not today. The rest of the family will be home soon and we've to arrange the funeral. I suggest you're gone before they get here."

I nodded. "We understand." I held out my hand as I rose unsteadily to my feet. "Frank, we cannot thank you enough, but I must stress that the subject of this conversation must remain a secret between the three of us. Please don't mention it to any of your family. When I can tell you more, I'll do so. Is that clear?"

He rose and faced me as Natalie took my arm. "I know what you're saying and I promise to keep quiet. I'm sorry too about what happened out there when you arrived but I think you can now appreciate what dad's going through. That should ease your pain a bit."

"I understand." I knew the damage inflicted on me by the old man would, for some time to come, be a constant reminder of the old boy's anguish and grief.

He walked us out to the car and waved as we drove away. I may have been mistaken but I thought I caught a glimpse of the old lady waving from the cottage doorway.

We drove in silence for a while then I put a hand on Natalie's arm. "Pull over into that gateway on the left."

She didn't question my demand and we coasted to a halt off the road. She killed the engine and only the tick of the cooling engine broke the silence. I could feel Natalie's eyes on me as I gazed vacantly through the windscreen.

"Okay, Carver, it's not just the pain turning your face grey, something's troubling you. What is it?"

I waited until I could gather my thoughts into a coherent rationale from the flood of images and suppositions. The more logical my thoughts, the more anxious I became.

"What are the odds it was not an accident?" I asked as I turned to watch her reaction.

She gave me a little grin but I could see she was not as confident as she was trying to appear. "Oh, come on, Sam! You said yourself he was drunk. I saw him too, remember? He most certainly was well under the influence."

I banged my hand on the dashboard in frustration. "I know, but he was not so drunk he could simply ride his bike into a bloody canal and drown."

"You don't know that. He may have had a lot more to drink after we saw him."

I shook my head. "I don't think so. I heard the landlord say he was not serving him any more. Okay, maybe he got some from somewhere else but I reckon it's unlikely." I wiped aimlessly at the condensation forming on the windscreen in front of me. "No! I am damned sure somebody else saw that helmet, and realising the significance, decided to do something about it. If they had to murder him, then they wanted to make sure nobody else could put two and two together."

Natalie didn't reply. I knew she was trying not to let her own thought processes be tainted by my wild suspicions and conjecture.

"You think I'm a bloody fool, don't you." I gave a sigh of resignation.

"No, Sam. I just feel you may be letting this whole thing get out of hand."

"Why? Surely it is a very real possibility that the guy was murdered to prevent him telling others where he'd found the helmet."

Natalie began to beat her fists gently on the steering wheel. One beat to each of her spoken words.

"Even if you're right, how the hell are you going to prove it?"

I cupped my hands and blew on them to warm them. "A postmortem."

Natalie gripped the wheel and stared at me in disbelief. "You can't be serious?"

"Why not?"

"For God's sake, Sam. That family has been through enough without you making it worse by holding up the funeral on a crazy notion only you believe in."

I grasped her arm. "But how the hell else are we going to find the truth? Look, if somebody in the pub saw the helmet and realised what it was, where did they get that knowledge? How could a big, strong lad like Norman fall off his bike and drown? I bet if we were able to drag that drain with a fine net, no way would we find the helmet. That helmet has been erased from the plot and so has the only person who knew where it came from."

"Frank knows," Natalie said quietly.

I felt a shiver of fear. "If Norman was tortured and talked before being killed, then the murderer would know that."

"Sam! Sam! Sam!" Natalie cried. "Slow down, for goodness sake! It is all conjecture. You've no proof for any of this and you're unlikely to get proof. Don't make a complete fool of yourself. Take a step back and look at the whole thing logically. The evidence, seen with your own eyes, is nothing more than a young lad who got drunk and ended his life in a tragic accident. No murders, no torture, in fact - nothing!"

I opened the door on my side and quickly scrambled out into the cold air.

"Sam!" Natalie pleaded as she too left the car and joined me as I leaned against a tree and stared into the nearby copse as if I might find the answer somewhere in its dark interior. I felt her arm slip through mine and I clasped it tightly to my body as if seeking reassurance that my suspicions were not those of a sprog intelligence officer but those of a rational and logical man.

"I know something is wrong," I said sharply. "I can feel it."

She sighed and rested her head on my shoulder. "Alright, do what you feel you've got to do but please don't give Janner the chance to crucify you. If you go down you'll drag Houseman with you and we cannot afford to lose either of you."

135

My head ached and I felt sick with the pain in my ribs. I raised her face to mine and kissed her cold lips. Cold they may have been but it lit a fire in me and swept all my doubts away.

"Come on, let's get back. I need to speak to Houseman. It is time we got the experts in."

When we got back to the section, I left Natalie in the main office and went through to find Houseman busy at his desk.

"How'd it go?" he asked. Then he saw the look on my face and the dried mud on my clothes. "Ahhh - not so good?"

"Not so good," I affirmed. "At the risk of being accused of overreacting, I'd say we've a real problem on our hands."

"Alright. Start at the beginning."

"I need to start at the end, sir. How does one get a funeral delayed for a special postmortem to be carried out on the deceased?"

"Bloody hell!" exclaimed Houseman. "Are you serious?"

"Absolutely, sir."

"Okay, you've shocked the hell out of me, now start at the beginning."

I related the full story of Norman Troutbridge and his demise, my subsequent beating at the hands of the old man and the information gleaned from Frank Troutbridge. I then told him of my suspicions and waited for him to toss my theories out of the window and me out of the door. He filled his cheeks with air and slowly let it whisper out through his pursed lips, all the time regarding me with the now familiar impassive expression.

"You know, Carver, if you're wrong, the repercussions for you would be minimal. For me, on the other hand, they would be catastrophic. I want to remain in a position where I can fight until this bloody war is over. I don't want to waste the effort I've expended up to this point. If I do what you're suggesting and it turns out to be a load of bollocks, Janner will have all the fuel he needs to light the pyre under both our arses. But, if you're right, we've a lead on a major security problem right here in our parish. More importantly, the other Troutbridge boy could be in danger." He tapped his fingers on the desk as he searched for the answers. Suddenly, he leapt to his feet.

"Right, that's it. This is beyond our capabilities. I reckon you've enough theories to get even the experts thinking. I'll report to the station commander and advise we let the security services in on what we know and what we suspect. How do you feel about it?"

"I think it is an excellent move, sir."

"Right! Collect your thoughts together and get them down on paper. Make out a full report from the mystery intruder to the death of Troutbridge. I know your suspicions will far outweigh any real evidence but, like you, I feel there is something here that needs sorting out. How soon can you get it typed up and ready?"

"I'll start now, sir. Problem is, I can't type and this whole thing is secret for the time being."

He grinned. "Well, I do believe Natalie can type. She knows all about the Troutbridge saga so you'd better fill her in on the rest as you make out the report. She's not exactly busy until we start putting tomorrow's op together."

"I'll see if we can get it all together before tomorrow morning, sir. We'll stick at it, even if it means working all night. If we can stir up a big enough hornets' nest, the security bods may move quickly."

"Let's hope so," he replied with feeling as he left the office.

I found Natalie in the main office and, as nobody else was around, we grabbed a cuppa and sat down in the rest area. I told her of my meeting with Houseman and of his suggestion that she help me.

"Suits me," she replied. "I may worry less if I know what you're up to."

"It will soon be out of my hands." Even I could hear the relief in my voice. "Houseman is asking Groupie to get the real intelligence types in. Once they take over, there will be no room for amateurs like me."

Her eyes met mine. "Does that mean we'll be able to spend a little more time together?"

I laughed. "Every spare minute we get. Well, we will if I survive my operation with Mason." All of a sudden I didn't feel like laughing.

"Don't say that sort of thing!" Natalie said sharply.

I could see the concern in her eyes. "Only thinking out aloud. Look here, if I can trip over a little kerb and damage my wrist, plus let an old man beat me to pulp, what chance do I stand against Hitler and his mob?"

She laughed. "You're such a failure, Carver. If they are unlucky enough to shoot you down they'll throw you back like a useless fish."

"You're probably right." I grinned ruefully. "Anyway, this is no time for nattering, time to start on that bloody report. How's your typing skills?"

"Best described as 'Banana Fingers Strikes Again'."

"Bloody marvellous!" I complained with little conviction. The more time we spent together on the report the better I'd like it. "Come on, let's make a start."

It was a long slog and it was three in the morning before we had four copies of a coherent report. She had been fantastic and without her help in getting my thoughts down on paper, my report would have been a shadow of the one now sitting on the desk before us.

We were drained and, having decided not to trust our report's confidentiality to the section secret registry, we placed each copy in a large envelope and I'd deliver them to Houseman's room in the mess. He'd not like being woken at such an ungodly hour but the sooner he saw the report the better. We destroyed the carbons and left the section.

It was yet another freezing Lincolnshire night and our breath burst from us in clouds of condensation. Outside the waafery, like a couple of naughty kids, we stole a long kiss.

"I love you, Carver."

"Not as much as I love you."

"You've always got to have the last word."

She blew me a silent kiss as she walked away up the path. I didn't move until the door had closed behind her. We'd known each other for such a short time but there was no doubt how I felt. I was in love and I could feel that warmth flooding back to me every time I was near her.

I sighed and headed for my lonely room. Well, I hoped it was a lonely room. Hammond had had enough time now to bugger off somewhere else. I knew with whom I'd like to share a room but the authors of King's Regulations had, in their wisdom, made it quite clear that the opposite sexes should be kept apart - especially when it came to sleeping accommodation. Miserable sods!

I was feeling totally knackered when I staggered into the section the next morning. Natalie was already there and looking as fresh as a daisy.

"You look awful," she said with a grin as I tottered back with a cuppa from the watchkeepers' office.

"Wish I could say the same about you," I whispered in reply.

"You really know how to flatter a girl, Carver."

I leered at her. "I know. All my conquests have told me so."

She laughed and quickly changed the subject. "Maximum effort tonight. We've to find twelve kites from 552 and sixteen from 629."

"Target?"

"Düsseldorf, and I hate to tell you but they're trying out the new route markers tonight."

I tried to appear nonchalant but even I could hear the rattle of my cup in its saucer.

"Mason flying?" I asked.

She nodded but deliberately didn't catch my eye. "Leading the main section."

"Has Houseman said I'm on tonight?"

"Not to us but I understand Command have requested an observer."

"Anybody volunteer?" I asked casually.

"Do pigs fly?"

"No, and neither should bloody intelligence officers if they have any sense." I replied with feeling.

The inner door opened and Janner strode in followed by Houseman. Janner paused momentarily when he saw me but, to my surprise, he took no further interest in me. I glance at Houseman but there was that impassive look again.

"Gather round, everybody!" called Janner.

Dave Jones, Hammond, Corporal Maudsley, ACs Vernon and Christian and three of the WAAFs joined Natalie and myself.

Janner puffed out his chest. "Right, I want a special effort from you all today as we will be observed by two senior officers from Command and the senior intelligence officer. They want to see how we do things here at West Fen. A good show will reflect well on the section."

I knew he meant it would reflect well on Wing Commander Janner.

He looked at his watch. "Briefing will be at sixteen-thirty but we'll have a run through at fifteen hundred." He finally seemed to notice me. "Ah, Carver," he said with a false bonhomie that fooled nobody. "You'll give a hand for a while but it will be essential for you to get some more sleep as you'll be flying tonight. You'll be supernumerary as an observer with Squadron Leader Mason and his crew."

"Jolly good show, sir!" I loudly acknowledged the pleasure my impending flight seemed to give him.

He paused for effect and then delivered the really bad news. "The target is Dusseldorf, Carver." He was literally purring with pleasure. "The Ruhr Valley, Carver."

"Thank you, sir," I answered brightly. "I knew it was somewhere east of Clacton."

His face darkened and the piggy eyes narrowed but, with an effort, he pulled himself together and decided to ignore my taunt. "Right everyone, let's get to it!"

He strode from the office as if he really knew what he was doing. Later, he really would know what he was doing – we'd have to make certain of that.

Houseman strolled over and steered me to the other end of the room. "You never learn, Carver."

"Sorry, sir."

"I know why Bourne fancies you, Carver. She sees something of herself in you. Bolshie, arrogant and lots of 'neck'." He regarded me seriously as he made the remark but I could see the laughter in his eyes.

"You can be very cutting at times, sir."

He laughed out loud and several heads turned in our direction. He lowered his voice. "I've passed on your report to the station commander and he was getting on to Command as I left his office. It is now up to them to try and get us a postmortem."

"I hope they do take notice, sir. I am even more convinced Troutbridge was murdered."

He nodded. "Fingers crossed." He turned and looked at the others beavering away collating and planning Janner's moment of glory. "Give Hammond a hand on flak and night fighters and then get off to bed for a couple of hours. Also familiarise yourself with the positioning and colours of the new markers. Make sure you know the time they are due to go down. Did you keep your flying kit from the sea search?"

"Yes, sir."

"Take it down to the locker rooms before you go to briefing. Then, after the briefing and meal, you can join your crew and get changed together. Oh, and Carver... good luck."

I joined Hammond as he worked at our section of the planning and, to my surprise, he kept his mind on the job. Houseman disappeared with Dave Jones to assemble the main briefing map on the wall of the briefing room next door. The other sections on the station would already have been notified of the target and everybody, from the station commander down, would be hard at work trying to get twenty-eight Lancasters and one hundred and ninety-six aircrew airborne with the right bombs and enough fuel to get them to the target. Tonight there would be at least one extra bod up there - me. I glanced at the sheet showing our payload for the night. 629 squadron were equipped with the Lancaster – Mark Three and, as the air war progressed, the poor old Lancaster was being cleared to carry a payload far beyond anything the designers had planned. Our load was going to be one thousand, four hundred and twenty four gallons of fuel plus one 4000lb 'Cookie' and two containers holding eleven 30lb incendiaries and twelve 4lb incendiaries. Bugger up the takeoff and you had a cocktail made in hell at the end of the runway.

When I changed my investigation to the planned route, I was surprised to see we were going to fly virtually straight to Düsseldorf with no feints north or south to confuse the German defences. Our entry over the Dutch coast would be slightly south of the Hook of Holland and, after a dogleg south to avoid potential collisions with all the other aircraft still approaching the target, we would exit the enemy coast near Walcheren. The total force would comprise 124 Lancasters, thirty-three Halifax and five Mosquitoes. The Pathfinder Mosquitoes were equipped with Oboe, a new ground-controlled radar blind bombing system and they would mark the target from low level. The main Pathfinders would back up the initial target indicators dropped by the Mosquitoes. They would also drop the trial 'route markers'. Not only was this the first time Bomber Command had used the new markers, it was also the first time Oboe-equipped Mosquitoes were to be used to carry out the low-level marking. It seemed I was going to be present at a double debut.

I dragged myself back to the job in hand but it gave me little comfort. The flak concentrations in the Ruhr Valley were horrific. Each indicator on the chart

Hammond was bringing up to date showed a mass of flak with barely a gap to fly into or out of Düsseldorf. Night fighter stations abounded and it seemed that no matter which way we went, we were going to get a pasting. I started to pick up a few remaining reports that dealt with specifics. Maybe it was better to ignore the big picture - it was too scary.

"Mr Carver, sir!"

I glanced up quickly. It was Sergeant Powell. "Telephone call for you, sir."

I went through to his little office and picked up the receiver. "Carver."

"Morning, Carver, Squadron Leader Mason. All set for tonight?"

"I've just seen the target, sir. Any chance I can stay here? I've got some library books I really must change - much more important than bombing Hitler."

I heard him chuckle. "Sorry, old boy, you're part of the crew now. See you at the briefing and then, after supper, we'll join the rest of the crew for kitting-out."

"Okay, sir. I just hope you'll cough up towards my library fine."

He laughed. "Just get some rest. It's going to be a long night. See you at briefing." The line went dead. My hand was shaking as I put down the phone. I really was getting the wind up. I rejoined Hammond.

"Bad news, I hope?" he grunted.

"Good news, actually," I lied. "It was Mason welcoming me aboard for this evening's little jolly."

He glanced up quickly to check whether or not the lightness of my tone belied my true feelings. I must have been a better actor than I thought, as he looked disappointed.

"What's this?" I asked, picking up a copy of a recent signal.

"What's what?" he asked irritably.

I handed him the signal. It was a very recent report of a possible new German night fighter airfield. The report said the Germans were experimenting with a new radar in the area and had established a makeshift airfield at a place called Gemert, a few miles north of Helmond in Holland. They'd begun to lay a temporary runway and a few mobile radar vehicles had been seen, but nothing yet had operated from there.

Hammond read the report and tossed it back on the desk. "Bloody thing isn't even ready. It's all a bit thin anyway."

"When did we receive the signal?"

"This morning, for Christ's sake!"

"If you take into account the length of time for agents to get the report to London and then for the powers-that-be to sit on it and cogitate before getting it out to us, the bloody thing could be operational by now."

He snatched the signal back off the desk. "Look, just fuck off and get your head down. I'll plot it with the rest of the bumph.

I needed no further encouragement. I felt jaded and tired and was made to feel even more miserable when I realised Natalie had gone over to the tower and I'd not see her before turning in. I possibly would not see her until I got back from Düsseldorf - if I got back from bloody Düsseldorf.

I looked around the room but everybody was busy. I felt really pissed off that nobody wished me luck as I headed off to bed.

Düsseldorf

CHAPTER ELEVEN

I awoke to the clamour of my alarm clock at fifteen thirty. At first I had a little difficulty in orientating myself. Two short naps instead of a good night's sleep were having a detrimental effect upon my little grey cells. They, like me, wanted to stay in bed.

When I finally got my thoughts together I didn't like the reality. I was actually going on a raid. Little old me, who didn't even like loud noises let alone big bangs, was going to play silly buggers with the real heroes. How could I have been such a prat to let myself get talked into such a stupid escapade? Then I thought of the hundreds who did this every night. You didn't hear them complain. Sure they moaned about the food and bitched about the constant shortage of hot water in the washrooms but I'd never once heard aircrew complain about their job. They were proud of the job they were doing. As for me? Oh well, if you can't take a joke you shouldn't have joined. Who was the cretin who first thought up that old service adage?

I swung my legs out of bed and winced as my warm feet hit the cold lino. I shivered and hoped it was just a reaction to the low temperature. Light still filtered greyly through the closed curtains and I found myself looking around the box-like room with a kind of fondness, as if it might be the last time I'd see it. Oh, bollocks, Carver, why were you blessed with such a vivid imagination? I leapt up, grabbed my towel and toilet bag and headed for the showers. If I was going to be shot down, I might as well be a clean prisoner - or corpse!

Fifty minutes later, having dropped my kit off at the aircrew locker rooms, I showed my twelve-fifty to the RAF police corporal on the door and strolled into the briefing room. I'd purposely not entered through the ops/intelligence section. I didn't want to face my colleagues this time. I was scared they'd see my fear

Most of the crews were already there and I could see Mason's crew, minus Ted and Mason, seated near the front of the room. Jock had obviously been keeping an eye out for me because he waved and pointed to a place next to him. They all hitched up the bench to make room as I sat down.

Tommy grinned and leaned forward across Jock. "Hi, Telly, looking forward to your big night out?"

"Just as long as you don't want an encore. I don't reckon my nerves could take any more. How do you silly buggers do it - night after night?"

Phil joined in. "What you see before you, Telly, is five quivering jellies trying hard to look like five big brave airmen."

I laughed. "Well, I hope the bloody briefing doesn't take too long. I can feel my resolve slipping."

Phil grinned. "Just don't let the old sphincter go, boy. That's when things really start slipping!"

They all chuckled and I felt a small slap on my back from one of the gunners. It was only a small gesture but it did wonders for my morale. I began to settle down to the job ahead of us.

Mason and Ted rushed in and gave me a hurried welcome. They'd just seen the station commander and the squadron COs arrive outside. Ted pulled out a packet of cigarettes and lit up. I stared at his hands in disbelief. On the back of the left hand, written in indelible pencil, was the word 'LEFT'. The word 'RIGHT' adorned the right hand. I glanced quickly at Jock and found him grinning at me. He'd been waiting for me to see the navigator's hands.

"Don't ask!" he warned me quietly. "He's done that ever since we were at OCU. It's his little superstition and we've never questioned it. We all like to hedge our bets one way or another."

I was going to reply when somebody shouted,

"Attention!"

We all scrambled to our feet as the station commander and the two squadron commanders strode down the aisle to the dais at the front of the room. The RAF policeman closed the doors behind them. The Groupie called for us to be seated and told us we could smoke. Ted grinned sheepishly at me and waggled his already lit cigarette behind his hand as the briefing began.

Wing Commander 'Bluey' Thompson, officer commanding 629 Squadron, opened the briefing with details of fuel loads, bomb loads, takeoff time and other generalities which had already been covered at earlier specialist briefings. As he talked my eyes were on the red tape on the main briefing map. It marked our outward and return tracks. The tape stretched from West Fen, across the North Sea, over Holland and into Germany. It ended in a sharp turn over Düsseldorf. It then back-tracked to the UK via a little bit of Belgium, a sizeable chunk of Holland, the North Sea and home to West Fen via Cromer on the Norfolk coast.

I was startled back into taking notice of the proceedings when I heard Thompson call. "Wing Commander Janner?" It was the turn of our section.

Janner rose from where he had been sitting with Houseman and three senior officers from Command HQ. He strutted importantly onto the dais, placed his notes on the lectern and picked up his long black pointer stick.

I made a mental note that Houseman would never be seen with notes. He addressed the crews with the latest intelligence in his head. He never ever used notes.

"Good afternoon, gentlemen." Janner stared around the packed room with an air of a pompous schoolmaster at assembly addressing a throng of grubby little schoolboys. If he was expecting us to chorus a suitable reply, he must have been very disappointed. We just sat there and waited for him to get on with it.

With his little bubble burst, Janner started hesitantly with general information on the target. Its status, in terms of industrial output, population numbers and its importance to the German war effort. He told us Düsseldorf had last been bombed on the night of the 23/24 January but because of complete cloud cover, the raid had not been a success. Only a few bombs hit Düsseldorf and they had landed in the southern suburbs. The flak that night had been heavy, concentrated in a barrage from 18,000 to 20,000 feet. Searchlights had been ineffective because of the thick cloud. He mentioned, as if in passing, light flak had also been in evidence.

For some inexplicable reason, as he came to the end of his rundown on the defences, the crews all cheered. I'd considered myself to be a lunatic for going on this raid, now I knew I was in good company. They were all raving bloody lunatics!

Janner was stressing the importance for our navigators to keep us on track, as the gaps between some of the most heavily defended areas were getting pretty tight. The Germans were pouring massive resources into anti-aircraft defences.

Then he came to the enemy night fighter defences. He warned us not to stray too near Rotterdam or Breda on the way out as the fighters were very effectively controlled by radar in those areas. On the way back we were to avoid the areas of Beek in Belgium plus Heikant, Turnhout and Bergen-op-Zoom in Holland. The Dutch coast defences were getting more dangerous with the advent of the fighters, controlled by radar, landing after intercepts on the bombers' outward leg, refuelling and getting back into the air to wait for their return. They orbited around radio or visual beacons like killer moths around a candle's flame.

Janner now moved on to the Pathfinder force's marking techniques for the night and to be aware of the clever decoys on the ground. Green route markers on the outward trip and OBOE-equipped Mosquitoes would open the raid with red target indicators. Red and yellow TIs would be dropped as back-ups by the main force Pathfinder Lancasters. Aiming points would be marked with green TIs bursting at 3,000, 6,000 and 12,000 feet. It all became a bit over my head after that and, when I looked around me, I could see puzzled faces among the crews. Then it dawned. Janner had gone beyond what was required of him for the briefing. He was out to impress the bigwigs but he was losing the respect of the airmen.

Suddenly, he had my full attention. "Tonight," he stated proudly as he looked around the room in an attempt to locate me. "Tonight is a double debut for the Pathfinder force. This will be the first time OBOE-equipped Mosquitoes will have been used for ground marking. The new ground-controlled radar blind-bombing system should make a big improvement in target-marking accuracy. Secondly, tonight will be the first trial of a new marker named 'Spot Fire - Red'. This first trial will be to use Spot Fire - Red as a final route marker. It will be dropped by the Pathfinder force at set intervals on the route into the target."

He consulted his notes and began to read, his half moons perched on the end of his nose. "Spot Fire is a 250 pound bomb case filled with a cotton wool sock impregnated with an alcohol mixture ..."

He got no further as a voice from the back shouted. "What a bloody waste of good booze!"

Hoots of laughter followed his shout and other ribald comments followed.

I could see Janner's face darkening as he fought to control his temper. The crews could see it too and they knew he was rattled. Nothing pleased them more than to see a senior officer lose his grip and he was now fair game.

A sharp, "Thank you, gentleman," from the station commander restored instant order.

Janner ran a nervous finger around his shirt collar as if it was too tight. The gesture was not lost on the crews. He was sweating and they knew it.

"As I was saying, before I was so rudely interrupted..."

It was a stupid and petulant thing to say and he got no further as many of those present made loud falsetto 'Ooooooo' noises and the room's occupants collapsed into gales of laughter.

This time Groupie stood but not before we all saw him stifle a smile. He raised his hands and, once more, there was an immediate silence. This was a man who commanded and had earned respect; attributes Janner would never aspire to.

"Gentlemen," said Groupie quietly. "This information is for your benefit. Any more interruptions and the perpetrators will be rostered for lots of extra onerous duties for the foreseeable future." He looked at us with eyebrows raised as if daring anyone to speak but we maintained a respectful silence. "Good," he said finally. He turned to Janner. "Carry on please, Wing Commander."

Janner wisely decided to get on with the rest of his briefing. He had learned not to tangle with the men in his audience. We were back to Spot Fire - Red.

"The bomb case bursts at a predetermined height and the sock is ejected to fall to the ground, where it will burn with a bright crimson flame for fifteen to twenty minutes."

So, that was my bit over and done with and I only vaguely registered Janner's information on decoys, enemy recognition signals which were, for some inexplicable reason, called 'sisters', leaflet dropping, convoys and balloons. Finally he laid down his pointer. "Any questions?"

Somebody asked for a little more info on the convoys. Not without good reason. If it had engines and flew, it was fair game to the gunners of the Royal Navy.

As Janner answered the question, I realised he had made no mention of the possible new night fighter field at Gemert. I glanced around to see if I could attract Houseman's attention but he couldn't see me from where he was sitting.

I felt Mason's hand on my arm. "What's up, Telly?"

"We had a signal warning of a possible new forward night fighter field in Holland. It is right on our outward track. I know we can't change the route but at least I thought the gunners might be interested."

Mason looked grim. "I'd like to know about Gemert too. Jog his bloody memory, Telly."

Bloody hell! This was not going to add to Janner's professional credibility. After his other problems with the briefing, this could be a bummer for him. Aw, sod it! It was my arse up there tonight, not his. I raised my hand and Janner frowned.

"Yes, Carver?" he responded carefully.

"I'm sorry, sir, but I didn't hear you mention Gemert."

There was total silence in the room and I heard the rustle of clothing as those seated at the front turned to look at me. Houseman appeared in my peripheral vision as he leaned forward. He was frowning.

Janner looked confused. "What about Gemert, Carver?"

I decided I'd better stand up, although I actually felt like crawling under the table to hide. Every eye in the room was on me. Oh well, in for a penny, in for a pound.

"Earlier today, sir, I saw a signal about a possible new forward night fighter airstrip at Gemert, just north of Helmond in Holland. It's right on our outward track and, although I realise we cannot change the route, I thought the gunners would like to know of the possible new threat in that area. Admittedly, it was earlier this afternoon when I saw the signal and it may have been up-dated since then and therefore no longer relevant to this briefing."

If anyone at this point had dropped a pin, the resounding crash would have deafened us all. I could feel my heart beating in my chest and the blood coursing through my veins. The silence was total.

A look of fury spread across Janner's face and he grasped the lectern with both hands. When he spoke, his voice was airy and flippant but dripping with sarcasm. "I must explain, gentlemen. Carver is coming with you tonight, in the role of observer. It will be his task to assess the new Spot Fire markers. Naturally, he's a little anxious."

"He's not the only bugger!" came a cry from the back. "What about bloody Gemert?"

Janner's face became suffused with rage and, in his confusion, his choice of words was fatal. "I know nothing of any new fighter airfield or this bloody place, Gemert. Might I suggest that Carver is making a mountain out of a molehill; as usual."

The room exploded into protestations and utterances of disbelief. "Why don't

144

you come instead, you smug bastard?" shouted Jimmy our mid-upper gunner.

Wing Commander Brady, OC 552, leapt onto the dais. "Silence," he roared.

As if by magic, the hubbub abruptly ceased. Janner stood as if rooted to the spot. His face was now ashen and his mouth moved as he struggled to say something. We watched with embarrassment as he fought to pull himself together. It seemed like a lifetime. Then he grabbed his notes from the lectern and strode from the room. The door to our section slammed behind him.

We were all stunned. Houseman stood and joined Brady on the dais. They had a short whispered conversation and then Houseman faced us all.

"Gentlemen. Somebody, somewhere, has dropped a colossal bollock and I'm as much responsible for this omission as anyone. He turned to me. "Carver?"

I rose to my feet.

"Carver. Pass on the contents of that signal to the crews - now."

I recited the text of the signal as I remembered it. To my embarrassment, as I sat down, I received a round of applause.

Houseman raised his hand for silence. Again there was an immediate response from the crews.

"Any more questions?" Houseman asked.

There were none and it was left to the Met man and the section leaders to wrap up the briefing.

"Attention!" Houseman called the room to stand as the senior officers left the room.

Mason grinned at me. "Well done, Telly, but I'm afraid things may be a little difficult for you over the next few days."

"Carver, a moment of your time." Houseman was at my shoulder.

We walked off to one side but I noticed that, as the other crews drifted out, Mason and his crew were going nowhere without me.

Houseman's face had that old impassive look. "This signal about Gemert. When did you see it?"

"Earlier this afternoon, sir, before I went back to the mess."

"What did you do with it?"

"Hammond had it and I asked him about it. He said I was to piss off and let him get on with his planning. He told me he'd include it in the final briefing plans."

Houseman sighed and his face looked strained and tired. "Well, in spite of the fact that my name will be crap, you were right to bring it to notice. The wing commander will now want your hide and I don't think I've ever seen behaviour like that at a briefing. You really know how to make life interesting."

"I'm sorry, sir, I just felt it ought to be included. I'd no intention of causing grief for you or anybody else, not even the wing commander, believe it or not."

He smiled grimly. "I don't think he'll ever believe that." He looked at his watch. "You'd better go or your crew will not get their bacon and eggs. Best of luck for tonight and I'll see you at debrief when you get back." He moved quickly to forestall my thanks and I rejoined Mason and the others.

"All sorted?" Mason asked.

"For now, sir," I sighed.

"What are you worried about, Telly?" laughed Jock. "They can't demote you, you're at the bottom as it is."

Bill Bedford put an arm around my shoulders. "He could join us in the peasants' mess."

"He's too posh," laughed Jimmy.

"Will you lot stop bloody gabbing, I want my sodding bacon and eggs," Tommy complained.

Mason pushed him towards the door. "Come on, lads, time we weren't here." He turned to the gunners. "See you in the locker room."

We headed off to the Officers' Mess for our meal, although by now I didn't feel like food. I was worried my performance on the forthcoming raid would not come up to scratch and I'd let down Mason and the crew. I was also facing problems in the section having reduced my commanding officer to a gibbering wreck in public. I think it could be summed up as professional suicide. There again, I wasn't a professional. I'd no intention of staying in the bloody RAF once the war was over. This was my temporary profession but, in spite of trying to convince myself I didn't care, I knew my pride wanted me to be a success, even if my job was temporary and no matter how alien it was to my character. Sod the bloody war. Nothing but bloody decisions!

After we had eaten, we went to our rooms and removed all identifying objects from our pockets. All letters, bills - anything that might, in the event of our being shot down, give the Germans intelligence on our squadron or airfield. It was already dark when we reached the aircrew locker rooms. Normally takeoffs were timed for dusk but this was going to be a night takeoff. The locker rooms were noisy with the nervous banter of men about to risk their lives. The haunted look in the eyes of some of them made me look away. We collected our parachutes and moved out to the vehicles taking us to the dispersals.

"Do we have D-DOG again, sir?" I asked Mason.

"Indeed we do. It's a good kite and I make such a scene if offered another, they've given up trying. We also know the ground crew well and they are good lads. It all counts towards my peace of mind."

I glanced hastily around me hoping desperately that Foghorn Fanny was having a night off. To my relief there was no voice booming 'Petal' from the darkness and our trip to the dispersal was uneventful. We slung our parachutes up into the fuselage through the rear door and formed a ritualistic line for a final pee on the edge of the pan. Mason was first into the aircraft and we had to manage with the weak glimmer from a couple of torches. Bill Bedford was the last in and he closed and secured the door. Before he disappeared into his cramped rear turret, he clapped me on the back.

"See you later, Telly."

"See you, Bill," I replied and groped my way up the fuselage and over the main spar. I stayed well back to let Jock and Mason go through their litany of checks.

Mason peered at the luminous dial of his watch. "Time to start engines." He called to the marshaller out of the open window by his shoulder and received a flash from a shielded torch in reply. The fuselage shook slightly as the first prop began to turn, then there was the familiar burst of sound as the engine caught and the fuselage began to vibrate - a vibration that would be with us for the next few hours. Soon all four Merlins were fired up and we got the signal to taxi. As we moved out onto the peritrack, Jock came on the intercom.

"Brake pressures are a bit low, Skip."

"Yeah, I'd noticed that. Rear gunner?"

"Yes, Skip?"

"Anything close behind us yet?"

"No, Skip."

"Right, I'll stop and let it build up but we'd better watch it."

We halted on the peritrack whilst the hydraulic pressure built up. No point in risking it.

"Skip, rear gunner."

"Go ahead."

"There's a Tilly coming up behind flashing its lights at us. He's coming round the port wing tip."

We craned to see out of the cockpit. The Tilly appeared and a figure jumped out as it stopped, ran round the nose of D-DOG, under the starboard wing tip and disappeared.

"Skip to mid upper."

"Skip?"

"Jimmy, hop down, open the door and see what the silly bugger wants."

"Roger, Skip." There was a pause and then a click as Jimmy's voice came back on the intercom.

"It's Houseman, the intelligence officer. He says that Command have changed their minds about Telly going with us. They want him off - now."

I could see the irritation in Mason's face as he turned to me but I forestalled him by putting both thumbs down and shaking my head.

Mason grinned. "Jimmy, tell him to fuck off, he's holding up the raid. I can't afford to waste any more time." As he spoke he eased the throttles open and we began to creep forward.

There was a pause then Jimmy came back on. "He's got the message, Skip and I don't think he was too pissed off because he was laughing. Door secured."

"Good old, Jake," Mason answered as we resumed our steady progress to the runway, following the blue lights of the peritrack. I watched Mason steer us by using the two outer throttles and purposely keeping off the brakes and I began to relax. I was with professionals who had just as much a desire to live as I had. Only bad luck could claim us and I felt that these professionals would do everything in their power to give us better odds. To my surprise I began to look forward to the trip and my breathing steadied. I was left wondering why Command had had a change of heart. What did they know that we didn't know? Ah shit! I was going to Düsseldorf and that was that.

We entered the runway just three minutes before the briefed takeoff time. I could dimly make out the runway controller's caravan and vehicles parked near it. There was always a small crowd to see the aircraft off, no matter the weather or time of day. There was a 'steady green' from the caravan.

"Here we go," warned Mason as he opened the throttles.

The lights of the runway stretched ahead of us like an infinite funnel and at first the lights swung slightly as Mason fought the torque of the huge propellers but finally the lights steadied and then blurred as our speed increased. The takeoff run seemed to go on forever and I could feel my body tense. I could see the red lights of the overshoot getting rapidly nearer and then, just when I thought we were going to run out of runway, Mason eased back the control column and we roared over the lights and the boundary hedge. There was a rumbling sound and then two thuds as the mainwheels came up and were locked away into the inner engine nacelles. It was totally dark and I had a sudden panic as I felt we'd stood still and were about to fall out of the sky. There were no visual references on the ground. No lights, no horizon - nothing. Just a black emptiness that seemed to swallow us up. I was just getting control of my brief panic when the intercom crackled into life.

"Rear gunner, Skip. Rear light OFF."

"Roger."

147

We ran through a patch of turbulence and I saw Mason's gloved hands caress the control column as he reminded D-DOG who was boss.

The intercom crackled. It was Bill again and his voice was high and strained. "Rear gunner, Skip. Combat over the field. I can see tracer and the kite behind us has an engine on fire."

Mason whipped his head around in a fruitless attempt to see the danger. "It's that bloody intruder again." He breathed heavily into his mask. He started to ease us over to port.

"He'll come from your seven o'clock and low." I said it without even thinking.

Mason's head jerked in my direction. "In that case I'm already turning the right way to give both gunners a clear sight. Gunners, did you hear that?"

"Got it, Skip."

"Right, Skip."

Mason began to tighten his turn to port and where we had been, seconds before, a stream of tracer lanced past.

"Fucking hell!" yelled Mason.

"Keep turning, Skip," yelled one of the gunners and the fuselage shook as they both opened up at the enemy behind us. The acrid smell of cordite filled the aircraft.

"I hit the bastard! - I hit the bastard!" It sounded like Bill Bedford.

"He's dropped off to starboard and I don't reckon he'll be back. Well done, Bill, you gave the bastard a headache." That had to be Jimmy from the mid upper turret.

"Keep your eyes skinned, lads," Mason grunted as he pulled our heavily laden aircraft into an even tighter turn. "Bloody hell!" he panted. "I never thought I'd have to start this manoeuvre so close to home."

There was a long, tense silence and it was Mason who broke that silence. "What happened to the other Lanc?"

"Rear gunner, Skip. I reckon he put the fire out. There was no crash or I'd have seen the fireworks. He certainly lost an engine but I reckon he got away with it."

Mason grunted. "I bloody well hope so. That was Tubby Payne following us. We went through HCU together." There was no need to reply as each of us silently willed the gods to look after Tubby Payne and his crew.

Mason peered at us over his shoulder. "Well done, Telly. How the hell did you know where he'd come from?"

"I was there the last time he paid us a visit, Skip. He chopped the first kite just off the deck and then zoomed to catch the next as it turned south away from Coningsby's circuit."

"Thank fuck for that!" said somebody over the intercom.

"Alright chaps, let's settle down." Mason was all businesslike again. Then he relented for a second more. "At least you two in the back will not have to test your guns over the sea - we already know they're working!" He ended the remark with a chuckle and then re-established the operational discipline with a terse, "No more chatter, lads."

We roared on into the night. The sky was calm and we shuddered only occasionally as we caught a lonely thermal or the slipstream of another aircraft. The high cloud had cleared and the moon now bathed us in a cold, unwelcoming light. Over the sea, cloud had filled in lower down and we'd be a perfect silhouette for enemy fighters but by the time we crossed the Dutch coast at Wassenhaar, the high cloud was back again and we plunged into the welcoming darkness. There was a little light flak over the coast but well south of our track. The last time I had looked at the altimeter we were at 19,000 feet and I was feeling more than a little chilly.

About every fifteen minutes Jock would climb off his 'dickey seat' and motion for me to sit for a spell. There was no conversation, just the mind-numbing roar of four Merlin engines. My face was getting sore from the pressure of the oxygen mask and I began to get itches it was impossible to scratch through the layers of the heavy flying suit. It was a relief when the monotony was broken by the terse course corrections given to Mason by Ted. We were just twenty miles from the target when there was a flurry of searchlights and heavy flak off to port. We could see an aircraft caught in the searchlights like a helpless, blinded moth. The flak converged and suddenly there was a huge blossom of red flame as the aircraft received a direct hit in the bomb bay. Trails of fire slowly drifted like fiery tendrils to the earth below. I pulled out my notepad and recorded the time that seven colleagues had died.

Jock saw me trying to write in the glow from his dim panel light. "Krefeld," was all he said.

"What the hell was he doing that far off course?" wondered Mason aloud.

"First marker going down, Skip." Phil was setting up his bombing panel in the nose.

"Got them," replied Mason. He turned to me. "We should now see the Spot Fires go down."

As if on his cue, a bright crimson spot of flame burst on to the ground ahead, shortly followed by another nearer the target and then another nearer to the target indicators falling on the target itself.

"Can't miss them, can you." Mason's eyes glinted above his oxygen mask in the diffused light from the searchlights bouncing off the high cloud above us.

Phil's voice came from the nose. "Bomb doors open - master switch on - bombs fused and selected."

Mason repeated the bomb aimer's instructions as the flak opened up with terrifying ferocity. I stared, as if hypnotised, at a box barrage directly ahead of us. We'd have to fly through it to reach the target and I couldn't see how we could do that and live.

"Right - right - steady - left - steady – steady," Phil intoned as he watched the target drifting into his bombsight.

The flak was now all around us and as the aircraft juddered and bucked, I could see Mason's gloved hands working hard on the control column to keep us on the bomb line through the turbulence of exploding flak. It seemed to go on forever.

"Bombs gone!" Phil finally called. There was relief in his voice. D-Dog leapt upwards as our load of death plummeted earthwards. "Bomb doors closed."

Mason flew straight and level for another thirty seconds so that the F24 camera in the nose could record the fall of our bombs. "Bugger this for a game of soldiers," he grunted as he finally threw us into a diving turn to starboard in an effort to get out of the flak and on course for home.

What happened next took us all by surprise. There was a massive explosion from somewhere aft and D-Dog's tail surged upwards and the nose shot down as we entered a vicious spiral dive to port. I was thrown up to the cockpit canopy with a bone jarring crash. I smashed my head on the armour plating at the back of Mason's seat and my senses swam. I was pinned to the Perspex canopy whilst fire and flak whirled around me, as if I was at the centre of a hellish, fiery vortex. I couldn't move. I was sucking greedily on my mask for oxygen and I fought to get my head down to try and orientate myself. Surely we must be going down. How the hell could I get to my parachute and out through the hatch in the nose when I was pinned like an impaled moth on a specimen board? My eyes finally located Jock. He was spread-eagled over his panel, desperately trying to claw himself into an upright position.

"Hang on lads," grunted Mason's voice. "Don't panic yet, we've got plenty of height."

How he managed to keep his orientation in all that negative 'G' I'll never know. He obviously did because suddenly the outside spiral stopped and, with the engines screaming a Rolls Royce soprano, the nose started to rise. I came down rapidly from my perch in the canopy and landed half on Mason and half on Jock. Without ceremony, Jock grabbed me and hurled me to the rear. I smashed my head again but it didn't seem to matter as we were nearly on an even keel and the engines were descending in pitch to their customary bellow. I stayed where I'd fallen, still sucking deeply on oxygen to try and clear my senses. I ached in every muscle and I felt as sick as a dog. I swallowed the rising bile. Things were bad enough without me puking all over the bloody place.

"Everybody check in," ordered Mason.

All but Bill Bedford, in the rear turret, answered. Mason rammed the nose down and I started to float again. He quickly explained his actions.

"We've lost 9,000 feet so I'll go down another couple of thousand so that we can come off oxygen. If Bill's hurt, he may not have oxygen." He glanced round at me. "Telly, get down to the back and check on Bill." He called to Phil in the nose. "Phil, pass Telly one of the portable oxygen sets just in case we've to climb again."

Phil's head appeared from the nose compartment and he handed a portable oxygen bottle to Jock. He, in turn, showed me how to connect my mask to it and how to attach the bottle to my parachute harness.

"The first aid kit is on the port side, just about opposite the fuselage entrance door." Jock told me ominously as he handed me a torch.

I nodded, unplugged my intercom lead and headed aft. I suddenly felt very alone and cut off without my electrical umbilical cord. I climbed over the main spar and scrambled down the back of the bomb bay roof towards the rear turret. I could see Jimmy's feet above my head in the mid-upper turret and I felt a little calmer at having company - no matter how remote. I turned my torch towards the rear turret and yelled with shock. It was not just a gasp of fear it was, to my shame, a full-bloodied howl of terror.

The sight that confronted me in the light of the torch chilled my blood to ice. Bill must have received the full impact of the close flak burst near our tail. He had somehow scrambled from the wreckage of his turret and back into the fuselage. He stood before me, his face smothered in blood. He had lost his flying helmet, revealing a massive wound to the right side of his head. A flap of skin hung down from the top of his skull to his lower cheek. I could see the white of bone shining through the blood. One arm dangled uselessly by his side. The other moved spasmodically as he reached out to me, his eyes pleading and frightened. His legs started to buckle and I grabbed him as he fell. His weight pushed me backwards and we fell in a heap on the metal floor. I managed to struggle from under his inert form and shone my torch to find his parachute stowage. I grabbed the chute and raised his head until it was cushioned by the pack. I could see the first aid kit and snatched it from its stowage. I had been taught basic first aid on the officers' course at Cosford but this was beyond my capabilities. I had to let Mason and the others know of Bill's condition.

I clawed my way up to Jimmy's turret and banged on his foot with my fist. When he glanced down in surprise I shone the torch on my blood-soaked glove. He nodded and I saw him click the intercom switch on his mask and begin talking. He gave me a thumbs up and I went back to Bill. Blood was oozing from the head wound and I decided that would be my first priority. I ripped open the first aid pack and found a shell dressing big enough to cover the wound but I knew I had to get the flap of skin back into place. It would help, along with the shell dressing, to prevent dust and dirt getting into the wound and infecting it. I found it impossible to hold the torch and treat Bill so, grabbing a roll of sticky aid tape, I lashed the torch to the side of my head outside my flying helmet. It seemed to work. Where I looked, the torch illuminated that area.

Bill's eyes were now failing to focus and I could tell, from the violent shudders coursing through his body, that he was in deep shock. If I tried to put the skin back before bandaging he was going to suffer even more pain. I rooted around in the pack - surely there must be morphine?

I found it in the form of a small tube like a toothpaste tube with a long nozzle. I removed the nozzle cover and saw the needle glint in the light of the torch. I had no idea how to administer it so I just shoved the needle into his thigh where the flying suit had been ripped away by shrapnel. I squeezed the tube until it was empty. The shivering slowed and finally stopped as his body began to relax. His hand grasped my wrist and squeezed it in appreciation. I'd killed the pain for now but it was a long way home. How many shots of morphine could I safely give him? With a Chinagraph pencil, I wrote the time of the injection on the unwounded part of his forehead. Now I had to dress the wound. It was all so unreal. It was dark, freezing cold and the roar of the engines made it impossible to think. I'd no visual references to our altitude and I began to feel sick again.

I started violently as a hand touched my shoulder. As I spun round, Jock's face loomed in the darkness. He took one look at Bill and I saw shock register in his eyes. I held up the empty morphine tube and pointed to the time written on Bill's forehead. Jock gave me a thumbs up and indicated for me to partially remove my flying helmet in order to clear an ear.

He placed his mouth close to my ear and shouted. "Can you cope here?"

I nodded but spread my hands in a helpless gesture at the same time.

"Just do your best," he shouted. "We've got a holed fuel tank and I can't stay back here - we've got to juggle the fuel to get home. I'll come back ..."

He got no further as the floor tilted sharply to the left and down and the mid-upper turret crashed into life, spewing cordite fumes into the cramped fuselage. I grabbed a piece of fuselage racking and held myself tight over Bill to stop him floating up under the negative 'G'.

Jock went flying into the darkness but it was impossible to see where he landed among the sharp metal projections of the fuselage and its equipment. I prayed he was unhurt. We really needed him. Then all hell let loose as cannon fire crashed into us from below and behind. Splinters of aircraft and shell shrapnel screamed and crashed into the dark hell of the plummeting aircraft. We were now under tremendous positive 'G' and I was crushing Bill to the floor but he was totally out of it and feeling nothing. Lucky bastard!

Jimmy, up in his turret, kept firing bursts at something out there in the darkness so he was still alive but I was beginning to fear for Jock. Then a hand grasped my ankle and Jock pulled himself up next to me. I turned to look at him and saw a huge gash on his cheek. It was bleeding profusely but as I opened my mouth to shout he just raised a hand and pointed forward. I nodded in return and he headed back to help Mason. Thank God he moved when he did. Where he had been lying another burst of cannon fire ripped through the floor and smashed into the top of the fuselage just inches from Jimmy's turret. It didn't seem to deter the gunner. He kept on firing and suddenly there was a glow in the sky out to starboard, which was extinguished as quickly as it appeared. I hoped it was the night fighter getting some of his own medicine.

As I began to get to grips with the situation again, I began to feel a burning sensation from the area of my buttocks and up into my back. I must have been hit in the last attack. I put a hand around to feel for damage and it came back red and sticky. I think it was at this point that I lost the plot completely. I was in a tin box, which was throwing itself all over the sky. It was dark, cold and the noise was hellish. In addition to the noise of the engines there was the scream of the slipstream through the myriad of holes punched into D-Dog by the enemy fighter. I had a severely wounded friend who desperately needed proper treatment but my hands would not stop shaking. I felt totally alone and an insidious fear began to creep into my mind that the rest of the crew had baled out and left me to die in the darkness. I began to come apart and I felt the first tears of helplessness prick my eyes. Angrily I wiped them away with a bloody hand and yelled into the dark hell around me,

"For God's sake, somebody help me!"

Suddenly a hand grasped my wrist and I snapped my head down to shine the torch onto Bill's face. His eyes were closed and he had to be unconscious, but the pressure of his hand was unmistakable on my wrist. Had he heard my cry for help? I doubted it. It must have been an involuntary muscular spasm, but I didn't give a shit - it made me feel better. I breathed deeply and, as the aircraft ceased its wild gyrations, I set about repairing the damage to Bill's head. I held the flap of skin in place with my left hand whilst I placed the shell dressing on the wound and tied the tapes around his head to hold it in place. A few more deep breaths and, after a bit of a struggle, I'd dressed his leg wound too. All I could do with his damaged arm was to immobilise it by taping it to his body. I checked his pulse. It was thin and a little fast but at least it was regular. The poor instructor, who'd so despaired of my first aid efforts at Cosford, would have been proud of me. I fell back exhausted onto the hard metal floor. The wind screamed through the holes next to my head but I didn't care. I was totally drained, both mentally and physically. The floor was relatively steady under my back and the roar of the engines in the darkness began to have a soporific effect. The thought passed through my head that I might be bleeding to death from the wound in my back. Strangely, I didn't care. I'd had enough. I slipped into blessed oblivion.

My head throbbed and I felt sick. I could feel my head cradled in somebody's arm. I hoped it was Natalie. She'd smooth away the aches in my body with those cool, gentle hands. I was rudely disabused of my ideal scenario by a sharp slap across the face and a rubber mask placed firmly over my nose and mouth. My head cleared a little as I breathed the oxygen and I came reluctantly back to reality.

My torch lit the face of Phil as he bent over me. His eyes were anxious so I gave him a thumbs up. I didn't feel that good but it was no use worrying him when we had Bill to consider. I rolled over to check the rear gunner and his eyes blinked rapidly in the light of the torch. I moved my head slightly. He seemed calm but both his eyes were turning blue and black with severe contusions. I hoped that was all it was. I felt his pulse - not bad considering.

Phil fiddled with something down by my chest and my spirits soared as I heard his voice in my helmet earphones. He'd found an intercom wander lead and we could communicate again.

"How's it going, Telly?"

"Great!" I lied happily. I didn't feel alone anymore.

He grinned and put his oxygen mask back over his mouth to speak. "Doesn't look like it, mate, but I'll take your word for it." He pointed at Bill and then up towards the front of the aircraft. "We've got to get him up to the rest bed if we can. Do you think he can stand being moved?"

"I don't know. He has a serious head wound and I don't want to move him unless it's absolutely essential."

Phil looked at me for a few moments then shrugged his shoulders. "Telly, you've both been out for a long time. We couldn't get to you as we've had plenty of problems up front. We've lost the starboard outer and nearly all the hydraulic pressure. We might have to belly in when we get back. If we have to do that it would be very dangerous for you to stay back here."

"Telly?" Mason's voice startled me. "Skipper here. Try to get yourself and Bill further forward as soon as possible. We're only an hour from base and I need everybody in their crash positions by then."

I looked at Phil in surprise. Only an hour from base?

He nodded sombrely. "I told you you'd been out for some time."

I clicked my mike. "Roger, Skip. If Phil can give me a hand we should be able to do it."

"Good man - get moving!"

There was little room to manoeuvre Bill in the narrow fuselage but finally, with me lifting him by his Mae West and Phil at his feet, we began to edge Bill towards the crash position by the main spar. Once more we couldn't communicate, as we'd had to unplug our intercom leads. As we struggled with Bill's inert body, I saw the sweat begin to bead on his forehead and the parts of his face not blue with bruises, were adopting a ghastly white pallor. His eyes opened and I could see the pain written there. It was clear he had other injuries - possibly internal. I motioned Phil to lower him gently to the floor. I put the chute back under his head and checked his pulse. It was very rapid and irregular. I wiped his mouth gently with my hand and he slipped back into unconsciousness. I began to get that helpless feeling again.

Phil indicated that he was going up front and I nodded in agreement. He was soon back with a thermos and a pack of bully beef sandwiches. He offered me a sandwich and I wolfed it down. He poured me a coffee from the thermos and it tasted like crap but it seemed to restore my will to continue. As I ate and drank, Phil was scribbling on a notepad. Finally he held it up to me and I read his message.

Undercart - U/S. Skip has offered crew chance to bale out over field. We all said 'No'.

He raised his eyebrows questioningly.

I shook my head, grabbed the pencil and wrote, *'Bill would never survive.'*

Phil read my note, shrugged and took the pencil from me. His reply read, *'You'll have to take a chance here. Good luck!'*

I nodded and shrugged. He clapped me on the shoulder and was gone.

I don't know how long I lay in the dark next to Bill. I knew I was cold and the vibration of the fuselage floor through my back set my teeth chattering. I finally lay on my side and waited for the whole bloody night to end - one way or the other.

After what seemed a lifetime the note of the engines changed and Jimmy squeezed past on the way to his crash position.

"Okay?" he mouthed. I nodded and he disappeared up front.

If we had no hydraulic pressure then I assumed we would have no flaps. That added up to a very high speed, wheels-up landing. I wrapped my arms around Bill, held him tightly to me and waited.

The crash, when it came, was violent beyond belief. It smashed the breath from my body - God knows what it did to Bill. The engines had died just before we first impacted with the earth. I guessed, in my stunned state, that we had landed on the grass to one side of the runway. The noise was incredible as we hit the ground yet again but this time we stayed there. I felt the bucking fuselage begin to slew to port. The swing became more severe and there was a deafening cracking and rending noise from the rear of the fuselage. Grass and mud showered in and covered us as I grimly hung on and waited for our uncontrolled juggernaut to skid to a halt. It did just that with a sudden violent deceleration that set my senses spinning. I crashed up against something with my shoulder and the pain was so excruciating, I lost my grip on Bill.

As I recovered my senses it was dark and there was an uncanny silence. Strangely I felt at total peace but my peace was short-lived. It was shattered by the sound of heavy vehicles outside in the darkness.

"Fucking 'ell, the whole tail unit has gone!" I recognised Jimmy's voice.

"Fuck the tail, see if you can locate Telly and Bill and let's get out of this fucking thing before it blows up." Ted Lowry was making sense.

"They're here - they're here!" Jimmy's voice again and I felt hands lifting wreckage off Bill and myself.

A new voice, one I didn't recognise, shouted. "Okay, lads, all out, leave it to us."

"We've two trapped and wounded here." Mason was in charge again.

"Okay, we'll take care of them. Just get yourselves out and over to the ambulance."

An arm slid under my shoulders. "Right, mate, where are you trapped?"

"I'm not," I croaked. "I've got a wound somewhere in my back and the other guy here is badly injured."

"Two stretchers!" called the man.

Light flooded into the wreckage and I could see a fireman silhouetted in the gaping hole where once the tail unit had been. It had been ripped off in the crazy slide to port and the whole rear fuselage was open to the night sky. There was a roar of engines and in the glow of vehicle lights, I could see foam flecking past the break in the fuselage. The fire crews were foaming the still hot engines.

I grabbed urgently at the arm of a new arrival who was helping to get me out of the wreckage. "I gave him morphine - the time is written on his forehead." I found I was slurring my words.

"Trying to be a bloody doctor now are we, young Carver?" I recognised the voice of the SMO and I waved a feeble greeting. The SMO raised his head and shouted to his men. "Get both over to sick quarters and I'll have a look at them there. Carver here seems pretty badly battered but the other chap will need to go to the hospital. Quick as you can, lads."

We were lifted onto stretchers and carried out into the cold Lincolnshire night. We must have been the last aircraft down as there were no runway lights and apart from the chaos and noise around the wreckage of D-Dog, the rest of the airfield was dark and quiet. The rest of the crew crowded around us as we were carried to the ambulance.

Mason put a hand on my shoulder and then burst out laughing. "Bloody hell, Telly, what the hell have you got on your head?"

I raised my hand and immediately felt the torch. It was still strapped to the side of my helmet. I grimaced and made a feeble attempt at humour. "No wonder I feel light-headed."

He laughed again. "You seem as daft as ever, Telly, so I guess you'll survive. We'll talk later. See you in sick quarters."

It was a quick ride to sick quarters and, when they carried us through the blackout curtains, I winced in the glare of the ceiling lights. A sergeant orderly and a young nurse worked on me. The SMO was with Bill in the next bay. I heard them wheeling the rear gunner away and when I heard the rear door of the building slam shut, I knew Bill was on his way to hospital.

The SMO appeared just as they had finally got me stripped naked. He gently rolled me over onto my side to inspect the wounds in my back. I heard a sharp intake of breath from the young nurse.

"Clean and dress the shrapnel wounds, nurse, but no dressing on this," the SMO ordered quietly. He came around the examination bed and stood in front of me. "You're a lucky young man, Carver. Apart from being peppered with bits of shrapnel, a cannon shell has travelled up your body from your left buttock to your shoulder. It has left a severe burn scar but no bleeding. The heat of the round must have cauterised the blood vessels as quickly as it burst them. A couple of inches difference in your position and it would have cut you in two. What bleeding there is, is from the shrapnel wounds and that is slight. Somebody up there loves you!"

There was a light knock on the door and the nurse crossed the room to open it. I heard Mason's voice. "Any chance we could see Pilot Officer Carver, nurse?"

"Come in, Sammy," called the SMO.

Unfortunately the first thing the crew saw when they came through the door was my naked arse.

"Bloody hell, Telly," laughed Mason. "I hope that bit wasn't your best bit 'cos it's looking a bit tatty."

"Thank you very much, sir," I started to laugh at the incongruity of the situation.

"Ah, now there's a surprise," Ted joked. "For once, the voice came from the other end. Are you sure he's an intelligence officer?"

"Bollocks to all of you." I found myself shaking with laughter.

Well, I thought it was laughter but the SMO saw something else. He ushered them quickly towards the door. "Right, lads, that's enough for now. You'll have to visit him in the morning."

Their parting good wishes had a puzzled air but they didn't argue and I heard the door close behind them.

I was still laughing.

"Nurse, the sedation please." The SMO's voice was quiet but urgent. I felt the sharp prick of a needle in the back of my hand and the last thing I heard was the SMO's voice.

"Time for rest, young Carver."

CHAPTER TWELVE

The next morning the medical orderly woke me but would not let me out of bed. I had to wash and shave in situ but the inconvenience was far outweighed by having my breakfast in bed. Luxury indeed!

The SMO came round about ten o'clock. "How are you feeling, young man?"

"Bit sore, sir, and a head like a bucket but ready to get back to work."

He shook his head and sighed. "What is it with you young chaps? You get the chance to have a lie in with room service and all you want to do is to get back to work."

"Don't get me wrong, sir. I'm very grateful but we've a lot on our plate at the moment and Squadron Leader Houseman will need my help."

The SMO's face became serious and I noticed he was unable to look me in the eye. "Jake is already here. He's outside, waiting to see you," he said quietly.

"Probably going to bollock me for going on the raid after the brass ordered me to stay behind. The way I feel, it probably would have been much wiser to have heeded their command!"

The SMO looked at me carefully and sat on the edge of the bed. "I'm afraid it is more than that and I want to make sure that you're mentally fit enough to take what he has to tell you. You had a rough trip last night. You were pretty badly injured and in a fair degree of shock." He paused and felt my pulse. " I need to know, Carver, if you can take yet another shock? I'm not a psychiatrist but I've no doubts as to the poor shape you were in last night. The unknown factor, as far as I'm concerned, is your ability to recuperate mentally."

"You obviously know what he's going to tell me, sir."

He nodded. "Some of it, yes."

I shrugged. "If you can't take a joke ..."

"You shouldn't have joined." He finished it for me with a despairing shake of his head.

"Precisely," I grinned. "Don't worry, sir, I'm not about to crack up. Last night was a little more exciting than I expected but I'm fine now. The question that's worrying me is, how's Bill?"

"He was operated on this morning and the reports are all good. You did a lot towards saving that man's life."

"I just wish I'd paid more attention in first aid classes," I replied bitterly.

"Nonsense, you did superbly well with what you had to hand. The fact that you refused to leave him says a lot about you, Carver."

"How the hell could I have left him on his own?"

"Some would have. The most important thing is, you didn't." He stood up. "As both you and Jake seem to be taking on the world at the moment, I'd better let him in."

As I waited for him to fetch Houseman, I tried to guess the nature of the bad news he was bringing. I just hoped it was not about the crew attacked on takeoff. I'd forgotten to ask about them.

The door opened and Houseman walked in. He grinned but I could see it was forced. "Carver, do you ever go anywhere without hurting yourself?"

"It seems not, sir. Some people attract interesting people and make friends. I attract nutters and shells. I think it must be a personality defect."

"How do you feel?" he asked quietly.

"Well enough to be told the bad news."

"Harry told you?"

"He said you had bad news but not what it was."

"He was a bit doubtful about your ability to take much more at the moment."

I sat up with difficulty. "I'm fine, sir. I ache all over and never want to see the inside of a bloody Lancaster again but let's get down to work. I assume it is work?"

He nodded and paused. Then he let me have it straight between the eyes. "The whole Troutbridge family were wiped out last night."

I began to think that I'd been wrong in telling the SMO I could take more shocks. I felt my heart lurch and, for a few seconds, I felt dizzy and sick. I breathed deeply and tried to get a grip of myself.

"All of them?" I asked hoarsely.

He nodded sombrely and walked over to the window to give me a chance to get myself together. I could still see the desolation in that family at their loss. The thin, careworn woman, trying to hide her grief as she comforted her half-crazed husband. Frank, kind and considerate, in spite of the loss of his brother. They'd been so real and I found it impossible to believe that they could all now be dead.

"How the hell did they die?" I whispered.

"German bombers."

"What?" I half yelled. "German bombers? Oh, come on, I'm not a bloody idiot!"

"Whoa, whoa!" Houseman walked quickly over and put a hand on my shoulder. "There was a raid on Coningsby and we think one of the bombers jettisoned his bomb load in panic when he was attacked by a night fighter. It was just bad luck the jettisoned load fell in a stick across the wood where the Troutbridge family lived."

"Bullshit, sir! ...and you know it!" I said savagely. "That was a determined effort to stop them talking." As soon as I said it I realised the stupidity of the statement. How could a bomber, in the dark, locate a small cottage and deliver a bomb with such accuracy as to blow it to bits. My thoughts raced and I grabbed his arm. "Sorry, sir, that was a stupid statement to make and I know it, but there is something seriously wrong somewhere."

He nodded. "Precisely. The two intelligence bods who arrived here yesterday are going out to the scene today. They should be able to tell us more this evening."

"Then I want to go with them," I said firmly as I struggled up from the bed.

He made no attempt to stop me. "I knew you'd say that. I've put Bourne on standby and she'll take the three of you out there in a staff car." He paused as I halted with dismay at the locker on the other side of the room. There was nothing in it. Of course not, my uniform was wrecked along with the flying kit. I turned to him helplessly as my mind refused to cope and I could see the conflict in his eyes. He wanted to tell me to get back into the bed but he knew he needed me out there at the scene.

He couldn't look at me when he spoke. "I've your best uniform outside. I'll send it in and, when you're ready, Bourne is waiting outside. She'll drive you down to the section to pick up the bods from the security service. One is a Wing Commander Face. The other is from Special Branch. His name is David Piper but I have no idea of his rank." He headed for the door. "I'll send somebody in with your uniform."

"Sir!" I called quickly.

He paused and turned.

"How did the crew fare that were attacked by the intruder?"

"They were hit in an engine but managed to put the fire out. Thankfully, they were a very experienced crew. They managed to stagger out over the North Sea, dump their bombs, make it back and land safely."

"Thank God!" I breathed a sigh of relief.

"Amen." Houseman smiled as he left the room.

I sat on the bed and tried to marshal my thoughts. I knew the official line on the death of the Troutbridge family was a load of balls and I bet the security guys knew that too. This whole thing had now become personal and I wanted revenge. I now had an aim and it was amazing what it did to clear my head and bolster my morale.

A medical orderly brought in a package containing my best uniform, a clean shirt, tie and shoes - even my dress cap. I'd nearly finished dressing when the SMO came back in.

"Back to the grindstone, Carver?"

"Afraid so, sir. It really was bad news and I'm going to make sure some bastard pays for it."

"I'm sorry," he said. He walked over and put a hand on my arm. "You're all fired up again, young man, but you'll find it will wear off after a while and that's when you'll know if you're really ready to take the job on again."

I grabbed my cap. "Thank you, sir. There is nothing more I'd like to do than to crawl back into that bed for a long sleep but we really do have a problem. Thank you for patching me up."

"That's what I seem to be doing an awful lot of these days," he remarked sadly. "We've not put dressings on your back and buttocks but keep a check to make sure no infection sets in. Okay?"

"Fine, sir, and thanks again."

"Get off with you, Carver." His eyes twinkled as he added offhandedly. "I see your girlfriend is waiting outside."

I sighed. "Not you too, sir. I expect better of a senior officer."

He guffawed. "It is all over the camp, Carver, or should I say - 'Petal'?"

"That's it!" I headed for the door. "I shall not darken your medical doorstep again!"

"I sincerely hope not, Carver." He was still laughing heartily as I closed the door behind me.

Bourne was standing beside a large Humber staff car and she looked quite smart in her best uniform. Well, as smart as Bourne would ever look! To my surprise she opened the car door and came to attention.

"Morning, Bourne, you're looking very smart."

"Good morning, sir."

I tried not to smile as she gave me a really first class parade ground salute. Then, in true Bourne fashion, she completely wrecked the whole scenario by patting my arse as I climbed in the car. I sincerely hoped the SMO was not watching.

"Can the leopard ever change its spots?" I asked as she settled into the driving seat.

"Not when you're as spotty as this one, sir."

I looked at her unattractive face and her bulky figure. Surprisingly it had a comforting effect and I felt a lot better. "Do you know, Bourne, I'm really pleased to see you."

She gunned us away from the kerb. "You smooth talking bastard," she laughed. "How are you feeling?"

"Bit bruised and knackered but I'll survive, thank you."

"Rough trip?"

"You could say that. I was pleased to hear that our rear gunner is going to be fine. He was in a pretty bad way."

"You're not going to volunteer for aircrew then, sir?"

"Not bloody likely. They have my admiration but from afar - the further away the better!"

"Your piece of stuff came to see you off last night."

I looked at her quickly. "I beg your pardon?"

"Granted," she countered. "I said, your lady friend, although she can't be your piece of stuff as she's a 'Henrietta', came to see you off last night. She waggled her little fingers at you as you took off but as it was dark you didn't see her."

"How do you know that?"

" 'Cos I was there as well. Actually, I gave her a lift over from the tower."

"That was kind of you," I answered truthfully.

"She's a bit of alright, isn't she?"

"Just keep your distance," I chuckled.

She cast a quick glance at me and grinned. "Do you know, if anybody else had said that, I'd have kicked the shit out of him."

"Well, don't try it on me, I'm hurting enough as it is."

She swept us around in a circle outside Intelligence and screeched to a halt.

"Wait here," I said as I struggled out. "We're going for a ride out to a place near Tumby."

"That's where the civvies got killed last night, isn't it?"

I looked at her in surprise. "How do you know that?"

"I'd done a run over to Coningsby and when I came back, I came the long way round by Revesby to give a couple of lads a lift. I passed all the fire engines and things out by the woods. The local copper said to watch out because the Jerries had dropped a load of butterfly bombs. He said they were all over the bloody place."

"Butterfly bombs?" I repeated. I was mystified, as they were only small anti-personnel bombs, not big enough to destroy a cottage and its inhabitants.

"As well as the big buggers," she added.

Now I understood. But as I ran into the section I was still mystified as to why the Germans should drop butterfly bombs.

Natalie was the only person in the section. "How's the hero?" she asked with a smile that told me what she really wanted to say.

"I'm fine. Thanks for coming to see me off last night."

"Bourne told you?" she sighed with exasperation.

"Bourne tells me everything," I said with a wink.

"I bet she didn't tell you what she said when the intruder appeared on the scene."

"Which was?"

Natalie smiled. "I think the shock of the attack took her by surprise because I distinctly heard her say, when the intruder opened fire, 'Oh God! Please, not Petal, he's all we've got!'"

I felt my face redden.

She laughed and whispered in an exaggerated conspiratorial tone, "Don't worry, your secret is safe with me. Anyway, at least she said it in the plural so I assume she recognises the fact that I've a share in you too."

Before I could answer the inner door opened and Houseman stuck his head into the room. "Ah! Carver, come through would you?"

I quickly squeezed Natalie's hand and followed Houseman to his office. Three men were waiting in the office. All three stood as we entered.

"Gentlemen," said Houseman, "I'd like you to meet Pilot Officer Carver."

Two of the men wore civilian clothes but the third man was in uniform and I recognised him as Squadron Leader Wareham, the station's senior provost officer. He gave me a small wave of greeting. I shook hands with the other two. The first, a tall man with white hair and a rather lugubrious face, introduced himself as Detective Chief Inspector David Piper of the Special Branch. He looked very laid back but his eyes met mine and damn nearly read my soul in the few seconds it took to shake hands.

Piper introduced me to the other man in civvies who actually turned out to be Wing Commander Face, but it was a true misnomer as he'd no memorable features, mannerisms, or even a recognisable accent. He was truly faceless. With his average height and nondescript clothes he almost blended into the office décor. His handshake, on the other hand, told me something quite different. He was a hard man and not to be underestimated. He looked me straight in the eye as he spoke.

"So you're the fly in the ointment, are you?" he asked me quite seriously.

"I hope you mean 'in the German ointment', sir."

He smiled. "Touchy too, I see." He waved us all to chairs and I noticed Houseman had found a couple of extra chairs from somewhere. I winced and had to bite my tongue against the pain as I lowered myself gingerly into the chair.

Face opened the proceedings. "Carver. You've certainly forced people to take notice. I am from MI5 and I think that will impress you enough for you to accept that we're taking serious notice of your theories. After last night's debacle, I think we can assume you're on the right track."

"Did we get an postmortem on Norman Troutbridge, sir?" I asked quickly.

"Steady on, young man, give me time. I was getting to that."

"Sorry, sir."

He grinned at Houseman. "I see what you mean."

Houseman had the decency to look sheepish as he glanced over at me. "I warned these gentlemen that you could be rather impetuous."

Face rose and stood with his back to the window. An old interrogation technique and I could no longer see his face clearly against the light through the window. "We obtained a warrant for the postmortem but we're still awaiting the result." He paused and then said quietly. "Sadly, after last night, there are no family objections to the delay to the funeral. There will now be eight funerals instead of just one."

I shook my head. "I should have done something instead of going waltzing off over Germany."

"I understand you had a rough night," Wareham said gently.

"For me, sir, but I think it was pretty average for the lads in the crew."

Houseman cut in. "Don't undersell yourself, Carver. I've already spoken with Sammy Mason and he said they would've lost their rear gunner if it hadn't been for you."

I felt uncomfortable as the others murmured their congratulations. I just wanted to get on with business. "Last night's raid on the cottage, sir?" I prompted.

"What about it?" asked Face.

I spread my hands in a gesture of helplessness. "The bombing couldn't have been planned or executed so accurately. Something stinks."

Face nodded. "We agree and we already have a team out at the site of the cottage. We'll soon know what actually happened. Although, purely for public consumption, it was a tragic accident. As far as the newspapers are concerned, the Troutbridge family were in the wrong place at the wrong time."

"When will we know the result of the postmortem, sir?" I asked.

He moved some papers aside on Houseman's desk and sat on the corner. "It has been a bit of a problem, actually. The body was found in a drain in the Boston police area but strangely, the incident comes under the jurisdiction of the Spilsby coroner. They of course have no facilities, but Boston still have to get their authorisation to carry out the postmortem." He indicated Piper. "I think the pressure put on the Spilsby coroner, by David here, speeded up the grinding of official gears."

"What's this I hear about butterfly bombs all over the Tumby area?" I asked.

Houseman seemed very surprised. "Bloody hell! Where did you hear that?"

"A very large person with a pronounced moustache and attitude," I answered.

"Bourne!" He sighed. "I don't believe it. How the hell does she know?"

"She drove past just after the raid last night. She told me on the way over."

"Bourne?" Piper asked Houseman. "Who is she? You did say 'she' didn't you?"

I laughed. "Yes, sir, he did. She may look like a character Boris Karloff would play, but she's a bloody rock. Totally loyal if you play the game. Don't play, and she'll reduce you to a gibbering wreck."

"Strewth!" exclaimed Face. "I hope we don't meet her. Powerful women scare the hell out of me!"

We all laughed at the look of dread on his face.

I couldn't resist thrusting the sword home. "I'm afraid she's waiting for us outside. She's my driver."

Face looked mystified. "Your driver? By God, Carver, you've got yourself organised. At this rate you'll be a group captain by the end of the year! Your powers seem unlimited."

Houseman interrupted the laughter. "Carver had an accident a few days ago, sir. We had to give him a driver and he picked Bourne. He's the only man who can handle her. She scares the shit out of me." He suddenly noticed the strapping had gone from my wrist. "Is your wrist okay now?"

"Not really, sir. It just hurts less than all the other bits."

"I think," Face remarked with feeling. "I'll stay well away from you, Carver. You seem to attract trouble."

"It just seems to find me, sir."

Face grinned and looked at his watch. "Right, I think we'd better get over to Tumby and see what the boffins have found in the wreckage of the cottage. When we get back, we can collate all the evidence and theories and try to agree on our next action. We should have the postmortem results by then, I hope."

Wareham moved to the door. "I don't think I can do much if I accompany you to Tumby, sir. If you'd like me to sit in on the debrief on your return, I'll be only too happy to do so."

"Fine, Tim, we'll see you later. I'll call you when we get back."

We walked out to the car and this time the section was full of personnel getting ready for the night's ops. They all stared at our little procession and their curiosity was palpable.

When we reached the car Bourne had the doors open and was standing to attention by the rear nearside door.

161

"You must be Bourne," said Face cordially.

"That's right, sir." She purred as she saluted, but she managed a little glance of surprise at me.

Face inclined his head to acknowledge her salute. "I understand you know your way to the bombed cottage?"

"Yes, sir."

"Good. In that case we'll do the talking and leave the driving to you."

"Thank you, sir," Bourne replied and I could see her weighing up the meaning of this soft approach. She looked wary, as if expecting something to follow, but nothing materialised. She seemed disappointed.

As he lowered himself into the rear seat, Face turned to look up at Bourne. "Whilst we do the talking, young lady, you'll hear things which are of an extremely confidential nature. Lives may depend on keeping our conversation exactly that - confidential. Do you see what I'm getting at?"

"Yes, sir. What conversation, sir?"

"That's my girl," laughed Face. Fortunately he didn't see Bourne grin at me over the roof of the car and place two fingers in her open mouth, as if making herself sick. I shook my head in warning.

Piper was already ensconced in the other rear seat and I turned to Houseman. "Are you not coming, sir?"

He was struggling to maintain his composure after catching sight of Bourne's little mime to me. "This is an operations and intelligence section, Carver. Somebody has to run the show!"

I lowered my voice. "What has happened to Wing Commander Janner?"

"I'll tell you when you get back." He turned quickly back into the section.

Bourne held my door and I prayed she wouldn't pat my arse as I climbed in. She restrained herself and we were soon smoothly on our way to Tumby.

I turned round in my seat. "What time was the raid that destroyed the cottage, sir?"

"About eleven o'clock," replied Face. "The butterfly bomb raid came about an hour later."

"You don't think the butterfly bombs were meant to delay our discovering what really happened?"

Face looked at me sharply. "By heck, Carver, you really have a suspicious mind. No, it really was a panic jettison by two Dorniers. Both were eventually shot down."

"What about the main bomber?" I asked.

"In and out without interception," Face answered.

"You've read the whole of my report, sir?"

"Every word, Carver."

"Then you'll know I met old man Troutbridge, his wife, and their son Frank."

He didn't answer and I saw Bourne's eyes move to the rear view mirror as she watched his reaction.

I carried on. "The old man was out of his mind with grief. So was the mother but she was holding back her own grief to help the old man. The son was a great chap and I think a lot smarter than young Norman - the first brother to be killed. They were just lovely people caught up in something that meant nothing to them." I tailed off into silence.

"Don't get too close, Carver." It was Piper who spoke the warning.

I didn't answer. I just felt a hollowness that was slowly becoming my constant companion. I felt Bourne glance over at me but she remained silent.

We arrived at the cottage and, as we drove down the track, I couldn't believe what I was seeing, or rather not seeing. There was no longer a cottage, just a huge crater. Army personnel were working with a mine detector on the back fringe of the wood. Obviously there were still some butterfly bombs around in the immediate area. There must be thousands in the fields and woods. Some poor bloody farmer, or farm worker, was going to get a leg blown off.

As we climbed from the car, there was a strong, rank smell. It was a strange smell to me and I could only imagine it to be the smell of spent explosives. There was not even a small piece of the cottage left. Just the odd brick and that dreadful crater. A middle-aged, bald-headed man, in overalls, Wellington boots and rubber gloves approached us.

"Morning, sir," he said to Piper

"Morning, Jack, what can you tell us?"

"No doubt about it, the cottage was deliberately blown up, along with a number of persons but not by an aerial bomb. As far as we can tell at the moment, explosives were buried under the floor of the cottage to give the impression of a deep penetration bomb. The evidence points to an explosive that is definitely not of German origin. Also, the crater is offline with the rest of the stick." He waved in the direction of another crater to the edge of the wood. "If you check back from that crater and the previous one, you'll see that this one is an 'oddie' - well off track."

Face looked at me. "Satisfied, Carver?"

"Yes, sir, but this is one situation where I wish I was wrong." I moved away to rummage through the rubble with a piece of stick. I could hear the mutter of their voices in the background as I sadly turned over clods of earth. Then I stopped and stooped to see more clearly. Something had glinted in the soil. I poked a clod away and there was a shard of silver trophy. I picked it up and could just make out a few letters engraved on the mangled surface. It was illegible but enough to tell me this was one of the old boy's trophies. The last time I'd seen them they were polished and standing proudly on the sideboard in the sitting room of the trim little cottage. I felt the tears begin to prick my eyes. Oh God, I was going to have to get a grip on myself. This whole thing had a long way to go and I was cracking up already. I rubbed my eyes furiously and threw the stick away. The old man, his family and all they had achieved had gone - vaporised in a searing explosion.

I turned back and saw Face and Piper watching me. They both looked worried and I knew I was the cause of their anxiety. I had better get my act together. I rejoined them as Piper lit up his pipe. The sweet smell of his tobacco was in sharp contrast to the acrid scent of death.

"Seen enough, young man?" he asked me quietly.

"Enough to last a lifetime, sir," I sighed and wiped a hand over my eyes.

"Right," said Face quickly. "Let's get back to West Fen."

Piper turned to locate Jack. "Full report, Jack, as soon as possible."

We drove back to West Fen in silence and I found the smell of Piper's tobacco soothing. The leather of the seats and the smell of tobacco reminded me of the library at my old school. The blended aroma of leather-bound books and tobacco smoke from the headmaster's pipe. It should not have been a pleasant memory because I was usually waiting in the library, senses heightened, awaiting the cane for some misdemeanour or other. I was beginning to scrape the barrel for solace.

Houseman met us back at the section, and to my surprise took us directly to Janner's office. He glanced over his shoulder at me as we approached the door, expecting my surprise. He waved us all in as he held the door.

I was astonished. The whole room had been re-vamped. The desk had gone and in its place were three tables put together to act as a kind of boardroom table. There were a number of chairs placed around the table and notepads, which I recognised as old signal pads, for the occupant of each place at the table. I turned and raised an eyebrow but Houseman gave me a slight shake of his head and helped us off with our greatcoats.

"I've had this room arranged for you as I know you'll have a lot to discuss." Houseman said.

Face walked over to warm his hands on the radiator. "Thank you, Jake. I'd appreciate your assistance as I think we're going to need Carver for some time. I'm now convinced we've a real problem right here on your doorstep. Carver's hypothesis was right. The Troutbridge family were deliberately killed and whoever did it has such good communications with the enemy they were able to organise a single aircraft raid to coincide with their destruction of the family." He sighed and patted his pockets but then clasped his hands firmly in front of him on the table - the sure sign of a man who had recently given up smoking. "They must have murdered the Troutbridge family and then blown up the cottage to try to cover the crime. They must also have had a very accurate means of target identification for such a precise fall of bombs. That means distinctive lights or, more likely, some form of radio beacon. They must have been pretty certain we would eventually realise the truth but at least their actions should have kept us off the scent for some time. Thanks to you, Carver, they were denied that breathing space."

We were all now sitting at the table and Houseman looked hopelessly at the rest of us.

"But where the hell are you going to start looking for the perpetrators?" he asked.

Face grunted. "How long is a piece of string?"

I leaned forward. "It had to have been somebody who was in the Red Lion that night when I first saw Norman Troutbridge."

"Not necessarily," argued Piper. "Anybody could have seen him before he got to the pub or even after he left. Had he been to any other pubs first?"

I nodded. "You're right, of course. He was already drunk when he got to the Red Lion. I am sorry, I'm not thinking straight."

Face gave me a long, hard look. "You've had a bit of a bashing yourself lately. Would you rather we postpone this meeting until you've had time to get some proper rest?"

I shook my head. "No way, sir. This is important and I want to catch the bastards who killed that family. They have to be linked to our mystery raider and he's killed a lot of good men."

"We don't know they are linked," said Piper quietly.

I sighed. "No, you're right. We've no proof, but I can feel it. All the tenuouselements we've identified are linked. I'm bloody sure of it."

Houseman doodled with a pencil on the pad in front of him. "We also have to try and get a line on the informant here on West Fen."

"You're convinced this agent exists?" asked Face.

Houseman nodded for me to answer the question.

"There has to be an agent here, sir," I said with confidence. "The night the mystery aircraft was orbiting Cornish's farm out beyond Eastville, he could not possibly have seen the runway lights come on. The weather was pretty bad and there was total radio silence. Yet, in spite of that, he suddenly shot off in this direction and managed to clobber two of our kites. He must have received a radio message. There can be no other explaination."

I must have raised my voice in exasperation because Face raised a hand. "Okay, Carver, I think we can all accept your reasoning on that. That reiterates your question about the perpetrators of the bomb, Jake. To find them will be a damn nearly impossible task, but where the hell do we start looking for an agent under our own noses?"

Before any of us could answer there was a knock at the door.

"Come in," called Houseman.

It was Max who stuck his head around the corner of the door. "Sorry, sir, but I think I've something you'd like to see."

"Come in, Shearing," said Houseman.

Max entered and to our surprise and no small amusement, he was carrying a bottle of brandy.

Houseman laughed and pointed at the bottle. "Well, I'm bloody pleased to see that for a start!"

Max looked embarrassed. "Sorry, sir, this is for Sam. Squadron Leader Mason and his crew have been given a seven-day stand down after last night and they've departed for the fleshpots of London. They brought this round for Sam with an accompanying letter." He pulled an envelope from his pocket and handed it to me.

I grinned. "Don't forget the brandy's mine too."

Max looked totally flustered. "Oh, Christ, sorry!" He put the bottle by me on the table and I placed the letter by the bottle.

"Aren't you going to open it?" asked Face with a grin.

Taken by surprise I blurted. "We haven't any glasses, sir."

They all laughed. "The letter, you clot," chortled Face.

It was my turn to be flustered. I grabbed the envelope and opened it. I unfolded the single sheet of paper and I could feel their eyes on me as I read the contents.

"Telly, this is for you. We squirreled it away to celebrate the end of our second tour, when it comes! Now we all feel you should have it for the efforts you made for Bill. Enjoy it!"

The letter had six signatures, each with a small and amusing comment. I glanced up to find the others waiting patiently. I felt I had to give an explanation.

"He says they were saving this for the end of their second tour but they want me to have it. Well, I'm going to put it away safely and bring it out when they do get to the end of their second tour. Then I can share it with them."

"Blast," said Piper with a sigh. "I was looking forward to a nip to warm my old bones. Ah well, c'est la vie."

"I think you mean, c'est la guerre," laughed Face.

Houseman caught my eye and he gave a slight nod. He understood what I was saying and he approved. He held out a key to me and nodded at the cabinets lining the wall. "Lock it in that cupboard until the happy day."

As I rose to lock the brandy away Houseman turned back to Max. "Right, Shearing, what have you got that will interest me?"

"I think it will interest you all, sir," replied Max as he unrolled a large aerial photograph and placed it on the table for us all to see. "I finally managed to get a bit of time to really study the recce done by Sam and yourself." He took a pen from his pocket to use as a pointer. "This is an area near Friskney, which is on the east coast not too far from here as the crow flies." We could see the flat marshlands pitted with water-filled holes that were immediately inland from the sea. Further inland we could see two sea defence banks and it was just beyond these that Max drew a circle with his pen. "Take a look at that, gentlemen."

Face and Houseman joined Piper and myself on Max's side of the table and we all peered intently at the photo.

"What the hell are we looking for?" asked Face after a long perusal of the area.

"An airstrip," answered Max.

Again we peered but with no success.

"Okay, Shearing, point it out." Houseman joined us in surrender.

Max pointed with his pen. "I've got another blowup on the way but I don't think we'll see it much clearer than this. Grain is already breaking up the picture even at this enlargement."

"I can't see a bloody thing," I complained.

Max pointed again. "Do you see these wheel tracks?" He was pointing to a long narrow field set back from the sea defence banking. It was the only field with trees and they formed a small copse in one corner of the area. A track ran from a small country lane down to the field.

"I can see a lighter area in the middle of the field," said Houseman slowly as he squinted at the image. Then he stabbed his finger on the field itself. "Ah, I can see a loop at the end of the track."

Max nodded. "See that dark line right in the corner of the field?"

We all nodded.

"That's a shadow," said Max. "The shadow formed by a structure such as a shed or a small hangar."

"I can't see any hangar or shed," complained Face.

"I'm not surprised, sir," answered Max. "You see, it is a 'blister' type building and it is probably covered with earth and grass as camouflage."

"Well, bugger me!" breathed Houseman.

Max continued. "You can also see where attempts have been made to harrow the grass across and along the field. It gives a nice contrasting square pattern. That in turn hides the wheel tracks made by an aircraft taking off, landing and turning at the end of the field to backtrack down the strip. Fortunately, the weather has been really bad and any attempt at harrowing would have resulted in the tractor pulling the harrows leaving ruts in the runway. One thing's for sure, the airstrip has been used at least twice just prior to the photo being taken."

We all gazed at the photo, trying hard to see what Max could see, but I don't think any one of us could have laid a hand on his heart and said he could interpret the scene as Max could see it.

Face returned to his chair and slumped in a dejected posture. "Well, Shearing, we're going to have to take your word for this - you're the expert."

Piper sat back and raised his eyes to the ceiling. "Now the problem is, how do we tackle them? Do we carry out a covert surveillance on the place and risk being spotted? Let's face it, it's bloody barren out there and they'd spot even the best surveillance team a mile away. On the other hand, if we raid the bloody place, we'll alert the other agents and the whole cell will close down and vanish into thin air."

"Further recce is out too," said Houseman. "We were stood off the coast at least a mile for that shot. Any closer and they will smell a rat."

Piper leaned over the photo. "There are no houses anywhere near we could use for cover either."

I had an idea. "May I use the phone, sir?" I asked Houseman.

"That brain of yours off at a tangent again, Carver?" he asked.

" 'Fraid so, sir."

"Help yourself." He pointed to the phone on the windowsill.

When the switchboard answered, I asked Trudi, who was on duty, to get me Stan Cornish's number. I seemed to stand there for an age but finally Trudi was back.

"You're through, sir."

"Hello?" It was Stan.

"Stan. How are you? It's Sam."

"Stan and Sam? We sound like a bloody music hall act," he joked.

"Maybe we could take it up after the war."

"Come on then, boy, what do you want, I haven't got all day."

I knew he was pulling my leg but I decided to get on with the job in hand. "Stan, was our friend there last night?"

There was a short pause and then he cottoned on. "Yes."

"How long?"

"Two."

"Minutes or laps?"

"Laps."

"Did you see friends?"

"No."

"Did he come back?"

"Oh, yes."

"You sound very positive."

"He was ill."

"Serious?"

"I'd say so."

I changed my tack. "Would it make sense for us to set a few snares tomorrow?"

He had no idea what I was talking about but he was prepared to accept that I did. "Aye, I don't see why not."

"Out Friskney way?"

"Who's paying for the fuel?"

"Me."

"In that case we can go to bloody Brighton, if you fancy it!"

"When the war is over, we will." I promised.

"What time tomorrow?" he asked.

"Very early."

"Bring your old clothes," he said. "Especially your wellies."

"Will do. Take care."

"God bless." He was gone.

Face looked at me with a puzzled frown. "What the hell was that all about and who were you talking to? Remember the security aspects, Carver."

I nodded. "That was Mr Cornish, sir - he's in my report. He said the mystery aircraft was around his area last night and, after two circuits, it headed in our direction. Shortly afterwards it returned with a very sick engine."

Houseman raised his hands in the air. "Oh, well done. Sammy's gunners must have given him a bit of his own back."

I nodded. "Bill reckoned he'd got a burst in."

Piper stood and filled his pipe. "I assume all the waffle about poaching was a Carver attempt to set up a covert surveillance of the suspected airstrip?"

I nodded. "Yes, sir. We can take Sam's tractor and trailer and stop off at that little copse in the corner of the picture to set a few snares. At least we should get a quick look at the structure we suspect is a hangar."

Max smiled. "I hate to disillusion you, Sam, but you don't look much like a farm labourer."

"I will by tomorrow. I didn't get a shave this morning and if I leave it until tomorrow it could look pretty scruffy. Anyway, Stan will fix me up somehow."

Piper lit his pipe with a match and puffed blue smoke up to the ceiling. "Well, we actually need to get a look and it would take some time to brief and organise a trained team."

Face looked at me with concern. "Carver, you realise how important it is that you don't spook our friends at the airstrip?"

"Perfectly, sir."

He looked me straight in the eye. "You do also realise, I hope, that if they even vaguely suspect your authenticity, they will kill you."

That was one thing that had not occurred to me but I couldn't let him see that. I returned his stare. "I'm sure that scenario will not arise, sir. Stan Cornish is a very resourceful man and I reckon that, with his help, we can pull off a reasonably competent surveillance without alerting the opposition."

Face stood up. "Right, let's stop at this point." He glanced at his watch. "I'll nip over and put Wareham in the picture, even if it's not the full picture. Then I'll get a team on standby to take the airstrip once you've made a positive report, Carver. Although we risk spooking the others, we cannot leave the raider to attack and kill our aircrews whilst we search for a needle in a haystack."

"I'll report back tomorrow, late afternoon, sir."

Piper and Face struggled into their coats. "Best of luck tomorrow, young man," said Piper as they left. I thanked him and waited for the door to close then I turned quickly to Houseman.

"What happened to the Wing Commander, sir?"

He waved Max and me back into our chairs. "He's been relieved of command. He's at this moment confined to the officers' mess until the brass decide what to do with him. The guys from Command were not impressed."

"I didn't intend to cause him all that trouble." I honestly meant it.

"Don't be stupid, Carver." Houseman snapped. "He was out to get you and at the risk of giving you a big head, you're more important to this section than he ever was. He was the one who insisted on taking the briefing, simply to impress. The fact that Hammond forgot to add in the info on Gemert from his part of the briefing was unfortunate and it could have been a disaster for any one of the crews. You rightly brought it to their attention. Don't blame yourself, you did what you had to do."

"What about Hammond?" I asked.

"He's had the bollocking of his life and a station commander's reprimand will be delivered in due course."

"Have I dropped you in the crap, sir?"

"To a degree, but I'm now the new OC, Ops and Intelligence, so watch your bloody self, Carver." He grinned as he said it. He turned to Max. "Well done, Shearing. You've given us all the ammo we needed to get things going with the security services. They are now in charge and I, thank God, can get back to being an intelligence officer. Counter-intelligence is not in my terms of reference."

"It all seems a bit involved, sir," said Max.

Houseman nodded. "It is and I'll leave the two of you together so that Carver can bring you up to date. I feel he's going to need a lot of help in the coming days and I

168

want you to lend a hand whenever you've a free moment from your normal duties." He stood and opened the door where he paused. He looked back at me and grinned. "Now I'm the boss, Carver, you can come and get your own bloody tea."

"I think I preferred you as second-in-command, sir. You were more humble!"

"Bollocks, Carver." He laughed as he disappeared to get on with, as he called it, his 'normal' job.

Max and I wandered out to get our tea. I winced as my back wound rubbed against my shirt.

"Were you badly hurt?" asked Max.

I shook my head. "Got burnt a bit but nothing really serious. It's just bloody sore that's all."

"What's this I hear about you getting beaten up?" he asked.

"Natalie?" I prompted.

He nodded. "She didn't say how, but I could tell she was very worried about you." He paused as I brewed our tea. "She thinks the world of you, you know?"

"Thank God she does," I said quietly. "I love the girl to bits."

"That's fantastic!" grinned Max, clapping me on the shoulder. "I'm really pleased for both of you."

"You don't think I should reconsider and succumb to the charms of Foghorn Fanny?"

"Jesus!" exclaimed Max. That was the nearest he ever came to swearing.

AC Christian passed us as he entered the corridor to the offices. I suddenly remembered we had very stupidly left the aerial photo pinned out on the table in Janner's old office. I ran into the corridor. Christian was just in the doorway of the office.

"Christian!"

He swung round. "Yes, sir?"

"Where are you going?"

He was about to give a sigh of impatience but decided not to when Max appeared behind me. Christian didn't like witnesses.

"Wing Commander Janner phoned to say he'd left some personal items in a drawer in his office, sir."

I strode down the corridor and closed the door in his face. "If we find anything we will send it over to the mess. Okay?"

There was a hint of a smirk on his face. "Very good, sir."

I watched him walk away along the corridor.

Max looked worried. "Do you think he saw the photo?"

"He saw it, but from that distance, he could have no idea where it was."

"Thank God for that." Max said it for both of us.

Sergeant Powell appeared at the top of the corridor. "Squadron Leader Houseman's compliments, Mr Carver. After you've briefed Mr Shearing, you're to get back to your room to rest."

"Haven't time, Sarge," I replied wearily.

"You must make time, sir. The SMO just called and said if you don't return to the mess, he'll confine you to SSQ for the next week."

I sighed. "Okay, Sarge, I'm going in a minute."

"Thank you, sir," he said as he disappeared.

"You'd better go," said Max. "You look awful."

"Thanks a lot, friend."

"Any time," Max grinned. "Brief me later. I've got a ton of urgent work to do and you need to get your head down, especially if you're to have a clear head for tomorrow."

I had to agree with Max so he went off to his work and I struggled into my greatcoat for the walk to the mess.

Natalie was not in the main briefing room but Dave Jones gave me a cheery wave as I stepped out into the freezing cold of the late afternoon. It was already getting dark and Lancasters were rumbling into life all over the airfield. I shivered at the sound and I was pleased I was not going with them.

Suddenly, a voice hissed with a decibel count equal to that of an express train letting off a head of steam. "Come on, Petal. Over here!"

I peered into the gloom with a sinking heart. "What the hell are you doing here?" I asked as Foghorn loomed into view

"I took the bigwigs to the mess and came back to wait for you seeing as you're a wounded hero and all that."

I felt a twinge of guilt. I really needed that lift to the mess as my legs were back to feeling like rubber and my head felt as if it was going to split in half. "That's very kind of you, Bourne," I said. "I really appreciate it." As hard as I tried my voice would not rise above that of a whisper. I tried to focus on the task of getting into the car but it all seemed like too much effort. I'm not sure what happened but the next thing I knew, I was being half carried up the steps into, not the mess, but sick quarters.

"What the hell?" I started to struggle.

"Shut your face, Petal, you need help." Foghorn grunted as she held me up with one hand and struggled to open the door with the other.

A male orderly ran forward as we staggered through the door. He looked at Foghorn and bridled. "What have you done to him?" There was a lilt to his voice that said much about his sexuality.

"Well! I bleedin' like that!" Foghorn exploded.

I stepped in quickly before she went over the top. "Thanks, Bourne, they'll manage from here. I really do appreciate your help." It was no lie on my part, as I felt cold and dizzy. God knows where I'd have been now if it hadn't have been for her.

"Don't let him give you an enema!" she said with feeling.

The orderly's prim little chin came up to verbally object but I'd had enough.

"For fuck's sake, get a doctor," I snapped.

"Right behind you." It was the SMO's voice. "Come on, Carver, time you were back in bed." He turned to Foghorn. "Thank you, young lady, you brought him to the right place."

"Thank you, sir." She purred with delight at the term 'young lady'. "I'll leave him in your tender care but make sure Jessie here doesn't tuck him in!" She glared at the orderly.

"Bourne!" I warned wearily.

"Yes, sir," she said and, in spite of her bulk, slipped silently out through the door and was gone.

As for me, I was soon in bed and the SMO gave me two tablets. "This will ensure you get at least eight hours sleep. Tomorrow you can stay in bed and get a bit of strength back."

"I can't," I protested. "I've got to be away early in the morning."

"For goodness sake, Carver, you need rest. I cannot be responsible for your mental and physical state if you'll not let me help you." There was an edge to his voice I had not heard before.

"Sir," I said quietly. "I've got to go or we may lose more crews to that bloody raider."

He looked at me for a long time and then sighed. "What time do you want Bourne to pick you up?"

"About seven, sir - in civvies and in my little car. I'll need my civvies from the mess."

"What did your last servant die of?" he asked with another sigh.

"Hard work, sir."

He cuffed me gently round the side of the head. "I can believe it. Now, get some sleep."

I needed no further bidding and was asleep in seconds.

CHAPTER THIRTEEN

We were on the road by half past seven the next morning. Both Bourne and myself were in civvies and the little Fiat hummed along towards the Cornish farm. Foghorn was in trousers and wearing something that looked like a donkey jacket. Under that she had a thick woollen roll neck sweater. I swear she could have passed as a Boston docker. She made me look totally overdressed in my sports jacket and flannels. I'd left my overcoat off as it was too much weight on my injured back. I began to wonder if my insistence on getting back to work was a good idea. My head pounded and I felt bruised and stiff all over. The wound to my back and buttocks was giving me hell. It was cold but I felt sticky with sweat.

"You sure you're alright?" Foghorn asked with an anxious little glance in my direction.

"Fine, thank you," I said shortly. "For God's sake stop worrying!"

She didn't reply and I knew I had actually offended her.

"Sorry, I'm fine as long as people leave me alone."

"Suit yourself, Petal." She was pissed off and we rode the rest of the way to the farm in silence.

Stan and Dog were waiting for us as we drove down the farm track. He opened the door on my side when we stopped. "Morning. How are things?" he asked.

I grabbed the top of the door and hauled myself slowly up from the seat to a standing position. Well, 'standing' was a euphemism for my actual stance but I persevered. "Bit dodgy," I said with a grunt.

"Dodgy?" he exclaimed. "You're a bloody wreck, boy!"

"He's a hero," said Foghorn with a smirk. She was still smarting from my bad manners in the car.

"Heroes usually win," Stan grunted. "If you're the winner, what the hell does the loser look like?"

"I don't know, he's in Germany," I answered shortly. I slammed the car door. "Now can we get on with the morning's task?"

Stan spread his legs and folded his arms. It was that stubborn stance of his and I knew I was in trouble.

"We could probably start right now if only I knew what we're supposed to be doing."

I mentally kicked myself. Of course, the poor chap had no idea what I wanted him to do and here I was, getting all het up, because I felt like death. I put a hand on his arm. "Is the kettle on?"

He nodded.

"Right," I said. "Let's have a cuppa and I'll explain, but we must get moving - time is short."

"Suits me." Stan moved off towards the house.

I called after him. "Stan, would you please ask Dog not to lead me by the wrist. I can't bend this morning and I'm too sore to be dragged into the house."

He didn't even turn around. "Dog!" was all he said and Dog promptly lost interest in me and followed his master into the house.

"See how easy it is when you know how?" whispered Foghorn.

"Bollocks," I replied with ill humour.

She was totally unmoved. "That is exactly what it takes," she answered as she followed Stan, leaving me out in the cold with my aches, pains and bad temper.

Seated in the back parlour with a hot and very sweet cup of tea, I began to feel somewhat better.

"Right, what do you want me to do?" asked Stan.

I set my cup and saucer back down on the table. "I want to take a quiet look at a field out near Friskney; about half way between Friskney and Wrangle Lowgate."

He was silent for a while and he looked at me intently. "Your mystery raider?"

I nodded. "We think so." I glanced at Foghorn.

"Do you want me to leave?" she asked and I could see the disappointment in her eyes.

I shook my head. "No, you'd better know what it's all about but the usual rules apply."

"Goes without saying, Petal."

Stan stifled a smile. "How do I fit into this? Although, from your phone call, I think I may have a rough idea."

I sat forward in my chair. "We need to get into a small copse which is in the corner of the field. The copse is next to the road and leads up to what we believe may be a concealed hangar."

"Shitty death!" exclaimed Foghorn but quickly shut up when I frowned in her direction.

I looked back at Stan. "Do you have any ideas as to what excuse we could use for being in that copse?"

He didn't even hesitate. "Setting snares. You suggested it yesterday."

I'd forgotten. "Fine, but I'm afraid I've no old clothes. Any chance you may be able to kit me out as a farm worker?"

He laughed. "With those hands and that pale face? You must be joking, although I see you had the sense not to shave this morning."

"At least I was able to remember something," I grinned. "I also remembered my Wellies."

"Those things are no good, they're too posh for a farm worker. What size are you?"

"Nine."

"Fine, I've got a spare pair. They're eight and a half so they'll pinch a bit."

He looked me up and down and scratched his chin. "We're about the same waist so I can give you some old corduroys but they will be miles too short. We'll have to tie them at the knee with binder twine, or tuck them in the wellies. A shirt with no collar, an old jacket and a topcoat should do it. There's an old topcoat in the barn. It's covered in mould but it should look authentic." He stared at my face. "We've got to darken your skin somehow."

"What about brown boot polish and some sort of cream?" suggested Foghorn.

Stan grinned. "Fantastic, I've got the boot polish if you've got the cream."

Foghorn gave him a wicked grin. "I'd have thought you'd have had a nice jar of Pond's face cream somewhere." She suddenly realised her faux pas and I could see her desperately wishing she'd kept her big mouth shut. She glanced quickly at me but I pretended not to notice the gaffe.

"What about headgear?" I asked quickly.

Stan seemed relieved the conversation was back to normal and he glanced out of the window. It had started to rain heavily. "An old sack, turned in at the corner to form a sort of hood," he said. "We all wear that in wet weather or when carrying wet bags and chaff from the threshing machine."

"Good," I said, finishing my tea. "Let's get the transformation under way."

It took a good hour but finally I was nearly ready. My face was sticky from the mixture of cream and boot polish but it seemed effective.

Stan entered with two short lengths of binder twine. "We'll tie these just below your knees." He reached down to tie them and the back of his hand just caught my inner thigh. I jerked slightly and saw him hesitate but he carried on. I felt bloody awful. There had been no need for that slight recoil. It was not his fault and I knew he had noticed my reaction.

He hid his feelings well. He stood up. "Okay, now nip out into the garden and ram your fingers into the muck and make sure you get plenty under your fingernails. I'll cut the tops off the fingers of a pair of old gloves to make you a pair of mittens."

"Are you sure I can't come on this trip," asked a glum Foghorn.

"Please," I pleaded. "I don't want to go through it all again"

"Spoilsport," she muttered. I left her to it and headed for the garden.

When I got back to the parlour, Stan gave me the mittens. "I thought we'd take the old Fordson and a trailer."

"Fine." I nodded my assent as I pulled out a map of the Friskney area. A few seconds was all it needed for Stan to know where we were going. I gave the map to Bourne for safekeeping and clapped my bemittened hands together. "Right, let's go."

"Dog, stay here with Rhoda," ordered Stan.

At least Foghorn looked a little happier. She loved that dog and he obviously thought the world of her. He'd not left her side since we arrived at the farm. Finally, with me looking more like a farm labourer than a farm labourer, we hitched up the Fordson to the trailer.

"See you later," I called to Foghorn as I climbed up beside Stan and sat on the mudguard. There was no protection from the elements and I could already feel the rain soaking through the cowled sack over my head.

She waved. "Take care, you pair of silly sods."

Stan opened the throttle and we were on our way.

We trundled the first mile in silence but finally Stan turned to me and watched me intently to see the effect of his words. "She's told you, hasn't she?" he shouted above the roar of the engine.

I wiped the rain from my face and nodded. "Yes."

"I'm not a bloody bum boy!" he shouted angrily.

I grabbed the mudguard as he swung right on to an even narrower lane. "Did I say you were?" I shouted back. "Look, Stan, I don't give a shit what you are. You've been a great help and I hope we'll always be friends." I paused and wiped more rain from my face. "This is not the time, nor the place for intimate discussions. Just take it for read I don't give a damn about your sexual orientation. That is your affair and is of no concern to me. I enjoy your company and that is all that matters."

He looked at me, rivulets of rain running down his face. "I've never done anything!" His eyes pleaded with me to believe him. The poor little sod was trapped in a situation he desperately hated. He must go through hell in that lonely farmhouse. No friends and an intelligence too acute to come to terms with his lot in life.

"Stan, just leave it," I ordered. "Just leave it for now."

He nodded and we roared on at a pedestrian pace in the direction of our mystery airstrip.

Sometime later, it seemed a very long time, Stan pointed across a dank and uninteresting, flat field. "There's your spinney."

I stared intently. There were no other trees for miles, just that one little copse. The narrow field looked like any other grass field in the area. I could see the second, inner sea wall, at the far end of the field. Any aircraft landing or taking off would only just clear the bank. At first, I could see no sign of a building but then, through the skeletal winter trees, I could just make out a large grass mound. As we passed a small gate about a hundred yards from the copse, I saw a red and white metal sign on the gate.

'AIR MINISTRY PROPERTY - KEEP OUT'

That was obviously for the locals. The airfield staff must have a twenty-four hour watch on the road. In the unlikely event of military vehicles coming down the road, the sign would quickly disappear.

Stan slowed the tractor as we came to the wood. He picked a place where we would not block the road and stopped. He left the engine running and climbed down. He opened a large toolbox bolted to the back of the tractor and removed several wire and wood rabbit snares. As he closed the box he spoke, just loud enough for me to hear.

"You're the village idiot. For God's sake, if we're challenged, don't speak!"

I nodded and we dropped into the ditch and scrambled up through the hedge into the wood. I shambled behind the little farmer, staring vacantly around me. The noise of the idling tractor became a faint murmur. The predominant noise now was our breathing and the sound of moisture dripping from the stark trees onto the dead leaves below. Stan stooped and began to set a snare. I crouched with him but he said nothing. As we rose, I stared in the direction of the mound, and that was what it still looked like - an earthen mound. No doors, no vehicles - nothing. I made a point of staring vacantly up into the trees and my heart skipped a beat. I could see a wire strung through the tops of the trees. An aerial? I quickly changed my line of sight and the hairs on my neck began their little dance. This was bloody dangerous.

Stan dropped quickly to the ground again and I joined him as he fixed another snare. Then the hairs on my neck went into alarm overdrive as I heard the distinctive sound of a Sten gun being cocked. There was no mistaking the sound and I could remember it well from my range training at Cosford. The Sten was a cheaply made submachine gun and devastating at close range. The 9mm rounds sprayed a deadly cone of death - when it didn't jam. I was not about to assume the certainty of the latter. I stayed crouched and desperately tried not to look in the direction of the sound, or even at Stan.

Stan reacted the right way. His head shot up and I could see the fear in his eyes. He rose slowly and started to raise his hands above his head. "Now, steady on, mayet," he said in a broad Lincolnshire accent to somebody behind me.

There was no response and Stan kicked me to bring me to my feet. In spite of my mouth being dry with fear, I managed a little saliva and, with my tongue, I pushed it over my lower lip to dribble down my chin. I left my mouth agape and slowly turned to face the enemy.

175

He was in the uniform of an RAF corporal and he was big, well over six feet. His eyes were a slate grey and he was obviously not impressed by what he saw. For some obscure reason I looked to see if his fingers were clear of the ammo ejection slot. They were. He knew what he was doing. I decided I needed a little more authenticity to my character so I stretched my gaping mouth into a huge stupid grin. I saw the distaste in his eyes.

"Can't you read?" he asked quietly. Too quietly for an RAF corporal. The words had a menace that dropped loudly into the steady patter of the rain.

"Noowaboddy neads to reead to ketch rabbits," replied Stan. I could only just decipher the heavy accent.

"There are no rabbits. We poisoned them all," replied the corporal. His speech was unaccented and precise.

"Wot's this then?" Stan pointed to the button – like rabbit droppings near where he'd placed the snare.

"We cannot kill them all." Again that precise form of speech. The corporal's eyes came back to me but by this time I had initiated a profound excavation of my right nostril with my filthy right index finger.

His eyes narrowed as he looked at me with undisguised loathing. "Get out of here - now!" he ordered. "Don't come back or you will be arrested. Is that clear?"

"If yow saya so, mayet," replied Stan, as if totally unfazed by our situation. He thumped me hard on the arm. "Cum on, yow daft bat, this bugger is in two minds wither to shoot us or not." He looked up at the corporal. "Can ay git me snares?"

"Just disappear." The corporal gestured towards the road with the Sten.

"Owt yow saya, mayet, special like yew've a bluddy gun." Stan headed for the road giving me a sharp kick as he did so. "Cum on, twat fayace!"

What made me do what I did next is still a mystery to me. Instead of following Stan, I walked slowly towards the corporal and stretched out my filthy left hand. He raised the Sten's stubby barrel to cover me. I reached out slowly and ran my finger lightly over the barrel cooler, my finger dropping into each hole. All the time I peered into his eyes and smiled my fool's smile. Then I turned slowly away from him and began to follow Stan. The farmer had stopped to watch my stupid little scenario. I could see the fear in his eyes. Just as I reached him, I turned and waved farewell to the corporal, who was watching us with a mixture of suspicion and abhorrence.

Stan gave me an almighty kick up the arse and I went sprawling. "Git up theer, yew bastard idiot."

I needed no more urging. I ran ahead and leapt aboard the tractor. Stan joined me and jerked us into motion. We roared away as fast as the old Fordson could manage.

We said nothing for the next three or four miles as we drove through the now even more intense rain and sleet. We were on a tiny lane, which ran beside a drain. A building was appearing up ahead. It was an isolated, large, wooden barn-like structure. No other farm buildings, just the shed. Stan swung the tractor and trailer over the little bridge leading to the shed.

"Open it up," he ordered curtly.

I jumped down and opened the doors. Apart from an old binder, the shed was empty.

"Unhitch the trailer," Stan shouted.

I did as I was told and he drove the tractor into the shed. He jumped down and moved to switch off the fuel supply. As he closed the doors behind us the tractor engine, starved of fuel, died. The rain hammered on the corrugated iron roof and the tractor ticked as it cooled.

"You fucking stupid, young bastard!" Stan shouted at me. "What the fuck were you playing at?"

I climbed up on the binder and sat on the seat. I removed the soaking sack and threw it tiredly onto the canvas bed, which carried the cut crop to the section where it was packed tight, bound with twine and the resulting sheaf tossed out to be stooked.

"I don't know, Stan. I honestly don't know."

"At a distance, you just about pass muster but close up you were taking a stupid bloody risk." He shook his head in disbelief. "I can't believe you did that. Have you got a fucking death wish or something?"

I sat dejectedly on the binder. I began to feel uneasy. Maybe I did have a death wish. It had been a stupid thing to do and I 'd no rational explanation for my action. I remained silent.

Stan paced the barn but every now and then stopped and peered through the gap in the doors.

"What the hell are you doing?" I finally asked.

"Do you think they won't check on us?" he asked in disbelief at my stupidity. He was right of course. He pointed back down the road. "They're bound to check that we've left the area. There are four different ways of getting back to my place so they'll have their work cut out. I suggest we stay here until nightfall."

"Nightfall!" I exploded. "Foghorn will be going frantic."

He didn't need to answer as we both heard it at the same time. I joined Stan at the crack in the doors in time to see a motorcycle coming fast along the fen road. It roared past the barn and riding it was the unmistakable form of the corporal. He didn't even look at the barn.

Stan turned and looked at me but there was no need for him to speak.

I felt ashamed of myself. "Sorry, Stan. You're right, we stay here."

He just nodded and we settled down to a very cold wait. We were wet through and the leaky barn didn't do anything to shelter us from the cold wind whipping in from the east.

We had a fright when we heard the motorcycle returning but it roared past. Once more the rider totally ignored the barn. We breathed a collective sigh of relief.

We left the barn once it was really dark and, although the rain had stopped, the wind was icy cold and it began to freeze. We were like frigid automatons when we finally arrived back at the farm.

Foghorn was waiting in the darkness by the front door as we walked stiffly back from the tractor shed. "Where the fuck have you been?" she demanded angrily.

"For Christ's sake, girl," said a very tired little farmer. "Let's get inside. Maybe then we can tell you all about it."

In the hall I raised a hand to silence her protest. "A large fire and a cup of tea are what we want, not bloody questions."

She realised the state we were in and soon had us by the roaring fire. Dog was going frantic trying to welcome both of us at once.

"I hope you don't mind, Stan," said Foghorn. "I filled the copper with water and lit the fire. I thought you'd both need a warm bath."

Stan put his arms around her, well as far as he could, and laid his head on her shoulder."You're a bloody marvel."

"I try," she said and winked at me over his shoulder. "I found two tin baths outside in the outhouse and I've put them in the back by the copper."

He took his arm from around her. "You'd better bring one in here." He looked embarrassed.

"Rubbish," I said quickly "I'm not a blushing violet and you're too tired to start anything, so let's just get on with it."

I ignored the surprise on Foghorn's face and gave Stan no more time to argue. I walked straight through to the utility room where the copper was situated. It was a sort of large cauldron, full of hot, steaming water, surrounded by bricks with a fire burning brightly beneath it. Foghorn followed and as soon as I started to undress, she whistled.

"Bollocks," I replied with a laugh. I just wanted her to get the bath filled.

"Well, Petal, we should see two if you keep whipping things off at that pace."

"I shall stop at the important bits, don't you worry."

"Second time you've been a spoilsport today," she quipped.

"Knickers!" I replied.

"I'm keeping those on," she retorted with a laugh.

"Thank God for that." I joined in her laughter. She began filling the two baths with a small bucket. Hot water from the copper and cold water from the pump in the corner.

"Now - out!" I said firmly as she finished filling the baths.

"Alright, I'm going. That makes it three times you've been a spoilsport now. I'm going right off you!" But she left and closed the door.

"And close the door properly," I shouted after her.

There was a snort of laughter and the door clicked properly shut.

I noticed Stan was still fully dressed. This was my chance to put him at ease.

"Come on, Stan, get 'em off, we haven't got all night!"

I was already totally naked and I stepped gingerly into my bath of hot water. I saw him quickly avert his eyes from my nakedness and he began to strip off his clothes. There wasn't an ounce of fat on the little guy. He had muscles where I'd never have muscles. His tanned face and arms were in sharp contrast to the whiteness of his torso and legs. I noticed as he slid into the water that he carefully shielded his genitals from my view. I smiled to myself. I knew I had no reason to fear that any embarrassment would arise to spoil our friendship and I felt a sense of relief. I sighed as I lay back in the bath and wallowed in the warmth of the water. Thank God Foghorn had foreseen our need.

Later, towelled dry and in dry clothes, we sat around the fire in the parlour. Houseman had joined us. He'd rushed over in response to Foghorn's phone call to the camp to tell him we were back. A job I should have done but my brain seemed to be on strike. I related the events and Stan added the extra bit that I'd sooner have left out. When we got to the bit where I'd touched the gun, Foghorn called me a 'silly bugger' but quickly apologised to Houseman for the indiscretion. She wisely kept quiet for the rest of the narrative.

Houseman rose as I finished. "May I use your phone, Mr Cornish?"

"Of course," replied Stan as he stood and opened the door to the hall. "It's down there. Will that small paraffin light be enough for you?"

"More than enough, thank you," Houseman said as he closed the door behind him.

As we sat in silence, we could hear the murmur of his voice above the crackling of the log on the open fire. Dog yawned and put his head on my knee. I guessed that Face had been waiting for Houseman's call. Well, now it was up to them. I'd done my bit. I felt my eyelids begin to droop as the effects of the warm bath, the roaring fire and the soft light of the paraffin lamp began to take their toll. I stifled a yawn and saw

Stan watching me. He smiled and nodded towards Foghorn. No wonder she had been quiet - she was fast asleep in her chair.

"What happens now?" Stan asked quietly.

"They'll send in a raiding party to take the airstrip and whoever is there. They were putting a team together last night."

Stan stared into the flames. "It's a rum do, isn't it? A bloody enemy airstrip right under our noses."

I yawned again. "I agree, but it's very isolated down there and what local would ask questions? Those that set up the airstrip must have known it couldn't last long. It was a planned short-term operation. Once they felt they'd pushed their luck as far as they dared, they would've closed the operation down and moved on. Thanks to you, we found it before they had time to move on and cover their tracks."

"Not soon enough though," he answered sadly. "A lot of young men died."

"That is the way it goes in war, Stan. You can never be sure what the enemy has up his sleeve."

"What happens to you now?" he asked glancing up from the flames.

"Back to normal, I hope. I'm not cut out for this counter espionage game. I value my life too much."

"Nothing wrong with that philosophy. You make the best of your life now because if you keep putting things off until another day, you're soon too old to enjoy that day. Time flies as you get older."

The door opened and Houseman came back into the room. He glanced at Foghorn slumped in her chair and smiled. "Sleeping Beauty," he whispered.

"You smooth talking little tinker," muttered Foghorn as she opened one baleful eye.

Houseman actually blushed with embarrassment and we laughed as he fought to find the words to reply but he failed. He too, with all his experience, had never before met anybody like Foghorn.

"Ahem!.....er... exactly." He fiddled with a pen in his tunic pocket. He managed to regain his composure. "The team's on its way. They are using a Special Air Service team. Face persuaded the army brass it would be good training for them."

"When will we know the result?" I asked, looking at my watch.

Houseman checked his watch too. "If we get back to the section, we can wait for the reports to come in. Wing Commander Face has promised to keep me posted. He sends you his congratulations."

"Nothing to do with me, sir. It was Stan here who did all the work. The disguises, the transport and the strategy - he was responsible for the lot. I just went along for the ride and played the village idiot. Seems I did a good job of that, though I feel it was simply good typecasting."

I saw Foghorn open her mouth.

"Don't even think it, Bourne," I warned.

Her mouth clamped shut and I saw a flicker of a smile cross Houseman's face. He turned to Stan. "He's right, Mr Cornish. You did far more than anybody could reasonably have expected of you. We're going to be heavily in your debt."

"Rubbish," exclaimed the farmer. "I'm pleased there was something I could do to help. It has certainly made life a lot more interesting than just farming. The only excitement I get here is the weather report on the wireless."

Houseman looked at him in silence for a few seconds. When he spoke there was no doubting the respect in his voice. "It was a bloody dangerous thing you did today. You're not a serviceman. Damn it, you're not even in the Home Guard! It was

179

unreasonable for us to even consider putting your life at risk. I'm afraid the responsibility for that must rest on Carver's shoulders. Thankfully, in spite of everything, you came up trumps. What we must never forget is that it could just as easily have gone the other way."

Stan stood as if to terminate the conversation. "I did what I felt was right and thankfully we were successful. I've a house full of people for the first time since my parents died. I've a promise of unlimited pints of beer from young Sam and a young lady who makes me laugh. What more rewards could a man want?"

Houseman smiled. "We're still grateful, Mr Cornish, and I know you'll be officially rewarded at a later date. Unfortunately, your houseguests must now vanish into the night. I'm afraid duty calls."

I shook myself fully awake and rose to my feet. I held out a hand to Cornish. "Thanks, Stan, for everything."

He took my hand. "It has been a pleasure, lad."

Foghorn hauled herself out of her chair and Dog, who had been laid across her feet, moved reluctantly with a faint groan of protest.

Houseman laughed. "I know how he feels."

We climbed into our cars and, with a little 'beep' on the horn, we took our leave of the farmer.

We were on the main road when Foghorn spoke. "Have you told Stan about 'you-know-what'?"

I watched a startled rabbit shoot across the road in the glimmer from the headlights. "We both understand the situation, if that's what you mean? What he is makes no difference to me. He's a grand little guy and I'm pleased I have him as a friend. He knows the situation as far as I'm concerned and I know there will never be any reason for him to feel uncomfortable with our friendship. What I'm trying to say is that we both know where we stand."

I heard her sigh. "I'm pleased about that. He's really sweet to me and treats me like his big sister. He's needed and longed for companionship all these years and at last he's finally got it. The nice thing is, the chap really deserves the break."

I didn't reply immediately. I just sat there and wondered at the complex woman by my side. I was seeing that other facet of her character that others seldom saw and most would never see. Here was a gentleness one would never know existed unless privy to a special moment like this. Gone were the loud voice, the coarse speech and the obscenities. For a few special seconds Foghorn was as feminine as she was ever going to be.

"You're a bit of an old softie, really," I said quietly.

"You tell anybody and I'll kick you in the trinkets," she said with a laugh.

I laughed with her. That special moment had been the briefest of glimpses through the occasional chink in her armour but I had enjoyed it. I tried out my best Jimmy Durante impression. "Dat's my girl!"

We roared with laughter the rest of the way back to West Fen.

It was around midnight when Face and Piper returned to the intelligence section. Both looked frozen to the marrow.

"How did it go, sir?" Houseman asked eagerly.

Face removed his gloves, shoved them in the pocket of his greatcoat and hung it on the hook behind the door. He said nothing until he had planted his backside firmly on the hot radiator under the window.

"Ahhh," he sighed. "These ruddy fens are so cold. That wind has got to be straight off the Russian steppes." We waited patiently and he grinned ruefully. "The element of surprise went well. The army lads were in quickly and quietly. There was a short and very one-sided firefight in which one of the enemy died. They also captured one Hawker Hurricane fighter."

"Brilliant!" exclaimed Houseman as he looked at me and rubbed his hands together with pleasure.

"That's the good news," Piper interjected quietly.

We looked at him in surprise. What could be wrong with that?

Face moved to a chair and wearily sat down. "The dead man was the only enemy at the site. It does not take a brilliant mind to appreciate that just one man couldn't have guarded the field and serviced all the aircraft's systems by himself. There has to be at least one other man, but where is he?"

"The dead man," I interrupted his thoughts. "Was he a big guy?"

He shook his head. " 'Fraid not. Bit of a titch actually."

"Did they find a motorcycle?" I pressed.

Again there was that shake of the head. "No motorcycle and I know what you're going to say next. You saw a big guy on a motorcycle?"

I nodded. "Yes, sir."

"Shit!" he muttered. "He must have left the area before we got there. Still, if he returns he'll run straight into an ambush. The SAS have the place under surveillance to nab anybody who comes near."

Piper glanced at Face, saw he had finished and took up the story. "We've a feeling that they were already about to pull out and close the site. Which leads me to suspect that the big guy made a quick getaway under some pretext or other and left the little guy to be the patsy."

"What makes you say that?" asked Houseman.

"The Hurricane," Piper replied. "According to my colleague here, it was knackered."

Houseman looked at Face who nodded. "Engine was shot to bits. Bloody miracle the pilot ever got it back to the strip. Mason's gunners earned their flying pay last night."

"Any chance the dead guy was the pilot?" I asked without real conviction.

Face shook his head. "I'm afraid not, Carver. He wore glasses with lenses like the bottom of a gin bottle."

There was a silence as we wrestled with our thoughts. One man was dead and at least one more on the run. Maybe he was not on the run. Maybe he knew nothing of the raid. One thing was for sure; the guy we'd seen with the Sten gun would never have fitted into the cramped cockpit of a Hurricane.

"Where did they get the Hurricane?" I asked.

Face shrugged. "Until we check out the engine and airframe serial numbers, we can't possibly know. It was probably damaged and captured in France when the Germans overran our airfields. Maybe it had crash-landed and the pilot was unable to destroy it before being taken prisoner. Who knows? They must have repaired the kite and flown it in during darkness. They didn't have much in the way of tools but by heck, they had plenty of ammo. Boxes and boxes of belted ammo for the machine guns although their avgas situation was getting critical, as was the diesel for their generator."

"What about radio kit?" asked Houseman.

"Not what we expected," replied Face. "There was a short range set plus the kit in the Hurricane. I checked the cockpit and made a quick check of the hangar but there was no evidence of a long range set or, more important, codebooks. That disappointed me. I really thought we would find something of that nature. It all points to the chap you saw getting out before the raid and taking the important bits with him."

"Now what, sir?" I asked.

"Well, somehow we're going to have to bring in a covert team to begin sifting through the records of the personnel on this station. Without a doubt, there is a source here passing information to the enemy. We'll insert a team to see what they can find. I'm afraid they will be known only to MI5 and Special Branch."

There was a sudden knock at the door and we all jumped.

"Who the hell is that at this time of night?" Piper grumbled as he glanced at his watch.

Houseman rose and headed for the door. "This place never sleeps." He opened the door. "Ah, Sergeant Powell, what can we do for you?"

"Telephone call for Wing Commander Face, sir. Thought I'd better check before putting it through."

"It's okay, Sarge. Tell the switchboard to put it through."

"Right away, sir."

Houseman resumed his seat and we waited for the telephone to ring. When it did, Face picked up the receiver.

"Face" He listened for some time and, as he sat there, he turned his head until his gaze rested on me. His eyes never left my face as he sat there with the receiver to his ear. Finally, he switched his gaze away and spoke into the phone. "Thank you very much." He replaced the receiver and returned his gaze to me. "Carver, that was the pathologist's report from the Norman Troutbridge postmortom."

He paused and looked tired but he shook his head as if to clear his thoughts. "I told them I wanted the results as soon as they came through, whatever the time of day. Norman Troutbridge didn't die in that canal or drain or whatever the bloody things are called. He did drown but the water in his lungs was domestic quality and not the crap one would get from the drain. He had four cracked ribs and all the fingers on his right hand had been forced backwards until they snapped. There were also burn marks on his genitals." He still stared at me. "You were right, Carver. He had been professionally and systematically tortured. His death must have been a relief after the torture he'd been put through."

"Poor bastard," muttered Houseman. "All because of a bloody helmet he was wearing as a joke."

"The fact his family had to die too completes the tragedy," I added.

Piper knocked his briar out in the ashtray. "He must have told them he'd discussed with his brother where he had actually found the helmet. That sealed the family's fate."

"How the hell do we find the bastards who did this?" I asked angrily.

"You don't, Carver," replied Face levelly. "That is now a job for David here and myself."

"So I can go back to being a real intelligence officer, sir?" I asked with a sigh of relief.

Face laughed. "I think so, Carver. You've done a superb job for us but I'm afraid you've now done all you can. It is our job now to uncover the cell operating locally and that takes trained personnel. I say that with no disrespect to you, young man."

"Thank you, sir." I knew he meant it.

Piper grinned. "More time with the girlfriend, eh?"

"You should be a mind reader, sir!"

Face stood and collected their coats from behind the door. He looked at me as he struggled into his coat. "We'll need a full report on yesterday's activities, Carver. I think I'd better send in a couple of my men to take it all down in the form of a statement." He held out his hand as I stood up from the table. "Thank you again - you did a great job. If you had not come up with your seemingly crazy theory, we would still be in the dark and more aircrew would be getting the chop."

He turned to Houseman. "You too, Jake. Thank God you had the nous to believe in this young officer. Your recce was the icing on the cake."

"Thank you, sir," replied Houseman. "I'll see you both out."

As they left Houseman said quietly, "Get yourself back to the mess and get some rest. I'll talk to you in the morning."

I suddenly felt completely exhausted. The wounds to my back were playing up and the headache was back with a vengeance. I glanced at my watch. It was four in the morning. Time to take Houseman's advice.

He was nowhere to be seen when I emerged into the night but there, on the parking space to one side of the path, was my little Fiat. Bourne was still huddled behind the wheel. I rapped on the window and she jerked awake.

"What on earth are you doing still here?" I asked in disbelief.

"Waiting for you, Petal. I knew you'd be tired so I stayed on to give you a lift back to the mess."

"Good God, girl, you should have been in bed ages ago. You must be bloody freezing out here?"

"Stop wittering on, I'm a big girl. Do get in, man, or are you going to stand out there all soddin' night?"

I climbed in as quickly as my stiff body would permit. "Thanks," I said quietly. "I really do appreciate you staying on."

She chuckled. "Don't go soft on me now, I didn't bring a hankie."

I sighed. "I give up with you."

She laughed. "Why should you be any different to the rest of the air force?"

There was nothing to say to that.

She dropped me off outside the mess with a quick. "Goodnight, Petal."

I tottered off to my room and having dumped my clothes in a heap on the floor, I crawled into bed. I was asleep before my head hit the pillow.

CHAPTER FOURTEEN

The next morning I was pleased to find Natalie already at work when I arrived in the section. I dumped my cap and coat and joined her by a chart table.

"Hi, need any help?"

She glanced up and smiled. "From what I've been hearing on the grapevine, it's you who's in need of a little help."

"Typical me, I'm afraid, always in the wrong place at the wrong time."

"How do you feel, really?" she asked, casting me an anxious look.

"Bit battered but at least I had a good sleep in spite of the little time I had in bed. Must have been last night's excitement."

She placed a hand over mine as I leaned on the table. "Is it true about the Troutbridge family?"

I nodded. "I'm afraid so."

She shook her head in disbelief. "How could a family be so unlucky? The poor lady was just about at the end of her tether when we saw her."

"It was sod all to do with luck," I said grimly. "Their fate was premeditated murder by a bunch of heartless bloody killers."

She looked up quickly and there was a frown on her face. "What are you talking about?"

I pretended to help her with her work as I quietly outlined the story to her.

She was silent for a long time. Then she asked the question I'd been asking myself. "Do you think the Red Lion is at the hub of all this?"

"I don't know," I sighed. "He could have been anywhere before we saw him. Still, it is academic now. I'm finished with all the cloak and dagger stuff, thank God!"

She looked at me and grinned. "Does that mean we can…?"

I grinned as I interrupted her. "From now on, we can have all our spare time together. Shall we start tonight?"

"I'm afraid not, Carver." Houseman's voice came from behind me and I spun round in surprise. He gave Natalie an apologetic smile. "Sorry, young lady, I'm afraid he's going to be busy for the rest of the day and well into the evening."

I sighed and smiled ruefully. "I don't suppose you're at all jealous of my liaison with Section Officer Cowen, sir? I can think of no other reason why you should keep knocking all our plans on the head."

"Of course I'm jealous, Carver, but I'm not responsible for this interruption to your pathetic attempts at romance. I've just had a call from our friends. It seems they are desirous of your services again and so I need you in my office for briefing."

"See you later?" I asked hopefully of Natalie.

"I'll be here all day and most of the night as both squadrons are on ops tonight. It seems we're both trapped."

Once we were seated in Houseman's office, he got down to business. "The two men coming to take your statement will be here about half eleven. I reckon it will take most of the day to complete the task."

"You said something about this evening, sir."

"Hold your horses, Carver, I'm coming to that. It seems the team out at Tumby has completed a thorough search of the cottage site. They have boxed all the evidence that may help them to identify the explosive used, where it came from and the placement of the charges. Wing Commander Face wants those boxes of evidence to be brought here for the night. They'll set up an incident room in the old Met Office hut."

"I gather from this that he wants me to collect the boxes?"

Houseman nodded. "Right first time. I've arranged for Bourne to drive you in a Tilly. The boxes will not be ready for collection until 18.00 hours so I've arranged for her to pick you up here at 17.00. By the way, the wing commander wanted me to stress that there will be no body tissue in the boxes. That is to be stored, what there is of it, in Boston mortuary."

I grimaced. "He's so thoughtful, for a wing commander."

He laughed. "Beware of thoughtful senior officers – they're likely to give you a shitty job."

I leaned conspiratorially towards him. "By the way, sir. How does it feel to be one of Bourne's favourite people? What was it she called you? 'Little tinker', wasn't it?"

He grinned. "You let that out of the bag, Carver, and I'll have you posted to bloody Iceland."

"Actually, sir, I was thinking of a little blackmail. You know, extra leave, nights off with Natalie - that sort of thing."

"Dream on, young man," he scoffed. "Now go and get Wing Commander Janner's old room into shape for your visitors. Anything you need, just ask Sergeant Powell."

I suddenly realised I knew nothing of Janner's fate since the briefing. "What exactly happened to Janner, sir?"

Houseman didn't look up. "He's confined to the mess until he can be disposed of somewhere else in this huge organisation called the Royal Air Force. Hammond and Jones were given the task of clearing out his office and he'll never return to this section."

I left to get on with the rest of the day and tried not to smirk with satisfaction.

Houseman had been right. The statement took six bloody hours and I was heartily sick of the whole exercise. They questioned me in detail and then laboriously wrote everything down in longhand. Every damned thing had to be exact and it was all very trying on my patience. The pain in my back had become intolerable and I began to get irritable with them. It was with great relief that I finally signed each page, top and bottom and the declaration at the end. I nearly cheered as they left the room. I was about to dash up the corridor for a few stolen moments with Natalie, when Sergeant Powell stuck his head round the door.

"Your transport is outside, sir."

"Oh, shit!"

Tom looked a bit pissed off so I quickly apologised, grabbed my cap and coat and headed outside to where Bourne was waiting.

As I limped towards the vehicle, pulling on my gloves, she leapt from her seat and whipped the passenger door open for me.

"Don't go over the top, please," I begged. "I'm not quite an invalid."

"In a nasty bloody mood, though," she said casually. "Face like a camel's arse with haemorrhoids."

"When did you last see a camel, Bourne?" I asked as I lowered myself carefully into my seat.

"Every day, sir. She's the warrant officer in charge of the Waafery. She's even got the two humps. Mind you they are on the front but she can spit fifty yards upwind."

I started to laugh in spite of my lousy mood. Trust Foghorn to put things into perspective.

We chatted amiably as we drove to Tumby and somehow the conversation turned to the subject of our respective experiences of childhood. I told her how, when I was small, my father always ensured that he and I shared the last hour before I went to bed. In the summer we would kick a ball on the lawn or cycle round the neighbourhood. In the winter we played table tennis or word games.

"My father used to play with me," Foghorn said quietly.

"Hey, that's nice. It seems we..." My voice tailed away as the timbre of her voice suddenly hit me. "Oh God, no!" I said as I turned to look at her. It was getting quite dark and I think I was pleased I couldn't see the expression on her face.

"From the age of seven," she added bitterly.

It was a long time before I could reply. I knew I had to say something but I was lost for a suitable response. "Could you not have told your mother?" I finally asked.

"I did, when I was twelve. She called me a lying little cow and beat the shit out of me. She then had me put in a home as being unmanageable."

"Hell, I'm sorry," I said quietly.

"Put it down to life's rich tapestry," she replied shortly.

"No wonder you're forever fighting authority. It seems nobody in authority was there for you when you needed them, but you can't fight them all forever. What happens when there are none left to fight?"

"Fight with myself, I suppose," she answered as she turned into the track leading to the cottage.

I decided to let it rest right there. I concentrated instead on the glimmer of torches as the last of the team prepared to depart.

"There is a ray of sunshine on the horizon," I started as Foghorn's announcement took me by surprise.

"That is?" I prompted her.

"Stan Cornish has said I can move in with him if we ever win this bloody war. He reckons we're two of a kind. He also reckons, mind you I think he's barmy, that I'll make a good farmer."

"Not a good wife?" I asked in a moment of rashness.

She guffawed. "Hardly likely, Petal - neither of us would know where to put what!"

I decided not to push my luck. "Well, I'm really pleased for both of you."

"We've got to win the war first," she replied as she braked the Tilly to a halt.

A hooded torch shone briefly on my face as I climbed from the vehicle. It was Jack.

"Hello, Carver. Just the two small boxes for you. The other stuff has already been despatched to Boston."

One of his men unlashed the tarpaulin covering the tailboard of the Tilly and stashed two small boxes in the back.

"Not much to show that a happy family once lived here," I said quietly.

"No, I'm afraid not," Jack agreed. "We think we've sufficient human remains, albeit fragmented, to confirm the presence of the entire family. The bits in your boxes are shreds of wire and bits of bomb which will give up some of the secret once we get them under a microscope, so please take care of them, young man. Goodnight."

We climbed back into the Tilly and waited until their Bedford lorry ground away down the track towards the road.

I suddenly opened my door. "Will you excuse me for a minute?"

"Yeah, of course, Petal," replied Bourne, failing to keep the surprise out of her voice.

It was now very dark but I groped my way to the edge of the crater. The only prayers I knew were from my childhood and they seemed totally inadequate. So I just stood there with my head bowed and hoped my thoughts would somehow reach the Troutbridge family - wherever they were now.

I don't know how long I stood there in the darkness, as I seemed to lose all sense of time. My mind and body were exhausted from my experiences over the last few days but I suddenly felt a deep sense of peace. I hoped it was God's way of telling me that the family were safe in that place we only believe exists when we're children. Maybe I still believed in a life after death. Maybe there was a heaven. There again, maybe I was just hedging my bets. The darkness seemed to envelop me and I became impervious to the cold. I could hear the wind sighing through the trees of the copse and the rattle of a recalcitrant dead leaf as it clung resolutely to a stark branch. I let my senses slide until I was totally engulfed by my newfound peace.

Then the nerve ends at the periphery of my senses began to pick up a faint rumbling in the distance. At first it gently stirred the night air but soon it became thunder as the first Lancaster bombers, heavily pregnant with death, began to claw their way into the night sky of Lincolnshire. My peace was shattered, as soon would be the peace of Germany. Suddenly, once more I could feel the cold and I shivered violently. I turned and picked my way carefully through the darkness and back to the Tilly.

"I've got an idea," I said as I closed the passenger door.

"Steady, Petal," laughed Bourne." The most dangerous thing in the world is an officer with an idea."

I ignored her. "We'll stop at the Red Lion in Revesby. Balls to service etiquette and all that crap. You and I are going to have a drink together."

"You don't get feelings of unbridled passion after a drink, do you?" Bourne pretended excitement.

"Certainly not!" I replied, matching her pretence. "I'm an officer and a gentleman."

"Bugger it," she sighed. "I'm just in the mood for a bit of rumpy-pumpy."

"You're disgusting," I laughed. "Anyway, I thought I wasn't on the menu as far as your tastes are concerned."

She was totally unfazed by the barb. "Any port in a storm, Petal."

"I still think you're disgusting."

"No, Petal," she grunted as we bumped off down the track. "The word is 'disappointed'."

When we arrived at the Red Lion we had an immediate problem - where to hide the Tilly from the ever prying eyes of the RAF Police.

"Stick it down there by the toilets," I directed Foghorn.

As we entered the pub, I saw a hissing pressurised lamp instead of the paraffin lamps that had been the only source of light during my last visit. After blinking a few times in the bright light, I was pleased to see that, once more, there were no service personnel in the pub. We received a brief and perfunctory visual interrogation by the locals present but they soon returned to their dominoes and darts. It looked as if the men playing dominoes were the same chaps I'd seen on my last visit. The males of Lincolnshire were definitely men of habit.

I bought a couple of pints of beer as Foghorn had given me a derisory look when I'd suggested a gin and tonic for her. As we sat down, I noticed I was facing a large mirror on the far wall. In it, I was able to check newcomers as they entered the bar but there was nobody to bother us. An officer drinking with an airwoman, both on duty, could have serious repercussions. Not that I gave a shit but it was all the hassle that followed such a breach of service etiquette. As more patrons arrived, I tired of watching my back and gave my full attention to Foghorn's bottomless archival abyss of jokes. Some were a bit near the knuckle and some were positively disgusting but on the whole she kept me pleasurably entertained. At one point I saw her glance up and frown towards the doorway behind me but when I glanced in the mirror, the doorway and passageway were empty again. Another pint later my bladder began to give warnings and I stood up from the table.

"Excuse me, I'm just going to the little boys' room."

I was surprised she didn't make a rude comment. She just nodded and seemed preoccupied with something. I thought little of it because it was typical of the mercurial Foghorn.

I shivered as I walked out into the night. It was freezing hard again and I could see the frost already whitening the tilt of the Tilly. I groped my way into the outside 'Gents' and was surprised to see a tiny paraffin lamp under the cistern. It provided very little light but I guessed it gave off enough heat to prevent the cistern freezing. I grinned to myself at the thought that maybe the light had been placed there to help gentlemen find their shrunken equipment on a cold night. Bloody hell, I was getting as bad as Foghorn.

I emptied my bladder and was just buttoning my flies when I got that prickly feeling again in the hairs on the back of my neck. I began to turn but it was too late. An arm clamped around my neck from behind. I felt the bulk of a body press me up against the back wall of the urinal and the pressure from the arm became intense. The musty smell of my assailant's clothing promptly vanished as I lost the ability to breathe. I tried a sweeping kick behind me but to no avail. The arm simply tightened even more. I tried dropping quickly to the ground to break the hold but it was a futile gesture as he was now holding me so high I was on tiptoe. I began to lose my vision and the blood was pounding in my head. I felt his left hand slide around to cup my jaw and, even in my semiconscious state, I knew what was coming next - a quick wrench up and to the left and my neck would snap like a dry twig. I wanted to cry out but it was impossible. I could feel tears beginning to flow down my cheeks as a total feeling of helplessness swept through me. Dear God, I didn't want to die. I felt the fingers of his left hand tense as he readied himself for the coup de grace. He began the movement. I heard him grunt as a loud crack echoed in the confines of the toilet and I knew no more.

If this was heaven then I hoped God had a decent fire ready as my bloody feet were freezing. Maybe I'd gone to the other place and the story of the great inferno was a crock of shit. I was also soaking wet and there was a rasping sound as if somebody had severe asthma. I'd a strange feeling it was me. A voice was hissing at me from afar. If it was St Peter, then the guy had better get his act together, as I couldn't hear a bloody thing he was saying. Then I thought I heard the name 'Petal' and my heart sank. Bloody hell; don't tell me they let people like Foghorn in here. What was heaven coming to? Trust them to lower the standards the very day I arrived here.

"Petal! For fuck's sake speak to me!"

"Arrrff!" I replied.

"Can you get up, you daft sod?" I knew that voice - it was definitely Foghorn.

"Arrrff!" I replied yet again. I was doing my best but my vocal chords didn't seem to be working as they should. I felt her place her arms under my armpits and slowly, with very little help from me, she got me to my feet. My head was spinning and I nearly took us both back down into the urinal. I grabbed the cistern pipe for support and, after a few seconds of serious concentration, the flame of the little paraffin lamp stopped hurtling around the piss house. Now, it just swayed from side to side.

"Arrrff!" I croaked and made a determined effort to get to the door but nearly went arse over tit. This time it was not from my reeling senses but because some prat was lying on the floor. Silly bugger must be pissed out of his brain. I stepped unsteadily over the inert form and continued my desperate trek to the door.

"Oi! Hang on a fuckin' minute," Foghorn hissed. "What are we going to do with him?"

I looked at her blankly but then a few seeds started to fall on fertile ground. I looked down at the man and tried to roll him over with my foot. The rule of opposite forces came into play - he stayed where he was and I reeled away, back in the direction of the urinal.

"Oh, for fuck's sake!" muttered Foghorn as she stooped and heaved the inert form face up.

"Arrrff!" I said in alarm. The last time I had seen that face, it had been behind a Sten gun in the wood at the airstrip. Not the last time actually, thinking about it. He'd been on the motorbike that had roared past the barn. Strangely, I seemed to have a need to get the facts straight. I shook my head to clear the lingering tendrils of fog that still clouded my brain. I motioned to Foghorn that we must pick him up and take him outside.

"Who the hell is he?" she hissed at me.

I could feel my vocal chords were not up to an oral response, so I raised one arm in a Nazi salute and put two fingers under my nose for a moustache. I thought she was going to crack up with mirth but then her eyes opened wide with shock.

"Shit!" she whispered and glanced back down at the inert form of my assailant. She soon got over her shock and ran to the door for a quick glance outside. All was clear. So, with her at his head and me at his feet, we struggled to haul the comatose giant outside. We finally dumped him by the tailgate of the Tilly. I had just untied the rear flap of the tilt when the pub door opened and voices boomed out into the night. I looked at Foghorn in alarm but her response was to throw me up against the Tilly and clamp her lips on mine in a frenzied kiss. I couldn't even manage an "Arrrff!"

The two men peered in our direction and laughed as they walked off into the night.

"Lucky bastard," I heard one say.

"Hope his cock don't snap off in this frost," laughed his friend.

Foghorn finally released me from our impromptu osculation and went back to hissing like a very pissed off snake. "Grab him, you daft twat. Don't just stand there with your mouth open."

"Arrrff!" I said with feeling.

We struggled to get the man over the tailboard and as we did so, I got a closer look at his face. It looked a very funny colour and I knew, without taking his pulse, he was as dead as a doornail. At last the seriousness of our situation got through to me and I started frantically searching the pub car park.

"What the hell are you looking for now - and don't say fuckin' 'Arrrff' again?" It was obvious Foghorn was getting more than a little pissed off.

I made a mime of riding a motorcycle.

She cottoned on immediately and it was her who found it in the yard behind the pub. We did have a problem though - there were two motorcycles. It never rains without it pours!

"Which one, Sherlock?" Foghorn sighed with impatience.

I peered in the darkness at the two bikes. The one our corpse had been riding the day he roared past the barn, when he was still alive and kicking, had been a powerful bike. Both the bikes in the pub yard were powerful but one of them I could see was a twin. He'd not been riding a twin.

"Arrrff!" I pointed and we wheeled the correct bike back to the Tilly. How we got the heavy bike into the back of the Tilly, already full with sample boxes and the body, I'll never know, but we did it. I slammed the tailgate shut and tied the tilt back into place.

"Bloody hell, Petal," Foghorn panted. "I'm knackered. You certainly know how to give a girl an exciting night out!"

"Arrrff!" I croaked.

She sighed and grinned. "Unfortunately, it is a big turn off when you insist on sounding like a bloody castrated walrus."

It must have been the sudden release of tension but for some inexplicable reason I began to laugh. Well, at least, I attempted to laugh.

"Arrff! arrrff! arrrff!" I croaked and shook with mirth.

It started Foghorn off and we collapsed up against the Tilly in paroxysms of laughter.

"What exactly is going on here?" asked a plummy voice from the darkness.

Foghorn recovered from surprise first and flicked on her hooded torch. In its dim beam we had a brief glimpse of three rings on a blue RAF greatcoat. Shit! What was a wing commander doing out here? Two other officers accompanied him. Their uniforms were immaculate so I knew they were definitely not aircrew. That meant they would be suffering from a serious lack of humour. They must be admin types billeted in the village.

"Put that light out!" snapped the senior officer. "Who the hell are you?"

I seemed to find this hilarious too. "Arrff! arrrff! arrrff!" I was off again.

Foghorn quickly stepped in. "Aircraftswoman Trenchard, sir. This is Pilot Officer Harris. He's recently had a tracheotomy and is only just out of hospital."

One of the minions decided to get in on the act. "Where are you stationed?"

Prissy bastard!

"We're part of the East Kirkby forward party, sir." Foghorn sounded very convincing.

"Right," snapped the wing commander. "Get in your vehicle and get back to your unit. I'll be in touch with your unit commander in the morning."

Thankfully they stalked off into the warmth of the pub. What a trio of wankers.

"Yes, sir," Foghorn answered meekly and raised two fingers in a very unladylike salute.

"Arrrff!" was all I could manage. I just wondered how long it would take for the penny to drop that Foghorn had given the names of two of the RAF's most senior officers. Thank God they'd not asked for any ID.

Foghorn had the same thought. "Good thing he didn't ask for our twelve-fifties. I don't think we could get three more in the back!"

"Arrrfff! arrrff!" I went into more strangled hoots of laughter.

Foghorn shone her torch in my face. "I think I preferred your posh accent, Petal. At least I could hold a conversation with you." She shone the torch up at the pub sign. "Pity this isn't the Rising Sun at Stickney."

"Arrrff?" What the hell was she going on about?

"You know," she gave me a wolfish grin. "Beware the Hun in the Sun?"

It was too much and I was still 'Arrrffing' when she pushed me into the passenger seat of the Tilly.

As we drove back to West Fen, I was frantically trying to think of plan to get us through the gate without the SPs looking in the back of the truck.

I need not have worried - Foghorn had it all under control. She swept up to the barrier with a screech of brakes. The corporal policeman was already mentally sharpening his pencil as he strode purposefully towards us. He was going to tear a strip off the prat driving the Tilly and, as Foghorn lowered her window, he stuck his head belligerently into the cab on her side. Poor sod! He never knew what hit him.

"What's yer cock, darlin'," she hollered into his face. "How about a quick gobble?"

The poor bastard turned whiter than his cap and, in his haste to extract his head from the cab, he smashed it on the top of the doorframe. His service cap fell into Foghorn's lap and he was trapped. He desperately wanted to escape from the dreaded Bourne but he couldn't really go without his cap.

"I'll settle for a quick snog, you shy little fellow." She smacked her lips in an obscene parody of expectation.

It was too much for our little 'snowdrop' - he ran for it. Hat or no hat, all he wanted was the sanctuary of the guardroom.

Foghorn leapt out and hurled his hat after him. "Do we have to open the fuckin' gate ourselves?" she screamed at his fleeing back.

He turned and, in one flowing movement, retrieved his cap from the road and swung the barrier up to let us through. Foghorn leapt back into the driving seat and accelerated through the gate in a crash of gears.

"Dead from their fuckin' gaiters up," she spat scornfully.

"Arrrff," I agreed wholeheartedly.

"Where to now, Petal?"

I made the sign of a cross.

"The church?" She was incredulous.

I shook my head violently and then wished I hadn't been so careless. I mimed my arm in a sling.

"Oh, sick quarters," she laughed and nodded to the rear of the truck. "Bit late for him, don't you think?"

I grinned as she suddenly started to shake with uncontrollable laughter. At least I thought it was laughter but then I saw what the SMO had seen in me after the crash - she was cracking up. I mimed for her to pull over and she wrenched us to a halt by the gas-training hut.

Her body shook violently and her teeth chattered. She was fighting for breath and the air rasped in her throat. I quickly grabbed her hand and held it in mine. I stroked her hand and made soothing noises. This was no time for another 'Arrrff!'

It was a good ten minutes before she wiped the tears from her face with her free hand. I was still hanging on to the other one and I think it was more to bolster my courage than hers.

"Thanks, Petal," she finally gasped. "Sorry to let the side down."

I just shook my head and pushed her hair back from her forehead. Her skin was cold and damp. She'd need help tonight. She started the engine and we drove slowly to sick quarters.

"How... you...feel?" I managed to speak at last.

"Shitty," was her reply. "But I'm pleased you've got at least three words back in your vocabulary."

"Must... have...SMO," I croaked.

She grinned as we braked to a halt. "Now you're just showing off."

I started to protest at her levity but she raised a hand to stop me. "Okay, the SMO it is."

I climbed out and joined her by the front of the Tilly. I put a restraining hand on her arm.

"How... did... you... know?" I was still croaking.

She gave me a puzzled look and then the penny dropped. She jerked a thumb in the direction of the back of the Tilly. "Oh, you mean Jack the Ripper in the back?"

I nodded.

"I saw him come in through the door but he suddenly stopped and went straight back out again. It looked a bit odd and I'd the strange idea he'd spotted you in the mirror and didn't want you to see him."

I nodded again. It was less painful than talking.

"So I followed you out and saw him creep out from behind the 'Gents' and follow you in. The rest, as they say, is history."

I squeezed her arm. "You...saved... my... life."

She put her hand over mine. "You're worth it, Petal." She disengaged my hand, as if suddenly embarrassed, and walked round to the back of the Tilly. She wrinkled her nose. "Bloody hell, what's that pong?"

I joined her and quickly turned away when the stench assailed my nostrils. "He... has... voided." I still croaked but it was getting better.

"Avoided what?" she asked with a puzzled frown.

"He... has...defecated." I tried to make myself clear.

"You mean he's shit himself?" She had such a way with words and I felt mirth, once more, beginning to bubble to the surface.

"Arrrff, arrrff, arrrff," I chortled.

"Oh, not again, Petal, I've had enough of that for one night."

We entered sick quarters and were met by one of the young nurses. I croaked a request to see the SMO.

"I'm sorry, sir," she said patiently, as if dealing with a total idiot, although she was keeping a wary eye on Foghorn. "I'm afraid he's not here. If it is your throat then possibly I can get one of the orderlies to look at it for you?"

"Look love," said Foghorn quietly. "It's nothing to do with his throat. Just get him the bloody SMO."

The nurse bridled. "Don't you speak to me like that."

I quickly raised my hand. "Give... me... phone."

She reluctantly placed the phone on the table and I managed to get Mr Bates.

Thank God, he was on duty. I croaked for him to get me the SMO and told him it was urgent. Good old Batey, he didn't even question my request - he just did it. I waited for a while and then I heard the receiver being picked up at the other end. It was the SMO.

"Yes, Carver, what's the panic?"

The nurse had departed in deep dudgeon so I could speak openly albeit huskily. "I've a corpse in the back of the Tilly, sir." I managed the sentence quite well.

There was a long silence and I heard the menace in his voice as he finally spoke. "Are you pissed, young man?"

"No, sir. Please understand - we need your help urgently."

"Alright, Carver, where are you?"

"Sick quarters, sir."

"I'm on my way."

He arrived just ten minutes later. He was pulling off his gloves as he bustled through the door. He raised a hand as I opened my mouth to speak. "No need to confirm things, Carver, I took a look in the back of the Tilly on the way in. Don't tell me you knocked the poor sod off his bike?"

I shook my head. "He's a German agent, sir."

I was not disappointed by his reaction. He jumped as if I'd kicked him somewhere nasty.

"Would you like to say that again?" he asked quietly.

"It's true, sir. He tried to kill me earlier this evening. If it had not been for Bourne here, I'd have been in the back of the Tilly instead of him."

He turned to Bourne. "Well, Bourne, you've threatened enough people with death - seems you finally got to prove they were not idle threats."

She grinned. "Ah, but this was in the line of duty, sir. The pilot officer was taken by surprise. Actually he was taken from the rear - if you'll excuse the expression, sir?"

What a bloody woman! A few minutes ago she had been on the verge of collapse and now she was cracking bloody awful jokes again. I envied her resilience.

The SMO opened the door of his office and nodded for me to enter. He turned to Foghorn.

"Bourne, stay here and I'll get somebody to bring you a cup of tea. How are you feeling?"

"Not too bad, sir."

"Okay. The police are going to need a statement from you later, but listen to me, young lady - if you feel at all off colour, you knock on my door. I mean that. Okay?"

"Yes, sir."

"Beddows!" shouted the SMO. "A cup of tea for the young lady in reception."

I wondered idly what the orderly's reaction would be when he saw the 'young lady!'

The SMO closed the office door and sat on the corner of his desk. "Before we start, Carver, who would you like present to hear your story?"

"Squadron Leader Wareham and Squadron Leader Houseman, sir."

He managed to get them both on the phone and announced that both officers were on their way over. He walked behind me and began inspecting my neck.

"Mmm.... You've a lot of bruising and your neck will become very stiff. In fact you may not be able to turn your head for some time. It will be bloody painful." He walked back to his desk and grinned at me. "You're really collecting the injuries, lad."

"Tell me about it, sir," I croaked ruefully. "Still, I can't complain, I'm still here, thanks to Bourne."

He shook his head. "Remarkable woman. I only had time for a quick check out there in the Tilly but she's broken his neck as clean as a whistle. He's a big bugger too. She must have the strength of an ox!"

I nodded. "He gave a quick grunt and that was that."

"Did you lose your voice for a while?" he asked.

"Yes, sir."

He grinned. "Well, sounding like a frog will give Bourne some entertainment at your expense! Don't worry, I doubt there will be any permanent damage."

There was a knock at the door.

"Come in, whoever you are." He winked at me. "This is going to give them a bloody shock!"

Wareham entered but before he could say a word, the SMO held up a hand. "Hang on a mo, Tim, let's wait until Jake gets here."

"Okay, Harry." Wareham sat on the edge of the examination couch. His eyes dropped to my still soaking trouser bottoms.

"Don't ask, sir," I croaked.

Wareham just grinned and shook his head in despair.

Then Houseman came through the door like a tornado. "What's up, Harry?" he panted. Then he caught sight of me. "What the hell have you done now, Carver?"

The SMO waved him to a chair. "For goodness sake, Jake, sit down. Carver has a remarkable story to tell but as he's a severely bruised voice box, I'll save him some of the pain by telling you why I've called you here at such short notice." He paused for effect and I could see he was really enjoying himself. He couldn't wait to see the reaction of the two men and he didn't beat about the bush. He cleared his throat. "Carver and Bourne have killed a German spy."

There was a stunned silence and Houseman was the first to react. "You're not serious, of course?"

"The body is in the back of the Tilly outside. In fact you passed the corpse on your way in." The SMO was really enjoying himself.

"Was that what that bloody awful smell was?" asked Wareham, wrinkling his nose in recollection.

"Bloody hell, Carver!" Houseman said in exasperation. "Tell me this is all a piss-take!"

I shook my head. "I'm afraid not, sir."

He winced at the sound of my croaky voice but I persevered.

"You remember me telling you about the big guy with the Sten at the airstrip?"

He nodded.

"He's the corpse in the back of the Tilly."

Houseman slumped back in his chair. "How the hell do you attract all the trouble, Carver? I simply asked you to collect a few boxes from Tumby and you kill a German agent." He kicked angrily at a chair. "I fucking well don't believe you. You've got to be pulling my pisser!"

At least he quietened down as I slowly croaked out my story. It took a long time but finally I finished and looked expectantly at them. They in turn looked at me as if I was a complete stranger.

"Where is Bourne now?" Wareham asked.

"Next door," answered the SMO. "She was trying to be manly about the whole thing but I didn't like the look of her."

"Who does?" Wareham laughed.

194

The SMO grinned and continued. "In spite of her outward reaction, she's had a hell of a shock and I'm going to keep her here for the night and sedate her."

"She did actually break down in the car." I told him.

"That settles it," said the SMO. "No question. She stays in tonight."

Wareham rose and stared at the table of medical instruments. "I'm afraid, yet again, this is all out of my realm. This is for MI5 and the Special Branch so I'd better get back and try to contact them."

The SMO glanced at his watch. "I must get on to the mortuary at Boston and make sure our corpse is bagged and tagged. I think I'd better give him a name and rank, just to keep them quiet until Face has a chance to work his magic on them."

Houseman rose. He seemed to have recovered from the shock. I'd been surprised how he'd used anger to combat his disbelief but he seemed back to normal.

"How are you feeling, Sam?" he asked quietly.

"It seems to get worse from day to day," I tried to joke.

The SMO headed for the door. "I'd better go and put something in Bourne's cocoa."

"Good idea," I answered without thinking.

"I'm pleased to hear you agree, Carver," he said, as he paused in the doorway. "Because I'm keeping you here too."

I jumped to my feet. "Oh no, sir," I protested. "I'm feeling fine. I'm just a bit tired, that's all."

"Exactly," he replied. "This time you'll remain here until I say you can go."

It was no good continuing the argument, as I'd have been talking to the closed door. Secretly, I felt relieved I wasn't going back to the loneliness of my room in the mess. At least others would be around if the nightmares got too bad.

Houseman put a hand on my shoulder. "See you in the morning, Sam."

The door whipped back open. "No, you'll not!" corrected the SMO firmly. "Nobody will see Carver or Bourne until I am satisfied they are fit to be seen. Do I make myself clear?"

Houseman held up a hand in defeat. "Alright, we hear you, Harry."

He and Wareham stepped quickly out of the door and disappeared.

"Right, Carver," sighed the SMO. "Go through to the single room on the other side of the corridor and get undressed. The orderly is already running a bath."

"Can I see Bourne before I get undressed, sir?"

"No, you bloody well cannot see Bourne," he said firmly. "She's already in another bath and will soon be tucked up in the WAAF ward."

I could see it was no good trying to argue with him. This time he was determined I'd not escape until I was, in his estimation, fit and well again.

An hour later I was between clean, starched white sheets again. I was spending more time in SSQ than in my own room and I fervently hoped it was not going to become a habit. I was beginning to doubt my powers of resolve. My two recent brushes with death were beginning to take their toll. I was edgy and tense and, in spite of the sedative, I slept little that night. Doubts, fears and nightmares vied for prominence in my thoughts and I spent a miserable night fighting them all.

CHAPTER FIFTEEN

The SMO had not been joking about having the last word on my release from sick quarters. He kept me in bed for the next two days and it was only because Face pleaded with him, that he finally relented and let them take my statement on the second day. On the third day I was allowed to sit out of bed and the fourth day I went for a short stroll. I read two books and listened to the wireless until I was sick to death of the plummy BBC voices. Surely real people didn't have such pretentious diction?

The only thing I looked forward to were the visits from Natalie. She was frequently on duty but occasionally managed to get away to see me. I waited avidly for her visits but they left me with mixed feelings. I daren't reveal my true feelings for her - I was afraid I'd scare her away. I'd known her for so little time but my feelings were no less intense. When she visited, we stole a few kisses and, from her body language, I knew there was so much more promised for the future. Whenever she left me to go back on duty I was desolate. I couldn't concentrate on a book or even force myself to listen to the wireless. She had sent my hopes soaring by suggesting it was time to meet her parents. If any girl in the past had suggested such a dramatic increase in a relationship, I'd have run a mile in the opposite direction. This time I welcomed the prospect with open arms. I already knew that Natalie was the girl with whom I wanted to spend the rest of my life. I kept looking into her eyes for signs I was rushing the relationship but all I saw was reciprocal signals of my own feelings.

Twice Houseman dropped in for a chat and brought me some magazines. He also brought me a small bottle of Scotch, which I had to hide from the SMO. The padre called too but we didn't exactly find a lot to talk about so he left looking rather disappointed.

I saw nothing of Foghorn. I knew she was in the building for the first two days because I heard her giving the male orderlies hell. Our statements had been taken separately too. I suppose that was to prevent collusion in the event we really had knocked somebody off his bike and had invented the whole story.

Around mid-morning on the fifth day, which was the Friday, the SMO said I could return to the officers' mess but I was to remain there. I'd resume normal duties on the following Monday.

Unfortunately, Nat had a forty-eight hour pass and so I was left kicking my heels in the mess.

Monday seemed to take forever but, after the most boring weekend of my life, I finally returned to work. Dave Jones was the first to welcome me back but my pleasure at his apparent enthusiasm for my return was slightly tempered by the fact that now we were back up to strength he could apply for leave.

Houseman spotted me just a few seconds later. "Morning, Carver. Nice to have you back in the fold. My office, if you please."

I glanced in dismay at Natalie who had only just got back in from experiencing the ghastly early morning milk train.

She grinned. "Don't worry, you can't be in trouble. You haven't been back long enough."

I grimaced as I followed Houseman out of the room. "I wish I had your confidence."

I settled myself into a chair in Houseman's office. At last I was going to be a real intelligence officer. I had an awful feeling it was going to be a bit of an anticlimax after my first few weeks. At least it would be more of a normal existence.

"How are you feeling?" asked Houseman.

"Ready to get back to the job I was supposed to be trained for, sir."

He regarded me carefully for a few seconds then dropped the bombshell. "Face and Piper were very impressed by your efforts and have asked the command intelligence officer if they can borrow you for a while. How do you feel about that?"

I looked at him in amazement. "Flattered, sir, but what the hell can I do for them now? They know as much as I do and I've come to a dead end. I've no clues as to who the local agent is or where the cell is located. I'm hardly going to be much of an asset, sir."

Houseman nodded. "I know how you must feel but let's face it, as an amateur, you did a bloody good job. They reckon you have special talents and I agree with them. It would be a shame to waste those talents in a mundane job here."

My disappointment must have shown.

"Oh, come on, Sam! You've a devious mind - a great asset in counter espionage."

"I also have a propensity for getting into trouble, sir. I reckon that is a serious handicap."

Houseman laughed. "There you go, running yourself down again. Anyway, I'm sorry but it makes no difference. Command have agreed to your detachment to MI5 until this affair either disappears or is brought to a satisfactory conclusion."

I sighed. "Where are they sending me, sir?"

"Nowhere, you're staying right here."

I looked at him in surprise. "At West Fen? Right here in the section?"

He nodded. "Had you worried there for a while, eh? Yes, you'll be based here but they want you to start investigating the area where young Troutbridge supposedly found the German parachutist's helmet. As you said before, or somebody did, if there was a helmet then there may be a parachute. Can you remember where the lad's brother said Norman had discovered the helmet?"

"Yes, sir. I should be able to find the exact spot, once I know where the Meacher farm is actually located. I think that was the name he mentioned."

He leaned back in his chair. "How are you going to explain your presence on the guy's land if he catches you there?"

I thought for a minute. "Well, there is no sense trying to do this covertly. We need to be seen doing something openly to allay any suspicions they may have about us being there in the first place. Maybe I could be a signals expert surveying the site for a new communications mast."

"You see!" he laughed. "You think on your bloody feet. I reckon that is a damned good cover. Run it past Wing Commander Face and, if he gives his blessing, take Max with you. He's already in the know and it would look very strange if you were there by yourself."

I nodded. "It will also give me the chance to meet some of the other local farmers and we can pull the same trick on each farm. We can tell them we're trying to find the ideal site for the mast and we're looking at farmland all over the local area.

That way, Meacher should not feel his land has been singled out for special attention."

"Sounds good," nodded Houseman. "Better get on the blower and tell Face your plan. Think you can get it across without revealing too much on an open phone?"

I smiled ruefully. "He thinks I talk in riddles at the best of time. He probably won't have a clue what I'm talking about but I'm sure he'll trust me and tell me to go ahead."

Houseman laughed. "Okay, you'd better get cracking."

Face didn't hesitate and gave me a free hand. An hour later I was briefing Max. I'd located Meacher's farm by the simple method of calling Stan Cornish. He seemed to know everybody and, without any questions as to why I wanted the information, he gave me the location of the farm. Using an Ordnance Survey map of the local area and using Stan's directions to the farm, we found the wood near where Frank Troutbridge had told me Norman had found the helmet. We decided to visit three other farms in that area in order to let the word spread that we had an interest in more than the Meacher farm. We knew that word on the local grapevine travelled faster than the speed of light and for once, we were pleased it did.

We signed a Tilly out from the MT section and headed for Tumby. We stopped near Mareham-le-Fen and visited a farmer there and then a couple more out on the flat fen land nearer Tumby Woodside. Finally, we drove slowly down a lane to the south of Tumby Woodside and there, just across the field from the road, we could see the wood. The wood marked the eastern boundary of the Meacher farm but the farmhouse was just visible about half a mile away across the field. There had to be a junction up ahead, turning off in the direction of the farmstead.

"Looks like a muddy old walk across that field," grumbled Max as he slowed the Tilly.

"I don't know so much. The OS map indicates a track up the side of this field."

"All the way to the wood?" he asked hopefully.

"Yes. In fact, I reckon the culvert must span the ditch that runs alongside the track from the road up to the boundary of the wood."

"Damn me! You're right, Sam," said Max and pointed to a farm track on our left. "And there's the ditch alongside the track."

Max eased the Tilly onto the track and we skidded and slewed our way slowly towards the wood. He stopped just short of the culvert under the small bridge connecting one field with its neighbour.

"Don't fancy reversing back down that track," said Max as he switched off the engine.

I opened my door. "I'm pleased we brought our wellingtons," I said with feeling as my feet sank into the mud.

I stood and looked around me. The wood was just stark, bare trees against a grey sky. There was not even a breath of wind and there were already the first hints of a foggy night ahead. There would be no ops tonight. A crow broke the silence with a harsh cry. I shivered and felt uneasy. I looked carefully around the ground in the immediate vicinity. This was the area where some of the butterfly bombs had fallen. Damned things could be anywhere. I started as Max slammed his door.

"Who the heck would want to live in this desolate place?" he asked.

I smiled to myself as I noticed Max was whispering. "There's no need to whisper," I laughed.

He grinned and raised his voice. "It's so damned spooky out here."

I shook my head. "I don't reckon we're cut out for this sort of job."

"I heartily agree," replied Max, rubbing his gloved hands together vigorously.

"Let's clear off back to camp. It may be a bit of a hole but at least it's better than this."

"Stop moaning," I chided. "Get the bloody clipboards out and we can start looking like we know what we're doing."

"Have you got the compass?" he asked.

"I certainly have, but haven't got much of a clue how to use it."

"Which way are we heading?" Max queried as he gazed about him.

"Well, the culvert looks quite clear now so the helmet must have been an afterthought. If an agent did land here, then he'd have buried the parachute and the wood must have been the obvious place. He'd have been scared and anxious to put as much distance as he could between himself and the drop zone. What I can't understand is why he didn't bury the helmet with the chute?" I paused as I caught Max grinning at me. "Now what?" I asked.

"You really are good at this game, aren't you?" he said.

"Bollocks!" I laughed with embarrassment. "Come on, we'll work away from the wood at first, just in case we're being watched. We can work our way slowly back later."

"What are we looking for exactly?"

"Disturbed earth," I replied. "If there was a parachute, then his friends will have been here to remove the evidence. They couldn't take a chance once they learned that Norman had told his brother about the helmet. I bet they wish they had done it sooner."

"Come on," sighed Max. "Let's get it over and done with."

We started a charade of pacing the ground and taking bearings with the compass. I'd borrowed it from the RAF Regiment lads on West Fen. They were the soldiers of the RAF and were responsible for the defence of the airfield.

The heavy soil clung to our boots and made the going heavy and tiring. The lone crow had been joined by some of his friends and they were now wheeling over the trees and cawing loudly.

Max looked up at them and whispered, "Do you think they are Jerry crows? You know, brought in to keep guard. They certainly blend in with the landscape. Do you think they are cawing in Kraut?"

I started to laugh. "Do wrap up, Shearing, and get on with the bloody job."

After an hour of diversionary tactics taking us away from the wood, we started to work our way slowly back towards it. We were about thirty yards from it when Max cocked his head in my direction and whispered.

"Can you see him?"

I only just stopped myself from turning in his direction. I forced myself to look at the compass.

"Where?" I said out of the corner of my mouth.

"Your four o'clock. About ten yards into the wood."

"Did you get that last reading as two-two-zero?" I called loudly. I was really disappointed. The hairs on the back of my neck had really let me down this time.

"Roger! Two-two-zero," he answered loudly.

I desperately wanted to take a peek but there was no way I could bring the move off without the guy knowing we had spotted him.

"How much bloody longer?" I asked loudly.

"Half an hour should do it," Max replied. "Problem is, this bloody wood is going to mask the signals from the west."

He had spoken loud enough for our watcher to hear and I turned naturally in that direction. At first I didn't see him, then I saw the paleness of his face slightly to the right of the trunk of a silver birch. I slowly moved my eyes away from him as if scanning for a break in the trees. My glimpse had been long enough to register a man of about five feet eight inches tall, wearing an old overcoat with string tied at the waist. His head was covered with a very battered trilby hat.

I raised my voice again as I moved to my left across the furrows. Bloody hell, I just hoped we wouldn't have to run for it. I had ten tons of Lincolnshire's best clinging to my Wellies.

"If they decide on this site then all those trees will have to come down. Pity really but it's the best place we've seen so far," I called to Max.

"He's coming out!" whispered Max.

It took me all my self-control not to turn and face the man. We were in a dodgy position and I didn't like the idea of him having the whip hand. Especially if he had a weapon.

"Can I help you, gentlemen?" The voice was unmistakably southern Irish.

We both spun round as if startled. Max actually overdid it and fell on his arse with a loud, "Sugar!"

The man glanced briefly at Max and then turned his full attention on me. He had a pale face for a countryman and the hairs of his eyebrows were pure blonde. It gave him a weak look but the pale, washed-out, grey eyes couldn't disguise the intensity of his stare.

"Bloody hell!" I exclaimed loudly and added a not entirely false nervous laugh. "You scared the shit out of us. Where the hell did you come from?"

He nodded in the general direction of the farmhouse. "Over there," he answered vaguely.

As Max scrambled to his feet I noticed him stagger again. Good old Max. The stagger had taken him just that little bit closer to our man. I smiled inwardly at the ploy from a so-called amateur and pulled the list of farms from my pocket.

"Ah!" I said, squinting at the list. "You must be Mr Meacher from Chapel Farm."

He gave a dry little laugh. "Hardly."

I made a play of confusion as I looked from him to Max and back again. "But if you came from the farm over there, I've got you down as Mr Peter Meacher. We were going to pay you a visit later."

He looked at me steadily. "My name is Sean Smith - Peter Meacher's foreman."

"A good Irish name, Smith," I joked.

He didn't even smile. "What are you doing on Mr Meacher's land?" he asked.

"Surveying, old boy," Max butted in, sounding like the pompous permanent commission types I'd met so many of during my short time in the service.

Smith looked at Max with contempt. He had not liked the 'old boy'. "Surveying for what?" he asked.

"Site for a new low frequency communications mast." Max sounded very knowledgeable.

"On whose authority?" Smith was good with the questions.

"The Air Ministry." I thought I'd better get my pennyworth in. "It comes under the Defence of the Realm Act - Clause Twenty-Four. Compulsory purchase of land."

He digested this for a moment. "What sort of mast?"

Now I was up the creek without a paddle. I knew sod all about communications and I was about to stall him with the Official Secrets Act, when Max came to our rescue.

"Fifty foot high, geodetic on a thirty square foot base and ten foot foundations."

I dared not look at Max or one of two things was going to happen. I'd register surprise at his knowledge or I'd burst out laughing. The desire to laugh was already nibbling at the peripheries of my self-control. I had no need to worry as Max was now in full stride.

"If it is decided to use a simple stay pylon with supporting guys, then I'm afraid most of your wood will have to come down." Max began to walk backwards towards the wood. "You see the guys have to be anchored a considerable distance from the base of the pylon and so...."

"Don't go in there!" Smith interrupted him urgently.

We both stared at him in surprise and I made a mental note of the area I had seen his eyes flit towards, then just as quickly look away. I estimated about ten feet into the edge of the wood.

"Why on earth not?" I asked.

"Butterfly bombs," said Smith quickly. "They're all over the area. The wood hasn't been cleared."

I strode towards the wood. "I don't think they will pose us any problems, Mr Smith. There's no undergrowth to conceal them and we're perfectly au fait with the butterfly bomb." I was now about five feet into the wood and I glanced quickly at the spot I had seen him look towards. There it was - disturbed earth. I whirled back to face him. "This is as far as we will have to go into your wood."

I walked back to join them. Smith looked relieved and, to my surprise, so did Max.

The Irishman's self-assurance quickly returned. "I do think it would have been more tactful if you had spoken to Mr Meacher before you trespassed on his land." It sounded so righteous I wanted to laugh again.

I nodded. "I agree, Mr Smith, but this is very urgent and we've so little time. Anyway, the whole matter of good etiquette is a formality only. Once the decision has been made, that's it. No questions and no redress. Whether you like it or not, your Mr Meacher will have a mast."

I saw him weighing the whole thing up in his mind. "What is the mast for, exactly?" Bless him - he was trying hard.

"Sorry, old boy," burbled Max, "Security and all that, you know."

There it was again - that flash of anger in the face. He really didn't like the 'old boy' bit. He was making a supreme effort to control himself, which indicated he didn't want to make waves. He wanted a low profile.

"Mr Meacher is up at the farm at present. I suggest you call and see him. I'm sure he'd like to know what is going on." With that, he abruptly turned on his heel and strode off, following the edge of the wood.

"Bye, old boy!" called Max cheerfully.

"Don't push it!" I whispered.

"Bit posh for a farm foreman, don't you think?" commented Max.

I nodded. "Words like 'tactful' don't normally drop into a simple countryman's vocabulary. He didn't want us in that bloody wood either, did he?"

"No," agreed Max. "Did you see anything in there?"

"Certainly did but we'll steer well clear of it because I don't trust our Mr Smith. I reckon once he's out of sight, he'll nip back here for another look."

"Did it look like somebody had dug something up?"

"Definitely."

"Then can we piss off," sighed Max. "I'm bloody freezing."

I shook my head. "We'd better do another half hour and then go see Meacher."

Max tried to remove some of the cloying mud sticking to his boots. "Makes sense, I suppose," he conceded reluctantly.

We dawdled around for another half an hour then climbed back into the Tilly. Max reversed down the track with difficulty but made it safely back out into the lane. Now for Mr Meacher.

I glanced at Max as he drove. "Where the hell did you get all that crap about low frequency masts? Geo-bloody-detic? What the hell's that when it's at home?"

Max laughed. "Same place you dragged the Defence of the Realm Act from, I shouldn't wonder."

"There is a Defence of the Realm Act," I protested. "That's how the government got the farmland on which to build all these bloody airfields."

"Clever old you!" Max replied. "Actually, I know nothing of masts and pylons but somebody had to say something. I suddenly thought of the Wellington bomber."

"What about it?"

"Well, the fuselage is built on the geodetic principle. I think the guy who designed it into aircraft construction is called Barnes Wallis. Anyway, it is a complex latticework, which is incredibly strong and can take a lot of punishment. I thought if it is good enough for the Wellington, it would be good enough for a mast. Sheer genius on my part, don't you think?"

"Modest sod."

"At least it got you into the wood."

I conceded the point. "It certainly did."

Max drummed his fingers on the steering wheel to some silent jazz riff going through his mind. "Looks like we've hit the nail on the head without even trying."

I shook my head. "Bit soon to tell yet, although I think our Mr Smith is worth another look."

"It will be interesting to meet his boss, Meacher."

I nodded. "I agree. No need to tell you we'd better go carefully. If they really are part of the cell, then they are very dangerous people. They have already killed a whole family in cold blood. One false move and we could have a very fatal accident in the Tilly."

"How did I get into this?" Max asked in disbelief.

"Same way as I did - you were volunteered."

"Ah well, it's all for King and Country," Max sighed.

I laughed. "Very patriotic … Look out, this is the farm."

Chapel Farm seemed an odd name for a farm that was a hell of a long way from the nearest chapel. It was a typical Lincolnshire red-bricked farmhouse with an untidy clutter of outbuildings. Again, as in the case of Stan's farm, it was well back from the road down a very bumpy track. The Tilly's springs complained as we drove slowly over the potholes. Poor old thing, it was not really designed for all this rough terrain.

Max braked to a halt at the entrance to the farmyard. We could proceed no further as our way was blocked by two of the biggest Alsatian dogs I had ever seen.

"Here, pussy, pussy!" said Max through his teeth as he quickly wound up the window.

"Big sods," I commented needlessly.

A tall man appeared from inside the house and shouted sharply at the dogs. They gave us a last longing look before they obediently trotted off into the house.

I wound down my window. "Is it safe to get out now?" I called.

The man beckoned. "Yes. Come on, you'll be fine."

"Said the spider to the fly," Max muttered.

We climbed out and the man met us half way across the yard. He was a rather imposing figure. Tall, with the countryman's tanned face. There was not an ounce of fat on the man and the thick leather belt at the waist of the old corduroys sat neatly in place. He had a shock of thick white hair, which made his blue eyes quite startling.

He held out a hand. "Afternoon, gentlemen. What can I do for the Air Force?" His voice was pleasant, with a faint accent I couldn't immediately identify - certainly not Lincolnshire. This was not the sort of man I was expecting to meet. I felt disappointed because I immediately liked the man.

"Mr Meacher?" I asked.

He nodded. "That's right."

I shook his hand. "My name is Pilot Officer James and this is my colleague, Flight Lieutenant Samuels." I hoped to hell we could remember the names. This was the problem with jumping in feet first without any preparation. "We're communications officers," I added rather pompously. I prayed Max would keep a straight face.

Meacher smiled. "Well, there is only one signal you're both transmitting at the moment and it is an SOS for a cup of tea."

I was even more puzzled. This was not the attitude I had braced myself for on the way over here. Still, I really could do with a cup of tea. Slogging around a very soggy ploughed field had certainly brought on a thirst.

"That's very kind of you, Mr Meacher, but we don't want to take up too much of your valuable time."

He waved a dismissive hand. "Come on in, I've got plenty of time for a cuppa. Anyway, I was just about to have my tea."

We followed him into the house, keeping a weather eye open for the dogs. He sensed our apprehension.

"Don't worry, they're friendly enough once they've seen you with me."

"I'm pleased about that," Max said with feeling.

The house was large and the first room we passed through was virtually empty of furniture. It had a red-tiled floor and no rugs. The next room was the living room. It was cluttered but clean and cosy. Both dogs lay on a colourful snip rug in front of the fire.

"Sit yourselves down. The kettle has just boiled so it will not take long to get a brew going."

He was quite comfortable with our presence and gave the impression that he had no idea we were going to pay him a visit. That confirmed my suspicion that Smith had not come back to the farm but had indeed doubled back to watch us at the wood.

"There we are," said Meacher as he handed us our tea. "Now, what can I do for you?"

I indicated that Max should do the explaining. I couldn't remember all that crap he'd waffled on about to Smith. I just hoped he had a good memory. I also wanted to be free to observe Meacher.

Max put his mug down on the table. "Mr Meacher, I'm afraid we've some good news and some bad news."

Meacher smiled at Max. "The bad news first, if you don't mind."

"We're going to have to build a communications mast on your land."

That didn't seem to be a problem to the farmer. "And what is the good news, young man?"

Max began inventing again. "You'll get a small monetary award as compensation."

Meacher stirred his tea slowly and fixed me with a direct gaze. "Where would you want to put this mast?"

I fished the map out of my pocket and spread it out on the bit of table not occupied by the farmer's simple repast. I pointed to the wood shown on the OS map. "Just here. It will be well away from the house but I'm afraid some of the wood will have to come down."

Meacher sipped his tea and nodded slowly. "I see no problem with that."

"We will need access to it at all times too, I'm afraid," I said quietly and watched his reaction.

"Again, no problem," he replied and looked as if he meant it.

As I watched him I suddenly began to have the feeling I'd seen him before. I tried to put face and place together but without success. I spotted a snapshot on the sideboard of a pretty young woman and a couple of children.

"Your daughter?" I asked nodding at the photo.

He laughed. "My wife."

"Oh, I'm sorry," I answered quickly, embarrassed at my gaffe. "Taken some years ago?"

"No." He smiled tolerantly at me. "It was taken just last year. Jeanette is thirty years my junior. Those are my children. Peter is now thirteen and Paula is eleven."

I could see, out of the corner of my eye, that Max was enjoying my embarrassment. "I'm sorry, Mr Meacher. It was very rude of me to pry."

"Nonsense, lad. It's only natural to be interested in a man's family. Are you married?"

I shook my head. "I'm afraid not."

"Me neither," said Max.

"You're both young. Believe me there is plenty of time. I didn't marry until I was fifty. It was a big change in my life, I'll tell you."

"Is she a Lincolnshire girl?" I asked.

"Good Lord, no," he laughed. "She'd be very upset at the very thought of it. She's a Norfolk girl, born and bred. She runs a farm in Norfolk."

I wanted to know why she was not here with him but I decided it was time to change the subject.

"We met your foreman when we were looking at the site for our mast."

He didn't even blink. In fact he looked pleased. "Ah, Sean. He lives over near Moorby. I've no tied cottages on this farm, so he has a place up in the woods in the back of beyond. He must be mad to live in such an isolated place but that's the Irish for you."

I felt that was enough for our first visit, so I rose to my feet and Max followed. "Thank you for the tea, Mr Meacher. You'll hear from the Air Ministry in due course. Thank you for being so understanding."

He rose to show us out. "Thank you for being honest with me about having to chop down most of my wood. Any time you're passing, drop in for a cuppa - the kettle is always on. Or, if you prefer it, I'm a bit of a dab hand at the old home-made wine."

"Oh no, not another one," laughed Max. "My uncle is into that. God knows what he puts in them but we've our own names for his potent brews. Nettle nitro-glycerine, Carrot Cordite, Peapod Powderkeg and Blackberry Bombshell. I learned my lesson about you chaps when I was just a lad. I'm surprised you survive your own brews."

Meacher laughed. "There is nothing like it for keeping out the cold."

"I'm not surprised," Max chortled as he climbed behind the wheel. "It puts fur on your tongue, so there is no reason it should not line your insides the same way."

Meacher laughed heartily. "By heck, young man, you wait till you've tried some of my wines. They are smoother than the finest Burgundy."

"That's probably where you ought to send them," Max replied, pulling a wry face.

Meacher turned to me and his face was full of humour and laughter. "Will you get this heretic out of here?"

I grabbed Max by the arm. "Willingly, Mr Meacher. I'll not bring him next time. I seem to spend my whole life apologising for his bad manners."

He held open the passenger door for me. "I look forward to seeing you both again."

Max pressed the starter and there was a grinding noise from under the bonnet. "Sounds like it needs a drop of your wine, Mr Meacher," Max laughed.

Meacher closed the door as the engine fired. "Away with you and take care," he called as we bumped off down the track.

I wound up the window and, for a couple of minutes, we drove in silence.

"Well, that was a bloody disappointment," Max said in disbelief.

"You're not joking. I was expecting hostility."

"Couldn't have been nicer."

"Even asked us to pop in any time," I said in disbelief.

"Bit different to his bloody foreman."

"He not a Lincolnshire man - Meacher I mean. I couldn't place his accent, could you?"

"Sounded a bit south-west England to me," replied Max.

"What, Devon?"

"Could be Dorset."

"Pleasant on the ear, anyway."

"He was altogether pleasant," said Max. "I really liked the guy."

"Me too. Now what?"

"God only knows," he replied. He slowed the Tilly as we entered a hamlet just before the turn off to West Fen. "Do you know the name of this place?" he asked.

"Not a clue," I replied, mystified by his question.

He grinned. "You're now in New York."

"You're kidding."

"No, I'm not. Over there is Boston and this, I kid you not, is New York. I'll show you on the map later. If they hadn't taken all the road signs down when they thought there was going to be an invasion, you could have seen the name for yourself."

I looked at the grey little hamlet in the fading light of the winter's day. What a godforsaken place. How the hell did people live here without going mad? Flat fields of black soil spread themselves out under the enormous expanse of the leaden sky. Grey, soggy and cold. I shivered. "You can bloody well keep it."

"No thanks," Max chuckled as we resumed the last couple of miles back to camp.

By the time we reached West Fen, the fog had really rolled in off the North Sea. Vague forms on foot and bicycles swerved out of our path as we groped our way to the section.

"No ops tonight," said Max, rubbing his hands.

205

"That will please the crews."

"Not really," said Max as he parked the Tilly. "Most just want to get it over with and find a safer hole to hide in for a while."

"What are you doing tonight?" I asked as I held the section door open for him.

"Working. Thanks to all this flitting around with you, I'm getting well behind with my own work. I've the sergeant to help me but it's a lot for him to cope with on his own. As much as I enjoy a break in the countryside, I wish you'd discourage Houseman from making me your partner."

I assured him I'd do my best and glanced around to see if Natalie was in the main room.

"Gone to tea, sir," whispered LAC Hoare with a straight face.

I couldn't help a smile. "You're too clever by half, Hoare, but thanks all the same."

"My pleasure, sir."

"Is the squadron leader in?"

He stopped writing and scratched his head. "I do believe he is, sir. I seem to remember him going through to his office with the two civvies – the two who have been hanging around here lately."

I looked at him carefully but he had the most innocent of looks on his face.

I kept a straight face. "And you'd like to know what they are doing here?"

"Me, sir?" the innocent look was still there. "How could you think such a thing?"

"Very easily, where you're concerned, Hoare."

"Thank you, sir. I'll remember that when you need my professional advice."

I laughed. "The only thing you can wax professionally and lyrically about are jellied eels - and no, I'll not satisfy your curiosity."

"How can we expect to win this war, sir, when you insist on keeping me in the dark and refusing to fortify your brain cells with the fruit of the gods."

I headed for the offices. "The only thing godlike about jellied eels, Hoare, is what one says when one first sees a plate of the bloody things - OH, GOD!"

"That is blasphemy!" he laughed.

I left him with the vision of two fingers, behind my back, giving a rude version of the Churchillian salute. His laughter followed me down the corridor. Not the way to behave with a junior airman but he knew his stuff. In fact he knew a hell of a lot more than I did about operational intelligence. I felt sorry for him because he always seemed to be teamed up with Christian, although it didn't seem to bother him. Come to think of it, nothing much bothered Hoare.

I knocked on Houseman's door and entered when he called.

Face and Piper were sitting around Houseman's desk and the room was full of smoke from Piper's briar pipe. They all nodded a greeting.

"Fruitful trip?" asked Houseman.

"Yes and no, sir," I replied as I pulled up a chair and joined them. I related the story of the helmet site and the disturbed earth. Piper became very interested when I told them of our meeting with Sean Smith.

"Did you ever see him at the Red Lion?" Piper asked.

I shook my head. "No, never, but you've just jogged my memory. I knew I'd seen Meacher somewhere before - he was one of the regular domino players."

"Did he recognise you when you went to the farm?" Face asked quickly.

"If he did, he certainly didn't show it."

"If he's a professional, he wouldn't have," Piper added dryly.

I tapped the arm of the chair with the fingers of my right hand and marshalled my thoughts.

"I know I'm not being professional when I say that I actually liked the man. He seemed very genuine and quickly volunteered information without being asked."

Piper smiled tolerantly. "Again, young Carver, if he's a professional, he'd not wait to be asked. As long as he was answering questions before being asked, he was in full control of the interview."

I shook my head in dismay. "Bloody hell, I've an awful lot to learn."

"Did you see any wife or children?" asked Houseman.

I shook my head. "No. He lives there alone and the way the house is cluttered but clean screams out 'man only'. There is a wife though. She's very young, very pretty and they were married when Meacher was fifty years old. She lives in Norfolk with their two children."

"Strange situation," muttered Piper. "Did he indicate a breakdown of the marriage?"

"No. He just said she ran a farm in Norfolk."

Face glanced quickly at Piper and turned back to me. "Carver, if you like Meacher, would you be prepared to get to know him better?"

"Hang on, sir!" objected Houseman. "You're putting an untrained man into the lion's den. I think that is a very dangerous thing to do."

"I know, Jake," replied Face with exasperation in his voice. "But who else could do it? Time is our greatest enemy and the only person who's au fait with the whole of this operation is Carver. He's already met our suspect and they got on well. Damn it all, Jake, the lad actually has an open invitation to call at the farm whenever he wants. I know we're cutting corners but I do think it is well worth the gamble."

Houseman looked at me and I could see he was worried. I could also see the sense in Face's argument.

"If you can spare me, sir, I don't mind giving it a go." I was not feeling like a hero but I knew they were up against it.

Houseman gave a little shake of his head but seemed to accept the situation, albeit reluctantly.

"What did the search teams manage to turn up at the airstrip, sir?" I asked Face.

"Apart from the dead agent and the stuff I mentioned before, not much else. We've questioned all the local farmers in and around that area and on the approach roads but there was nothing they could tell us. As far as they were concerned the sign said 'Keep Out' and they did just that. They all noticed the motorbike but even on that subject their evidence varied. Some said it 'barked' and some said it 'purred' but sod all else. Ask them what the bloke looked like riding it and all you got was a blank stare."

I thought for a moment and then the seed of an idea began to propagate in my mind. "The bloke Foghorn topped had a bike that, in the words of your witnesses, 'barked'. That is how I knew which one to bring with us. The bike we left behind was a twin."

Piper opened a notebook and flipped through the pages until he found what he was looking for.

"You're right. The bike you brought back in the Tilly was a Norton 16H - a model built especially for the armed forces. I saw it had a four-stroke engine but I can only guess at it being about 350cc. As you say, it was not a twin."

Suddenly, a kaleidoscope of images began to flash through my mind. I thumped the desk in frustration. "Shit! Shit! Shit!" I muttered as I slammed my fist repeatedly on the desk.

The others watched me in amazement as I fought to bring the images into a coherent mental scenario. I fought with myself in silence as the others watched me with frowns on their faces. Then it all began to slot into place.

"Why would our man be going to the Red Lion?" I asked them.

Face shrugged. "We can only assume to meet one or more of the cell."

"Why?" I insisted.

"To warn the others the airstrip had been blown?" Piper suggested.

"Exactly!" I replied eagerly. "Who would need to be warned?"

Face began to sense my excitement and he leaned forward to answer my question. "The contact who gets the info from West Fen or the courier or even the…" He paused and fixed me with an intense stare. "You saw somebody, didn't you?"

I rubbed a hand over my eyes as if to erase the remnants of the mental fog. "When Foghorn and myself went into the pub, we were the only service personnel in there. I remember being pleased because I was breaking the rules and I had no desire to get Bourne into trouble."

Houseman grinned as if to break the tension. "I do think you could have chosen a more tactful phrase."

We all laughed and it was as if laughter was the trigger to clear away the last of the fog. I could see the inside of the Red Lion and hear the sounds. There were the clicks and scraping of the dominoes, the wireless playing quietly somewhere and, outside, the sound of a motorcycle arriving. I remember glancing up when I heard the outside door open and catching sight of a uniformed figure as it passed the open door to the public bar and went through to the snug. I remembered the sudden uneasy feeling that Bourne and I were about to be rumbled. It was a great relief when the man carried on after only the briefest of glances in the room where we sat. His greatcoat had been open and I had caught a brief glimpse of his tunic jacket.

"Who wears a largish white or silver insignia where RAF pilots normally have their wings?" I asked as I fought to retain the image in my mind.

"Poles," replied Houseman without any hesitation. "The Polish airmen who fly with the RAF are still in the Polish Air Force. They wear their own form of insignia and it has a little chain attached. Some actually wear the RAF wings too but over the other breast pocket."

I nodded slowly. "That's it. I saw something glint and it could have been a chain."

Face stood and then sat gingerly on the hot radiator. He quickly changed his mind and went back to his chair. He stared at me with a worried frown on his face. "What are you getting at, Carver?"

I thumped the table in exasperation. "I don't really know, for Christ's sake!" I stood up and faced them. "The motorcycle I heard when the Polish guy arrived, if he was Polish, was a twin. It had that unmistakable smooth roar. When the guy who tried to kill me arrived, I heard his motorbike and it was definitely not a twin. It was a four-stroke side valve or something like that. The noise was harsh." I turned to Piper. "What did your witnesses say?"

He clapped a hand to his forehead. "Oh shit! I see what you're getting at. Some said it purred and others said it barked."

I thumped the desk again. "Precisely!" Then my excitement began to fade rapidly when I realised what a ridiculously slim thread connected my surmise with reality. "I'm sorry, gentlemen. I'm afraid I got a bit carried away."

Piper toyed with his box of matches. He kept opening the tray as if expecting to see something untoward in there. He finally removed a match and began a studious investigation of his right ear. "As tenuous as your scenario seems, young Carver, it is all we've got to go on," said the Special Branch man. "It is a connection of sorts and it could indeed have been a meeting between our mystery pilot and his handler."

"Did you see the Pole again?" asked Face.

I shook my head. "Events put the mockers on that, sir. All I can tell you is that his bike was still there when we grabbed the other one."

"Where are the Poles stationed around here?" asked Face.

Houseman shrugged. "No idea, sir, but I'm sure you could find out much quicker than me."

Face nodded. "I'll get on to it." He stood and put a hand on my shoulder. "Carver, you seem to have this ability to pull nothing out of the hat but turn it into something before our very eyes. If you can make your magic stick with this, we'll grab the bloody lot."

I didn't reply. I suddenly felt totally whacked. My back was killing me and my throat ached. Just a few seconds ago I had been firing on all four cylinders, now I felt totally drained of all energy.

Houseman looked at me and frowned. "Are you alright, Sam?"

I nodded and climbed wearily to my feet. "I'm a bit tired, sir. I'm getting so bloody frustrated at always being that little bit too late. If I had been on the ball, I'd have remembered that bloody Pole."

Face turned on me quickly. "Don't talk rot, Carver. Intelligence is all about putting a jigsaw together but somebody has hidden some of the pieces to make it more difficult. You've done a damned good job so far - we don't expect miracles."

Piper rose from his chair and began to don his overcoat. "Would you recognise this chap again?"

"The Pole?" I asked and he nodded. "Yes, I'm sure I would, sir."

He turned to Face. "In that case, once you find where the Poles are stationed as aircrew, we can pop Carver into their midst, under some pretext or other, and see if he can flush the bugger out."

My heart sank. All I wanted to do was rest and here he was volunteering me again. I saw Houseman watching me carefully.

"That, gentlemen, would be up to Carver here."

Face spread his arms in a helpless gesture and spoke as if I wasn't there. "What options do we have, Jake? Only Carver can identify our man. It is a slender thread but if Carver's right, he's the only person who can point the finger at him."

I tried to shrug off the lassitude that was threatening to engulf me. "I'll have a go, sir, but not tonight, eh?"

Face laughed. "Sorry, Carver, you look all in. I know we're asking a lot of you but we really do need you to stick with this. Go and get some rest and I'll contact you tomorrow, once I know where the Poles are. This could actually explain the gaps in the attacks. He can only fly from the strip when he's not on his normal duties. It looks as if we've a part-time freelance on our hands."

That wrapped up our meeting and Houseman and I saw them off into the foggy night. We walked back into the section and sat in the rest area in the main office. Paula Tyde, who was duty watchkeeper, brought us a couple of mugs of coffee.

Houseman sipped his coffee and watched me over the rim of the mug. "Are you sure you can take this thing on?"

"Yes, sir, I think I'd like to see it through to the end."

"It's playing hell with your health, young man. You've been through a lot just lately."

"It's playing hell with the romantic aspects of my life too, sir," I replied bitterly.

"Natalie?" he grinned.

"Natalie." I nodded grimly.

Houseman looked away to the far end of the room as if intentionally avoiding my eye.

"When there is a break in the proceedings," he said quietly, "I'll try to get you both a spot of leave at the same time. You've earned it."

I suddenly felt a lot better. "Blimey, sir, do you mean that?"

He laughed. "By heck, that brought you back to life! Yes, I'm perfectly serious. That night you were on ops, she spent the whole damned night watching the situation board. When it became obvious you were overdue, I thought she was going to come apart. Then we received the news you were on your way in but badly shot up. She asked if she could go to the tower to see you land. I'm afraid I refused her permission. If Sammy had got it wrong on the approach and spread you all over the airfield, she'd have witnessed something she'd never forget for the rest of her life. So I kept her busy until news filtered through that you were down safely, albeit a bit tattered at the edges. I missed her for a while but then found her outside having a quiet weep."

I looked at him and I knew I was the luckiest officer in intelligence to have Houseman for my boss.

"Thank you for telling me, sir. I really appreciate it as neither Nat or myself are very good at telling each other how we feel."

"Wait until you've been married a few years," warned Houseman. "You'll know what each other is thinking without saying a word. It is quite uncanny and not a little disconcerting."

As we laughed and chatted I began to relax. I slowly realised this was not an impromptu chat at all. Houseman had worked his magic yet again. The strain and tension had gone and now I just felt very, very tired.

That night I slept the sleep of the dead.

CHAPTER SIXTEEN

Next morning, as soon as I arrived in the section, Sergeant Powell buttonholed me.

"Secret signal for you in the safe, sir."

I had spent so little time in the section, I had already forgotten the combination of the safe but Nat came to my rescue.

"You're looking distinctly better," she said as she opened the safe door and stood to one side.

I grinned. "I feel much better after last night. Still a bit stiff but I reckon I'll survive." I removed the signal from the safe and signed the receipt book. "More bloody work," I said, tapping the signal thoughtfully with my pen.

"Are you still playing 'spies'?" Nat asked. Her tone was light but I could sense a thinly veiled anxiety.

"Afraid so. Not much longer though." I closed and locked the safe door before I turned and led her to a quiet corner of the room. "Where would you like to go if we both managed to get a spot of leave at the same time?" I asked quietly.

Her blue eyes regarded me steadily for a few moments and I saw a faint smile playing fitfully at the corners of her mouth. "Bed," she said.

With that one word she had totally wrong-footed me. To my embarrassment, I felt my cheeks begin to colour. I tried hard to regain the high ground. "I thought young ladies were supposed to save themselves for marriage" I countered.

"Not this young lady, Carver. The way you keep being shot, battered and half-murdered, I reckon we'd better get down to it while you're still in a halfway fit state. The chances are you'll succumb to something dire before we get the chance to marry."

"Oh, so you do want to marry me?" I quipped.

"Of course I do, you great twit - ever since you walked through that damned door looking every inch the perfect officer - all polished and shining."

"My smart uniform did the trick, huh?"

"I was talking about your face."

"You're so nice to me."

"I know," she said without hesitation.

"Do you know how much I love you?" I asked.

She grinned. "You'd better love me a lot if I'm to let you have your evil way with me."

I was lost for words. No woman had ever spoken so directly to me before, especially about sex. From her, the remark was explicit but not crude. She was just being honest and I loved her even more when I realised she was comfortable enough with me to make such a remark. I decided not to try a smart rejoinder.

"So, where would you like to go?" I asked her.

"My home."

I looked at her in surprise. "Your home? How on earth can we indulge ourselves in unbridled passion if your parents are there?"

211

"It is a large house and where there's a will there's a way."

I shrugged. "Okay, we go to your home. Where is it? You did tell me but I've forgotten."

"Stoke Fleming in Devon. It is just up the coast from Dartmouth."

"Dartmouth!" I exclaimed. "How come you're not in the Wrens?"

"All through my childhood I was surrounded by the Royal Navy. The last thing I wanted to do was join their ranks."

"Their loss is my gain."

She laughed. "Flatterer."

"I'm serious," I replied and lightly touched her hand.

"Can I continue with my story, Carver?" she asked with a grin.

"Sorry, I thought you'd finished. I hope you're not going to make a saga out of it as I've a lot of work to do!" I ducked as she aimed a playful clout at my head. I held up my hands in mock surrender. "Okay. I'm all ears."

"I had noticed a pachydermatous resemblance."

I looked at her and grinned. "Isn't that a dirty word for an elephant?"

She was all innocence. "also It actually means 'thick-skinned'."

I sighed. "You really know how to hurt a man."

She tilted her head to one side. "I think my father is going to like you. He too, is very good at playing the hard-done-by male."

"What's his profession?"

"He's retired. He used to work for the Foreign Office but I've no idea what he did there. He was frequently away from home but my mother did a great job of bringing me up. In fact we ended up more like sisters than mother and daughter. She was forty-one when I was born and dad was fifty-five but, in spite of the disparity in our ages, we've always been a close family and I love them both deeply. I know you'll like them."

"But will they like me?" I asked and I was only half joking when I said it.

She laughed. "They will view you with great suspicion at first but, once they know you're the man I am going to marry, they will accept you and spoil you until it hurts."

I pulled her to me. "I think I could get accustomed to that." I could feel the warmth of her body and all I could see in her eyes was the reflection of my love for her. There was no doubt any more. She was as much in love with me as I was with her.

I heard Houseman's voice in the corridor outside as he shouted something to Tom Powell. We had managed to step apart before the door opened and he walked in. He glanced at us and there was a small smile on his face. He just nodded in the direction of his office.

I sighed and grinned at Nat. "Duty calls."

She smiled and I felt her fingers brush the back of my hand. "It always does when there's a war on." She went back to her work and I followed Houseman to his office. The spell had been broken.

In his office, Houseman watched me open the signal. It was from Face and it listed the RAF stations in Lincolnshire hosting Polish squadrons. I read it and passed it to Houseman.

"Where the hell do I start? It will be like looking for the proverbial needle in a haystack."

There was a light knock on the door.

"Enter!" called Houseman and salvation walked in the door in the shape of the author of the signal.

"Morning Jake, morning Carver," Face said cheerfully as he nodded at the signal in Houseman's hand. "I see you got my list."

Houseman handed me back the signal.

I nodded. "Yes, sir, but I'm going to need some expert help to try and formulate a plan of visits. Which ones will be our priority?"

"Where are the bases again?" asked Houseman as he peered over my shoulder.

"Swinderby, Hemswell, Ingham, Faldingworth and Kirton-in-Lindsey." I read them out for him.

"Most of those are bomber squadrons," remarked Houseman. "Mind you, that does not mean a Wellington pilot couldn't fly a Hurricane."

Face eased himself into a chair. "The first thought that comes to me is that all those airfields are a fairish way from Friskney. They are all up in the Lincoln area. There again, that could explain the infrequency of the attacks."

I tapped the signal with my finger. "Which one of these bases has an operational role that would give a pilot reasonable freedom to disappear without attracting too much attention?"

"None more than the other," Houseman answered. "Bombers or fighters are at the beck and call of every whim from their respective commands. You know yourself how the situation can change from one minute to the next."

There was a knock at the door and Sergeant Powell walked in. He pulled up short. "Oh, I'm sorry, sir, I thought you were alone."

"Okay, Sarge, what is it?"

Tom handed him a sheaf of papers. "I must have your signature on these, sir. I need to get them on the mail run to Grantham."

Houseman quickly perused the papers and signed. As he handed them back he popped Tom a quick question. "Sarge, what do you know about the Polish Air Force in Lincolnshire?"

Tom screwed up his eyes as he concentrated on the surprise question. "Well, sir, I was at Swinderby in 1940 when the first of them arrived from Bramcote. Good lads but compared with our lot, a bit erratic. They had only two things in mind - fighting and fu........ahem.....sex, sir."

Face laughed. "I've heard they're a lusty lot!"

Tom grinned. "Lusty, sir? They are like penises with legs. Nothing and nobody was safe. If it breathed and had at least two legs, it was fair game."

I laughed. "Sounds like a posting for Bourne."

A look of horror crossed Tom's face. "No way, sir! I said 'two legs'. That one is an animal - must have at least four."

"What about the Poles around here, Sarge?" Face was laughing but steered Tom back on track.

Tom shook his head. "None round here, sir. The nearest would be Faldingworth or somewhere like that." He paused and then said in a matter of fact voice, "If you don't count those at Sutton Bridge."

There was a sudden and very long silence as Houseman, Face and myself exchanged surprised glances.

Tom looked uncomfortable. "Did I say something wrong, sir?"

"Just the opposite, Sarge," Houseman hurried to reassure him. "In fact you may have saved us a lot of valuable time. What do you know about the Polish squadron at Sutton Bridge?"

Tom shook his head. "There's no Polish squadron there, sir, just two Polish captains as flying instructors on Hurricanes and Spitfires. Polish fighter squadrons, working up to operational readiness or on refresher courses, go there for gunnery and air combat training. They had to post in a couple of native Poles as half of their countrymen passing through the the school couldn't even speak English. They've got a couple of Czechs and a Froggie there too."

Face looked at Tom in amazement. "How do you know all this, Sarge?"

"I spent a four month detachment there, sir."

Face smiled wryly. "So much for our superb intelligence machine. Just shows how important bits can drop through the net."

"Is that all, sir?" asked Tom as he headed for the door.

Houseman nodded. "Yes, Sarge, and thank you very much for your help but what we've just talked about is confidential, okay?"

"Of course, sir," Tom assured Houseman as he closed the door behind him.

"Well, I'll be buggered," exclaimed Face. "Sutton - bloody - Bridge! That's about twenty miles south-east of Boston." He raised his eyes to the roof as he did a quick mental calculation. "That's about thirty miles from Friskney."

"Wouldn't take long on a powerful motorbike," added Houseman.

Face headed for the door. "I'll use the phone next door and get some info on the pilots at Sutton Bridge."

Houseman waited for the door to close behind Face. "Looks like a detachment to Sutton Bridge for you, young man."

"Why could it not have been an airfield somewhere off these bloody fens?" I moaned.

He laughed. "The flatter the better. Aeroplanes have a nasty habit of trying to fly through hills."

I thought for a few seconds and then voiced those thoughts. "What cover can I use at Sutton Bridge?"

Houseman waved a dismissive hand. "Don't worry about that, we'll think of something. The most important factor is time. The sooner you're in position, the better." He glanced at his watch. "I've kept the station commander up to date but I'd better give him a ring with this latest development."

After a short pause, he was finally connected with the Groupie. "Sutton Bridge, sir."

That was all he said. He listened for a while then smiled and gave me a thumbs-up. "Thank you, sir. That would speed things up enormously."

He replaced the receiver. "A bit more good luck has come our way. Groupie knows the station commander at Sutton Bridge. He'll arrange, along with Wing Commander Face, a cover story for your detachment. He agrees that we should get you in there ASAP."

I tried to ease myself into a more comfortable position but my back and buttocks felt as if they were on fire again.

"You feeling okay?" Houseman asked with a frown.

"Fine, sir. I just get twinges now and then." I could hardly confess that the thought of coming face to face with the bastard who had shot down our aircraft filled me with unease. He'd nearly killed Sammy Mason's lads and myself. This had become personal and I was worried how I might react. Would I recognise the guy? It had only been a fleeting glimpse in the mirror. For sure, he'd not seen my face well enough to know me again. Could I meet him and control myself sufficiently so as not to give the game away? The doubts flashed through my mind but before I could even attempt to rationalise them, Face barged back into the office.

"The info will be telexed here in code as soon as they have it." He fished around in his briefcase and eventually handed me a stack of photographs. "Take a look at those, Carver. I brought them with me to see if we can jog your memory."

I studied the photos depicting Polish insignia and uniforms. I pointed to the silver eagle with the wreath. "That is all I can recognise, sir."

Face stroked his chin. "You said he was wearing his greatcoat, didn't you?"

I nodded.

"Did the greatcoat have a flash at the top of the sleeve?"

"No idea, sir. I only caught a glimpse."

Face pondered for a minute. "Mmm, I'm not even sure they have flashes on their greatcoats but they certainly do on their tunic. At the top of the sleeve there is the word 'POLAND' embroidered in a flash. The letters are light blue on a grey blue background. Well, at least the officers have the flash and if our man is a captain, then he's the equivalent of a flight lieutenant. They are not actually in the RAF. They are not 'Free Poles' like the 'Free French'. They actually form part of the armed forces of the sovereign state of the Republic of Poland with their government temporarily located in London. Their full title is Polskie Siły Powietrzne and they are the Polish Air Force, not the Royal Air Force."

"Well," I said as I stood to ease the pain in my back. "If there are only two of them at Sutton Bridge, I shouldn't have my work cut out identifying our man."

"You're sure he didn't see you?" stressed Face.

"Pretty certain, sir. He'd have seen my uniform but to see my face in the mirror in that dim light, he'd have needed x-ray eyes."

"Okay," Face murmured. "Now we've to find a cover story for your visit."

Houseman rose. "Actually, sir, the station commander would like to see you. He's an idea to discuss with you."

Face grabbed his cap. "Right, I'd better get over there." He paused in the doorway. "I've just had a thought, Jake. If these Poles are such sex maniacs, then Carver ought to have a pretty girl with him. Might put them off their guard a bit."

Houseman and I looked at each other and burst out laughing. It was Houseman who spoke our thoughts aloud.

"Well, that rules Bourne out."

"What about the young lady in the outer office?" asked Face.

Houseman groaned. "Oh no, not Natalie again. The rest of the staff are going to get really pissed off at the extra work for them when I take her out of the system."

Face grinned. "Just tell them it is in the interests of national security." He swept out of the door before Houseman could reply.

Houseman looked at me and smiled ruefully. "Ah, well, at least the lovebirds will be together for a few hours."

"You're not expecting me to complain, are you, sir?"

Houseman pointed to the door. "Bugger off, Carver. Go pack a bag and warn Natalie to do the same. I've a feeling you'll soon be on your way."

"Any chance of that leave when we get back, sir?" I asked with a straight face.

He grinned. "I'll think about it. Now, bugger off."

Just two hours later, Natalie and I had our orders. We were to pick up a Tilly from MT the following morning and drive down to Sutton Bridge. Face was having the identification letters on the Tilly changed to hide the fact that we were from West Fen and part of Five Group. It had been arranged that our cover was that of two officers from the RAF Film Unit making a recce into a possible film about advanced flying training facilities in the RAF. As RAF Sutton Bridge was the last posting for many before joining their first operational squadron, it fitted the bill nicely. A Flying Officer Browning, who had the unenviable secondary duty of Station Press Officer, would escort us around.Despite our protest that we knew nothing about film making, Face insisted we could busk it for the few hours we would be there. I only wished I had his confidence in our acting abilities.

The next morning dawned bright and clear as we headed down to Sutton Bridge. Boston looked so much better by daylight and the Stump was quite impressive.

Natalie nodded as we passed a working windmill on the way into town. "We must come and take a proper look at that sometime. Also, I'd imagine the church must be something to see too."

I nodded. "We'll bring Max with us and he can try out the organ."

She looked at me in surprise. "Max can play the organ?"

"Haven't you heard him?"

"Nope. He doesn't go anywhere near the piano in the mess."

I shrugged. "I suppose once a mess member is known as a pianist, he'd be on call every time there was a piss up."

A sign caught my eye and I laughed. "To the Docks," I read aloud. "What sort of docks do they have in this place? It is well upriver from what I've seen of it from the air. Surely not much gets in here?"

"Plenty of reasonable size stuff," Nat replied. "Last autumn, I cycled down to the riverside, with a couple of the other girls. We saw a couple of large ships come up to the docks. We had quite a laugh when some lads on an RAF Air Sea Rescue launch whistled after us. They sounded their hooter or whatever you call it."

"Are they based in Boston dock?" I asked.

Natalie eased the Tilly through the market place. "Yes. They only have the one launch. They are billeted in town but RAF Coningsby is their parent station."

"Nice job if you can get it," I remarked.

Natalie cast a quick glance in my direction. "Surely you don't mean that? Probably great in the summer when most aircrew survive if they manage to live through the ditching. Winter is another story altogether. Think of the terrible cargoes they sometimes have to bring back. Not only do they have bad weather to contend with but they also have to get very close to the enemy coast. They have to contend with minefields, enemy seaplanes sent to sink them or capture them and God knows what else. I reckon you've to be of a certain mentality to volunteer for their job."

I grimaced. "You're quite right. It was a stupid thing to say."

We drove in companionable silence through Kirton and Sutterton and crossed the River Welland at Fosdyke. Weird and wonderful names to a man from Sussex but they were just small villages, each one seemingly empty of life. Where were all the people? Probably out in the fields, as everywhere I looked, it was agricultural land with hardly a tree in sight. Even the sun, shining from a clear blue sky, didn't do a thing to brighten the view. I was pleased when Nat finally eased up to the barrier at the entrance to RAF Sutton Bridge.

We were spot on time and, as I made to get out of the vehicle, a short, wiry and very young flying officer ran from the guardroom. The officer held out his hand and hastily pushed his glasses back up his beaky nose.

"Hi, you must be Carver."

"That's right." I held out my ID card.

He only gave it a cursory glance as he was far more interested in Natalie. He raised an eyebrow to encourage an introduction.

"Section Officer Natalie Cowen," I said politely.

He rushed around the other side of the Tilly and grabbed her hand like a drowning man. I was already beginning to harbour an intense dislike of the little shit.

"Natalie!" he enthused, totally over the top. "I'm Kit Browning and I'm the station adjutant. How welcome you are. A pretty girl is indeed a rare sight here at Ess - Bee."

'Ess - Bee?' What a crock of crap! This guy was a supercharged turd. I thought for one minute he was going to kiss her hand but I think he saw the look in my eye and decided that discretion was the better part of valour. Like me, he had no brevet but, unlike me, he had adopted the now familiar patter of aircrew. I decided to steer well clear of him if we went to the mess. I bet he went down like a fart in church.

Natalie, out of sight of Browning as he leaned through the door, made a very rude two-fingered gesture, to indicate how she was really feeling.

"Thank you, Kit," she cooed. "It is so nice to meet a real gentleman."

I swear the little runt grew three feet in point five of a second. Good move, Nat. Anything we wanted from now on, she'd only have to ask and he'd fall over himself to oblige. He pointed now towards the rear of the guardroom.

"Look, park the old Tilly round the back and we'll use the boss's Humber. The boss and I are like that." He twisted two fingers together. "He sits in the chair and I run the station."

Bullshit was the one and only word that entered my mind at that moment. The Humber was down to our Groupie being a mate of the boss here and if 'Gravy' Browning here ran the station, then we'd all better start learning how to speak Kraut.

When we reached the Humber he opened the front passenger door for Nat. His eyes nearly ended up like fried eggs on the inside of his glasses when she brazenly flashed him a bit of leg. He literally ran round to get behind the wheel and I was left to scramble into the back before we roared off at high speed.

"Is this a training film you're making?" he asked, doing a very bad impression of a racing driver as he wrestled needlessly with the wheel.

Natalie looked suitably shocked. "Kit, how could you think such a thing? This will be a feature film to run in cinemas all over the country. The folks at home will be able to see how we train our pilots."

"Wow, jolly interesting," he enthused.

I waited and finally, inevitably from a twat like him, it came and he didn't disappoint me.

"Want any local stars?" he asked jovially. "I'm free any time, you know."

"Really?" I said before I could stop myself. "How does the station run without you?"

"Delegation, old boy - delegation," he crowed.

I tried to work that out. He was only one rank higher than me and the same rank as Nat. That didn't leave too many officers junior to him on a station this size. This was a guy with a serious ego problem! He was still prattling on when I heard him say something that made my heart sink.

"Bit of 'slap' and I'm all yours," he whinnied.

It was the word 'slap' that caused me consternation. It was show business talk for 'make up'. That's all we needed - a bloody professional.

I phrased my question carefully. "You know something of show business, Gra...er...Kit?"

"Amateur dramatics, old boy," he gushed. "I'm the male star of all our station club productions."

"I bet you are," I answered, only just keeping the contempt out of my voice. "Do a lot of comedy, do you?"

From where I was sitting, I could only see Nat in rear profile but it was enough to see her jaw muscles tense as she fought to keep laughter at bay. Gravy was oblivious to the fact I was taking the piss.

"Do you have any foreign pilots here?" Nat asked casually, once she'd recovered.

"You bet we do," Browning replied as we swept to a halt outside a Nissen hut, which, from the sign on the end wall, declared itself to be the Operations Centre. He switched off the engine. "Free French, Czechs, Poles, Canucks, Aussies - you name 'em, we train 'em."

Strewth! Was he going to be a prat all day? Also, I was not too sure that the Canadians and the Aussies would take kindly to being called 'foreigners'.

He hustled us into the ops centre and shouted out to a tall, slender flight lieutenant who was making himself a cup of coffee on a table at the rear of the room. "Hey up, Richie, old boy - Hollywood's here!"

The officer turned and surveyed us over the rim of his coffee mug. He sipped tentatively on the hot liquid and smacked his lips appreciatively before placing the mug on the counter in front of him.

"Hi, Richie Holland, Duty Ops. I heard you were coming from none other than the stationmaster and wingco flying. What can I do for you?"

I made our introductions and started my spiel. "We're doing a quick recce to sort out possible locations for a film on RAF Training Command. The producer decided that this was an ideal location because you do live firing - perfect for the action shots. We would appreciate your help in pointing us in the right direction and keeping us out of trouble."

"No problem," replied Richie and I noticed he had the decency to keep his eyes on me and not ogle Nat. More than I could say for 'Gravy' Browning.

Richie took another sip of his coffee. "I've already detailed a couple of student pilots to escort you around and explain things, so what would you like to see first?"

"Some good and interesting faces," Nat interjected casually.

"Here I am, babe!" crowed Browning, throwing his arms out wide and falling to one knee. Any minute now I was really going to have to kick him in the balls.

Richie gave him a disdainful glance. "Browning, why don't you pop along and rustle up a few spare bods?"

"Of course, old boy," Browning yapped. He turned to Nat. "See you later, my lovely."

Nat blew him a kiss and I thought the poor bastard was going to ejaculate on the spot. He leapt from the room like a scalded cat.

Richie sighed. "Every bloody station has one but we've the worst - him!"

"Ours is a wing commander," I responded with a grin. "Well, he was. He's no longer with us, thank God!"

"Bloody hell!" exclaimed Richie. "At least we can sit on that little shit when he gets out of hand but a wing commander - that's bloody dangerous!" He made us coffee and we chatted idly for a while then he glanced at his watch. "Bring your coffees through to the despatch room. A flight of three Hurricanes is going off in a minute on a live firing exercise. They will mix it with a bit of dog fighting and then meet up with the drogue aircraft for the live shoot. Each aircraft has a different colour painted on their ammo so that we can identify and count the hits when the target tug drops his drogue. The flight will comprise an instructor and two students."

"Has anybody ever shot the target tug down by mistake?" laughed Nat.

"I'm afraid so," Richie grinned wryly. "Once they get up there, students can have a rush of blood and testosterone. A fatal cocktail from the tug pilot's point of view."

Nat put a hand to her mouth in shock. "I was only joking."

"I wish I was," Richie answered grimly. He brightened up. "Right, let's see what we can offer in the way of picture opportunities."

He led us through into the main ops room. Like ops rooms everywhere, the walls were covered with large charts, maps, flight safety posters, standing orders and instructions of all kinds. We'd entered the room from a door at the rear and were now behind the counter on which lay all the Form 700s for the aircraft out on the flights. A warrant officer and a flight sergeant were busy keeping the state board up to date with aircraft availability.

Richie pointed to the counter. "This should be a good place to come to once you've filmed a briefing. Here, the instructors and students sign the 700s for their aircraft. The F700 is signed by all the aircraft tradesmen and should leave a kite snag free. Sounds good but these kites are worked to death and we're often desperate to meet operational requirements. A kite may actually have a snag, but if that snag poses no danger, we 'red line' it in the F700 for the attention of the pilots. Also in there are the fuel and weapon loads. Think it will be of interest?"

I nodded. "It will make good close ups and help build the tension."

Nat gave me a quick admiring glance. Oh yes, Carver was getting quite good at the bullshit.

"Who did you say makes up this flight?" Nat asked casually.

Richie glanced at the state board, which we had pointedly ignored. "The instructor is Jerzy Giedrovski, one of the Polish guys and he's leading two pilot officer students."

I dare not look at Nat. Only two Polish guys on the station and we were already about to meet one of them. I started chewing at my nails as we waited and Nat gave me a nudge with her elbow.

"Stop, or you'll reach your knuckles."

"What?" asked Richie, half turning from the state board.

"Just telling my partner to stop chewing his nails," replied Nat. "He recently stopped smoking."

Richie smiled politely and went back to work checking all was ready for the impending sortie.

Suddenly, the door opened and two youngsters walked in, each wearing a thick flying suit and Mae West. They had their maps stuffed casually into the top of their flying boots but no matter how hard they tried to look like steely-eyed fighter pilots, they still looked like a couple of schoolboys. Bloody hell! If the pilots were starting to look younger, I must be ageing fast!

The door opened again and Nat and I waited with bated breath.

He was about five feet eight or nine inches tall and had jet black, wavy hair. He was wearing the customary winter flying suit plus Mae West and carried his helmet, oxygen mask and goggles in his left hand. At first he didn't seem to notice Nat and myself.

"Have you signed yet?" he asked the student pilots as he pulled out a pen to sign for his own aircraft.

"Not yet, sir," replied one of the lads as he laboriously checked out his own F700.

219

"Please! You bloody move, yes? We don't have a full day for just you two." He glanced up and, unseen by the two students, winked at the flight sergeant. It was then that he first noticed us. Actually, he gave the impression of seeing only Nat. I was of no interest to him but he was to me. I could feel my heart begin to pump harder as the adrenaline flowed into my system. I knew I was looking at the man I had seen fleetingly in the Red Lion.

He smiled at Nat and his handsome face, spoilt slightly by a nose that was a little too large, seemed to light up. His eyes were a peculiar icy grey and the smile did nothing to melt their inherent coldness.

"Good morning, madam," he said to Natalie.

"Good morning, captain." She smiled broadly as she replied.

For a fraction of a second his smile wavered and he glanced quickly at me for the first time. There was no hint of recognition but Nat had blundered badly. There was nothing on his flying suit to indicate his status so how did she know his rank?

I stepped forward quickly to try to mend the breach in our cover. I smiled and held out my hand. "Captain Giedrovski? Flight Lieutenant Holland told us to expect you and we've been waiting to meet you."

He reluctantly shook my hand. The smile was back but it had still lost its way somewhere between his mouth and his eyes.

I plugged on. "My colleague and I are from the RAF Film Unit. We've been briefed to make a film about advanced flying training with special emphasis on the valuable role played by foreign instructors. We were ordered to make contact with yourself and your countryman, plus the two Czechs. I hope you and the others will not object to becoming film stars for a short while?"

His eyes widened slightly but he still smiled. "You think I'll make like a good film star?" he asked quietly.

I was tempted to tell him he stood no chance with a conk like his.

"I'm sure you will," Nat answered enthusiastically.

He gave a slight bow from the waist in her direction. "In that case, I'll be happy to do this for you. When do you make your film?"

I took over. "At the moment we're filming at Cranwell but, if this recce goes well, we should be ready in about a week's time."

He nodded. "God willing, I'll still be here."

He turned to the flight sergeant and tapped the F700 for his aircraft. "Flight, I see I've a full fuel load."

"That's right, sir," confirmed the NCO after a quick check of the F700.

Giedrovski looked up at Richie. "In that case, can I change my flight profile?"

"Depends what you want, Jez."

The Pole thought for a second. "I think I stay up there. I not come back with the first two students. Send next two students early and I wait over range area." He nodded at the two young students. "These two must wait for debrief when I land with second flight."

Richie nodded. "Sounds good. I'll make sure the second pair are airborne early although you've got plenty of fuel - even after thrashing around in a dogfight."

The Pole nodded. "Thank you, Richie." He turned to Nat. "I look forward to being your Charlie Chaplin."

We both called out our thanks as he led the two students out and over to the three Hurricanes waiting on the flight line.

As the door closed behind them, Nat turned to look at me. She raised a questioning eyebrow and I nodded. Her face turned white and I quickly squeezed her

220

hand.

"Mind if we walk out and watch them takeoff?" I asked Richie, trying to keep my voice casual.

"Be my guest." I lifted the hatchway in the counter and we strolled out through the door. The three Hurricanes were parked some way away from the building. Their tails were towards us and the red 'Aircraft Armed' signs emphasised the prudence of having the guns pointing away from the buildings. Three airmen helped the pilots to strap in and soon the Merlin engines burst into life. The propwash flattened the grass and the scent of burnt avgas filled our nostrils. The nearest aircraft roared as the chocks were pulled away from its wheels and it began to taxi across our front towards the runway. The other two aircraft quickly followed and all three zigzagged as the pilots swung their aircraft to improve their view beyond the nose. As the lead aircraft passed, I realised the pilot was Giedrovski. His oxygen mask hung loosely to one side and, as he passed, he turned his head to look directly at us. His eyes found mine and he gave a small grin. His gaze still locked with mine, he slowly raised his right hand over the rim of the cockpit and my blood froze. He had formed an imaginary pistol with the shape of his hand and he pointed the two extended fingers of the barrel in my direction. He made a sharp motion of imaginary recoil and I saw his mouth open wide in silent laughter. The bastard knew exactly who we were and what we were doing at Sutton bridge. He'd not been fooled by my explanation. Nat's slip had been all the warning he needed.

As the three Hurricanes taxied away, Nat grabbed my arm. "He knows, Sam, he knows."

I wrenched away from her and ran back into the ops room. Richie looked up in surprise at my haste and I motioned him into the back office. I closed the door and grabbed his arm.

"You've got to stop those aircraft taking off!" In my panic I was half shouting.

He shook my hand from his arm and stepped back away from me. His face registered a mixture of alarm and anger. "What the hell are you going on about?" he asked angrily?

I tried again. "We're not from any bloody film unit, we're intelligence officers and you must stop those kites."

"And my cock's a kipper!" he replied scornfully.

I grabbed the phone off the desk. "Call your station commander, now. He knows who we really are and we must stop Giedrovski getting airborne."

It was a fruitless and tardy plea. The windowpanes rattled in their metal frames as the three Hurricanes roared into the sky and turned towards the Wash.

"Oh, fucking forget it!" I slammed the phone back down on the desk and slumped into a chair.

Richie quickly opened the door. "Flight! Ask the young lady to come in here."

Natalie looked totally dejected as Richie closed the door behind her. I rose and guided her down into my chair. Richie picked up the phone and asked to be connected with the station commander's office. He stood for a while and then turned to look at me as he checked our true identity. His eyes widened in surprise as he listened. He finally slammed down the phone and ran into the main office. As I followed, I saw him flick a switch on a squawk box.

"Tower? - Ops here. Recall Red Flight immediately. No questions, this is an emergency."

The door opened and Browning appeared with two very reluctant aircrew in tow.

"Here we are," he called brightly. "Two future stars of the silver screen."

"Get out, you fucking prat!" hissed Richie and Browning scuttled away, pushing his two baffled 'volunteers' in front of him.

Richie rounded on me. "Why the hell were we not told about all this bloody cloak and dagger shit?"

"I'm sorry, Richie," I replied. "It was a case of 'need to know'. I'm afraid our bosses made the decision."

"Ops from tower." The squawk box burst into life.

Richie flicked the switch. "Go ahead, tower."

"Sorry, old man, can't make contact with Red Flight. We're getting no answer from Red Leader but we did get a garbled squawk from one of the others."

"Could you make out anything from the transmission?" Richie's voice was tense.

"All we got was a burst of static and what sounded like the word 'downed' or something like that."

"Hold one, tower." Richie spun round to the flight sergeant. "Flight, who are the two pilots in Blue Flight due to join Giedrovski on the range?"

"Moss and Barber, sir."

"Get them airborne, now!" He turned back to the squawk box. "Any bearing on that transmission, tower?"

"No, I'm afraid not. All I can tell you is that they headed due north from here out over the Wash and the range."

The door crashed open as the flight sergeant and two young pilots dashed into the room. The two youngsters were still struggling into their flying kit and looked startled by all the panic. The flight sergeant rushed out through the door to the airfield.

Richie turned back to me. "Are you sure he knows that all that film unit stuff was a load of balls?"

"I've no doubts at all." I was already beginning to think along the same lines as Richie.

Richie turned back to the two youngsters. "Right! Get airborne. Head due north to the practice and range area. Start looking for wreckage, oil or even dinghies."

"Oh God, no," I heard Nat whisper.

"What's going on, sir?" asked one of the pilots.

"Just get fucking airborne, now!" Richie yelled and the two lads ran from the room.

There was a sound of engines starting up out on the flight line. The flight sergeant must have warned the ground crews to start the engines to enable the pilots to scramble without delay. We waited without speaking until the sound of the two Hurricanes faded into the distance. The squawk box stayed stubbornly silent for what seemed an eternity but then it crackled into life.

"Ops - Tower."

"Go ahead, tower," snapped Richie.

"Blue Two reports wreckage and oil just off Seal Sand."

"Oh, fucking hell!" I smashed my fist down on the counter in fury. This is what happened when amateurs like me tried to do the professionals' job.

"Blue One now reports a dinghy in the water about two miles off Hunstanton. A lifeboat is already on its way to the position of the dinghy. What the hell is going on, Richie?"

"You've heard and seen nothing, okay?" snapped Richie.

"Okay, old boy, keep your shirt on. We'll keep you posted."

They kept their word and it was bad news all the way down the line. The lifeboat crew, in touch by radio, informed the tower they had found a badly wounded survivor in the dinghy. They had also found the pilot of the other Hurricane floating among the wreckage of his aircraft. He was dead.

Richie had informed the station commander of events and he arrived in a rush, accompanied by a wing commander. They listened while Richie filled them in on events to date and I had the impression they were trying hard not to look at me.

The station commander, a group captain, was a short stocky man with red hair. He had the pugnacious look of a boxer. The wing commander was average height and build but there was nothing average about the number of ribbons on his chest. This officer had been around and he was still only a young man.

The group captain nodded for me to join him outside. The wing commander came too.

"What went wrong, Pilot Officer Carver?" asked the group captain. He was standing with his arms folded across his chest and his legs wide apart. His chin jutted aggressively forward as if tempting me to throw the first punch.

"He saw through us straight away, sir. I'm sorry but he was just too smart to be taken in by our cover story."

I wasn't going to let Nat take the blame.

"Brilliant. Now one of my young men is dead and another in a pretty bad way. My unit has also lost three very valuable Hurricanes. I think the whole thing has been a bloody shambles. I'm going to have a serious chat about you with Group Captain Edmunds at West Fen." He sighed and his tone mellowed, "There again, I'm as much to blame for letting this bloody affair go ahead without taking advice."

"I'm afraid my bosses decided we had to act quickly, sir," I said quietly. "I'm sorry about the way things turned out but, in spite of today's tragedy, it is possible a lot of other lives may have been saved."

"Why all this interest in Jez Giedrovski?" asked the wing commander. "He's a bloody good pilot and a natural instructor."

The station commander held up a hand. "Don't ask that question because even I don't know the answer. I was just asked to play host while this chap and his colleague took a quiet look at our foreign instructors. I had no idea everything would turn tits up like this." He looked out across the airfield and then turned back to me. "Right, Carver, you started this mess, you'd better get back in there and see if you can salvage something from the day."

"Thank you, sir. I really am sorry about the way things turned out."

"Not half as much as I am," he replied curtly as they strode back into the building.

"Keep me posted, Holland," called the wing commander as they headed back to SHQ.

Richie looked at me and, for the first time since the panic began, he smiled ruefully. "I didn't hear him screaming so I imagine they are not going to send you to the gibbet?"

"Nothing is certain, yet," I shook my head sadly.

"It was all my fault," said Nat quietly.

"That's nonsense," I said quickly. "We were just not ready for him. Why did he have to be the first bloody guy we met?"

Richie put a hand on Nat's shoulder. "There will be time for recriminations later. More important is finding out exactly what happened. The lifeboat coxswain wanted to tell the tower over the radio what happened. They were actually exercising in the area and saw it all. Al, the officer in the watchtower, shut him up quick and told him to talk to nobody until the authorities have seen him." He paused and looked at us expectantly. "You're the 'authorities' aren't you?"

I pulled myself together. He was right. The job may have gone badly but there was still work to do. "Sorry, Richie, feeling a bit sorry for myself. Where do we find the lifeboat crew?"

He looked at a piece of paper on the table. "Shit, can't read my own writing.... here we are...the lifeboat was taking the injured pilot into King's Lynn docks for transfer to the hospital there. The body will be off-loaded there too. They're probably now heading back home to Hunstanton. I suggest you get over there smartish and debrief the crew before the story is all over the town."

Nat and I headed for the door. "Thanks, Richie. Sorry to spoil your day."

"Just get the bastard!" was all he said.

We had to run the whole way to where we'd left the car. No bloody Browning now we actually needed him.

Nat drove like a woman possessed and we were soon searching Hunstanton for the lifeboat station. We quickly found it and, as we pulled up in a screech of brakes, the crew were hosing down the boat and stowing their gear.

A small slim man, wearing a thick blue woollen jumper came over as we climbed out of the Tilly. He looked to be in his late sixties and his face was the colour and texture of a walnut, topped by a healthy growth of thick, grey hair.

"I suppose you're the authorities I've been hearing about?" he said in a broad Norfolk accent. Any other time I'd have found it charming but now I just wanted information.

"That's right," I answered sharply. "What happened out there?"

He looked at me steadily. "Have you got anything to say you're who you say you are?" he asked loudly. " 'Cos, if you haven't, you can bugger off."

Bad start, Carver. I raised a placating hand and fished my 1250 out with the other. "I'm sorry. I'm Sam and this is Natalie. Please, we really need to know what happened."

He looked somewhat mollified and fixed me with his sharp, grey eyes and lowered his shaggy, grey eyebrows. "He shot 'em both down."

"Who did?" I prompted.

"The other bloody Hurricane," he replied as if I was a complete idiot. Actually, the way I was behaving, he was not far off the mark.

"Tell us exactly what you saw," I said quietly.

He scratched his head. "Well, they came out over the coast from the direction of Sutton Bridge in a formation like one at the front and two, side by side, behind him."

"Vic formation," I prompted.

"If you say so, boy," he replied. "Then the one at the front suddenly pulls up, rolls over the other two until he's dropped down behind 'em and then he opened fire. The one on the left just nosed straight down into the water. The one on the right tried to turn away but he was already on fire. He was too low to jump so he put her down on the water. The old boy managed it, in spite of him being in a hell of a mess."

"What happened to the one who did the shooting?" asked Nat.

The coxswain pointed. "He cut across just to the north of the town and out over Brancaster Bay - he'd be just a touch north of east."

"I understand you took the injured pilot to King's Lynn?" I was still looking in the direction Giedrovski had flown.

"Aye, and the other one."

224

I turned back to him. "I must stress that it is imperative that you and your crew keep this to yourselves. You can understand the mess we've got on our hands after this?"

"You should have seen the bloody mess my lads had on their hands when they pulled the dead lad out of the water," he replied bitterly.

I decided it was time to go. I was behaving like a bloody idiot and I was only alienating the man even more. I put out my hand. "Thank you for your help. We really do appreciate it."

He hesitated but finally shook my hand. "Just get the bastard," he said as he returned to his crew.

Another one who wanted us to 'get the bastard!' and I wished I knew how we would ever do that. Giedrovski had literally flown the coop and it was not difficult to guess where he had gone. I remembered how he had made sure his tanks were full of fuel.

We drove back to West Fen at a more sedate pace. Nat was still feeling guilty for the slip that had triggered the warning in our quarry.

"Forget it," I said. "We're bloody amateurs and he was a pro. He's a dedicated man, with far more fire in his belly than you or I are ever likely to have, even if we live to be a hundred years old. He could have just flown away, leaving them wondering where the hell he'd gone, but not our man Giedrovski. He had to add two more to his score as a final gesture. It was a last two fingers to the enemy."

We drove on in silence, each with our thoughts. The predominant thought in my mind was that, at last, for me it was all over. The airstrip was no more and the pilot had gone. There was still the suspicion of an agent at West Fen and the Meacher farm was probably not what it seemed but that was a problem for the professionals.

"That's that," I said, half to myself.

Nat reached out and took my hand. "Thank God for that."

I squeezed her hand. "We should now get that leave Houseman promised us."

She dropped a gear and thrust her foot down hard on the accelerator. "Then let's not waste time," she replied grimly. We flew back to West Fen!

CHAPTER SEVENTEEN

The next two days were taken up by a full debrief on the debacle at Sutton Bridge. Natalie kept blaming herself but, as Face explained, Giedrovski must have intended making a move before long. Unfortunately the circumstances had been just right for him the day we visited Sutton Bridge and our slip had inadvertently forced his hand.

I could still see the arrogant gesture and the smirk on his face as he'd taxied past leading the two unsuspecting youngsters. In moments of private contemplation, I had discovered a previously unsuspected rage as I thought of the good men he had betrayed and killed. I had flights of fancy as I dreamed of the unlikely day we would meet again. I'd feel no compassion - I just wanted the chance to kill him in cold blood and watch his face as I took his life slowly and painfully. How I was going to achieve that dream? I'd no idea. I'd never see the man again and I was deluding myself if I thought I could handle him in physical combat. Maybe Bourne could. Now there was a thought!

At least one of my dreams did come true. Houseman kept his promise and Nat and I went on leave at last. Clutching our travel warrants we boarded the early morning train out of Boston station. Nat had called her parents the previous evening and her father had promised he'd be waiting for us at Kingswear station. Although officially retired, her father worked for the Admiralty as a civilian - hence he had a petrol allowance for his old Lanchester car.

The rail journey from Lincolnshire to Devon seemed interminable. There were frequent delays and the trains were crowded. It was already dark when we steamed into Kingswear station. We waited until a crowd of sailors had noisily detrained into the darkness before we made our own way down the platform. My back wound was throbbing again and I had a nightmare of a headache. I suddenly realised I could go no further and I dropped our bags onto the platform.

"Are you okay, Sam?" asked Nat anxiously.

I took a deep breath and coughed as I took in a lungful of sulphurous smoke from the panting engine at the head of the train. I wiped my eyes. "I'm fine - just need a rest."

Then, as if plucked from the cutting room floor of Ealing Studios, the steam rolling over the platform swirled away on a sudden eddy of cold air from the River Dart, leaving the indistinct shadow of a tall man standing perfectly still in the gloom. Only the absence of dramatic music marred the tableau. We heard the sigh of the wind, the asthmatic wheezing of the engine and the fading laughter of the departing sailors but it was hardly the same effect. I shivered as another gust of cold wind, carrying the damp, sour scent of the sea, blew away the last tendrils of steam.

"Dad!" Nat ran forward and the shadowy figure opened his arms to embrace her.

"Hello, Beanpole!" The man laughed as he clasped her to him. I couldn't see his face in the darkness but I knew his eyes were looking at me over her shoulder. He swung Nat off her feet and stood her to one side. He held out a hand. "This must be

226

Sam."

"Good evening, sir," I replied as I shook his hand. He took me by the arm and slipped his other arm through Nat's.

"Jack!" he shouted down the platform.

A small, elderly porter quickly emerged from the darkness as if he'd been awaiting the summons.

"Yes, Mr Cowen?"

"Could you pop these bags into my car, Jack - it's out front."

"Certainly, sir." The little man whipped the bags away into the darkness.

Cowen crossed the platform and opened the door to the waiting room. He ushered us through the blackout curtain and we blinked in the light from the gas lamp. There was a cheery fire in the small fireplace, giving the austere room a token ambience of welcome.

It was not only the sudden light that made me blink. I had to blink hard a couple more times to make sure I was not dreaming. There, standing with her back to the fire, was the most beautiful elderly lady I had ever seen. Her hands were clasped behind her back and her whole posture was that of self-assurance and dignity. Her light grey hair seemed to take on the warm glow from the fire behind her, creating a surreal frame to her beautiful face. She was tall and wore a simple long dark coat with a tasteful batik scarf draped loosely around her neck. Her eyes and face lit up when she saw Natalie and she strode forward in an elegant sweeping motion.

"Hello, darling," she said as she hugged Nat to her. Her voice was low and husky. It was the voice of a much younger woman but she had to be at least seventy years old.

Nat gently freed herself from her mother's arms and walked over to me. She hooked her arm through mine. "Mummy, this is Sam." She said it simply enough but I felt myself colour slightly as I heard the pride in her voice.

Mrs Cowen stood stock still for a few seconds, her head tilted slightly to one side as she looked at me. From a person other than her, the stance and steady gaze would have been offensive. From her, it was simply a contemplative survey whilst she made up her mind about me. To my relief she seemed to like what she saw.

She walked forward and opened her arms. "Hello, Sam, welcome to Devon." She offered each cheek in turn for a kiss. Her hands rested lightly on my shoulders for the embrace and I felt her grip tighten momentarily in welcome. She finally stepped back, held me at arms length and smiled. "Natalie has told us so much about you in her letters, I feel we know you already. She's been at pains to stress how you have an innate ability to end up in hospital at the drop of a hat."

I grinned. "I'm afraid I'm a little accident prone at the moment but I'm hoping to rectify the situation."

Cowen laughed. "I jolly well hope so, young man. Wartime is not the best time to be accident-prone. There are enough dangers without creating a few yourself."

I turned to get a better look at him. Even in the yellow light of the gas lamps, he was a handsome man. His hair was white and cut short. He had a small white military moustache that contrasted well with his ruddy complexion. His grey eyes were smiling and I knew why Natalie was so beautiful. With parents like these, she'd had a head start over the competition.

I smiled at him. "Your daughter constantly reminds me to think before I act. Maybe I should take her advice"

"Whatever next?" he laughed. "Old Beanpole giving out advice? She's never taken any, so how on earth dare she have the nerve to hand it out?"

"Ah, but look at the advice you were constantly dishing out," Nat protested and tapped a finger playfully on his chest. "Your advice was all the 'no boys' and 'no booze' variety - both of which could have been popular pursuits of mine. You were a rotten old spoil sport."

Cowen laughed and fixed me with his grey eyes. "Well, Beanpole, I think you've found a pursuit of which I'll approve." It was not said rudely or with flattery. He made it a simple statement and backed its validity with his unwavering stare. He left me in no doubt that I'd passed the initial inspection and was welcome in the Cowen home. I saw a happy little smile pass between Nat and her mother.

I returned his gaze. "Thank you, sir. That was a very kind thing to say."

"Good Lord, boy!" he exclaimed. "Let's get the formalities out of the way. I'm Matthew and my wife is Amanda. I had enough of formality in the Foreign Office. You're here for one week and during that week, our home is your home. No formalities - just enjoy yourself. We will. We don't get young people around the place now Beanpole's in the air force."

"Pop!" exclaimed Nat. "I do think it is time 'Beanpole' was confined to the Nostalgia Box in the attic. If that name ever gets out back at West Fen, my life will be hell."

"Sorry, Poppet," Cowen laughed. "You've always been 'Beanpole' to me and so you shall remain."

She hugged him to her. "Okay, you old so-and-so. I suppose it would not be home if you called me anything else."

Cowen kissed the top of her head, untangled one of his arms from Nat's embrace and held it out to his wife. "Come along, my dear, we must get these two tired souls home for supper."

My stomach rumbled loudly, as if on cue.

The others roared with laughter and Amanda grabbed my arm. "Oh, you poor soul, let's go before you expire on the spot."

There was the roar of a truck entering the station forecourt as we emerged into the cold night. It screeched to a halt and a crowd of sailors poured over the tailboard. I had a feeling of déjà vue. Boston station, darkness, the press of uniforms - it was all there. A shiver coursed through my body and Nat's mother tightened her grip on my arm.

"Relax, Sam," she said quietly. "You're here now. No more war for a whole week."

I tried to see her face in the darkness but only the outline of her face was there and I could read nothing from that.

The Lanchester stood gleaming softly in the fitful light of the moon, now casting quick gleams through the gaps in the scudding clouds. I sat in the front with Matthew and the two women sat in the back. It was only a short journey to the ferry but a long wait to be transported to the Dartmouth side of the river. Once across, it didn't take long to reach the dark and seemingly deserted village of Stoke Fleming. We turned into a narrow gravel drive and pulled up in front of a large old house, its dark shadow thrusting up into the night sky. We climbed out of the car and Matthew pulled a chain by the front door of the house. Somewhere, a bell jangled faintly. We didn't have to wait long before the door opened and a stout figure planted itself firmly in the portal.

"Hello, Mrs Simmons," called Matthew. "Only us."

"Oh, that's alright then," replied Mrs Simmons, whoever she was. Then, to my utter disbelief, I distinctly heard the unmistakable sound of a shotgun breech being broken to make it safe. Before I could express my disbelief verbally, Matthew reached my side and gripped my arm in a warning gesture. He put his mouth close to my ear.

"Our housekeeper has a morbid fear of German raiders from the sea. At night, here or at her own home, she sleeps with her deceased husband's twelve bore under her bed. When we leave her alone at night, she arms herself to the teeth. I know we have the commandos just along the coast but I reckon that Jerry would stand a better chance against them than Mrs Simmons."

"I heard that, Matthew Cowen!" called out Mrs Simmons as she opened the door fully. "Just you stop telling tales out of school!"

"She also has unbelievable powers of hearing," chuckled Matthew.

Mrs Simmons ushered us into the hall and closed the door before she switched on the light, leaving us all shielding our eyes from the sudden brightness. I saw Mrs Simmons, stout and ruddy, deftly slip the cartridges from the shotgun and drop them into the pocket of her flowered pinafore. The gun she stashed in a boot cupboard near the front door.

Nat introduced me and the housekeeper looked at me hard for a few seconds but then seemed to make up her mind.

"You look like a nice chap, Mr Carver, but you're awful thin. Come along, all of you," she commanded as she bustled off down the hall. "Supper is ready in the dining room."

What a supper it was too. I suddenly realised how poorly fed we were at West Fen. However, my pleasure at our present repast was tempered by the fact that the Cowens had probably used up most of their ration coupons for this day.

After supper, we moved through to the drawing room for coffee. We chatted about the progress of the war and the Cowens seemed genuinely interested in our anecdotes of service life. It was altogether a warm and convivial evening around a huge log fire. A style of life I had begun to think had vanished forever.

It was just after ten o'clock when Mrs Simmons popped her head around the door. "Is that all, Mrs Cowen?"

Amanda glanced at her watch. "Good heavens, is that the time? Of course, Mrs Simmons, you get off home."

"Thank you, ma'am. Good night all."

I called after her just before the door closed and she looked back in surprise. "Thank you for the lovely supper, Mrs Simmons," I said quietly.

A big smile spread over the old girl's lined features and she winked at Nat. "I think I'm in love with him already!" she said as she closed the door behind her.

Matthew laughed as he passed me a scotch from the cabinet. "Crafty move that, Sam. I guarantee tomorrow will see the biggest damned apple dumplings you've ever seen in your life. That is her speciality - if she likes you."

Nat looked surprised. "You've never mentioned that before. She's never made apple dumplings for any of my friends in the past."

"I'm afraid, my darling," chuckled Amanda, "that could be an indication as to her views on your past friends."

Nat grinned ruefully. "Some of them were a bit 'prattish', I suppose."

"Prattish?" asked Amanda with a laugh. "Where on earth is that in the English dictionary?"

"I'm afraid it is only to be found in military dictionaries, my dear." Matthew answered the question for us as he leaned over and turned on the radio for the news. It was the usual stuff and I sank further back into my chair as the tension seeped out of my muscles. The drone of the newsreader's voice and the fine old malt had a very soporific effect and I drifted off into a deep sleep.

I've no idea how long I slept but when I awoke, the room was empty and what had been a roaring fire in the hearth was now just dying embers. I was about to get to my feet when the door opened quietly.

"Ah, so you're awake at last?" said Matthew as he entered. He was carrying a battered old brass bucket full of cut logs. "We thought we'd let you sleep for a while. The ladies have gone to bed and I've locked up. These are for the fire tomorrow - they dry out nicely in here overnight." He looked at his fob watch. "Time we were in bed too. It gets damned cold down here once the fire had died."

I felt an apology was required. "I'm so sorry I was so rude."

"What? Going to sleep, you mean?"

I nodded.

"Rubbish, my boy. I know what it is like in the services. I had four years of the last lot."

"Which service?" I asked.

"Army. Royal Artillery. Started as a private and ended up as a captain. In spite of the horror of the trenches, I liked being an officer and decided to stay on in peacetime. You know, make a career of it."

"It sounds as if it didn't work out that way," I said carefully.

He glanced at me and smiled. "Beanpole said you were pretty astute when it came to people's feelings." He prodded the embers with a poker. "No, you're right, it didn't work out. When the dying was over, they wanted their exclusive club back. Grammar school boys from the wrong background were no longer welcome in the mess."

I stared into the revitalised embers. "I think things will be different once this war is over. Something tells me that serving men and women are putting up with the injustices just long enough to see us win the war. Do you know, NCO aircrews in the RAF fly the same planes and fly as many sorties as the officers but, on some of the pre-war built stations, the officers live in good permanent messes with batmen and all the mod cons. The NCOs, on the other hand, live in Nissen huts dispersed all over the ruddy local countryside. It seems in Fighter Command, things are even worse. During the Battle of Britain, officer pilots were billeted in comfortable requisitioned manor houses, well away from the airfields and the inevitable raids whilst the NCO pilots very often had to live in tents on the airfield. No safe haven for them. Damn it! They didn't even have the luxury of hot water! It is all going to happen again, you know. The old brigade is not going to want twenty-seven year old group captains around once the dangerous stuff is over. That would wreck their cushy career plans."

I looked up at Matthew as I stressed my point and continued. "There is no doubt in my mind that there will be a drastic change of government when this war is won. A lot of very disgruntled and unfairly treated men, who volunteered to fight for their country, will be determined to see a dramatic change in our class system. In fact I fear that Winston's lot will be out on their ear and look at the prats just waiting in the wings!"

"God forbid," Matthew sighed. "But I fear you're right. I'm not a communist or a rebel of any kind but I'll enjoy a certain satisfaction when it happens. Problem is, the first thing the socialists will do is give their Russian friends all our military and technological secrets. Even when the war is over, we'll find the going hard."

"What did you do after leaving the army?" I asked after a slight pause.

He grinned. "I went back to college and became an architect. In a way I should be grateful to the army because, if I'd stayed and made a career of it, things could have been very different. My old colonel, the one who turned down my application for a commission in the regiment, retired here to Dartmouth. All he could afford on his pension was a poky little flat. He died a lonely, sad old man. I went to his funeral but nobody else from the regiment was there. Being an old Etonian probably meant something in the army but it means sod all down here. I, in the meantime, had prospered. Maybe if I'd stayed in the army, I too would have become a lonely, sad old man. I'm pleased to see a different type of chap in the forces these days, Sam. You're a different breed - not afraid to question or to answer back."

I smiled. "I suppose we're a generation that accepts military discipline as a necessity to win the war but I think the old boys have got a shock coming when peace finally arrives."

He nodded. "I shall enjoy that." He glanced at his watch. "Now, it is time for bed."

In my room, a small fire burned in the hearth and an ornamental fireguard protected the rug from sparks. I quickly undressed, turned out the light and slid into the huge bed with its feather mattress. I could hear the soothing sound of the sea in the distance and that, combined with the flickering patterns of the firelight on the ceiling, lulled me into a deep and untroubled sleep.

The next morning dawned bright but windy. I could hear the wind making its noisy passage around the bulk of the old house, protesting at the detours forced upon it by the high gables and eyebrow windows. I slipped out of bed and shivered as I pulled on a dressing gown which had been hung over the back of a chair near the now dead fireplace. I walked to the window, pulled back the curtains and stopped in surprise. The view was stunning. White fluffy clouds were hastening across an azure blue sky. The sea, invisible in the darkness last night when we arrived, was now in full view with its turbulent green flecked with a myriad whitecaps. The house stood on the edge of a huge cliff with only the garden between the house and a sheer drop into the sea below. A small convoy was battering a slow passage through the waves about a mile offshore. Occasionally, one of the heavily laden little coasters would bury its stubby bow into a wave and the forepeak would disappear in a rainbow haze of spray. That would be lovely weather to the seasoned crews but what must it be like in the bigger ships on the arctic convoys? Gales, ice and U-boats. Thank God I'd joined the RAF. My reverie was interrupted by a knock at the door.

"I've just run a bath for you, sir," called Mrs Simmons.

"Thank you, I'm on my way."

"Breakfast at eight-thirty, sir."

I heard her head off along the landing. She was whistling an old music hall ditty and I wondered idly if she knew the lyric the RAF lads sang to the tune. I hoped not! I took a quick bath, dressed and headed downstairs.

Nat met me in the hall. "Come on, slowcoach! Time for breakfast. We're waiting in the dining room." She kissed me quickly on the cheek. "Just think, a whole week together. So, no wasting time in bed. Well, don't take that too literally!" She grinned and kissed me again.

"Hussy!" I said and pulled her to me. I kissed her long and hard. I could feel her tremble in my arms and I held her even tighter. I could feel the hunger in me as she moulded her body to mine. It was obvious that hunger was making itself felt in the inevitable way and she pressed her lower body hard into my groin. I had to force myself to release her and, as she buried her face in my shoulder, I could hear the breath rasping in my throat. My breathing eventually slowed and she raised her head.

She kissed me lightly on my chin and smiled up at me. "I know what we would both like to do but I'm afraid we're expected in the dining room."

"Good thing, really," I replied hoarsely. "If we'd continued down that road, it would have led to us both being banished back to West Fen for doing something extremely anti-social on the stairs."

She gave a mischievous giggle. "I'm all of a quiver at the thought."

"Anyway!" I said, holding her at arm's length. "What sort of girlfriend are you, leaving me to snore my head off and embarrass myself in front of your father?"

She smiled. "That was mother's idea. She thought you and dad should have a little time alone together."

I took her hand and we headed down the hall to the dining room. "I like your father. He's a bit like my own father but my dad was never a professional man - just a good father and I still love him to bits. Everything in my life I owe to my parents. Mother is the strong one but dad makes up for lack of expertise by having the nature of a saint. You'll like him, I'm sure."

"When will I get to meet them?" she asked.

"The next time Houseman grants us both leave at the same time."

"Not this year then" she said with a sigh.

"Don't be so pessimistic. Where there's a will there's a way!"

She laughed as she opened the door to the dining room. "I've my fingers, eyes, arms and legs all crossed."

"Don't blame me if you fall flat on your face," I replied and smartly hopped out of the way of her quick jab of the elbow towards my ribs.

"Oh no!" exclaimed Matthew as he rose from his chair at the table. "They've only been here a few hours and they're already fighting."

Nat pulled a face at her father. "Just a lovers' biff! … if you'll excuse the pun. For a junior officer, he can be very rude."

"Thank God for that," replied Matthew. "I like a man who keeps his woman in her place."

"Careful, darling," warned Amanda, pausing in the process of buttering her toast and waving her knife in his direction. "Don't say anything you may regret in the divorce courts."

Matthew winked at me. "As you can see, I've not been permitted to practise what I preach."

Breakfast continued in pretty much the same fashion. The banter was light and we discussed nothing of earth-shattering importance. It was not long before Nat and myself took our leave. We soon shrugged ourselves into warm clothing and set off to explore the glorious morning.

We headed off along the cliff path towards Dartmouth. A naval destroyer was now cleaving its way through heavy seas off Start Bay. It had an air of importance, unlike the poor old tramp steamer in the distance, straining its way across the horizon with black smoke belching out of its stubby funnel.

"I bet he's popular in a convoy," laughed Nat.

"Probably that's why he's on his own - nobody will have him in their convoy."

"Oh, don't say that!" Nat protested. "I'll have to feel sorry for the poor little thing all day and ruin our outing."

I hugged her to me. "You great softie."

We walked, still entwined, the whole way to Dartmouth. We ate an indifferent lunch in a riverside hotel and then caught the bus to Totnes.

There was a party of young sailors on the bus and I suddenly realised the huge gulf that existed between the different arms of our country's military. These lads spoke a totally different language to us. Words like 'tickler', 'scuttles', 'swine' and 'liberty' rolled off their tongues like a foreign language, which, to most people, it was. Still, it was fascinating and the journey soon passed.

We walked around Totnes for a while but, instead of waiting for another bus, we managed to scrounge a lift back in a naval supply truck. We then puffed our breathless way back up the hill out of Dartmouth towards Stoke Fleming. It was a relief to see the cliffs again.

"My God!" I gasped. "I'm totally out of condition."

"Me too," panted Nat. "It is all that work and no play at West Fen."

I looked at her in the dying light of the winter's day. "I like the way you brought up the word 'play'."

She slid her arm around my waist. "You spend so much time chasing German spies, we get very little chance to 'play'"

I stopped walking and pulled her to me. "So where, if you're so desperate for my body, are we going to 'play', as you call it, without your parents playing gooseberry?"

She sighed. "All I ever wanted was a Romeo to sweep me off my feet but what do I get? I get a man who cannot find his way from his room, across a landing, up seven steps and into the lady's chamber."

I looked up into the sky, hamming up a perplexed frown. "Those were very precise directions. I mean, a chap could possibly construe it as an invitation - even a tryst."

She giggled. "You catch on fast."

"You're definitely a hussy," I replied primly, keeping a straight face.

"If you call me that again, Carver, I shall withdraw all favours."

"Not after that invitation, you don't."

She pulled my face down to hers and cupped my face in her hands. "I love you, Carver."

I traced the line of her lips with my finger. "I love you, Cowen."

We jumped as the loud 'Whoop, whoop, whoop!' of a ship's siren sliced in from the sea. We turned to see a destroyer, probably the same one we had seen earlier, hurrying back along the coast.

"Do you think the bridge party have the binoculars on us?" laughed Nat.

"We'll soon see," I said as I grabbed her and pressed my lips to hers.

The siren went mad.

Nat pulled herself from my grasp. She was helpless with laughter. "Cheeky blighters!" she gasped. "It's not just Ma and Pa playing gooseberry, it's the whole damned Royal Navy!"

We waved to the destroyer and received another blast on the siren. In my heart I wished her and her crew well - wherever they were going.

It was totally dark by the time we got back to the house. Matthew and Amanda were in the drawing room, already sipping pre-dinner Martinis.

"Ah, the wanderers return," exclaimed Matthew as he rose from his chair. "Have a nice day?"

"It was lovely," Nat replied as she warmed her hands by the fire.

Amanda laughed. "It has certainly brought the colour to your cheeks. Wherever did you go on such a windy day?"

I told her of our trip into Dartmouth and then on to Totnes.

She smiled in recollection. "Oh, you should have been here before the war. We would take the steamer up to Totnes and have a lovely picnic by the side of the river.

Then we would have a little doze and Natalie would play football and cricket with the boys. She never once played with the other little girls. We were afraid she was going to grow up to be a bit of a tomboy but look at her now!"

I did just that. I looked at my Natalie and I felt a tightness in my chest. I also felt a frisson of fear at the depth of my love. She seemed to sense my gaze. She rose and came over to me, putting her arm through mine. "Come on, it is time we bathed and changed for dinner. If we're late, Mrs Simmons will kill us."

"Good point," agreed Matthew. "The last thing we want is a stroppy Mrs Simmons."

The dinner was well worth all the effort of washing and dressing. It was superb. Mrs Simmons or the Cowens knew somebody in the right places. That dinner would have used up a month's supply of coupons. Mrs Simmons insisted on serving me rather than me helping myself. She loaded my plate until there was no room for more and Matthew had been right about the apple dumplings.

"You need building up, young man," she said in answer to my protests.

"If you build me up any more, Mrs Simmons, I'll have to buy another uniform. This one is already getting a bit tight across the midriff."

My words were lost on her. Her response was to place another enormous apple dumpling and custard in front of me.

In spite of the excellent meal and wine I did manage to stay awake. Matthew was an excellent raconteur and he dispelled any notion that architects were a boring lot. His anecdotes were interesting and humorous and it was impossible not to listen and to enjoy them. His stories were interspersed with some from Amanda, who added to the superb evening with her tales of amateur dramatics. She was a member of a club in Dartmouth and I was in no doubt she was an accomplished actress. She had the voice, poise and looks, plus a flair for comedic delivery and timing that kept us in stitches.

At last, about eleven, we fell into a companionable silence, each with our own thoughts as we stared into the dying embers. Amanda broke the silence. She rose, smoothing her dress with her hands.

"I think it is time for me to turn in."

"Me too," yawned Nat as she too rose from her chair and stretched her arms above her head.

"Another early start tomorrow, Carver, no excuses."

I groaned. "Dear God! How can I have fallen in love with a sadist?"

I realised how easily the word 'love' had slipped from my lips. I felt a little embarrassed at the gaffe in front of her parents. I saw a little smile on Matthew's face as he exchanged glances with Amanda. It was Amanda who laughed and quickly put me at my ease.

"Other than the fact you called my daughter a sadist, that was a lovely thing to say, Sam."

I smiled wryly. "I'm sorry if I sounded a bit soppy."

Amanda threw up her arms in protest. "Oh, you men! You're so frightened to reveal your true feelings. Let yourself go, Sam. We ladies love to hear those words of endearment. Do you know how Matthew proposed? We'd been to a show and dinner in the West End of London. Just as he was about to pay the bill, he turned to me and, in a very matter of fact way I must add, said he liked me rather a lot and thought we ought to get married! He actually called me 'old thing'. I felt like a veteran car or his favourite horse." She spread her arms in disbelief.

Nat and I roared with laughter whilst poor Matthew smiled ruefully and looked distinctly uncomfortable.

"I thought you said you were going to bed, my dear," he finally protested.

"We are now," laughed Amanda. "That was my parting shot."

She linked her arm with Nat's and they crossed over to where I had just risen politely from my chair. Both women kissed me but it was Amanda who put her hand on my arm.

"We love our daughter very much, Sam. Try not to live your life too dangerously as we're beginning to love you too and we cannot afford to lose either of you."

It was a lovely thing to say and in my confusion I murmured something in reply but they were already closing the door behind them.

I turned to Matthew. "You've a very loving and caring wife, sir."

He waved me back down into my chair. "I'm a lucky man, Sam. I've a beautiful wife and a beautiful daughter. A daughter that thinks the world of you, young man. I've watched you closely and I'm sure you're genuine when you say you love her."

I nodded slowly. "With every fibre of my body. I think I loved her from the very minute I bumped into her in the doorway at West Fen."

He laughed. "I hope you did because that is where she said she fell in love with you." He leaned forward and reached out to shake my hand. "You're going to make a fine son-in-law, Sam."

I found it difficult to reply. The warmth of his acceptance of me into the family was very moving. He realised the problem I was having with my emotions and he released my hand. He rose slowly to his feet. "Now I must retire." I made to stand but he waved me back down. "No, you stay here for a few moments longer. I know how little time you and Natalie get to spend together and wartime has a habit of snatching people away." He walked over and opened the door. He turned and looked at me with a perfectly straight face but there was a twinkle in his eye. "Don't step on the fourth step of the seven - it makes a dreadful noise."

The door closed quietly behind him.

I sat quietly in my chair. Only the light from the ornate standard lamp lit the area of the room in which I sat. I felt warmth flood through my body. I thought of my own father. Would he have reacted in the same way if a potential suitor had visited my sister? I thought not. Dad, bless him, was old fashioned and Mum would have certainly acted like a Victorian chaperone. Was this what war did to people? Did it make everybody want to live for today? I sighed. What the hell did it matter? I rose and opened the door into the hall but the only sound was the loud tick of the grandfather clock at the bottom of the stairs. I returned, switched off the standard lamp and quietly closed the drawing room door. I moved silently and slowly up the stairs to my room.

I took my time as I washed and even more time cleaning my teeth. What the hell was wrong with me? Then the truth dawned. I was bloody nervous. The time had come to fulfil every dream and deepest wish I'd harboured since the day I met Natalie and here I was, behaving like a callow teenager on his first date. Get a grip, Carver. I slipped my dressing gown on over my pyjamas and moved silently out onto the landing. I moved along to the short flight of steps and took great pains to avoid the fourth. I hesitated outside the door to Nat's room. Should I knock or just walk in? Oh, bloody hell, what an amateur! I started slightly as the door opened noiselessly and the soft light from the room cast shadows on the wall behind me.

"Are you going to stand there all night?" Nat asked as she stifled a giggle.

"Just plucking up a bit of courage." I had to slap a hand over my own mouth as mirth bubbled to the surface. This was supposed to be the most romantic moment in our lives but it was rapidly turning into a bloody pantomime.

Nat grabbed my arm. "For goodness sake, you clot, come on in before you wake Ma and Pa."

She pulled me into the room and closed the door. To my surprise she led me over to the window. The heavy curtains were closed and there was a window seat covered in the same material. She pressed me down onto the seat and then moved over to switch off the bedside light. She returned and opened the curtains.

The view was like something one conjures up when reading a romantic novel. The moon shone from a cloudless sky and glistened on the sea. Nat sat down beside me and snuggled into my shoulder. I closed my arm around her and I could smell the freshness of her hair as it bunched up against my face.

"Isn't it a beautiful view?" she whispered.

"Stupendous," I admitted.

"I used to sit here as a little girl and dream about all the exotic lands beyond the horizon."

I hugged her tighter. "I used to read books and go to sleep dreaming of adventures in faraway places. You never know, we may have met up somewhere in our dreams."

She raised her head and placed a hand on my cheek. "My dreams came true the day I met you."

I couldn't reply. My throat was tight with emotion and love. I took her hand and led her to the bed. As she stood before me, I gently lifted her nightdress over her head. She raised her arms to help me and I let the silky material fall soundlessly to the floor. She was now totally naked. I could see the smoothness of her skin in the soft glow of moonlight filtering through the large window. I ran my finger from her lips, down under her chin and between her breasts. She trembled as my finger traced the contours of her stomach but I let my finger move on until I felt the soft, damp, triangle of hair.

She reached down and untied the cord of my dressing gown. She eased it off my shoulders and it joined her discarded nightdress on the floor. My pyjama jacket soon followed. I shivered with ecstasy as her cool fingers brushed the skin of my torso. She undid the cord at my waist and the last vestige of concealment left my body. Those same cool fingers began to trace their way down my chest and waist. I was trembling as her touch stopped at the hair surrounding my hardness. I lowered my mouth to her left nipple. I traced its outline with my tongue and felt it stiffen and mirror my own hardness. I ran my tongue down until I felt the moist warmth of her. She gasped and moved her fingers gently through my hair, pressing my mouth tighter to her body.

I felt I could wait no longer. I had never before in my life felt such an intense emotion. It totally overwhelmed my normal senses - nothing could penetrate the sheer intensity of desire that coursed through my brain. I slipped an arm behind her knees and one around her neck. She lay back in my arms as I gently lowered her to the bed. Her knees were drawn up and her thighs apart. I wanted to take her there and then but I knew this was different to anything I had known before. This was not to be the quick fulfilment of a callow lover. This was to be the culmination of weeks of unfulfilled love. It was to be savoured. I lay down beside her and caressed her proud breasts. I could feel her heart beating hard and fast and I knew mine was echoing its intensity. Only love was keeping the reins on our emotions when it was obvious we both wanted to take each other in a frenzy of passion. We slowly explored each other's body in the flickering light of the dying fire and the cold light of the moon. When finally I took her, it was a long and gentle coming together with, even at the supreme climax, a gentleness that surprised us both.

236

We spent the whole night completely engrossed in our love. It was the arrival of a cold and sunny dawn that eventually sent me reluctantly back to my own room. I quickly bathed and dressed. My feelings were still so aroused I found it impossible to rest so I crept downstairs and, pausing only to slip into my greatcoat, I left the house and walked to the bottom of the garden. It was cold in spite of the early morning sun and I shivered as I walked past the summerhouse and on to the garden bench at the edge of the cliff. To my surprise, Matthew was already sitting there. He too was bundled up against the cold.

"Morning, Sam." He patted the bench for me to sit beside him.

"You're out early." I blew on my already cold hands.

He nodded, stretched his legs out in front of him and breathed deeply on the cold air. "I just love mornings like this. It seems a shame to waste it by staying in bed."

I decided not to reply. I could think of a perfectly good reason this morning to stay in bed and to hell with the beautiful day. There was something I needed to say though and I waited until I had it worked out in my mind.

"You remember you kindly said I'd make a very good son-in-law?"

He chuckled. "I remember."

"Well, I'd very much like to become your son-in-law," I replied quietly.

He turned to look at me with a small smile. "Are you asking for my daughter's hand in marriage?"

I laughed. "No question about it."

"How does Beanpole feel about it - or need I ask?"

"She's all for it."

"Funny," he said, stroking his chin. "The last thing Amanda said last night was 'I hope Natalie and Sam make a go of it.' I wholeheartedly agreed with her. When do we start planning for the big day?"

I sighed. "We haven't decided. The war gets in the way of everything but she insists we should not let it stop us from doing what we want to do. She's suggesting a September wedding."

"How do you feel about that?" he asked, watching me intently and I found it difficult to meet his gaze.

"I'd marry tomorrow but obviously we must make it a real wedding. Something we can all remember for the rest of our lives."

He chuckled. "I hope the old bank balance can take it!"

We sat in silence for a few moments and finally he put a hand on my arm. "Come on, Sam, spit it out. What's troubling you?"

I looked at him in surprise and he smiled. "You wear your heart on your sleeve, young man. I'd hate to have you as a bridge partner."

I decide to be absolutely straight with him. "Matthew, I love Nat so much and I now know how much she reciprocates that love. If anything were to happen to me, I know it would kill her. Life is so bloody uncertain in wartime and I want her to be happy for the rest of her life, not grieving for a dead husband."

"Why are you talking about dying, Sam?" he asked earnestly. "Surely your job is a pretty safe post?"

"It should be from now on, I suppose." I had not intended to say it aloud.

He stood and walked to the edge of the cliff. He didn't turn round when he spoke. "Is there something you and Beanpole are not telling us, Sam? Or maybe it is something you can't tell us?" He turned to face me. "Which is it?" he asked quietly.

"There was something I was involved in but it is over now. You're right, I shouldn't be worrying about death. Nat is right too, we should not let Hitler spoil our love."

"That sounds more like the man I thought you were. Whatever your fears, Sam, it is all too late. My daughter loves you deeply and no matter what fears you may have, your biggest worry should be not to break her heart by worrying about the future. None of us can predict that and in wartime your priority should be your present happiness. As you say, the future is very unpredictable."

"Matthew!... Sam!" It was Amanda calling from the house.

Matthew trotted back to the summerhouse. "Yes, dear? We're in the garden."

"There is a phone call for Sam, dear. The man says it is urgent."

"He's on his way," Matthew shouted as I joined him.

I felt disquiet. Why the hell should anybody want to phone me here? I was on leave for Christ's sake. Then I had the dreadful thought it might be bad news of my family.

"I'd better go and see who it is."

"I hope it is nothing serious." Matthew's face was anxious.

"Probably Hitler has decided to surrender to me personally," I joked as I set off at a trot for the house.

"If it is him, tell him to piss off until you're back off leave," he shouted after me.

I ran into the hallway and Amanda was there. She too looked anxious as she held out the receiver.

I nodded my thanks. "Carver!"

It was Houseman. "Sorry to do this to you, Sam. Wing Commander Face wants you like yesterday. I'm afraid your leave is cancelled immediately."

I bit my lip to prevent an involuntary expletive embarrassing me in front of Amanda. "Any idea what it is all about, sir?"

"Sorry, Sam, not on the phone, anyway I don't know the full story. A car will collect you at midday. Bring all your clobber with you as, according to Face, you'll not be returning to Devon for some time. I'm sorry, boy, I can say no more. Needless to say, it is really very urgent." The line went dead.

Amanda took my hand. "Oh, Sam, not so soon, surely?"

I shook my head in despair. "I'm afraid so. I must be ready to leave by midday."

I heard footsteps on the stairs and glanced up. Nat had overheard our conversation and, although she was smiling, I could see the disappointment on her face.

"I do wish you were not so important, Carver. It's like trying to tie down an eel."

I gave an angry shrug. "I must be the most indispensable little pilot officer in the whole ruddy air force."

Amanda reached up and kissed my cheek. "I'm so sorry, Sam, but we must expect these things in wartime. Come along, Mrs Simmons is waiting to serve breakfast."

"That sounds good!" said Matthew as he entered and removed his duffel coat. He was about to head for the dining room when he saw our faces. "Oh Lord! Something wrong?"

Nat sighed. "Sam has just received immediate orders to return to duty. His leave has been cancelled."

"Bad luck, lad," Matthew said quietly. I knew he'd like to say more but he knew the rules - obey the last order and moan about it later.

Nat linked her arm in mine. "Come on, at least the condemned man can eat a hearty breakfast."

I am sure I was not the only one to hear the catch in her voice.

Breakfast was a subdued affair and even the normally irrepressible Mrs Simmons had little to say but, just as we were about to rise from the table, the housekeeper leaned over me and murmured in my ear.

"I've made up a nice fire up in Miss Natalie's room, sir. Perhaps you'd both like a quiet morning alone until your car arrives?"

I smiled my thanks and she squeezed my arm in reply.

"That woman is a treasure," I said to Amanda after the housekeeper had left the room.

"Nobody in this house will disagree with that statement." Amanda smiled.

The rest of the morning passed quietly. I sat with Nat on the window seat in her room and, in spite of having so much to say to each other, we sat for the most part in companionable silence. Everything we really needed to say we had said last night. It was enough just to sit there and watch the sea merge with the sky like a huge seascape in oils. It was a view I didn't want to leave behind me so soon.

Mrs Simmons had packed my things for me and, when a large military staff car of American origin roared up the drive, she was ready with my case, cap and greatcoat. She was also carrying a large brown paper carrier bag.

She tapped the bag. "A little snack for your journey, sir."

I gave her a big kiss on both cheeks. "You're very kind, Mrs Simmons."

She actually blushed and was lost for words - a very rare event.

Nat and her parents fussed around me as my WRAC driver, a young girl private, held the rear door open and saluted. Somehow she didn't do it with the saucy panache of old Foghorn. She also lacked Foghorn's bulk. She looked too petite to drive such a big car.

"May I sit in the front with you?" I asked her.

She looked pleasantly surprised. "Of course, sir."

As she closed the rear door I'd already got the front door open. She moved round and climbed in behind the wheel. I smiled to myself when I noticed she had two large cushionsat her back to help her reach the pedals.

I turned to Nat and found her fighting back the tears so I decided to make a quick exit. I shook Matthew's hand, kissed Amanda on both cheeks and kissesd Nat lightly on the nose.

"See you back at West Fen," I said quietly.

She nodded miserably. "Okay, darling. Be careful - whatever it is they want you for this time."

I grinned. "Houseman's probably lost the paperclips!"

She smiled weakly and wiped her eyes. "Clear off, Carver."

I jumped into the car, closed the door and wound the window down. I was going to say goodbye but a damned great lump formed in my throat and I decided not to risk opening my mouth. Instead I made it a quick wave and managed to avoid spoiling the hero's farewell by bursting into tears. As we roared off down the drive, I turned in my seat to get a last glimpse but they were already hidden from view by a huge yew tree. I slumped into my seat.

"What time will we get to West Fen?" I asked my driver.

She gave me a puzzled frown before she gave her full attention back to the road. "I don't know where West Fen is, sir. I'm taking you to Oxfordshire. Woodstock, actually."

"Woodstock!" I exploded. "What the hell is there at bloody Woodstock?"

"Blenheim Palace?" it was said without a glimmer of a smile.

In my misery, I was about to reprimand her for being a smart arse but I realised she was serious. Blenheim Palace. Winston Churchill's birthplace. What the hell was going on? I slumped even further into my seat. I was totally pissed off with the RAF and the silly buggers in charge. I was so engrossed in my own misery and self-pity, the driver and I exchanged not one word during the rest of the trip.

CHAPTER EIGHTEEN

I have no recollection of that trip to Woodstock. I must have slept the whole way. The first I knew of our imminent arrival was a nudge in the ribs from the WRAC driver.

"Better have your ID ready, sir."

I stared about me in confusion. It was already dark and I could just catch the odd glimpse of stone cottages in the glimmer from the hooded headlamps. I sat up straighter and hauled my senses back together as we swung to a halt by a guard post, positioned between two huge stone pillars. Bloody hell, this really must be Blenheim Palace. Who the hell would want me here?

The guard took our IDs into his little hut and spoke to somebody on the phone. He was obviously satisfied, as he emerged and directed us through the grounds to the entrance we required. As we drove off, he threw up a salute that would have made a guardsman proud. Maybe he was a guardsman

We drove slowly through the parkland and I thought I saw the glimmer of a lake off to our right. Finally, we braked to a halt by a flight of stone steps leading up to a large oak door. The guard at the gate was obviously on the ball because there, waiting on the steps, was the unmistakable figure of Wing Commander Face. The WRAC handed me my bag from the boot and I ran up the steps and saluted.

"Good evening, sir." I hoped my real feelings were not obvious in my voice.

Face gave an irritable wave of his hand at my gesture towards service etiquette and held out his hand. "Evening, Carver. Sorry to end your leave but something has cropped up and I'm afraid we need you even more than that lovely girlfriend of yours needs you."

I shook his hand. "In that case, sir, it must be of national importance and a matter of life and death."

He smiled. "Ah, it's that serious between you two, eh?"

"Absolutely, sir."

He closed the door and we moved through the blackout curtain. "I'm pleased for you, Carver. She's not just lovely, she strikes me as being very intelligent too. A rare commodity I'd have thought."

I decided not to reply to that and I knew the retort Nat would have given to his statement.

We showed our IDs yet again at another security post at the bottom of a huge flight of stone stairs. By the time we reached the top, we were both breathing hard. I tried to convince myself that my lack of stamina was down to the tiring journey from Devon. Face led the way into a large room and closed the double doors behind us. I dropped my bag but kept my hat on as there was a rather senior army officer waiting for us. He stood with his back to the huge open fireplace and it was the profusion of red on his lapels that made me decide to keep this formal for a while. He had to be at least a general.

"Dump your hat and coat, Carver," the army officer said quietly. "Come and warm your backside. It is freezing out there."

I did as I was ordered and walked towards my 'general'.

Face quickly put me right before I showed my ignorance of army ranks. "Carver, this is Brigadier Franklin. He's with a rather specialised unit that we'll tell you about later. Brigadier Franklin is very much involved in the matter that has brought you here tonight."

I shook hands with Franklin. He was very tall with greying hair. His angular face was handsome in spite of the scar tissue above his right eye. He saw my eyes flicker to the scar and his small, grey moustache moved a little as he smiled.

"Dunkirk. Should have kept my bloody head down."

"I imagine it is not easy for a man of your stature to keep his head down, sir," I replied.

He laughed. "You've got it in one. Shove my head down and my arse goes up. Bound to get hit somewhere vital!"

We laughed and I'd already warmed to this man. Would I still like him when he came clean as to why I had been recalled off leave?

Face pushed another easy chair nearer the fire. "Sit here, Carver. Blenheim's a beautiful place to have one's HQ but bloody chilly."

I looked at him in astonishment. "This is your HQ?"

He nodded. "Well, part of our organisation is here. The main HQ staff came here after our old HQ was bombed in September 1940. Later they moved to Wormwood Scrubs prison for a few weeks and are now just off Piccadilly. My little branch was permitted to stay here in the country. Much more civilised."

We settled back in our chairs and I saw a slight nod from Franklin for Face to open the evening's proceedings. Face steepled his fingers under his chin and looked at me carefully. He wasted no time with formalities. "We've found your pilot!"

My head snapped up and I felt a tingle of excitement.

"Dead, I hope?"

Face shook his head. "He's very much alive."

"But you have him?"

Again that shake of the head. "No. That is the minus in the equation. The plus is, we know where he is. The real problem will be getting our hands on him."

"That is a very big minus, sir."

Franklin looked into the flames of the fire. "He's in Holland."

I nodded. "I'm sure you were not surprised by that. He had full tanks when he left Sutton Bridge. So that is the end of that - the bastard will never be brought to justice."

Franklin turned to look at me. "We could, with a bit of effort and a bit of luck, bring him to justice, as you say."

There was a long silence and I suddenly began to get a nasty feeling as to how we were going to do that. Actually it was 'who' not 'how' that concerned me. I'd not just been invited to dinner and the indecent haste to get me here was ringing alarm bells in my brain. I looked at them both in turn, as if to glean something from their expressions but they just looked straight back at me. It was as if they were doing a final mental assessment as to my suitability for the job in hand. Why didn't they just come out with it? Yet again, I had the feeling I was about to be put in a situation for which I had no training. Fear was spreading its insidious tentacles through my mind but that fear was tempered by the excitement of being in at the kill. I'd give anything to wipe the contempt off that bastard Giedrovski's face. I decided it was time to stop buggering about. I raised my eyes and looked in the direction of the large mahogany table in the middle of the room. I stood and walked towards it.

242

"I think the formalities are over, gentlemen. You'd better tell me what you have in store for me. I'm damned sure I'm not going to like it but let's not beat about the bush any more."

They exchanged glances and, as they stood, it was Franklin who spoke. "You said he was a touchy young bastard, James."

Face grinned. "Cheeky young bugger too."

I smiled grimly. "But I'm all you've got?"

Face sighed. "I'm afraid so but don't get too cocky, You haven't heard the rest of the story."

We watched as Franklin opened up the large chart on the table and I recognised the north coast of Holland.

"Friesland?" I asked.

Face nodded and placed a finger on a town about twenty kilometres inland from Harlingen.

"Leeuwarden," he said.

"Why there?" I asked.

Franklin shrugged. "We don't know why but that is where he is, or at least he was two days ago."

"Are you sure it is Giedrovski?" I prompted.

Franklin glanced at Face and it was the wing commander who answered. "Actually, no, we're not sure."

I looked at them in disbelief and he held up his hands to stop me opening my mouth.

"Having said that, we've evidence that suggests Leeuwarden is his present location." He turned to Franklin. "Is it possible we can tell him how much we know and how we got that information?"

Franklin nodded. "I think it is only fair that we tell him everything but we'd better sit down, it's a long story."

Face nodded and we moved back to the comfortable chairs around the fire.

"You'd better start from the beginning, James," said Franklin.

Face settled back in his chair. "How familiar are you with the workings of MI5?" he asked me.

I thought for a second. "I know that MI5 is responsible for the security of the British armed forces and counter-intelligence in this country. That's all, I'm afraid."

"Broadly speaking, you're correct. So therefore I am sure you're beginning to wonder why we're so interested in somebody who has already flown the nest. Somebody who, to all intents and purposes, is out of our jurisdiction?"

I nodded.

"The role of overseas intelligence gathering and espionage is the responsibility of another arm of the security services, called the Special Operations Executive. Needless to say, as we too are one of the departments under the overall control of the Security Committee, there has been a clash of personalities and operational procedures between our two organisations - even jealousy, for goodness sake! Now a situation has arisen which is dividing us even more. Neither organisation likes interference from the other but, due to certain intelligence coming our way, we believe that SOE operations in Holland have been seriously compromised. In spite of our, admittedly flimsy, evidence being accepted by some of their junior officers and operators, the commander of SOE's Dutch Section, over at Norgeby House in Baker Street, refuses to accept they have a problem. We're pretty sure that every agent they insert into Holland is immediately arrested. The German Abwehr is forcing the captured wireless operators to send fake messages and disinformation back to the SOE here in this country."

"But surely there must be a safety code, known only to the operators, which guards against that very scenario?" I protested.

Face nodded. "There are such safety codes and these codes have been used but SOE's hierarchy will not listen, especially when the suspicion of their authenticity comes from us. We've tried to tell them but they insist they are getting first class stuff from their agents and to get our noses out of their trough."

Franklin joined in. "The Germans, of course, will make sure the SOE are getting good stuff. If they keep dangling a good carrot they will keep catching the best of the donkeys."

I nodded. "Okay, sir, if that is the case, how do you know your own intelligence is authentic and not just a crock of shit sent by the Abwehr?"

Franklin's voice was a little sharp as he replied. "Because, Carver, our codes and triggers have been in place in all transmissions."

Then a thought occurred to me. "Hey, hang on a minute. If your operational commitment is to the internal security of this country, how come you're 'talking' to agents in Holland?"

Face held up a hand to stop my flow. "Carver, slow down. The brigadier told you this was a long tale."

"Sorry, sir," I apologised but I was getting impatient. Nice to know all the details but I was more interested to know where I came into the plot.

Face stood and paced for a while then he sat back on the arm of his chair. "When we suspected SOE's efforts in Holland had been compromised and they refused to listen to our suspicions, our bosses here decided to do something about the situation. A secret meeting was arranged with the Prime Minister himself and we told him of our fears. He came to the same conclusion. There has to be an enemy agent at a high level in the SOE. The PM immediately agreed on our setting up our own secret programme to prove, once and for all, that SOE in Holland has been compromised. So, unknown to SOE, we inserted a team of three men into the Leeuwarden area – a wireless operator and two minders. They have been there three months and have confirmed our worst fears. SOE in Holland only exists as a ghost operation run by the Abwehr. Not one of the SOE agents remains at large. Every time they send in a new agent, he's met, not by the Dutch Resistance, but by the Germans. SOE have a traitor in Holland who's passing all the information from London intended for the Resistance movement to his friends in the Abwehr and the Sicherheitsdienst. Normally, these two organisations are great rivals but they are working together this time and very effectively too."

Face paused and sighed. "We're about to deliver the bombshell to the PM and we're going to be very unpopular with SOE. Our team has done a fantastic job and we must extract them before their luck runs out or collaborators betray them. They'll be in even greater danger once SOE knows they are there."

"Brave men," I said quietly.

Franklin looked at me steadily. "They are three men from my unit - a sergeant and two corporals. The sergeant is the wireless operator and the two corporals his minders. They are trained to look after themselves and they have managed to avoid detection for a whole three months."

I waited to see if he'd tell me more and finally, as if sensing my interest and after a quick glance at Face, he continued. "My unit is a very special unit, Carver. Very, very few people even know we exist and we intend the situation to stay that way.

We're called unofficially and rather dramatically, the Phantoms. Not too long ago, General Montgomery complained that his intelligence was often days old and, being General Montgomery, he wanted something done to rectify the situation. The fresher his intelligence on the enemy, the sooner he could react and, not only that, he could react in a way that would minimise his casualties. So, my unit was formed to operate behind enemy lines, in uniform, to gather intelligence and relay it immediately back to his HQ. A sort of very highly trained forward reconnaissance unit. Albeit, so far forward as to be behind the enemy lines."

"In uniform?" I expressed my amazement. "Your casualties must be high."

"Surprisingly, no. We operate in uniform to prevent the enemy shooting us on the spot as spies." He suddenly grinned. "No, Carver, the men in Holland are not in uniform. They volunteered for this special operation with no doubts in their minds as to what would happen to them if they were captured. They are three very special men."

"You're telling me," I said with feeling. "What still puzzles me is how they have evaded capture when they must have help from the Dutch Resistance"

Face nodded. "I know what you're saying and I'll try to answer your question simply. The traitor we believe is based in The Hague. The main resistance groups are in the west and south of Holland but, up in Friesland, there is a small splinter group, who are fully aware of the traitor in the main organisation and avoid it like the plague. They have also avoided all contact feelers put out by SOE. Their only contact with this country's intelligence service has been this small, illicit operation. There have been no leaks or even the suspicion of a leak, so that little group in Friesland has complete faith in our security."

I shook my head in disbelief and turned to Franklin. "Your men are living on borrowed time, sir."

He nodded. "Don't I know it, but the delay in getting them out has had its plus points. It was my team who sent us the information about Giedrovski, well, at least the chap we think is Giedrovski. You see, the Dutch civilian telephone engineers in Leeuwarden have set up a secret room with a covert switchboard, manned twenty-four hours a day by volunteers. They monitor all the German military phone lines, including those linking the civilian houses commandeered as billets for the personnel from the airfield at Leeuwarden. They overheard a conversation between two pilots from the group commanded by a Major Helmut Lent." He consulted a small notepad. "Ah, here we are. The group is called the Fourth Staffel of the Second Nachtjagd Geschwader. One of the pilots carelessly asked the other, on an open line, if he'd seen the British fighter aircraft in one of the hangers. His friend said he hadn't but he'd had the pleasure of meeting the pilot - a real hero of the Fatherland. He mentioned no name but I think we can pretty well be sure Giedrovski is about to be presented with one of Germany's top decorations."

"I hope it chokes the bastard!" I muttered.

"Precisely," replied Face. "We were lucky that the Dutch thought it a strange enough conversation and put a priority on its onward transmission. They gave the message to the local KP - I think it stands for Knok Ploeg and means Fighting Group. It is an even smaller splinter group of these chaps who are looking after the brigadier's lads. Anyway, they passed on the message to our wireless operator and he transmitted it to the Phantom's HQ as a priority. You see? If the brigadier's men had been extracted we would have missed this vital piece of information. I think you'll agree, it is too much of a coincidence."

I didn't reply immediately. I was thinking of all the bloody heroes fighting behind the scenes to make sure we won this war. The Dutch were taking a hell of a risk but the three army lads were sitting on a powder keg. How far did the traitor's evil tendrils stretch out from his base in The Hague? I decided it was time for the dénouement!

"Where do I come into this?" I asked carefully.

Face didn't beat about the bush. In fact he didn't even have the decency to look in the slightest bit uncomfortable as he replied. "We want you to go to Holland and bring Giedrovski out."

In spite of feeling as if somebody had kicked me in the balls, I was determined not to let the shock show. I saw an anxious look flash between the two senior officers at my lack of reaction. Actually, it was taking all my willpower to prevent me jumping to my feet and legging it out of the room. What the fuck was going on? I was no agent and I'd had no training. Bloody hell! We'd been over this before. More important, I was no bloody hero. Their whole preoccupation was with secrecy and double-dealing whereas all I wanted to do was get back to West Fen and do the job for which I'd been half-trained. Bollocks! I just wanted to get back to Nat. What did they expect me to do? Catch a bus to Cloggieland, introduce myself to the Luftwaffe and ask to be introduced to the German agent? Now there was an expert. He'd infiltrated the RAF, killed the enemy from within and got away without a scratch - just what he'd been trained to do, and he believed in it enough to risk his life to bring it off. How the hell could I be expected to take on a man like that? Anyway, why would they not be happy with just a corpse? I would be - as long as it was Giedrovski's.

As the thoughts raced through my confused brain, I had locked eyes with Face and he was beginning to look uncomfortable. Strangely, that gave me a perverse sense of satisfaction and it had the effect of tempering my heightened feelings of anger and bewilderment. I needed to take control of the situation and the best way I knew was to wrong-foot them. So I was perfectly calm when I finally responded.

"How exactly do we go about this little adventure?" I asked quietly.

Franklin jumped to his feet. "Hold it right there, Carver. Do you fully understand what we've just proposed?"

I nodded. "Yes, sir."

"This is no bloody game, Carver, and it's no Boy Scouts adventure. We've just made a very dangerous proposition to you and you just sit there as if we'd asked you out to dinner. You worry me!"

I was pleased to see him rattled. Face was easy but this guy was a strong-minded bastard and a professional down to his toes. I leaned back in my chair quite satisfied with myself.

"I'm sorry, sir, what do you expect me to do? If I protest, where will that get me? You've obviously talked this through with the wing commander and his colleagues and you must think I'm the man for the job. Believe me, I'd like to tell you to stuff the whole idea up your arse and walk out of this Cloud-cuckoo-land."

To my surprise Franklin burst out laughing "Thank God for that! You do have feelings. Sorry, Carver, James here knows you, I don't, but I am beginning to think we've the right man for the job."

Face looked relieved. "You're the only one we can send who could positively identify Giedrovski. He may have changed his appearance but why should he? As far as he's concerned, he's home and dry. You also have all the inside information on the man and I think you have the motivation. You saw what it's like for seven young men to be blown out of the sky."

His ploy worked. I had a sudden flashback to that night when I'd stood with Nat on the tower. I could also see the two kids at Sutton Bridge. Oh yes, in spite of a perverse admiration, I wanted to kill that bastard with my bare hands.

Franklin waved us back over to the table. He pointed to a lake, the southern edge of which ended up about five kilometres from the northern coast of the Ijsselmeer. I bent over the table to read the name of the lake.

"Tjeukemeer?" I tried my best at the pronunciation.

"That's right," replied Franklin. "That is where we intend to drop you off when we extract my three lads."

"I don't like the sound of the word 'drop'!" I said, carefully.

Face laughed. "Don't worry, no parachutes. We intend using a seaplane."

"Like a Sunderland or a Catalina?" I asked, with a tinge of apprehension, thinking the lake a bit small for such large aircraft.

Face shook his head. "Those are flying boats, we're talking of something much smaller."

"Such as?" I asked.

"Fokker," he replied.

"I only asked. There is no need to be rude," I answered, with a grin.

Franklin laughed. "The old ones are always the best, as we keep saying."

Face grinned. "It is a Fokker T-Eight. Two engines, cruises at about one hundred and thirty and, with full tanks, it has a range of about one thousand and seven hundred miles."

"Where did you get it?" I asked.

"When the Germans invaded Holland, the Dutch navy flew eight over to this country, initially to Calshot. In June of 1940, the Dutch crews and the eight aircraft were incorporated into RAF Coastal Command at Pembroke Dock, where they were used on convoy escort duties. They lost a couple on active service and later, because of lack of spares, they were taken out of service. One has been kept airworthy by robbing the others for spares."

I looked at them both carefully as I posed my next question. "Has this lake, or even the idea, been used before?"

Franklin looked away and left a very uncomfortable Face to answer my question.

"Yes, it has actually, in the October of 1940. The same type of aircraft was used to pick up four agents but the operation had been compromised and the agents were arrested. The pilot just managed to get the aircraft back off the lake by the skin of his teeth. He had been under very heavy fire."

I looked at him and nodded. "Thank you for being honest."

He put a hand on my arm. "Don't make it more difficult for me than it is, Sam."

For the first time I realised how hard he was finding it to send me in as an untrained agent. He was an honourable man and now I knew his true feelings.

"Who will be the pilot?" I asked.

Face consulted his notes. "A Lieutenant Gerrit Bouma. Leeuwarden is his home town and he knows the area and the lake like the back of his hand. He was the pilot who made the last disastrous trip. The other crewmember will be a Lieutenant Jan Kramer. He's also a native of the area and will act as gunner and help Bouma with the navigation. Excuse me a moment." He picked up the telephone. "Corporal, send coffee and biscuits to my room. Knock and leave the tray in the corridor."

"Thank God for that!" said Franklin as Face replaced the receiver. "I'm parched."

"Sorry it can't be anything stronger," Face apologised.

"How do I get from the lake to Leeuwarden?" I asked, getting back to the point.

Face sorted through the maps and pulled out a town map for Leeuwarden. "You'll be met by Dutch agents and they will get you to the town, or city I believe it is to the Dutch. Once there, you'll be taken to a street with the unlikely name of Mr P.J Troelstraweg. It is the main route from the centre of the city to Leeuwarden airfield. A number of houses on that street are used to house essential personnel from the airfield. Number 87 houses the medics and the Gruppenkommandeur, Major Lent, has his quarters in 86. Numbers 97 and 98 are used as an officer's mess, or Kasino as they call it. Behind the mess is a large civilian hospital, part of which is used by the Germans."

"Do we know for certain that Giedrovski will be billeted there?" I asked.

Franklin took over. "We must assume he'll be there. The RAF has bombed the airfield a few times and, if he's such a bloody hero, you can bet he'll be at a safe billet in the town. That is the area where the German pilots are billeted and he's a pilot."

I nodded slowly. "Okay, let's take it a little further. I spot my villain - excellent! Now for the difficult bit. How the hell do I get him to come with me? I'm no strong-arm type and, having seen him, I know he'd make mincemeat of me."

"You don't do a thing," was Face's reply. "Your job is to simply point the finger, taking care not to compromise your own identity. The Dutch KP will make the snatch. How they intend to do that, we've no idea. All we can plan is your insertion and extraction."

"When do I go in?"

"Three nights from now." He said it without looking at me.

I looked at them both in amazement. "How the hell can I be ready in that time?"

Franklin stepped in. "You have to be. There is no time to train you in damn all other than your identity. You'll be travelling as Henk Visser."

I fought with my anger. "Henk Visser? Good name that. It rhymes with 'pisser' and this sounds to be a right pisser to me, sir. Who is bloody Visser when he's around?"

"He's dead," replied Face shortly. "You'll be an undertaker's assistant."

"Pretty apt bloody job by the sound of it," I muttered.

Franklin rounded on me angrily. "I don't give a flying fuck what you think, Carver. We don't like this any more than you do but we're desperate. You'd better get your attitude sorted out because other lives depend upon you obeying orders to the letter. You fuck up and a lot of good people will die, including some very brave Dutch civilians. If those people die because of your bloody arrogance, then you had better hope the Gestapo get you too, because I'll rip your guts out with my own hands if you come back here."

There was a long silence. I stood by the map, unable to bring myself to even look at Franklin. I could hear his breathing - it was harsh and fast. Face seemed stunned into total immobility.

A knock at the door broke the silence. "Coffee, sir." There was the sound of a tray being placed on the floor and then footsteps departing down the corridor. Silence reigned again.

"Carver, get the tray," Franklin ordered as he strode back to the fireplace.

I walked to the doors, opened them and picked up the tray. I placed it on a small table by the fireplace and went back to close the doors. Face poured the coffee in silence. I helped myself to sugar and chose a rather fancy biscuit. I got a childish pleasure from stealing the best bloody biscuit off the plate. It seemed I was desperate for satisfaction, no matter how trivial. There was a loud snap as Franklin bit angrily into his biscuit and Face busied himself by noisily clanking his spoon against the bone china cup as he stirred his coffee.

Oh, fuck it. Surely there were better things to do than sit here with a couple of petulant old farts. No, I was the petulant one and they were just pissed off with me. I tried to ratify the situation.

"Where do I leave from?"

Face leapt in, relieved no doubt at the chance to end the silence. "Quite near West Fen, actually - Boston docks."

"Can this seaplane get into Boston?"

"No. The pilot intends to use the cut from the Wash to the dock, which I think is called 'The Haven.' Takeoff will be at the turn of the tide, just before dusk. You'll be taken out to the mooring by an RAF Air Sea Rescue launch from 1109 Marine Craft Unit based near the entrance to the dock. That is also where you'll return with your 'package'."

I nodded. "What about my identity training?"

Franklin took over. "Tomorrow morning, 07.00, in this room. You'll also be given a short familiarisation with small arms. Best to be on the safe side."

I tried a little joke. "Nobody is safe anywhere around me when I've a gun in my hand."

"Then make sure you're pointing it at a fucking German," Franklin snapped in reply. He turned to Face. "Have we finished for tonight?"

The wing commander nodded. "I think that is enough for this session."

"Good," replied Franklin brusquely. "I'll say goodnight." He left the room without a backward glance, the doors closing quietly behind him.

I sighed. "Sorry, sir, I made a real balls up of that."

Face began to fold the maps and place them in a large safe by his desk. "I'm sure he'll get over it, Carver. He's a very hard man with high expectations of the men who serve in his unit. As far as he's concerned, until this operation is over, you're one of his men. The problem is, you're not the sort of material he's used to. You're too sensitive and you've a penchant for letting people know exactly what you're thinking. Anyway, that is the least of our problems. We need to get you in and out of Holland as soon as possible. We must not delay our findings on the SOE debacle any longer than necessary because any more delay could mean SOE sending more agents to a certain death, whilst we struggle to get Giedrovski out." He glanced at his watch and, picking up the phone, called his duty corporal and told him to have my transport ready at the door. "I'll walk you back to the main entrance," he said as he put down the receiver. "Your driver will take you to a billet I've organised for you in the village. Get a good night's sleep and be here sharp at 07.00, okay?"

I nodded and, having collected my bag and outdoor clothes, we walked to the main entrance. As I made to take my leave of him, Face touched my arm.

"Don't let us down, Carver. We need that bastard back to answer a lot of unanswered questions. We may be able to turn him although, being realistic, I've little hope of that eventuality. I'll not sleep until I discover the size of that bloody cell in Lincolnshire and find out how the hell we let it get through the net in the first place."

"I won't let you down, sir."

I wished I could believe my own rash statement. He needed to believe it because, in the harsh light of the hallway, I could see the strain etched on his face.

"Good man."

I paused and watched him start wearily up the stairs and I then went out into the night.

I spent a sleepless night in an uncomfortable bed in the pretty little cottage that was my billet for the night. I just wanted to be back in Devon with Nat, sharing the moonlight, the sea and our love. Instead I lay in the darkness, my mind racing with the improbables of my present situation. It had to be a bad dream but I stayed awake all night, so I knew it was no dream.

The next morning, back at Blenheim, a fussy little man with a bald head fitted me out with clothing to transform my appearance into that of a native of north Holland. I discovered he either didn't care for jokes that early in the morning or he was a humourless bastard at the best of times. All I said was I was pleased I was not expected to wear clogs. He flounced out the room as if I'd made an improper suggestion. Face, who had supervised my fitting, laughed at my expression.

"I think he likes you," he said, giving me a dirty grin.

"You could have fooled me!" I replied as I folded up my civilian gear and put it into the battered suitcase I'd take with me to Holland.

Face handed me a full set of papers. They looked authentic but what did I know about false papers? There was an Ausweiss, a labour card and a special pass for being out after curfew in the town of Leeuwarden. I raised my eyes at that one.

Face responded. "Very few people are allowed out after curfew but as an undertaker's assistant, you'll be one of those privileged few."

"You guys think of everything." It was genuine admiration on my part.

"Not us, Carver," replied Face. "Our Dutch friends in Leeuwarden supplied us with all the intelligence necessary to produce the papers and passes. The only problem is, the Germans tend to change the authorisation stamps pretty frequently. Just pray they have not been changed since we made that set. It would be curtains for you if you were stopped by a patrol."

I felt no reply was necessary!

Face paced the room and halted by one of the huge windows. Last night the curtains had been closed but now they were drawn back to reveal a superb view across parkland to the lake. Up on a distant rise there was what looked like a monument of some sort.

Face suddenly crossed over to me and gripped my arm. "Carver, I cannot tell you how important it is that you've no contact with anybody other than the cadre of Dutch agents assigned to help you. In Leeuwarden prison there are SS personnel who are guards and torturers. Some of them are actually Dutch and Belgian nationals serving in the special SS national brigades. They are reputed to be more cruel than the Germans - it seems they have much more to prove. There are collaborators everywhere who will shop you the minute they know you exist. Remember, if you're caught, you'll betray all the men and women who are working so hard for us over there. That is not a reflection on your resilience. The SS and Gestapo are sadists and professional killers - very few can withstand the torture."

I looked thoughtfully out of the window. "What do you think my chances are of getting in there, grabbing Giedrovski and getting out again?"

Face didn't reply for a long time but then he turned away and slumped into a chair by the fire.

"You know I cannot answer that, Carver."

I nodded and walked over to the table and looked idly at the map of Friesland. "Do you have the operation timetable yet, sir?"

Before he could answer, the door opened and Brigadier Franklin walked in. He pulled a file from his briefcase and tossed it on the table. "Good morning, James -

Carver." He threw his cap into a chair and pointed to the file. "Operations orders for you, Carver. Have you been kitted out?"

"Yes, sir."

"How about small arms training?"

"Today at 14.00, sir."

"Good." He turned to Face. "Right, James, let us get him briefed and sorted."

I could feel the coldness in his manner. After last night, he had changed his original feelings towards me. Once more he regretted having to use an amateur for the job but obviously somebody higher up the chain of command thought otherwise. I too regretted that I'd been chosen for the operation but I was all he had. I began to get the fire back in my belly. I was going to prove this arrogant bloody hero wrong and stuff his doubts down his bloody throat.

Face joined us at the table and Franklin opened the file.

"Right, Carver! You'll take off from Boston at 16.00 hours this Wednesday, that is the day after tomorrow. You'll be flown to the lake and handed over to your guides. My three men will return in the same aircraft. That same night you'll be escorted to Leeuwarden or at least within striking distance of the place. You'll have a further three days and two nights to go for the snatch. On the following Saturday, at 22.00 hours, you'll be airlifted back out from the lake - hopefully with your target. RAF Mosquitoes will make diversionary raids on Leeuwarden airfield, both on the night you arrive and the night you depart to coincide with your ETA and ETD. Hopefully, all that traffic and bombing will help confuse the radar operators and keep heads down."

He opened his briefcase and pulled out a small cardboard box. "In here are enough small hypodermics, filled with a powerful sedative, to keep your man quiet for a total of forty-eight hours. Read the instructions carefully as an overdose can kill. We want him alive - remember?"

"I remember, sir."

"Fine. You'll rendezvous with the Dutch aircrew at the Marine Craft Unit in Boston docks, at 14.00 hours on Wednesday. Your pilot will brief you as to his intentions for getting you in and getting you out. A reception committee will be awaiting your return to Boston early on the Sunday morning. If things go wrong, the seaplane will return again on the Sunday night at the same time but without the advantage of diversionary raids. That will be the last flight. We cannot ask the Dutch aircrew to do more than that. If you're still at liberty with the target and you miss that final rendezvous, kill the target and the resistance will attempt to get you out. Do you understand?"

"Yes, sir."

He looked around the room and patted his pockets as if checking for something, but I was pleased to see it was simply a gesture to cover the fact that he was nervous. He knew he was sending me on what was, to all intents and purposes, a one way trip.

We shook hands quickly. "That's it then, Carver. Good luck. We will not meet again." He turned to Face. "See you at lunch, James."

Face nodded and the brigadier left as quickly and as quietly as he had arrived.

I stared at the closed door and the anger in me began to build. "The bastard's written me off, hasn't he?" I said to Face.

He didn't reply.

"He doesn't give a fuck for me or the target. All he's interested in is getting his own guys back out of Holland."

Face watched me carefully but he still didn't respond. I felt my rage increasing.

"Well, fuck him. I'll find that bastard Giedrovski and I'll bring him back here if it is the last thing I do. I'll march the bastard into that stiff-necked fucking pongo's office and make him eat his own fucking regimental badge."

Face picked up his folder, removed the pages and threw them on to the fire. He watched them burn and then turned to face me. He was expressionless. "Read your orders, remember them and then burn them before you leave this office. Just remember, Carver, this operation does not officially exist. If you don't return, nobody will know what happened to you. It may even be necessary to post you AWOL to cover up any debacle that may occur."

He swept up the charts, stuffed them in his safe and locked the safe door. "Use your time on the firing range wisely, Carver. Also, ensure you know your identity cover off by heart - again before you leave this office. Your driver will be at your billet tomorrow morning at 07.00 hours to return you to West Fen." He held out his hand. "Good luck, Carver."

I returned the handshake. "Thank you, sir."

That was it. He headed out of the door without another word.

So, now he was pissed off with me too. Not half as pissed off as I was with the bloody lot of them. I hoped my anger would see me through this bloody bodge-job because I doubted my courage or expertise were up to the job.

I sat for the next couple of hours and memorised my cover. Some cover, when I couldn't even speak a word of Dutch. I threw the notes on the fire in disgust and watched as they shrivelled into a grey ash and hoped that it was not symbolic of the coming operation. I picked up my suitcase of Dutch civvies and my papers. I took a last look around the room and headed for the exit. Maybe I could vent my spleen on the range targets

Even that was denied me. My shots were anywhere but on the bloody target and the point thirty-eight revolver seemed to have a mind of its own.

The army sergeant instructor took the weapon from me and began to clean it. He chose his words carefully. "When my squaddies do that bad with their rifles, I tell them not to worry because they still have their bayonets." He looked up at me with a pitying expression on his pockmarked face. "You, sir, will only have a pistol. So far, nobody at the War Office has invented, or even given thought to, a method of fixing a bayonet to a pistol. This leaves you with only one alternative, sir."

"And that is, sergeant?"

"Kick the enemy violently in the bollocks, sir."

"And if the enemy is ten yards away, sergeant?"

"Kick yourself in the bollocks, sir. It might take your mind off the bullet heading your way."

"You're very kind, sergeant."

"I do my best, sir," he replied, wryly.

That evening I was stuck in my bloody billet. I couldn't go out and leave my case of clothes and papers behind because of the security considerations. If I went out and just left the clothes behind, what would happen if I had an accident? Carrying two different identifications would take a little explaining away. So, I sat in my little room and read. I was still reading when my transport arrived the next morning.

CHAPTER NINETEEN

The next day I was back at West Fen just after lunch. I dumped my bag and suitcase in the mess and strolled down to the section. I'd intended using my bike but it had been pinched by one of many nefarious types stationed in Bomber Command. Still, it was a nice morning and I enjoyed the exercise. I pushed open the door to the main office and pulled up short as the first person I saw was Natalie. She grinned when she saw the shock on my face.

"What the hell are you doing here?" I asked in disbelief. "You've got at least a couple of days' leave to go."

She pushed the door closed behind me. "Life was not the same without you so I asked Houseman if I could come back early."

"Does he know where I've been?"

"I suppose so. The security services can't just keep kidnapping you without his permission."

"Hi, Sam, how's it going? I hope you've given up your life of leisure and decided to come back to work."

I grinned at Dave Jones. "I wish I was back for good, this place is a holiday camp."

"Cheeky bastard!"

Hammond, who looked totally pissed off at seeing me back, was not echoing Dave's cheeky rejoinder. I was about to goad him into making a comment when Nat caught my eye. She shook her head slightly and I took the hint. I'd leave him to stew in his own juices. I looked around and realised that most of the staff were on duty. All four airmen were present, as were the three WAAFs.

"Something special going on?" I asked Nat.

"Maximum effort tonight on Hamburg."

"Both squadrons?"

She nodded.

"Ah, Carver, you've deigned to return!"

I turned at the sound of Houseman's voice. "Not for long though, sir."

He gave a tight little smile. "Got a minute?"

I followed him to his office and was about to tell him what was happening when he held up a hand to stop me.

"Don't even start, Sam. I know with whom you've spent the last few hours but I don't know where. I am also not privy to what happened there. All I know is that you're going to be detached somewhere for a few days. I am not allowed to know where."

"That's why they snatched me off leave, sir."

"When will you be back?"

I sighed. "If all goes well, early Sunday morning."

He toyed with some papers on his desk. "Are you being asked to do something stupid?"

"No, sir. I'm being told to do something stupid."

He looked at me carefully. "You're having a rough time of it, aren't you?"

I dropped my eyes before he could see my true feelings mirrored there. "Just a bit, sir."

He paused for a long time and I thought he was going to express his own views on the way I was being used but suddenly he was my commanding officer again. He stood up. "I can only wish you luck, Carver."

I stood. "Thank you, sir."

"Good man," he said quietly and sat back down at his desk. I was dismissed.

As I passed through the watchkeepers' office, Paula Tyde approached and handed me a folded piece of paper. "From Section Officer Cowen, sir."

I opened the note and it was to tell me she'd had to go over to the tower on urgent business and hoped I could make it to the debriefs later. It would be our only chance to meet. I thought back to how happy I had been just a couple of days ago. Now I was going back into the twilight world of espionage, deeper into it than I could ever have imagined. Worse than that, there was only a slim chance I'd survive. I felt the tendrils of fear starting again and I shook myself mentally to chase the demons away.

I spent the next hour trying to help Dave Jones but my lack of experience and my lack of concentration made me more of a hindrance than a help. Finally, he tactfully suggested that I was in need of some fresh air. I took the hint and left him to get on with his job.

I walked aimlessly around the camp but became irritated by constantly having to return salutes from those who had more important things to do. Then I remembered I had to be at Boston docks the following afternoon, so I nipped into the MT section and fixed up transport with the MTO. I'd no written orders to show him but he didn't give me a hard time.

"I'm sure you'd like Bourne again," he said, without looking up from signing my transport order.

I watched him carefully for some reaction but I was disappointed. He seemed perfectly serious. "If she's available."

He finally cracked and gave me a wry smile. "She's always available when she knows it's you she's going to drive. I must say, she's changed a hell of a lot since you arrived at West Fen. She's still a bloody horror but I do believe she's mellowing."

I laughed. "Don't let her lull you into a false sense of security."

He grinned as he looked up from the paperwork. "What time do you want picking up to come back here?"

His question took me by surprise. "Ah, I won't need picking up, thanks."

"Not joining the merchant navy, are you?"

"No, no," I answered quickly. "Just spending a few days with the ASR boys. All part of Five Group's new strategy - letting junior officers see the big picture, or something like that."

He regarded me carefully. "Are you going out to sea with them?"

"I hope so."

"Don't be too eager, young man. Those bloody boats are powered by aero engines and run on high-octane aviation fuel. One tracer round in the wrong place and the poor buggers fry. They have flak mattresses around the vital bits but it's no real protection. "

"That is the least of my troubles," I grimaced. "I get sick on wet grass!"

"Ah, I feel I may never see you again. Is there anything you'd like to leave to me

254

in your will?"

I gave him a malicious grin. "I leave to you, not my worldly goods and chattels, but one month's holiday in Skegness with Bourne."

He held out my MT requisition. "I've just gone right off you, pal. Piss off and if you meet the Navy in Boston, keep your arse tight up against the bulkhead."

"Just my bloody luck to meet one called Able Seaman Bulkhead, then what do I do?"

"Think of Nelson and pray it's not your turn in the barrel!"

His laughter followed me out but my own humour quickly faded as I strolled towards the main gate. I felt nervy and dejected so I kept on walking, straight out of the gate and on into the village.

It was the first time I'd been in the village itself. Actually, it was not even a village, more like a hamlet. There was a small shop but no pub. There wasn't even a church in which I could while away some time.

An old man, obviously well into his eighties, emerged from the shop. He was slightly bent with age but his eyes were still sharp and determined to miss nothing.

"You lost?" he asked, in that flat Lincolnshire accent.

"No, not at all," I replied, taken by surprise. "Just passing an hour but not having much luck at finding a diversion."

"Time must be important to you chaps."

His remark puzzled me at first and then I realised he thought I was aircrew. I opened my greatcoat and showed him my tunic, bereft of flying brevets. "I'm just a pen pusher."

"No less important," he replied, leaning on his stick. "I reckon a lot of folks had to push pens before those planes came to West Fen."

I smiled at the logic. "That's true."

He changed tack. "You live on the camp?"

I nodded.

"Married?" That direct Lincolnshire approach again.

"Not yet but I will be as soon as this blasted war is over."

He glanced down the street as if looking for somebody. "I'm on my own, now. The wife died two years back. Funny, I always thought I'd go first."

"Still miss her?" I asked, quietly.

His head came up sharply as if checking me out for unsolicited sympathy. He seemed satisfied the question was seriously intended and he grinned. "Haven't had a decent cup of tea since."

In spite of my gloom I burst out laughing.

"Fancy a cup?" he asked.

"Are you offering?"

"Certainly am. Mind you, I don't have none of that fancy bone china you officers are used to."

"We're not exactly that grand at West Fen."

"Come on then - you'll get a mug and like it."

We walked to the very edge of the little village and entered the garden gate of a small red-bricked cottage. It had a rose arbour around the door, which, like the windows, needed a lick of paint, but I could see the garden would be a picture in spring and summer. Even now it was neat and tidy, with a few colourful shrubs to brighten his winter days.

Inside, it was not as tidy as Stan Cornish's farmhouse but it was clean and, in spite of his earlier comment, he made a superb mug of tea. I found myself eyeing four medals in a display case on the mantelpiece.

"Yours?" I asked.

His face clouded. "My son's. I was never in the forces."

I began to realise I had opened an old wound and I wished I'd kept my mouth shut.

"He was killed in 1917."

"France?" I asked, although I didn't want to go down this road.

He nodded. "Aye. He was killed on the tenth of May, just two days after his twenty-first birthday. According to his mate, who came to see us when he came home on leave, Harold was a company runner. He'd just come back to the front line with some orders from command headquarters for his sector commander. He took the orders into the sector bunker and a bloody great Jerry shell hit it fair and square. Everybody in and around the bunker were blown to bits. He was our only child."

I sat silently in my chair. The old man's face began to crumple and his hand shook as he put his mug on the table.

"Young man," he said quietly but with a suppressed hatred that disturbed me. "If you can do anything in this war to kill a German, do it for me. Kill every bastard you can lay your hands on. Do it for me, boy!"

I stood up and walked to the window. I suddenly realised I could see our section just beyond the security fence. It was only a couple of hundred yards away but partially hidden by a red phone box on the other side of the road from the cottage. I turned to face the old man. He sat gripping the arms of his chair and the tears streamed from his eyes.

I crouched in front of him. "If I get the chance, I'll do it for you and for your son." I don't know if he heard me and when I placed my hands over his gnarled hands, there was no response. He was totally lost in his own grief and there was nothing I could do. I quietly let myself out of the cottage and, as I closed the door behind me, I heard the full flood of anguish burst from him in sobs that tore at my heart. As I walked off down the street I realised I didn't even know the old boy's name.

By the time I got back to the mess the light was beginning to fade and the air trembled with the thunder of Merlin engines as the squadrons taxied for takeoff. I paused as a crescendo of noise told me the first Lanc was on its way down the runway. I watched it claw its way into the air, tuck its mighty wheels up into its nacelles and bank away to the south. It still gave me a thrill to see all that power and death in close harmony. I stayed until the last one headed out into the darkening sky. Strangely, I had no feelings whatsoever for the inhabitants of Hamburg. In a few hours, many of them were going to die but I felt no sorrow.

I went to my room and began to go over my cover again. I knew I had it off pat but what the hell was the point? As soon as I opened my mouth the whole charade would be over. I was going to be totally reliant on the Dutch aircrew to get me through the radar, flak and fighters. Then it would be the turn of my Dutch guides. How were they going to react when they knew I was a complete amateur? Why should they risk their lives for me? If I managed to survive all that, we still had to get back out again. The more I put the operation together in my brain, the more impossible became the odds. I flopped back on my bed with a profound feeling of helplessness.

I was still awake when the aircraft returned in the early morning but I stayed on

256

my bed. I felt I didn't want to see Nat again until this was all over. I knew I was scared to see her or let her see me in my present state. I curled up on my bed and tried to blank out the doubts and fears but I was fighting a losing battle.

I was pleased when the first glimmers of light came through the curtains. I sat at my little table and wrote a letter to Nat. In it, I told her how much I loved her and what she meant to me. I also told her that if she received the letter, then I was already dead. After I had sealed it, I sat and stared at it for a long time but I knew that in the event of me not coming back, I wanted her to know why I had avoided her last night and today. I felt tired, jaded and ill. Even the act of taking a shower and putting on clean clothes did nothing to revitalise my flagging spirits. I took a walk up to reception but Mr Bates wasn't there so I put the envelope in another and addressed that to Bates. Inside I jotted a quick note that he was to give the letter to Nat if I was not back by Monday night. Later I relented and actually phoned Nat but Dave Jones told me she was out of the section.

The time seemed to crawl by but at 13.00 hours I was waiting outside the mess when Foghorn pulled up in a Tilly. I threw my suitcase into the back and climbed into the passenger seat. She let the clutch out and gave me a puzzled look.

"I've got Boston docks on my chitty, Petal. What you doing then, running away to sea?"

Even her doubtful humour was a welcome relief and I found myself smiling. "You'd like that, wouldn't you?"

"You wouldn't though, Petal. All those funny sailor boys? You wouldn't like that."

I laughed but chose not to reply. The way the conversation was heading, this could get smutty.

"Did you know it was legal after being at sea for ninety days?"

"What is?" I was stupid enough to ask.

"A bit of bum with the cabin boy," she replied, with a dead straight face as we roared out through the main gate.

"You're disgusting."

"I feel for the cabin boy," she replied.

"Sounds like, after ninety days at sea, so do most of the crew!"

"Now who's being disgusting?" she cried.

"You started it," I protested. "And keep your eyes on the road, these bloody drains scare the hell out of me."

"Can't you tell me why you're going to Boston?"

I sighed. "I am spending a few days with the ASR unit."

She looked disappointed. "Oh, they're not real sailors so I don't suppose they'll have cabin boys."

"I'm only there for a few days, so the disgusting scenario you've conjured up in that cesspool you call a mind will not even arise."

She laughed and so did I. Frankly, I was enjoying the stupid banter. It took my mind off the days ahead, if only for the short drive to Boston.

"Stan sends you his best wishes," she suddenly announced.

"When did you see him?"

"I've been over there a few times while you've been spending dirty leaves with your Henrietta."

I decided to leave Nat out of the conversation but was interested in Foghorn's visits to the Cornish farmstead. "How is he?" I asked.

"Full of it. He seems to have had a new lease of life. The old boy is really good to me and, apart from you, Petal, I reckon he's the best bloke I've ever known. Mind you, I have to smile to myself when he opens doors for me and stands up when I walk into the room."

"Stan is a polite little guy - you should be honoured."

"I am, Petal, I am. He treats me like a lady, even if I don't look like one. I know what I am and you both know what I am but you two are the only men I feel comfortable with."

"Any chance there could be a little romance starting here?" I asked.

She checked me out with a quick glance but decided I was serious. "Not in the true sense of the word, but we both know we're misfits and seem to find something..... oh, I don't have the brains to find the words to explain."

"Empathy," I prompted.

"Don't know what it means," she smiled. "But it sounds right."

"I'm pleased. You both deserve a break."

She chuckled. "Thanks, Petal."

We roared into Boston and she slowed with a curse as an old cattle truck ground across our bows.

I commented on the fact that there seemed to be more people than usual on the streets.

"Market day," she told me. "All the old ploughboys are in for the stock sales. You can't hear yourself think for moaning farmers and farting sheep."

"Not necessarily in that order," I added.

She hooted with laughter and it was infectious. When we finally arrived at the entrance to the docks, we were still laughing. The policeman on duty at the gates gave us an odd look but, after checking our IDs, he directed us through the docks to 1109 Marine Craft Unit. Foghorn pulled up and I hopped out to retrieve my bag. I walked round to her window and she gave me a strange look.

"Now what have I done wrong?" I protested.

"Nothing, Petal, but you're up to something. You looked worried to death when I picked you up."

"Maybe I was worried in case I was going to be the cabin boy"

She didn't even smile. "You just take care of yourself, Petal - stay safe."

I was going to make some fatuous reply but she let the clutch out with a jerk and roared away. Her arm waved briefly out of the window and then she was gone.

The Marine Craft Unit HQ was based in a large hut on the dockside. I pushed open the door and looked around the interior. It was obviously used for resting, working and messing. There were battered armchairs and trestle tables strewn around the room. The walls were covered in a mixture of official service orders, safety posters and pin-ups. There seemed to be nobody around.

"Hello!" I called.

"Hang on a minute, will you?" The voice came from a small office at the end of the hut. Suddenly, there was a loud crash. "Shit!"

I waited and finally the office door opened and out walked a very young pilot officer in RAF uniform but with the addition of a thick, white rollneck sweater and Wellington boots. He was frowning and sucking his knuckles. His curly black hair emphasised his rather pink, youthful face.

"Problem?" I asked.

"Bloody useless filing cabinet! Anything bloody Coningsby don't want they dump on us. Bastards actually try to make us feel as if they are doing us a favour."

"Why Coningsby?"

"Parent unit, old boy."

"Ah, yes." I remembered I had already been given that information.

He stared at me for a moment and then clicked his fingers as if a light had suddenly dawned.

"You're our 'Joe'!"

"Sorry?" I was mystified.

"Isn't that what you guys are called? Nobody is allowed to know your name so you're known to all and sundry as 'Joe'."

His enthusiasm was admirable but more than a little disconcerting. Then the penny dropped. The whole unit must be wondering who I was and what was I up to. It was only natural they were curious. They had orders to take me, dressed in civvies, out to the seaplane, which had a Dutch crew. It would be pretty obvious we were not going for a little jolly up the coast to Skegness!

I smiled. "Something like that."

He glanced at his watch. "The boss and the lads will be back soon. They're down the river mooring your seaplane. A couple of the lads will stay on board as guards until we take you out there later. The plane's crew will be coming back with the boss."

"Who is your boss?"

"Flight Lieutenant Locke - Ralph Locke. Nice chap but a hard taskmaster. Do your job well and he's a gentleman. Get it wrong and he can be a real bastard."

"And you're......?" I asked.

"Oops! Sorry, I'm Davy Conway. Very new and learning fast."

I gave a wry grin. "Aren't we all." I cocked my head to listen as the deep rumbling of engines rattled the glass in the windows.

Conway glanced at his watch. "That's our boat, they're earlier than I thought."

"Your boat sounds powerful."

He grinned. "She's one of the early boats and has three Napier Sealion engines which can be very temperamental. She does around thirty-six knots and can be a bit of a handful in rough water."

"Does she run on aviation fuel?" I was remembering the remark made by the MTO.

"Certainly does," he called as he ran to the door. "Sorry, got to take the lines."

I followed at a slower pace and saw him grab a line thrown by a young airman in a duffel coat standing in the rakish bows. Conway tied it expertly around a bollard on the jetty as the boat slid alongside and the engines died.

The boat was long and narrow with a small wheelhouse, which was swathed in some sort of fabric armour. There was a gun turret just forward of the wheelhouse and another towards the stern. By that turret stood two men in flying clothing and Mae Wests. One of them was a huge guy with blonde hair. He was enormous - at least six-three and with the girth of a sumo wrestler. His colleague, who was of medium build with dark hair, was minute by comparison.

I turned as a flight lieutenant, wearing duffel coat and old flying boots, leapt nimbly ashore. His red hair was sticking out from under a battered officer's cap. He called to the two aircrew on the stern.

"This way, lads, but watch the gap. We don't want you to disappear into the water at this time of the year, it's bloody freezing."

They both stepped carefully ashore over the gap between the boat and the quayside. We followed Locke as he hurried towards the unit hut and it was then that he noticed me.

"Ah, you must be the cargo."

My esteem in the service was getting lower by the minute. I was now simply 'the cargo'.

"I'm very delicate cargo so handle me with care."

He grinned. "Picky bugger, eh?" He held out his hand. "I'm not allowed to know who you are but my name is Ralph Locke. I command this shambles."

I looked around me. "Shambles or not, there are a lot of aircrew on the east coast who are very relieved to know you're here."

"That's kind of you. We might even give you a biscuit with your cup of coffee for those kind words. Come on, let's get inside and I'll introduce you to your chauffeur and his mate."

I glanced at the two Dutchmen and couldn't stop myself from staring at the big guy. I could now see he had a small blond moustache and his blue eyes were surrounded by the wrinkles one associates with a person who laughs a lot. This guy certainly liked his food or his beer. Only good living could be responsible for his ample girth. He had to duck his head as we entered the hut and the room seemed so much smaller once he was inside.

Locke told the Dutchmen to dump their kit in the corner. "One of the lads will organise some coffee for now," he added. "We will rustle up a fry-up for you later."

Once divested of their flying kit, the two Dutchmen looked expectantly at me. Locke led me forward and introduced them. First he pointed at the giant.

"This is your pilot, Lieutenant Gerrit Bouma and this is Lieutenant Jan Kramer. I think I've remembered the names correctly."

"You've remembered them perfectly," rumbled the giant as he shook my hand. I winced as my hand disappeared into his huge paw but his shake was just firm and I was thankful I was not going to have to count my fingers! I stared at the two men uncomfortably as I realised I couldn't give them my name. Bouma came to my rescue.

"We're not allowed to know your real name so just tell us what will do for now."

"Call me Joe."

"Okay, Joe, I am very pleased to meet you." I received a little bow from the waist.

"Hi, Joe." Kramer stuck out his hand.

As I shook his hand I noticed that everything about the smaller guy was dark. He had dark hair, dark skin and dark, slightly oriental eyes. I suspected his ancestors originated from Dutch Indonesia.

"When your coffee arrives," announced Locke. "I'll take you across the way for your briefing. The harbour master has let me borrow an office for a couple of hours. This place is always buzzing and the boat will have engineers swarming all over it as we're having trouble with one of the engines. Over there, in the office, you'll be undisturbed and there is no chance of anybody earwigging your conversation."

"Thanks, that was very thoughtful of you." I was very impressed by Ralph Locke's efficiency. As if on cue a young airman arrived with the coffee.

Locke headed for the door. "Right, let's go."

The small office was sparsely furnished but at least it was warm. Locke ensured we were settled and left us to it.

Bouma cleared his throat and opened the briefing. "How do you feel about this trip?" he asked.

"Shit scared!" I'd already decided he was the kind of guy who would take no bullshit.

He grinned. "Me too. So, let's get to work and try to make the odds a little more in our favour."

He opened out two charts. One covered an area from the east coast of England to encompass most of Holland. The smaller chart covered just a small part of Friesland and I could immediately see the lake that was our destination. It was down in the bottom right hand corner.

"Okay," said Bouma. "Let's start at the beginning. We will takeoff at 16.00 hours. By 18.00 we should be approaching the Dutch coast here near the island of Texel." He pointed to the southernmost island of the chain stretching up through the Waddenzee. He then pointed to the third island in the chain. "Here, on Terschelling, there is a tracking radar and another down here at Den Helder. The one on Ameland we can ignore. These are all part of the huge and complex radar shield they call Himmelbett. I think that is a four-poster bed in your language but I think it can also mean a blanket in the sky. Anyway, their Freya early warning radars have a range of about eighty to ninety miles and the Wurzburg tracking radars go out to about fifty miles. To try to avoid detection, we're going to fly the whole trip at ultra low level. That is not so bad as long as the weather stays good and, so far, the met men are predicting a calm, clear moonlit night."

He took a drink of his coffee before he continued. "When we approach the coast the big problem will be the flak ships. They move about so we can never be sure where they are. All being well, we will slip through the gap between Texel and Vlieland, curve to the south-east to bring us into the Ijsselmeer. Next, we slip slightly north of east and cross the coast at Lemmer. That will put us just five kilometres from the south-west tip of Tjeukemeer."

I stared at the map as if hypnotised. It was actually going to happen. I think that up to that point, I'd felt it all to be a bad dream from which I'd awake and discover the whole charade a figment of my overactive imagination. Now, standing by my side, were two perfectly real and sane men taking the whole thing very seriously. They had a job to do and, as professionals, they were going to do it to the best of their ability. The problem was, they thought I, like them, was a professional. They were not privy to the fact that I was a rank amateur dabbling in a deadly game for professionals only.

It was Kramer who broke my train of thought and brought me back to the job in hand. "All clear so far, Joe?" he asked.

I tried to take the panic out of my voice. "Ah, yes…perfectly clear."

"Good." Bouma sounded relieved as he opened a notebook. "The pick up point, for the three men coming out and where you disembark, is on the northern edge of the lake. So, as long as the wind has not risen, I'll curve to the right for a while then make my approach over Echten, which is here on the southern shore of the lake. If I touch down about half way along the lake, it will be a straight taxi in to meet the boat near the north shore."

I cleared my throat. "Are there German units in the area?"

Bouma laughed. "Of course. The nearest will be at Sloten but our biggest worry is the Schnellboot."

"Schnellboot?" I asked.

Bouma nodded. "It is like a small E-Boat, with which I am sure you're familiar. It is very fast and heavily armed for such a small vessel. It is not based permanently on Tjeukemeer but uses the canals to move from lake to lake. If it is on our lake, as long as we can keep the time spent on the water to an absolute minimum, we should be in and out before they can react. Better still, let us hope it is on one of the other lakes."

"Amen to that," I said, offering up a quick prayer to that effect.

Jan Kramer put a hand on my arm. "Joe, we both come from that area and we know it like the back of our hands. Even if the weather turns out different to that forecast, as long as we can get a brief fix on something on the ground, we can position ourselves to land, even if it is a bit foggy."

I put on a brave smile. "I'm pleased to hear that, Jan."

He laughed. "You feel better, eh?"

"Oh, much better." Somehow, my assurance didn't ring true.

Bouma laughed heartily and got back down to business. "Now, when you come to disembark, it is very easy. You slide the canopy forward just in front of the rear gun and step out on to the wing. From the trailing edge of the wing, there is a float strut studded with footholds. You go down this and get into the boat from the float." He scratched his head. "We understand that you'll be bringing back cargo which, according to our other briefing, will be inert."

I nodded. "That's the plan. I sincerely hope that, if we get that far, the cargo is, as you say - inert!"

Bouma's ample girth shook as he laughed. "If it isn't, we will use a large wrench to ensure 'inertness'!" Faulty English it may have been but I wholeheartedly agreed with the sentiment.

Bouma resumed and I realised that these guys had worked on every eventuality and I had done nothing other than to get myself into a lather. "Jan has made a harness from an old parachute to help you get the cargo aboard. You'll fix the harness to the cargo and, whilst Jan pulls from up on the wing, you'll push. Hopefully, it should be quite easy, although you'll have to contend with the swaying of the aircraft and the propwash."

Eternal bloody optimists, these guys! Bouma closed his notebook. "If I should be incapacitated in any way, Jan will take over and fly the sortie, which means you'll have to carry out some of his duties. On the way out he'll show you how to use the machine gun in the rear of the aircraft."

I remembered how Franklin had taken offence at my flippant remark about my prowess with a pistol. This was even more bloody dangerous but I decided to keep my mouth shut. I just nodded to bolster their misapprehension that I too was a professional.

"Any questions, Joe?" Bouma asked as he folded the charts.

"I don't think so other than I don't suppose you know who is meeting me?"

Bouma shook his head. "We've been told only what is necessary for us to carry out our part of the operation. If we're shot down and captured, it is better we know as little as possible."

"Fair enough," I replied.

Jan opened the door. "Okay, let's go and get the bacon and eggs we were promised."

Locke was as good as his word and I enjoyed the biggest fry-up I'd had since the war started. What do they say about the condemned man eating a hearty meal?

I turned to Conway who had joined us for his duty meal. "Coningsby may be a bit stingy on your equipment but they do you proud on the catering front."

"I'm afraid that's wishful thinking," he made a grimace. "Actually, a lot of this is given to us by the locals. They seem to have adopted the unit."

I looked around the hut. "Do you all sleep here?"

"Only the duty crew. Our permanent quarters are in civvy digs. The Skipper and myself have a place just outside the dock gates and the rest of the lads are billeted in St John's Road."

"You've a strange life," mused Bouma. "You're serving in the RAF but spend all your time at sea and live in civilian houses."

Davy nodded. "Yeah, we're a bit of a bastard operation and nobody really wants to know us. Mind you, that suits us down to the ground."

"Davy!" Locke called from the office.

"Yes, boss?"

"Nip out and see how Chiefy is getting on with number two engine."

"He's finished. I checked before I came in to eat. It's as right as it's ever going to be - his words not mine."

"Okay, but get him to put one of the lads on checking that stern gland on number two propshaft. I know it's difficult to see but it was weeping earlier and I don't want it to get worse."

"Okay, boss," called Davy as he rose to his feet. "Actually," he confided quietly, "He wants me out of the way so that he can have a quiet word with you chaps. See you later."

As he disappeared Locke strode in and sat at the table. The two Dutchmen had lit up their cigarettes and looked totally at ease. I was beginning to get distinctly shaky. Either they were good actors, very brave or just unimaginative.

"Right, Joe," Locke said. "We need to get you out to the boat without attracting unwanted attention. So, once you've changed into your civvies for the trip, we'll stick your RAF cap back on your head and wrap you up in a spare duffel coat. Wellington boots should round off the disguise until we're under way and heading out to the floatplane."

"Bloody hell!" I said. "I'd not even considered that problem."

He gave me a hard look. "The docks employ a lot of labourers. Even if they're not enemy agents, they're nosy buggers. The last thing we want is one of them blabbing off in the pub that a civvy has gone out on the launch and not returned."

It was obvious he thought I should start getting my act together and he was right. I needed a good kick up the arse. I was not tuned in to what was expected of me. I was just going with the ebb and flow of the very capable people surrounding me. So far, I had contributed sod all to the operation, just hoping I could busk my way through. It was about time I woke up and began to face reality. I glanced up and saw Bouma watching me through a haze of cigarette smoke and I could see the first signs of doubt in his eyes. As he spoke, he picked a shred of tobacco from his top lip.

"Stay sharp, Joe. A lot of people on the other side are risking their lives to help you. You cannot afford to give them anything less than one hundred percent. Lives depend on it."

I held up my hands. "Sorry, folks. Poor choice of words on my part." I glanced at my watch. "It's time I got changed."

"Use my office," said Locke. "I'll get the disguise ready."

As I changed into my Dutch civvies, I wished I had not eaten so much. My nerves were beginning to jangle and I was beginning to feel nauseous. Then I recalled that supercilious smirk on Giedrovski's face as he'd taxied past in the Hurricane. I wanted to see that bastard pay for what he'd done in the name of the bloody Fatherland. My anger acted like a palliative to my fear and the nausea faded to just a knot in the pit of my stomach. Like the number two engine on the boat, I was as ready as I was ever going to be!

Back in the main office, I donned the duffel coat, the cap and the Wellington boots. I then did a last check of my papers and the contents of my little suitcase. Gerrit and Jan were back in their flying kit and Jan handed me a Mae West. He spoke quietly although we were on our own.

"Better get this on. We don't want you to drown before you get a chance to take a look at our homeland."

Gerrit Bouma put an arm around my shoulders. It was a bit like being crushed by a grizzly bear. "Let's go fuck the Krauts!"

Who could disagree with the man?

The launch engines were already rumbling impatiently as we climbed aboard. Wisps of smoke and steam eddied up from below the stern transom. With three extras and Bouma's bulk, it was a little crowded in the wheelhouse.

"Let go for'ard!" called Locke.

An airman whipped the bowline off its bollard and leapt nimbly aboard. The tide was slack but enough to turn the bows away from the jetty. Locke let her swing until we were facing seawards.

"Let go stern!"

The last line snaked aboard and the engines went from a rumble to a muted roar and I felt the deck surge under my feet.

I moved over to stand by the flight sergeant coxswain. "You've got a lot of power here, Flight."

"As long as they keep going, sir," he grunted.

I was beginning to get the feeling that Napier Sealion engines were not the most reliable. Maybe that was why the boat had three of the brutes - the designer had hedged his bets.

There was no more conversation in the wheelhouse until Bouma suddenly pointed ahead.

"There she is!" he said and I could hear the pride in his voice. This was a man who loved his aircraft. I followed the Dutchmen out onto the deck.

One thing I could safely say about Bouma's aircraft, it was not an ugly Fokker! In fact it looked strong and purposeful. The fuselage looked positively roomy. The upper surface of the bulbous nose was extensively glazed and the cockpit glazing extended right back to the trailing edge of the mid-mounted wing. The two large radial engines looked powerful but seemed rather let down by the puny looking two-bladed props. The whole shebang rested on two huge floats, braced from the wing roots and the engine nacelles. I actually liked the look of the machine but my vision was rapidly fading into a blur as tears flooded my eyes. The wind was cutting in from the North Sea and I swear it was colder than the Russian steppes.

"Bloody hell!" I stammered through chattering teeth. "I'm bloody freezing."

Bouma laughed at my discomfort and clouted me on the shoulder. "Wait till you get to where we're going. This will feel like summer!"

I realised that I'd soon have to relinquish the duffel coat. All I'd have between me and the elements in Holland, were a vest, a shirt, a pullover and an overcoat. None were what one might call 'high quality'. I was going to freeze to death before I got anywhere near bloody Leeuwarden!

"Shit!" cursed Locke, who had joined us on deck.

"What's the matter?" I mumbled through lips which were quickly beginning to have a mind of their own.

"Bloody sightseers!" He nodded towards the small group of people on the far

264

bank. "The word must have got around that there was a strange plane on the river. You'll have to keep your disguise on and the crew can bring it back."

At least the sightseers had ensured I'd not freeze to death for a few more hours.

The two airmen left on board the floatplane as guards had descended onto one of the floats. Locke conned the launch gently across the front of the two floats and then turned to Bouma and Kramer.

"I'll keep her here until you're ready to start your engines."

"Good idea," agreed Bouma. The Dutchman turned to me. "We will board by the front of the floats. Not the usual way but best under the circumstances. You'll have to take care as you move around the struts."

I needed no more warning. I stepped gingerly down onto the starboard float, helped by one of Locke's crew. That left me with a dodgy and slippery three feet until I could grasp a strut for support. It may only have been three feet but it felt like a mile and I was very relieved to reach a handhold. I managed to make it to the rear strut, which had built in footholds giving access to the upper surface of the wing.

Meanwhile, Jan had done the same on the port float. Being familiar with the craft, he had already climbed into the open rear cockpit, dumped his kit and was back out on the trailing edge of the starboard wing to guide me the final few feet. I managed to get on to the wing but then snagged my duffel coat on the handgrips of the machine gun as I climbed into the cockpit. In spite of the cold I was now bathed in sweat and paused for a second to get my breath back. There was a reasonable amount of room in the cockpit. I could see the control yoke and it looked like a large wheel with about a quarter segment cut out from the top. Down to the right of the pilot's seat was the entrance to the glazed nose section. I looked around for seats in the rear section but there were none. I started as Jan punched my shoulder.

"Your case, Joe."

I took it from him. "No seats?" Holland was a long way!

"No seats," he confirmed. "We had to make as much room as possible for the three guys coming home with us. Also, your cargo will need to be in a reclining position so we took out everything that was not absolutely necessary. Now we've room." He reached under the machine gun and pulled out a yellow one-man dinghy pack. "You can sit on this - more comfortable than the floor."

He leapt back out on to the wing and I pressed myself to one side as Bouma, once more looking like an over-padded monster, squeezed past me. He was breathing heavily from the exertion of getting aboard.

"Okay," he panted as he dropped into his seat. "Let's get this show on the road!" He waved a hand and I heard the launch engines roar as Locke moved out of the way. I peered over the side and saw Jan, on the rear of the starboard float, waiting to slip the mooring rope from the temporary buoy.

Bouma began throwing switches and looked to be pumping something on the instrument panel. After a last quick check around the cockpit he flicked the starter switch for the port engine. It began to whirr and cough reluctantly but finally burst into life. The smell of burnt fuel and oil spilled into the cockpit on the propwash. A few more throaty coughs and the starboard engine joined its mate in a harmony of power.

Jan reappeared and climbed in having slipped the mooring line. Bouma opened up the throttles and we headed towards the sea and into the wind for takeoff. He gave the launch, which was now stood off to one side, a quick wave and we received a casual salute from Locke in reply. There was nothing else to keep us there.

Bouma pushed both throttles fully forward and we began our takeoff run. I

265

braced myself as the floatplane gathered speed and began to porpoise slightly on the water. The takeoff run seemed to take ages but at last Bouma gave the yoke a short, hard pull and we broke contact with the water. He held the aircraft low as we gathered speed and the noise of the engines dulled a little as Jan slammed the canopy shut.

As we headed out of the estuary, still low, we passed a couple of coasters at anchor. They must have had to wait until we had taken off before they could enter the Haven. Somebody, somewhere, had a lot of 'pull'. I decided I had to be the most important little pilot officer in the air force to get that sort of priority.

Jan slipped a spare helmet over my head and plugged me into the intercom. "Better make yourself comfortable. We've a long way to go and it will get very cold. We're staying low so it will be a bit bumpy too." He glanced up at the sky. "No clouds so we should have moonlight to help us stay low. It will soon be dark so let's hope the met men have got it right for once."

I nodded and eased myself down on to the dinghy pack. My back seemed to find every metal projection in the fuselage and I knew it was going to be a long and uncomfortable trip.

The floor suddenly came up and my head snapped down as the aircraft jerked violently upwards. It quickly returned to steady flight.

"Sorry folks!" laughed Bouma. "Just scared the shit out of a trawler."

The guy was a born comedian but I was not laughing. I just wanted my heart to get back to its normal rhythm.

As promised, Jan took me through the operating procedure for the machine gun. I finally yanked on the cocking handles and fired a test burst. I saw no splashes in the water so I guess I was such a bad shot I had actually 'missed' the North Sea!

Darkness eventually descended but we roared on with the moonlight glittering off the water as it flashed past just a few feet below our floats. I could see the outline of Jan as he leaned on the machine gun to the rear. He looked totally relaxed and not a bit worried about what lay ahead.

Bouma, in spite of our proximity to the sea, lounged in his seat with just the constant twitching of his hands on the yoke betraying the fierce concentration needed to stop us from ploughing into the water.

At about 18.00 there was a sudden burst of flak and searchlight activity over to starboard.

"Spoof raid on Den Helder going in," Bouma called.

"Let's hope they get the Leeuwarden one right too," Jan replied, switching his gaze away from the flashes.

"Keep your eyes peeled," warned Bouma. "We're about to enter the Eierlandse Gap into the Waddenzee."

I stood up just in time to see an island out to our right and another to our left. We could only have been about thirty to forty feet off the water and it gave the impression of great speed but I knew we were only flying at about one-twenty.

"Texel to the right and Vlieland to the left," announced Bouma. "Let's hope we're not spotted by any bloody ships."

I watched the islands disappear to our rear.

"Thirty minutes and we should be there," Jan told me as he headed for the nose position. "Just keep a good look out astern, okay? If you see anything out there even remotely like another plane, shoot at it. You may not hit it but there is every chance you may scare the shit out of it."

I ignored his little joke but strained my eyes into the sky behind us. Glancing down, there was just sea again. I bent my legs slightly to take up the bumping from the turbulence. Just over fifteen minutes later, I could see land out to port.

"Stavoren," reported Jan.

"Roger," Bouma answered curtly.

A few more minutes' flying and he banked the aircraft gently to port on a new course. I could see the land closing in on us from both sides. We flashed in over the coast and a small town.

"Lemmer," Jan's clipped tones.

"Roger."

We curved gently to the left and I could see the moonlight shining on the waters of a large lake. Our lake?

"Tjeukemeer dead ahead," Jan confirmed.

A burst of fire and flak lit up the sky due north of our position.

"Mosquitoes going in on Leeuwarden," called Bouma, as he eased back the throttles and dropped some flap. The airframe quivered with the drag and the nose dropped.

"Don't forget the island, Gerrit," warned Jan.

"Okay, I see it - off to our left, yes?"

"Affirmative."

We were now throttled right back and gliding down towards the centre of the lake. At the last minute, Bouma used a burst of power to ease us gently on to the surface of the water. We slowed somewhat but he kept up a fast taxi towards the northern shore.

"Got the torch ready, Jan?" asked Bouma.

"Roger."

"If it doesn't look right we fuck off, okay?"

"Roger."

Suddenly, there were three short and one long flashes of light dead ahead. I saw light reflect from Jan's face as he replied. The response was three long and one short flashes from the shore.

"Correct answer," called Jan.

"Roger," replied Bouma. "Eyes peeled for the boat!"

I glanced out at the two engines clattering away each side of me. Surely every bloody German for miles around could hear us?

"Boat off to starboard at one o'clock!" Jan shouted.

"Got him," Bouma throttled right back.

Jan hurried up out of the nose and opened the rear canopy and clamshell. He trained the machine gun on the boat, his face white and tense in the moonlight. The boat bumped up against a float.

"Quick, Joe - off, off, off!" urged Jan as he pushed me, without ceremony, out and on to the wing. I eased backwards and, with my foot, groped for the first foothold on the strut. I started as a hand grabbed my foot and guided it on to the first of the steps. My legs were shaking and I was already frozen to the marrow. The wing was slippery and the propwash threatened to blow me off my precarious perch and into the freezing water. I clung on for grim death and finally groped my way down and on to the float.

The man who had helped me had a blackened face and his teeth gleamed whitely as he helped me down into the boat. Satisfied I was safe and sound, he hauled himself up the strut to the wing. My little suitcase flew through the air and landed in the bottom of the boat. Two other men quickly followed the first up the strut and into the aircraft. Only a man at the oars and myself remained in the boat. He pulled us away from the aircraft as the engines roared up to full power and it began to surge down the lake on its way back to England. I watched it lift from the lake with the water streaming from the floats looking for all the world like mercury in the bright moonlight. Even after the aircraft had disappeared and the sound of its engines had faded, I still stared in the direction it had taken. In that direction was home and it suddenly seemed a long way away.

To the north, the flashes of flame and the crump of explosions died away, leaving just the faint squeak of oiled rowlocks as my mystery oarsman rowed us towards the shore. We entered a narrow channel through some tall reeds and scraped ashore on a small shingle beach. The oarsman motioned for me to disembark and followed me out on to the beach as three other men appeared like spectres from the darkness. I was ignored as the four of them lifted the boat from the water and concealed it in the reeds.

As I stood there, feeling like a spare prick at a wedding, another figure materialised from the reeds. He was so well wrapped up against the cold his features were invisible. One thing was for sure; he was a big guy.

"Do you come from Cheltenham?" he whispered with a strong accent.

I stared at the buffoon in total amazement. What the fuck was he babbling about? Then, from the reeds, I heard the unmistakable click of a rifle bolt as it chambered a round.

Amazing what it did for my memory. Of course, the bloody passwords! "No, I come from Devizes," I replied, feeling a total arsehole.

"Hesitate like that again my friend and you'll not be going any further into Holland."

"Sorry," I whispered.

He looked at me shivering like a Sunday tea jelly with delirium tremens and called out quietly in Dutch. A young man appeared carrying a large, black overcoat.

"Here, put this on before you freeze to death. Don't they think of anything back there in England?"

I didn't reply. I just shrugged gratefully into the coat. It smelt rather dubious but I was not about to complain. I already felt warmer.

He took me by the arm. "We must get out of the area. The Schnellboot is not around this evening but you never know where the bastards are. You follow me. We don't speak and, if we run into a patrol, act dumb. Actually, you seem to be doing a good job in that respect already."

I was going to give the arrogant bastard a mouthful but, as usual, I was too late as he was already disappearing into the darkness. We emerged from the reeds and finally into a narrow lane bordered by dykes. To my dismay he began a fast trot and I staggered after him, cursing Face and Franklin to hell. I've no idea how long we kept up the trot but I think my guide called a halt when he realised there was a distinct danger the Germans would hear my wheezing lungs in Berlin. We slowed to a fast walk.

"My name is Piet," he said quite easily without any sign of breathlessness. "Of course, it is not my real name but at least you've something to identify me."

"I'm Henk," I gasped, the freezing night air searing my lung tissue.

"I'm sure you are."

He was a right supercilious bastard and I'd had enough. Fuck him, fuck Holland and fuck 'em all. I threw my suitcase down and stepped into the middle of the road.

"What are you doing? " he hissed.

"I'm going to break your fucking neck, you arrogant bastard."

To my astonishment the words came out quite clearly, with not a hint of breathlessness. There wasn't even a tremor in my voice. My rage had an icy calm, which, at any other time, would have disturbed me, but I'd no thoughts for that now. I was angry and fed up to the back teeth and some bastard was going to pay. This long, lanky twat was the nearest and he was the one going to get the full effect of one pissed off little pilot officer.

My sudden icy calm was not lost on my guide. He stepped quickly away from me and drew a revolver from the pocket of his coat. I heard the hammer click as he cocked the weapon with his thumb. I stared at the bastard with hatred pouring from every pore. He watched me steadily enough but there was disbelief and fear on his face. The moon was shining from behind me and it was so bright, I could now see his long face and pinched features. He had thick, shaggy eyebrows, which seemed to exaggerate his surprise and consternation.

We stood in total impasse for a very long time. I still felt perfectly calm and, in the silence, I could hear my heart beating powerfully and slowly. I was at total peace yet I wanted to kill. Maybe, at last, I had found my true vocation. I watched uncertainty flitting across his face. The bastard could stand there all night for all I cared. I could - no problem. Finally he spoke.

"I think we had better start again."

There was a hint of a question in his voice but I didn't even consider answering. Let the twat talk.

The gun wavered in his hand. "I'm going to lower my gun and we must talk. The way things are, there is no point in going further and the whole operation comes to an end right here. I'll have to kill you because you'll be of no further use to anybody."

Honest bastard, but I still stared.

"For God's sake," he hissed. "Do something or I'll shoot you where you stand."

I contemplated the situation. I was here to pick up a murderer, not kill the bloody people that were here to help me. I suddenly stooped and picked up my suitcase. The movement made him jump backwards but I just turned my back on him and continued in the direction we had been heading before I had thrown my teddy bear in the corner.

He eventually caught up with me but I noticed he stayed well over on the other side of the lane. He was not going to trust me yet.

"If you'll not talk are you prepared to listen?" he asked.

I gave him a curt nod.

"There has been no time to plan for your arrival or even plan your operation here. We feel our little organisation has been put in danger. In fact we feel we may have been sacrificed in order that you complete your mission."

"Do you know why I'm here?"

"Of course."

My voice was harsh. "But you've no plans."

"Of course we've plans," his voice was angry. "But they are makeshift and untried. We've had no time to plan alternatives, escape routes - nothing."

"What are the plans?"

"You'll be told when you reach Leeuwarden."

I noticed he said 'you' not 'we'. "Are you not taking me all the way?"

"No. We're just approaching the village of Haskerhome. We will head east and then north, using small roads to get you around Joure. Then we head towards Joure to pick up the road to a village called Akmarijp. Once I've set you on that road, you'll make your way to the village and wait by the belltower in the churchyard. Your next guide will meet you there."

A churchyard seemed an ominous meeting place but I reminded myself I was in their hands. My rage had gone and I could feel the cold again. I stopped and looked at the flash of flak and the probing searchlights on the coast behind us. There was a drone of aircraft high in the night sky.

"Your bombers heading for Germany." My guide was getting quite talkative. "They fight their way out and they fight all the way back. The Ijsselmeer is a watery grave for many of your airmen."

As if to illustrate his words, there was a burst of flame high up in the sky to the south. It slowly trailed its fiery way to earth like a dying comet. There was a huge mushroom of flame on the ground - the sound of the explosion reached us much later. If ever I needed a reminder as to why I was here, I'd just seen it.

I felt my guide's hand on my arm. "Come on, Henk, we must move more quickly."

Henk, eh? It seemed I was finally one of the team. We trudged on until we came to a little road branching off to the right.

Piet pointed. "Okay, that is the road to Akmarijp. If your contact has not appeared by 21.00, make your way to the village of Terkaple. It is only about another one and a half kilometres further along the road. Find the little flower shop, go round the back and knock on the door. They will hide you until we can get the operation back on track."

"Okay," I murmured and glanced around me. We seemed to be in the middle of nowhere. I put out my hand. "Thanks, Piet. Sorry about our bad start."

He shook my hand and I could see his small smile. "It was my fault as much as yours, Henk. Good luck." He released my hand and walked away without a backward glance.

I sighed and began my trek to a village, the name of which I couldn't even pronounce.

CHAPTER TWENTY

At least the walk to Akmarijp kept me warm and it was not long before I found myself approaching a scattering of houses on the left of the road. There were no lights and the village was ominously quiet in the moonlight. I could imagine German troops behind every garden hedge, all waiting to ambush me. A dog barked somewhere but it brought no response from the invisible inhabitants. As the houses became more numerous, I could hear my footsteps echoing from the facades of the buildings and there was no grass for me to walk on to deaden the sound. I was relieved to see the church looming up ahead on the left. I eased the gate open and stepped into the churchyard. It seemed I had arrived before my guide. I looked up at the church silhouetted against the moonlit sky and shivered. My earlier courage had dissipated and I was becoming edgy again. I slid into the shadow of the church and waited.

Only one vehicle passed during my vigil, a small jeep affair with a distinctive sounding engine. It was after curfew so it had to be German. I sank deeper into the shadows and listened with relief as its engine note faded away on the now frosty air. I could see a white rime forming on the gravestones. Bloody hell, it was really getting cold.

I've no idea how long I stood there but suddenly, after what seemed an age, my already overactive nervous system twanged into overdrive as I just detected an audible 'click' from the churchyard gate. I tensed in the shadows.

At first I didn't see her. She seemed to blend with the shadows but, as she moved stealthily past my position, I could see her long hair protruding from a rather silly but practical woolly hat. She slipped by me without a sound and melted away into the darkness. If she was my guide, where the hell was she going? If she was not my guide, why was she creeping about in a bloody churchyard? I decided to follow. As I rounded the corner of the church, I saw a strange 'A' frame structure sticking up into the night. The girl was stood by the structure looking around as if searching for something or somebody. She had to be looking for me.

I called quietly from the shadows. "Looking for somebody?"

She immediately dropped into a crouch and, although I couldn't see it, I knew she had a weapon pointing directly at me. She couldn't see me but she had unerringly pinpointed my voice. I decided it very wise to stay put!

"Do you come from Cheltenham?" she whispered.

Oh, bloody hell, here we go again! It sounded so inane but I had to play the silly game or risk being shot.

"No, from Devizes."

She was by my side in an instant. "What the hell are you doing over here? You're supposed to be by the bell tower."

I didn't answer for a second, as I was startled to hear her unmistakable American accent and as far as I was concerned, I'd been by the bloody bell tower!

"Isn't that the bell tower?" I asked, pointing back to the bulk of the church.

"No, you asshole!" she hissed and pointed to the structure in the middle of the graveyard. "That is the bell tower. They are unique to this area of Holland. For Christ's sake, didn't they give you a proper briefing?"

I bridled. "Everybody seemed to be in a bit of a hurry back home and your lot were not exactly snailing it. I think they cut a few corners."

She sat on a gravestone. "You've caused more than a little panic, I can tell you. We haven't had time to put much of an operation together but we'll do our best."

I decided introductions were overdue. "I'm Henk."

She laughed. "You don't sound much like a 'Henk'."

"Don't you bloody start!" I grunted in reply.

She gave that delightful laugh again. "I'm Annie."

"Not your real name, of course?"

"You bet your life on it!"

"How did you get that American accent?"

"I am an American, you clown! I lost my parents in '38. My father's parents are Dutch and I came over here to live with them. I stayed and went underground when the Krauts invaded. I wanted to join the Resistance but it was not as easy as I'd thought it would be. That was pretty fortunate for me because all the agents sent out from England and the original Resistance groups have all been compromised. We're a very elite little group that operates in even smaller cells. Nobody knows anybody outside his or her own cell. That way, if you're captured, no matter what torture the Krauts inflict, you've no information to give outside your own cell."

"Has it worked?"

"So far, but your mission is stretching both our resources and the integrity of our security."

"Sorry," I murmured. "But we really want what I've come to collect."

She stood. "In that case, we'd better get going. Did a vehicle pass here a while back?"

"Yes. A jeep of some kind."

"Mmmm," she mused. "Strange - it was a Kubelwagen and they don't usually come anywhere near here."

"I thought there were Germans everywhere?"

"Yeah, near the cities and the coast but this area is sparsely populated so we don't see too much of them. Don't worry, if you're disappointed, you'll soon see plenty in Leeuwarden!"

"I'd rather not make their acquaintance, thank you."

"You're going to have to come face to face with some, otherwise you're not going to get near your man."

"You know why I'm here?"

She nodded. "The full story."

"What do you think of my chances?"

"You really want to know?" she asked, quietly.

I sighed. "No, not really. I guess I'll just have to busk it."

She laughed. "You're either one great professional with ice in his veins or you're a goddam clown."

"You're familiar with the circus?"

"No." She sounded puzzled.

"Thank God for that, " I replied.

She stifled a giggle. "Oh, boy! This job is going to be a barrel of laughs - I don't think. Come on, hero! As they say in the best movies - let's get the hell out of here!"

"Can I ask how old you are?" I whispered as we moved out from the shadows.

272

"Twenty-four. Does that scare you?"

"Not if you know what you're doing."

I heard her give a soft giggle. "Thanks for the vote of confidence, asshole!"

"You're welcome. How far do we have to travel tonight?" I asked as we moved out on to the road.

"We're going as far as Goutum tonight. That's about three and a half kilometres from the centre of Leeuwarden. So, we've to cover just over twenty Ks tonight."

"Bloody hell! My feet are killing me already."

"Calm down, hero. A local farmer has hidden a couple of cycles for us just up the road."

"Well, at least my feet won't suffer."

She laughed. "Your ass ain't gonna be too healthy though."

"Thank you for that."

"You're welcome."

We found the bikes behind a barn near the village of Terkaple. Annie leapt on hers and began to pedal away down the road. I leapt on mine and, to my consternation, found it hard to pedal and it rode rather oddly.

"Hang on a minute," I hissed after her. "There's something wrong with this bloody thing."

She stopped and looked back as I pedalled unsteadily up to her. "What's wrong with it?" she asked impatiently.

"I can hardly pedal the bloody thing. I think the tyres are flat."

I heard that delightful laugh again. "Listen, pal, you're in Holland now. This is a pretty backward area and there are no luxuries like pneumatic tyres, especially since the Germans came. All you have on your rims is a kind of padding inside leather - a sort of cushion."

I sighed. "Bloody hell, what is this dump?"

Her voice hardened. "Think yourself lucky, hero. The locals have had all their transport commandeered or stolen by the Krauts. These bikes are a great sacrifice by that farmer. Remember, this is an occupied country and life is hard so, whatever they give you, appreciate it. For them it will always be a sacrifice."

I felt a complete arsehole. "Sorry, I guess I just don't appreciate the situation. My country is still free and, although times are hard, it is impossible for us to fully appreciate what the people of occupied Europe are going through."

"You soon will," she replied, as she pedalled away.

I've no idea what time it was when we reached Goutum. My brain had gone numb along with my arse. My legs felt like lead and my lungs were burning from inhaling the freezing night air. It was now so cold; the whole countryside was white and shone like quicksilver in the moonlight.

Annie suddenly turned off into a farmyard just before we reached Goutum itself. A dog barked loudly from one of the outhouses but was quickly stilled by a man's deep voice. The same voice called softly from the shadows.

"Annie?"

"Ja, Klaas."

A figure moved from the shadows and took her bike from her. They spoke quietly together in Dutch and then the man came over and relieved me of my machine of torture.

"Welcome. Annie will take you into the house."

I could just make out a grey beard. His hair too was grey and it protruded untidily from under a small peaked cap. He was a short man but his voice seemed to come from somewhere in his boots. He rumbled rather than spoke.

"Thank you," I whispered over my shoulder and followed Annie into the house.

The light from the paraffin lamps hurt my eyes and I shielded them with my hand for a few seconds. The room, which I took to be the living room, was immaculate. There were plants everywhere and, although the furniture was dark and heavy, glass cabinets and shelves, carrying a beautiful display of china and glassware, broke its angular and serious tone. A large fire burned in the huge inglenook style fireplace and a large black cooking pot hung over the flames on a chain and hook arrangement. The heat made my frozen ears, nose and fingers ache in a way I had not experienced since I was a kid. I could feel my lungs thawing out but they stopped working altogether for a few seconds when I got my first real look at Annie. She literally took my breath away. She was beautiful. Not just pretty but really beautiful. She had removed the woolly hat and her long dark hair made a perfect frame for her delicate features. Her cheeks and the tip of her nose were still pink from the cold but it simply gave her a homely look without detracting from her beauty. Her eyes were large and brown and they were regarding me with amusement. Her figure was enough for a red-blooded male to die for. Even I was affected!

"Easy there, feller, your horns are beginning to show!"

I cringed inwardly at being caught out thinking thoughts that were just a dream and totally impractical under present circumstances.

I grinned. "I'm sorry, but you're a very beautiful lady."

"That from a Limey is a compliment indeed. I thought you guys were reserved and shy"

"Don't believe the Hollywood picture of the English. We can be hot stuff when aroused."

"But not out there, tonight, huh?" rumbled a deep voice behind me.

I spun round and came face to face with a bear of a man. I'd initially thought he was a smallish man but that had been in the dark. He was actually built like the proverbial outhouse. He too had removed his cap and his hair looked like a demented skein of grey steel wool. His beard was in desperate need of a trim but his eyes were alert and humorous. This guy had once been the archetypal blonde-haired Frieslander.

"Sit!" he commanded and, like two domestic pets, Annie and I sat.

He then opened a door to another room and said something in Dutch. A small rotund lady, in her late sixties and with hair as unruly as the man's, entered the room and joined us. She looked nervous but her smile was warm. I rose to meet her.

The bear rumbled into speech again and held out his hand.

"I am Klaas and this is my wife, Grietje."

"Henk," I said, shaking his hand. I gave Grietje a small bow from the waist and she beamed happily at me. She beckoned me to follow her to the big pot suspended over the fire. She lifted the lid and motioned for me to sniff the aroma from the pot. I did and my stomach, as it had on the station in Kingswear, rumbled in a fair imitation of a Victorian sludge pump. It was so loud they all heard it and they collapsed with laughter.

Klaas wiped his eyes on his sleeve. "I think you sit, boy. Time to eat."

It was a delicious supper and we ate more or less in silence. Grietje fussed over me like an old mother hen but I finally had to raise a hand to stop her ladling yet more stew on to my plate. I was full of food, the room was warm and I could feel my eyes beginning to close.

Klaas took me by the arm and led me to a small bedroom at the top of the house. It was freezing up there away from the roaring fire in the room downstairs but at least there was a stone hot water bottle in the bed.

"Sleep!" commanded Klaas and who was I to argue? It had been a long day.

The next morning, Klaas woke me about six. I joined the others in the living room and ate a hearty breakfast. As I sat there watching the fire dancing in the grate, the war seemed a long way away. I was having difficulty getting my mind around the problems ahead. I should have been planning some sort of strategy but all I could do was watch the flickering flames. Earlier, Annie had gone outside with Klaas but she returned and flopped into a chair on the other side of the fireplace.

"Klaas is going to take you into Leeuwarden in his horse and trap. He'll deliver some milk to a couple of places on the way and then to a couple in the city. He'll eventually drop you off at the undertaker's. If you get stopped just act dumb, it is your only chance. Last night, after you'd gone to bed, I took a look at your papers and they are very good."

I glanced at my jacket hung on the back of the door and decided I'd stay very close to those papers from now on.

A smile flitted across her face as if she was reading my thoughts.

"Late this afternoon, it has been arranged for you to get a look at Mr. P.J. Troelstraweg. It is a hell of a name so what say we call it PJT from now on?"

"Sounds good to me."

"Okay. You'll be travelling with the old guy who collects the food refuse from the German Kasino and the hospital. It is used in the swill to feed the pigs. The idea is that you get a look at the street in daylight to help you get your bearings. It will be your briefing that will trigger the snatch, so make sure you know that street like the back of your hand."

"Is he still there?"

"How the hell should I know?" she sighed with impatience. "You're the only one who knows what he looks like. Come on, feller, wake up will you?"

I felt my cheeks redden. "Sorry."

She stared at me for a long time and I knew she had just realised she was dealing with an amateur. She obviously decided to make the best of a bad job because she resumed the briefing.

"Once you identify the target, a four man team will be briefed and move in for the snatch. Using the drugs you've hopefully brought with you, the target will be sedated and brought out of the city in a coffin. It will be a long haul back to the lake but the Germans seem to feel nervous around coffins so we just hope they stay nervous and you stay lucky."

"You make it sound easy."

She laughed bitterly. "Nothing here is easy. There are as many collaborators as there are resistance fighters. Our small group has been lucky so far but it can only be a matter of time before some bastard infiltrates the cell and shops us to the Krauts."

"You're playing a very dangerous game," I remarked and I meant it as a display of my admiration for her and her colleagues. But of course I'd got it wrong - again!

"It's not a fucking game, mister!" she snapped. "If you think it is then you'd better haul ass and don't bother coming back."

"For Christ's sake, don't be so bloody touchy." I was getting pissed off with all these fucking heroes. "I didn't mean it that way and you should bloody well know it. I'm not here as a volunteer but you are. I was simply making a comment with reference to your bravery and long-term safety. I only have to stick it out for a few days - you're here until the end of the war or until that mole gets into your

275

organisation. I am under no illusions as to the dangers involved so don't treat me as if I'm some sort of unfeeling bastard."

She raised her hand to stop me. "Okay, okay. I'm sorry but you've an infuriating flippant manner that does you no favours. It's not a sin to show your true feelings but I guess that is the British way, huh?"

"If you really want to know, I'm scared to death. I'm completely out of my depth and totally reliant on you and your friends. What do you want me to do, go around wringing my hands and wailing?"

She laughed. "You left out the tearing of your raiment."

"Balls!" I replied.

"Attaboy!" Somehow, from her, it sounded like the first faint praise.

The door opened and Klaas stomped in. He was wrapped up like a mummy in layer upon layer of clothes. "You ready?"

I nodded and stood to get my coat and case.

Grietje came in from the kitchen carrying a large coat, some woollen gloves and a huge scarf. She gestured for me to put them on over the coat I'd been given at the lakeside. She put the finishing touches to my outfit by winding the scarf firmly around my neck and lower face and tucking the ends into the coat. I held out my hand to thank her but she pulled my head down to her level and gave me a big kiss on my forehead.

"Come," rumbled Klaas. "Before my wife run away with you. That very bad. She go - no hot food!" I'd not have liked to lay a bet on whether or not he was serious!

I followed him outside and climbed up into the trap. The horse looked a little old and a bit scruffy but it farted heartily enough, so I guessed it had the stamina to make Leeuwarden.

The sky was leaden and the first flakes of snow began to fall. It was going to be a cold trip and I'd soon appreciate the extra clothing. I glanced round at the milk churns in the rear of the trap. At least I couldn't say my life was not varied. Fledgling intelligence officer to spy and rapidly back down the ladder to bloody milkman. Hey ho, nobody said life was easy.

Annie and Grietje waved us away as we clanked and rumbled our way out on to the road. To my surprise, the tatty old nag began an easy trot and we fair bustled along. The clop of hooves interspersed with frequent farts. Only I could be guaranteed to unerringly find myself behind the most flatulent equine in Holland.

Klaas and I exchanged not a word - it was too bloody cold. We kept our scarves firmly over our lower face and tried to ignore the tears as the biting wind and the snowflakes stung our eyes. To think I'd complained of cold, old Lincolnshire. Compared to this, it was sub-tropical!

We stopped twice to drop off a milk churn but saw and spoke to nobody. Klaas just put the churn on a wooden platform by the gate and we moved on. Eventually we reached the southern suburbs of the city. Actually, I was disappointed. For a city it was quite small and I had expected something bigger.

I stiffened in my seat as I suddenly spotted two soldiers, in unfamiliar uniforms, standing by a motorcycle and sidecar. My first Germans. We eyed them and they eyed us but it was obvious they had no interest in us. The horse farted again as if to pass on our unspoken thoughts. One of the Germans laughed and threw his cigarette into the gutter. I had the feeling he was telling his mate he was not sure if it was the horse or the 'cloggies' that had broken wind. I thought I caught a snippet of his remark, which included a word that sounded something like 'arsemusic'. I wasn't surprised - it sounded so descriptively Germanic.

By the time we stopped to drop off another churn at a bakery at the Oostergrachtswal, a street running alongside one of the many canals, we looked like a couple of snowmen. I was now seeing more Germans but they, like us, had their heads down as they protected their faces from the biting wind and snow. As Klaas carried the churn into the bakery, I distinctly heard a metallic clank. Either there was a lot of iron in Dutch milk or that churn was being used for something else. I decided I didn't want to know.

Klaas came straight back out again and jumped up into his seat. I nodded towards a large building behind us - on the other side of the canal.

"What's that place, Klaas?"

"Prison."

I wished I hadn't asked.

"How much further to the undertaker's?"

"You see the tower?" Klaas pointed and for a second I thought I'd got a touch of the leans, then I realised it was the tower. It had a distinct attitude problem but not as bad as the Tower of Pisa.

"This is the Oldehove," Klaas explained. He gave a slight nod towards another large building.

"Here very careful, please. That is Burmania House. It is Headquarters for Wehrmacht, SS and Gestapo."

"What about the undertaker's?" I asked again and damned nearly fell off the trap when he pointed to a rather drab establishment on our left. Bloody hell, the Gestapo and their friends only had to look out of the window and there was the funeral parlour.

"Undertaker is busy man," Klaas said bitterly as he hauled our methane-propelled nag to a halt.

As we scrambled stiffly down, the door to the undertaker's opened and there, framed in the doorway, was the most archetypal undertaker I'd ever seen. He was tall and had, in keeping with his profession as depicted in cartoons and horror films, a long lugubrious face. He was rather like an exaggerated Fernandel. Dressed entirely in black, he seemed to hover rather than stand in the doorway. He gave me a slight bow and beckoned me into the shop. I felt like a fly accepting a dubious invitation from the spider.

As I shook the snow from my overcoat, Klaas brought my little case into the shop and wished me luck before he set off for the return journey to the farm. He'd done his job well and another stage of the unlikely charade was completed without incident. I turned back to my new host and was staggered by the transformation. Gone was the slight deferential stoop and gone too was the doleful graveyard expression. His great long face had lit up with a big beaming grin.

He held out his hand. "Hello. I say bugger Cheltenham and bugger Devizes - what do you say?"

I took the cue and grasped his hand. "Fuck 'em all!"

He burst out laughing and I sighed with relief. Somebody else who didn't give a toss for the rules. I knew I was going to like him.

He ushered me upstairs to the living accommodation and lifted a coffeepot from the stove. He poured coffee into two blue enamel mugs and took a bottle of something from a shelf. He added a generous measure from the bottle to each of the mugs and handed one to me.

"Good health, Henk. I believe that is your name?"

"Good health to you too." I took a welcome swig from my mug and damned nearly choked. God knows what he had put in the coffee but it tasted like paint stripper. After a few seconds, I felt my innards take on a glow as if I had my own personal internal fire.

"Good stuff, yes?" he grinned.

"Fantastic," I replied hoarsely, still fighting for breath.

He took a huge swig from his own mug without a flinch. "My name is Wim de Jong. It is my real name. As I actually live here it would be pointless me giving you a false name. Just don't get caught, eh?"

"I'll do my best," I promised. I was feeling much more confident but I had a feeling it was due more to the contents of the mug than his reassuring presence.

We sat down and chatted. The more I talked with Wim, the more I liked the man.

He lived alone as his wife had moved to the countryside and was living with her brother. Wim's life was too dangerous to risk incriminating his wife simply by association. His wife didn't like the arrangement but, without any sign of mawkishness, he said he loved her too much to have it any other way. He hadn't mentioned children but, on the sideboard, I saw a photo of two young boys. I estimated Wim to be about fifty so the boys would now be around twenty. He saw my glance at the photo.

"They are both in England. They got away in a fishing boat with six of their friends and are now doing their bit to free our country. What they are doing I've no idea but I know they are safe and I cannot wait to see them again. It was a long time after their escape before news filtered through that they had been successful in their escape. I was so worried during that time but for my wife it was worse. I think she aged a hundred years during that long wait for news."

"Maybe I can look them up when I get back?"

I suddenly realised I believed I'd get back. It must have been something to do with the coffee! Wim brought me back to the present.

"Later this afternoon, you'll go with the man who collects the pig swill from the German Kasino and from Saint Bonifatius's hospital. I've some old clothes for you and you'll work with him. He'll hang around in Mr. P.J. Troelstraweg, for as long as he dares, around the time the duty pilots are changing over. If your man is billeted in that area, he'll have been assigned to one of the first five houses on the left as you approach the city from the airfield. They are on the same side as the hospital. I am afraid you're going to have little time to take a good look at anybody. If you stare at them they will become suspicious of you and Gurbe will not be able to hang around for too long. You must keep moving all the time and walk as if you're there for a purpose. Don't look unsure or hesitate. If you do, you'll immediately attract attention."

I toyed with the mug in my hand. "You make it sound impossible."

He nodded. "If you really want to know the truth, I think it is impossible, but I want to stress one thing, Henk. If the operation does fail, don't be disappointed or blame yourself. Everybody, both back in England and over here, knows the chance of success is remote. You've been set an impossible task." He looked at my dejected posture. "Come on, Henk, time to find you some different clothes. Gurbe will be here about three o'clock."

At least it took my mind off his pessimistic views on my chances. He was right, of course. We couldn't be certain the target was billeted here. Damn it! we didn't even know if the target was actually Giedrovski !

After a simple lunch, I spent the rest of the day memorising a plan of the oddly named street, Mr P.J. Troelstraweg. Wim was busy downstairs. He'd explained that only one of his staff was a member of the Resistance. He'd make sure they were all out of the building when Gurbe arrived.

Three o'clock on the dot, there was the sound of horses' hooves as Gurbe pulled his dray to a halt outside the undertaker's. He had two horses and the dray was laden with empty fifty-gallon drums, each with one end removed. These were the swill containers. To think that, just a few hours ago, I thought milkman would be as low as I could get in my varied career.

Now, just a short time later I was already demoted to pig swill collector. Maybe the Dutch were taking the piss

Gurbe was about seventy years old. He was a thin, spare man but, as I was soon to find out, as strong as an ox. His face was heavily weathered although his eyes were bright and alert. The immediate problem was that Gurbe spoke no English. So far I'd been lucky but now there was going to be a distinct communications problem. It didn't seem to bother Wim.

"Gurbe is very sharp. Just make signs and he'll know what you want."

I checked the two hypodermics I had removed from my case. On our way back to Gurbe's farm, we were going to drop off the hypos with the leader of the snatch squad. I'd stay at Gurbe's that night and he'd return me to the undertaker's the next morning. They'd decided that a swill cart, visiting the undertaker's twice in one day, would be considered pretty unusual and might attract the notice of the Germans. It could, God forbid, arouse tangential suspicions as to what was actually going into the swill!

Gurbe and I set off on time and once more I was horse-powered. After just a few yards, I began to wonder what the Dutch fed to their horses, because these two also had a severe problem with flatulence. With methane up front and pigswill to the rear, this was going to be a very malodorous trip.

We worked steadily, collecting the small bins of swill from cafes and restaurants. We were slowly filling up our collection of oil drums and already four of them had large wooden lids floating on the surface of the contents to prevent it slopping all over the place. It was 16.45 and getting dark when we finally turned into the entrance road to the hospital off PJT. Gurbe nodded to the house on our left.

"Kommandant."

I nodded. So that was where Gruppenkommandeur Major Helmut Lent lived. Pity I couldn't just ring the bell and introduce myself. I could see it now..."Excuse me, old boy, do you have a chappie called Giedrovski on your staff? You do? I'd like to stick one of these hypos in him and take him home with me - hope you don't mind. Jolly good show."

Gurbe jogged me out of my reverie with his elbow. He'd reined the horses to a halt and was nodding for me to get down. I clambered down, pointed back the way we had come and raised my eyebrows. He nodded and held up his gloved hand showing me five stiff fingers. He repeated the signal twice more and pointed up the road past the hospital. I knew I had fifteen minutes before he'd pick me up at the end of the exit road from the hospital. I nodded that I understood and, remembering Wim's advice, I strode purposefully away and into the main street.

I passed the front of Number 86, Lent's house. The house looked quiet and innocuous. Number 88 seemed unimportant but then I noticed a sign indicating that number 90 was the Gruppe HQ. On past 92 and 94 until I reached 96 and 98 which, together, housed the officers' Kasino. I glanced up the narrow exit road from the hospital but it was deserted. The light was beginning to fade and although it had stopped snowing, the wet slush made the pavement slippery. I walked on until I reached the far end of the row of commandeered houses and began to retrace my steps. I hadn't seen a soul. The street was totally deserted and only a couple of vehicles had passed along the main road. In spite of my dejection at so little action, I kept up my purposeful stride towards the hospital exit road. I glanced surreptitiously at my watch but already ten minutes had elapsed. This was going to be a total waste of time. Somehow my helpers were going to have to get me out near the airfield or into a position where I could keep a longer watch. This nonsense of loitering for a few minutes, in the hope of spotting Giedrovski, was a waste of time. But how the hell could we do it any differently?

I was still deep in thought as I swung into the hospital road. My head was down against the wind but I was still walking determinedly, as if on a very important errand. It was because my head was down that I failed to see the German officer hurrying the other way. Right on the junction of the pavement, we crashed into each other with a bone-jarring crunch. I heard the sharp exhalation of breath as he recoiled in pain.

"Gottverdammt!" he grunted.

"Fucking hell!" I muttered, rubbing my forehead where the peak of his cap had smashed into me. It was because I was dazed, that the enormity of my involuntary expletive didn't immediately trigger an alarm. Finally I began to get myself together and my head snapped up as realisation dawned and my heart went cold. It was nearly dark and his face was screwed up in pain but there was no mistaking it. I was looking Giedrovski straight in the face.

It is difficult to describe the events that followed. I saw his eyes widen in shock as he realised my verbal response had been in English. They opened even wider when he saw the shock of recognition on my face. Then his eyes narrowed quickly as he too began to get hold of his senses. From the new angle of his body, I knew his hand was going to the pistol in the holster at his waist. I'd only seconds to react and I didn't have a clue what to do.

Thank God for the mysterious powers of adrenaline. I acted automatically as fear hit me like a cold shower. I'd used the tactic at school when older and bigger boys had tried to bully me. I kicked him, with all the strength I could muster, right between the legs. He went down like a ton of bricks and his pistol clattered into the road. He began to vomit noisily into the gutter. I looked round in total panic. So far there was nobody else around but for how much longer? Also, the bastard was not going to stay incapacitated for long. He was going to be one very pissed off and dangerous Kraut if I didn't soon do something. Then I remembered the hypos in my pocket. I fumbled one out and broke the cover off the needle. I hesitated for just one millisecond before I muttered, "Oh, fuck it!" and plunged it into the side of his neck. As I pressed the plunger I had the thought that he might choke on his vomit but panic was now in total control of my every move. I threw the hypo over the hedge, grabbed his pistol from the road and, holding it by the barrel, I smacked him smartly on the back of the head with the butt as a sort of insurance.

"Now get up, you bastard," I grunted.

I was panting and gasping for breath as if I'd run a marathon. Fear had completely taken over and I looked around wildly, as if hoping to conjure up a fairy godmother who would spirit away the prostrate body in a puff of smoke and glitter. Unfortunately, that happens only in pantomimes but there was hope yet as this operation was rapidly turning into a bloody pantomime.

As if on cue, the Big Bad Wolf came out of a small gate from the side of the Kasino. He was tall with a handsome face and he was pulling on his gloves as he strolled onto my stage. His uniform was black and I could see the unmistakable Death's Head emblems on his lapels. No thick greatcoat for this guy. He was SS and he was prepared to face anything head on, including the freezing Dutch weather. His cap was set at a rakish angle on the back of his head and he oozed arrogance.

Luckily for me, there was one little flaw in his armour - he was pissed. A few too many Schnapps had blunted his senses but, in spite of his puzzled smile, he was soon going to put two and two together and Little Red Riding Hood was really going to be in the shit!

For the moment, he took in the body and the pool of vomit and beamed happily at me. He was making a 'tut-tutting' sound like a two-stroke puritan. He had found a fellow piss artist but this one was just a simple Luftwaffe peasant, unable to take his booze.

As for me, I just opened my arms in a helpless shrug that would have put a Frenchman to shame.

He removed his cap as he bent over the prostrate body. It was all the invitation I needed and I put the Luger to good use once more. I hit him hard on the back of his skull but terror had given me a strength I didn't normally possess and I felt the butt smash through the bone of his skull. Something splattered my face as he slumped over the other body.

Enough was enough. There was nothing I could do now. I'd blown the whole operation and all I could do was get away from the area before I had a pile of dead German military that would keep Wim busy for a month. I began to run in the direction of the hospital and, just at that moment, Gurbe and his outfit came plodding round the corner. His head jerked up as I ran towards him but he relaxed when he saw it was me.

I jumped up on to the dray. "Go! Go! Go!" I whispered urgently and pointed to the bodies. He was going to have to drive up on to the pavement to get round them.

His startled face turned to me. "Ja? Ja?" His eyebrows were raised in a questioning mime.

"Ja, bloody ja!" I panted. I wished the silly old bugger would get a move on.

To my horror, he flicked the horses into motion and, handing me the reins, jumped on to the dray. He quickly cleared an area in the middle of the drums and scrambled back, just in time to stop the horses trampling the bodies into the asphalt. He looked around quickly, making sucking noises through his teeth. Satisfied it was clear, he leapt down and beckoned for me to do the same. The man had to be bloody mad! I just wanted those horses to fart us away out of town.

I reluctantly joined him in the road and he shoved an empty drum to one side on the dray and nodded for me to move its neighbour. I did as he asked but I was now so scared, I was shivering uncontrollably. Gurbe grabbed the SS guy's feet and nodded for me to grab the other end. It was all like a dream - a very bad dream. Fortunately I now possessed a new found strength, fuelled by all the adrenaline speeding around my body. That, plus the old man's wiry strength, ensured the SS man was quickly up on the dray and out of sight in the middle of the bins.

Next, it was Giedrovski's turn. He went up just as easily and Gurbe quickly pushed the outer drums back into place. He gave me a big grin and pushed his cap to the back of his head. As we moved back to our seats at the front, he wiped his perspiring forehead with a rather grubby handkerchief.

At this point one of the horses decided to open its bowels and a steaming pile of horse dung plopped into the road. As if to confirm my growing fears that Gurbe was as batty as a fruitcake, he leapt back down into the street and began scooping up the steaming shit in his hands. Poor old bastard had cracked! Then I saw what he intended to do and, dropping all sense of decorum, I leapt down and began to help him scoop up the crap. The old boy was a quick thinker because he was using the crap to hide the pool of vomit and blood. It made an excellent short-term camouflage. We leapt back up on to the dray and he edged the horses out into PJT. A small truck had pulled up by the front of the Kasino and five Luftwaffe officers were climbing down into the road. I wanted to look back to see if they were watching but there were no shouts and the truck eventually overtook us on its way into town. In spite of the freezing cold wind I was bathed in sweat. The sweat was already beginning to cool and I knew I'd be in deep trouble if I couldn't soon get into dry clothes. My lungs were burning as I greedily sucked in the cold air. My panic was causing my breathing to be fast and shallow. Gurbe on the other hand was totally unaffected. In fact he turned and gave me another big grin. The old sod was actually enjoying himself! My shaking became more pronounced and I'd given up all pretence at normality as spasms wracked my body. Gurbe looked at me anxiously and then suddenly turned the horses into a narrow street that led into a sort of courtyard. He reined in the horses, held up five fingers and jumped to the ground. He went to the third small house and his knock was answered by the frail voice of an elderly lady.

"Gurbe," he replied gruffly.

The door opened and he slipped inside.

I sat in the darkness with the foul smell of the bins on the dray behind me and the rank smell of the steaming horses in front of me. I didn't smell too pleasant either! In fact it was a close tie between the horses and me.

Then I heard a sound that actually stilled my shivering. It was the sound of heavy boots on the cobbled courtyard and they were getting nearer. It sounded as if there were at least six of them and my worst fear it was a German patrol was confirmed by the 'clink' of military equipment. A hooded torch bobbed round the corner on the far side of the courtyard and I heard the sharp bark of laughter. The soldier carrying the torch suddenly sensed my presence and the torch flicked up to light the horses.

Now my crazy body went into total reverse. Sweat began to bead on my forehead as fear took over once more. This had to be the end. I couldn't speak the language and although I had a curfew pass, mine said I was an undertaker. Even if I could speak the language it would be hard to convince them I freelanced at night as a pigswill specialist! I decided to try the moron act, which should be easy for me. I fell back to the trick I'd used in the copse at the airstrip. Germans didn't seem to like nosepickers. I rammed my stinking index finger up my right nostril and probed deeply. The torch flicked up and caught me full in the face. I shielded my eyes with one hand but kept my finger firmly up my nose in search of God knows what. I heard a snort of disgust and somebody made a remark in German that brought a ripple of coarse laughter from his colleagues. The one with the torch stepped forward and held out his hand.

"Nachtpasse!"

I removed my finger from my nose and pulled my forged papers from my pocket. I held out the lot for him to take his pick. As he did so he got a whiff of my hands.

"Ach!" he spat as he recoiled in disgust. He cursed me long and loud in German but at least he had lost interest in the papers. Finally, with a spiteful crack across my ankles with his rifle, he switched the torch off and they marched away into the darkness.

As for me, I just felt dizzy and sick. All my energy seemed to drain from my body and I slumped backwards into a heap on the dray. I couldn't think any more and

I didn't care any more. I'd had it!

It was Gurbe, thumping me and pointing to the house that brought me back to my senses. He helped me down from the dray and let me into the house. In the hallway there was a little pile of clothes and he mimed for me to put them on. He went back out to the horses whilst I changed. The clothes smelt a bit musty and were about two sizes too big but at least they were dry. Nobody emerged from the doors leading off the hall so I just left my damp clothes in a pile where the dry ones had been and closed the door quietly behind me.

Gurber was stood on the dray, in the centre of the bins, and he motioned for me to help him with the two Germans. We heaved the dead SS officer into a bin that already had a small amount of swill at the bottom. The stench was pretty foul but he wasn't going to complain.

Giedrovski we put in a dry bin. I felt the pulse in his neck and was relieved to discover that, not only did he still have one, but also that it was steady. I tried to remember how much time one hypo would give us but my mind was in turmoil and I gave up the struggle. We'd have to take a chance on him waking, as I daren't risk an overdose.

We put the outer bins back in position and headed out into the main street. I felt much warmer now and my nerves were getting back to normal after the encounter with the German patrol. Later, we were stopped by another patrol but they only looked at Gurbe's papers and seemed satisfied with his curfew pass. They left me alone. I think the stench from the bins was getting to them. They quickly waved us on and once more I knew the laughter was aimed at our perceived status in life. At least it seemed there was no emergency out yet for the two officers.

We finally arrived at Gurbe's farm. There was no doubting it was a pig farm because, in spite of our on-board stench, I'd been overpowered by the smell of pig shit for the last mile. The wind may be cold but nobody said it had to be fresh!

The farm was situated close to the tiny village of Wirdum. Naturally, the place was in complete darkness as we turned into the track leading to the farm.

As soon as we stopped, Gurbe unhitched the horses and led them into the stable. He brought each horse a bucket of water and put some feed in the racks. He insisted we groomed them and rubbed them down as they ate. The horses were far more important to his survival than the two Germans, hence the priority treatment.

Satisfied the horses were settled, we transferred our attention to the SS officer and Giedrovski. The dead SS officer we carried into a cart shed and hid him under a tarpaulin. We hauled Giedrovski up into a loft over the stable. Gurbe lit a small oil stove and placed it well out of the German's reach. He tied Giedrovski to a stout post that supported the roof. I tied the legs together and also bound the hands behind the post. A gag was thrust into his mouth to round off our security precautions. If he awoke, he'd still be totally incapacitated. I was still worried about him choking but what alternative did we have? I reckoned, with luck, he'd be out for at least another four hours.

I was shattered by the time we finally stood in the farmhouse. It was furnished in traditional Dutch style - heavy and dark. The same description could have applied to Gurbe's wife! She was a very large lady and, although in her late seventies, was no shrinking violet!

"Geesje," she boomed with a welcoming smile that was rich in warmth but seriously short on teeth.

"Henk," I replied and winced as she wrapped her huge arms around me and planted a big kiss on each of my cheeks. She then held me at arm's length and looked me up and down. I'm sure my appearance did nothing to prompt her next reaction.

"Winston Churchill!" she roared.

Ah, now there she had me. I was rather short on famous Dutchmen, especially politicians and I didn't think a cry of 'Van Gogh' would really cut the mustard in the popularity stakes. I decided to keep quiet and just grin inanely in the hope that she'd release me. It seemed to do the trick although her smile faded a little and, as she spoke to Gurbe, I had the feeling she was saying. "What a wanker!"

She regained some of her spirit and we sat down to a supper of meats and cheeses, washed down with a bitter tasting black coffee. Once more my spirits were revived and I relaxed in the fragile security of the farmstead.

After the meal, I settled on a big old sofa and stretched out my legs in front of the fire. I was just beginning to doze when Gurbe tapped my arm, pointed to my Dutch fob watch and indicated one hour. He mimed somebody riding a cycle.

"Annie," he said and left the room.

The fact that Annie would be here gave my morale another boost.

Geesje the Great had quickly washed up and now regarded me rather in the manner of a cat eyeing a mouse. I could see the mental cogs in her brain grinding into motion and I'd a feeling the resultant brainwave would not be to my advantage. I started as she clapped her hands together and trotted over to an old writing bureau. She opened a small drawer and returned triumphant, clutching a pack of cards. I was hauled unceremoniously to my feet and dragged to the table. I groaned inwardly as there was nothing I hated more than playing cards.

She tried me with several games but I'd no idea how to play real cards. As she spoke no English, other than 'Winston Churchill', we were at an impasse. Then, in an effort to salvage and uphold the pride of the English, I'd a flash of inspiration. After a short familiarisation with the scant rules we settled down to play the only card game I knew – Snap!

The scene must have been like something from a ward in a hospital for the seriously bewildered. The silence of the old house was punctuated by the sound of cards and fists hitting the table followed by screams of "Snap!" This was invariably followed by hoots of laughter. Geesje was a wily old bird and, in an endeavour to nobble me, she doled out regular and liberal shots of Dutch gin. My lips steadily became numb and, by the time Gurbe came back, I was screaming "Nab!"

Geesje, for some reason, was screaming "Schnapps!

Maybe it was the release of tension but I was enjoying myself immensely.

Of course it had to come to an end. We had two German officers out in the farmyard - one dead and one drugged. Reality was never going to be far away. I smelt the cold of the night emanating from Gurbe's overcoat as he bent over me. He tapped my watch again.

"Annie," he said, as he gratefully accepted a large mug of ersatz coffee from Geesje.

The fun had gone out of our game of cards so I sat and stared at the fire until a quiet knock on the door jolted me from my reverie.

Annie was breathless, her face red from exertion and the cold night air. She kissed Geesje and shrugged off her coat. She moved to the fireplace to warm her hands and spoke over her shoulder.

"Boy! Do you know how to throw the smelly stuff in the fan!"

"Sorry," I said quietly. "I'd no choice. We literally bumped into each other."

"Why the hell could you not have just walked on by?" she asked and she was angry. "You knew the rules. You point the finger and leave the snatch to us."

I was beginning to get pissed off again. It seemed it was always my bloody fault.

"Because," I snapped back, "he recognised me and was fucking well going to shoot me. Now you may be a gung-ho fucking Yank, with the mouth to go with the image, but get sensible, girl – I'd no choice. In fact, if it hadn't have been for old Gurbe here, things would have been a lot worse. I was in a state of shock and not thinking any more. So, we're in the shit but you seem to have all the fucking answers, so get solving and get me and my target out of this shithole."

She locked eyes with me and anger blazed from hers but the fire slowly faded and she flopped into a chair with a sigh. "Sorry, kid. I guess Gurbe's story was a little scarce on detail. I was not aware of all the facts. My first impression was you'd wanted to be the hero and had done it all by yourself."

"Look," I said earnestly. "Once and for all, I want you to file away in your shit file, this bloody silly idea that I want to be a hero. All I want to do is get the job done and get home. To incapacitate one guy and kill another is not something I do before dinner every day."

Her head came up fast. "Kill a guy! What the hell are you talking about?"

"You don't know?"

She shook her head angrily. "Of course I don't know. Gurbe just said you'd got your man and could I come straight away."

I sighed. "I'm afraid there is a little more to it than that. I was stood in the middle of the road with Giedrovski spark out at my feet, when an SS guy popped up from the Kasino like a Jack in the Box."

She looked aghast. "For Pete's sake!"

"I'm afraid that, in my panic, I was a little over zealous. I only intended to knock him out but I'm afraid I smashed his skull in with Giedrovski's Luger." I gave an involuntary shiver.

She noticed and reached out to lay a hand on my arm. "Where is he?" she asked quietly.

"Under a tarpaulin in one of the sheds."

"What about Giedrovski, or whatever you call him?"

"In the stable loft."

I saw her start to protest.

"It's okay," I reassured her. "Gurbe lit a stove up there to make sure he doesn't freeze and we've immobilised him. Even if he comes round, about all he'll be able to do is break wind."

She sighed and shook her head helplessly. "You realise Gurbe has signed both his own and his wife's death warrant by bringing him here? If we don't succeed in getting the bastard out, we'd better make sure he doesn't live to tell his tale. If the Germans get him back alive, he'll know exactly where he's been and Gurbe and his wife will be shot."

I nodded. "I know what you're saying but the old guy took charge and had both Germans on the dray in seconds. If it had been up to me, we would have legged it. There would have been a hell of a hue and cry and I'd have lost all hope of getting Giedrovski. Old Gurbe showed not a shred of fear and he brought us straight here to the farm. I don't think he even thought about the danger."

"Oh, he thought about it," replied Annie. "He thought about it and weighed up the situation. To him, you're somebody who is risking his life to help Holland. That was all the motivation he needed to lay his life on the line. These people are a proud people who love their country and they'll willingly give their own lives to help those who come to help them in their struggle. You may not feel like a hero but, to them, that is exactly what you are, so don't let them down."

"Have you ever felt inadequate?" I asked miserably.

She laughed. "You've the nerve to ask an American girl if she feels inadequate? Just a few minutes ago you were adamant I knew everything and had the big mouth to match."

I cringed. "Any chance of an apology being accepted?"

She laughed. "Only a grovelling one!"

"Okay, I'm grovelling."

"I'm honoured."

"So you should be," I smiled. " I don't make a habit of this."

She took my hand and smiled. "You should, humility suits you."

I gave her a guarded look because I was afraid my feelings would show. She was beautiful and she was brave. She was only twenty-four years old but had the self-assurance and wisdom of a much older person. Maybe it was the isolation I felt at being in a strange and hostile land but I was drawn towards her, both emotionally and physically. I knew if I spent too much time in her company, I was going to fall in love with two women. I decided to break the spell before my heart leapt out and sat on my sleeve.

"How long do you think we've got before our two Germans are missed and the panic begins?"

She removed her hand from mine and sat back in her chair. "I'd think the alarm bells are already beginning to ring."

"Saturday night is going to be a long time coming."

"We've already made an attempt to sort out that problem."

I didn't fail to notice it was a guarded statement. "How?"

"Well, when the three agents left on your seaplane, they had to take their radio with them and that was our only link with England. They promised they would request a radio drop for us when they were debriefed. Nevertheless, we do have a radio at a secret location and we've already sent an urgent message to London, asking them to reschedule your pick up for tomorrow night, Friday."

This was great news. "What did they say?"

She hesitated and looked away. "We don't know."

I began to get a nasty feeling. "What do you mean, you don't know?"

She finally looked me right in the eye. "We don't know the range of our radio. It's an old Dutch army model, not one of the modern sets sent from England. Those all went to the real Resistance and they are all now in German hands, including the codes. Before the agents left, they gave us a simple code to use in the event we were able to get a radio. Nobody else knows the code, so they would be sure it was us and not the real Resistance trying to make contact."

She paused for some sort of reaction but I could sense there was more and I'd a feeling I wasn't going to like it.

"There is another problem," she continued, her eyes still on mine as if defying me to criticise. "Our radio does not receive and we cannot get a replacement valve. It does however transmit but of course we don't know how far. It should, according to the spec, have the range to reach England but we cannot be sure of that. It is old and more than a little battered."

I shook my head in disbelief but nothing would be gained by me blowing my top. "Let me get this straight," I said. "Tomorrow, we're going to move Giedrovski south to the lake and keep him hidden until the seaplane arrives. Okay, assuming we get him all the way there without German patrols insisting we open the coffin, we cannot be sure England has received the message. So, if the seaplane fails to appear tomorrow night, we've to keep a very visible hearse at the lake for another twenty-four hours. Now, accuse me of being picky if you like but are we not pushing our luck a little here?"

Gurbe and his wife had pulled up a couple of chairs and were looking a bit like a couple of spectators at a tennis match. First they looked anxiously at me as I spoke and then looked earnestly at Annie as she replied. They hadn't a clue what we were saying but you'd never have known it, as they nodded sagely at every remark. The whole thing was getting more bizarre by the minute.

"He's not going by hearse," replied Annie. "We've had to change that plan too. Gurbe has an old barrel organ in his barn. Tonight we're going to remove the innards and make a compartment for Giedrovski. We will transport him to the lake inside Gurbe's barrel organ."

Did I say bizarre by the minute? Make that by the second! I didn't dare reply. If I had opened my mouth at that stage it would have been to collapse into maniacal laughter. So, I just stood up and headed for the hall and my warm clothes.

"Where are you going?" she shouted in surprise.

"I can feel a bloody tune coming on," I grunted as I headed out into the night.

CHAPTER TWENTY-ONE

I was still angry when I reached the barn but it was no good throwing a tantrum. These people were doing their best in very dangerous and difficult circumstances. I felt my anger dissipate as reality sank into my confused mind. The only thing to do was keep everybody happy and make the best of what we had available to us. Maybe the radio would not reach England but at least they'd quickly adapted to the new circumstances and done their best to get the show back on the road.

Annie and Gurbe joined me as I climbed the steps to the loft. In the glow from the paraffin stove I could see that Giedrovski was awake. He was still dopey and disorientated but he was recovering fast. He blinked owlishly in the light of Annie's torch. She spoke quickly in Dutch to Gurbe and he disappeared down the ladder.

"I've asked Gurbe to get some water and a little food for our prisoner. Geesje will feed him whilst we get to work on the barrel organ."

We went back downstairs and found the barrel organ covered by a tarpaulin. Cosmetically, the organ looked in a pretty good condition but the innards were totally shot. The wooden frame and pipes had suffered badly in the damp barn.

For the next three hours we worked solidly to make a compartment inside the organ, big enough for Giedrovski to lie down in relative comfort. We had decided that Geesje, Gurbe and myself would travel on the dray. Annie would travel some way ahead of us on her bike. Hopefully she'd get prior warning of any roadblocks or patrols. We'd add some more furniture from the house to make it look as if we were moving house. Departure would be just before dawn for the long trip to the village of Ouwsterhaule, which was about two and a half kilometres north of the lake. We'd hide up in a deserted farmstead on the far side of the village. It was isolated enough to give us good cover but its poor state of preservation would make any story of our moving in look distinctly suspect. We'd make our way on foot to the northern shore of the lake for the pick up.

I had protested at having Giedrovski on his feet and awake for the last stage to the lake but I realised there was no practical alternative. If he gave us a hard time during the walk, we'd have to render him insensible and carry him on some sort of litter.

It was four in the morning before we'd finished the barrel organ modifications. We loaded it on to the dray with a sack hoist and lashed it down tightly with rope. We collected a few chairs, a small table and a few more bits of furniture from the house and piled them around the barrel organ. We finished off our Trojan horse by covering the load with a large tarpaulin and pushed the dray back into the shed. I was shattered but I nipped upstairs to see how Geesje was getting on with our prisoner. He was fully awake now and his eyes burned with hatred when I entered the loft.

Geesje had fed him and was watching him like a huge, hungry praying mantis. Any excuse and she'd tear his arms off. He made an effort to struggle out of his bonds but he'd no chance of succeeding and he knew it. It was a futile display of bravado to try to save a little face. Geesje soon put a stop to the proceedings by whacking him hard across the side of the head with a hand like a side of ham. The disorientated look came back into his eyes.

I made a mime of sleeping to indicate that it was time Geesje turned in for what little of the night remained. She shook her head and pointed for me to go. I tried everything I knew but she was having none of it. She was going to stay here with the prisoner and that was that. She settled down into swathes of blankets and clutched a bottle, the contents of which had a miraculous visible effect on her demeanour every time she took a swig - which was often! I just gave in and returned to the warmth of the farmhouse.

When I entered the living room, Annie was already asleep in one of the armchairs so I dropped into its neighbour and fell sound asleep. For once there were no dreams, not even of Nat.

It seemed like only minutes later when Gurbe shook me awake. Surely it was not yet time to go but when I looked at my watch it was already six o'clock. Time to move out.

Geesje had made us quite a breakfast and we washed it down with lots of hot coffee. Lord knows when we would eat again.

Giedrovski didn't struggle as we helped him down the steep steps from the loft but he certainly put up a fight when he saw the compartment in the barrel organ. Geesje soon sorted him out with another great clout around the side of his head. She beamed happily at me. The lady was enjoying herself immensely.

We retied Giedrovski's hands and feet and laid him on his side in the compartment. I placed a small sack of straw under his head to act as a pillow and covered him with blankets to keep out the bitterly cold air. As we screwed the back of the organ back into place I suddenly had a mild panic attack.

"What if we see a patrol in the distance and I've to give him a shot to keep him quiet. How the hell am I going to get at him?"

Annie spoke to Gurbe and he grinned. He pulled me around to the other side of the organ and tugged at a decorative carving on the lower section. To my surprise, it slid to one side, exposing the upper arm and neck of our captive.

I laughed. "Oh, neat!"

Annie was just as surprised. "The old guy must have done that after we went to bed."

I looked at the old man but he looked as fresh as a daisy. I shook my head in wonderment.

"That means he's had no sleep at all!"

She nodded. "I guess not. He's one hell of a guy."

"Ask him what he'll do with the dead SS guy."

She spoke to Gurbe and he laughed, put his arm around his ample wife and whispered in her ear. Geesje cracked up and began interspersing her guffaws with porcine grunts. They were convulsed with laughter. I raised a questioning eyebrow at Annie but she shrugged and shook her head. Then I think we both got it at the same time and we looked at each other in horror. I began to feel sick and, even in the low light of the lantern, I could see her face turn ashen. She turned to Gurbe and spoke quietly. He stopped laughing just long enough to gasp a reply before once more cracking up with mirth.

I looked at her intently. "What did he say?"

She swallowed noisily. "He said the pigs had a more nourishing breakfast than we did."

"Oh, Christ!" It was all I could say as I felt the bile rising in my throat. They'd chopped up the SS officer and fed him to the pigs. I looked at Gurbe and his wife as they finally ran out of steam and were wiping their eyes. They looked just like anybody's grandparents, gentle and kind. It seemed impossible that these two amiable old people could have carried out such a barbarous act. Was this what war was doing to us all?

Then I opened my eyes and let myself recognise the hatred these people had for those who had invaded their land. The Germans were already committing inhuman crimes against the Dutch population and the Dutch wanted revenge. Gurbe and Geesje were no different. They had no guns or sophisticated equipment but they would use whatever was at hand to do their bit against the invader. I could hear the contented grunts of the pigs and I knew we had little to fear. There would be nothing left of our SS officer.

I decided right there and then that we had to succeed. I'd not risk the lives of these two brave old souls without making sure I made their safety my priority.

Gurbe made a clicking noise with his tongue and motioned for me to help him. He snuffed out the lantern and opened the shed doors. The horses were already in their collars and bridles and it was a simple matter to lead them to the dray and hitch them into the shafts.

"See you later, kid," Annie called softly as she pedalled away into the freezing cold dawn.

Gurbe motioned me to get aboard and I sat with him up front whilst Geesje sat at the back, her legs dangling over the back of the dray. Seconds later we were clattering noisily down the farm track to the road.

Just after dawn, as we came to the Tee junction in Reduzum, a Kubelwagen and a half-track truck, full of troops, swept across our front. They had come from the direction of Wijtgaard and were heading at speed towards Jirnsum. The two officers in the Kubelwagen glanced curiously at us but the troops in the half-track looked frozen stiff and paid us little interest. Not even Annie, who was waiting for us at the junction, raised their attention level.

"Do you think they know something we don't know?" I murmured down to her as she sat on her bike.

She shook her head and looked anxious. "Lord knows. I just hope they haven't outguessed us and headed for the lake."

I wished she hadn't said that and I felt nervously for the hypos in my pocket.

We set off again but made frequent stops to rest the horses. To my surprise and relief, we saw little of the Germans. A Fieseler Storch spotter aircraft circled and hovered over in the direction of Sneek but it came nowhere near us. It was with a great sigh of relief that we reached the deserted farm. It was 16.00 hours and already getting dark again. Annie was waiting in the gloom and helped us back the dray into the dilapidated barn. Gurbe unhitched the horses and led them into the ramshackle stables next door. He'd brought feed and straw to make them as comfortable as possible and he and Geesje set about bedding them down.

"What happened to the previous occupants?" I asked Annie.

"They left just before the Germans invaded. We thought it would look natural for a family to arrive as if taking over. Unfortunately the house has been robbed of anything of value. They've even ripped out the fireplaces."

Bang went any notions I may have had of hot coffee and food. I glanced round as Gurbe came into the barn. He looked anxious and spoke urgently to Annie. He kept glancing up at the sky. It had been a very cold day but at least the hazy sun had helped our morale.

Annie came over to me and now she looked worried. "Gurbe reckons he can smell fog."

I was about to make an impatient reply to the effect that one cannot smell fog but one look at the old guy's face stopped me in my tracks. He was an old countryman and they often knew the fickle weather much better than any trained meteorologist. If Gurbe said he smelt fog then I knew he was serious. Everything pointed to it. We were close to a water mass, there was no wind and there had been that hazy sun.

"Shit! That's all we need." I cursed our luck. "It makes for good cover but no good for seaplanes."

"Yeah, I know." Annie sounded weary. "Come on, no good worrying. Let's give Giedrovski some more fluids and get him ready."

The next hour seemed like an eternity and my heart sank as quickly as the nightfall. Gurbe had been right about the fog. It seemed to rise up out of the ground. First, as darkness fell, it hovered just a few feet above the ground, only the tops of the bushes protruded from the grey veil. Then it seemed to sweep up in triumph at the distress it was causing us and it blotted out the moon. Visibility was less than twenty yards. There would be no seaplane tonight. I said as much to Annie as we stood dejectedly in the barn doorway.

"Okay, maybe not but we've to go through with the move to the lake. The fog could suddenly clear and then where would we be?"

"But we don't even know the bloody plane is coming," I replied in exasperation. "Even if it does, the pilot will not even be able to see the lake, let alone land on the bloody thing."

She was adamant. "Nevertheless, we move out at 18.00 hours."

I'd only known her a few hours but already I could recognise that defiant tone in her voice. She was not going to change her mind.

"Okay, you're the boss," I conceded.

To my surprise, she suddenly leaned over and gave me a gentle kiss on my cheek. She squeezed my hand and gave that special little chuckle of hers. "That's the nicest thing you've said to me."

I was a little taken aback by the gesture and I felt a flood of pleasure at her touch.

I grinned. "My driver back home is always telling me I'm a smooth talking bastard."

She laughed. "Seems like a nice guy."

"Gal," I corrected her. "Gal, not guy, although she's probably more masculine than most of the men on the unit."

She slipped her arm through mine. "Only you could pick somebody like that. Nothing uncomplicated or easy for you."

I held her arm tight to my side and grinned in the darkness. "Would you want me any other way?"

"I love it when you talk dirty." There was that chuckle again.

Time to change the subject, Carver! "Where are the two G's?" I asked, peering into the gloom of the barn.

"Stretched out and fast asleep in a couple of chairs they've taken off the dray."

I stared wistfully out into the fog. "I wish I could take you all home with me."

She sighed. "They'd be like fish out of water if you took them away from their surroundings and their friends."

"What about you?" I asked her quietly.

There was a long silence and then she said it so quickly I nearly missed it.

"Maybe it's time I got out."

I stood perfectly still. "Say that again."

She moved away from me and sat on an old hay turner. "There have been a lot of arrests recently. The Abwehr and the Sicherheitsdienst, normally bitter rivals, are actually working together from their headquarters in The Hague. There is a traitor out here and he's high up in the organisation but London will not listen. Maybe the three guys who were out here will be able to provide the proof to shake those dozy bastards at SOE. Our little group cannot carry on much longer; we don't have the resources. Last night Wim advised me to get out before it is too late."

"Do you want to come tonight?"

She looked around her and sighed. "Yeah, I guess so. There is nothing left for me here. I've been pushing my luck for a long time now. I reckon it is time I had a rest."

"What about Gurbe and Geesje?"

She glanced into the darkness. "I discussed it with them this morning and they agreed I should go as soon as an opportunity presented itself. They'll not be coming to the lake. If there are any patrols in the area then they'll get just you and me but, if we look like being caught, we must kill Giedrovski."

"Sounds good to me," I said softly. "But you'd better kill me too. If I'm caught and tortured, I'll sure as hell talk eventually. I'm no hero and I couldn't bear it if I thought I was responsible for the death of those two old folks."

"You mean that?" she asked with a catch in her voice.

"You bet I do."

We were silent for a long time but eventually she raised her watch close to her face to see the luminous dial. "We'd better get Giedrovski out of his hidey hole and get going."

Gurbe heard us moving about and struggled to his feet. I waved him back down but he ignored me. He helped us get the back off the barrel organ and he quickly cut the ropes binding Giedrovski's ankles. The poor bastard couldn't walk at first but he was finally able to stagger upright. Annie rooted around in some old sacks on a shelf at the rear of the barn and came back with a 9mm Browning automatic.

"Where the hell did that come from?" I asked in surprise.

"The guys who were here earlier to make sure the boat was in place left it here for us. They knew we'd need to persuade our friend here to co-operate." She turned and put the barrel of the Browning to the base of Giedrovski's skull. "If you don't do exactly as we tell you, you bastard, you're one dead hero. Understand?"

He nodded but his whole heart wasn't in it so she rapped him smartly on the temple with the gun. This time there was more vigour in the nod. In fact, he was so eager to please, his bloody head nearly came off his shoulders. He turned to look at me and I had to force myself to hold his stare. The eyes were malevolent and burning with hatred, a long way from the cocksure grin he'd given me at Sutton Bridge. I knew that as long as he was conscious we were going to have to watch him like a hawk.

Annie stooped and tied a length of rope between his ankles. He'd be able to take about a third of a normal pace. I checked the rope around his wrists and was satisfied he was as secure as we could make him. Then he began to struggle and shake his head up and down.

Annie grinned. "I think he wants to say something."

I nodded and quickly removed his gag. He took in great gulps of air before he

292

spoke.

"I need to urinate or would you rather I did it in my pants?"

Annie laughed. "Sounds like an excuse to get somebody to hold your dick."

"Well don't look at me," I replied with feeling.

"Why not untie me, for Christ's sake, I only need a piss." He was tired, in pain, uncomfortable, disorientated and naturally very angry.

Gurbe said something in Dutch to Annie and she handed him the Browning. Gurbe pressed it to Giedrovski's forehead. The German moved slowly and carefully as they left the barn. He knew Gurbe was simply waiting for the slightest excuse to shoot him.

"You ready?" Annie asked me.

"As much as I'll ever be." I tapped my pockets to check the hypos and made sure I had the torch in the event the seaplane actually made it to the lake.

As we neared the door, Gurbe pushed Giedrovski back into the barn. The old Dutchman grinned and crooked his little finger as a sign that our German hero was not too well endowed.

Annie laughed. "So much for the Master Race!"

Strangely, the obscene gesture seemed to have an effect on Giedrovski that was out of all proportion. He tried to lunge forward but Gurbe pulled him up short. The German's face was contorted with fury and there were flecks of saliva at the corners of his mouth.

"You'll all soon be arrested and I personally will have the greatest pleasure in escorting you to the basement of Leeuwarden prison. You'll wish you had never been born."

Gurbe didn't understand the words but he did his own loose interpretation and smacked the German smartly over the bridge of the nose with the Browning. Blood and snot flew everywhere as Giedrovski slumped to his knees.

Shit! I hoped he could still breathe through his nose because I didn't want him out there without a gag. I yanked his head back by the hair and thrust the gag into his mouth. His eyes blazed again but I was relieved to discover he could still breathe. Once the swelling started then the situation could change. We were going to have to watch him for any signs he was suffocating.

Annie hugged and kissed Gurbe and Geesje. I received a bone-crushing embrace from Geesje and the mandatory big wet kiss. Gurbe began by shaking my hand but suddenly he threw his arms round me and hugged me. He said something I couldn't understand and, when he finally let me go, I turned to Annie for a translation. I saw her swallow quickly before she replied.

"He says that when the war is over, you're to come back to Holland. You've a special place in their hearts and that they are now blessed with a son."

I looked at the old couple as they stood there in the gloom. They looked so homely and I knew the sacrifices they had made to feed me and to transport our prisoner. I also remembered that they had dismembered a man and fed him to their pigs. My emotions were confused but I embraced them both again. These were the real heroes in Holland.

Without another word, we left them in the barn. Tomorrow they would return to the farm and, if the plane failed to turn up, we would have to spend a cold night in the barn.

We turned left at the end of the village and, although a couple of dogs barked, we saw nobody or even a glimmer of light from the houses. About another kilometre further on we turned right and it was now less than two kilometres to the lake. Visibility was zero. The fog was a real pea-souper. Our outer clothes were beaded with water droplets and it was an anxious time as we groped our way forwards. We'd have no warning of a patrol, roadblock or ambush and, although the fog blanketed most of the noise we were making, we'd still give plenty of notice of our approach.

Suddenly Annie held up a hand and I yanked the German to a halt. She disappeared into the fog and I waited anxiously for her to reappear. I need not have worried as she was soon back.

"We're there," she whispered. "The boat is where it should be and we should be able to manage it between us."

We moved cautiously forward as the road petered out into a track. Soon we were in among the bushes and the reeds. I tied Giedrovski firmly to a small tree and helped Annie drag the boat onto the water. We returned to fetch our prisoner and sat him in the stern of the boat. I picked up the oars and made to sit but Annie put out a restraining hand.

"Let me - I'm used to rowing."

I didn't argue. Ten minutes on a seaside boating lake as a ten-year-old was no great training for our present situation. I looked at Giedrovski and slid a hypodermic from the tin in my pocket as I leaned towards him.

"Time for bye-byes."

I should have been more careful. He suddenly lunged forward taking me totally by surprise. I damned nearly went into the lake but managed to stay on board and grabbed despairingly for his neck. I finally got an arm round his throat but had no way of raising his sleeve to give him the injection.

Annie half fell forward and managed to yank his sleeve up to expose a little of his arm. I plunged the hypo into the area of his upper wrist. He fought like a madman for a few seconds but finally went limp. I'd no idea how much I'd managed to get into him because the hypo had gone overboard in his last desperate attempts to stay conscious.

"Did he get the dose?" Annie asked anxiously.

"Some, but I don't think he got the lot."

"How long do you think he'll be out?"

"No idea. Let's hope it was enough."

Annie was about to reply but quickly held up a warning hand as we heard movement on the shore behind us. We sat stock-still and hoped it was an animal. We heard the noise again but this time it was much closer and we knew it was no animal. This was somebody in a hurry. Annie tossed the Browning to me and crouched to give me a field of fire. Giedrovski was already a shapeless bundle in the bottom of the boat.

"Annie!" It was a loud whisper from the darkness.

"Hell! It's Gurbe," whispered Annie. She shipped the oars and, taking the painter, slipped over the transom and secured the boat to a bush. Good thinking, girl! I'd have hated to drift off into the fog.

She disappeared into the murk and I heard the low murmur of voices. When she reappeared, I could hear the anxiety in her voice. "A German patrol turned up at the farm after we'd left. The patrol was making a lot of noise so Gurbe and Geesje had plenty of warning. Geesje took the horses into a field at the rear of the farm and Gurbe kept watch. The patrol peered into the barn and looked under the tarpaulin at the barrel organ but fortunately, the old folks had screwed the back into place. The patrol also had a quick look at the house but finally cleared off in the direction of Ouwster-

Nijega - a village on the road that runs parallel to the road we used to get here. If they are coming to the lake, then they'll arrive here just one kilometre to the right of our position. Let's pray they decide to check around the western side of the goddam lake and not come this way."

"Where's Gurbe now?"

"Gone back to collect his wife and horses. He wants to get rid of the barrel organ."

"God go with him," I said quietly.

"Amen," whispered Annie as she climbed back into the boat.

We sat quietly in the fog, our breath vaporising in the cold air. The only sounds were the lapping of the water against the hull of the dinghy and the lonely cry of some water bird far away across the lake. My nerves were getting as tight as a bow string and I knew, as I watched Annie fiddling nervously with the oars, it was not just me who was feeling the pressure. She needed a rest and I was pleased she'd elected to come back on the seaplane.

A sound disturbed the silence of the fog and darkness. It was so faint I had to strain to pick it up again. There it was again - the sound of an aircraft. It seemed to come from the east but the blanketing effect of the fog made it difficult to be sure of the direction. It did nothing to raise my hopes. There'd be plenty of aircraft up there tonight. Up high there would be no fog but down here it was a different story. I felt the gentle kiss on my right cheek from the first suspicion of a breeze.

"Did you hear what I thought I heard?" Annie whispered.

"Could be, but let's face it, nothing special in the sound of an aircraft around here."

We started as the crump and thud of explosions came from the north. My spirits rose but were quickly stifled by the fog.

"Sounds like a raid on Leeuwarden," I whispered. "Looks like your message got through but the fog has screwed it all up." I felt sick at the thought we'd been so close. I stared desperately at the thick, milky mass that surrounded us. The breeze had begun to blow the fog along the surface of the lake but it was going to take a good stiff wind to clear it away. No aircraft could land in this. I thumped my right fist into my left palm in suppressed anger.

"Fuck the bastard fog!"

As I spoke, another sound alerted my senses. It was a weird sound - one I couldn't identify. There was a deep rhythmic sound accompanied by a subdued rushing of air.

"What the hell's that?" I whispered angrily and with no little trepidation.

Annie didn't reply. Her back was to me as she prepared to row. Her head was tilted to one side as she tried to locate the direction of the sound, which was getting louder. Then it was upon us and I swear the two floats, which passed either side of the boat, were no more than five feet above our heads.

Annie gave a stifled scream and I thought my heart had stopped. There was a sudden roar of aero engines going to maximum power and then a sound like an empty metal drum smashing into the water. The engines roared again and there was another loud smack of sound, then silence.

Annie needed no urging to start rowing and we began to move blindly out onto the lake. I could now hear the aircraft's engines heading back towards us through the fog but how the hell were we going to locate each other? There was also another factor that worried me. If the pilot kept coming in our direction, there was every chance he'd end up running us down or running aground. I still couldn't understand how the mad, brave bastard had managed to get the kite down in one piece. I tensed as the noise of the engines became deafening.

Suddenly, there was the Fokker, damned nearly right on top of us. We careened off the starboard float and I caught a brief glimpse of a torch flashing from the nose section. They must have seen or felt us collide with the float and the aircraft began to turn back towards us but it was soon out of sight. At least he should have just missed the shore. The noise of the engines suddenly died to a rackety clatter as the crew decided to let us find them. It was marginally safer that way.

I thought of the patrol that was supposed to be in the area. This racket would have them heading in this direction as fast as their legs could carry them.

The aircraft finally loomed up out of the fog and we managed to get ourselves around to the starboard float and I grabbed a strut. It was wet and slippery but I managed to hold on, although I nearly lost my grip as something snaked past my head. When my heart steadied I realised it was the harness Jan had made for the inert Giedrovski. It was a hell of a struggle to get the harness around the German but, in spite of my frozen fingers and his dead weight, fear enabled me to complete the impossible. I flashed my torch upwards and the line went taut. To my surprise, the unconscious German rose easily up towards the trailing edge of the wing. I hopped onto the float to steady him and guided him upwards as I climbed the stepped strut.

As I hauled myself up onto the wing I realised why Giedrovski had ascended so easily. It was Bouma who stood on the wing and I realised that, without his strength, Jan and I would never have managed it. He grinned in the soft glow of moonlight now filtering through the fog.

Giedrovski was unceremoniously dumped through the rear hatch and Bouma waved for me to follow but stopped when Annie materialised out of the fog and joined us on the wing. There was no time for questions and he bundled her into the cockpit, albeit with a little more care than he had shown the German. He clambered in next and headed forward to take over the controls. I quickly followed and was surprised to see an extra crewmember manning the rear machine gun. Jan saw me as he climbed from behind the controls to let Bouma back into his rightful place. He gave me a thumbs up and threw me a spare helmet before he headed for the nose of the aircraft.

As I plugged the intercom lead into a fuselage socket the engines roared to full power. My heart skipped a beat as I heard what sounded like backfiring. Then a couple of Perspex panels in the canopy shattered and shards flew around the cockpit. Shit, somebody out there was firing at us and it had to be the patrol but they were firing blind and not too effectively. The gunner had ducked below the cockpit coaming as the gunfire ripped into us but now he was up and hosing fire from the machine gun towards the invisible shore. At least it would help keep their heads down until we were out of range. We were now beginning to porpoise a little on the surface of the water as Bouma drove us headlong through the fog to try to gain flying speed. The engines were screaming at full throttle and, as brave and as competent Bouma might be, I was beginning to have doubts that we could ever make it safely off the water.

Then, as if from nowhere, a light of searing intensity burst directly into the cockpit, blinding us all. How the hell could the light stay with us like this? And then the penny dropped. The bloody Schnellboot. It was cutting in from our starboard side and we were like a moth in the flame of a candle, fluttering helplessly and soon to be cremated in the flame. Heavy calibre fire lanced out towards us and even the Schnellboot's searchlight couldn't subdue the intensity of the vicious tracer. The noise was mind-numbing as the cannon rounds screamed through the cockpit. The rear clamshell of the cockpit glazing shattered into a million shards and our gunner spun round as if struck by a mighty blow and crashed to the floor. Blood glistened everywhere in the blinding light but the screaming engines had drowned any noise the dying man may have made.

I threw myself to the floor as once more cannon fire lashed into us. I rolled over to look towards Bouma's position and saw him yank the control column back into his ample stomach. Through the nose Perspex and in the light from the boat I saw bushes flash by just under the nose and they could only have been just inches under the floats. Surely we'd not run out of lake - it was too bloody big.

We seemed to stagger as if the aircraft was on the point of stalling but then, on the lake behind us, a huge red flash of flame and fire replaced the blinding white light of the searchlight. The ensuing explosion nearly tore away our already precarious hold on the air but we finally burst out of the top of the fog layer into brilliant moonlight.

I slumped back down onto the cockpit floor and didn't have the strength to rise. My legs were shaking and my mouth was dry. In my confused state I tried to work out what had happened to the Schnellboot. We'd fired nothing in return and then I remembered the bushes and the penny dropped. The island... the bloody island! Jan had warned Bouma not to forget it the night we landed. The crazy bastard had taken a hell of a risk but, for a man who knew the local area so well, a calculated risk. In the heat of the chase, the Germans had forgotten the small island in the middle of the lake. We'd hopped over it but the Schnellboot didn't have our ability to fly and had hit the island at full power. Either Bouma was brilliant or stark raving mad. Probably a little of both.

Jan clambered past me to go to the aid of the gunner but one quick look was all he needed. He pulled a canopy cover from out of the back of the fuselage and covered the corpse. He then crouched in front of me and helped me into a sitting position. We couldn't talk, as the intercom lead had pulled the helmet from my head when I'd dived to the floor. I was shaking violently and it was not just from the freezing night air, which was whipping around the cockpit through the shattered rear clamshell cover. He put his hands on my shoulders and just squatted there until the shaking subsided. I gave him a small smile of thanks and he rummaged around until he found the flying helmet and slipped it over my head.

"Hi there. Better now?" His voice was like a tonic to my shattered senses.

I nodded. "Thanks to you two crazy bastards. How the hell did Bouma get down in that fog?"

He shrugged. "We managed to get a quick fix through a gap in the fog over Heerenveen. We actually spotted the windmill so Gerrit flew due east for a few seconds. Then he turned due south and started to let down. We counted the seconds we thought it should take and he came down the last few feet. We damned nearly hit the shore but God was with us."

"I was with you," roared Bouma over the intercom. "God had nothing to do with it."

"Don't tempt fate," advised Jan. "We're not yet home!"

"We won't get home either unless you come and do something about my foot," replied the pilot and I now detected pain in his voice.

Jan gave me a startled look and shot forward to investigate.

My problem was to try and focus my mind. Then it was all there and I whipped round to look at the prostrate form of Giedrovski. Oh shit! Don't let the bastard be dead or all this was for nothing. I crawled past Annie's legs and my heart lurched when I saw Giedrovski was covered in blood. I frantically groped for his wrist and his pulse. I breathed a sigh of relief. His pulse was strong and steady. The blood was from the poor bloody gunner. The blood had still to congeal and it was being flecked around in the slipstream that howled through the cannon holes in the fuselage. I could feel the freezing slipstream tugging at my clothes as it seemed to penetrate to my very soul.

I could now check on Annie. She was leaning back against the fuselage, her legs stretched out in front of her. Her head was down with her chin on her chest and I began to smile. It looked as if she couldn't wait for that rest she had been talking about. Then I felt a cold hand on my heart. I could remember her screaming when we were hit by the first burst of cannon fire. After that, I'd been so preoccupied with survival, I'd forgotten both Annie and Giedrovski. I grabbed her gloved hand and pulled up the sleeve of her jacket to get at her pulse. I could feel nothing there so I tried the pulse in her neck but again, nothing. I could see no marks or wounds and I began to cling to the desperate hope that I was wrong and she was still alive. I found what looked like a canvas engine cover and I folded it to make a pillow to go between the cold metal of the fuselage and her head. I slipped my hand behind her head to ease it forward and I instantly recoiled in horror. Where my hand should have felt the hardness of her skull, I'd encountered a soggy mush. I stared wildly at my hand and saw it was covered in a mixture of blood and grey matter. Again I recoiled and vomited violently on to the tarpaulin covering the body of the gunner. I stayed kneeling, with my head pressed hard against the vibrating floor of the Fokker, and totally came apart mentally. I beat my fists on the floor and I could feel myself rocking to and fro in shock and grief.

"Annie, oh Annie!" I could hear myself crying her name over and over again. I began to sob as all the tension of the last few hours finally ripped me apart. As I cried Annie's name I could hear somebody calling my name but it wasn't Annie's voice.

"Go away! Go away!" I screamed at the alien voice, trying to prevent it intruding on my grief. I desperately wanted my grief to be an illusion. I wanted to wake up from this nightmare to see only normality but the alien voice was insistent. Then I realised the voice was not calling my name, it was calling for Joe. Joe? Who the hell was Joe? I fought against the voice. I wanted to grieve alone.

The sudden shock of pain as Jan slapped me violently on each side of my face, brought me back to reality. It was still a nightmare but at least I was back to understanding what was happening to me.

Jan held my face in his hands and stared intently into my eyes. He removed one of his hands from my cheek and switched on the intercom on his oxygen mask.

"Are you back with us now?"

I nodded feebly.

"You were screaming on the intercom."

I pointed to Annie's body.

He glanced briefly and I saw the shock register on his face but then his eyes were back on me.

"Gerrit has taken a hit in his right foot. I've dressed it the best I can but he's in a lot of pain and he's lost a lot of blood. Obviously I cannot give him morphine but the stubborn bastard will not let me take over."

"You fly like a fairy. This is a man's aeroplane," Bouma yelled over the intercom.

There was a quick retort from Jan in Dutch and Bouma roared with laughter but he suddenly stopped laughing and I could hear anxiety in his voice. "Oh, oh! We've a problem."

Jan looked forward with a worried frown. "What problem?"

We're losing fuel."

Jan slapped me on the shoulder. "You stay with us now, okay?"

I did my best to give him a reassuring grin as he disappeared up front to check the fuel state. The bloody boat must have holed one of our fuel tanks. I comforted myself with the thought that at least when we ditched we would be in an aircraft designed to land on water. I just hoped we could get close to the English coast because I imagined all hell had been let loose in Holland and they'd do everything they could to get Giedrovski back. I glanced at the now white and unnatural waxy colour of the dead girl's face and I felt the grief welling back up in me but I managed to get a rein on my feelings. I decided to move up next to Bouma and see if there was anything I could do. Anything to postpone the nightmare that was hovering on the edge of my consciousness.

Bouma glanced over his shoulder at me as I moved to his side, one hand bracing myself on the back of his seat and the other on the canopy rim. I could see the fog had cleared away and below was the sea glistening in the moonlight.

"How's the wound?" I asked.

He shrugged. "Bloody painful and I am beginning to feel tired but we will make it back to England."

"I hate to spoil your dreams, Gerrit," called Jan from the nose section. "I'm afraid we will not make England."

Bouma cursed silently then keyed his mike. "Tell me the bad news."

"At the present rate of fuel consumption, you'll have to put down about thirty miles from the English coast."

Bouma gave one of his shrugs. "Well, the old crate will float well enough, unless they've holed a float. What more can you want?"

I grinned in spite of my anxiety. The big guy was so calm about it all. I recalled old Gurbe's reaction at the sight of the bodies of the two Germans lying in the street. I'd been in a blue funk but he'd stayed totally calm and rescued the whole operation. Wim and the others had been so confident when all I could do was gripe. Thank God for the Dutch!

I stooped to check the dressing on Bouma's foot but Jan had done a very professional job, better than I'd done on poor Bill Bedford. I took in the irregular shape and the size of the dressing and I hoped we were not going to have to wait too long for rescue or Bouma was going to lose his foot. I glanced up at him and saw that, in spite of the freezing temperature in the aircraft, his forehead was beaded with perspiration. He was suffering a great more than he was admitting.

I huddled down on the floor next to Bouma's seat - I felt safer there. We roared on and at some point I fell asleep or lost consciousness. To anybody watching there was no tangible difference. I prefer to say that I fell asleep.

It was Jan who finally awoke me. "Joe, only another ten minutes and we've to go down. There should be no problems but it may be a little rough. I suggest you get down the back and brace yourself."

I nodded and climbed shakily to my feet. I tried not to look at Annie's face as I squeezed myself into a spot for the landing. The thought crossed my mind that I should be getting Giedrovski into a safer position but I just didn't give a shit what happened to the bastard. I listened eagerly to the roar of the engines. The longer they roared the nearer we would be to home. The beat was still steady and I'd seen Bouma lean the mixture as much as he dared to try and get the last drop of fuel to count.

Then the port engine faltered, picked up and died altogether. The nose dipped as Bouma traded height for speed and I heard Jan's voice sending out a mayday signal. He had to send the signal or nobody would know where we were. The problem was, it was also alerting the Germans to our actual position. I just hoped our lads would get there first. Then the starboard engine coughed into silence. We glided down with just the eerie sound of the slipstream as it played and cavorted through the cannon holes in the fuselage.

"Brace! Brace!" called Bouma and seconds later we hit the water.

To my surprise it was quite a smooth landing. We rocked and skipped a couple of times but finally the Fokker settled and we ploughed to a halt.

Jan scrambled out of the rear hatch carrying what looked like a large canvas bag on a length of rope. He disappeared from view over the trailing edge of the wing.

"He's gone to drop the sea anchor to keep us into wind," Bouma explained. His voice seemed to echo loudly in the fuselage after the tinny timbre of the intercom.

I peered ahead. "How far are we from the coast?"

Bouma looked surprised. "Thirty miles, of course. When Jan says thirty miles, he means thirty miles. He may be a lousy pilot but he's a superb navigator and engineer." He grinned at me but he looked pale and just about all in.

"How are you feeling?" I asked anxiously.

"I'll live," he rumbled but the strength had gone from his voice and I hoped fervently we would not be out here too long.

"How about you? How are you feeling now?" he enquired.

I bent my legs slightly to help absorb the rolling of the seaplane. "Not too bad. I just hope I don't get seasick!"

He laughed but then winced with pain. "You're so typically English. One minute you're crying over the death of someone you only met yesterday. The next minute you're afraid you'll get seasick! I'll never understand the English."

I looked him straight in the eye. "I'll never understand the Dutch but I think I'll love your people for the rest of my life."

The big man quickly turned away and I saw him struggling to contain his emotions. Three times that night he'd been within a whisker of death. He'd lost a fellow crewmember and he knew Annie was dead. The stress on him must have been immense and I'd nearly spoilt his macho image by speaking my mind. The big guy was not as unfeeling as he tried to make out and I'd unwittingly called his bluff. I wished he'd been able to meet Annie - he'd have liked her.

"If I'd not persuaded her to come, she'd still be alive." I said the words half to myself.

He looked at me quickly. "You don't know that! Was she in the Resistance?"

I nodded. "A very special little cadre. They were totally isolated, even from the main Resistance groups."

"For how long?"

"Since the Germans invaded."

"If she's been working for the Resistance since the Germans invaded, then she was lucky to live this long. Don't blame yourself, Joe."

I winced at the name, Joe. "Can I tell you my real name now?" I asked him.

He chuckled. "Why not?"

I put out my hand. "I'm Sam."

He shook my hand. "God go with you, Sam."

"I thought you didn't believe in God."

"Don't you ever ...?" he struggled for the right words.

"Hedge my bets?" I prompted.

"Exactly." He passed a shaking hand over his eyes. "Now I am going to faint."

He damned well did too and his head crashed forward onto the instrument panel. I grabbed for his pulse and found it fast and thready. I stared forward through the windscreen as if I could conjure up the magical vision of an ASR launch coming to our rescue. Bouma desperately needed blood. Without a transfusion soon, he was going to die. I heard Jan moving around in the back of the aircraft and then he joined me. He leaned quickly over Bouma and then turned anxiously to me.

"It's okay," I assured him. "But we must get help soon."

He looked at his watch. "We've been on the water for just thirty minutes. It will be at least another thirty before the launch gets here."

We sat in silence for a while but then I found I had to stand up. Sitting down in the rolling aircraft was making me feel queasy. Thirty-five minutes had passed when I thought I detected a familiar sound.

I made a motion with my hand to attract Jan's attention. "Do you hear aircraft engines?"

We moved to the open rear cockpit and looked out into the moonlight. There was the unmistakable sound of aircraft engines and they were close. It sounded as if they were flying a search pattern.

"Could it be a Walrus?" I asked.

His face was grim. "No way. That's a bloody German. Could be a Heinkel floatplane out looking for us. They must have sent something out to chase us. They would never have got fighters off because fog covered all the land-based airfields. They must have got a loose fix on our mayday and come to reclaim our friend here." He nodded down at Giedrovski.

Bloody hell, I'd forgotten him again and I glanced at the German's recumbent figure in alarm. That bloody sedative couldn't have lasted this long. I stared hard at him. His face was not that well lit by the moonlight but enough for me to suddenly detect a slight movement of his eyelids. Worse, I saw an infinitesimal change in the posture of his upper body.

For once I didn't hesitate. I lashed out with my right leg and kicked him smack on the point of his jaw. His head smashed back against the fuselage wall and his eyes flew open. They stayed open just long enough for me to see the pain reflected there. A second later they were closed as he sank into unconsciousness.

"What the hell are you doing?" Jan yelled as I lurched forward again.

I yanked my arm from his grasp and rolled Giedrovski over onto his face with my foot. We both saw the shards of rope. The bastard had used the jagged edge of a hole in the fuselage, made by a cannon shell, to sever the ropes that bound him. That was not all. Half concealed under his body was Annie's Browning and he'd somehow opened the emergency kit and added a flare pistol and a couple of flares to his armoury. The bastard had been very busy and I cursed myself for my stupidity. Another few minutes and we would have all been dead. I was so bloody angry, I kicked the bastard again and again in the head. I'd have killed him if Jan had not pulled me away.

"Hey, Joe. You need him alive or all this will have been a waste of time." He began to rebind the German's wrists.

I took a deep breath and listened for the Heinkel but the sound had faded. Somehow they had missed us but, if he was carrying out a square search, he'd be back. I'd no sooner had the thought, when I heard aero engines returning.

301

"The bastard's coming back." I found myself, for some inexplicable reason, whispering.

"That's no Heinkel," Jan shouted as he clambered out onto the wing. "That's a launch and he's coming from the right direction. Give me the torch, quick!"

I handed him the torch and then I saw a phosphorous bow wave roaring towards us from dead ahead. Jan flashed the torch and the engine note died as the coxswain cut the power and the launch finally rumbled up to stand off our starboard side. We rocked as his wake caught up with him.

"Good to see you," called a voice I recognised as Ralph Locke.

"Not as pleased as we are to see you," I called down to him.

"We didn't expect you until tomorrow night. What happened, get fed up?"

"Too much excitement. I wanted to come home."

He laughed and his voice echoed over the moonlit water. "Well, get a bloody move on, will you? I don't like sitting here like this, making a juicy target for any Jerry following up your mayday."

Jan took over. "We've two dead, one badly wounded and unconscious and one just unconscious. We'll need your help."

Locke's voice was subdued when he replied. "I see what you mean about all the excitement." He began to give orders to manoeuvre the boat closer.

"Hold it!" Jan yelled. "I've got a sea anchor out - it will snag your props." He leapt down onto the float and began to haul on the anchor. A young airman somehow managed to safely jump the gap between the launch and the aircraft float. He'd an axe in his hand and, with one quick movement, he cut through the anchor rope.

"No time for that, mate," he said apologetically to Jan.

The launch crew took over and we were soon aboard and in the relative warmth of the wheelhouse. The bodies of the gunner and Annie were lashed to the deck down near the stern. Giedrovski was lowered down a small hatch. His face was a bloody mess from my kicks but he was wide awake again and hating with a vengeance. Jan and I were hovering around the unconscious Bouma, who was on a stretcher on the floor of the wheelhouse, when we were pushed aside by a youngster in the ubiquitous duffel coat and wellingtons.

"Can you help him?" I snapped.

He took a stethoscope from the pocket of his duffel coat. "Only if you get out of the fucking way, old boy."

Locke put a hand on my shoulder. "When there is a real doctor available we bring him along in addition to our usual medical orderly. We can't cope with some of the wounds and having a doc on board is saving a lot of lives." He turned to the coxswain. "Okay, let's go home."

The engines roared as the coxswain wound up the power. I sank tiredly onto a bench seat. It was damned nearly impossible to stand up to the shocks as the boat pounded through the waves at high speed. I cupped my hands around my mouth and shouted at Locke.

"What will happen to our plane?"

He braced himself against the heaving of the boat. "The Navy will come out, at first light and tow it in or sink it."

I slumped back up against the bulkhead and hoped they would salvage our old Fokker. She had done her best and deserved to soldier on.

"Skipper!" yelled the coxswain as he pointed out to port.

In the sky there was a flower of flame and it was slowly arcing towards the surface of the sea. Just before it impacted, it broke up into several trails of fire which were extinguished the instant they hit the water.

"What was that?" I tried to make myself heard above the noise of the engines.

"Hopefully a Jerry," yelled Locke. "They scrambled a Beaufighter when they received your mayday. The Jerries listen out for distress calls and home in on the transmissions. Looking at your cargo I'd imagine you're a very important target. The Beaufighter was waiting to nobble anybody who came near. I think the lads up there just saved us from a strafing."

Nevertheless, he kept a long watch, just in case it had been the Beaufighter going down. Finally he put down his binoculars and put his mouth close to my ear. "Looks like you had a pretty rough trip."

I found I couldn't answer. It was the sudden knowledge that it was all over. Now I knew I was safe I began to come apart again. I began to shake violently and I buried my head in my hands to try and stop the tremors coursing through my body. I clenched my teeth hard together to stop them chattering but it was no good. My senses began to swim and I felt as if I was sinking into a maelstrom. I sensed my vision ebbing and the light fading as I was sucked down into the blackness of hell. I only just heard Locke's urgent call.

"Doc!"

I felt strong hands grab me but I remembered no more of the voyage back to Boston.

CHAPTER TWENTY-TWO

The week following my return from Holland was a kaleidoscope of jumbled memories and dreams, some too painful to recollect without my body sinking into uncontrolled spasms. At times I could neither see nor sense a defining line between what was reality and what were dreams. I seemed to recall Brigadier Franklin being at Boston docks but I couldn't swear to it. Somehow I was transported to a hospital. How I got there I'll never know. I just opened my eyes and found myself there. Clean sheets, flowers on the bedside locker and the sun shining through the windows. It was heaven-sent relief after all the nightmares.

At first I didn't dare move. I was scared it would all disappear and I'd topple back into the dark depths of my personal hell. Finally, I plucked up the courage to move an arm and slide back the bed covers. I looked down and discovered I'd been bathed and dressed in a pair of striped pyjamas that were certainly not my own. I became more courageous and lowered my feet to the floor. To my relief it was not an illusion but I quickly began to lose my new-found feeling of well being as my head began to pound and I felt all the energy desert my body. I sat on the edge of the bed and waited for the room to stop spinning. Behind me, I heard the door open.

"Ah, you're awake at last but where do you think you're going?"

I didn't dare turn my head so I waited for the owner of the voice to drift into my line of sight. It was worth the wait because she was really pretty. Dark brown hair in a bun and grey eyes that surveyed me with a hint of amusement as she waited for an answer.

"I was heading for the loo but I'm afraid my gyros packed in and stranded me here on the edge of the bed."

She lifted my legs and swung me back into bed. I let my head sink back on the pillow and felt the room begin to stabilise.

"Sorry," I murmured.

"Don't apologise but I'm afraid you're going to have the humiliation of a bottle for a little while yet."

"Where am I?"

"A clinic in Oxford," she replied as she tidied my bed.

"Oxford?"

She laughed. "You're suffering from a variety of maladies but deafness is not one of them."

"How did I get here?"

"No idea. I wasn't on shift when you arrived and we don't ask questions when we've patients from 'The Big House' as we call it."

I lay quietly and tried to figure it all out but suddenly Annie's face slid into my mental photo album and I could clearly see the waxy death mask of what had been such a beautiful young girl. I shivered violently.

The nurse was quickly by my side. "Pain?"

I shook my head. "Not really."

She sat on the edge of the bed, took my left hand and grasped it in both of hers. "Somebody walk over your grave?" she asked quietly, watching me intently.

I looked deep into those grey eyes. "Somebody else's grave."

Her eyes clouded. "I've no idea what you've been up to but I do know that you've just about come to the end of your mental tether. You must try to confine the bad thoughts to the back of your mind or learn to accept them. You're a young man and you've a lot of living to do yet."

I let my chin sink to my chest and closed my eyes. "Some don't get the chance, do they?"

She squeezed my hand. "No. You're one of the lucky ones."

I thought again of Annie and the young Dutch gunner. The Troutbridge family, too, crept into my reverie. All of them wanted to live but they were not given the choice. I was still here fighting with their ghosts.

"I hope you're right," I said wearily.

She raised a hand and smoothed the hair from my eyes. "Of course I'm right. Now, settle back and I'll let the doctor know you're back with us. Are you hungry?"

I shook my head. "Not hungry but I could murder a cup of tea."

She laughed lightly and hurried from the room, stepping aside briefly to let a doctor enter my room.

He was tall and in his forties but a pretty unremarkable sort of man.

"How are you feeling, Carver?" he asked.

"A bit rough, sir."

"No need for formalities. My name is Charles and I am a civilian doctor. Laughton is my surname but I hasten to add I'm no relation to the famous actor."

"You mean I've escaped the clutches of the RAF?"

He grinned. "Not exactly but you'll not be required for duty for some time. You've had a pretty tough experience and I'm afraid you're not the mental stalwart you probably thought you were."

"I've never entertained any illusions in that direction."

"Then I'm afraid somebody should have told your masters. I've had you sedated for some time to give you a chance to get yourself together. Are you still having nightmares?"

I nodded. "All the time."

He fiddled with a pen in the top pocket of his white coat. "When you were admitted you were mentally exhausted. I can only guess at the cause of your state but, as I'm retained by the occupants of a large house not too far from here, I can make an educated guess. Getting you back to fitness for duty is going to be a long haul."

"You seem to have made up your mind that I'm some sort of weakling," I was feeling slightly nettled by his apparent doubts as to my sanity.

He looked at me keenly. "I've had ten days to study you closely and I can assure you I know my job."

"Ten days?" I was puzzled and not a little shocked.

"You were brought in here on the Saturday morning, which was ten days ago. You've been in that bed from that day."

I slowly shook my head. "I'm sorry, I didn't realise."

He stood up. "That's okay. As I said, you've had a rough time and I want you to take another two days' of bed rest before I begin my work on you. I'll also be able to let the circling vultures in before they all have apoplexy."

I gave him a puzzled look and he drew a piece of paper from his pocket. He raised his reading glasses from where they dangled at the end of a chain. "A Brigadier

Franklin and a Wing Commander Face are both pestering me to give them access to you. I've told them they must wait for at least two more days."

I smiled. "I appreciate your efforts. I really don't feel up to seeing either of them. All they want from me are details of the very things that are the source of my nightmares. I don't think I'm ready for that yet. When I can accept them, then Franklin and Face can share them with me but not until then."

He watched me for a while and then smiled. "You're already talking good sense. Don't worry, nobody will be allowed near you until you say otherwise. Is there anything I can get you to help relieve the boredom of being confined to bed?"

"Let me see my fiancée?"

He shook his head. "I'm afraid that is where your masters have me over a barrel. I can say what goes medically but I'm afraid they control all other aspects. Every time I stray from my brief they begin quoting the Official Secrets Act. No contest!"

"I understand." I didn't understand but there was damned all I could do about it. I broke off my confused thinking as the nurse returned carrying a large mug of tea.

"Jenny," said Laughton. "I'll leave Sam in your capable hands."

He left and Jenny helped me into a sitting position. I already felt a little better and I was certainly looking forward to being in the hands of the pretty Jenny.

I languished in bed for another three days. The bad thoughts were still with me but I was now getting them more into perspective. Sounds good, but it was still a bloody effort to come to terms with the death of Annie. One night I found myself crying uncontrollably because I was already beginning to forget what she had looked like. Soon I'd have nothing tangible to help me retain her memory.

The violent tremors that had wracked my body were becoming less frequent although my hands still shook when memories encroached into my train of thought. I also found I was unable to eat more than a few morsels at each meal. The lack of nourishment was beginning to manifest itself in the scrawny figure that confronted me in the bathroom mirror. On the fourth day, as if to put me off food for the rest of my life, the door to my room was filled with the figures of Tweedledum and Tweedledee.

"Carver!" exclaimed Face. "You're looking fine."

I grimaced. "And I thought senior officers didn't lie."

"You're not that gullible," growled Franklin as he pulled up a chair. It was the only chair in the place and poor old Face was left standing in the middle of the room looking very uncomfortable.

I patted the edge of my bed. "Take a pew, sir."

"Ah, thank you." He sat gingerly and gave me his most innocent look. "Fancy a bit of a debrief?"

It was said so casually but I could see they were both panting to get at the full story of the Dutch operation.

I sighed. "Might as well get on with it, I suppose." I saw Franklin's face stiffen at my flippant remark. He still didn't like me.

"In your own words," he said.

I talked for two hours. They were forced to ask me question after question, as I was tending to gloss over certain aspects of the story but they understandably wanted it all in detail. In a strange way I found it cathartic to tell the story. I'd problems when I came to Annie's death. I kept my face neutral but, under the bedclothes, I had to clench my hands between my thighs to stop them shaking.

There was a long silence when I came to the end of my story. Face had been taking notes but Franklin had simply listened. I'd no doubts his mental notebook was just as full as Face's little pocket book.

"What's happened to Giedrovski?" I broke the silence.

Face looked at Franklin and the brigadier answered my question but his eyes evaded mine.

"He's said nothing and, as we snatched him, we can't use him as a double. He'll be given a summary trial and executed."

I felt a frisson of fear at the cold and premeditated response but the feeling lasted only a few seconds. I could still see the mushroom of flame that had cremated seven young aircrew at West Fen.

"How's Bouma?" I was suddenly concerned for the big Dutchman.

"He'll probably lose his foot," replied Face and he quickly held up a hand at my look of alarm.

"Don't worry. Both Bouma and his colleague will be decorated for their part in the operation."

"He's an incredible pilot," I said with sadness. "I wouldn't be here if it weren't for those two men."

Face grinned. "If Bader can fly a Spitfire with two tin legs then I'm sure a tin foot will not keep Bouma on the ground."

I cheered at the thought. "Better keep him off bloody seaplanes or the thing will rust."

They both laughed and I saw a change in Franklin. He was now able to look me in the eye and I could detect a grudging respect. I may have been a little unconventional for his taste but I'd given him an operational success and I'd earned his approval. He stood and put a hand on my shoulder.

"You did a fine job, Carver. Even if we get nothing of value from Giedrovski, you brought him back to pay for his crimes. According to reports we're getting from Germany, Hitler is so bloody mad at the loss of his 'hero', he's sending anybody and everybody connected with the operation to the Russian front. It has badly shaken the confidence of the Abwehr and the Sicherheitsdienst. They thought they'd Holland sewn up and yet you went in, kidnapped a hero of the Fatherland and brought him safely back to England. The Dutchmen are not the only ones who are to be decorated."

Somehow I didn't give a shit for a medal. I'd fumbled my way through. It had been the dedication of the Dutch cell that had ensured a success. "What about those in Holland who helped me. Are they still safe?"

His eyes held mine. "No news is good news and we've heard nothing."

It was comfort of a kind. I turned to Face. "Is there any chance I can now contact Section Officer Cowen, sir?"

He shook his head. "I'm sorry, Sam, I can't let you do that yet. Please bear with us a little longer. I've told her privately that you're safe and well but that is all we can do for the moment. I'm afraid you'll now have to formulate a cover story to allay suspicions at West Fen. Sorry, my boy, but that is how it must be."

We engaged in small talk for a while but I could see they were eager to get away and they soon took their leave.

The next week was a concerted effort to get me back on my feet. I progressed from walks in the grounds to a short walk in the city. There were uniforms everywhere and at first I felt out of place, as my borrowed clothes were all civilian, supplied by those I now called 'The Blenheim Bunch'. Then came the day when a brand new uniform arrived, courtesy of the wing commander and I was surprised at the pride I felt when I next walked into the city. The thin little bands on my sleeves didn't rate much attention but I felt I belonged. At times, whilst in the city, I was tempted to pick up the phone and call Nat but I knew I wouldn't break the rules.

Another three weeks went by and I was becoming crazy with boredom but at last the great day arrived. I was going back to West Fen and Nat.

As I packed my little bag I found myself shaking. Here, whenever the demons crept from their lair, experts were on hand to help me. At West Fen I'd be on my own. I wouldn't be able to tell Nat anything and I'd have to resolve the nightmares myself.

Doc Laughton walked me down to reception. "I'm sorry to see you go, Sam. I've enjoyed our conversations."

"Have you learned anything new from those conversations?" I asked him seriously.

"I always do, Sam. No case is the same. You each have your own terrors and, even in war, the root cause is seldom the same. How do you honestly feel now?"

I paused and looked out of the window at a squirrel hopping around in a frantic search for the last of his winter store. I knew how he felt. I was still searching for the answer to Annie's death. I was restored physically but mentally I still had a way to go.

"I'm fine now, thank you," I lied. "Just the occasional bad dream and the odd headache."

He opened the outside door for me but, strangely, he put an arm across the door to prevent me passing. "I hope this is not going to be a nightmare," he said with a straight face. "I was assured, by Wing Commander Face, that if introduced gently, there should be no severe or lasting effects. I hope his judgement was sound." He dropped his arm.

Mystified, I walked out into the warm April sun. There was a perfectly ordinary RAF Hillman utility parked on the drive but there, to my utter surprise, in all her ugly glory, stood Foghorn.

I ran down the steps and, although she did her best with a cracking parade ground salute, I wrecked it all by throwing my arms around her and hugging her. I think only Doc Laughton saw us but I didn't care. At last, a link with home. It was only old Foghorn and home may only be West Fen, but I was desperate to re-establish links with what passed as normality.

"Cor! You alright, Petal?" Foghorn gasped as I released her.

"Never better, Bourne." I breathed in the spring air.

"Is your sap rising or are you just pleased to see me?"

"I'm very pleased to see you, Bourne."

She gave me a lascivious wink. "Want me to stop off somewhere quiet on the way home?"

I coughed loudly and glanced up quickly to see if Laughton had heard her remark. I need not have worried. He was so convulsed with laughter he was past hearing anything. I grabbed her and pushed her into the vehicle. "Let's get out of here before they detain us both."

We roared down the drive and launched ourselves into the streets of Oxford. Soon we were into the countryside and I marvelled at the greenery already appearing on the hedgerows.

"By heck, doesn't the advent spring make everything look better?" I remarked as I watched mother nature struggling out from under her winter mantle.

Foghorn laughed. "West Fen still looks the same so don't get too excited."

"Don't be such a wet blanket," I protested. "At least I'm bloody free again. This is how a convict must feel on his release from prison."

"You mean you feel like getting your end away."

"Don't be disgusting," I laughed.

"What were you doing in a bloody clinic anyway?"

I glanced at her. "You don't expect an answer to that, do you?"

She sighed. "The wing commander told me not to ask, but you know me, can't keep my nose out of other people's affairs. Why is it that everything about you is so secret?"

"You'll get to know one day but for now keep your snout out of the trough."

She grinned. "I love it when you talk dirty."

It was like having a bucket of cold water thrown in my face. Annie had used those very words and I felt my throat restrict as I fought the tears. Oh God! I had a long way to go yet.

"You alright, Petal?" asked Foghorn quietly.

"Yes, fine," I finally gasped.

"Do you want me to stop for a few minutes?"

I looked out of the window and the beauty of the countryside had vanished. All I could see was the charnel house that had been the cockpit of the seaplane and I shivered.

"No, thank you. Let's just get home."

She was right about West Fen. The sun was shining and the hedgerows were showing a hint of buds but it still looked desolate and temporary. The huge expanse of sky was still there, broken only by the black rectangles of the hangars and the water towers. The irregular shapes of the Lancasters merged into the green of the grass and the blue of the sky. The circuit was busy with aircraft returning from night flying tests and, judging by the number, it was going to be a busy night for the squadrons.

Still, this was where my love was and I couldn't wait to see her. Bourne dropped me off at the section and promised to take my bag to the officers' mess. Before I could open the door to the section, it was opened by Houseman. He held out his hand.

"Welcome back, Carver."

"Thank you, sir," I replied as I returned the handshake.

He closed the door behind him and glanced up and down the corridor. "When you get inside, say 'hello' to everybody and then make your way to the wing commander's old office. Cowen is waiting there for you. Face told me you were coming back this morning and I thought you two would like to be alone for a few minutes. Okay?"

I looked at him and felt a strange emotion. I was closer to this man than any other in my life. He seemed to anticipate the needs of others and he did it without a fuss.

"Thank you, sir. That was really thoughtful of you."

He clapped a hand on my shoulder, opened the door and motioned me through ahead of him. "Good to have you back."

There was a roar of welcome from the others as I entered the room but I noticed Hammond didn't join in. I promised Max and Dave Jones that I'd soon be back and went through to find Nat.

I opened the door to Janner's old office and there she was. She'd heard the racket from the outer office and the watchkeepers welcoming me back as I came through their room. She stood facing the door with her back to the window, the sunlight forming a halo around her hair. It was a long time before we broke apart and held each other at arm's length.

"Hi, Carver," she whispered and I saw the moisture in her eyes.

"Hi, Cowen." I felt the tears in my own eyes.

She grinned. "When we're married will you still keep going off like this?"

"Oh, all the time, I'm afraid. I'll be off saving the world every five minutes."

"Did you save it this time?"

I changed my viewpoint to look out of the window. "I helped to save a bit of the world but not some of the people in it."

She detected the sadness in my voice. "One day you'll be able to tell me all about it. I was getting worried about your extended detachment but Wing Commander Face, God bless him, finally called to tell me you were safe. It made life a little more bearable."

I kissed her gently and held her to me. "I'll not be leaving you again. From now on we will work as a team and then, once we're married, we'll enjoy the rest of our lives together. I refuse to be parted from you again."

There was a quiet knock at the door and Houseman gave us a few more seconds before he walked in. "Homecoming over, young man. Time you and I had a chat."

I squeezed Nat's hand. "See you sometime later."

I followed Houseman to his office. As he sat, he waved me into a chair. "Okay, I don't know the full story of the last few weeks but I've been assured that you've had a pretty rough time. Looking at you, Carver, I'd say that was an understatement. You look like death. Still, at least there is one bit of good news for you. You're no longer an Acting Pilot Officer, your substantive rank has come through."

"Any more pay, sir?"

He laughed. "I'm afraid not. Anyway, you still don't know how to do the bloody job. You're supposed to be a working intelligence officer but you keep being sidetracked. I hope we can now have you working full time at the job you were posted here to do."

"Are you sure I'll be able to withstand the heady stuff that comes with high promotion?"

He grinned. "We all had to start somewhere."

He spent a few minutes briefing me on what had happened during my absence and discussed the best way to integrate me back into the working roster. As we talked, I felt he was moving gradually towards something more specific. Finally there was a short silence and he must have decided the time was ripe. He sighed, stood up and walked to the window.

"There is no easy way to tell you this," he said quietly.

"Tell me what, sir?"

He paused. "The bottle of brandy is yours."

I stared at his back for a few seconds before the penny dropped and it was as if I'd been kicked in the guts. I felt the tremors starting in my hands but kept them under control.

"Squadron Leader Mason, sir?" I asked quietly.

I saw him nod and his shoulders slumped. "Yes. Went down on the final trip of their second tour. It should have been a milk run but they just disappeared. We've heard nothing since. No notice that they are dead or if they are POWs - nothing." His voice fell and I knew Sammy Mason and his crew's death had hit him hard.

"Under the circumstances I think you and I should share the bottle, sir. At least we can drink to their memory. You can drink to a friend and I can drink to the crew that brought me home."

He nodded and sat back at his desk. His face was grey and there were black shadows under his eyes. The loss of Sammy Mason would be a constant reminder to Houseman of how lucky he himself had been to survive two tours of operational flying. At least he knew he'd not have to go back but I suspected that very thought would make him feel guilty in some way. He'd survived when so many had died.

His head snapped back up and he was the old Houseman again. "Do you want the rest of the day off to get organised?"

"No, sir. I'd rather stay here until the squadrons takeoff."

"Super. Join Jones and give him a hand."

I laughed as I stood up. "I hope I make a better job of it than the last time I tried to help him."

"I suspect you had other things on your mind," Houseman replied quietly. "Oh, by the way, I understand you now have a new room mate. I believe Shearing moved in whilst you were away."

I felt a wave of relief sweep through me. No more dark nights with only the nightmares for company. "Great, sir," I replied as I closed the door behind me. There was a bounce in my step as I walked off down the corridor.

I worked with Dave for the remainder of the day and I learned a lot from him. He was a joker but very professional when it came to doing the job. I attended the main briefing and then watched the aircraft takeoff. The target was Essen and the news from the Met men had not been good. I silently wished them luck.

Later, in the early hours of the morning, I glanced at the State Board and saw my prayers had been answered. All the crews, from both squadrons, had returned safely. Essen had been clear of cloud cover and although the target marking had confused the crews, they seemed to have given the city a real pasting.

I walked back to the mess with Max and we chatted as I unpacked my bag. He'd organised his side of the room and I found his presence reassuring.

"I'd better warn you, Max, I am still having the odd nightmare. If I do, just try to ignore me."

He looked up and his face was serious. "I don't know what you've been up to, Sam, but did anybody tell you that you look dreadful?"

I paused in sorting out my locker. "Yes, Houseman did. Do I look that bad?"

"You look washed out and you jump at the slightest noise. What the hell have they done to you?"

I thought about my reply for a few seconds. "I should look a picture of health. I've just spent a few weeks in hospital."

His eyes narrowed. "What?"

I sat on the edge of my bed and clasped my hands together between my knees. "I did something that was out of my league and watched three people die. The Germans killed two and I killed the other one. It seems I found it all a bit difficult to accept mentally. They decided to keep me in hospital until the shakes and the nightmares stopped."

"Bloody hell!" he said quietly. Then he rose and put a hand on my shoulder. "Okay, you're back in the fold and among friends. If you need help or a shoulder to cry on, I'm here. Does Nat know about the stint in hospital?"

"No, and I don't want her to know. I shouldn't have told you but I needed to unload on somebody and I know I can trust you."

Max sat back on his bed. "Okay. If you have the screaming habdabs, I promise not to complain to the mess manager."

I laughed. "Sounds good to me."

"If we're on Stand Down tomorrow night, how about we cram Nat into the MG and go out for a drink?"

"At the risk of repeating myself, that sounds good to me."

Next morning, as we groped our way to work in the fog, it was obvious that whatever command had planned for Five Group that night, the brass was going to be disappointed. As the day progressed, the wind from the North Sea failed to materialise to blow away the thick fog. By 14.00 all ops were scrubbed.

Nat and myself had pinned the target photos from the previous night's raid on the board in the Intelligence Library and sure enough, the crews had plastered Essen. There seemed to be widespread damage in the centre and the western half of the city. Of course, there had to be a negative side to temper the success. Twenty-three aircraft had been lost from the total taking part in the raid. That was an attrition level of 6.1% or, put another way, one hundred and sixty-one men had been killed, injured or taken prisoner. It seems our squadrons had been lucky.

At seven o'clock that evening, with Nat somehow crushed with me into the passenger seat of the MG, we arrived at Revesby Red Lion. It had been a nightmare journey in the fog and there had been no decision to come to the Red Lion. We'd just seemed to gravitate that way.

I hesitated momentarily outside the front door. I could hear voices and laughter from inside but the pub now had too many bad memories.

"Something wrong?" Nat gently squeezed my arm.

"No, it's fine," I replied but I'm sure she felt the small tremor pass through my body.

When we pushed our way through the blackout curtain, we found the bar packed with RAF men and women. There were all ranks in there and the press continued out into the corridor.

"Excuse me," a deep voice spoke and its owner placed a hand on my arm. "I've a seat, a pint and a hand of dominoes waiting for me in there."

"Sorry," I replied and moved to one side to let him through.

"Well now, if it isn't the trespassing signals expert."

I looked up in alarm and found myself pressed up against Peter Meacher. He was smiling and looked genuinely pleased to see me.

I glanced quickly at Max and Nat. Max was in the know but not Nat. I need not have worried. She looked puzzled but knew when to keep quiet. I quickly regained my composure.

"Hello, Mr Meacher. Nice to meet you again."

"Are you alone?" he asked, glancing around.

I pointed to Max and Nat. "No. I'm with my friends."

He craned to see over the press of drinkers. "If you like to follow me, I might be able to get you all a seat in our domino corner. We guard it jealously from strangers but friends are always welcome."

I glanced at Max and Nat and they nodded. I smiled. "Lead on."

Meacher was true to his word and found enough room for the four of us to cram ourselves into the corner where he was about to play dominoes with his farmer friends. He seemed to manoeuvre things effortlessly to ensure I was sitting next to him. The move was done expertly and I'd never have noticed if it had it been executed by anybody else but Meacher. He was a different kettle of fish and I was wary of his every move. He was now able to see Max for the first time.

"Ah, Signals are here in force. Is this young lady also in Signals?"

I crossed my fingers but I needn't have worried, Nat had already cottoned on.

She gave him that special smile of hers that could melt a man's resolve at a thousand yards.

"I'm afraid I'm not so brainy. I work in the stores receiving, documenting and issuing aircraft spares. Very boring."

Meacher smiled gently. "But essential."

Nat gave him that smile again. "I like to think so."

I stepped in to reinforce our previous bogus identities before Nat ran out of ideas. The problem was I couldn't remember the bloody false names we had used on our visit to the farm. I decided to play for time.

"Nat," I said, indicating the farmer. "This is Mr Meacher. We carried out a survey for a new radio mast on his farm. Mr Meacher this is Natalie Smith."

Nat backed up a bit at the name 'Smith' but shook his hand. Now for the difficult bit! How the hell could I warn Nat of our false names? I needn't have worried.

Meacher put a hand on my arm. "Let me see. You're Pilot Officer James and your colleague is Flight Lieutenant Samuels."

Thank God he had a damned good memory. The names sounded right.

"Well done," I said, trying to keep the relief out of my voice. "You remembered."

He then introduced us to his three friends at the domino table. Their names meant nothing to us and it was obvious they'd no interest in us. One of them shuffled the dominoes impatiently with his large careworn hands and the game began. They played for a while and we chatted in a rather stilted way, scared stiff we would make a mistake in front of Meacher. As for the farmer, his mind didn't seem to be on the game and twice he was rebuked by his friends for careless play. Finally, he handed over to another man and turned his attention to us.

"You've not been over to see your mast."

I thought quickly. "We're just the surveyors. Design and construction are the tasks of others. Anyway, I imagine the fewer of us on your farm, the better you like it."

He looked straight at me and didn't even blink. "Why do you say that?"

I had unwittingly entered dangerous ground. I thought fast. "We make such a bloody mess and never clean up afterwards."

His eyes stayed on mine for a few more seconds and then they moved away as he gave a small smile. "They certainly did make a mess of one end of my wood."

Obviously Face's men had made sure they got a good look at the place where we suspected the agent's parachute had been buried.

"Sorry about that." I sounded so sincere.

He returned his unwavering gaze back to me and that small smile was still there. His shoulders seemed to drop suddenly as if in resignation. It was as if he had made a difficult decision.

"I'd like you to visit me tomorrow." He said it quietly and I got the impression the invitation didn't extend to Nat and Max. I tried to keep the surprise out of my voice.

"I'd like that very much."

Before I could say any more, he stood up, turning his flat cap in his hands. He looked down at me but I could see nothing in his eyes.

"Good. Give me a ring just before you set off." He made polite farewells to Max and Nat and pushed his way out through the crowd. I could see the questions already forming on Nat's lips but I held up a warning finger.

"Later," I cautioned. "Now, how about we get down to some serious drinking?"

They agreed and we did. I had no nightmares that night.

313

CHAPTER TWENTY-THREE

Next morning, I managed to see Houseman at breakfast in the mess. I told him of Meacher's request to see me.

He didn't hesitate. "I'll get on to Face as soon as I get into the office." He grinned. "It seems you're not finished with this business yet."

I sighed. "I wish I'd kept my bloody mouth shut."

"A lot of aircrew will be pleased you spoke out when you did. You've saved many lives by opening your mouth and expressing your thoughts when you did."

I gave him a wry smile. "They'll never know, sir."

"What does it matter? You removed a very dangerous cuckoo from the nest." He glanced at his watch. "Come on, we'd better get started. The sooner Face knows about this the sooner we will have his decision."

Houseman wasted no time. As soon as we reached the section he was on the phone to Wing Commander Face. They spoke for a while and then Face asked to speak to me.

"What's his game?" he asked me bluntly.

"No idea, sir. He took me by surprise too."

"He's on his own at the farm, isn't he?"

"Yes, sir."

There was a pause. "He doesn't bloody fancy you, does he?"

I laughed. "I don't think Meacher is that way inclined, sir. His ideology may be askew but I'm sure he's straight sexually. No, it is something more than that."

"Like what, Carver? You must give me a clue." He sounded impatient.

"I can't give you a clue, sir. Although, having said that, maybe I had the impression he knew something. It was as if he was extending a challenge."

"Carver, I don't like this," muttered Face.

I decided to change tack to give him time to think. "How are the surveillance team doing, sir?"

He cursed. "On Meacher? Nothing - bloody nothing. Smith is a different kettle of fish. His background stops at Fishguard. We've even tried the Garda but without any success. Mind you, the guys we spoke to were not exactly helpful. In fact I had the impression they would like to see the Germans win the war. Why do we have to have such shits on our bloody doorstep? I wish they'd all fuck off to America, although the Irish and Sicilian gangs are already well on their way to ruining that bloody country."

I smiled to myself. Somebody in Ireland had really rattled his cage. "So there's nothing to tie Smith in with any others in the cell, sir?"

"No. We must find that link or we'll have to arrest him and lose the others. It's so bloody frustrating."

"Give me your blessing to meet Meacher today and maybe I might find that link. At least I've an invitation, sir. Who knows what I might see or hear?"

There was a short silence before Face replied with a question. "Do you have a weapon, Carver?"

"No, sir." I began to realise how hasty I had been to volunteer to stick my head in the lion's mouth. "Do you think I need to be armed?" I asked anxiously.

"Who knows, Carver. It seems strange that he should ask you over to the farm. If he suspects your cover then surely he'd be unlikely to extend you an invitation."

I could think of nothing to say so I waited. Houseman and I looked at each other. I tried to keep my own face expressionless but he had an anxious frown on his face.

"Right, Carver." Face had made up his mind. "Get Jake to arrange for somebody to authorise you a weapon from the armoury. I suggest a 9mm Browning. They can jam but they make less of a bulge than a Smith Wesson. Make sure you can get at it quickly. I don't like the idea of you going alone but if he emphasised the point, you'd better go along with it. All I can do is have a small back-up team nearby. If they hear shots then they'll come running but that is all the security I can give you."

"Thanks for that anyway, sir."

"Good man. Best of luck and call me as soon as you get back. I want to know what the hell is going on over there." The line went dead.

When I told Houseman Face wanted me to have a weapon, he looked shocked.

"Bloody hell, Carver, what are you getting yourself into now? Do you know how to use a handgun?"

"Bang one in the upper body to slow them down and that gives you time to pick the bit between the eyes to make sure they go down for good." I grinned as I remembered the words of my instructor at Blenheim.

Houseman looked at me and there was a flash of anger on his face. "Whatever happened to the young man who came through that door just over three months ago? I'll not ask where you learned that little gem. I think I'd rather not know." By the time he had finished speaking the anger had gone but it had been replaced with a sadness that disturbed me. Had I changed that much? Surely I was still the same flippant old Carver? I didn't need to get a second opinion. I knew just how much I had changed since I arrive at West Fen.

Houseman picked up the phone from his desk. "I'll get the station commander to authorise the weapon. At least nobody will argue with him. How many rounds do you want?"

"A dozen or so, sir. If I don't put a stop to my target after two, I'm a dead duck. Pointless carrying more really."

"Maybe so but I'll get you three full clips. In the meantime you'd better get down to MT and collect a vehicle. I'll phone ahead and warn the MTO you're on your way. I'll have the weapon here by the time you get back." He was already making the connection when I left his office.

Nat smiled as I entered the main office. "At last! Back to the real job, eh?"

Her smile faded when she saw the look on my face. "Oh, no," she said quietly. "Now where?"

"Just local. Got to tie up a few loose ends, that's all."

"You're going to meet that man?"

I didn't answer and she took my silence as confirmation.

"Well, just be careful, Sam."

I laid my hand on her arm and spoke quietly. "I'll be back before tea."

She smiled but she couldn't hide the anxiety in her eyes. "That's great. The squadrons are due to takeoff at 16.30. See you over at the tower, if you like?"

"What's the target?"

"Duisburg."

315

"Strewth, don't they ever get an easy target?"

She shrugged. "Tell me what you consider to be an easy target."

"Sorry, stupid thing to say. I'll see you at the tower."

I called Meacher from the mess and he wasted no words. "See you at eleven o'clock." I didn't even get the chance to reply. I glanced at my watch and realised I'd better get a move on.

It was just about eleven o'clock when I eased the Tilly up the bumpy track to Meacher's farm. He was already waiting for me by the stables. The two Alsatian dogs were nowhere to be seen. I drove up to him and switched off the engine.

"Good morning, Mr Meacher."

"Good morning, Mr James."

He smiled as he said the word, 'Mr'.

"The name is Sam," I replied, giving him the chance to offer his Christian name but he declined to do so.

"It's a lovely day. Let's walk," he suggested.

We paused momentarily as two Spitfires, one damned nearly glued to the tail of the other, roared over the farm. They were no more than fifty feet from the ground. The leading aircraft reared up on its starboard wing as the pilot hauled it round in a tight turn. Then it flicked back to the left, well beyond dead centre, its port wing seemingly skimming the tops of the few trees near the farm. Finally the two aircraft zoomed upwards into the blue of the sky. They were soon lost to view and the sound of the screaming Merlins faded to be replaced by the protesting squawks of the local crows and jackdaws.

Meacher looked at me and smiled. "The master and his pupil," he said.

"You think so?" I asked in surprise.

He nodded. "Did you notice the sudden and violent movements of the lead aircraft? The tailing aircraft was flown precisely and smoothly and I bet his propeller hardly moved a degree from the tail of the first aircraft. Not only that, the pilot of the rear aircraft even had time to glance down at us here in the farmyard. He was a real professional." He sighed. "Beautiful but very deadly."

"You seem to know a lot about aircraft, Mr Meacher."

He smiled. "I've lived in Lincolnshire for a long time, Sam. I think every native of this county knows something about aircraft. All day and all night there is the sound of aircraft."

As we cleared the farm buildings and moved out into the open, I could see two men working a couple of fields away. They looked to be repairing a fence or stringing barbed wire but it was too far away for me to be certain. Meacher followed my gaze.

"Germans," he said.

I stopped in my tracks. "What?"

He laughed. "German prisoners of war from the camp at Moorby, Sam. I've two working here full-time. Wolfgang Kline and Hans Weber. Nice chaps and good workers. Germans from an Italian camp in the English countryside."

"I'm sorry?" I was puzzled by the remark.

He picked up a stick from the ground and swished it at the long grass. "The first POWs at Moorby were Italians. They were billeted in tents until they'd built the camp that would house them. I'd imagine an approaching Lincolnshire winter would have been all the incentive they needed to build it well and quickly. The Italians left and now I believe it is an all-German POW camp. Those two are brought out in the morning and picked up in the evening. They bring their own rations every day but I'm given coffee and sugar to last them the week."

"Are they always unguarded?" I asked.

He nodded. "They are all trusted men. Where would they go if they did abscond? Have you ever heard of a German prisoner escaping from this island?"

I shook my head. "No, I haven't, now you come to mention it."

We walked in silence for a while and then he played his ace.

"How was Holland?" he asked quietly.

This is where the film hero plays a cool hand and keeps his composure. Sure they do. They've read the script and know what's coming next. I didn't have that advantage and I failed miserably on all counts. I actually missed a step as I walked and couldn't stop my head from snapping up to look at Meacher in alarm. My hands were behind my back. Not the ideal place for me to reach my gun.

He laughed and put a hand on my shoulder. "That was just a shot in the dark but I do believe I hit the target."

I was dumbstruck and I was also appreciating the vulnerability of my situation. We were totally alone. He may be an elderly man but he was fit and strong. My youth would be no advantage.

He sensed my anxiety and I felt his hand close tighter on my shoulder. "Relax, Sam. I've no intention of harming you. In fact, I want to help you."

"Who are you?" It was the best I could do for the moment.

He steered me over to an old cattle water trough by the hedgerow. It was empty and he pressed me down to sit alongside him on the wide rim. "A German agent," he replied without drama.

My own mind was in a whirl. This had to be another of my nightmares and I was hallucinating!

He removed his hand from my shoulder. "I came to this country at the age of eighteen - back in 1897. I'd been trained as an agent by the then rather inept German intelligence service. I remained here as a sleeper until 1914, when they reactivated me. I was working on a farm on the Hampshire coast. It was owned by a sympathiser to the Kaiser's cause. By this time I spoke perfect English and was of value to my country, passing information on shipping and troop movements. At the end of the war I thought Germany had forgotten all about me but when this war looked inevitable, the new Abwehr re-established contact with me and I became one of Admiral Canaris's agents." He paused and I tried desperately to get my thoughts together. Why was he telling me all this?

"How did you end up here?" At least I finally managed to say something.

"Via Norfolk," he replied. "In 1923 my employer in Hampshire died so I had to find another post. I answered an advertisement for a herdsman in Norfolk and actually got the job. That was when I met my wife. It was what they call a whirlwind romance and we were married the following year. I was forty-nine and she was just twenty. We had a son the next year followed by a daughter two years later. It seemed fine for the first few years but we slowly grew apart and the situation became really acrimonious. She turned the children against me and made my life impossible. My former employer had left me a sizeable amount of money and when I heard of a tenancy going here, I took the opportunity to start a new life."

"When was that?"

"In 1930. It was a fortuitous move as far as my bosses in Germany were concerned. When the Nazis came to power and began to modernise the intelligence services, they suddenly discovered they had a field agent right in the middle of the RAF's main concentration of airfields in Lincolnshire."

317

"Why are you telling me this and why did you make that remark about Holland?"

He shielded his eyes with a hand to watch a Lancaster drone overhead. When the silence returned he put a hand on my arm. "I had no idea you were involved in the snatch of our pilot in Holland but I'd already sensed you were not what you seemed. If you were not a signals officer then you had to be with the security services and probably knew about Giedrovski. The question was just a wild guess on my part but your reaction told me you knew all about the Dutch snatch. I received a radio message telling me he'd been taken and that I should be prepared to move. They expected him to be tortured to reveal what he knew. I was pretty sure he'd not talk, no matter what he was subjected to in the way of persuasion. He's an ardent Nazi and a very cool customer."

"He'll soon be a very dead ardent Nazi." I failed to keep the pleasure out of my voice.

His hand closed tightly on my arm and he turned me so that I faced him. "Sam....Sam! Don't let this war taint you with its hatred. You don't belong in this game."

I remained silent and waited for him to elaborate a little more but instead he stood up.

"Come on, let's go back to the house and have a civilised cup of tea and then you can place me under arrest." He grinned at me and I still couldn't find it in my heart to dislike the man. "It should give your career a big boost," he added.

I found myself smiling in return. "Bugger my career, I just want to be a civilian." As I made the reply I suddenly remembered how proud I had been back in Oxford in my new uniform. I decided this was not the time to start asking myself questions about my future.

As we approached the farm, I glanced idly in the direction we had seen the two POWs but they were no longer to be seen.

"I still don't know why you're doing this." I pressed him to answer.

He too looked into the distance. "There have been many things that have caused me to become disillusioned with my role in this war but the straw that broke the camel's back was the fate of the Troutbridge family."

I took a sharp breath. Now we were getting down to it. "Were you responsible for that?" I had asked the question but I knew the answer before he even opened his mouth.

"Sam, I'm an agent and I've worked hard for my country but to kill an innocent family in cold blood over a silly bloody helmet - that is not my way. Then there was the quality of the agents sent in to help. If the idiot who came in that night had hidden the helmet with his parachute, then the situation with the Troutbridge boy would never have arisen. The agent landed well but he was disturbed, possibly by poachers. He panicked and, when they had gone, he hurriedly buried the chute and started to get out of the area, only to discover he was still wearing the bloody helmet. He just rammed it into the culvert in his panic. I ask you, Sam, is that the action of a professional?"

"Hardly," I replied. I just wanted him to get on with the story. "Where is that agent now?"

"Believe me, Sam, when I tell you I've no idea. He was supposed to meet Giedrovski at the Red Lion one night but he didn't show. The pilot was sure he was around as he'd heard a motorcycle enter the pub yard but the agent didn't arrive in the back bar. We've not heard from him since."

"Did he work at the secret airstrip?"

Meacher paused slightly before he answered. "Yes. He was a first class mechanic but not the brightest of men."

It was my turn to hit hard and fast. "Who killed the Troutbridge family?"

"Smith."

He gave me the name without any hesitation and left me hanging out to dry with no follow-up question. I'd not expected such a direct response but there was only one question to ask now.

"Where does he fit into all this?"

"IRA sympathiser who hates the English. He offered his services to the Abwehr in 1939. They trained him in Germany and then sent him here as my foreman. A rather grand title for a farmer who has just two old labourers and two POWs."

"He must have had help."

"The two men from the airstrip. I tried to stop them and actually contacted Berlin but I was told to shut up. It was all so unnecessary. The act itself and the thought of Smith and his cronies being given power if we win this war, horrified me."

I glanced at him as we entered the shelter of the farm buildings and he misinterpreted my thoughts.

"They will be given local powers as part of the occupying power." He said it so easily.

I let that ride although it had been interesting to hear him say 'if we win this war'. "Where is Smith now?" I asked.

We both jerked with shock as the lower half of one of the stable doors flew open and crashed up against the wall.

"Here." Smith stood framed in the doorway. He'd a gun in his right hand and his face was white with rage. Although he'd answered me, his grey eyes were fixed on Meacher. "You traitorous bastard!" he shouted at the farmer. As he screamed the words, I saw the gun jerk round towards the farmer and I hit Meacher hard with my shoulder. The gun fired as we crashed to the ground and I distinctly heard the bullet smack into the farmer's body. There was another crack from the gun as I kept rolling and the bullet fanned the air close to my head. I felt my face sting with pain as the bullet impacted with the ground and filled the air with razor sharp shards of stone. I still rolled frantically across the yard in a desperate attempt to find cover but all I could see was a farm cart in the shed. Yet another round just missed me as I threw myself into the shed and the scant cover of the cart.

At least it was fairly dark in the old building and Smith was in the sun. He'd have great difficulty in spotting me in the shadows. I struggled to get the Browning out of my pocket and eased the safety catch off. I winced as a bullet whipped a large sliver of wood from the cartwheel near my face. It sliced down my cheek before bouncing off my hand. My cheek felt as if it was on fire and my eyes began to water. I rubbed furiously at my eyes to clear away the tears and then I thought I caught a glimpse of Smith at the far end of the stable. How the fuck did he get there? I fired a snap shot in that direction and promptly received return fire from just inside the stable doorway. This time a shower of brick dust came from the wall to my rear. I was baffled and trapped. I'd no way out. I could see Meacher's body lying in the sunshine. A chicken was absently pecking near his feet and another by his outstretched hand.

Smith's next move took me totally by surprise. He launched himself from the doorway of the stable, his lips drawn back in what I took to be a rictus of hatred. He was screaming and he fired just one shot as he came but I now had a clear view. I fired two quick shots into his chest. That brought him up sharp and I had plenty of time to go for the one between his eyes. Actually my third shot entered his right eye and a splatter of blood and brains hit the cream painted wood of the stable door. Smith's body teetered upright for a couple of seconds and then he pitched forward onto his face.

That was when I saw the pitchfork sticking out of his back.

I stared in disbelief from my cover. What the fuck was going on? No wonder the bastard had come steaming out of the door screaming his bloody head off. Anybody would have done the same with eight inches, times two, of Scunthorpe's best steel rammed into their vital organs. As I lay in the shadows, I wondered if I dare break cover. The problem was answered for me by the sound of a vehicle approaching at speed. It slithered to a halt by the farm gate. Doors slammed and there was a crash of a tailboard going down. Somebody began shouting orders.

"Spread out and watch your backs."

Footsteps echoed back as men ran to encircle the farmyard.

"Anybody there?" shouted the voice again.

Before I could reply, somebody shouted from close to the end of the cart shed. "Two men down, sir. Both in the farmyard between stables and sheds."

"Do not approach!"

Whoever was in charge was efficient and taking no chances. I decided it was my turn.

"Hello, out there. Who are you?"

"Backup. Identify yourself."

"Carver."

"Do you think it is safe to show yourself, Carver?"

"I think so. There's been no movement since the guy went down with the pitchfork in his back."

"Pitchfork?" He sounded incredulous. "Who was doing the shooting?"

"Me and the guy killed with the pitchfork."

There was a pause and then the team began to check in.

"Number One - all clear, sir."

"Number Two - all clear, sir."

It ended with Number Eight. Good old Face, he'd come up trumps with these lads.

"Okay, Carver. You can come out now."

I climbed stiffly to my feet but kept the Browning in my hand down by my leg. I was met by a very young man wearing black coveralls. He was also wearing a black beret but with no badge. He glanced quickly at the Browning but said nothing. He walked over to Smith, yanked the pitchfork out of the Irishman and rolled him over on to his back. He whistled approvingly and turned to me.

"Hey, neat shot, Carver."

"Beginner's luck. Anyway, the bastard was already dying when I hit him."

"Who is he?"

"Irishman named Smith who worked for the other dead guy."

He glanced around the farmyard, shielding his eyes against the sun. He seemed satisfied everything was under control and turned his gaze back to me.

"Now for the big question," he said. "Who used the pitchfork?"

I shrugged. "I've no idea and that's the truth. I thought I saw movement up at the end of the stables just before Smith copped it. Actually, I thought he had gone out the back and was trying to get round behind me but when I fired in that direction, Smith fired back from the doorway. Having said that, I was so pepped up I could have

320

imagined it."

He scratched his chin. "Who else lives here?"

I nodded to Meacher's body. "Only he lived here and his name is Meacher. He has two old part-time labourers and two POWs. I saw the two POWs across the field earlier."

"Where are they now?"

"No idea."

Then I thought I heard a small sigh and I spun round and looked at Meacher. His eyes were open and he was trying to speak. I began running towards him and shouting over my shoulder. "Christ's sake! Do you have medics with you?"

"Certainly do. They're waiting up the road a bit."

He cupped his hands and shouted. "signallers!"

"Sir?"

Another young man, in similar garb to his leader, appeared around the corner at a gallop. He had a large field wireless strapped to his back, its aerial whipping around as he ran.

"Call the medics in - now!" ordered the team leader.

I knelt by Meacher and placed my hand under his head. "Don't talk, Mr Meacher. Save your energy - the medics are on their way. We all thought you were dead."

He winced but managed a small smile. "If it had not been for you, I would have been dead. My fault. I let my guard down too soon."

I scanned his jacket and could find just the one bullet hole in the right side of his chest. It didn't look life threatening but it may have nicked a lung. I talked quietly to him until the medics arrived with the field ambulance. If this was Face's idea of a small team, I'd love to see the sort he organised for a major crisis!

Meacher was soon on a stretcher and away to hospital in the ambulance, guarded by two of the team. The rest of the men finally reported in but they'd found nobody else around the farmyard or in the house. It seemed that Meacher had pitchforks that turned murderous all by themselves. The medics were now cleaning up the wounds to my face and I tried not to move my head as I thanked the team leader.

"Thanks for riding to the rescue. My name is Sam, by the way."

He gave an apologetic twist of his lips. "I know who you are, Sam, but I'm afraid I can't give you my name. I'm sure you understand"

I nodded. "Perfectly. Thanks to all your men too."

He turned to his men and quickly briefed them on what to guard around the farm until the search teams arrived. He then turned to me and nodded at the body of the Irishman. "Where does he live?"

"Place called Moorby. All I know is that he lived in an isolated cottage, somewhere in the woods up there."

"Married? Family?"

"I don't think so."

"Right. I'll take just one of my guys and try to find the cottage. The sooner we get a guard on that the better."

"May I come with you?" I asked.

He studied me for a moment. "I don't see why not. We're a bit stretched to cover two places."

I had an idea. "Look, hang on here. I may be able to find out the location of Smith's cottage."

"How?"

I laughed. "Phone a friend who knows everybody."

He frowned. "Mind if I come with you? I can't let you chatter on the phone without me being there."

I started for the house. "I understand. Come on, let's make that call."

We entered the house cautiously as I had already warned him of the Alsatians but we need not have feared the dogs as they were in a pen in the back garden. I picked up the phone from the sideboard in the living room and asked the operator for Stan Cornish's number. It seemed to ring for a very long time and, thinking he must be somewhere down across the fields, I went to hang up. As I went to return the receiver to its rest I heard a 'click' and the sound of Stan's voice. He didn't sound pleased.

"Stan?" I shouted. "Sam Carver here."

"Bloody hell, boy, you certainly know when to call at a bad time."

"Why, what's wrong?" I asked quickly.

"My bloody chimney caught fire and I was up on the roof with a stirrup pump."

"Christ! Get back to it before the bloody house burns down."

"No, no, it's okay. Just got a bloody mess to clean up in the living room. How are you, boy? I haven't heard from you for ages."

"I've been away, Stan. Look, how about meeting me at the Lancaster Arms tomorrow night?"

"Suits me." He sounded delighted and I decided to get down to business.

"Stan - do you know a Sean Smith? He works for a farmer out here at Tumby called Meacher."

"Yeah. Bloody Irishman with a chip on his shoulder a mile wide. He lives out at Moorby. His cottage is hidden from the road though and not easy to find. You need the track on the left that goes off on the apex of the second of the 'S' bends, just after the POW camp. You know the road don't you - the road from Revesby to Horncastle?"

"I know it. Did he have a wife or family?"

There was a long pause and I knew what was coming. "You made a slip there, boy. You asked me 'did' he have a wife or family. That means he's dead."

I shook my head in anger at my stupid mistake. "Stan, just don't ask questions and remember that bit of paper you signed."

I heard him sigh. "Alright, boy. No he wasn't married and he had no family. The way he carried on I doubt if he even had a mother or father!"

"I take it you didn't like him?"

"He was a nasty, arrogant bastard."

I laughed. "Take care, Stan."

"You too, lad."

I replaced the receiver and turned to the team leader. He was frowning again.

"Who was that?" he asked.

"Probably the most useful man in Lincolnshire. Definitely one of the nicest guys I've ever met and totally trustworthy."

He headed for the door. "I'll take your word for it."

We used my Tilly for the trip and headed for Revesby. Just before the Red Lion we turned left towards Moorby and Horncastle. A little way up the road, on the right, we passed a compound with rows of military style huts and a large water tower. I nodded to it as we passed.

"That must be the POW camp where Meacher's two Germans come from."

The team leader glanced across me and studied the compound. "Maybe we should check on their whereabouts. Problem is we need to secure that bloody cottage."

"Surely we will be able to check the Gate Log, or whatever they have. That will tell us what time they went out and what time they returned," I suggested.

He nodded. "You're right. That can wait."

We found the cottage without any difficulty, thanks to Stan's directions. It certainly was isolated and it looked pretty dilapidated. The garden was overgrown and an air of neglect hung over the whole place. We looked under the boot scraper and under a couple of old flowerpots but we found no sign of a key. Obviously Smith was not as trusting as most of the people of Lincolnshire. So we kicked down the door.

The interior was worse than the exterior. It was filthy. Dirty clothes and dirty pots littered each of the three downstairs rooms and the bed in the only furnished bedroom was disgusting. No sheets and the blankets looked as if they had not been washed for months. A chamber pot, brimming with rank-smelling urine, stood on the bare wood floor in the middle of the room. An odour of stale perspiration pervaded the whole place.

My young companion wrinkled his nose in disgust. "We'll take a quick look around but I think we'll leave the pleasure of the search to the teams."

"You do a quick search," I replied. "I'm going outside for some fresh air."

I was still out there when the search team arrived. It had turned chilly but I just didn't fancy going back in that stinking bloody cottage. I'd sat in the Tilly for two hours and I felt stiff and jaded. I soon cheered up when the first person to climb stiffly from the Search Party's vehicle was David Piper.

He stretched his long, lanky frame and peered over at me. "You never cease to surprise me, young Carver. Are you just naturally dangerous to be with or are you making up your own personal body count?"

"Don't blame me. I just do what I'm told," I laughed.

He glanced around the garden and finally let his eyes linger on the cottage. "Bit of a shit hole this, isn't it? Couldn't you find something better?"

"Wait until you get inside."

"That bad?"

"That bad. Where is the other half of the duo?"

He grinned. "Face, you mean?"

I nodded.

"He's at the farm."

"Does he want me over there?" I asked.

"No. He's leading the rummage. He told me to tell you to be at your section at midnight tonight. We've a lot to talk about."

Then the team leader came out of the cottage and Piper pointed with the stem of his pipe. "Think you could detour by way of the farm and drop him off? He and his lads will need to get back to their depot."

"Okay, no problem. Enjoy your rummage through the cottage," I said as a parting gesture.

"Piss off, Carver. I'll see you later."

My last view of him was in the rear view mirror of the Tilly as he wearily pulled on his overalls.

I dropped the young leader off at the farm and headed back to West Fen. I wondered at the way my love life seemed doomed to failure. "Bugger the war!" I shouted out of the driver's window and scared the shit out of a brace of partridge. As I wound the window back into place, something dug into my hip. I reached into my tunic jacket pocket to investigate the source of the pain and found the Browning. It had the smell of freshly fired cordite and I found the odour nauseating. I thrust it into the large pocket of my greatcoat. Out of sight - out of mind!

I stopped off at the mess to get cleaned up and put on my battledress uniform. I left my dirty uniform with Mr Bates and he promised to get it sponged and pressed. I was getting through uniforms at a fair old pace.

A couple of hours later, when I strolled into the section, I found the place empty except for Hammond. He glanced up but said nothing.

"Where are the others?" I asked.

"Duty supper."

I wandered into the watchkeepers' office and found Trudi at the switchboard. She was knitting but quickly folded it up and put it in a bag at her feet. She looked a little shocked at the wound on my cheek.

"It's okay, Sarge," I said. "I know it's spring out there but you're still going to need that jumper."

She smiled. "It's for my boyfriend."

"Aircrew?"

She nodded and I could see a mixture of pride and fear in her eyes. "He's on Beaufighters - a night fighter squadron."

"He's got a tough job."

I glanced idly through the signals on the desk but took in none of the information. All I could think of was how long would it take Nat to eat supper.

"What time are the squadrons due back?"

"About 23.00, sir."

I glanced at my watch. It was 20.30. Where was Nat? I wandered aimlessly into the corridor and walked down to Janner's old office. I opened the door and found the blackout curtains were not in place. I quickly closed the door and groped my way over to the window. I had to get the blackout in place before I could turn on the lights. As I drew the curtains something began to niggle at the back of my brain. I tried to focus on the niggle but I could find no obvious reason for my feeling of disquiet. Eventually, after switching on the light and arranging a few chairs around the table, I headed back out and strolled down to the intelligence library. Nat walked in just after me.

"Hi!" she called. "Trudi said you were back here somewhere." Her eyes narrowed when she saw the marks on my face. "Now what have you been up to?"

"Nothing," I grinned. I looked round quickly. "Have we got time for a quick clinch?"

"No," she said firmly. "Keep your mind on the job and what girl wants to be offered - what did you call it - a clinch?"

"Spoil sport."

"Mind you, if on the way back to the Waafery we happen upon a quiet spot, I may relent."

"Sounds good but by the time you've finished the debriefs, I'll be ensconced with Houseman and the dreaded duo."

She looked concerned. "Why, what happened?"

"It all got a bit messy," I answered her quietly.

She walked over and laid a cool hand on my cheek. She traced the outline of the cuts and scratches with her finger. "When does it ever go any other way for you, Sam?"

I shrugged. "Up to now? - not often. At least we now have some of the answers to some of the questions."

She now ran her finger lightly over my lips. "Are you ever going to come back to us and lead a normal life?"

I shrugged and took both her hands in mine. "We're nearly there, kid. Just hang on a bit longer."

She smiled. "I think I'll have that kiss now. I may have to wait some time before I see you again."

I needed no further bidding but we had only just drawn apart and were still breathless when Houseman bustled into the room. He was no fool and he knew damned well what we had been up to but he pretended not to have noticed.

"Carver, there you are. I received a rather curt message from Wing Commander Face requesting the use of the conference room and my presence there tonight at midnight. Now what have you done?"

"Received a nice surprise with a twist in the tail, sir."

"Oh, no...don't start those riddles of yours again, and what the hell happened to your face?"

"Mind if I tell you later?" I asked him quietly.

He glanced quickly at Nat then back to me. "Of course not. Have you eaten?"

"No, sir."

"Well you'd better get over to the mess and get yourself a duty supper. From what the wing commander said, it could be a very long night."

I sensed it was not just good advice - it was an order.

"See you," Nat laughed.

I grinned ruefully and followed Houseman. I heard a tinkle of laughter from her as I made a rude gesture behind my back.

Houseman half turned his head as we walked along the corridor. "When you've had supper, get straight down to the conference room. Get some notes down because I sense you're going to be asked a lot of questions. Get it all straight in your mind."

"Fine, sir."

He glanced round to check my face. "How did you get those injuries?"

"Somebody shot at me, sir."

He stopped abruptly and I cannoned into him. "What the hell did you get yourself into this time?" He then held up his hand and shook his head. "No, I don't want to know. I'll wait until we're all together later. Go and get your bloody supper. At least you should be safe from trouble there!"

The squadrons were beginning to return as I walked back from supper. The air vibrated with the noise of engines joining the circuit and I could see the navigation lights floating down to merge with the runway lights.

I was surprised to find Face and Piper already in the section. They'd just arrived and both looked tired and dirty. We all trooped through to the conference room, divested ourselves of hats and coats and took our seats around the table. Piper stoked up his briar as Face opened the proceedings.

"Carver, you've done it again."

"I didn't do anything, sir. Meacher took charge from the moment I arrived and had me wrong-footed right from the start. His admission to being a German agent took me totally by surprise. How is he by the way?"

"He was lucky and will recover."

Secretly, I was pleased with the news.

325

"How exactly did he broach the subject?" Piper asked me, puffing on his briar.

"He asked me how I'd got on in Holland."

There was a stunned silence. The news had badly shaken Face and Piper but Houseman didn't even know I'd been to Holland. His face was a picture!

Face was the first to recover. "Say that again and say it slowly."

I licked my lips. "He asked me how things had gone in Holland."

"He knew all about the Dutch operation?" Face's voice had risen an octave.

I shook my head. "Not exactly. He'd been told that Giedrovski had been snatched and to keep his eyes and ears open. His question was just a shot in the dark but I'm afraid my reaction gave the game away."

"Bloody hell!" breathed Face.

"Have you any thoughts on why he picked you for his confession?" asked Piper.

"No idea, but I'm sure he made up his mind the night before when we met him in the Red Lion. I'm certain that was when he'd decided he'd had enough."

Piper chuffed out a cloud of sweet-smelling smoke. "Fine, but let's start at the point when you arrived at the farm, shall we?"

So I related the whole story, blow by blow and shot by shot. When I'd finished Houseman was watching me with a mixture of amazement and confusion. He kept perfectly still and perfectly quiet but I knew his brain was working overtime.

"So, who stuck the pitchfork in Smith?" asked Face.

I shrugged. "It had to be one of the two POWs. They were nowhere to be seen when we arrived back at the farmyard but that doesn't mean they weren't there. I'm sure somebody was at the far end of the stable block between Meacher being shot and Smith making his charge from the doorway. Of course, we now know he was already dying before I shot him. Did you find the POWs?"

Piper nodded. "Yes. The team who came to your rescue found them hiding in the woods across the fields from the farm. Naturally they've denied all knowledge of the events. They said they heard shooting from the farm and decided they were best out of it."

I shook my head and toyed with my pen. "I can't buy that, sir. Who the hell else could it have been if it was not one of them?"

"But why would the POWs want to kill Smith?" Houseman had decided to join the party.

"Precisely," agreed Face and they all looked at me expectantly.

"Sorry, gentlemen. You're the professionals. You find the answers because I don't even know where to start. What about evidence turned up by the search teams?"

"So far we've found nothing at the farm," replied Face. "No radios, no code pads. Mind you, it will take us at least a week to tear the place apart."

I turned to Piper. "What about the cottage?"

He tapped his pipe out into an ashtray. "There we were a little luckier. We actually found a transmitter receiver quite cleverly hidden under the floorboards but therein lies another mystery. It was a short range model and certainly not powerful enough to reach Germany or even France."

Face butted in. "Which leaves us thinking that it was simply a relay radio. The main long range radio must be somewhere else but not that far away."

"But you found a radio at the airstrip, didn't you?" I asked.

Face nodded. "We did but again it was short range. In fact it was an identical model to that found in the cottage."

I thought for a moment. "So it is reasonable to suggest that Smith was passing information to the airstrip?"

"Could have been," agreed Piper. "But where was he getting his up-to-date information? Nobody would get away with a radio on the bases where the attacks have taken place and all the phone lines on camp are closed down from before the first briefing until the kites are well on their way."

I turned to Face. "What about the investigations into our hypothesis that we may have an agent here at West Fen, sir?"

He looked disappointed. "Nothing so far. Everybody checks out."

"God, it's like looking for a needle in a haystack." Houseman sighed and nobody in the room disagreed with him.

There was a long silence as we sat quietly around the table, each of us with our own thoughts.

Finally it was Face who decided on a new line of attack and he spoke to me - his voice quiet. "What if we were to give you access to Meacher. Do you think he'd open up to you?"

I shrugged. "No idea, sir, but it is worth a try. For some reason he trusts me."

Face turned to Piper. "What do you think, David?"

Piper tapped his pen thoughtfully on his chin.

"What have we to lose? It could be worth a try. To date we've got bugger all out of Giedrovski."

"Okay," replied Face. "We will go with that." He turned back to me. "I'll arrange for you to visit him at Latchmere House as soon as we get him out of hospital. Let's say the day after tomorrow?"

"Latchmere House?" I queried.

"Camp 020," said Face quickly. "Our interrogation centre at Ham Common. I'll send transport for you. I'll also have a couple of our psychological boffins take your statement. They may be able to see more than we can at this stage."

I glanced at Houseman and he looked away quickly. I knew he was wondering how the hell I'd got myself into so much trouble. I half expected him to do what he usually did when he needed to think and was playing for time. He'd stand up and look out of the window with his arms behind his back. Tonight he couldn't do that as the blackout curtains were drawn and...........

"Shitty death!" The others stared at me and I realised I'd uttered the expletive out aloud.

"I beg your pardon?" Face laughed at my embarrassment.

I stood up. "Sorry about that but something has been niggling at me since I came into this room earlier today." I stopped as I struggled to find the words to persuade them I was not talking crap.

"Go on." Piper smiled tolerantly at me.

I took a deep breath. "Shortly before I left for Holland, I took a walk in the village and met an old guy who had lost a son in the fourteen-eighteen war. He was kind enough to ask me in for a cup of tea. A habit of Squadron Leader Houseman's just reminded me of something. When he's trying to find the answer to a problem, he stands, deep in thought, over there in front of the window. I did just that in the old man's cottage and from his window I could see this section."

They just looked at me and waited. So far I was not making much of an impression.

I plugged on. "Between the old man's cottage and this section there is a telephone box."

There was an even longer pause.

"I'm afraid you've lost me," Face finally admitted.

327

Houseman looked at me carefully. Once more there was disbelief on his face and his disbelief was even more apparent in his voice. "I'm with him all the way, sir, but you're not going to like what he's about to suggest."

"Which is?" Face was getting irritable.

Houseman stood. "He's saying that somebody could have signalled from this section to somebody waiting in the public phone box. He in turn would phone the cell's radio operator and he in turn would inform the airstrip. Maybe he could even communicate directly with the aircraft. That is what you're saying, isn't it, Carver?"

I nodded. "Yes, sir."

Piper placed his now cold briar gently on the table and leaned back in his chair. His voice was barely audible. "Which in turn implies that the enemy agent is a member of this section."

There was a stunned silence. Nobody, including me, could reconcile themselves to that scenario.

Face jumped to his feet as Houseman slumped back into his own chair. Add a little music and we had a party game.

"Surely," protested Face, "there is a police guard on the phone box to prevent calls once the target is known?"

Houseman shook his head. "Wareham's men keep an eye open to prevent service personnel using the box but West Fen is too far from a police station to warrant a civilian police presence. Coningsby and Woodhall Spa phone boxes can be isolated at its exchange but for some reason, West Fen's phones cannot be switched off in the same way. Wareham's lads keep an eye on the box to prevent service personnel from making calls but the odd civilian could slip through the net. Anyway, how often would the agent be there? Pretty infrequently I'd imagine."

I decided to stir things up a little more. "How could the cell know about the operations at other stations the rogue aircraft attacked? Does it mean there are agents there too?"

I swear Face turned a whiter shade of white.

Houseman answered for me. "That information could come from here just as easily. We've access to the operations of other squadrons in the group for planning the various waves of attack."

Face began to look a little better. For a while there I think he had visions of enemy agents in every intelligence section in the command. It would have destroyed MI5's credibility overnight.

Piper leaned over and put a hand on my arm. "Carver, as you seem to be the expert at frightening scenarios, any thoughts on who the traitor might be?"

I paused to give the matter some thought but realised I was beginning to form opinions based on my dislike for certain members of the section. That was no way to make an educated assessment.

"No, sir. None."

"Jake?"

"Nobody springs instantly to mind although we must not forget who occupied this office before we turned it into a temporary conference room."

Face exploded. "Oh, come on, Jake. I know he was an arrogant, autocratic prat but I don't think he had the nous to be an enemy agent. He was too mercurial. The first time he lost his temper he'd have given the whole game away. No, I am damned sure that Janner is not our man."

Piper laughed. "I've just realised that there is only one man who couldn't possibly be our agent." He jerked a thumb in my direction. "Carver here is the only person posted in after the attacks started. Damn it, Jake, it could even be you."

I saw Houseman's face tighten but he kept his voice very quiet when he replied. "You're a big chap, David, but don't ever suggest that again."

There was confusion on Piper's face. "I'm sorry, Jake, it was meant as a joke. It seems it was in bad taste."

I think, by the time he had made his apology, Houseman had already forgotten all about the matter.

Face took charge and outlined his plan of action. The service records of all personnel in the section would be gone over with a fine-toothed comb. He'd inform the station commander of events to date. I'd visit Meacher and they would continue to sift through the farm and the cottage for further clues. When he'd finished, Piper made his excuses and left, as he had to be back in London for a conference that very morning and it was already three o'clock.

Face declined to brief me on my visit with Meacher. "I want you to go in there with an open mind, Carver. You've a way of getting to people and I don't want your talents to be influenced by suggestions from me. You know what the man is. Try to think of a strategy on the hoof. If he's down, try to lift his morale. If he's cagey, try taunting him - that sometimes works. Get him angry and he may say something he didn't mean to. If he's a bit too light-hearted, remind him of the rope waiting for him at Wandsworth Prison. Those are the only guidelines I can give you."

"Will it come to that?" I asked quietly.

"Why not? He's been an agent a long time. How many deaths has he been responsible for - no matter how indirectly?"

I could give him no answer to that.

Face tapped the table. "Do you know how many we've hanged so far?"

I shook my head.

He closed his eyes and began ticking off on his fingers. "Let's see.....at Pentonville we disposed of Kieboom, Waldberg, Meier and Job. At Wandsworth it was Winter, Scott-Ford, Timmerman and Dronkers. Those are just the ones I can remember. The cruel twist is that if the Germans somehow manage to win this war, they will judge me and my associates as war criminals and it will be us dancing at the end of a rope."

"Do you sleep well?" asked Houseman who had listened with a sad expression on his face.

"Like a top!" laughed Face. "The more of the bastards we kill, the happier I become." He suddenly turned to me and the laughter had gone. In its place was a look I didn't care for and I knew I was seeing the real Face. "How much did you hate Giedrovski?"

"What do you mean, sir? The past tense does not apply. I still hate the bastard and I'd love to see him strung up although that sounds too good a death for him."

"Ah, but he'll not be strung up, Carver. He's destined for a meeting with a firing squad."

"Why the different method of execution?"

"Because he's a member of the German armed forces and not a civilian recruited by the German intelligence services. In fact he's now in the Tower of London and being held in a cell on the top floor of Waterloo Barracks. The east end of 'E' Block to be precise. The Scots Guards have the honour of guarding him until he takes his walk with destiny. He's shown nothing but arrogance and has been totally unbending in his determination not to reveal the cell. He was given a general court-martial in camera and found guilty of espionage. He'll be shot early tomorrow morning."

329

He paused and walked over to the window and I realised he didn't want to see Houseman's face when he made his next remark. "Carver, I want you to attend the execution. You'll be taken to see Meacher immediately afterwards and should be back here in time for dinner. What do you say?"

I saw Houseman's face stiffen and his mouth opened slightly but he decided to keep quiet. His gaze was impassive and I could read nothing there.

"Refusal is not really an option, is it, sir?"

Face didn't reply. I knew he wanted me to see Giedrovski die. It would put me in the right frame of mind to meet Meacher. Face knew I had a soft spot for the farmer and he knew I didn't want to see the man go the same way as Giedrovski.

I took a deep breath. "When do I leave, sir?"

"You'll be collected from the mess at 15.00 hours this afternoon and driven to Waterloo barracks. A room has been reserved for you in the officers' mess."

Oh, fucking marvellous. Here we go again. Tonight I'd planned to take Nat to meet Stan Cornish at the Lancaster Arms. Instead I'd be in the fucking Tower of London. What did I need a room for? Did he think I was going to have a good night's sleep knowing I was going to have to attend an execution? I'd get as much sleep on a bench on the embankment. I wanted to see Giedrovski dead but I also wanted to spend time with the girl who was my sole reason for living. Oh, fuck the bloody war and fuck Face!

Face turned and saw my barely controlled anger but just ignored it. He'd a war to fight and temperamental little pilot officers had no say in the way he fought his war. He walked over to the table and began to close his briefcase.

"See if you can get Meacher to open up a bit more about his wife. She doesn't seem to figure highly in his life these days but one never knows. Slot her into the conversation and see what evolves." He turned to Houseman. "Thank you, Jake. Sorry to steal your star officer again. I'll see myself out."

Houseman and I sat for a while after the door had closed behind Face. There wasn't even the sound of a Merlin out on the airfield to break the silence.

I finally looked up at my boss. "Sorry, sir. I guess I'm really a bloody nuisance to you and the section."

He sighed and leaned forward on the table, his face cupped in his hands. "Don't be stupid, Sam. You started all this and thank God you did. Who the hell would have thought we had a traitor in our own section? If it had not been for you, we would never have even suspected such a thing. What worries me is the effect it is having on you. I fear for you, my lad. You've been though a lot here but to send you into enemy occupied territory with no training was sheer madness. You must be the luckiest man on this planet to survive that experience."

I decided he ought to know just a little more about that trip. "I was lucky, sir. Two others were killed as we made our way out. One was a beautiful, intelligent American girl who was a real professional. It was no fault of hers she was killed - just bad luck. If I'd sat in the same place in the aircraft then I'd have died instead." I thought about old Gurbe and his wife. "I just hope those we left behind survived."

Houseman held up a hand. "Don't tell me any more. The less I know the better until we bring this affair to a close." He glanced at his watch. "You'd better get back to the mess and catch some sleep."

"What about you, sir?"

He yawned. "I might as well stay. The first of tomorrow's ops signals will be in shortly."

"I'll stay and give you a hand, sir."

He stood up. "No way, Carver, you get to bed." He started for the door but turned when he realised I had not followed. I could feel his eyes on the back of my head. The tension was back with me and I knew I'd have even more demons to face tonight if I tried to sleep. I needed to be occupied.

Houseman seemed to sense my reluctance to leave and I'm sure he knew the reason.

"Okay," he said quietly. "You can help if you'd rather."

I rose and he held the door open for me. "You worry me, Sam. You must draw back soon or I can see you going under. It has all been too much - too soon."

I gave him a wry smile. "If you can't take a joke...

"You shouldn't have joined." He finished for me and we laughed together but our mirth sounded hollow and I decided to put it down to the acoustic properties of the corridor. I was unable to face the truth.

I was still in the section when Nat came on duty. I told her I was being sent away, yet again. I could see the disappointment in her eyes but she smiled and squeezed my hand.

"How long this time?"

"Should be back tomorrow evening in time for dinner."

"You're not going off with Bourne again, are you?"

"Bloody hell, no. I'm being chauffeured by one of Face's lot."

She sighed. I seem to spend all my time wishing you luck, Carver. How much luck can a guy have?"

"No problems this time. I'm simply going to interview somebody."

"Doesn't that need luck?"

"More than you'd imagine, especially as I don't even know what I'm doing. Mind you I seem to have had that problem from the day I left Harrow and came here."

She laughed. "I think that is the secret of your success. You don't know what you're doing which results in nobody being able to predict your next move. I reckon that is a canny skill for an intelligence officer."

Maybe she had a point. Anyway, I dawdled around the place for a while in the pretence that I was helping her when all the time all I really wanted to do was gather her up in my arms and never let her go. Finally she laid a hand on my arm.

"For goodness sake, Sam, go away and get some sleep or something. I can't work with you here. Have you told Stan you won't be at the Lancaster Arms tonight?"

I clapped a hand to my forehead. "My brain is so full of you, I'd forgotten. I'll call him from the mess. See you for dinner or duty supper tomorrow."

"I'll hold you to that," she replied as she pushed me firmly out of the door.

I called Stan and he sounded disappointed but I told him I'd contact him as soon as I got back and we would arrange another evening. That seemed to mollify him and he wished me luck before he rang off.

I went to my room and packed a small bag for my overnight stay. I looked at my greatcoat hanging in the locker but decided there was a definite improvement in the weather and I'd take a chance and leave it behind.

Mr Bates was in the foyer when I eventually ambled out to wait for my transport.

"Going on your travels again, Mr Carver, sir?"

"I'm afraid so, Mr Bates."

"No overcoat?" It was said reprovingly and with a frown.

"I think the weather is changing. Anyway, I'll be in a vehicle most of the time."

He waved a warning finger. "You should heed the old Lincolnshire adage, sir. "Nary cast a clout till May is out."

"Sounds like you can't belt the wife until June."

"Droll, sir, very droll, but it is not as absurd as it seems. I don't remove my long johns or my flannel vest until the beginning of the month of June."

"When do you start wearing them?"

"The first week of November, sir."

"Bloody hell, Mr Bates, they must be a bit ripe after seven months."

He started to smile but it turned into a full belly laugh. He finally wiped his eyes with his handkerchief and gave me a wry smile. "Like a lamb to the slaughter, eh, sir?"

"I imagine it's not often somebody gets one over on you, Mr Bates."

"I like to think not, sir." He fiddled with the silver inkwell on the reception desk before he resumed the conversation. "May I be so bold, sir, as to offer you an invitation?" The old boy looked uncomfortable and I was quick to put him at his ease.

"An invitation from you, Mr Bates, would be accepted with alacrity."

He smiled. "Well, sir, I couldn't help noticing that you've formed a close relationship with Miss Cowen. I wondered if you and your lady would like to join Mrs Bates and myself for tea one Sunday?"

I looked at him in amazement. "We would love to, Mr Bates. That's very kind of you."

He looked pleased. "It will be our pleasure, sir. We've not asked anyone for such a long time." There was a sad inflection in his voice as he spoke the last words of the sentence.

"Was this a regular event in the past?" I asked quietly, as I suspected I already knew the reason for the sadness.

"It was, sir, but I'm afraid that making friends with the aircrews can be a very short friendship. My wife found it particularly distressing. Each time it happened it was like losing one of our family."

I smiled. "Do you think I'll be a better bet?"

He grinned. "Oh, I do hope so, sir."

"Take it as read, Mr Bates. When I get back we will fix up a date."

"I look forward to it, sir."

A horn tooted outside and I saw a Humber staff car with a WAAF driver waiting at the kerb.

"Bye, Mr Bates - keep the teapot hot."

He shouted something in reply but I was already on my way.

When we arrived in London I was taken straight to The Tower. I was welcomed by a young army captain and escorted to the officers' mess where a cold supper awaited me. Later a batman showed me to my room. The army seemed to do things in style. I was exhausted after so long without sleep and was relieved to have a deep, dreamless sleep.

My alarm went off at 05.30 and an hour later, the young army captain appeared once more and escorted me to a small office. Here he briefed me on what was about to take place and I could see that he was mystified as to why I was there. He was tactful enough not to ask. He informed me that I was not speak to anybody or make notes. I'd simply be escorted to the place where the execution was to take place, witness the execution itself and then be escorted to my car for the journey to Latchmere House. I signed a document to the effect that I understood and would comply with the orders.

At 07.00 we walked out into a cold, wet morning. It seemed Mr Bates had been right with his warning about 'casting clouts'. As we walked around the base of a round tower, which formed a corner of the inner wall, I saw, on my right, abutting the inner wall, a long, low building of sectional construction. To my surprise, it seemed that this nondescript little shack was our destination.

The captain opened a door in the far end and I permitted myself an ironic little smile when I saw the sign on the door - 'Miniature Rifle Range'. There were already four other officers and two civilians present when we arrived and we were quickly followed by an eight-strong firing squad. The army SNCO in charge of the party quickly and efficiently arranged his men into their positions and the range fell silent. Only the slightest signs of fidgeting from the riflemen betrayed their true feelings.

Finally, Giedrovski was led in. Following behind, among the small entourage, was a priest, but something told me the German would have no need of his services.

As the group walked slowly past our little gathering, Giedrovski suddenly stopped and turned. The others, taken by surprise, cannoned into him, which ensured that any hopes of a dignified exit for the enemy agent had just gone down the pan. I realised that I was the cause of Giedrovski's sudden about turn.

He stared at me for a few seconds, a little smile hovering on his lips. The smile became a broad grin as he raised his cuffed hands and pointed an index finger at me. His thumb moved in the gesture he had used once before - he was cocking the hammer of an imaginary gun. His hands jerked upwards as if from the recoil and his grin seemed to grow even larger as he held the pose.

I shook my head slightly and I looked pointedly at the firing squad. I returned my eyes to his and it was my turn to smile. His own smile faltered slightly as he lowered his arms and jerked his escort into motion.

In spite of my satisfaction, I felt a cold sensation pass down the length of my spine. He had repeated the gesture I had first seen at Sutton Bridge. He was an arrogant bastard but he was a brave bastard.

The charge was read out and his hands re-cuffed behind his back. A wooden post, the full height of the range in length, had been fixed to the ceiling and the floor and he was tied to this in the classic pose of the firing squad victim. He tried to refuse the blindfold but they blindfolded him anyway. Too much eye contact with the members of the firing squad was not conducive to good shooting. A circle of white lint, about five inches across, was pinned to his overalls to cover the area of the heart. All was ready.

Somehow I expected him to make some final grand gesture but at 07.45 precisely, eight shots crashed out as one in the confined space of the range and Giedrovski was smashed backwards against the post. His body then slumped forwards and down as far as his bonds permitted. The cordite fumes were strong and bitter but I felt totally unmoved. No satisfaction, no shock. In fact, nothing.

We followed the others outside and most of them lit up cigarettes. My escort ushered me straight to the guardroom and booked me out of the Tower. My case was already in the Humber and I was whisked away before I could even thank the man. So much for that. If it was supposed to have had an emotional effect upon me, to prepare me and put me on my mettle for my meeting with Meacher, it had failed miserably.

When we arrived at Latchmere House, I was signed in and handed a visitor's pass. My escort this time was a middle-aged civilian who led me to an office with rather pleasant views.

Here I was introduced to another faceless civilian who seemed to get great pleasure in not introducing himself. As he seemed so full of his own importance, I decided he was a 'Gerald'. He explained, in his pompous way, that he was the Deputy

Head of 'B' Division and responsible for investigating all threats to the nation's security. He said it in a way that implied he, and he alone, was responsible for our national security.

Needless to say, I took an instant dislike to the man, as he seemed to regard me as a minion who had become too important for such a lowly station in life. All the time he gave me the impression that somebody much more senior than he, had insisted upon my interview with Meacher and his nose had been put out of joint

My reaction to the man was to become monosyllabic and unhelpful. He rather pointlessly instructed me to watch what I said to Meacher and finally admitted he thought the whole episode to be totally unorthodox and dangerous. At last the self-important little prig given me the chance to bring him down a peg or two.

"Why, if you're so against the meeting have you agreed to let me see Meacher?" I asked.

"That is nothing to do with you, Pilot Officer," he snapped.

"You mean you've discovered you're not as important as you thought you were?" I goaded him.

His face turned white with anger and he walked to the door and damned nearly wrenched it off its hinges. "Mathern!"

My escort returned. "Yes, sir?"

"Take this junior officer to the interview room and stay with him at all times. He's not to be left alone with the prisoner. Is that clear?"

"Bollocks!" I replied before my escort could get a word in.

'Gerald' spun round. "What did you say, Carver?" Every one of the five words dripped with vitriol.

Just in case he liked me to talk dirty, I repeated the word. "Bollocks!"

'Gerald' brought himself to what a serviceman would call 'the position of attention'.

"Mathern, escort this officer to your office and await further instructions.

"Stay where you are, Mathern," I countermanded. He thought I was an uppity, sprog officer? Okay, then I'd show him how fucking 'uppity' I could really be. I leaned on 'Gerald's' desk and he took a pace backwards, alarm on his face.

"Meacher will not say a word if anybody else is present in that interview room. He's no fool and he knows you'll be listening in, so he'll already be guarded in what he says. Mathern's presence will inhibit him even more."

'Gerald' ignored me. "Carry on, Mathern."

At least I had a parting shot. "Do you have a direct line to the Prime Minister?" I asked him. "My handler does and you can bet your bottom dollar this was not just his idea."

'Gerald' made as if to respond but bit his lip. He was damned nearly about to choke.

I turned to Mathern. "I think he's trying to say 'Carry on, Mathern' but something must have got stuck in his throat - probably his pride."

As I followed him back to his office, I saw a hint of a smile break through Mathern's impassive countenance. I flopped into a chair and wondered what the fuck I was doing here.

"Tea?" Mathern asked as if we were about to have a jolly little picnic.

"Thank you. Two sugars and a fairy cake." I failed to hide my irritation.

Mathern smiled pleasantly. "I think my ration will extend to that."

I stared in amazement as he spooned two sugars into my tea and, pulling an old biscuit tin from a cupboard, produced a bloody fairy cake! I glanced up at this quiet

334

civilian and saw him watching me intently. There was a real twinkle of amusement in his eyes and I began to laugh.

"Sorry, Mr Mathern, I'm afraid I've just about had enough. I apologise for being so rude to you when you were simply offering me hospitality. I'm afraid I was taking my anger and frustration out on you. I hope you'll forgive me."

"I understand, Mr Carver. I've no doubt you'll win this little contest but I'm afraid a little face-saving ploy will now be brought into operation. Don't be surprised if we've a long wait."

I sipped appreciatively on my tea. "If you can continue to serve up tea of this quality, I don't mind if we stay here all day."

He smiled. "Thank you, Mr Carver."

Mathern was right about the long wait. He busied himself at his desk and I slumped in my chair, tapping my feet to the rhythm of a popular song that was flitting through my mind. We sat there for an hour or more but at last the phone rang. Mathern picked up the receiver.

"Mathern." He listened for a while and then glanced at me. He gave me a conspiratorial wink. "At once, sir." He rose as he replaced the receiver. "Please follow me, Mr Carver."

We walked endless corridors until we came to a guard sitting at a table by an iron door. He checked our passes and unlocked the door.

"Fourth door on the left, sir." He pointed up the corridor.

The door clanged shut behind us as we headed for Interview Room Four.

Mathern opened the door. "You've a visitor, Mr Meacher." He beckoned me to enter as he slipped out and closed the door behind me.

Meacher had risen to his feet. At first there was a frown on his face but when he saw me, he grinned and held out his left hand. His right arm was in a sling and he winced as he moved forward to greet me. "Sam, it's good to see you."

I returned the smile and shook his hand. His greeting was warm and friendly and I was surprised at just how pleased I was to see him again. He waved to one of the two utility-looking wooden chairs.

"Please, Sam. Take a seat."

He took the other chair and we sat facing each other across the small table. He was still grinning happily and I felt like a fish out of water. Here I was, as green as grass, facing probably the most successful agent the Germans had ever had and I hadn't a bloody clue what to say next. I made a feeble effort to redress the situation.

"How are they treating you?"

He shrugged. "Other than the threats of Cell Fourteen, very well, thank you."

I was puzzled. "Cell Fourteen, what's that?"

Meacher chuckled. "Oh, Sam, how did you ever become a counter-espionage agent?"

I smiled ruefully. "For your information, I'm not an agent. I'm involved in this purely by chance. I'm afraid you confessed to a rank amateur. God knows what I'm doing here but I really am pleased to see you looking so well. I thought Smith had killed you."

His smile disappeared and he looked down at the table. "You saved my life, Sam. You know you could have taken that bullet."

I felt uncomfortable. "He was a lousy shot."

He shook his head. "He was a very good shot but he did prefer helpless targets. His speciality was the shot to the base of the skull. He liked that."

"Such as the Troutbridge family?"

He nodded but said nothing more.

"How are you feeling?" I nodded at the sling.

"Fine really. It hurts a little but I can live with it. At least I'm still alive."

I nodded sagely but was acutely embarrassed to find I had no more material to carry on the pretence. We just sat there. Him relaxed and confident. Me, stiff and uncomfortable.

He leaned forward across the table. "You know, Sam, I really don't know if you're as green as you seem or whether it is just a clever act."

"It's no act. I'm as green as I look."

"A man who enters occupied Holland, snatches a very professional German agent and delivers him back here is not green, Sam."

"Beginner's luck?" I raised my eyebrows.

He laughed. "I don't think so."

I sat up straight in my chair and decided I must take charge of the meeting. This was getting too much like my confessional, not his!

"Do you have anything to tell me about your activities? They'll be taking it all down, of course." I nodded in the general direction of the ceiling where I assumed the microphones to be concealed.

He laughed. "Are you always so honest?"

"I try to be."

The smile disappeared as if turned off with a switch and his face became hard. "Then get out of this game now," he said shortly. "You're a nice chap, Sam. This is a dirty game and it is not for you. I don't think you want to spend your life dealing with the constant lies, duplicity and dishonesty. You'll lose your innate innocence and that would be a shame."

"Too late, Mr Meacher."

"Peter."

"Too late, Peter."

"There's still time."

I took a deep breath. "Only if you tell me the rest of the story. The sooner I finish this job, the sooner I can take your advice."

He sat back in his chair. "Okay, Sam, fire away."

I looked him straight in the eye. "Who killed Smith?"

His surprise was genuine. "You did. After I went down I was still semi-conscious for a while and I heard your shots."

I shook my head. "Not me, Peter. Oh yes, I shot him three times but he was already dying."

He looked perplexed and I continued. "He had a pitchfork rammed into his back by somebody who'd got round behind him in the stable."

His head dropped and I could see he was doing some quick thinking.

I forced the pace. "How about the two POWs?"

His head snapped up. "They were in the field repairing the fence. You saw them yourself."

"They were not there when we came back."

I noticed with dismay that his air of confidence was back. "They would have moved to the forty acre. That was the next fence they were due to repair."

"Where is the forty acre?"

"Next to the wood where you've erected your mast."

Shit! That tied in with the report they had been found hiding in the wood.

"Where were your other two labourers?"

"Both at home I suppose. They only come in when I need them. They are both well past retiring age."

I decided to try another tack. "We found the radio." I threw the remark in casually but it seemed to have no effect - he just remained impassive. I decided to go a step further and watched him closely as I made my next revelation.

"Smith had it concealed under the floorboards in his cottage."

I was rewarded by a barely perceptible flash of relief in his eyes. My friend Peter was not yet about to tell us all he knew.

"Was it Smith who transmitted to Giedrovski at the airstrip?"

He paused for a second as if confused. "Ah, yes."

"What was Giedrovski's real name?"

That brought his head back up and there was a strange look on his face - part surprise and part fear.

I tried to spur him on. "I watched them shoot him just a few hours ago."

His shoulders slumped. "Oberleutnant Christian Krebs."

I kept my eyes on him as I replied. "I hated the bastard, Peter, but he was a brave man."

He raised his eyes to mine and there was a fire there I'd not seen before. My Mr Meacher was a proud man.

"He was a brave man, Sam. He lived with the constant fear of discovery by the Poles. If they'd found out he was an agent, they would not have handed him over to the British authorities. He'd have been tortured and executed by the Poles themselves. He'd lived the life of a Pole for some years and had trained as a pilot with the Polish Air Force. It was his own idea to make for England with the refugees. He knew how desperate you were for pilots and he knew it would only be a matter of time before he could be in a position to do a lot of damage. His sole aim in life was to serve his country."

"Are you proud of what you did, Peter?"

"Of course I am. To remain undiscovered for so long was no mean feat. I assure you, Sam, if it had not been for the murder of the Troutbridge family, I'd have had no doubts about carrying on with my role."

I stood and walked over to the barred window. The grounds of the centre looked peaceful and calm. "It would only have been a matter of weeks, Peter. We were already on to you. Smith was certainly under suspicion and we knew about the buried parachute."

He grinned. "Your mast really was a phoney?"

I returned the grin. "I'm afraid so."

He clapped his hands. "I knew it! I told Smith I had my suspicions but he said you were two typically snotty Brits - all stiff upper lip and as thick as pig shit. You were no threat to anybody but yourselves. His words not mine."

Time to strike again. "Where does your wife fit into all this?"

He looked down at his hands clasped on the desk in front of him. "If you'd met my wife, you'd not ask that question. My wife is still an attractive woman but she does not have the intelligence to spell the word 'espionage' let alone be involved in that sort of thing. She's unimaginative and suspicious of strangers which is pretty much endemic in the natives of Norfolk. God knows why she married me, other than to find a father for the family she needed so desperately."

"Did she know about or even suspect you for what you were?"

"My wife would not know a spy if one jumped out and bit her on the arse." He suddenly laughed heartily as if at some secret joke.

"What's so funny?"

He got control of himself again but he was still grinning. "Sam, if you knew the number of times I bit her arse whilst making love, you too would see the funny side of the remark."

I joined in his laughter and I knew the interview was over. I knew he was hiding an awful lot from us but I couldn't dislike the man. How could I criticise him for his actions? He'd done what any Englishman would have done if the roles had been reversed. In the silence that followed our laughter, he gave the first signs that he was worried about his ultimate fate.

"What happens to me now, Sam?"

I felt a desire to say all the right things to reassure him but I knew he'd see through the platitudes. "Well, Peter, you cannot be used as a double agent and I'm damned sure you'd never agree to that anyway."

"So I go the same way as Krebs?"

I shook my head. "He was military. That's why he faced a firing squad. For you it would be the hangman."

He gave a little smile. "How correct our two countries are, Sam."

"Maybe, if it had not been for Hitler, our two countries could have done great things together?" I suggested.

He shook his head. "I'm afraid we needed somebody like Hitler, Sam. Our country was destitute and the occupying forces after the First World War did nothing to help us get back our pride. The French in particular were bastards."

"The French have always been bastards," I replied.

"Sam...Sam," he chided me with a small smile on his face. "You're talking about one of your allies."

I shrugged. "The English have always disliked the French. They will remain our allies just as long as we're useful to them. After that, they'll ally themselves to whoever who pays the most. The French are sad bastards. Always have been and always will be."

He sighed. "You surprise me, Sam. I didn't think you had a nasty thought in your body."

I grinned. "A lot of people make that mistake."

"Do you feel this way about all your allies?"

"No, just the Frogs. Hitler got it all wrong, you know. If he'd invaded France instead of Poland, I'm damned sure the people of this country, as long as they knew he was coming no further, would not have lifted a finger to help the French."

Meacher walked over to me and put a hand on my shoulder. "Don't spoil my image of you, Sam. You're too cynical for your tender years."

Time for a last quick stab before I departed. "Who is the agent at West Fen?"

I saw him suppress a smile and I knew I was going to get little from this man. "I've no idea. All I know is that he'd pass information to our agent as he waited in the phone booth near the camp. He'd place small cards in the window of his department. It was a very simple and crude code but effective. The agent would use a small pair of binoculars to see the colour and shape of the cards. When it was dark, a box, fitted with a battery and a number of coloured bulbs, would be used. There was just the security fence and a small field between the airfield building and the phone box, so little chance of anybody just passing and spotting what was going on."

"Who was the agent in the phone box?"

He shook his head. "Probably one of the men from the airstrip. I really don't know."

I looked at him carefully. "Any idea what the building housed, you know, the one sending out the signals?"

"No, I'm afraid I don't." He looked totally innocent but I knew he was lying.

I sighed. "It doesn't matter." My heart sank. I knew exactly which building.

He sat on the corner of the table. "Look, Sam, you've cracked our cell, the airstrip is finished and you got the pilot. It is only a matter of time before you find your agent at West Fen. The whole business is finished."

I nodded. "Thank God! Perhaps I can get back to normal and marry my young lady."

"Was that her with you at the Red Lion that night we had the chat?"

I nodded.

"She's very pretty. I wish you years of happiness, Sam."

"Thank you, Peter. I hope all goes well for you but I'm afraid I've no control over your future." I moved my chair back neatly under the table. "I think it is time I was getting back to West Fen. Is there anything you want me to do for you, Peter?"

He shook his head. "No. You've been more than generous as it is. I'd expected hostility from you but all you've given me is understanding and friendship. Whatever happens, I'll always value that." He held out his hand. "Goodbye, Sam."

As I shook his hand, I still could not see an enemy agent. He was a fine man for his age and even the events of the last few days had failed to dim the brightness in his eyes.

He suddenly increased the pressure of his grip on my hand. "What happened to Brunner?" he asked quietly.

"Brunner?" I frowned.

"The agent from the airstrip who didn't arrive at the Red Lion."

I looked straight into his eyes. "Oh, he did arrive at the Red Lion but, before he could talk to the pilot, he recognised me from our unfortunate meeting at the airstrip. He tried to kill me."

He looked at me in disbelief. "You killed him?"

I shook my head. "No. A young lady I know killed him for me. She snapped his neck."

The description 'young lady' was stretching credibility a bit but I knew Foghorn wouldn't mind.

"Your future wife?" He looked shocked.

"No, just another young lady I know."

He released my hand. "You live a charmed life, young man."

I sighed. "Everybody keeps telling me that. I hope they're right." I walked over and knocked on the door to be let out. It was Mathern who answered my knock. I turned to Meacher.

"Goodbye, Peter."

I saw the first sign of emotion on his face but he was quick to regain control of his feelings.

"Goodbye, Sam."

Mathern closed the door behind us and it was the last time I'd see Peter Meacher.

When we arrived back at Mathern's office, I was pleasantly surprised to see Face waiting for me.

"You seem to have cornered the market in magic carpets, sir."

He laughed. "Just a Humber, Carver. How did it go?"

I strolled over to the window and looked up at the blue sky. "Did you find a radio at the farm?" I asked him.

"Not at the farm. Just the one at the cottage."

I turned to face him. "In that case you'd better search the farm again."

He slumped into a chair. "Carver, we've searched that farm from top to bottom. Not even a piece of straw has remained unturned. There is no radio and no incriminating evidence to suggest that there has ever been a radio there. Why are you so positive we've missed something?"

"Because he told me, that day at the farm when he was talking about his disgust at what Smith and his cronies were proposing to do to the Troutbridge family, that he'd contacted Berlin for help. How did he do that if he didn't have a radio at the farm? Smith's radio had insufficient range to reach Berlin."

Face's shoulders slumped. "Shit! Did you mention this in your report?"

"Yes, sir. Word for word."

"Well, obviously we all failed to pick it up. Oh, sod it!" He picked up the phone and was soon giving orders for the search of the farm to be intensified. He spoke to me as he replaced the receiver.

"You'd better get back to West Fen."

"Okay, sir."

He stopped me just as I reached the door. "Oh, Carver. Try some of your tangential thinking on the possible identity of our in-house traitor. You might come up with something we old plodders have missed."

I nodded and Mathern escorted me back to my car for the trip back to West Fen.

CHAPTER TWENTY-FOUR

It was around 18.00 when I got back to my room in the mess and I felt edgy and unsettled. I went out to the phone in reception and called the section. There was a maximum effort again so Nat would be on duty until they got back. Even Mr Bates was absent from his desk. The thought of drinking in the mess bar had no appeal so I went back to my room, grabbed my greatcoat and went out into the evening.

I spotted the little Fiat parked in the corner of the mess parking area and I knew I still had the keys in my pocket but a trip to the Lancaster Arms could hardly be classed as a duty trip. Ah, what the hell. I climbed into the little car, turned the ignition key and pressed the starter to be rewarded with the sound of a seriously depleted battery. No way was the damned thing going to start.

"Got trouble, old boy?"

The voice made me jump. I glanced up to see a couple of flight lieutenants peering in through the driver's window.

I wound the window down. "Bloody flat battery."

"No problem," shouted the nearest. "Put her in second and let the clutch out when I yell."

They both disappeared around the back of the Fiat and the next thing I knew I was rolling swiftly out of the car park and on to the road.

"Now!" yelled a voice from behind.

I let in the clutch and, after a few stutters, the engine burst into life.

One of my saviours reappeared at the window and he was out of breath. "For Pete's sake, don't switch off again until she's had a good run."

I nodded. "Thanks a lot. I owe you one. The name's Sam Carver and next time you see me in the bar the beer is on me."

He laughed. "What a gentleman you are."

I watched them as they trotted off in the direction of the hangars. I was pretty sure the one who had spoken was one of the engineering officers on the station.

Fine! Here I was, money in my pocket and a set of wheels just waiting to roll but where the hell did I want to go? Did I really want to drink by myself? The answer was no. Then an idea surfaced and I drove off the camp to the phone box in the village. I placed the floor mat from the footwell on to the accelerator to keep the revs up on the engine whilst I made my call. As I waited for an answer I looked over at the intelligence centre but there were no signs from Janner's window. Who the hell could be hiding a secret like that?

"Hello?" The voice sounded sleepy.

"You're not in bed I hope, Cornish?"

"Is that you, young Carver?"

"Who else?"

"For your information, I was in a deep sleep in front of the fire. Some of us have a hard day's work to complete before we can put our feet up."

"Poor old sod," I laughed. "Fancy a pint?"

"What a stupid question from a so-called intelligence officer."

"Right, get your coat on. I'll be with you in about twenty minutes."

"I'll be ready. Drive carefully."

As I got back in the car I glanced at the little cottage in which I'd had tea with the old man. One day, I'd call round and tell him that two of his hated Germans were dead. That might cheer him up a little. That would have to wait until another day. Tonight I was going to have a few beers and relax.

When I arrived at the farm, Stan was waiting on the roadside at the entrance to his drive.

"By hell! You're keen," I laughed as he climbed in.

"Didn't want you to waste drinking time, that's all. Come on, get a move on."

When we walked into the Lancaster Arms, the Army and the Land Girls were there in force but there were very few of our lads.

Ethel saw us as we entered. "By heck, Stan, you keep some funny company. Watch him, he'll have you signed up and taking the King's shilling before you know what's hit you."

Stan laughed. "Ethel, if they're that bloody desperate, we'd better start taking German lessons."

Harry appeared with a tray of empties. "She can't even speak our own bloody language, let alone German."

Ethel took a swipe at him with a tea towel she had in her hand. "It doesn't matter what tongue I speak in, Harry Woods, you'll always get the rough edge of it."

Harry roared with laughter as he headed into the kitchen. Ethel looked around the crush in the bar. "Look, you two, go through into our sitting room and I'll bring you a couple of pints in there. You can't hear yourself think in here."

We thanked her and wandered through to their private quarters. There was no sign of the two young boys I'd seen on my previous visit. Ethel was soon through with our beer and we settled down in a couple of chairs in front of the fire.

Stan took a sip of his beer and shook his head. "You look worn out, boy."

I wiped beer froth from my upper lip. "Knackered is the word, Stan."

He paused and then spoke carefully as he put his glass on the table. "They say Peter Meacher, from Chapel Farm, has been arrested."

I looked at him but didn't reply.

He tried again. "Also, from what I hear, it seems that Irish bastard, Smith, has disappeared."

I didn't respond straight away but I remembered how we would have still been groping about in the dark if it had not been for this little chap. I was about to break every rule in the security book.

"Smith is dead, as you've already guessed, our mystery pilot is dead and Meacher is in custody."

"Bloody hell!" He breathed the words quietly.

"I've not told you that and if it gets out I'll personally shoot you."

The little man looked away quickly but not before I had seen the hurt in his eyes. I was such a twat. There had been no need for that warning. "I'm sorry, Stan. I didn't mean it as it sounded. You know what I was trying to say. I just didn't say it very well."

He ran a hand through his unruly hair. "I know, boy. I know what you meant. I shouldn't be so touchy."

We sipped our beer in silence for a while and I could see him struggling with his curiosity. He finally lost the struggle and leaned towards me. "What were Smith and

Meacher up to?"

"Espionage. I don't think I need tell you that."

"Did they have wirelesses and codes and things?"

I smiled at the childlike eagerness of his question. "Indeed they did. Smith's radio was very cleverly concealed under the floorboards of his cottage."

"That was his forte," replied Stan casually.

"What was?"

"Woodwork."

"Oh, I see."

"Will you let me see the cottage sometime, Sam?" He looked uncomfortable with his request.

I laughed. "Why are you so interested?"

He shrugged. "Well, it's a bit like Boys Own really. Who would have thought Peter Meacher was a spy? Smith? Well, I could have believed anything of that twat but Meacher seemed a decent enough chap. I'd never have suspected him of being a fifth columnist."

"He was more than that, Stan. He was a very professional German spy and had been spying for them since the First World War."

"Bloody hell!" He sat back in astonishment.

I was not enjoying my beer as much as I had expected and it was then that I made a very strange decision. "Do you really want to see the cottage?"

"Yes, I do."

I drained my glass. "Drink up, then. No time like the present."

He quickly downed the rest of his pint. "What, at this time of night? We won't be able to see a bloody thing."

"Yes we will. The search team will still be there."

"Then how the hell will I get in?" he asked in dismay.

I was already heading for the door. "I'll think of something."

I drove the little Fiat as fast as I dared in the puny light from the hooded headlights. We arrived at Revesby and did a quick left and then right on to the Moorby road. We passed the blacked-out POW camp and were soon bouncing down the track through the woods to the cottage. I braked to a halt as an armed soldier stepped out into the headlights and another appeared at my window. I wound down the window and a torch shone in my face.

"May I ask what you're doing here, sir?"

"I thought the search team would still be here."

"I'm afraid they left at about 19.00 hours, sir."

"Shit!" A bloody wasted journey.

"Who are you, sir? May I see your identity card?"

As I passed my ID through the window I saw the light of a torch coming towards us from the cottage.

"What's going on, Corporal?"

I sighed with relief as I recognised Piper's voice.

"A Pilot Officer Carver, sir."

"Sam?" Piper called in surprise as he came forward. "What on earth are you doing here?"

"To be honest, sir, I don't really know. I think I just wanted to show Stan the cottage."

Piper stooped to peer in the car. "Ah, Mr Cornish, isn't it?"

"Yes, sir," replied Stan. I liked the 'sir'. He was playing it the right way.

343

To my relief, Piper straightened up and spoke to the corporal. "It's okay, I know both of these gentlemen. I'll take care of them."

We followed him into the cottage and waited for him to turn up the oil lamp in the living room. It was now much tidier than on my previous visit. Everything had been taken apart for examination and even sections of the floorboards were still loose. There were lighter patches on the wallpaper where pictures had once hung.

Stan looked around him. "Not very house proud, was he?"

Piper laughed. "You should have seen it when we first got here. Damned place needed fumigating before we could get down to work."

"How come you're here on your own, sir?" I asked Piper.

He sighed. "Like you, Sam, I don't really know. We've been through this place several times, from top to bottom but we've found nothing new. There has to be more than a short range..." He glanced at Stan and then at me.

"It's okay, sir," I reassured him. "I'd trust this little man with my life."

The little farmer gave me a look I'll never forget. I think it was the highest praise he'd ever received. I put a hand on his shoulder. "Anyway, I'm bigger than he is!"

Piper grinned and continued. "There has to be a more powerful radio transmitter somewhere around here."

"I think you'll find it at the farm, sir."

He looked at me in surprise and I realised that he'd not been in touch with Face. I told him about my meeting with Meacher and why I suspected the radio to be there and not here at the cottage.

"Sounds good, Sam. I think you're probably right. Do you know I could've gone home hours ago if I'd been given that information earlier? Oh, well, at least I'll not come steaming back here tomorrow and waste more time."

Stan idly unrolled a print depicting a typically Irish scene of mountains and a little white thatched cottage. A woman in bright clothes leaned over the bottom half of an open stable door. Idyllic, romantic and totally unrepresentative. The print had been removed from its frame during the search and now the empty frame was propped up on the mantelpiece.

"I think it would be much easier to hide the radio at the farm than in here. Plus, I'd have expected the radio to have been with the main agent and that surely was Meacher?" I surmised.

"I agree with you, Sam." Piper nodded but he was quietly watching Stan as the farmer moved slowly around the room.

"Did you find any suspicious woodwork or carpentry?" asked Stan.

Piper glanced quickly at me before returning his gaze to Stan. "Why do you ask, Mr Cornish?"

"Because he might have been a bastard but he was a superb carpenter." Stan had picked up the picture frame from the mantelpiece. He hefted it in his hand and then replaced it on the mantelpiece. "If it was possible to do anything with wood, Smith was your man." Stan looked at us as if willing us to understand.

Piper sighed. "Well, the radio we did find took a lot of unearthing and you're right, Mr Cornish, excellent carpentry made sure our task was not an easy one."

Stan didn't seem to be listening. He had gone back to the picture frame and was twisting it around in his hands, as if testing its strength.

"Funny," he said, almost to himself. Then, without warning, he smashed the frame down on the edge of the table. There was a loud crack and the frame split across one corner.

"What the hell?" shouted Piper as he moved forward. He'd travelled just two feet before he jerked to a stunned halt and we both watched as Stan pointed to a roll of stiff paper jutting out from the smashed frame.

"Hold it, Mr Cornish!" Piper pulled on a pair of gloves. We watched as he eased the tube of paper from a section of the hollowed out frame. He held the roll gingerly by the edges.

"How the hell did you know about that?" Piper looked at Stan in amazement.

"Frame was too light for its size," Stan replied. "A solid moulding of that size should have been much heavier. It had to have been hollowed out. I told you he was a good carpenter."

Piper scratched his head. "Well, I'll be buggered."

I glanced at Stan and grinned. He reddened slightly and he knew why I was grinning but he kept his composure.

Piper carefully eased open the tightly rolled paper in order to read the contents. I saw his jaw stiffen and his eyes narrow. I could see that the stiff paper was, in fact, three tightly rolled photographs. Each print was about eight by six inches.

"Oh, my God!" whispered Piper as he finally saw the content of the shots. He stared at each photo for a long time but finally moved over to the table and pressed them flat on the surface for us to see.

"Oh, bloody hell." Stan was also shocked into whispering.

I couldn't even speak. The content of the photos made me feel sick. Each print was of a naked man with a naked girl. The man was fat and in his middle fifties but the girl could only have been seven or eight years of age. She looked terrified at what the man was doing to her and forcing her to do to him. It was the most revolting thing I'd ever seen in my life.

"Who is that dirty bastard?" Stan's voice was tight with anger and disgust.

I looked at Piper and he nodded his consent for me to answer. "It is an RAF officer named Janner." I could hear the anger in my own voice.

Piper was the first to regain his composure. He gently took the photographs from the table and placed them in his briefcase. He turned to pick up the remains of the broken frame and spoke to Stan.

"I'm afraid, Mr Cornish, you're in for a long night. I must ask you to accompany us back to West Fen." He turned to me. "Sam, take Mr Cornish direct to SHQ and wait outside. I'll clear his entry at the guardroom. I'll also contact Wareham, Houseman and the Station Commander. I think it is best we meet well away from your section."

We walked out to the vehicles and Piper threw the picture frame on to the back seat of his car. "Let me go first," he instructed as he climbed into the driving seat and pressed the starter. "I need to organise a pass for Mr Cornish."

We followed his dim taillights down the track and let him surge ahead until he was lost from view. We drove in silence for a while but I could feel Stan bursting with curiosity.

"As we've to stay away from your section, does that mean that dirty bastard was one of yours?" I could hear the disbelief in his voice.

I'd no right to breach security but I trusted the little guy and he'd a right to know what was going on. "He was my boss at one time, until he got the push."

"They should push the dirty bugger all the way to the Witham and drown the bastard."

"Easy, Stan," I tried to calm him. "We know where he is and he'll be punished."

"I bloody well hope so."

I glanced at him in surprise. There was a viciousness there I had not heard before. I began to think that maybe I didn't know this little man as well as I thought I did.

When we arrived at West Fen, Piper had primed the policeman on the gate and there was already a temporary pass waiting for Stan. He didn't even have to get out of the car to sign for it. I drove round to the front of SHQ and switched off the engine. We sat in silence apart from the lonely muttering of a Merlin being run up out on the airfield.

"Eerie bloody place," Stan said with a shiver.

"It can be much worse, believe me."

Hooded headlights swept up behind us and blinked out as the engine of the vehicle died.

I climbed out and was met by the station commander. He slammed his car door and walked towards me. "Is that you, Carver?"

"Yes, sir. I also have Mr Cornish with me."

I couldn't see his face in the dark but I sensed his hesitation but he knew a civilian would not be here unless Piper had agreed.

"Okay, let's get inside. Piper has gone to pick up Jake Houseman and Tim Wareham."

The policeman on duty at the desk inside SHQ checked our passes and we walked down the corridor to Groupie's little conference room. Just as we were removing our coats, Piper arrived with Houseman and Wareham. We settled into chairs around the table and Groupie opened the proceedings.

"Right, Mr Piper. What's all the panic?"

Piper gave a quick résumé of our meeting at the cottage and Stan's discovery of the photographs. He removed the photos from his briefcase and handed them to Groupie. I saw he'd placed them in acetate envelopes.

The Groupie's sense of self-control was legendary on the station but this time he failed the test. His eyes widened in shock and he actually gave an audible gasp. He handed them on to Houseman in silence. I don't think he could find any words to prepare Jake for the shock.

"My God!" Houseman flicked through the photos quickly and passed them on to Wareham.

The provost officer looked at them for a long time. His face was white when he finally spoke. "Yesterday I was going through the records of the intelligence staff on this station. In 1937, Squadron Leader Janner, as he was then, was on the staff of the RAF College at Cranwell. He was suddenly posted to the Middle East because of, and I quote, 'a misdemeanour.' No explanation was given as to what that misdemeanour was but I'm sure the college commandant at that time will know the reason for the posting. I've arranged to talk to him tomorrow and I fear that Mr Janner was already known for this sort of thing."

"Where is Janner now?" asked Piper.

"Five Group HQ," answered Groupie. "They thought they could keep an eye on him there. He, of course, is in his element. All those senior officers? Just up his street."

"So Janner was being blackmailed into revealing our secret ops orders and targets to the local cell?" Houseman's voice shook with anger.

Piper nodded. "Certainly looks like it."

"What happens now?" asked Houseman.

Piper put the photos back into his briefcase and rose to his feet. "I've already notified the Special Investigation Branch to have him placed under immediate Mess Arrest." He glanced at his watch. "They should be detaining him about now and I'll need a statement from Mr Cornish and young Carver here. I wonder if your lads could do that for me, Tim?"

Wareham nodded. "No problem, David." He too rose and headed for the door. "I'll get somebody round here right away or Mr Cornish will never get home to bed."

"What about me, sir?" I joked.

He paused at the door. "I think the two words which come instantly to mind, young Carver, are 'tough' and 'cheese'. You're paid for this job but Mr Cornish has a farm to run."

I made a face as he closed the door behind him. "Nobody understands me."

Houseman laughed. "Oh, but we do, Carver, only too well!"

Groupie stood and walked round the table to where Stan was sitting. He put a hand on the farmer's shoulder.

"Mr Cornish, I've heard a lot about you and I know we owe you a debt of gratitude for helping us find the airstrip. You took a big risk, along with Carver here, in carrying out that recce. It took a lot of guts to do that and it was far beyond what should be expected of a civilian in wartime."

Stan tried to joke to cover his embarrassment. "I only went along to keep young Carver out of trouble, sir."

Groupie laughed. "Don't go anywhere near Carver, Mr Cornish. He's a magnet for trouble."

I grinned ruefully. "May I remind you, sir, this was all your idea? I just came here, minding my own business and look what you landed me with."

Groupie laughed and went back to his chair. "You may remind me, Carver, but it'll do you damn all good." His grin faded and he looked at me seriously. "I understand that more congratulations are due to you. I heard all about your foreign holiday. Superb job. Sorry about the casualties."

I glanced at Stan and he was justifiably puzzled. I turned back to Groupie. "Thank you, sir. I saw the final results of the trip this morning." I felt uncomfortable as I failed to hide the tremor that passed through me.

He nodded slowly. "So I gather. I also understand you saw our other friend. What did you think of him?"

I thought for a few seconds but I knew I was going to be honest with him. "It may seem strange to you, sir, but I actually like him."

I saw Houseman's head jerk up to look at me but I carried on. "He's a very intelligent man and I'm afraid we'll only get to know what he wants us to know. He's still loyal to his country and I know he's holding out on certain aspects of his role over here."

Groupie stroked his chin. "Mm...so you think the others are wasting their time with him?"

"Yes, sir."

He looked at me intently for a while and then turned to Houseman. "Jake, do you need this young man tomorrow?"

Houseman looked puzzled. "No, sir. He still has a long way to go before he gets to know the job but all these diversions are not helping." He looked at me and shook his head. "Having said that, I reckon we owe him a lot."

Groupie nodded. "In that case, Carver, I want you to take the next couple of days off as unofficial leave. You look all in and I'm damned sure you need a little time to get over what you witnessed this morning. I suggest you get away and get plenty of rest. Where is your home?"

"Near Brighton, sir."

As I answered Groupie, I looked at Houseman and raised an eyebrow.

"No," he replied without even batting an eyelid. "She's going down to Grantham tomorrow on a course that will last two days."

"Who is?" asked Groupie, looking puzzled.

Houseman remained impassive. "I'll explain later, sir. Anyway, Carver, it is peace and quiet you need." There was not even the trace of a smile on his face but his eyes said it all.

"If it's peace and quiet he needs he can stay at my place." Stan looked uncomfortable as the three of us looked at him in surprise.

Groupie looked at me. "What do you say to that, Carver?"

I looked at Stan's face and I knew what I had to say. "Sounds just the job to me, sir." The look on Stan's face told me I'd said the right thing.

Groupie stood and collected his coat from the coat stand. "I must get on. The squadrons should be starting to drift back soon. Stay here by all means. Wareham's lads will want you here for the statements. I'll see you tomorrow, Jake."

We all stood as Groupie left the room.

Houseman cocked his head to one side. "Sound like the first ones are back already."

I could now 'read' the sound of the Merlins. The engine note would change as the pilot selected the prop pitch for landing and adjusted the power as the wheels and flaps came down. I waited for the first one to cross the boundary fence and listened to the mighty Merlins popping and banging as the pilot throttled back on round out. I even heard the squeal of the main wheel tyres.

"The first of many, I hope," said Houseman with feeling.

Stan had been watching us both carefully. When he spoke there was surprise in his voice. "Do you know something?" he asked.

We both looked at him in surprise but said nothing.

Stan struggled to pluck up the courage to finish what he'd started. He decided he'd gone too far to pull out now. "You both love this war." He really had gone the whole way. It was a dangerous thing to say to a man.

I opened my mouth to protest but Houseman raised a hand to stop me. He sat back in his chair. "I know what you're saying, Mr Cornish, but it's not quite as straightforward as that. We don't love the war, but we do revel in the challenges. How is one tested on one's mettle in peacetime? Success in business maybe? Or even success in sport? In this game you're tested on what some call courage but what I call pigheadedness. Carver here hates war and so do I, but I've a love for aeroplanes that could, if I let it, equal the love I have for my wife. I love the atmosphere of organised chaos and the camaraderie. As I listened to that Lanc landing, I could feel the relief of the crew at still being alive but knowing that relief is tempered by the knowledge that they may have to go out again tomorrow night and the night after that." He paused as another Lanc roared overhead. "Can you understand what I'm saying, Mr Cornish?"

Stan nodded. "Yes, I think I can, but what I can't understand is why, even when events are at their most dangerous, you have to push it that little bit harder. Sam here, for instance, when he walked back to that chap at the airstrip and stroked the bloody barrel of the machine gun ... I nearly died on the spot. It was as if he needed to push himself that little bit more."

Houseman looked at me and shook his head. "I think Sam is a special case, Mr Cornish."

Stan laughed. "I think he's a nut case."

Houseman rose and joined in the laughter. "I agree with you, Mr Cornish. Then again, he's needed your help and you've always been there for him. Don't tell me you're not enjoying your role in all this cloak and dagger stuff"

Stan grinned. "Best time I've had in years."

Houseman put a hand on Stan's shoulder. "In that case, you should not be so surprised at our reaction to this unreal life we're forced to lead."

"I'm learning by the minute, sir," replied Stan soberly.

After we had made our statements to Wareham's men, Stan and I stopped off at the mess for me to collect my toilet articles and a change of clothes. As I drove us off the station I asked casually "How many bedrooms do you have?"

"Only one furnished."

There was an awkward silence and then he started to laugh. "Don't worry, boy, I only have a single bed and there's not room for two in that. I've a spare mattress and you can sleep on the floor in the living room. It'll be warmer there. I keep the fire in all night."

I began to relax and although I couldn't spend the two days with Nat, I knew I'd enjoy myself at the farm and Houseman was right, I needed the rest. I looked at the little man's silhouette in the first light of the false dawn. "You did a superb job tonight, you know."

I saw his silhouette change as he turned to face me. "Beginner's luck."

"That's my excuse."

He laughed. "You are a bloody excuse. An excuse for what ...I've no idea. Now put your foot down, I've got to be at work in an hour's time."

"You're not working this morning surely?" I protested.

"I'm a farmer, boy. Farmers work from six in the morning until it's too dark to work. I'm not a gentleman farmer, living a life of leisure whilst others do the work for a pittance."

"Do I detect a socialist note creeping in here?"

"Bollocks!"

We were still laughing when I braked to a halt outside the farmhouse. Dog gave us his usual frantic welcome and had to be removed from the sitting room when he insisted on sitting on the mattress Stan had provided for me.

Whilst I was having a quick wash and settling into my bed in front of the fire, Stan was upstairs changing into his working clothes. He came down in his old corduroys, held up with broad braces, a collarless shirt and waistcoat. I looked up at him. "Are you sure you wouldn't like me to give you a hand today?"

He laughed as he headed out of the door. "You'd be more of a hindrance than a help. Just get some sleep."

My two days at the farm did me a power of good. The first day I slept soundly until three in the afternoon when Dog woke me by licking my face. I helped Stan knock up a dinner and we spent the rest of the evening chatting and drinking home made wine. Whether it was the wine or the good company I'm not sure, but I slept soundly again until ten the next morning. After lunch, or dinner as Stan insisted on calling it, I helped out on the farm for a couple of hours but had to give it up when I began to fail, both mentally and physically. I was much better employed preparing the evening meal. I'd intended making the suggestion that we go to the Lancaster Arms that evening but Stan dropped off to sleep in his chair after the meal and I didn't have the heart to disturb him. For me it was another undisturbed night of rest.

The following morning I rose at six o'clock, as I wanted to get back to camp early and get changed for work. After breakfast I threw my bag into the car and turned to the little farmer.

"I don't think I need to tell you how much I've appreciated the last couple of days, Stan."

He looked pleased. "It has been a pleasure having you here. Dog will take another couple of days getting back to normal after all the fuss you've given him."

I looked up at the farmhouse. It looked solid and welcoming. "You know, you're a very lucky man, Stan."

He turned and followed my gaze. "I suppose I am really. It just makes me sad when I think what my life could have been."

"Be thankful for what you have, my friend," I said quietly.

He turned back to me. "Aye, you're right I suppose." He rubbed his hands together vigorously. "Now get along with you. I've work to do."

I smiled at his way of not making a fuss of farewells. "See you, Stan!" I shouted out of the window as I slipped the clutch on the little Fiat. He just waved and headed for the barn.

I was in the section by eight o'clock but it was pretty quiet. Tom Powell was pinning up changes to the Bulletin Board.

"Morning, Sarge. Quiet this morning. Where is everybody?"

He glanced around. "Morning, sir. Yes, we've a stand down. No ops for two days. You certainly know when to come back to work!"

I grinned. "Takes a lot of training to be good at avoiding work."

"Modest as ever," called Nat from behind me.

I turned and she was smiling as she slipped off her coat. Spring was knocking on nature's door, but it was still chilly in the mornings. As she walked towards me, I marvelled again at the way she could still look beautiful, even when wearing the shapeless WAAF uniform. I also saw, out of the corner of my eye, Tom Powell quickly gather up his bits and pieces and head tactfully back to his office. The word was obviously out about Nat and me.

"Report to the Intelligence Library at once!" I grinned as I said it.

"Sorry, aircrew already in there."

"Main briefing room then."

"Our airmen are bumpering the floor." She tossed her head and watched me out of her eye corners.

"Alright then, the bloody broom cupboard!" I was desperate.

"Oh, that's nice, Carver," she laughed. "You're so romantic."

I sighed in frustration. "I try. God, how I try!"

She placed her hands on my shoulders and rocked me gently backwards and forwards. "Well don't, you might burst something."

"Chance would be a fine thing."

"Carver! You're disgusting." She started sorting out coloured pins from a map drawer. "Have you heard the latest gossip?" she asked.

"No, I've heard nothing for two days. I've been catching up on my shuteye at Stan's farm."

She nodded. "Houseman told me you were skiving off with the blessing of the station commander. I don't think he was being serious."

I jumped up and sat on the edge of the map table. "Come on then, girl, what's the

350

hot gossip?"

"Hammond has gone AWOL."

"He's probably pissed in the bottom of a ditch and can't get out. When did he disappear?"

"Failed to turn up for duty about three days ago." I could see she was actually concerned.

"Has he taken his stuff from his room?" I asked.

She shook her head. "Not according to the RAF police."

"Who knows he's missing... from the section I mean?"

"Just the officers, so far."

I decided to put a toe in the water. "Have you heard anything of Janner since he left?"

She looked at me in surprise. "What made you dig him up again?"

So they had not been told yet. I decided to do a quick cover up. "Oh, nothing – just another guy I couldn't stand. Which reminds me, where's Christian?"

"With the others bumpering the floor in the briefing room."

The outer door opened and Houseman rushed in. "Ah, the return of the prodigal son. Morning, Carver - Morning, Natalie."

"Morning, sir," I replied as I hopped off the table and headed for his office.

Houseman laughed. "You see, Natalie, I don't even need to tell him any more. He's very perceptive."

Natalie smiled and called out loudly enough for me to hear as I exited through the door. "He just responds well to kindness, sir."

I gave her a two-fingered response behind my back.

"Dreadful manners though," Houseman remarked dryly.

Once settled into his office he took a file from his safe and opened it on his desk.

"Wing Commander Janner's file from his interview with David Piper and his gang."

"He denied everything, of course," I remarked with a grin.

"Oh, absolutely," replied Houseman. "Then they showed him the photos. That stopped him in his tracks but, once he'd recovered from the shock, he did the usual bluster. Said they were fakes and insisted on an interview with the AOC. Piper pointed out that the AOC had actually authorised his arrest and that the photos had been tested by their lab and had been pronounced authentic and untouched in any way."

"Checkmate."

"The word required begins with 'C' but it should have been 'collapse'," Houseman corrected me. "He folded and started blubbing about how he had been drugged and forced into the act without being aware of what he was doing. It didn't wash of course, because you saw the photos and it was obvious he was enjoying every minute."

"How did he get trapped in the first place?"

"He met an Irish lady in Boston. She took him home and that is how it started. Ring a bell?"

"Smith?"

He nodded. "Exactly. She was Smith's younger sister. She actually let the perverted bastard interfere with her little daughter, all in the grand cause of the IRA. I don't think they knew who he was at that stage. They just knew they had a senior officer. What a piece of luck when he finally boasted he was in charge of the intelligence section at West Fen. He dovetailed nicely into the airstrip operation."

"So he signalled the information from his own office window?" I said and couldn't keep the incredulity out of my voice.

Houseman gave me a long and hard look and I could tell he was going to enjoy the next few seconds. "No, not at all," he said with a straight face.

"What?" I nearly yelled the question.

He placed his elbows on the table and leaned towards me. "Smith and his cronies didn't think him trustworthy enough so they made sure they got somebody else to keep an eye on him. Somebody who'd use his office for passing signals and Janner would turn a blind eye."

I stared at him in amazement. "Two bloody agents in the same section? Oh, come on, sir, that's bloody impossible!"

He just shook his head.

I wracked my brain to find another traitor and suddenly I had him. "Christian," I said in triumph.

Houseman didn't even blink. "Why do you say that?"

I found myself huffing and puffing trying to find a reasonable cause to think Christian could be a traitor. "He just doesn't fit in," I finally announced feebly.

Houseman sat motionless. "How many times have I told you, Carver, not to let your heart rule your head?"

I remained silent, ashamed of my lack of ability to justify my choice of Christian as a traitor.

Houseman shook his head and raised a cautionary finger. "You just elected Christian to the status of traitor simply because you hate his guts. I must confess, so do I. He's an arrogant little shit but I'm afraid he's not our man."

I sighed. "You'd better put me out of my misery, sir."

He paused and then dropped the bombshell. "Hammond."

I wiped a hand over my eyes. "Not another bloody pervert?"

Houseman shook his head. "No, an altogether different kettle of fish. It seems our man, Hammond, is in debt up to his eyeballs. At the end of each month he has a colossal mess bill but always manages to pay it. He's also a compulsive gambler and poker player. If his winnings paid off the mess bill there would have been no grounds for suspicion but it seems he's a heavy loser. So, where did the money come from? According to Janner, a gentleman would meet Hammond in Boston on the third Wednesday of every month, work permitting, and hand him a considerable amount of cash. How could he do this, you may ask? He simply did it because he didn't give a shit. As long as the bills were paid he'd sell the information."

"Now he's AWOL," I added quietly.

Houseman sighed. "I'm afraid so. Would you like to make a stab at when he went AWOL?"

I shook my head.

"The day after you shot Smith," he replied.

I looked at him and watched his reaction. "In that case, he's dead."

I just got that impassive look of his. "Why do you say that?"

"He took nothing from his room. He's been killed to tie up the loose ends."

"By whom?" Houseman asked carefully.

"By the same people who killed Smith."

"Supposition," he replied dryly.

I placed my hands palms down on the table. "Look, sir, Smith was killed for the same reason. His killer thought Meacher was already dead. Fine, get rid of Smith before he could be captured alive and be made to talk. Janner was out of the way for now but of possible use later. That left Hammond out on a limb. A pisshead and gambler who couldn't be trusted. The mess bill business would eventually be spotted and, being Hammond, he'd have squawked like a chicken with its head in the fox's mouth. They've tidied everything up. He's dead."

"Who exactly has done the tidying up, as you put it?"

"How the fuck should I know? Why does everybody think that I've all the fucking answers?" I exploded and immediately regretted my outburst.

Houseman said nothing. There was just that impassive expression that gave nothing away.

I stood up. "I'm sorry, sir, that was totally uncalled for. I'm out of my depth again and the whole situation has really got to me. I apologise for my outburst."

He motioned me back into my chair. "Sit down, Sam, sit down." He waited until I was back in my chair before he spoke and when he did, I knew he'd already forgiven me my little tantrum.

"Last night, I had a call from David Piper. He told me you'd be refreshed after your rest and maybe that brain of yours could put a different slant on the whole affair. He was right, wasn't he?"

I managed a small smile. "It seems he was, sir."

He nodded. "So, what are your thoughts on this affair as it stands at the moment?"

I assembled my thoughts and used the time to regain my composure.

"The cell is not finished, sir. There is a professional still out there, plus a radio operator. What I cannot understand is why they didn't find a radio at the farm? When I spoke to Meacher about finding a radio, he actually looked relieved when I told him we'd found it at the cottage. There has to be a radio at that farm!"

Houseman tapped the table with his pencil. "Sorry, Sam, no radio. Face and Piper both say the farm is clean."

I tried another tack. "Surely all airwaves must be monitored or something, in order to detect any unofficial transmissions?"

Houseman nodded. "Indeed, according to Face, the odd rogue transmission has originated in this area, but it was short and in code. No time to get a fix on its location."

"Have there been any more transmissions since Meacher and Smith were removed from the scene?"

"There you've got me. I've no idea. You must ask Face that question."

I started in my chair as the telephone rang. Houseman picked up the receiver and sat listening for some time. His eyes came up from the file in front of him and met mine. "Thank you," he said quietly and put the receiver back on its rest. He brought his right hand up to his nose and massaged the bridge. His eyes were closed and he had that tired look again. He spoke after a long pause.

"They've found Hammond."

"Dead?" I asked but I already knew the answer.

"Very," he replied. "At least three or four days."

"Where?"

"Place called Moorby."

"Moorby!" I exclaimed. "What was he doing out there? Also, how the hell did he get out there?"

Houseman sighed. "I too can get pissed off by too many questions, Carver."

I backed off quickly. "I'm sorry, sir, but can I ask just one more?"

He nodded and slumped back in his chair.

353

"How did he die?" I asked him.

"He hanged himself."

I shook my head. "I can't believe that, sir. Hammond didn't have the guts to do that. Take my word for it, he was murdered."

Houseman gave a sardonic laugh. "By hell, Carver, when you get your teeth into something you're like a bloody terrier."

I ignored him. "When did they find him?"

"Just now. Two young boys playing in the woods found the body. His ID and a letter were in his pocket. The kids got an adult to phone the guardroom. That was Wareham on the phone."

"Can I go out there?"

He sighed. "Will you stop asking bloody questions if I say 'yes'?"

I grinned as I leapt to my feet. "Nary another query will pass my lips, sir."

"Then piss off. I'll pass your thoughts on to Face and Piper. No doubt they'll be on their way here as soon as I tell them of Hammond's demise."

I headed for the door but he stopped me. "Carver, better not go in the Fiat. This had better look official. I'll call MT and get transport for you. Wareham has already gone up there or you could've had a lift with him."

He picked up the phone and I saw a small smile appear on his lips. "MT? George? - Jake Houseman here. Any chance Pilot Officer Carver could have his girlfriend and a vehicle? Ah, thank you, George. Yes, right away please, at the intelligence centre." He replaced the receiver and grinned at me. "Bourne is being despatched post haste with your chariot."

I grimaced. "You're very kind, sir."

He laughed. "I know I am, Carver. I'm especially kind seeing as you're now quite capable of driving yourself. Now piss off!"

CHAPTER TWENTY-FIVE

Twenty minutes later, Foghorn and I were belting down the seven-mile straight. From the rocking of the Tilly and her antics at the wheel, I decided the Lincolnshire County Council had a serious subsidence problem with their fenland roads. It was akin to riding a roller coaster.

"What's this place, Moorby?" Foghorn was as blunt as usual.

I decided to build up the suspense. "Very small village."

"Then why are we busting our arses to get there?"

I tired of the suspense. "We're going to see a corpse."

"Fuckin' hell!" The car veered momentarily as she corrected the sudden divergence in our course.

"Nicely put, as usual," I laughed.

"Are you bleedin' serious, Petal?" Her eyebrows were somewhere up near her hairline.

"Perfectly. Well, I'm going to see a corpse. You don't have to."

"Who is it?"

"One of the officers from my section. Guy called Hammond. The usual 'keep your trap shut' rules apply."

"Oh, the pisshead."

I glanced at her in surprise. "You knew him?"

"Every bugger knew him, Petal. He's had more lifts back to camp, in the back of MT trucks, than I've had hot dinners. You'd find him staggering about all over the bloody neighbourhood."

I nodded. "He certainly liked his pop."

She braked to a halt at the New Bolingbroke level crossing as a steam locomotive hauled countless flatbed wagons across our bows. On each flatbed there was a tank or a couple of Bren gun carriers. The irregular pattern was repeated all the way along the train. Finally the guard's van passed and the guard waved from his platform at the rear of the van. Foghorn gave him a little 'toot' on the horn in reply.

The signalman came down from his box and opened the gates to let us on our way.

A convoy of RAF lorries laden with bombs impeded our progress out near Revesby but we were soon scanning the roadside as we neared Moorby, looking for clues as to the scene of Hammond's demise. We saw three cars, an ambulance and a solitary, rather elderly police constable in a dip in the road by The Royal Oak, a small public house.

"Dis am de place, Massa!" Bourne muttered as she braked to a halt.

The constable wheeled his bicycle slowly towards the car. He looked a morose old boy but his uniform was well pressed and his cape was neatly folded over his shoulder. He propped his bike up against the nearby fence and leaned down to look into the car.

"You another for the body?" He asked the question with an air that did nothing to disguise the fact that he didn't give a shit one way or the other.

"That's right, constable," I replied whilst Foghorn fixed him with her best leer.

He tried hard not to look at her and fixed his eyes steadfastly on mine. "Past the pub and into the trees. You'll find some of your police there and they'll direct you to the body."

"Thank you," I replied as I climbed out. I leaned back into the Tilly and tapped Foghorn on the shoulder. "Do you want to come with me?"

She didn't even look at me, she was too engrossed with the poor old policeman.

"No thank you, Petal. I think I'll try to get the constable into those other trees, over there. He looks like a bit of rumpy-pumpy would do him a power of good."

The poor chap tried to laugh but his face ended up like a death's head rictus! I felt sorry for him. He was going to have a difficult couple of hours. Nothing in his training could have prepared him for the likes of Foghorn.

By the time I reached the actual scene, having been guided there by the two RAF policemen, Hammond had been cut down. Two ambulancemen were strapping his body to a stretcher as I approached the group. A tall civilian and a police inspector accompanied our provost officer.

Wareham glanced up at my approach. "Morning, Carver. Bad business, eh?"

I nodded. "Any doubt in your mind he committed suicide, sir?"

Wareham looked at me intently. "Why on earth should you ask me that?"

No sense in pissing about. "I think he was murdered, sir."

He sighed. "Another of your hunches?"

"I'm afraid so, sir."

Wareham turned to a tall, bald-headed man with half moon spectacles. He was carrying a small Gladstone bag and he turned to peer at me over the half moons.

Wareham nodded in my direction. "Dr Potter, I'd like you to meet Pilot Officer Sam Carver. He claims to be an amateur but he has an uncanny knack of hitting the nail on the head without even trying."

Potter nodded a welcome. "I think he's done it again."

Wareham looked at him in surprise. "I'm sorry, what did you say?"

Potter stooped to pick up a piece of rope from the grass. He held it out to display the noose. "What do you think of that for a tidy bit of knotting?"

Wareham shrugged. "Very neat?"

Potter nodded. "Exactly. It's too perfect for a man who still has the smell of whisky about him. No way could that man, in the state he must have been in, have climbed into the tree, tied such a perfect noose and then thrown himself off the branch. He must have been as pissed as a parrot. He'd have had trouble walking, let alone climb a ruddy tree."

The police inspector pointed to the base of the tree. "In addition to that, Dr Potter, I think the amount of flattened grass also lends credence to the supposition that there were more persons here than just the dead man."

Wareham turned to him. "Surely the boys who discovered the body would have been responsible for some of that?"

The inspector shook his head. "They saw the body from a distance and they ran for their lives. You saw how careful we were not to disturb the scene. That flattened grass was already there. I think your man is right."

"Shit!" cursed Wareham. "Why is nothing ever simple in this job?"

Potter clapped a hand on Wareham's shoulder and picked up his Gladstone bag. "Don't worry, old boy, I'll arrange the postmortom. That should help us to come to a proper conclusion. Bye for now."

We watched him stride away, whistling happily to himself.

Wareham called his lads over and instructed them to guard the area until the civilian forensic team and the SIB investigators had gone over the scene.

Just as we reached the road, a car swept past and then screeched to a halt. It reversed rapidly and stopped. "Damned nearly missed you!" Face called as he scrambled out, followed by Piper.

I glanced at my watch. "How the heck did you get here so soon, sir?"

"We were only over at Grantham, having a few more words with your friend Janner, when I got Tim's message. I hear you've had another of your famous theories, Carver?"

Wareham answered for me. "It looks as if he's right too. Well, at least he has the doctor on his side. He's gone off to get the postmortom under way."

Piper puffed on his briar. "Got a murderer for us yet, Sam?"

I smiled sheepishly. "I'm afraid not, sir."

Face walked round to the back of the car and opened the boot. He took out a pair of wellingtons and began to remove his shoes. "You'd better show us where it happened," he puffed with the effort of bending.

The police inspector led us back into the trees and, as we walked, he explained the circumstances of the discovery of the body.

Piper grunted. "Bit of a shock for the boys."

The inspector grinned. "It might do the little devils a bit of good. They're both a pain in the neck around here. Always where they shouldn't be and up to everything they ought not to be."

We stopped a little way from the tree for Face and Piper to get an overall impression before we moved in closer.

Face cleared his throat. "What do you think, David?"

Piper frowned. "Was this flattening of the grass caused by the boys, the doctor and the ambulance crew?"

The police inspector nodded. "The outer area, yes. The grass immediately under the tree we tried to keep as it was. We actually pulled the body to one side with an old broken branch, in order to prevent further interference with the ground under the tree as we cut him down."

Face looked approvingly at the inspector. "Good thinking."

Piper wandered off on another path. His head was down as he carefully studied the ground. He was some way off when he finally straightened up and sighed. "Carver's right, I'm afraid. There are distinct marks here where the heels of somebody's shoes have been dragged over the ground. They must have carried him the last bit. Was there an abnormal amount of mud around the heels of his shoes?"

The inspector nodded. "First thing Dr Potter noticed. He's a sharp old bird. I think he knew it was a murder scene right from the start but he said nothing until this young officer arrived." He nodded in my direction.

Face sighed. "That's it then."

Piper nodded. "I'm afraid so."

Face turned to the inspector. "Had he been to that little pub we just passed?"

"Not as far as we can gather. The landlady said she gets very few RAF types. Most of her customers are the guards from the POW camp. I think it's a bit out in the wilds for the RAF. She was certain there had been no RAF personnel in for at least two weeks."

"But who the fuck is doing the killing?" Face was getting impatient with our lack of progress and it was beginning to show. We simply followed him back to the road in silence as none of us could answer the question.

When we reached the cars, I noticed the elderly constable was now some way away down the lane. He was casting uneasy glances in the direction of Foghorn, who was sitting in our Tilly and smirking happily to herself. I walked over and tapped on the window and she wound it down.

"Nothing doing?" I nodded at the constable.

She grinned. "Poor old sod, he's only a 'special'. I don't reckon he knows what a blow-job is."

I smothered a grin. "You should be locked up."

Her grin spread wickedly. "Funny, that's what he said."

I shook my head and rejoined the others.

"There's bugger all else we can do here," Face was saying. "The teams can get on with the forensics and let us know the results later. We might as well get back to West Fen and take a closer look at the stuff taken from Hammond's room. He turned to me. "Carver, you can follow us back and we'll impose upon Jake's hospitality and use the conference room again."

We climbed into our cars and Foghorn waited until they turned around in the direction of West Fen. We were already pointing the right way and followed behind as they set off. It began to rain heavily and we dropped back a little to cut down the effect of the spray from the car in front. The woods either side of the road looked dark and forbidding, even with their new spring foliage.

"What a bloody awful place to die," Foghorn muttered.

"I couldn't agree more."

I wrapped my greatcoat tighter around my body and felt uneasy. I seemed to be getting more than my fair share of death these days. I glanced up as we neared the POW camp. Smoke drifted up from the chimneys of the huts but it didn't rise in the heavy air. It drifted low across the road and its acrid odour filled the car.

Foghorn nodded at the camp. "I bet they're pleased they're out of the war."

"Maybe, at least most of them will be, although I suppose there are a few hardened souls who would like to get back and fight for the Fatherland."

"Have any actually tried to escape?"

I shrugged. "I've no idea."

"What's that big tower?" Foghorn was full of questions today.

I looked over at the huge tower that dominated the camp compound. "Water tower, I suppose." I replied idly.

The camp passed out of sight as we headed on for Revesby. Then the thought struck me like a lightening bolt.

"Stop the car!" I was yelling and waving my arms. Then I realised my mistake as she slammed on the brakes. "No! No! Blow your bloody hooter - stop them for fuck's sake." I jabbed my finger in the direction of the car in front, now rapidly fading into the rain.

"Make your bloody mind up, Petal." She gunned the engine and charged after Face and Piper, blowing the horn, which sounded about as raucous as a duck with laryngitis.

"Not much of a bloody horn!" I shouted above the roar of the engine.

"As the art mistress said to the bishop." She only just managed to shout the riposte before she had to stand on the brakes to avoid ramming into the back of the other car. We slithered to a halt just inches from their bumper.

"Shit!" she panted. "Amazing what effect even a little horn can have."

For once I didn't find her funny. Face was already climbing out of the passenger seat when I ran forward to meet him.

"What the hell is going on, Carver?"

I yanked open the rear passenger door of his car and ducked inside. "Get back in out of the rain, sir. I've just had an idea."

He got back in the car but he wasn't looking too happy.

Piper had switched off the engine and was half-turned in his seat, watching me. "Don't tell me," he sighed. "Carver's had another bloody hunch."

"Wouldn't you know it!" Face muttered as he wiped the rain from his forehead. "Come on, Sherlock, out with it."

Now I was sitting in the car and having caused all the fuss, my confidence began to desert me. For Christ's sake, it had only been a slender notion in the first place and now it seemed pathetically scant on substance. Nevertheless, I had to give it a go.

"What would it take to convince you both that the German POWs, from Meacher's farm, murdered Hammond?"

"Proof," Face demanded.

"Okay," I continued. "Let us assume for now that they did. Is it fair to assume they'd have to have had orders from a higher authority to carry out the act?"

Piper nodded. "In order to go along with your fantasy, I'll say 'yes' to that. Mind you, they could have acted as freelances. Maybe they are werewolves in disguise?"

"Are you taking the piss, sir?"

"Yes, I am, Carver, but carry on and let us see what you're getting at."

I leaned forward in my seat. "If they needed to get clearance for the hit, who did they get it from and how did they get it?"

They both remained silent. This was going to be hard work.

"Look, I'm sure that Smith was taken out on the spur of the moment. I reckon the shooting of Meacher took them by surprise. They had a pretty good idea Smith would be captured and they had to get rid of him quick. Now they have two more weak cards in the pack. Hammond is a piss artist and Janner a coward. Funnily enough, I reckon Janner being a coward has saved his skin. His weakness and new position in Five Group HQ meant he was still of value to the cell. The only remaining fly in the ointment was poor old Hammond. He'd shop them as soon as they stopped coming up with the ever-increasing amounts of cash to settle his debts. He was also a worry to Janner. If Hammond went down, Janner knew he'd go down with him. What a boost it would be to Janner's morale if Hammond were to commit suicide. He'd not be able to resist the tempting offer of more kids and he'd be in the perfect place to give the cell all they wanted." I paused to take stock and the other two just stared at the rain running down the windscreen. Their frowns boosted my confidence. At last I had them thinking.

Face threw his gloves on to the dashboard as if in disgust as he spoke. "Go on, Carver. Don't stop when you're getting to the good bit."

I caught Piper's eyes on me in the rear view mirror and I spoke as if to him only. I needed eye contact to get the next bit across. "If we've now agreed to my hypothesis, let's look at something that will sound even more fantastic. After the death of Smith, your search teams found no radio at the farm and we already had possession of the radio from Smith's cottage. So, if our two POWs needed authority, and I'm damned sure they would, how did they get their orders? I can see only two ways and I don't think you're going to like either." I took a deep breath and leaned back in my seat but my eyes remained locked with Piper's eyes. "Either they got their orders from a high ranker in the cell, somebody we don't know about, or they got the authorisation for the hit direct from Berlin - by radio!"

Face flung the passenger door open and climbed out into the rain. He didn't say a word - just slammed the door closed and walked off up the road, head down and hands thrust deep into his raincoat pockets. I made a move to go after him but Piper reached over the back of his seat and restrained me.

"Don't worry, Carver... Yes, it's something you said but I know him when he goes off like that - he needs time and space to think. Bloody hell, I can see what you're going to say next and I find it a preposterous supposition but I can also see how it could be a reality. We've been through the records of all the contacts and acquaintances of both Meacher and Smith. We found nothing on any of them to cause alarm. I'd bet my pension that there are no more agents remaining in this cell. Your POWs have no chance to meet with or contact any strangers without arousing the suspicion of the locals. If there is still a radio at the farm, as you suspect, there is no way they could get to the farm to use the radio, as they have been reassigned to another farmer." He paused and peered through the windscreen as Face loomed up at the side of the car. "I think, young Carver, we are about to see if my colleague has drawn the same conclusions." He leaned over and opened the passenger door to let Face into the car.

The wing commander slumped into his seat and closed the door gently. He was breathing hard and he waited for a few moments to get his breath back. He pulled out a handkerchief and began dry the rain from his face. He didn't turn to look at me when he spoke but when he did, it was without any preamble. "You think there is a covert radio transmitter in the POW camp."

Again Piper's eyes flicked to the mirror as I spoke.

"Yes, sir."

"God! You're so bloody plausible, Carver. Next you'll have me thinking Snow White is another bloody Mata Hari."

I kept my voice serious as I tried to break the tension that had built up in the car. "Well, she did have some very strange mates down in the forest, sir, and I don't think that guy Dopey was as daft as he looked!"

To my relief they both laughed and I knew we were back to work.

"Can we visit the camp?" I asked.

Face shook his head. "Not without the permission of the army."

"Surely they'd let us in for a quick look?"

"No way!" He said it with a finality that was depressing.

"Surely we could ask the camp commander a few discreet questions?" I was pushing it now.

"Like what?" It was Piper this time.

"Like where are they working now? Where were they on each day of last week? Maybe grab some of their footwear to see if it matches up with anything in the woods where we found Hammond. Any fucking thing, sir. Just let's give it a try."

Piper sighed. "We'll have to interrogate them later anyway, even if it is just to eliminate them from our enquiries." He turned to Face and gave a rueful grin. "I suppose it would save us some time if we could do some of the spade work now"

Face shook his head. "Bloody hell, you're getting as bad as Carver."

Piper grinned. "Maybe he has something that's catching."

Face sighed and turned to me. "Carver, if we all get court martialled for this, I'll personally see that you end up in the bloody Tower of London."

"It is the tower at the camp that interests me," I replied half to myself.

"Oh, Christ!" muttered Piper. "He's off again." Nevertheless, he started the engine and turned the car around. As we passed a surprised Foghorn, I beckoned her

360

to follow us back to the POW camp. We pulled into the approach road to the camp and stopped at the gate. Two armed sentries were on duty and one approached us through a small gate in the fence whilst the other unslung his Lee Enfield in a businesslike manner.

The first sentry spotted Face's uniform and saluted. "What can I do for you, sir?"

"We would like to see the camp commandant." Face made his request friendly and the sentry responded favourably.

"May I ask your names and have your identity cards, sir?"

He wrote down our names on a small pad and slipped our IDs under a bulldog clip at the top of the pad. "What unit, sir?"

"Provost Branch," answered Face without hesitation. He handed the sentry a piece of paper. "Ask your commandant to call that number. They will verify my identity. These gentlemen are my colleagues."

We waited whilst the sentry returned to the inside of the wire. He entered the little guard hut and we saw him crank the handle of a field telephone. He spoke into the receiver but he kept his eyes on us the whole time. He nodded, replaced the receiver and came back to the car. He handed back our IDs.

"The commandant will be here in a moment, sir. He was not expecting you and I'm afraid he's rather busy with the area commander's inspection."

"Area commander?" asked Face with a puzzled look.

"Colonel Vickers, sir." The sentry marched off back to his place inside the wire.

"Area commander, eh?" grinned Face. "Could be our lucky day. We might be able to circumvent a few of the rules if we can get straight to the big cheese today. You're a jammy young sod, Carver. Trust you to pick the day when the boss is here on his inspection." He switched his gaze to a rather elderly army captain, resplendent in best uniform complete with Sam Browne and swagger stick, who was approaching the gate. The sentry saluted and pointed to our car.

"Better meet him half way, in more ways than one," Face muttered as he climbed from the car.

We joined him in the rain and trotted over to the wire. At a nod from the captain we were allowed into the little guard post but I noticed both guards had their rifles across their bodies. The captain saluted Face. "Captain Townley, sir. Can I help you, gentlemen?"

Face handed over his ID and we followed suit. Face glanced at the sentries. "Is it possible we could discuss that somewhere a little more private?"

Townley didn't reply. Piper's card raised one of the captain's eyebrows and he glanced quickly at the Special Branch man but handed back the cards without comment. He was tall with an angular face. He must have seen action in the last war as he had a chest full of medal ribbons. This was one man who was not going to be baffled by a bit of bullshit. His pale eyes regarded us for a few seconds before he made up his mind.

"How about we talk in your car, sir?"

We were not going to just amble in past this guy.

By the time the four of us were crushed into the Humber, it was impossible to see out through the condensation covering the windows. Face looked uncomfortable but I was relieved to see he intended to keep cool. Upset Townley and there would be days of form filling before we got back here. Face leaned over the back of the front seat.

"We're desperate to have a quick look at the camp compound. We've just come from the scene of a murder, just up the road in the woods by the Royal Oak. We

361

suspect that the murderers came from this camp."

Townley didn't move a muscle. "Why should that be of interest to the RAF Provost Branch? I'd have thought it would have been of more interest to MI5 or the CID?"

Face sighed. "We're MI5. That is why I gave your sentry a number for you to call. I didn't think it wise to announce who we were in front of your guards."

Townley tapped his gloved hand with his swagger stick. "Who was murdered?"

"An RAF officer from a nearby airfield," Piper answered for Face.

"Who, among my prisoners, do you suspect of being involved in this murder?"

Face wiped the condensation from his window. "Kline and Weber."

Townley looked up quickly. "The same two men who were interviewed a little while ago about another murder?"

Face and Piper both nodded.

"Do you have authorisation from the area commander?"

Face sighed. "I'm afraid not, Captain, but as he's here on his inspection, we thought we may be able to cut a few corners. It really is very urgent that we follow up a new line of investigation."

Townley looked a little surprised that we knew about the inspection but he soon regained his composure and climbed from the car. "I hope you don't mind a wait, gentlemen. First, I must verify your credentials. Secondly, I'll ask the area commander if he has any reservations as to you entering the camp. It may take some time." He saluted and headed off into the rain.

Piper took out his briar and began to fill it with tobacco. "He's a good officer, don't you think? He's totally unfazed by your rank, James, and the bit about MI5 left him absolutely unimpressed. He's a tough nut for an old soldier and he's not going to be a walkover."

Face sighed. "Just our bloody luck. Why couldn't we have had a good, old fashioned 'yes' man?"

We waited nearly half an hour in the steamed up car. Face was getting impatient and I feared he would blow and ruin our chances but we were finally rewarded by one of the sentries coming to escort us back to the guard post.

Townley was waiting for us. "The area commander has agreed to see you and your colleagues, sir, but I must ask you if you're prepared to submit yourselves to a body search?"

Face nodded. "Of course, we would expect nothing less."

He wouldn't but I bloody well would. I suddenly remembered I still had the bloody Browning in my greatcoat pocket. Every time I threw on the coat, I'd feel its weight bump against my hip and I kept telling myself to return it to the armoury but here I was, still carrying it around. Hell's bells, I was breaching security every time I opened my mouth and now I was breaking all the rules on firearms safety. I was pretty sure that a huge spanner would fall in the works if I were found trying to take a firearm into a POW camp. I had to do something quickly.

"May I get your papers from the car, sir?" I asked Face, with what I hoped was enough emphasis in my voice to alert him to the fact I had a problem.

He gave me a peculiar look but nodded and I dashed back to the car. I slipped the Browning under the passenger seat and returned with Face's briefcase. He and Piper were already submitting themselves to a thorough search and I was about to get the same treatment.

Satisfied with the search, Townley nodded to one of the sentries. "Open the inner gate, Private."

We followed him as he trotted quickly through the rain at a speed that did credit to his advanced years. He led us into a hut that served as a general office, with a sergeant and three privates sitting at their desks. We signed in and then he led us through to the corridor and on to an office towards the rear of the building. He opened the door and waved us in.

"The visitors, sir," he announced as he followed us in and closed the door.

We were faced by the epitome of the Colonel Blimp cartoon character. He was indeed a colonel and it was obvious, from the tension on his tunic buttons, he was no martyr to wartime rationing. He too was in full uniform and, to my surprise, wearing what looked like a pair of highly polished riding boots. He was sitting behind the desk, which according to the nameplate, belonged to Captain Townley. The colonel's hands were locked together and resting on his ample stomach. He made no effort to rise as we entered. In fact I think, because of his girth, he'd have had great difficulty in getting up out of the chair.

Face extended a hand. "Colonel Vickers, I believe. How nice to meet you. I am Wing Commander Face and this is Chief Inspector Piper of the Special Branch. At the rear there is Pilot Officer Carver."

Vickers didn't even glance at me. Junior officers were of no importance to such a great man. He actually shook Face's hand but remained in the chair. Face's reaction told me he had not liked the handshake. Looking at our colonel, I'd imagine it had been like clutching a wet haddock.

"What exactly can I do for you, gentlemen?"

Bloody hell! The voice fitted the Colonel Blimp type perfectly. It was the 'brandy and cigar' voice with a slight lisp, beloved by music hall comedians doing jokes about senior army officers.

"We've just left the scene of a murder." Face was obviously not going to beat about the bush with this prat.

"Good God!" spluttered Colonel Blimp.

Face belted on. "I understand you're the area commander?"

"No, not exactly, old boy." Vickers was already on the defensive. "I'm standing in, actually. The regular chap is off sick for a few weeks. My patch is up north but I was asked to step in until the chap's better."

"Ah, damned tricky." It was all Face said but I could see Vickers dying to show us he was still the man in charge. He was about to play right into Face's hands. Vickers would start asking the questions and Face could then manipulate him. Feed him enough and he'd do just what Face wanted him to do and all the time he'd think he'd thought of it himself.

"Who has been murdered?" Vickers had taken the bait.

"Sadly, one of our officers." Face said it with such a tragic expression, I was hard pressed not to burst out laughing. Piper eyed me carefully as he tried to make up his mind whether or not I'd be able to retain my composure.

"Good God! Damned bad luck. One of your own chaps, was he?" Vickers was spluttering again and I actually saw a globule of saliva fly from his lips and land on Face's greatcoat. I felt mirth bubbling to the surface but I was still under control. At least I was until, just as Face opened his mouth to reply, the colonel's stomach gurgled in protest at all the excitement.

It was too much for me. I whirled round and grabbed at the door to make my escape before the explosion came.

"Excuse me," I managed with a strangled gasp.

I think I might have got myself under control but Face totally ruined any chance

I might have had of regaining my composure. As I closed the door, I heard his excuse for my rapid departure.

"Poor chap," he said, his voice laden with concern. "Overcome with grief."

I hurtled down the corridor until I found the toilets. I dashed in and stuffed my handkerchief into my mouth to prevent the explosion of laughter I knew was on its way. The tears rolled down my face and I was glad of them when the door suddenly opened and Townley walked in. I hurriedly bent over the sink and splashed cold water on my face.

"Are you okay?" His voice was gentle but alarm bells began to ring in my head. It was not a gentleness born of solicitude or sympathy.

"Fine, thank you." I quickly dried my face on my handkerchief and turned to face him. He had placed himself firmly between me and the door. "He was a close friend," I tried.

"Bollocks," he replied without a flicker of expression in his face. "You were pissing yourself with laughter."

I looked at him carefully and I knew our assessment of him had been right on target. This was not just an old timer in a backwater posting. He was still sharp and took his job seriously. I was, not for the first time, lost for words.

He removed his hat and perched his backside on the edge of a sink. "Right, young man, I think it's about time you came clean. Why exactly are you here and don't give me the flattering bullshit your boss is using in there." He jerked his head in the direction of his office.

I sighed. "Can I first apologise for being party to underestimating you?"

He gave a slight smile. "Apology accepted. We're not all like Colonel Vickers. A regular area commander would never have let you through the gate without prior permission from HQ. I'd have reacted in the same way." He paused as he pulled out a cigarette case. He offered me one but I declined. He lit the cigarette and inhaled a huge lungful of smoke. "Right," he said as he exhaled the smoke. "Let us hear your story."

I nodded. "The wing commander is telling the truth. We've just left a murder scene but we think… well, that is … I think … the murderers are here in this camp."

He looked at me through narrowed eyes as smoke drifted in front of his face. "Go on."

"Two of your prisoners, Kline and Weber, once worked for a farmer called Meacher."

He nodded. "Right. They were also interrogated by the security services and given the 'all clear'."

"Tell me about them."

He shrugged. "What can I say? They are two model POWs. They work hard on their outside assignments and have never given us a spot of trouble. In fact they do a lot of work here in the camp too."

"Such as?" I asked but my heart was sinking.

"They were responsible for modifying and decorating the prisoner messing facilities. Damn it! They now live better than my guards. They started a large kitchen garden plot by their hut and grow most types of vegetables to supplement their rations. They fixed the ablution block so that the POWs have decent showers. What else can I say? They are both superb craftsmen and model prisoners."

I walked over and looked at my reflection in a mirror over one of the washbasins. "So, if we asked permission to search their hut or quarters, we would find nothing?"

He nodded. "Nothing. Prisoners are thoroughly searched on their return from work to prevent contraband entering the camp. We let them get away with a few cigarettes or other little luxuries but we limit our leniency. Too much contraband can undermine morale if it's used to give one POW undue power over the other prisoners."

"Do you have any hard cases here?"

"Three difficult cases but not necessarily hard. They are ex U-boat men but they're soon to be transferred to Camp 21 up in Scotland at Cumrie."

"Do they have anything to do with Kline and Weber?"

"Quite the opposite. In fact Kline and Weber get on well with all the other POWs but make no particular friends of any of them. They don't have to mix if they don't want to, either. As trusted prisoners, in charge of that section of huts, both men have their own single rooms."

Well, so much for the great Carver theory but still, the remark made by Foghorn made me uneasy. I tried another tack. "Did they ever carry out a task which you thought was unnecessary or pointless?"

He shook his head. "Not that I can think of."

I sighed. "Okay, I guess I've been on the wrong track. We'd better rescue my boss and the civilian before they talk themselves into a corner."

As we walked out of the toilets, I had just one more question to ask. I turned to face Townley.

"What was their trade in the German army?"

He thought for a minute. "Ah, just a minute ... yes, now I remember, they were both signals NCOs with a Panzer division."

Suddenly, my morale had received a real shot in the arm.

Face, followed by Piper, emerged into the corridor. Face gave me a suspicious look when he saw I had Townley in tow. "Ah, Carver. Colonel Vickers has given us permission to have a look around the camp. I believe you're to escort us, Captain."

"Fine, sir," replied Townley but I could see he didn't really feel it was at all fine.

Nevertheless, he opened a door leading into the compound. "If you would follow me, gentlemen."

"How many prisoners?" asked Piper, looking at the rows of accommodation huts.

"One thousand and twenty."

"Guards?" asked Face.

"One hundred exactly." Townley answered over his shoulder.

"What regiment?" asked Face.

"No particular regiment. Most of them are conscientious objectors. I think they prefer this to the Pioneer Corps."

I looked up at the large brick tower. "I assume this is the water tower?"

Townley nodded and then looked keenly at me. "Funny you should mention the tower. I suppose that was one job on which I felt we should have brought in a civilian contractor."

"What job?" My blood began to race again.

"Lightning conductor," replied Townley. "Works and Bricks decided it should have a conductor and Kline and Weber volunteered to do the job. The previous commandant gave them the materials and they fitted it. I took over the day they finished the job."

I strolled over to the tower. "Which hut is home to Kline and Weber?"

Townley pointed to a hut about twenty feet from the base of the tower. "That one."

Between the tower and the hut was a large vegetable patch.

"Where are Kline and Weber now?" I suddenly realised I'd taken charge. I glanced at Face and Piper but they seemed happy to give me my head.

Townley strolled quickly back to the administration hut and tapped on the window of the office. It was the sergeant who opened the window.

"Get me the Outside Task Allocation Sheet," ordered Townley. He retrieved the sheet from the sergeant and scanned its contents. "They are at the Benton farm just up the road," he called.

"Do they often work there?"

"Only for the last ten days."

"Do you know the Bentons?" Piper decided to join in.

Townley nodded. "Very much so. They keep a room free to accommodate the area commander and his batman when the AC comes on his inspections." There was a pregnant pause and, for the first time since we arrived, Townley actually laughed. "Sorry, I must make myself clear. The Colonel has the room and his batman sleeps on the landing outside his door."

"Thank God for that!" chuckled Face. "I hope the Bentons get paid for this service?"

"Oh yes. I think it is five shillings for the colonel per night and tuppence for the batman."

Piper laughed. "Hardly a sum of sufficient import to give Mr Benton the incentive to quit farming."

"Indeed," agreed Townley. By this time I had walked over to the tower. "Are there any other prisoners in the Kline and Weber hut at the moment?"

"No," replied Townley. "The prisoners from this section who are not working are on the sports field."

"Good." I looked around and we appeared to be unobserved by anybody other than the perimeter guards. I walked forward and looked at the thick cable that formed the lightning conductor. "Do you have a penknife?" I asked Townley.

He shook his head and turned towards the perimeter fence. "Guard, throw me your bayonet - carefully!"

The surprised guard pulled his bayonet from its frog on his webbing belt and tossed it over the wire. Townley retrieved it and passed it to me.

I took a deep breath and mentally crossed my fingers as I gently prised part of the conductor away from the tower brickwork with the point of the bayonet. I took a look and my heart skipped a beat. "Would you all come and take a look at this?" I called to the others.

Face motioned Townley to take the first look. He stooped to peer at the point where I'd eased the cable away with the bayonet.

"Good Lord!" he breathed quietly.

Face and Piper both pushed forward to get a look and both gave me a look of astonishment.

"Is it what I think it is?" I asked them, trying to keep the excitement out of my voice.

Face nodded. "Aerial cable." He glanced upwards. "And I bet it goes all the way to the top."

I pointed to the immaculate garden. "And I bet it goes under that garden and up into the hut."

"How the hell can it?" protested Townley. "We physically check the huts for any

366

signs of illicit equipment. We would see the cable."

I took the shortest distance from the cable on the tower to the wall of the hut. It was timber-framed. I prodded carefully at one of the wooden supports and finally struck gold. Putty flaked away from the wood and there was the cable nestling in a carved out channel. The channel had been cut, the cable hidden in the channel and the whole thing disguised with putty. A quick coat of paint had completed the camouflage.

"Did Kline and Weber volunteer to paint the outside of the huts too?" I asked Townley.

From the look on his face, I already knew the answer.

Face sighed. "Captain, this hut is out of bounds to all POWs as of now. I want you to send a squad of guards to arrest Kline and Weber and hold them here, in your isolation cells, until I can arrange transport to carry them for interrogation. In the meantime, I need a phone to get a search party up here."

Townley looked ashen. "I just don't believe this."

Piper put a hand on the captain's shoulder. "Not your fault, Captain. They're a very clever little gang and have run us ragged for some time. The last thing you'd expect in your POW camp is a long range radio transmitter, but I'm afraid that is what you've got here."

"But how the hell can they hide something as big as that?" Townley protested.

Piper removed his hand and puffed at his briar. "I think we will find it in pieces all over the hut. They assemble it when they need to use it. All the bits will be cleverly disguised as every day items and only our trained experts will be able to spot them. As I said, Captain, nobody can blame you or your men."

Things moved fast from that point. Face was continually on the phone for the next hour. Colonel Vickers had huffed, puffed and retired back into Townley's office, no doubt desperately seeking somebody to blame.

We watched Kline and Weber brought in under armed guard in separate trucks and placed in separate huts until the teams arrived from London.

I sighed and looked at Piper. "Does this mean I've to write yet more bloody statements?"

He laughed. "Serves you right, Carver. You shouldn't be such a bloody clever clogs. What the heck made you think of that tower?"

I shook my head. "I'm not sure but I do remember you, or the wing commander, saying that the German long range sets needed an aerial at least thirty feet in length. Well, when Foghorn brought the tower to my notice I suddenly realised the significance of the height. Allied with my suspicion that it could only be the POWs doing the killing, I decided it was not beyond the realms of possibility that they were using the POW camp as the perfect cover."

"The bastards must have had a lot of luck for all this to come together," Piper mused.

"How do you think they got the radio in?" I asked him.

"The essentials, such as valves, probably up their backsides. The rest they could have made with the tools they have available in the camp. Things such as the radio chassis for example. We'll soon know."

To my surprise, the orderly room sergeant began pulling the blackout curtains and I realised it was already getting dark. I glanced at my watch. "Bloody hell! Time flies when you're enjoying yourself."

Piper too glanced at his watch. "You might as well bugger off. We'll be here most of the night. Go and see that lovely girlfriend of yours before somebody else grabs her."

For one horrible moment I thought he was referring to Foghorn. Oh, hell! Foghorn! She'd been sitting outside in the car for hours.

I grabbed my hat. "You're right, sir. I just hope my other 'girlfriend' is still in a frame of mind to drive me back."

"Don't worry about her, sir," called the sergeant. "We fed and watered her at regular intervals. She's told me enough dirty jokes to keep the mess happy for weeks."

Sure enough, it was a very contented Foghorn who greeted me when I reached the car.

"Ready to go at last, Petal?" She yawned and scratched herself in a very unladylike place.

"Sorry we took so long."

She started the engine. "What was all the panic?"

"We've just got the murderers, thanks partly to you, actually."

"Thanks to me?"

"In a roundabout way. It's a long story and I'll tell you later. I just want to get back and have my dinner. I'm ravenous."

She grimaced. "I'll be in time for duty supper or something."

"That bad?"

"How many ways are there to cook bully beef?" she asked.

"I though you ate it in sandwiches."

"Not in the airmen's mess, Petal. They fry it, batter it, grill it and make a soddin' hash of it. One day some twat is going to serve it with custard and call it 'pudding'."

I laughed. "Never mind, we've come to the end of our little problem. Now it will be celebrations all round. I'll tell you what, we'll all go out for a meal and a jolly good piss up. How about that?"

She gave me that evil grin of hers. "If you get pissed, Petal, will you try to have your evil way with me?"

I laughed. "If I do, I won't be trying very hard."

"Just my bloody luck," she yelled in mock protest. "Nothing is very hard when they get near me."

It was time to change the conversation before it got too much for me to handle. So we chatted about where we would hold our celebration and decided, if we could get the transport, Lincoln would be just the place. I was looking forward to it already.

368

CHAPTER TWENTY-SIX

The next few days were spent tying up loose ends and completing statements. The search parties discovered the radio transmitter and all its relevant parts and we now had the missing link in their communications chain. Kline and Weber had said nothing since their arrest but enough forensic evidence was now turning up to convict them for the murder of Hammond, if not for that of Smith.

The following weekend, Nat and I both had a forty-eight hour pass and we made damned sure nothing was going to spoil this one. We borrowed Max's MG and headed off early Saturday morning for the Lincolnshire coast. Not a wise choice as it turned out. Skegness looked bleak and ghastly with mobs of navy recruits and army types everywhere. We drove past a holiday camp that now bore the grand title of HMS Royal Arthur. Although the sun shone, it was a cold wind that blew in off the North Sea. The even more dilapidated and deserted Mablethorpe made our next decision for us. No more coast, we would head inland. To our surprise, we found a hotel in the little market town of Spilsby, only about twenty miles from West Fen. It was just across the street from the parish church. The statue of Sir John Franklin, who, it seemed, perished trying to discover the North West Passage, dominated the nearby market square. The one building that stood out from the starkness of the others, was the ivy-clad façade of the grammar school.

The hotel itself was not exactly the Ritz but a large fire blazed in the hearth of the lounge and our room was quite adequate. Once more, we were surrounded by service personnel but this time, there were also countless Irishmen. No doubt labourers employed on the construction of the new airfields at East Kirkby and Little Steeping. After my experiences with Smith, I was not enamoured of the Irish and, in spite of the smiles and merriment, I found them shallow and, after a couple of drinks, belligerent. I also decided, by the time Nat and I had retreated to our room, that if anyone else sang bloody 'Danny Boy' in my presence again, I'd cheerfully strangle the bastard.

It was still quite early and we discovered that if we left the lights off and just sat in the flicker of the flames from the open fire, we could almost forget the war, the Irish and the rather tatty décor. I pulled a chair close to the fire and Nat sat on the floor with her head in my lap.

I gently ran my fingers through her long hair and immediately began to feel a welcome calm descend upon me. Over the last couple of months I'd become edgy and I'd not been sleeping well. Even when I did finally drift off, I frequently awoke with a violent start - the reaction to a sudden vision of Annie, lolling back with a bloody pulp where her skull should be, or the sound made by the bullets ripping into Giedrovski's body in the dingy rifle range. The strange and disturbing thing was, since we had cracked the cell and all that nonsense was over, the dreams had intensified. I'd often find my hands shaking for no apparent reason and I'd developed a twitch in my left eye that would not go away. I'd find myself anxious and nervy when there was no reason for being that way. That night though, as I sat there in the firelight, I did, for the first time in ages, feel myself relax. In fact I slipped into a deep sleep, right there in the chair. When I finally awoke it was one o'clock in the morning and Nat was trying not to disturb me as she added coal to the dying fire. She placed a gentle hand on the inside of my thigh.

"Welcome back, Sleeping Beauty."

I placed my hand over hers. "Some Romeo I turned out to be. Here I am with the most beautiful girl in the world and I fall asleep."

She laid her head on my knee. "We've the rest of the night."

I pushed my chair back and joined her on the carpet in front of the fire. "Indeed we have," I whispered.

I think at some point we did move to the bed but my memory became hazy as we made love again and again. It was as if we would never get another chance. In spite of the joy I felt, as we took our lovemaking to new heights of emotion, I had a subliminal feeling of disquiet. Surely all this was too good to last? Tragedy had spread its dark mantle over my every move, when all I wanted to do was to do my job and have time to love this beautiful girl in my arms. Surely, now it was all over, Nat and I could, within the constraints of wartime, live a 'normal' life? Was that too much to ask?

I tried to hide my fears as we fought to assuage our doubts and lose ourselves in passion. Tonight was our night and finally the fears evaporated as we both fell into a deep and exhausted sleep.

The next morning, as we ate breakfast, Nat was quiet and only toyed with her food.

"Tired, kitten?" I asked as I reached across the table and took her hand in mine.

She smiled but I saw the fear in her eyes. "It is too perfect, Sam. I am so scared it won't last. I don't mean I'll ever stop loving you but surely nobody deserves such a feeling of intense love. It's almost unreal. and it scares me."

"Why?"

"I'm afraid of losing you." Her voice was just a whisper.

I squeezed her hand. "The way I'm going to stick to you for the rest of our lives, you're going to have to be pretty bloody careless to lose me."

She smiled ruefully. "Do you ever take anything seriously?"

I nodded and whispered my reply. "Yes...you."

Her eyes were moist with tears and I leaned over and stroked her cheek. I was so happy I was close to tears myself. Time to get control before I let the side down.

"Hey!" I said. "It's Sunday."

She took my cue. "So what?"

"Let's go to church."

She looked surprised. "What on earth brought that on?"

"Well, if we intend to marry, we'd better start showing a bit of interest in religion. Par for the course, isn't it?"

"I don't think that is a very honourable motive for our suddenly swelling the congregation, Carver." She glanced at her watch. "Anyway, I'd imagine we're too late for Holy Communion. Saints get up early around here!"

"How do you know all this about the church?"

She tossed her head to clear her hair from her face. "I go every Sunday if I can. The Church of England padre is quite nice, so I go to his little church at the back of the guardroom."

I sighed. "I haven't been to church since I was confirmed."

"Slacker."

"More like 'slider'," I corrected her. I pushed my chair back from the table. "Shall we have a last walk around the town before we head for parts unknown?"

"Why not," she agreed. "How about a drive to Lincoln. I'd love to see the inside of the cathedral."

"Done. I'll go and pay the bill and ask them to keep our bags behind reception until we're ready to leave."

The sun was shining as we strolled out of the hotel and into the market place. The only sound was that of a little Tiger Moth biplane. It was flying quite high and battling with a strong headwind. Nat had been watching it for some time.

"Do you know, I reckon we could overtake that thing in Max's MG."

I nodded. "No doubt about it but I bet he's having more fun."

"Oh, thank you, Carver!" She punched me hard on the arm.

"I didn't mean it like that, you clot." I looked deep into her eyes and grinned. "Oh, I don't know though."

She aimed a playful kick at my ankle and, as I hopped quickly out of range, a voice called out from just behind us.

"Miss Cowen, that is hardly appropriate behaviour for a young lady."

We turned in surprise to see Mr Bates, smartly dressed in a dark overcoat and a Homburg hat, which he raised with a gloved hand.

"Hello, Mr Bates!" I exclaimed in both surprise and pleasure. "What are you doing here?"

"No, sir, wrong question to the wrong man. I live here. Surely it is I who should be asking you what you're doing here?"

Nat winked at him. "I'm afraid we're enjoying a romantic tryst, Mr Bates."

He didn't even blink. "A most suitable pursuit, young lady. It seems all the rage these days."

"You're not shocked?" she teased him.

He grinned. "Not at all, miss, although I'll admit to being a little envious but envy is one of the less interesting of the deadly sins. I seem to miss out on all the interesting ones."

Nat slipped her arm through his. "You're too nice to sin."

Bates sighed. "It is a cross I seem to have to bear. I'm sure even a little sin would do me the power of good."

"I'm not sure I like all this talk of the church and sin," I complained.

Bates clapped his gloved hands together. "Then we will change the subject. We will change it into an invitation to the 'Bates Manor' this afternoon. I did mention my intention to offer an invitation to Miss Cowen and yourself, sir. We now have the perfect opportunity to make that invitation for today. Shall we say 16.00?"

I looked at Nat and she nodded. "You're on, Mr Bates. Are you sure Mrs Bates will be happy to receive visitors at such short notice?"

"Positive, sir," he assured me. "We will see you at 'Llamedos', on the Partney road, at 16.00."

I frowned. "Welsh name?"

He smiled. "Hardly, sir, but you'll understand when you see the sign." He raised his hat again to Nat and gave a slight bow. "Sixteen hundred then. I'm looking forward to it immensely." He hurried off, no doubt to alert Mrs Bates.

Nat watched the departing figure. "I think he's a lovely man."

I nodded. "He certainly is. I wonder where he got that quaint gentlemanly manner? Hardly Lincolnshire style."

Nat shook her head. "No idea but I cannot imagine him being any other way."

Now we had accepted Mr Bates' invitation to tea, there was insufficient time to visit Lincoln, so we took a drive out into the Wolds instead.

We visited Somersby, the birthplace of Alfred Lord Tennyson. It turned out to be a bit of a disappointment, but at least the wolds, now looking splendid with the trees covered in many shades of spring greenery, made up for Somersby. We had the hood down on the MG and the birds were so frantic with the excitement of the season, we could hear them singing and chattering their hearts out above the noise of the engine.

We came to a narrow road that ran along the top of a ridge. Each side of the road, the ground sloped steeply away only to rise again a couple of fields distant. We could see the sun glistening on the sea out in the direction of Skegness and occasionally we glimpsed Lincoln cathedral, majestic on its distant hill. I stopped the car on the grass verge and looked at the landscape as it stretched away to the north.

"Bates was right," I said as Nat's head came to rest on my shoulder. "Lincolnshire is a beautiful county if you know where to look."

Nat just murmured something and I felt her hand slide gently between my legs. I leaned back, as far as I could in the cramped little car, as she slowly unbuttoned my trousers.

"I don't think you'd better go any further, love," shouted a voice from the other side of the hedge. "You might get a round of applause when you finish him off!"

I quickly doubled forward and tried to get my stiff pride and joy back into my trousers. I though Nat was going to pass out with shock and embarrassment.

As I gathered my thoughts and my genitals, I peered through the hedge but all I could see was a grassy bank. Then the voice spoke again and it came from above our heads.

"Up here, mate."

I looked up to see two ruddy faced men, in their fifties, peering down over the hedge. They wore dark blue uniforms and berets. One had a set of headphones clamped over his ears. Then I recognised the badge on one of the berets. We had only tried to get passionate just feet from an Observer Corps post.

"Thanks for the warning." It was all I could think of to say.

"That's alright, mate," replied one of the men. "I didn't mind but I thought it might overexcite my mate here." He jerked a thumb at his grinning companion.

Nat was squirming with embarrassment so I thought it was time we took our leave. I started the engine and, as we began to move, I gave them a farewell wave.

"Keep your hands off his gearstick, love!" was the parting shot from one of the observers and we heard their laughter, like the birds, over the noise of the MG. We both had very red faces and it was not from the fresh Lincolnshire air!

Our visit to the Bates house, later that day, was a perfect end to our short holiday. We duly read 'Llamedos' backwards and thought it far more original than 'Dunroamin'. It was very much an indicator of the Bates sense of humour.

Mrs Bates, to our delight and surprise, was as erudite and amusing as her husband. We enjoyed a wonderful Sunday tea and then we actually accompanied them to the big Methodist chapel at the bottom of the High Street. I'd not been to a Methodist service before and I found it much less of a dirge than the Church of England proceedings. For once I actually recognised the hymns and, with judicious use of my hymnbook, I sang heartily along without any feeling of embarrassment - much to Nat's amusement.

Later, back at 'Llamedos', we had yet more food with Mr Bates and his wife.

This time it was supper and I'd not eaten so much food for months. It seemed Mr Bates had friends among the local farmers and was favoured occasionally with a few little 'extras'.

It was late when we finally took our leave and reluctantly headed back to West Fen. I drove with Nat's head resting on my shoulder and, to my surprise, in spite of the jarring of the MG's suspension on the terrible roads, she was soon fast asleep. I had to shake her awake at the guardroom barrier.

"Was that the beginning of my dream?" she asked sleepily as we drove slowly to the Waafery.

"Just the beginning of the beginning," I murmured. "The beginning of the rest of our lives."

Next morning, Monday, it was all hands to the pumps as Command demanded maximum effort from both squadrons. For the next three nights, they flew operations without a break. Losses were about par for the course - heavy! One morning a crew would be there, laughing and joking at lunch or the briefing. The next, their hut was being cleared out and their personal effects packed for return to their grieving families.

On the Wednesday, I found myself up on the dais and actually presenting part of the briefing. It wasn't much but it was a start and I was amazed to see the crews listening as intently to me as they did to Houseman. Since Janner's demise, Houseman had made a special effort to get Nat up to scratch for briefings and, whilst I had pursued other avenues of intelligence, she had become an old hand on the platform.

That same Wednesday I had my final meeting with Face and Piper. Houseman was there, of course, and we listened as the two men related the detailed story of our local cell. It was still under investigation but they were pretty much sure it was all over. They had come to the conclusion that Hammond had willingly supplied information to the cell via Smith. Smith, using an old BSA motorcycle they had found hidden in the woods, would position himself in the phone box and read the cryptic visual signals displayed in the window of Janner's office. In Hammond's locker they had found a small box, fitted with a series of switches and coloured bulbs. It was powered by a dry cell battery. Once darkness had fallen, the box would be positioned outside the blackout curtain and used to send messages. Nobody would see it from inside the room and the lights were so dim, it was impossible to see them from the road without binoculars. Smith would read the message and then phone the cottage. The signal would go out over the short-range radio to the airstrip, or even direct to the Hurricane if it was already in the air. Coded clicks on the mike would be enough to give revised takeoff times. The pilot would then have to decide whether to abort his attack or loiter out of range until the new takeoff time. They assumed Meacher had manned the cottage radio as, although Smith was well known in the village, nobody could recall ever having seen Meacher. It had been a simple strategy, its success boosted beyond their wildest dreams by the weaknesses of two of our own officers.

The cell had known that discovery was always a possibility and so the main radio had been secreted in the last place the security services would ever think of looking - the POW camp. Kline and Weber, on their outside jobs, were of little use to the Abwehr but at least they could report troop activity in the area and identify them by their badges. They might also pick up something from the farm labourers with whom they worked. Mainly, it seemed they simply reported on morale. Their real value was as the main radio link with Berlin.

Face and Piper finally sat back in their chairs - their story over. We sat in silence, each with our own thoughts. It was Houseman who broke the silence.

"If Carver here had not been able to recognise a Merlin from a Daimler, we would probably have been none the wiser. The covert airstrip couldn't have lasted much longer but long enough to kill a lot more of our crews. Damn it, it could even have been moved to another area. Difficult but possible."

Piper nodded. "That's true. We must also thank the incompetent sod who parachuted in that night and, instead of burying his helmet with the parachute, threw it into the culvert. Without that, we would have had no clues as to where to begin our search for the cell."

I wiped a tired hand over my eyes. It had been a busy day getting the briefing together and, before long, the first aircraft would be returning. Yet more overtired aircrew to debrief when all they wanted to do was get to bed. I raised my head and saw Houseman watching me closely.

"Twenty-three dead," I said quietly.

"What?" Face looked up in surprise.

"Twenty-three people have died, including the seven aircrew on that first night." I couldn't keep the weariness out of my voice.

Now Face was looking at me intently. "In wartime, Carver, it is not wise to count the dead, you'll always run out of fingers. Very bad for morale!"

I returned his stare but finally I let my eyes drop away from his. I was not made of the same mettle as Face, Piper and Houseman. Earlier and in private, Face had kindly asked me if I'd like to join his staff. He didn't quite hide his relief when I declined his offer. He knew I was already feeling the strain and there would be a lot more of the same before the war was over.

Houseman's head jerked up as the first murmurings of Merlins could be heard in the distance. Time to go to work. Face and Piper rose and Face walked over to shake my hand.

"You're a good man, Carver, and I'm sorry you had such a hard a baptism of fire so soon. It has taken its toll of you but I hope you can now settle down to your real job. I know our loss is Jake's gain."

I smiled. "He may not think that once he sees what a cock up I can make when I really try!"

He clapped me on the shoulder. "There is a decoration coming your way. I'm not allowed to tell you what it is until it has been promulgated. One thing I can tell you. You'll no longer feel out of place when in the company of all these young, bemedalled aircrew chaps. The problem is, you'll have to invent a story because you'll never be able to talk about what really happened until after the war."

Piper's farewell took me totally by surprise. He walked over to me and put both hands on my shoulder. "I didn't know about the medal, young Carver, but by God you've earned it. Take care of yourself and that lovely girlfriend of yours."

I laughed. "I assure you I'll do my best on both counts, sir."

He shook my hand. "Good lad."

They picked up their briefcases and headed for the door.

"Goodnight, Jake," called Face over his shoulder. "We'll now get out of your hair for good. Thanks for all your help." Their voices faded as they headed off down the corridor. I went to follow them but Houseman stopped me.

"Sam, congratulations on the gong, whatever it is."

"Probably the VD and scar, sir."

He grinned. "The penalty for all indiscriminate wickdippers." Then he remembered Nat and realised what he was inferring. He began to get very red in the face. "Damn it, Sam... I promise you, I meant nothing untoward...oh, bloody hell! - what a crass thing to say."

I burst out laughing. "Have you finished spluttering and farting, we've work to do."

He leapt out of his chair. "For Pete's sake, let's go, before I make an even bigger clown of myself."

CHAPTER TWENTY-SEVEN

Both squadrons were stood down for the following weekend and Houseman, who had taken charge of the arrangements for my little 'return to the fold' party, had booked a table at the White Hart hotel in Lincoln. He knew the place well from frequent visits during his squadron days and had booked us in as a party of seven.

There would be Houseman, Max, Foghorn and Stan, plus Nat and myself. Dave Jones, having earwigged us planning the party, volunteered to drive us and promised to stay sober. This was all very well but transport, as always, was a problem. Max volunteered to collect Stan but we really needed a vehicle that would get us there en masse. Salvation came in the form of a squadron leader on 552 Squadron. He offered us his tank-like Humber shooting brake. It was very generous of him but, as he said, having the vehicle was one thing - filling it with petrol was another. Max and myself took a risk and siphoned the service fuel from my little Fiat. Let's face it, I'd finished with it. No more special duties, no more Fiat. We managed to collect about three gallons from the Fiat and scrounged the rest from guys in the mess. We calculated we had just enough to get there and back, without detours!

Early Saturday evening, we assembled outside the guardroom. Stan, looking very smart in sports jacket and flannels, was already waiting with Max, who, like Dave, Houseman and myself, was in uniform. Nat and Foghorn, on the other hand, were in civvies. Nat looked stunning and, to my surprise, Foghorn was wearing a smart grey two-piece costume. One of the girls in the WAAF block must have done her hair for her because it had been cut short and styled. She was also wearing just a hint of makeup. She actually looked very nice - for Foghorn.

She saw me looking at her. "Strewth, Petal, you're looking at me as if I were an old banger that's just had a respray."

Nat laughed. "Take no notice, he's very rude."

"I think you look nice," I protested, but then I saw that glint in her eye and decided to stop her before she got into her stride.

"Don't even think about it," I warned her. "Tonight we're on our best behaviour."

"Damn that!" Stan protested with a laugh. "I might as well go back home. I thought this was my chance to live it up for once."

Foghorn rushed over and pushed him into the car. "Your time has come, my lover, I'm all yours." She heaved her bulk in next to him.

Houseman laughed. "If we don't have a good time it won't be her fault."

"That's what I'm afraid of," I muttered as I climbed into the car.

I need not have feared for the success of the evening. The food was quite good and the mixture of rank and backgrounds caused no problems. For me, the pleasure of the evening was seeing the obvious delight on the faces of both Foghorn and Stan. He and Houseman got on like a house on fire and Foghorn, well, she simply got on with everybody. Dave Jones turned to me at one point and made a rather surprising observation.

"I've no idea what you've been up to, Sam, but you certainly met some great people on the way."

I looked across the table at Stan. "You're right. For starters, we couldn't have done the job without that little chap."

"How the hell did you tame the dreaded Bourne?" Dave asked in awe.

I grinned and looked him straight in the eye so as not to miss his reaction. "She saved my life. Believe me, she's a long way from being tame, thank God."

His eyes widened briefly in surprise. "It was really that serious?"

I nodded. "I'm only too happy to see the end of it all. I don't think I could have taken much more."

Dave grinned and raised his glass. "In that case, welcome back."

I drank heartily to that!

When we eventually struggled out into the night, we all groaned with frustration. The fog was so thick you could have cut it with a knife. Even the mighty cathedral was invisible.

Houseman cursed. "Just our luck. I don't suppose the Humber is fitted with nav aids?"

Dave sighed. "I'm afraid it will be Mark One eyeball. I had enough trouble getting us here in the dark but this will make those bloody great dykes seem even more dangerous."

Foghorn came to the rescue. "Look, I'll drive. I know the route like the back of my hand. I know I've had a few but I'm not pi... er... drunk."

Houseman put his hand on her arm. "Are you sure you're okay?"

She nodded. "Yes, sir. No problem."

"Okay," he agreed. "You've been promoted from gunner to pilot."

As we walked down the steep cobbled street to the car, there was no sound. The fog muffled even our footsteps. I stopped and held up my hand.

"What do you hear?" I whispered.

They all crowded close to me and cocked their heads to one side.

"Eff all!" It was a typical Foghorn response.

It was Stan who had the answer. "No aircraft," he whispered. "I can't remember a night when I haven't heard a plane."

We stood like seven statues in the moist air. Each of us afraid to break the silence. Then, somewhere near at hand, a cat mewed. It was a plaintive sound and, for some unaccountable reason, I shivered.

Nat squeezed my arm. "Time we went home, folks."

The spell was broken and suddenly we could hear the sounds of a train shunting wagons down by Brayford Pool. A factory hooter wailed mournfully. We were cocooned in our sphere of nature's cotton wool but life was still going on out there somewhere.

We eventually found the car and used our handkerchiefs to wipe the moisture from the outside of the windows. Foghorn drove carefully through the deserted streets and somehow found the road out of the city. I couldn't see more than a few feet ahead of the bonnet but she seemed to know exactly where she was going. Then the evening began to go wrong.

Just as we were leaving Lincoln, Foghorn suddenly slammed on the brakes.

"What the hell?" Houseman exclaimed as he grabbed the dashboard.

"Coppers," grunted Foghorn and wound down her window.

"Evening, miss." An elderly special leaned into the car. "Where are you heading for?"

"RAF West Fen, near Boston." Houseman leaned across Foghorn and got in quick before her natural dislike of policemen could reveal itself.

The constable shone his torch briefly on the rest of us and seemed satisfied. "Then I'm afraid you'll have to go via Horncastle, sir. An RAF Queen Mary has overturned on the Metheringham to Billinghay stretch. Nothing can get through and won't for some time."

"Is that the road through Bardney?" Foghorn asked sweetly.

"It is, miss." The special touched his cap politely. "Take it slowly though, the road is very twisty."

"We will," called Houseman. "Thank you, constable."

We headed back into the darkness. The hooded headlamps were now even more useless in the thick fog. As we groped our way through Bardney, Foghorn rubbed furiously at the condensation on the screen.

"If I could be sure of finding it, there's a road off this one that cuts through to Woodhall Spa." She sounded doubtful.

"Forget it," Houseman was firm. "This road is bad enough in this fog. Anything smaller than this would be murder for you. We don't mind how long it takes us, just get us there in one piece."

"How's the fuel situation?" Max called from the back.

Foghorn peered at the instrument. "Not bad. At this speed we'll get a lot further on the bit we have in the tank. We should make it, even with the detour. When we get to Horncastle, there's a road through Moorby and Revesby. Our problems will be over once we're on the seven-mile straight."

Houseman laughed. "You're the pilot. I don't even know the road in daylight."

Deserted Horncastle, what bit we saw of it, looked like a ghost town. The market square was empty and we saw not a soul. We motored slowly back out into the bleak countryside and Foghorn only spotted the road off to Moorby at the last minute. She swerved hard left to get back on track.

"Sorry, folks." She wiped her eyes with the back of her hand. She was really beginning to feel the strain of the journey.

Dave Jones was fast asleep and Nat too had succumbed to the tiring drive. She had her head on my shoulder and I could feel her warm breath gently on my cheek as she breathed evenly in her sleep. Stan and Max were chattering away in the back. It must have been pretty uncomfortable back there.

Then things went from bad to worse as the headlights flickered on and off a couple of times, then died altogether.

Foghorn braked quickly to a halt. "Shit," I heard her breathe quietly. "Anybody got a torch?"

Houseman pulled one from his greatcoat pocket but it was so feeble it was going to be useless if we wanted to see to make repairs.

"Oh, well," Foghorn sighed. "Time to use the old sixth sense."

I sat up quickly. "Surely you can't drive without headlights, especially in this clag?"

"Any other suggestions, Petal?"

"'Fraid not," I conceded.

"Righty ho, then," she laughed. "Here we bloody well go. I couldn't see anything with the lights on so I don't suppose it will be much worse with 'em off. Just pray no silly bugger, especially the local copper, is coming the other way."

Nat mumbled something in her sleep and I tightened my arm around her shoulders.

As we crawled along, Houseman was peering out of the open window on his side of the car. If Foghorn got too near the edge of the road, he'd call out a warning. The converse applied if she went too far the other way. Then, just as we neared Moorby, the fog thinned a little. It was still a pea-souper but at least we could now see about twenty yards in front of the bonnet. I recognised the dip in the road near the Royal Oak but I could see nothing of the pub itself. We crawled up the far side of the dip and around the sharp right hand bend at the top. Dark trees now hemmed us in on both sides. It was a forbidding scene.

"Shitty death!" Foghorn yelled as she slammed on the brakes and we all lurched forward. Nat and Dave Jones were now wide awake.

The hooded lights of another car had swept into the road right across our path. We couldn't blame the other driver, as we were showing no lights at all. There was no way he could have seen us.

Houseman let out a rush of breath. "Christ! That was close."

Foghorn quickly jerked us back into motion. "Well, at least we can tag on behind until he turns off. He has the very thing we lack - lights."

Nat was still half asleep. "Did we nearly crash, or something?"

I pulled her to me. "If it hadn't been for 'Hawkeye' up there at the wheel, we would have crashed. I only saw a brief glimpse of something."

Foghorn butted in. "Oh, shit! Now where's the silly bugger going?"

The car in front had suddenly turned right onto a small lane. As Foghorn braked to a halt, realisation hit me like a thunderclap. I turned urgently to Stan.

"Where does that lane lead to, Stan?"

"It goes to Mareham-le-Fen. It's a tiny road though, barely enough room for one car."

I whipped my arm from around Nat and thumped the back of the front seat. "Get after that car, quick!"

"What the... began Houseman.

Foghorn stalled him as she shot off in pursuit. "Don't ask questions, sir, you know what he's like."

Houseman turned round in his seat. "What's eating you, Sam?"

I licked my lips as a shiver of excitement passed through my body. "I've just realised where that car was coming from when we nearly hit it."

Houseman just looked at me as he waited for me to enlighten him.

Stan spoke for me. "Smith's cottage."

"Exactly." I turned round to face the little farmer. "Who would be using that track at this time of the night?"

He shrugged. "Only poachers or maybe your search team has come back for something."

I shook my head. "No way. They've finished and handed the cottage back to the estate that rented it out. Do you really think it was poachers?"

"Very unlikely."

Foghorn broke in. "I've got him again."

I leaned forward eagerly. "It will be interesting to see where he goes next."

"Any chance I can be let in on the secret?" asked Dave. He couldn't keep the bewilderment from his voice.

I grasped the seat back. "Only if he goes where I think he's going."

Houseman turned back to me as realisation dawned and I could hear the tension in his voice. "You can't be serious, Sam."

"We'll see, sir." It was all I could say.

The other driver was completely oblivious to our presence behind him as he drove steadily and carefully. We entered Mareham-le Fen from the north. It was a tiny village and, as far as we could see in the blackout, it was as bleak as Horncastle.

"He's going right," Foghorn yelled. "Shit, that's the main road and we've got no lights."

I began to feel a surge in excitement and confidence. "That way goes to Tumby, right?"

"Spot on, Petal."

"Are you prepared to go on without lights?" I asked her quietly.

She turned and gave me that wicked leer. "For you, Petal - anything!"

She was as good as her word and followed the other car out onto the main road, accelerating a little as the fog eased just a little more. I hardly dared breathe for the next few minutes and my tension seemed to transmit itself to the others in the car. They too peered forward anxiously through the windscreen but only Stan and myself knew where the excitement would become dangerous. I think I gave an audible gasp as the car suddenly turned left up a track.

"The Meacher Farm." I could barely get the words out.

Foghorn parked on the grass just inside the track and switched off the engine. She rubbed furiously at her tired eyes. "Now what?" she asked.

"Damned if I know," I replied helplessly.

Houseman peered into the darkness. "Who is at the farm?"

I shrugged. "Nobody as far as I know. The search teams have all gone and it, like the cottage, was handed back to landlords. There should be nobody there. Especially anybody who also has a connection with Smith's cottage."

"The lease is back on the market," added Stan.

"New tenant?" suggested Max.

I shook my head. "Not at this bloody time of the night and don't forget it came from Smith's cottage. No, it is all too much of a coincidence."

Houseman opened his door and jumped out. "Okay, let's get going if we're going to do something." He turned to Dave Jones. "David! Head in the direction of Tumby village and find a phone. Knock the whole bloody place up if you have to. Call the RAF Police at West Fen and insist on talking to Wareham. Tell him what's going on and ask him to inform the station commander. Tell him we're at Meacher's farm - he'll know what you're talking about. Ask him to send armed assistance. It may all be a waste of time but I think Sam is right and we dare not ignore what is happening. I'm afraid you'll have to leg it to the village. We daren't risk starting the engine and alerting whoever is at the farm."

Stan grabbed Dave's arm. "The nearest place is Albert Hodgson's farm. He was in the last war so he won't hesitate to help you. Just tell him you know me."

"Thanks, Stan," Dave whispered and set off at a trot. He was quickly swallowed up by the fog.

Houseman turned to the rest of us. "Okay, Sam and myself will go forward to try and find out what is going on. The rest of you can come with us until we get close to the house, then I want you to stay put until we give you the all clear or shout for you to scatter. If you get that response, run like hell and hide up until you hear the police arriving. Don't show yourselves to anybody from the farm. Is that understood?" He searched out Stan. "Mr Cornish, as a civilian, I am quite happy for you to remain here by the car if you'd like to stay out of things."

Stan quietly closed the car door nearest to him. "No way, sir, I'm not missing this for anything."

Even though it was pitch dark, I could tell from Houseman's tone that he was smiling.

"Now how did I know you'd say that? In that case, I'd like you to stay with Max and look after the two ladies."

He turned to me. "Come on, Sam, let's go and see what the bugger's up to."

"Hang on a minute." I ran back to the car and groped in the back for my greatcoat. I breathed a sigh of relief when my hand contacted the cold metal of the Browning. Bloody hell, I'd only left it in my greatcoat, in an unattended car and on a pitch black car park in the middle of Lincoln. Not a good move, Carver! I just kept forgetting the damned thing and nobody had asked me to return it to the armoury. I checked the mag and slammed it back into the butt. I shoved the gun into my pocket along with a spare clip and rejoined the others.

"Sorry, sir," I apologised to Houseman but I didn't tell him why I'd returned to the car.

We set off, walking on the grass verge at each side of the track. It was quieter that way and the fog muffled the rustle of our clothing.

Houseman halted us at the end of the stable block. "Max, I want you and the others to stay here until we can let you know what is going on. Sam and myself will try to get closer."

I followed him as he slipped from stable door to stable door. At each door we paused to listen. So far so good but my nerves were at fever pitch. It was all probably going to be an anticlimax but I was enjoying the excitement that came with my heightened senses.

We stopped at the far end of the stables and Houseman gripped my arm. "See that?" he whispered. I peered past him into the darkness and towards the cart shed. There was a glimmer of light, possibly from a small lantern, high up in the open-fronted building. There was also the occasional metallic sound as if somebody was using tools. We watched for a good fifteen minutes and then the light descended. Whoever it was had been up a ladder. I tried to remember what had been in that bay of the shed the day I met Meacher. It took a while but then it came back to me - a threshing machine, sheeted over with a tarpaulin. The lantern moved across the farmyard to the house. There was a brief flash of light, as the door opened, and then total darkness as the door was closed.

Houseman spoke quietly. "What do you make of that?"

"He was working on the threshing machine. At least that was what was in the shed the last time I was here."

We crept quietly forward until we reached the bay. It was Houseman who bumped into the ladder, propped up against the threshing machine. "Shit!" I could hear him rubbing his knee.

I edged around him and carefully climbed the ladder. I found myself at the rear of the machine where four box-like structures moved on cams to push the threshed straw out and down into the elevator. I recalled Stan telling me the structures were called 'straw-walkers' and I could feel that somebody had removed the side panel of one of the hollow boxes. I groped blindly in the darkness but I could feel nothing inside the box. Whoever had been up the ladder had removed something and taken it into the house.

"Find anything?" Houseman was impatient as I climbed down.

"Nothing. Whatever it was up there has been removed."

"Bugger!"

I could share his frustration as I peered across the yard. "Any way we can get a peek into the house?"

"Not with the bloody blackout curtains," he grumbled.

As we stood there, frozen into immobility by indecision, I began to feel the sensation I'd felt in the woods at the airstrip. The same sensation that had prompted me to go back to the gunman and touch the barrel of the Sten. My every nerve began to tingle and I could feel my heart pounding in my chest. I knew exactly what I was going to do next.

I broke the silence. "There is only one way we can find out what is going on."

Houseman paused before he spoke and there was a wariness in his voice. "I don't like the way you said that, Carver. I reckon you've got a thistle up your arse again. Tell me what you're thinking and I'll tell you what a stupid idea it is."

"We walk straight in."

"Definitely a stupid idea. Much better if we wait for back-up."

"What if they make a move to leave?"

"Then we stop them," he replied but I could hear the doubt in his voice.

"If we're going to catch them red-handed, with whatever it is they've taken from the farm, we've got to act now, sir."

Houseman sighed in the darkness. "Bloody hell, I thought ops were bloody dangerous. What is it about you, Carver, that attracts trouble?"

"No idea, sir. Shall we go?"

"Lead on."

I laughed quietly. "Would you not rather lead, sir, being senior officer and all that?"

"Not bloody likely. Your idea - you lead."

Giving up all pretence of secrecy and concealment, I strode out across the yard with Houseman following a little way behind. We passed a small Austin Ruby parked in the yard as I led us up to the front of the house. I hammered loudly on the thick oak door and I heard the echo of an empty house. We waited a few seconds and I was sure I heard movement and low voices back towards the living room area. Shit! Why had we not considered there might be more than one person here? I tensed as I heard footsteps approaching. They echoed eerily on the mosaic tiles I remembered seeing in the hall. I sensed Houseman step slightly to one side of the door and I clasped my hand over the Browning. I thumbed back the safety catch. As the door opened, a soft light spilled down the hallway from the living room.

"Yes?"

I couldn't answer immediately and I knew Houseman was as shocked as I was. The last thing I'd expected was a woman but there was no doubt that, standing before us, with only the dim light to aid our vision, was a quite beautiful woman.

Houseman was the first to recover. "Good evening. So sorry to trouble you, ma'am, but we thought the farm was deserted and were rather surprised to see a car turn into the drive. We'd reached Tumby before we realised the significance and popped back to check if everything was in order."

I glanced at him and he was smiling pleasantly. Without any effort he'd covered the time we'd spent skulking in the yard. Even I wanted to believe him.

She smiled in return but, having seen our uniforms, she was wary. "I'm afraid my estranged husband, who used to live here, was a bigger idiot than I thought. You probably know he's been arrested and is in prison? Well, we popped over from Norfolk today to pick up a few bits and pieces he left for us. The police have finished with them so we decided to take what we wanted and dump the rest. There were not many things my husband possessed that I could possibly want but it was something we had to do."

"We?" Houseman asked innocently.

She inclined her head in the direction of the living room. "I have Peter and Paula with me - my son and daughter."

There was an embarrassed silence for a few seconds, then Houseman spoke amiably enough but it was more of an order than a request. "Do you mind if we come in? You must understand, some very unusual things have gone on here at the farm and we'd like to make sure you and the children come to no harm."

She hesitated for just a millisecond. "Of course." She opened the door wider and I noticed she raised her voice. "Do come in." That had warned the kids we were on our way in and I knew we were getting on to very dangerous ground - kids or no kids.

We followed her down the hall and into the living room. We blinked in the light from the lantern that stood on an upturned crate in the middle of the otherwise empty room. Two holdalls and a large suitcase were on the floor. The boy, Peter, was sitting on the suitcase whilst the girl stood by the empty and cold fireplace. People say that kids are smart. I agree to a certain extent but there is one thing kids cannot do as well as adults - look innocent. They try too hard and look too innocent. These two were no exception to the rule. From their faces and reaction, they had been up to something. There was that hostile, sulky look with the slightly jutting lower lip. Good looking kids but spoilt brats.

"Would you mind if we took a look in your bags?" I asked. "We've no warrant with us but the police will be here soon and then, I'm afraid, my request will become an order."

The children seemed to tense slightly and their eyes moved to watch their mother. Both kids had flaxen hair and the same facial bone structure of their father. If I'd met them in the street I think I'd have known they were Meacher's kids.

"Is that really necessary?" She gave a little laugh as she asked the question. "It's only trinkets and things."

I thought a threshing machine was a strange place to keep one's trinkets!

Houseman took over. "Sam is right, Mrs Meacher. I'm afraid it is a rude request but necessary. The police will be here soon and they will have a warrant."

She just failed to control her composure when she heard my name. It was an infinitesimal flicker in her expression but she knew my name. Now where the hell had she heard that? I gripped the Browning just a little tighter.

She moved forward and picked up one of the holdalls. She placed it by the lantern on the upturned crate. She turned to her son. "Peter, let the officer look in the suitcase."

He looked at her in amazement but she stood quite still and expressionless. He rose with seeming reluctance and joined his mother by the crate. The girl too moved to her mother's side.

I stooped and flicked open the locks on the suitcase. The lid seemed to be jammed but it suddenly flew open and, after a quick look and a concerted effort to close my mouth, I straightened and faced her. In spite of trying hard not to show my feelings, there was a tremor in my voice I couldn't fully control.

"Would you like to tell me what this is in the suitcase?"

She shrugged. "Some sort of wireless set, I suppose."

"You suppose?" I was incredulous at her calmness.

She was angry. "Well, I don't know anything about the damn things. This is what happens when you listen to a damn fool. My husband told me where the radio was and asked me to retrieve it and destroy it. It seems he kept it here as a spare. If it were found, then he'd hang. So far, he feels he's done enough in the way of co-operation to limit his punishment to a prison sentence."

I watched her carefully. "So you've been to see him in Brixton prison?"

She didn't even hesitate. "Yes, of course. He asked to see me."

Wrong reply lady! I thought it but I said nothing.

She spread her hands in a helpless gesture. "For goodness sake, he may be a total bastard but he's father to my two children. As far as we're concerned he may as well be dead. We haven't seen him for years then, right out of the blue, we discover he's a spy. Obviously that is why he didn't want us around him. I know he's a traitor but I did love him once, even if it was for only a short time. I'm afraid this was a foolish gesture to keep a foolish man alive. God knows, he doesn't deserve it."

I'd not thought Meacher a fool and now I knew how clever he'd really been. Once he knew we were closing in, he'd used me to save him from the gallows and to convince us the cell was finished. He'd sacrificed himself and Smith to save the remnants of the cell. How wrong could she be? Mr Peter Meacher was a clever bastard and he'd played me like a bloody yo-yo. He'd been right. I shouldn't have been in the game but my callowness had been the instrument of his success. I felt sick to the stomach at how easily I'd let myself be used - by both bloody sides.

Houseman closed the suitcase with his foot. "You realise we will have to hold you here until the police arrive?"

She nodded.

He walked to the outer door and called into the night. "Okay, Max, you can all come in." When he returned he spoke to Mrs Meacher. "We've two ladies with us. I'd like the children to go with them. They will be perfectly safe."

She suddenly stooped and wrapped her arms around her children. She held them close for a while and then straightened up. I was surprised to see no sign of tears in her eyes. The two children were also expressionless.

Max and the others came carefully into the living room. There was the damp smell of fog on their clothes.

"Natalie," said Houseman. "I want you and Bourne to take the children to the car and wait there for the police." He sounded confident but I knew he was worried that either Dave had not found a phone or maybe he had but West Fen had not believed him.

"Come on, love." Bourne held out a hand but the girl ignored it. At least she went without protest. The boy, Peter, began to follow.

"Don't forget your bag," Mrs Meacher called and he picked up the holdall from the floor. The girl took one of the handles and they carried it between them as they followed Nat and Foghorn.

"I'll stay with them," volunteered Stan as he left the room.

It was done so neatly that neither Houseman, Max nor myself realised what she'd done until I turned quickly to face her.

"What was in that bag?" I asked sharply.

"Just their night things," she answered me as she opened the holdall on the crate.

Alarm bells jangled a warning in my brain. "But you said you'd only popped over for the day. Why would they need night clothes?"

I knew something was dreadfully wrong and the hairs on my neck went into overdrive. I began to reach for the Browning but helplessness flooded through me as I saw her reach into the holdall.

"Oh, fuck!" Max grunted as he flung himself backwards into the hallway but

384

Houseman was standing as if hypnotised as her hands emerged from the holdall, grasping the deadly shape of a Schmeisser sub machine gun. The Browning was barely half way out of my pocket and I knew she'd rip us apart with the Schmeisser before I could even fire a round. I looked desperately at the stubby barrel of the sub machine gun as it began to swing up and around in my direction. There was just one way to go - forwards. I threw myself in a headlong dive at the crate, hoping it was empty. It was and as I hit it, the lantern flew in an arc through the air to crash into the corner of the room. Luck was with us. Instead of the lantern bursting into a mass of flame, it simply snuffed out and plunged us into darkness. The crate had hit the Meacher woman hard across the front of her legs and I heard her quick intake of breath but, as I rolled frantically to one side, a burst of fire ripped from the Schmeisser. Splinters from the floor lanced into my face and I heard Houseman grunt with pain. As I lay stunned up against the wall, I heard Foghorn scream outside in the yard.

"Oh, you fuckin' little bast...!" She never finished. Her cry was rent asunder by the sharp crack of two powerful explosions. The glass in the windows shattered into shards and flew into the darkened room. Then I heard a sound that chilled me to the marrow. I heard Nat scream my name. She screamed just the once and then there was silence.

I yanked the Browning up and fired a shot where Mrs Meacher had been but as my hearing began to recover from the blasts, I heard footsteps running down the passage at the rear of the house that led to the back door. Time for a quick human inventory check.

"Sir, you okay?"

"No," panted Houseman. "She hit me in the legs. I can't move. Where the hell did you get that gun?"

I couldn't believe it! He was injured and yet he still wanted to know where I'd got the gun!

"Don't ask, it's a long story." I turned towards the hallway. "Max?" There was no reply so I called louder. "Max!"

"Outside the window, Sam."

I breathed a sigh of relief at the sound of his voice. "Are you okay?"

"I'm afraid not. I missed the bullets on the way out but copped the shrapnel out here from the grenades."

" Grenades?" I coughed as the cordite got to my lungs.

"'Fraid so, Sam." His voice shook with emotion. "The kids had them in the holdall. They pulled the pins and ran." I heard his voice break with anguish. "Sam, it's bloody carnage out here."

I screamed in panic. "Nat! Nat!.... are you okay?"

Nothing - just a terrible silence.

I screamed again. "Bourne!"

"Sam," Max's voice was tight with pain. "You're wasting your time." I heard him sob. "I'm so sorry, Sam."

I felt a stab of pain behind my eyes and my chest hurt as if something alien was trying to claw its way out. I sucked eagerly for oxygen but it seemed a pointless exercise as it did nothing to assuage the pain. I wanted to run outside to help Nat but it would mean leaving the man who had done so much for me. To stay here with just a Browning against a Schmeisser was suicide. I wanted to scream Nat's name again. Maybe she was unconscious? Even as the hope entered my brain I knew I was wasting my time with false hopes. I felt myself beginning to shake and my heart felt as if it would burst.

Then, suddenly the energy I needed was there. The same calmness that had descended upon me that night in Holland was back again. I knew what I had to do and I was going to do it. My pulse rate had slowed and I could no longer hear my heart pounding in my chest. I rose slowly to my feet and Houseman heard the movement.

"Wait for help, Sam." His voice was full of pain.

"No fucking way, boss - no fucking way."

I slipped silently into the passage leading to the back door. I reached the door but when I went to open it, much to my surprise, it was locked. My new-found calmness nearly deserted me at that point but I tried the door again. The handle rattled slightly as I tried to turn it and I felt the muscles in my back spasm in fear. I threw myself backwards into the passage and smashed my head on the wall as I went down. I was only just in time as a burst of fire ripped into the door where I'd been standing.

Shit! She was still in the house. I could just see the staircase on my left. No way was I going up there - certain suicide. I tiptoed back into the living room.

I peered into the darkness. "Where are you, sir?"

"Over by the door." Houseman's voice sounded weak.

I groped my way in the direction of his voice and ran my hands up his body until I had him under the arms. "Think you can bear it if I try to drag you outside?"

"We can only try, Sam."

I took a deep breath and began to pull and nearly stopped as I heard him gasp with pain.

"For fuck's sake, don't stop," he muttered through his clenched teeth. "Just get it over with."

I eventually got him outside and discovered the moon was beginning to make its presence felt through the fog. I started as a shadow loomed up from where it had been crouching by the wounded and prone figure of Max.

I grabbed at the shadow. "Stan, is that you?"

He stumbled into me and put his hands on my arms. He held me and was desperately trying to tell me something but he was incapable of coherent thought. Speech was totally beyond him. His face was a mask of shock, the eyes wide with pain and there were dark flecks of blood on his face.

I peered around him to where Max lay. "Max, can you get as far as the cart sheds over there?"

"If I crawl, yes."

I broke Stan's hold on my arms. "Stan, help Max over to the sheds, as quick as you can and then stay there. Don't come out until I call, okay?"

He nodded and stooped to get a hold on Max. He began dragging him across the yard and I waited for a burst of fire from an upstairs window but all remained quiet. What was she doing? Maybe she didn't have a lot of ammo. Join the fucking club, missus, neither did I.

I managed to get Houseman to the relative safety of the sheds when a thought occurred to me. I ran back towards the house, zigzagging across the open ground as the moon was now getting very bright and we could no longer rely on the cover of darkness. I slid along the wall until I came to one of the smashed windows. I put my hand carefully through and ran it around the inside of the frame. Ah, there it was - a small round metallic bump. I ran my hand higher and found another. Screws! The search team must have screwed all the windows shut and forgotten to remove the screws when they'd finished with the property. If they had sealed the windows, then it was a damned good bet they'd sealed the back door. I hadn't known that and I bet

386

neither had Mrs Meacher.

I moved to return to the sheds but now I could see the still and prostrate forms of Nat and Foghorn. From where I crouched they looked like two rag dolls. Their limbs were in positions that no living person could physically achieve and I knew they were both dead.

Strangely, I felt no more grief - that would come later. All that burned in me now was the desire for revenge. I wanted a terrible revenge. Those pitiful bodies were the fuel for that burning desire and my cup of revenge was going to overflow with the blood of Mrs Fucking Meacher.

I tore my eyes from the bodies and loped across to where I'd seen Meacher's tractor. There had to be fuel around here somewhere. I found it in a large tank at the end of the sheds. I turned the tap at the end of the tank. Shit! It was paraffin. I needed petrol.

"Sam! What are you looking for?"

I jumped at the voice. I hadn't heard the little farmer approach. "I need to find where Meacher stored his petrol."

He pointed deeper into the shed. "It's back here. There are a few cans too."

"Help me fill some cans?" I asked.

His voice was calm. "Try to stop me."

"You getting it together again?" I asked him quietly.

"Just stop asking bloody fool questions and tell me what to do."

"How many cans do we have?"

"Five one gallon cans."

"Okay. Give me a hand to fill them. Do you have any matches?"

He nodded.

"Any old bottles around the place?" I asked, looking around.

"Bound to be some in the stables for giving drenches to the horses." He shot off to find the bottles and was back before I'd filled the third can.

"Molotov cocktails?" There was a sound of childish glee in his voice.

I grinned at him. "Exactly!"

He grinned back wolfishly in the moonlight. Like mine, his grief had gone. Like me, it had been replaced by madness.

"Shit!" I blurted out as I spotted a movement by the front door and grabbed for the Browning. I banged off a couple of shots and got a burst of Hitler's best in return. It went wide and I found myself muttering to myself.

"Stay where you are, Mrs Meacher, ma'am. You'll come out when I fucking well say you can come out."

We finished filling the cans and Stan ripped some pieces from an old sack to use as wicks for the Molotov cocktails.

I nodded at him and glanced towards the house. "Right, you murdering cow, let's be having you."

Making a detour around to the blind end of the house, we got our cans into position. We removed the screw caps from each can and leapt forward to throw them through the broken windows. We could hear the petrol 'chugging' from the cans as they hit the floor in the empty room.

I gripped Stan's arm. "Two in the other room and one in the hall."

Again we sprinted forward and heaved our cans through the other window and I tossed the final one into the hall. The smell of petrol was heavy on the damp night air. Mrs Meacher must have realised what was about to happen and, after a crash of breaking glass, a burst of fire came from an upstairs window but it did no more than make us jump.

"Okay, Stan, light the blue touchpaper and stand well clear." I began to chuckle with delightful anticipation. She was going to fry. The murdering bitch was going to fry!

The next bit was going to be tricky. I was going to run across the open yard, now well lit by the moon, with a Molotov in each hand. I was going to be a perfect target and if she hit one of the bottles, she'd literally cook my goose.

Stan lit the wicks and I zigzagged away across the yard. She began to fire the minute I left the cover of the sheds. I heard rounds smacking into the ground around me and one or two plucked eagerly at my sleeve but I was able to launch the bottles in a flower of flame before she hit me. Two rounds got me in the lower left thigh and the third took a chunk out of my right hip. Strangely, there was no pain for the first few seconds and my impetus took me safely back to the sheds before I collapsed in agony.

Sam dropped to his knees by my side. "Sam, are you hit?"

"'Fraid so, mate."

I felt his arm go under my head. "Not you too, Sam, not you. Please God, not all my friends in one night." He'd whispered the plea and I don't think he meant me to hear it.

I gritted my teeth. "Don't worry, Stan, I'm not going to die yet. Help me up, she'll be coming out soon."

He managed to get me back on my feet although my legs were not doing a very good job of keeping me upright. I changed the mag on the Browning and slammed the new one into its home in the butt. I propped myself up against a roof support and waited. As I looked at the flames, I thought I'd overdone the hallway but it was not long before I saw movement beyond the flames.

"Here she comes, Stan!"

"Blow the fucking cow to smithereens." It was a savage and vicious whisper from such a normally gentle man.

She must have known it was useless but she came running through the boiling smoke and flame, the Schmeisser spitting death as only Schmeissers do. Some of the rounds came pretty close but finally she was in the doorway, silhouetted against the flames like a moth against a candle.

I raised the Browning and aimed slightly low. When the barrel kicked up I'd hit the spot I wanted to hit. I squeezed the trigger and the Browning bucked in my hands. The round took her high in the chest and the impact momentarily stopped her in her tracks. It may only have been momentarily but it was long enough for her hair to ignite. A writhing halo of fire surrounded her head but she didn't even whimper. She squeezed off another burst and I replied with another aimed shot. This time my Blenheim instructor would have been really proud of me - it was straight between the eyes. I was getting good at this. She began to topple.

"Mummy! Mummy!" We spun round as the daughter hurtled from the sanctuary of the end stables stall and ran towards her mother.

I didn't even hesitate. I gave her two rounds in the back. The murdering little shit pitched forward as her mother pitched backwards. It was like a fiery satanic sequence dance. The mother backwards, to be engulfed by the flames and the daughter forwards to smash face down on the cobbles.

"One to go," muttered Stan as he took a long-handled hedging knife from where it hung on the wall with a collection of scythes.

We ducked as there was a sudden burst of fire but it was just the spare Schmeisser mag going off in the heat of the fire. She must have taped it to the one in the gun for a quick mag change. Above the crackle of the flames I heard the sound of vehicle engines racing down the farm track. I grabbed Stan's arm.

"Come on, my old friend, we don't have much time." We slipped away from the light of the blazing farmhouse and into the shadows.

It didn't take long to find him. He was hiding on top of the threshing machine. I waved him down with the Browning and he dropped to the ground. In spite of the carnage outside, he was quite calm. In fact he had a supercilious little smile on his face.

"Mummy's little boy, eh?" I goaded him.

He bridled. "I am my father's son and he's a great man."

I smiled at him. "Daddy will soon be dangling on the end of a rope but mother was the real commander of the cell, wasn't she?"

His chin went up a fraction. "If you're so clever, I don't need to answer that question." The little bastard had the gall to look down his nose at me.

"Your mother is dead and so is your sister. Was it all worth it?"

The chin went up a little more. "Of course it was but you'd never understand."

I stared at him with contempt. "How right you are, sunshine."

He raised his hands above his head. "Now I am your prisoner. Better late than never as far as you're concerned." The smirk was even more prominent on his arrogant face.

I listened to the shouts now echoing around the farmyard. The police were here and somebody was yelling for an ambulance. I wondered idly if anybody had thought to bring one with them. I could feel my wounds throbbing and I was beginning to feel woozy and faint.

I groaned with pain. "Hurry up, Stan - I can't wait much longer."

The arrogance began to drain from the kid's face, to be replace with the first flickerings of alarm. His mouth started to tremble. "I am your prisoner. I've surrendered. Under the Geneva Convention you cannot harm me."

Stan's voice was just a whisper. "You seem to know all about Geneva, boy, but what did you know of Rhoda?"

The boy was silent and his eyes darted from Stan to me.

"What about Natalie?" I joined in.

He said nothing but now his eyes were frantically darting from side to side as if seeking a route to escape.

Without any warning, Stan rammed the blade of hedging knife forward and it sank up to the haft in the boy's stomach. His eyes opened wide in panic and fear. Then the pain got to him. His eyelids snapped down and his lips drew back from his teeth in a grimace as the agony hit home.

"That was for Rhoda." Stan was still whispering and he was fighting back the tears. He grunted as he wrenched the knife from the boy's body.

He slammed it forward again. "...and that's for Natalie." He wrenched the knife out again and blood gushed from the boy's mouth. Stan threw the hedging knife out into the yard.

I watched with detachment as the boy struggled to speak but he finally sank to his knees and pitched forward on his face. I could hear Stan sobbing but I could do nothing to help him. I was anxious to tell him I was sorry for ruining his dream but I was fighting to stay conscious. All I wanted to do was sink to the ground and go to sleep. I wanted to join Nat. Was there another life? God! I hoped so. This one had been a shit. I felt my legs going from under me and, as I began to fall, I waited detachedly for the impact with the floor but, strangely, I remained as if suspended in mid air.

"Get that stretcher under him." The voice was calm and authoritative. I felt myself being lowered on to my back and I was carried out into the glow of the still burning farmhouse.

"Hope Jerry doesn't turn up and decide to use us as a target." The voice came from the head of the stretcher as they lowered me to the ground. I felt hands using a knife or scissors to cut away my trousers. I winced as bandages were applied to my thighs and, as I felt somebody pinch my arm, I knew a shot of morphine was next.

"Hold it!" I tried to yell but it came out as a hoarse whisper.

A voice spoke close to my ear. "Take it easy, old son, you'll soon be in a nice warm hospital bed."

"I want to see Nat and Foghorn," I whispered.

"What the hell is he on about?"

"He wants to see the girls." It was Max's voice. It sounded down at my level so he too must be on a stretcher.

"Not a good idea." It was a cultured voice. Had to be the Doctor.

"Just a last look," I pleaded. I tried to raise myself from the stretcher.

"Okay, okay…" A hand pressed me back down. "Take him over there."

They lowered me next to the blanket covered bodies. Somebody's hands went under my shoulders and raised me up into a sitting position. Another airman undid the top of the blankets and lowered them slightly. The tears began to stream from my eyes and down my cheeks, the salt of the tears smarting in the flesh wounds to my face.

Nat looked unharmed but her face was already waxlike and cold. The beauty had already faded and I was left with no one to grieve for. This was not my Nat, she'd gone for ever.

Foghorn had some shrapnel wounds to her face but she too was already just a memory. This shapeless bundle was not the woman who had once terrorised us all but whom I had come to love in a strange way. She'd so much enjoyed her 'posh night out' as she'd called it. It had been her 'special' night and the first she'd been able to enjoy with other people who had accepted her as an equal. Now there would be no new life with Stan at the farm and I was responsible. I'd destroyed the woman who was to have been the rest of my life and I'd ended the dreams of the person who had trusted me when she abhorred all others. It was time for me to die too. There was nothing left for me to live for in this world. I began to shake uncontrollably and I could feel the sobs beginning to tear me apart.

"Give him the shot now." It was the cultured voice again.

"Nat, oh, Nat," I whispered as my senses faded into what I hoped was the welcoming embrace of death.

CHAPTER TWENTY-EIGHT

I awoke in yet another hospital bed. I'd no idea how much time had elapsed since the debacle at the farm. There were the usual hospital noises outside the door of my room and the lusty singing of a blackbird outside the open window. The spring air wafted in with the bird's song and there was the scent of blossom. I listened to the bird. He was happy and free and his mood was reflected in the power of his song. I felt the tears begin again. I seemed to spend all my bloody life blubbing these days. It was strange really and a bit of a paradox. All the RAF types in books and films seemed to be heroes to a man. They flinched at nothing, not even death. Maybe they'd done their killing at a distance Mine had all been too bloody close and there was sod all heroic about death. I eased the bedclothes down to look at my legs. They were heavily bandaged and hurt like hell but at least they were still there.

The door opened and a sandy-haired young man walked in. He had blue eyes in a face that was a mass of freckles. He wore the obligatory white coat and the ubiquitous stethoscope around his neck.

"Good afternoon, Sam. I'm Dr Chas McDonald." He'd a pleasant Highlands accent and looked friendly enough but I could find no response to his announcement.

It seemed to make little difference to him. "How are you feeling?"

I licked my dry lips. "Okay, I guess. Legs hurt but not too bad."

"Well, that's only to be expected. We took six slugs out of your legs but you must have somebody up there looking after you as all the damage was limited to muscle tissue and we got all the lead out without any complications. You're going to be a bit stiff-legged for a while but you'll soon be back to normal."

I tried in vain to envisage a return to his ethereal notion of normality. "How's Jake Houseman, Max and Stan?" I asked.

"Squadron Leader Houseman did not have your luck. He has some wounds in his right leg and he copped a round in the left side of his pelvis. He's in theatre now but we can only do so much here. We'll have to transfer him for the remedial surgery he'll need to get him back on his feet. Shearing's wounds, like yours, were not that bad. In fact he got off a lot lighter than you did. Who was the other chap you mentioned?"

"Stan - Stan Cornish. A little civilian guy in his sixties."

He looked at me with a puzzled expression. "I'm sorry, we've no patient by that name."

I struggled into a sitting position. "You must have! I know he wasn't wounded but the little chap needed help, probably more than I did."

McDonald shook his head. "Sorry, I haven't even heard of him. He certainly didn't come in the ambulance with the rest of you."

I felt myself becoming extremely agitated. "Where are we?"

"Boston General Hospital."

I began to swing my legs out of bed and he rushed forward to restrain me.

"Hey! Hang on a minute. No way can you get out of bed. You've just had general anaesthetic and you must rest."

I shoved him furiously out of my way. "Where are my fucking clothes?"

He began to lose his rag. "Did you hear what I said, Carver?"

I hauled myself to my feet with the help of the headboard. I wished I hadn't as the room oscillated from side to side and I began to pour with sweat. I spoke through my gritted teeth.

"I'm going to ask you just one more time. Where are my clothes?"

I heard the door open but I was past caring as to the identity of the new arrival. I was expending all my energy in just staying on my feet. I knew the voice though.

"Alright, young man, I'll deal with Carver."

I sensed rather than saw McDonald leave the room and then strong hands were helping me back on the bed. I looked up into the face of Harry Jameson, our SMO from West Fen.

"Now you've made me upset him, Carver. What the hell has got into you now?"

I gripped his arm. "I need to get out of here, sir. I need to check on a civilian who has been helping us. He was with us at the farm but he didn't turn up here with the rest of us. I don't know where he is or what has happened to him." My voice was so strained, I barely recognised it as my own.

Jameson held me firmly down on the bed by placing his hands on my shoulders. "Look, stay here and don't move. I'll check with Shearing - maybe he knows something. If he doesn't know where your friend is then I'll pop down the corridor and see the registrar. I'll be back in a couple of minutes, okay?"

I nodded my thanks, as I was unable to speak.

He stepped back, grinned and raised a finger as if to a pet dog. "Sit and stay!" he ordered.

I nodded again but I couldn't raise a smile.

"Good man."

He headed for the door and then turned. The smile had gone from his face and he spoke gently. "I'm terribly sorry about Natalie, Sam."

I just stared at him, helpless in my grief.

He closed the door quietly behind him.

I lay back on the bed and stared at the ceiling. I had to find the little farmer. The last I remembered of him were his sobs in the darkness of the cart shed. Surely they'd looked after him? We'd both been temporarily insane with grief and hatred. He too had lost the person who was going to be his future. My grief was tearing me apart but I was in the armed forces. I was supposed to be able to handle death and grief. It was part of the job. It was a different story for somebody like Stan. He was a solitary man who'd been thrust into the war. To him, it had been exciting and a big change in his life but war always brought grief and I knew he couldn't handle that grief alone.

Jameson returned and he looked worried. "Shearing has no recollection of your friend Cornish after the cavalry arrived. I called Wareham and neither he, nor his men, saw any other survivors other than Jake, Shearing and yourself."

I struggled upright again. "I've got to go to his home. He must be there. Oh, God, I hope he's there. Would you try his telephone number for me, sir?"

"Of course." Jameson seemed prepared to go along with me for now.

I wrote the number down and he went off to find a phone. He was soon back.

"The phone seems to be disconnected."

"In that case, I must go out there, sir."

He raised a placating hand. "Look, let me ask the local police to go round there."

I shook my head. "It would be no good, sir. If he saw the civilian police arriving at the farm, I'm sure he'd run."

"Why the heck would he do that?"

I took a deep breath. "Because, last night at the farm, he killed a thirteen-year-old boy."

"Oh, shit!" Jameson breathed. "What the hell went on out there?"

"The boy and his sister killed Nat and Bourne. Stan and I killed both the kids. I shot the girl twice in the back and howled with glee as I did it. She was just eleven years old."

Jameson dropped on to the bedside chair. He rubbed a hand over his eyes as if trying to obliterate what I'd told him. He finally looked up at me and I could see the sadness in his eyes.

"A Wing Commander Face called me at West Fen and asked me to get over here as soon as I could. He wanted me to see if you were fit enough to talk about what happened last night." He looked at his watch. "He'll be here in about an hour's time."

I closed my eyes as helplessness flooded over me. "I must get to see Stan Cornish before I see Face. The little chap is going to need help with his story. If he tells the absolute truth, which he will because he could never tell a lie, he'll be in deep trouble. It doesn't matter a damn about me but he's too good a man to have to pay for a moment of madness. We were both out of our minds."

Jameson stood and headed for the door.

"Where are you going, sir?" I asked in alarm.

"To find you some clothes." It was all he said as he hurried from the room.

God only knows where he found them but he returned with a pair of blue overalls and a donkey jacket. He threw them on the bed. "Get dressed. We haven't much time."

"How am I going to get to the farm?" I asked as I struggled to pull the overalls up over my bandages.

"I'm taking you." He quickly held up a restraining hand. "Don't say a word or I may change my mind."

We left the hospital by the back door. I could hardly walk but he half carried me to his car and helped me into the passenger seat. As we drove out of the car park, I glanced up at the hospital and saw McDonald watching from one of the windows. He turned quickly away and disappeared.

Jameson drove fast but expertly and we were soon bumping down the track to Stan's farm. I peered anxiously through the windscreen. I felt weak and confused but this began to turn to alarm, as there was no Dog bounding out to meet us. The farm looked normal. The chickens were pecking around the yard and a farm cat arched its back as it stretched in the warm but weak sunlight. The sky to the west was black with an approaching storm.

Then my breath caught in my throat. The farmhouse door was open and a couple of chickens were actually in the hall. No way would the fastidious farmer permit that.

"I don't like the look of that open door," Jameson muttered thoughtfully as he switched off the engine.

"Nor me." I tried to keep my voice steady when all the time I wanted to scream the farmer's name.

As I waited to be helped from the car, I willed Stan to appear around the corner of the barn and stand there with that defiant stance I knew so well.

"Please, Stan, show yourself." I whispered the words to myself.

Even the sound of the slamming of the car doors brought no response and I glanced skywards as the first heavy drops of rain began to fall. The sun had gone and a grey, bleak aspect settled like a mantle over the farm. Jameson helped me towards the house, shooing chickens out of the way as I hobbled slowly across the yard.

"Stan!" I tried to shout but my throat was constricted with fear.

"Mr Cornish!" Jameson tried where I'd failed but there was no reply.

We slowly advanced down the hall and found the door to the little sitting room wide open. The mess on the floor was evidence that the chickens had been in here. There was no fire in the hearth, just cold, grey ashes and the kettle hung silently on its hook.

"Oh, Jesus," I whispered hoarsely. "He hasn't been here for hours."

"Maybe he's with friends," Jameson suggested half-heartedly.

"He doesn't have any," I replied bitterly. I looked towards the back parlour where we'd taken a bath. I pointed to the closed door. "Can you help me over there, sir?"

I was breathless with the effort by the time we reached the door. I hesitated a few seconds before I pushed it open and hobbled into the room. I gave a small cry of anguish. In the middle of the room was an osier basket and in it lay the inert form of Dog. He looked to be sleeping but already his fur lacked the lustre I knew so well from constantly stroking him. Just like Nat, death had reduced a natural vitality to an unnatural calm. I stooped and touched the fur but recoiled at the stiffness.

Jameson leant over the dog for a few seconds and then straightened up. "Poison," he announced quietly. He watched me anxiously as tears welled from my eyes. The basket and Dog blurred as if the tears were attempting to hide from me the source of my sorrow.

Jameson took my arm. "Come on, Sam, there's nothing for you here."

"The barn," I whispered.

"You stay in the car. I'll check the barn." He spoke quickly and I knew he too feared what was in the barn.

"No, sir, I must come with you."

It seemed to take an age to cross the farmyard and the storm was now heavy. The tears, pouring down my face, became indistinguishable from the rain. Finally we stood before the large sliding door. Neither of us moved for some time but finally Jameson broke the silence.

"Are you sure you want to go through with this?"

I nodded. "Let's get it over with."

He heaved the door open and, wiping the tears and rain from my eyes, I peered into the gloom.

Stan was there, or at least what had been Stan was there. His slight body hung slackly from the noose around his neck. Where once there had been alert blue eyes and a ready smile, there was just a grotesque black mask. The face was black in death and the swollen tongue hung slackly from the twisted mouth. There was a dark patch on the front of the grey flannel trousers where he had urinated in death.

"Oh, my God." Jameson's hand under my arm tightened.

I stared at the corpse, desperately trying to see the vital little man whose life I'd ruined. If I had not, in the urgency of youth, turned up at the farm that fateful day, he'd still be alive. He didn't have much of a life before I arrived on the scene but at least he had a life. I'd taken that from him in the most horrific way. He must have slid away into the darkness at the farm and, somehow, made it back here. He'd have been terrified and torn apart by grief. He must have decided, during the long trek home, to end his life. If there was a life on the other side, he had taken his only loyal friend with him - Dog.

394

I turned quickly away and stumbled out into the yard. My chest felt as if there was an iron bar crushing the very breath from my body. I felt Jameson's arm go around my shoulders but it seemed to make the constriction worse and I shrugged away from him.

A familiar sound began to make itself felt in my frantic brain and I turned my head in the direction of the sound.

It was low, very low. The four Merlins were roaring lustily, as if mocking my grief. The black fuselage grew bigger as it roared in at less than a hundred feet. Vortices spiralled back from the tips of the props as it forged its way through the moist air. Rain sluiced in a fine spray from the trailing edges of the wings. I could see two men in the cockpit, both staring intently ahead. The port wing dipped slightly as the Lanc began a curve to the north. I could now see the white face of the mid-upper gunner as he stared down at us in the farmyard. For the first time in my life, the Lancaster was obscene - a thing of death. Merlins had started this chain of events and here they were again - in at the death. The pain in my chest burst into a blossom of anguish, fear and pain. I fell to my knees in the mud and threw my head back to the leaden sky.

"Leave me alone! Leave me alone!" I screamed at the departing harbinger of death. My throat tightened and I barely managed to croak my final plea as I fell, face forward, into the mud.

"Oh, God! Just leave me alone."

CHAPTER TWENTY-NINE

I must have slept as we passed through the leafy streets of Woodhall Spa and the red-bricked village of Coningsby but I was wide awake by the time we came to the turn off to Frithville. I pulled myself upright and gripped the back of the seat in front of me. I strained forward to get my first glimpse. Then I saw the water tower rearing up against the blue sky and I knew we were there.

We roared past the guardroom but the two SPs on the barrier didn't even look up. The little phone box appeared and I glanced across at the security fence and the Intelligence Section beyond. Nat would be there, beavering away at the night fighter and flak concentrations. Houseman would be preparing his briefing for the night's ops and Tom Powell would be bashing away at his typewriter. Dave Jones would be whistling tunelessly as he put the routing tape up on the main briefing board.

Now the airfield itself was in sight. The flat expanse of green and grey stretched away across the flat fen, to be halted only where it met the blue vault of the horizon. The monotony was broken by the stark blackness of the hangars and the Lancasters dotted around on their dispersals. Sammy Mason's D-DOG was on her usual dispersal by the roadside. He'd obviously got a new kite because this one was pristine, even down to the new red and white stripes on the fin. It was probably straight from the factory at Castle Bromwich. An airman, stripped to the waist as he worked in the hot sun, sat astride the top of the fuselage, polishing the Perspex of the mid-upper turret. He waved but he could have been waving to the WAAF driving the tractor towing the bomb trolleys. On one of the trolleys was the unmistakable boiler-like shape of the 4,000lb 'Cookie'. A fuel bowser was tucked up against D-DOG's starboard wing, one of its hoses snaking up to where a corporal knelt on the upper surface. He was waiting whilst a colleague struggled to open a filler cap to one of the tanks. I saw the corporal laughing as his friend fought with the recalcitrant cap.

A sudden flash of light on the far side of the airfield grabbed my attention. The huge propeller blades on the port outer of a Lancaster were kicking round and catching the sunlight. There was a sudden burst of blue smoke as the engine fired and the blades blurred into a disc of light. I couldn't hear the sound of the engine over the noise of our vehicle but the hairs on the back of my neck tingled and I felt the quickening of my heartbeat.

I wanted to see so much more but my driver had no reason to stop and the last glimpse I had of West Fen was of a small truck with its tilt removed. It was careering around the peritrack towards the ops centre. Standing in the back were seven young men. They had the sleeves of their blue shirts rolled up to the elbow but were still wearing their Mae Wests. Each had a leather helmet, with goggles and oxygen mask, clutched in one hand whilst hanging on to the exposed tilt hoops with the other. They were laughing, so I guessed their NFT had gone well. One of them took his life in his hands and let go the hoop to wave. I wanted to return the wave but it was impossible. Then I thought I glimpsed a wave from the truck's driver and my heart sang - it had to be Foghorn, bless her! I struggled to turn in my seat to keep the airfield in sight but we were already speeding on towards Boston. I struggled again in my frustration.

There was a sharp crack and a stinging pain in my right cheek.

"Sit still, you loopy old bastard, or you'll get another."

My eyes watered from the slap and the humiliation but I raised my face to my assailant.

"Oh, bloody hell, he's starting to blub again." She waddled back to her seat at the front of the minibus.

"I'm not surprised, Trace," replied the other care assistant. "You don't half clout him sometimes. You don't know your own strength."

Big fat Tracy turned in her seat and gave me a contemptuous glare and then screwed her bulk back to peer out through the windscreen. "Snotty-nosed, old git. His posh accent gets right up my bleedin' nose. He always gets wound up when we come this way. For Christ's sake, it's only bloody ploughed fields!"

The driver, whom I'd not seen before, glanced at me in the rear view mirror. "Who is the old boy?" he asked. "He seems harmless to me."

Tracy hooted with laughter. "Dunno about harmless but he's a bleedin' nutter. I was looking at his notes the other day and he's been in the home since the war."

The driver's eyes met mine again in the mirror and, just for a second, I thought I saw kindness there.

"Since the war? Jesus! - Poor old boy. Over fifty years in that bloody place and I'd be a nutter."

"Bollocks, you soft git!" Tracy lit up another of her foul smelling cigarettes. Her husband was a long-distance lorry driver and brought them back from France.

Lily turned in her seat to look at me before she spoke. "He was a hero, you know. He's got some medals and one of them is the highest one you can get."

Tracy gave a liquid cough as she laughed. "He ain't got 'em no more. My Darren nicked 'em and flogged 'em to a bloke in Lincoln - up Steep Hill or somewhere."

Once more I felt the tears begin to flow freely down my cheeks. I wanted to jump up and smash the fat cow's head to a pulp but these days, my legs refused to move. They were always cold and useless. I was permanently in a wheelchair when I wasn't in bed. More humiliating was the fact I was strapped to the chair by my wrists. Why? Where the hell was I going? I wanted to shout but my voice had left me long ago. So I cried silently in bitter frustration as I realised her sadistic thirteen-year-old son had stolen my last tangible link with West Fen. He was always in my room and I'd hear visitors say how nice it was to see a young boy give his free time to the infirm and the elderly. What a load of bollocks! When nobody was looking, he'd bend my fingers back until they were about to snap. For Christ's sake, the bloody arthritis was bad enough without the little bastard's extra ministrations. I'd open my mouth in a silent scream of pain and he'd be convulsed with laughter, opening his mouth in a parody of my own gaping mouth.

It was taking so long to die. If there was a God, why had he taken so many of my friends and left me alive? As I aged I became weaker and even more incapable of fighting back against the fat slug taking up two seats at the front of the bus. She coughed with laughter again as she finished an obscene joke.

"Oooh, you are a one, Trace!" simpered Lily the Lackey.

I could feel the tears smarting as they dried on my cheeks. I locked eyes with the kindly driver again and fought back at the fat slug with the only weapon I had left - I pissed in my pants. Let the fat cow deal with that when we got to Boston hospital. It would mean another beating when we got back to the home but what the hell, maybe one day she'd go too far and kill me.

Could I ever be so lucky?

Glossary

AP	Air Publication. Updateable info on all things RAF
ASF	Aircraft Servicing Flight
ASR	Air Sea Rescue
AWOL	Absent Without Leave
BATMAN	Officer's personal servant
BOD	Person
BUMPERING	Polishing lino floors with weighted buffer
'D' RING	Chrome handle – pulled to open parachute
ETA	Estimated Time of Arrival
ETD	Estimated Time of Departure
FLAK	Anti-aircraft gunfire
FORM 700	Aircraft serviceability record
GARDENING	Dropping sea mines from the air
GROUPIE	Group Captain
HQ	Headquarters
IRONS	Knife, Fork, Spoon, carried everywhere by all airmen (other ranks)
MAE WEST	Aircrew lifejacket
MO	Medical Officer
MI5	Military intelligence
MT SECTION	Motor Transport Pool
MTO	Officer in charge of MT Section
NFT	Night Flying Test

PRU	Photographic Reconnaissance Unit
PRANG	Aircraft crash
QFE	Barometric pressure set on altimeter sub-scale
RHUBARB	Freelance interdiction attacks on random enemy targets
SCHNELLBOOT	Fast, shallow draught, heavy armed motor boat
SMO	Senior Medical Officer
SSQ	Station Sick Quarters
SHQ	Station Headquarters
SNAILING	Moving slowly
SNOWDROP OR SP	RAF policeman
SPERRBRECHER	Heavily armed German flak ship
SQUADDY	Soldier
STATION MASTER	Slang for RAF Station Commander
TANNOY	Public address system
TILLY	Hillman utility vehicle
TWELVE-FIFTY	Form 1250. RAF personal identification card
TWO-FIVE-TWO	Form issued as charge for offences against RAF law
WAAF	Member of Women's Auxiliary Air Force
WINGCO	Wing Commander
YOKE	Control Column